ISBN 978-0-276-44220-9

www.readersdigest.co.uk

The Reader's Digest Association Limited, 11 Westferry Circus, Canary Wharf, London E14 4HE

of **love** & **life**

Three novels selected and condensed
by **Reader's Digest**

The Reader's Digest Association Limited, London

CONTENTS

STANDOFF
SANDRA BROWN

TV reporter Tiel McCoy is driving to New Mexico for a well-earned vacation when she hears on the radio news that the teenage daughter of a well-known millionaire has been kidnapped. Eager not to miss out on this story, Tiel stops at a convenience store in a small town called Rojo Flats and calls her editor—only to stumble upon the scoop of a lifetime.

Chapter 1

'I JUST HEARD the news bulletin on my car radio.'

Tiel McCoy didn't begin this telephone conversation with any super-
fluous chitchat. That was her opening statement the instant Gully said
hello. No preamble was necessary. Truth be known, he had probably
been expecting her call.

But he played dumb anyway. 'That you, Tiel? Enjoying your vacation
so far?'

Her vacation had officially begun that morning when she left Dallas
and headed west on Interstate 20. She had driven as far as Abilene,
where she stopped to visit her uncle Pete, who'd lived in a nursing home
there for the past five years. They had shared a lunch of soggy fish sticks
and canned English peas. She'd asked if there was anything she could do
for him while she was there, like write a letter or buy a magazine. He
had smiled at her sadly and thanked her for coming, then gave himself
over to an attendant who'd tucked him in for his nap like a child.

Outside, Tiel had gratefully inhaled the scorching, gritty West Texas
air in the hope of eradicating the smell of age and resignation which had
permeated the nursing home. She had been relieved the family obliga-
tion was behind her, but felt guilty for the relief. By an act of will she
shook off her despair and reminded herself that she was on vacation.

It wasn't even officially summer yet, but it was unseasonably warm for
May. There'd been no shade in which to park at the nursing home; con-
sequently her car's interior had been so hot she could have baked cook-
ies on the dashboard. She flipped on the air conditioning full blast and
found a radio station that played something other than country music.

'I'm going to have a wonderful time. The time away will be good for me. I'll feel a lot better for having done it.' She repeated this internal dialogue like a catechism, trying to convince herself of the truth of it. She had approached the vacation as though it were equivalent to taking a bad-tasting laxative.

Heat waves made the highway appear to ripple, and the undulating movement was hypnotic. The driving became mindless. Her mind drifted. The radio provided background noise of which Tiel was barely aware. But hearing the news bulletin, everything accelerated—the car, Tiel's heart rate, her mind.

Immediately she fished her cellphone from her large leather satchel and placed the call to Gully's direct line. Again declining any unnecessary conversation, she said to him now, 'Give me the skinny.'

'What's the radio putting out?'

'That earlier today a high-school student in Fort Worth kidnapped Russell Dendy's daughter.'

'That's about the gist of it,' Gully confirmed.

'The gist, but I want details.'

'You're on vacation, Tiel.'

'I'm coming back. Next exit, I'll make a U-turn.' She consulted her dashboard clock. 'I'll be at the station by—'

'Hold on, hold on. Where're you at, exactly?'

'About fifty miles west of Abilene.'

'Hmm.'

'What, Gully?' Her palms had become damp. She experienced the familiar tickle in her belly that only happened when she was following a hot lead to a super story.

'You're on your way to Angel Fire, right?'

'Right.'

'Northeastern part of New Mexico . . . Yeah, there it is.' He must have been reading a highway map as he spoke. 'Naw, never mind. You don't want this assignment, Tiel. It would take you out of your way.'

He was baiting her, and she knew it, but in this instance she didn't mind being baited. She wanted a piece of this story. The kidnapping of Russell Dendy's daughter was big news, and it promised to become even bigger news before it was over. 'I don't mind taking a detour. Tell me where to go.'

'Well,' he hedged, 'only if you're sure.'

'I'm sure.'

'OK then. Not too far in front of you is a turnoff onto state highway two-oh-eight. Take it south to San Angelo. On the south side of San Angelo you're gonna intersect with—'

'Gully, how far out of my way is this detour going to take me?'

'I thought you didn't care.'

'I don't. I'd just like to know. Rough estimate.'

'Well, let's see. Give or take . . . about three hundred miles from where you are now.'

'Three hundred round trip?' she asked faintly.

'One way.'

She expelled a long sigh, but was careful not to let him hear it. 'You said two-oh-eight south to San Angelo, then what?'

She steered with her knee, held the phone with her left hand and took notes with her right. The car was on cruise control, but her brain was in overdrive. Journalistic juices were pumping faster than the pistons in her engine. Thoughts of long pleasant evenings in a porch rocker were swapped for those of sound bites and interviews.

But she was getting ahead of herself. She lacked pertinent facts. When she asked for them, Gully turned mulish on her. 'Not now, Tiel. By the time you get where you're going, I'll have a lot more info.'

Frustrated and irked with him for being so stingy with the details, she asked, 'What's the name of the town again?'

'Hera.'

The highways were arrow-straight, flanked by endless prairie with an occasional herd of cattle grazing in irrigated pastures. Oil wells were silhouetted against a cloudless horizon. Frequently a tumbleweed rolled across the roadway in front of her. Once she got beyond San Angelo, she rarely saw another vehicle.

Funny, she thought, the way things turn out.

Ordinarily she would have elected to fly to New Mexico. But days ago she had decided to drive to Angel Fire, not only so she could visit Uncle Pete along the way, but also to get herself into a holiday frame of mind. The long drive would give her time to decompress, begin the period of rest and relaxation before she even reached the mountain resort, so that when she did arrive, she would already be in vacation mode.

At home in Dallas, she moved with the speed of light, always in a rush, always working under a deadline. This morning, once she had put the metropolitan sprawl behind her, she had begun to anticipate the idyllic days awaiting her. She had daydreamed of clear, gurgling streams, hikes along trails lined with aspens, cool, crisp air, and lazy mornings spent with a cup of coffee and a fiction best seller.

There would be no schedule to keep, nothing but hours in which to be lazy. Tiel McCoy was way past due to engage in some unabashed ennui. She'd already postponed this vacation three times.

'Use 'em or lose 'em,' Gully had told her of the vacation days she had accumulated.

He had lectured her on how her performance, as well as her disposition, would greatly improve if she gave herself a breather. This from the man who hadn't taken more than a few vacation days in the past forty-something years—counting the week required to have his gall bladder removed.

When she reminded him of this, he had scowled at her. 'Precisely. You want to wind up an ugly, shrivelled, pathetic relic like me?' Then he'd really hit the nail on the head. 'Taking a vacation isn't going to jeopardise your chances. That job'll still be up for grabs when you get back.'

Miffed at him for homing in on the real reason behind her reluctance to leave work for any period of time, she had grudgingly consented to going away for a week. The reservations had been made, the trip scheduled. But every schedule should have a little bit of flexibility built in.

And if flexibility was ever called for, it was when Russell Dendy's daughter was allegedly kidnapped.

Tiel held the payphone's sticky receiver between the pads of her thumb and index finger, loath to touch any more of the surface than necessary. 'OK, Gully, I'm here. Well, near, at least. Actually, I'm lost.'

He cackled. 'Too excited to concentrate on where you're going?'

'You said yourself, the place isn't even on most maps.'

Her sense of humour had worn off hours ago, about the time she'd lost all feeling in her butt. Since talking to him, she had stopped only once, and then only out of extreme necessity. She was hungry, thirsty, tired, cranky, achy, and none too fresh. A shower would be bliss.

Gully didn't improve her mood any by asking, 'How'd you manage to get lost?'

'I lost my sense of direction after the sun went down. The landscape looks the same from every angle out here. I'm calling from a convenience store in a town with a population of eight hundred and twenty-three, according to the city-limit sign. The town is called Rojo something.'

'Flats. Rojo Flats.'

Naturally Gully knew the full name of this obscure hamlet. He probably knew the mayor's name. Gully knew everything.

The TV station where Tiel worked had a news director, but the man with the title conducted business from inside a carpeted office and was more a bean counter and administrator than a hands-on boss.

The man in the trenches, the one who dealt directly with the reporters, writers, photographers and editors, the one who coordinated schedules and listened to sob stories and chewed ass when ass-chewing was called for, the one who actually ran the news operation, was the assignments editor, Gully.

He'd been at the station when it signed on in the early fifties, and had mandated that they would have to carry him out of the place feet first. He would die before he retired. He worked a sixteen-hour day, had a colourful vocabulary, an extensive repertoire of yarns about bygone days in broadcast news, and seemingly no life beyond the newsroom. His first name was Yarborough, but only a few living persons knew that. Everyone else knew him strictly as Gully.

'Are you going to give me this mysterious assignment or not?'

He wouldn't be rushed. 'What happened to your vacation plans?'

'Nothing. I'm still on vacation. I'm just postponing the start of it, that's all.'

'What's the new boyfriend gonna say?'

'I've told you a thousand times, there is no new boyfriend.' He laughed his chain-smoker's laugh that said he knew she was lying, and that she knew he knew.

'Got your notepad?' he asked suddenly.

'Uh, yeah.' Whatever germs had been teeming on the telephone were probably living within her now. Reconciled to that, she propped the receiver on her shoulder and held it there with her cheek while she removed a notepad and pen from her satchel and placed them on the narrow metal ledge beneath the wall-mounted telephone. 'Shoot.'

'The boy's name is Ronald Davison,' Gully began.

'I heard that much on the radio.'

'Goes by Ronnie. Senior year, same as the Dendy girl. Never in trouble until today. After homeroom this morning, he boogied out of the student parking lot in his Toyota pick-up with Sabra Dendy riding shotgun.'

'Russ Dendy's child.'

'His one and only.'

'Is the FBI on it?'

'FBI. Texas Rangers. You name it. If it wears a badge, it's working this one. Everybody's claiming jurisdiction and wants in on the action.'

Tiel took a moment to absorb the broad scope of this story. The short hallway in which the payphone was located led to the public rest rooms. One had a cowgirl in a fringed skirt stencilled in blue paint on the door. The other, predictably, had a cowpoke in chaps and ten-gallon hat, twirling a lasso above his head.

Glancing down the hall, Tiel spotted the real thing coming into the store. Tall, slender, Stetson pulled down low on his forehead. He nodded towards the store's cashier, whose frizzy, overpermed hair had been dyed an unflattering shade of ochre.

Nearer to Tiel was an elderly couple browsing for souvenirs, apparently in no hurry to return to their Winnebago—at least Tiel assumed the Winnebago outside belonged to them.

The couple then joined Tiel in the hallway, moving towards their respective rest rooms. 'Don't dally, Gladys,' the man said. His white legs were virtually hairless and looked ridiculously thin in his baggy khaki shorts and thick-soled athletic shoes.

'You mind your business, and I'll mind mine,' she retorted smartly. Another time, Tiel would have thought the elderly couple cute and endearing. But she was thoughtfully reading what she'd taken down almost verbatim from Gully.

'You said "riding shotgun". Strange choice of words, Gully.'

'Can you keep a secret?' He lowered his voice significantly. 'Because my ass will be grass if this gets out before our next newscast. We've scooped every other station and newspaper.'

Tiel's scalp began to tingle, as it did when she knew she was hearing something no other reporter had heard, when she had uncovered the element that would set her story apart from all the others, when her exclusive had the potential of winning her a journalism prize. Or of guaranteeing her the coveted spot on *Nine Live*.

'Who would I tell, Gully? I'm sharing space with a cowboy buying a six-pack of Bud, a sassy granny and her husband, and two non-English-speaking Mexicans.' The pair had since come into the store. She'd overheard them speaking Spanish while heating packaged burritos in a microwave oven.

Gully said, 'Linda—'

'Linda? She got the story?'

'You're on vacation, remember?'

'A vacation you urged me to take!' Tiel exclaimed.

Linda Harper was another reporter, a darned good reporter, and Tiel's unspoken rival. It stung that Gully had assigned Linda to cover such a plum of a story, which rightfully should have belonged to her. At least that's the way she saw it.

'You want to hear this or not?' he asked cantankerously.

'Go ahead.'

The elderly man emerged from the men's room. He moved to the end of the hall, where he paused to wait for his wife. To kill time, he took a camcorder from a nylon airline bag and began tinkering with it.

Gully said, 'Linda interviewed Sabra Dendy's best friend this afternoon. Hold on to your hat. The Dendy girl is pregnant with Ronnie Davison's kid. Eight months gone. They've been hiding it.'

'You're kidding! And the Dendys didn't know?'

'According to the friend, nobody did. That is, not until last night. The kids broke the news to their parents, and Russ Dendy went ape.'

Tiel's mind was already racing ahead, filling in the blanks. 'So this isn't a kidnapping. It's a contemporary Romeo and Juliet.'

'I didn't say that.'

'But . . .?'

'But that'd be my first guess. A view shared by Sabra Dendy's best friend and confidante. She claims Ronnie Davison is crazy about Sabra and wouldn't harm a hair on her head. Said Russell Dendy has been fighting this romance for more than a year. Nobody's good enough for his daughter, they're too young, college is a must, and so forth. You get the picture.'

'I do.' And what was wrong with the picture was that Tiel McCoy wasn't in it and Linda Harper was. Damn! Of all times to go on vacation.

'I'm coming back tonight, Gully.'

'No.'

'I think you sent me on this wild-goose chase so it would be impossible for me to return.'

'Not true. Listen to me, Tiel. We've got it covered. Bob's working the manhunt—law enforcement angle. Linda's on the kids' friends, teachers and families. Steve's practically moved into the Dendys' mansion, so he'll be there if a ransom call comes in, which I don't expect. And, bottom line, those kids'll probably turn up before you could get back to Dallas anyway.'

'So what am I doing out here in the middle of freaking nowhere?'

The old man with the camcorder shot her a curious glance over his shoulder.

'Listen,' Gully hissed. 'The friend? Sabra mentioned to her that she and Ronnie might hightail it to Mexico.'

'Where in Mexico?'

'She didn't know. Or wouldn't say. But she did say that Ronnie's dad—his real dad; his mom's remarried—is sympathetic to their predicament. A while back he offered his help if they ever needed it. Now, you're gonna feel really bad about yelling at me when I tell you where he hangs his hat.'

'Hera.'

'Satisfied?'

She should have apologised, but she didn't. Gully understood. 'Who else knows about this?'

'Nobody. But they will. It works to our advantage that Hera is a one-horse town, not on any beaten path.'

'Tell me about it,' she muttered.

'When word gets out, it'll take everybody a while to get there, even by helicopter. You've got a definite head start.'

'Gully, I love you!' she said excitedly. 'Direct me out of here.'

The elderly lady emerged from the ladies' room and rejoined her husband. She admonished him for fiddling with the camcorder and ordered him to put it back in the tote bag before he broke it.

'Like you're an expert with video cameras,' the old man retorted.

'I took the time to read the instruction book. You didn't.'

Tiel poked her finger in her ear so she could hear Gully better. 'What's the dad's name? Davison, I presume.'

'I've got an address and phone number.'

Tiel wrote down the information as fast as he reeled it off. 'Do I have an appointment with him?'

'Working on it. I'm dispatching a chopper with a photographer.'

'Kip, if he's available.'

'Y'all can meet in Hera. You'll do the interview tomorrow as soon as it's arranged with Davison. Then you can continue on your merry way.'

'Unless there's more story there.'

'Uh-uh. That's the condition, Tiel.' She envisioned him stubbornly shaking his head. 'You do this bit, then you're off to Angel Fire. Period. End of discussion.'

'Whatever you say.' She could easily agree now, then argue about it later if events warranted.

'OK, let's see. Outta Rojo Flats . . .' The map must have been right there on his desk, because within seconds he was giving her further directions. 'Shouldn't take you long to get there. You're not sleepy, are you?'

She was never more wide awake than when pursuing a story. Her problem was shutting her mind off and going to sleep. 'I'll buy something caffeinated to take along.'

'Check in with me as soon as you get there. I've got you a room reserved at the only motel.' Changing subjects, he asked, 'Is the new boyfriend going to be pissed?'

'For the last time, Gully, there is no new boyfriend.'

She hung up and placed another call—to her new boyfriend.

Joseph Marcus was as much a workaholic as she was. He was scheduled to fly out early the next day, so she predicted he would be working late at his desk, putting things in order prior to being away for several days.

She was right. He answered his office phone on the second ring.

'Do you get paid overtime?' she teased.

'Tiel? Hi. I'm glad you called.'

'It's after hours. I was afraid you wouldn't answer.'

'Reflex. Where are you?'

'The end of nowhere.'

'Everything OK? You haven't had car trouble or anything?'

'No, everything's great. I called for a couple of reasons. First, because I miss you.'

This was the tack to take. Establish that the trip was still on. Establish that it was being delayed, not derailed. Assure him that everything was cool, then inform him of the slight wrinkle in their plans for a romantic getaway.

'You saw me just last night.'

'But only briefly, and it's been a long day. Secondly, I called to remind you to throw a swimsuit into your suitcase.'

After a pause, he said, 'Actually, Tiel, it's good that you called. I needed to talk to you.'

Something in the tone of his voice prevented her from prattling on. She stopped talking and waited for him to fill the silence that yawned between them.

'I could have called you on your cellphone today, but this isn't the sort of thing . . . The fact is . . . And I'm sorry as hell about this . . . but I'm afraid I can't get away tomorrow.'

She'd been holding her breath. Now she released it, relieved. His change of plans alleviated her guilt over having to change them herself.

'I know how much you'd looked forward to this trip. And so had I,' he rushed to add.

'Let me make this easier on you, Joseph.' Meekly she confessed. 'The truth is, I was calling to say that I need another couple of days before I can get to Angel Fire. So I'm fine with a short postponement. Would your schedule allow us to meet on, say, Tuesday instead of tomorrow?'

'You don't understand, Tiel. I can't meet you at all.'

Tiel stared at the countless perforations in the metal surrounding the telephone. She stared so long without blinking that the tiny holes ran together. 'Oh. I see. That is disappointing. Well—'

'It's been very tense around here. My wife found my airline ticket and—'

'Excuse me?'

'I said my wife found—'

'You're married?'

'Well . . . yeah. I thought you knew.'

'No.' Her facial muscles felt stiff and inflexible. 'You have failed to mention a Mrs Marcus.'

'Because my marriage has nothing to do with you, with us. It hasn't been a *real* marriage for a long time. Once I've explained my situation at home to you, you'll understand.'

'You're married.' This time it was a statement, not a question.

'Tiel, listen—'

'No, no, I'm not going to listen, Joseph. What I'm going to do is hang up on you.'

The receiver she had been reluctant even to touch she now clung to long after replacing it on the hook. She leaned against the payphone, her forehead pressing against the perforated metal.

Married. He had seemed too good to be true, and he was. Good-looking, charming, friendly, witty, athletic, successful and financially secure Joseph Marcus was married. If not for an airline ticket she would have had an affair with a married man.

She swallowed a surge of nausea and took a moment to compose herself. Later she would lick her wounded ego, berate herself for being a fool, and curse him to hell and back. But right now she had work to do.

Joseph's revelation had left her reeling with disbelief. She was furious beyond measure. She was terribly hurt, but more than anything she was embarrassed by her gullibility. All the more reason not to let the bastard affect her work performance.

Work was her panacea, her life support. When she was happy, she worked. Sad, she worked. Sick, she worked. Work was the cure for all her ills. Work was the remedy for everything . . . even heartbreak so profound you thought you'd die.

She knew that first-hand.

She gathered up her pride, along with her notes on the Dendy story and Gully's directions to Hera, Texas, and ordered herself to mobilise.

Compared to the dimness of the hallway, the fluorescent lighting in the store seemed inordinately bright. The cowboy had left. The elderly couple were browsing through the array of magazines. The two Spanish-speaking men were eating their burritos and talking quietly together.

Tiel sensed their lingering gazes as she went past them on her way to the refrigerated cabinets. One said something to the other that caused him to snicker. It was easy to guess the nature of the comment. Thankfully, her Spanish was rusty.

She slid open the door to the fridge and selected a six-pack of high-voltage cola for the road, before debating whether or not to buy a bag of chocolate-covered caramels. Just because a man she had been dating for weeks had turned out to be married didn't mean she should use that as an excuse to binge. On the other hand, if ever she deserved a treat—

The security camera in the corner of the ceiling exploded, sending pieces of glass and metal flying.

Instinctively Tiel recoiled from the deafening noise. But the camera hadn't exploded on its own. A young man had entered the store and fired a pistol at it. The gunman then aimed his weapon at the cashier, who screeched a high note before the sound seemed to freeze inside her throat.

'This is a holdup,' he said melodramatically, and somewhat need-lessly, since it was apparent what it was.

To the young woman who had accompanied him into the store, he said, 'Sabra, watch the others. If anyone moves, warn me.'

'OK, Ronnie.'

Well, I might die, Tiel thought. *But at least I'll get my story.*

And she wouldn't be going to Hera to get it. It had come to her.

Chapter 2

'YOU!' RONNIE DAVISON pointed the pistol at Tiel. 'Come over here. Lie down on the floor.' Incapable of moving, she only gaped at him. 'Now!'

Dropping her six-pack of colas and her satchel, she scrambled over to the indicated spot and lay face down as instructed. Now that her initial shock had worn off, she bit her tongue to keep from asking him why he was compounding a kidnapping with an armed robbery. Perhaps she shouldn't reveal that she was a reporter and knew his and his accomplice's identities.

'Get over here and lie down,' he ordered the elderly couple. 'You two.' He pointed the gun at the Mexicans. 'Move it!'

The old people complied without argument. The Mexican men remained where they were. 'I'll shoot you if you don't get over here!' Ronnie shouted.

Keeping her head down and addressing her words to the floor, Tiel said, 'They don't speak English.'

'Shut up!'

Ronnie Davison broke the language barrier and made himself understood by motioning with the pistol. Moving slowly, reluctantly, the men joined Tiel and the elderly couple on the floor.

'Put your hands behind your head.'

Tiel and the others did as he asked.

Over the years, Tiel had covered dozens of stories wherein innocent bystanders were found at the scene, lying face down, dead, executed for no other reason except that they had been in the wrong place at the wrong time. Was this to be how her life ended?

Strangely, she wasn't so much afraid as angry. There were goals she had yet to reach. Think of the stories she would miss covering if her life ended now. *Nine Live* would go to Linda Harper by default, and that was so unfair.

And not all her dreams were career-orientated. She and other single friends joked about their biological clocks, but in private she anguished over its incessant tick. If she died tonight, having a child would be just one of many dreams left unfulfilled.

Then there was the other thing. The big thing. The powerful guilt that fuelled her ambition. She hadn't done enough yet to make up for that. She hadn't yet atoned for harsh words spoken angrily and flippantly, which, tragically, had been prophetic. She must live to make restitution for that.

She held her breath, waiting for death.

But Davison's attention was on something else. 'You, in the corner,' the young man shouted. 'Now! Or I'll kill the old folks.'

Tiel raised her head only high enough to glance into the fish-eye mirror mounted in the corner at the ceiling. Her assumption had been wrong. The cowboy hadn't left. She watched him calmly replace a paperback on the revolving rack. As he sauntered down the aisle, he removed his hat and set it on a shelf. Tiel experienced a flurry of recognition, but she attributed it to having seen him when he came into the store.

The eyes he kept trained on Ronnie Davison had a tracery of fine lines at the corners. Unsmiling lips. The face said *Don't mess with me.* Nervously Ronnie shifted the pistol from one hand to the other until the cowboy was stretched out alongside one of the Mexican men, his hands clasped on the back of his head.

While all this was going on, the cashier had been emptying the cash drawer into a plastic grocery bag. From what Tiel could discern, there was an appreciable amount of money in the bag Sabra Dendy took from the cashier.

'I've got the money, Ronnie,' said the daughter of one of Fort Worth's richest men.

'OK then.' He hesitated as though unsure about what to do next. 'You,' he said, addressing the terrified cashier. 'Lie down with the rest of them.'

She might have weighed ninety pounds sopping wet and was a stranger to sunscreen. The skin hanging loosely from her bony arms looked like leather, Tiel noticed as the tiny woman lay down beside her. Little hiccups of terror erupted from her spasmodically.

Everyone had his or her own way of reacting to fear. The elderly couple had disobeyed Ronnie's orders to keep both hands behind their heads. The man's right hand was tightly clasping his wife's left.

This is it, Tiel thought. *He'll kill us now.*

She closed her eyes and tried to pray.

When the scream rent the silence, Tiel thought for certain it had originated from the cashier. She glanced quickly at the woman beside her, to see what unspeakable torture had been inflicted. But the woman was still blubbering, not screaming.

It was Sabra Dendy who had screamed, and that first startling sound was followed by, 'Oh my God! *Ronnie!*'

The boy rushed over to her. 'Sabra? What's the matter? What's happening?'

'I think it's . . . Oh Lord.'

Tiel couldn't help herself. She raised her head to see what was going on. The girl was whimpering and staring aghast at the puddle of fluid between her feet.

'Her water broke.'

Ronnie whipped his head round and glared at Tiel. 'What?'

'Her water broke.' She repeated the statement with more composure than she felt. Actually her heart was hammering. This might be the spark that set him off and caused him to bring things to a swift conclusion, such as shooting them all and then dealing with his girlfriend's crisis.

'That's right, young man.' Unafraid, the elderly woman sat up and addressed him with the temerity she had demonstrated when lecturing her husband about fiddling with the video camera. 'Her baby's coming.'

'Ronnie?' Sabra lowered herself to the floor until she was sitting back on her heels. 'What are we going to do?'

Clearly the girl was frightened. Neither she nor Ronnie seemed adept at armed robbery. Or at childbirth, for that matter. Taking courage from the older lady, Tiel also sat up. 'I suggest—'

'You shut up,' Ronnie shouted. 'Everybody just shut up!'

He kept his pistol aimed at them as he knelt down beside Sabra. 'Are they right? This means the baby's coming?'

'I think so.' She nodded, shaking loose tears and sending them rolling down her cheeks. 'I'm sorry.'

'It's OK. How much time . . . How long before it's born?'

'I don't know. It varies, I think.'

'Does it hurt?'

A fresh batch of tears formed in her eyes. 'It's been hurting for a couple of hours.'

'A couple of hours!' he cried in alarm. 'Why didn't you tell me?'

'If she's been in labour—'

'I told you to shut up!' he yelled at Tiel.

'If she's been in labour for a while,' she said persistently, keeping her eyes steadfastly on his, 'you'd better get medical attention. Immediately.'

'No,' Sabra said hastily. 'I'm OK. I'm—'

A pain seized her. Her face contorted. She gasped for breath.

Ronnie studied Sabra's face, raking his teeth across his lower lip. His gun hand wavered.

One of the Mexican men—the shorter of the two—surged to his feet and lunged towards the couple.

'No!' Tiel shouted.

The cowboy made a grab for the Mexican's leg, but missed.

Ronnie fired the pistol.

The bullet shattered the glass door of the refrigerated compartment, making a horrific sound and puncturing a plastic gallon jug. Everything nearby was showered with glass and milk.

The Mexican man drew up short. Before he came to a complete rest, inertia caused his body to rock slightly forward, then back, as though his boots had become stuck to the floor.

'Stay back or I'll shoot you!' Ronnie's face was congested with blood. A common language wasn't required to get his message across. The man's taller friend spoke to him softly and urgently in Spanish. He backed away until he reached his starting point, then sat down again.

Tiel glared at him. 'Save your machismo for another time, OK? I don't want to get killed because of it.'

Although the words were unknown to him, he caught her drift. His dark eyes smouldered resentment over being dressed down by a woman, but she didn't care.

Tiel turned back to the young couple. Sabra was now lying on her side, her knees drawn up to her chest. For the moment she was quiet.

By contrast, Ronnie looked on the verge of losing all self-control. Tiel didn't believe that, in the span of a single afternoon, he could have been transformed from a student who'd never been in trouble into a cold-blooded killer. She didn't think the boy had it in him to kill anyone, even in self-defence. If he had wanted to hit the man who had charged him, he could have easily. Instead he appeared upset that he'd had to fire the pistol. Tiel guessed that he had intentionally missed the man and fired the gun only to underscore his threat.

Or she could be entirely, terribly wrong.

According to Gully's information, Ronnie Davison came from a broken home. His real father lived far away, so visits couldn't have been too frequent. Ronnie lived with his mother and stepfather. What if little

Ronnie had had a problem with those arrangements? What if he had been concealing murderous impulses as successfully as he and Sabra had concealed her pregnancy? He was desperate, and desperation was a dangerous motivator.

For speaking out, she would probably be the first one he shot. But she couldn't just lie there and die without at least trying to avoid it. 'If you care anything for this girl . . .'

'I've told you before to shut up.'

'I'm only trying to prevent a disaster, Ronnie.' Since he and Sabra had addressed each other, he wouldn't wonder how she knew his name. 'If you don't get help for Sabra, you're going to regret it for the rest of your life. She needs medical assistance.'

'Don't listen to her, Ronnie,' Sabra said weakly. 'I'll be OK if I can just rest for a while.'

'I could take you to a hospital. There's got to be one fairly close.'

'No!' Sabra sat up and gripped his shoulders. 'He'd find out. He'd come after us. No. We're driving straight through to Mexico tonight. Now that we've got some money, we can make it.'

'I could call my dad . . .'

She shook her head. 'Daddy could've got to him by now. Bribed him or something. We're on our own, Ronnie. Let's get out of here.' But as she struggled to get up, another pain seized her and she gripped her distended abdomen.

Before Tiel had time to process the command of her brain, she was on her feet.

'Hey!' Ronnie shouted. 'Get back down.'

Tiel ignored him, moved past him and crouched down beside the suffering girl. 'Sabra?' She took her hand. 'Squeeze my hand until the pain passes. That might help.'

Sabra grasped her hand so hard Tiel feared the bones would be ground to meal. But she endured it, and together they rode out the contraction. When the girl's features began to relax, Tiel whispered, 'Better now?'

'Hmm.' Then with a trace of panic, 'Where's Ronnie?'

'He's right here. I think you should urge him to call nine-one-one for you.'

'No.'

'But you're at risk and so is your baby.'

'He would find us. He'd catch us.'

'Who?' Tiel asked, although she knew. Russell Dendy. He had the reputation of being a ruthless businessman. From what she knew of him, Tiel couldn't imagine him being any less unyielding in his personal relationships.

Ronnie said brusquely, 'Get back with the others, lady. This is none of your business.'

'You made it my business when you waved a pistol at me and threatened my life.'

'Look, lady . . .'

He faltered when a car pulled off the highway and into the parking lot. Its headlights swept the front of the store.

'Damn! Hey, lady!' He walked over to the cashier and nudged her with the toe of his shoe. 'Get up. Turn off the lights and lock the door.'

The woman came to her feet unsteadily. 'I'm not supposed to close until eleven. That's still ten minutes.'

If circumstances hadn't been so tense, Tiel would have laughed at her blind adherence to the rules.

The car rolled to a stop at one of the gas pumps. Ronnie said, 'Do it now. Before he gets out of his car.' She went behind the counter, her mules slapping against her heels. At the flip of a switch, the lights outside were extinguished.

'Now lock the door.'

She click-clacked over to a control panel behind the counter and threw a switch. The cowboy and the two Mexicans were still lying face down on the floor, hands on their heads. They couldn't be seen by the man approaching the door. Tiel and Sabra were also out of sight between two rows of shelves.

Ronnie duckwalked to the elderly lady and grabbed her arm, lifting her to her feet.

'No!' her husband cried. 'Leave her alone.'

'Shut up!' Ronnie ordered. 'If anybody moves, I'm going to shoot her.'

'He's not going to shoot me, Vern,' she said to her husband. 'I'll be all right, as long as everyone stays calm.'

The woman followed Ronnie's instructions and crouched down with him behind a cylindrical cold-drink cooler. From above the rim, he had a clear view to the door.

The customer tested the door, discovered it locked, and called out. 'Donna! You in there? How come you shut off the lights?'

Donna, cringing behind the counter, remained mute.

The customer peered through the glass. 'There you are,' he said, spotting her. 'What gives?'

'Answer him,' Ronnie instructed her in a whisper.

'I'm . . . s-sick,' she said, loud enough to carry through the door.

'Open up. All I need is ten dollars' worth o' gas and a six-pack o' Miller Lite.'

'I cain't,' she called out tearfully.

'Come on, Donna. It ain't quite 'leven yet. Open the door.'

'I cain't.' She unravelled at the same time her voice rose to a fully fledged scream. 'He's gotta gun and he's gonna kill us all.' She dropped down behind the counter.

Tiel was thinking that if Ronnie didn't shoot Donna the cashier, she just might.

The man at the door backed away, then stumbled as he turned and ran for his car. Tyres screeched as the vehicle shot backwards, then spun round and pulled onto the highway.

The old man was chanting, 'Don't hurt my wife. I beg you, please don't hurt Gladys. Don't hurt my Gladys.'

'Hush, Vern. I'm all right.'

Ronnie was angrily yelling at Donna. 'Why'd you do that? That guy will call the police. We'll be trapped here.'

His voice was tearing with frustration and fear. Tiel thought that he was probably as scared as the rest of them.

The girl was in the grip of another contraction. 'Squeeze my hand, Sabra. Breathe.' Isn't that what women in labour were supposed to do?

'Hey! Hey!' Ronnie shouted suddenly. 'Where do you think you're going? Get back over there and lie down. Hey, *I mean it!*'

Now wasn't the time to be provoking the rattled young man, and Tiel intended to tell whoever was doing so to cut it out. She glanced up, but the reproach died unspoken when the cowboy knelt down on the other side of Sabra.

'Get away from her!' Ronnie jammed the barrel of the pistol against the cowboy's temple, but it was ignored and so were the young man's shouted threats. Hands that looked accustomed to handling tack and fence posts were placed on the girl's abdomen. They kneaded it gently.

'I can help her.' His voice was scratchy, like he hadn't spoken in a long time. He looked up at Ronnie. 'They call me Doc.'

'You're a doctor?' Tiel asked.

His calm gaze moved to her, and he repeated, 'I can help her.'

Chapter 3

'YOU ARE NOT touching her,' Ronnie said fiercely.

The man called Doc continued to press the girl's abdomen. 'She's in the first or second stage of labour. Without knowing how much she's dilated, it's hard to gauge how close she is to delivering. But her pains are coming frequently, so I'm guessing—'

'Guessing?'

Ignoring Ronnie, Doc patted Sabra's shoulder reassuringly. 'Is this your first baby?'

'Yes, sir.'

'You can call me Doc. How long since you first started noticing the pains?'

'At first I just felt funny, you know? Well, I guess you don't.'

He smiled. 'I have no personal experience of it, no. Describe to me how it felt.'

'Like right before a period. Sort of.'

'Pressure down there? And twinges like a bad case of cramps?'

'Yes. Real bad. And a backache. I thought I was just tired from riding in the pick-up so long, but it got worse.' Her eyes moved to Ronnie, who was hovering over Doc's broad shoulders. He was hanging on every word, but he kept the pistol trained on the people who were lined up like matchsticks on the floor.

'When did these symptoms start?' Doc asked.

'About three o'clock this afternoon.'

Ronnie groaned. 'Eight hours? Why didn't you tell me?'

Her eyes began to fill with tears again. 'Because it would have ruined our plans. I wanted to be with you no matter what.'

'Shh.' Tiel patted her hand. 'Crying will only make you feel worse. Think about the baby coming. It can't be much longer now.' She looked across at Doc. 'Can it?'

'Hard to say with first babies.'

'Your best guess?'

'Two, three hours.' He stood up and faced off with Ronnie. 'She's going to deliver tonight. She needs a hospital, a delivery room and medical personnel. The baby will also need attention immediately after it's born. That's the situation. What are you going to do about it?'

Sabra cried out with another pain. Doc dropped down beside her and monitored the contraction by placing his hands on her abdomen. The steep frown between his eyebrows alerted Tiel to trouble. 'What?' she asked.

He shook his head, indicating that he didn't want to discuss it in front of the girl. But Sabra Dendy was no dummy. She picked up on his concern. 'Something's wrong, isn't it?'

To his credit, Doc didn't talk down to her. 'Not wrong, Sabra. Just more complicated. Do you know what breech means?'

'That's when the baby . . .' Sabra paused to swallow hard. 'When the baby is upside down.'

He nodded. 'I think your baby is in the wrong position.'

She began to whimper. 'What can you do?'

'Sometimes it isn't necessary to do anything. The baby will turn on its own.'

'What's the worst that can happen?'

Doc looked up at Ronnie, who'd asked the question. 'A Caesarean section is done, sparing the mother and child a gruelling, possibly life-threatening delivery. Knowing that, will you let someone call nine-one-one and get Sabra some help?'

'No!' the girl cried. 'I won't go to a hospital. I won't!'

Doc took her hand. 'Your baby could die, Sabra.'

'You can help me.'

'I'm not equipped.'

'Sabra, please listen to him,' Tiel urged. 'He knows what he's talking about. Take Doc's advice. Let us call nine-one-one.'

'No,' she said, shaking her head stubbornly. 'You don't understand. My daddy swore that neither I nor Ronnie would ever see our baby after it's born. He's going to give it away. He said the baby would mean no more to him than an unwanted puppy he would take to the dog pound. When he says something, he means it. He'll take our baby, and we'll never see it. He'll keep us apart too. He said he would, and he will.' She began to sob.

'Oh my,' Gladys murmured. 'Poor things.'

Tiel glanced over her shoulder at the others. Vern and Gladys were sitting up now, huddled together, his arms protectively round her. Both were looking on sorrowfully.

The two Mexican men were talking softly together, their hostile eyes darting about. Tiel hoped they weren't plotting another attempt to overthrow Ronnie. Donna, the cashier, was still lying on the floor face down, but she muttered, 'Poor things, my ass. Almost killed me.'

Ronnie, having reached a decision, looked at Doc and said, 'Sabra wants you to help her.'

He looked as though he were about to argue. Then, maybe because time was a factor, he changed his mind. 'All right. For the time being, I'll do what I can, starting with an internal examination.'

'You mean her . . .'

'Yes. That's what I mean. I need to know how far the labour has progressed. Find something for me to sterilise my hands with.'

'I've got some antibacterial hand wash,' Tiel told him.

'Good. Thanks.'

She made to get up, but Ronnie halted her. 'Get it and come right back. Remember, I'm watching.'

She returned to the spot where she had dropped her satchel and retrieved the plastic container of hand wash. Then, getting Vern's attention, she mimicked holding a video camera up to her eye. At first he looked perplexed, but Gladys nudged him in the ribs and whispered in his ear. Nodding vigorously, he hitched his chin in the direction of the magazine rack. Tiel remembered that they had been browsing there when the robbery commenced.

She returned with the bottle of hand wash and handed it to Doc. 'Shouldn't she have something beneath her?'

'We've got some bed pads in the RV.'

'Gladys!' Vern exclaimed, mortified by his wife's admission.

'They would be perfect,' Tiel said, remembering the disposable protective pads she'd seen on Uncle Pete's bed in the nursing home. They prevented the staff from having to change the bedding each time a resident had an accident. 'I'll go get them.'

'Not you,' Ronnie said. 'But the old man can go. She,' he added, pointing the pistol at Gladys, 'stays here.'

Vern levered his rickety body up off the floor, dusted off his shorts and moved to the door. 'Well, I can't walk through glass.'

Ronnie instructed Donna to unlock the door, which she did.

At the door Ronnie and the elderly man exchanged a meaningful look. 'Don't worry, I'll be back,' the old man assured him. 'I wouldn't do anything to jeopardise my wife's life.' And, although Ronnie Davison was fifty pounds heavier and half a foot taller, he issued him a warning. 'If you harm her, I'll kill you.'

Ronnie pushed open the door and Vern slipped through. His attempt at a jog was unintentionally comical. Tiel watched his progress across the parking lot until he reached the Winnebago.

She looked at Doc. 'What else would be helpful to you?'

'Gloves. Some vinegar. And gauze. And a packet of disposable baby wipes.'

'Standard distilled vinegar?'

'Yes.' After a brief pause, he remarked, 'You're awfully cool under pressure.'

'Thanks.' They watched the girl, who, for the moment, seemed to be asleep. Tiel asked softly, 'Is this going to end badly?'

His lips compressed into a grim line. 'Not if I can help it.'

'Hey, what are you two whispering about?'

Tiel looked up at Ronnie. 'Doc needs some gloves. I was about to ask Donna if the store stocks them.'

'OK, go ahead.'

She left Sabra's side and moved to the counter. Donna was standing behind it, waiting to unlock the door when Vern returned. She regarded Tiel suspiciously. 'What do you want?'

'Donna, please remain calm. Hysteria will only worsen the situation. For the time being we're all safe.'

'Safe? Ha!'

'Do you carry any latex gloves in the store? The kind a doctor wears.'

She shook her frizzy, permed head. 'Dishwashing gloves. That's it. Over with the household cleansers.'

'Thanks. Stay cool, Donna.'

As Tiel moved past Gladys, she leaned down and whispered, 'Is there a tape in your video camera?'

The old lady nodded. 'Two hours' worth. Rewound, too.'

'If I can get it to you—'

'Hey!' Ronnie shouted. 'What are you whispering about now?'

'She's afraid for her husband. I was reassuring her.'

'There he is now,' Gladys said, pointing at the door.

Donna threw the bolt and Vern came tottering in. From his Winnebago, in addition to the pads he'd gone for, Vern had brought two pillows, two quilts, two clean bedsheets and several bath towels. Ronnie gave the go-ahead for Tiel to make a pallet, which she did while Sabra leaned heavily against Doc.

Tiel used only one of the sheets, saving the spare for later, should the need for it arise. When she was finished, Doc laid the girl down on the bedding. She settled on it gratefully. Tiel placed one of the disposable pads beneath her hips.

Tiel then asked Ronnie's permission to shop the aisles, where she found several bottles of vinegar, a box of sterile gauze pads and a packet of disposable baby wipes. She gathered them up. She also managed to pass the tote bag back to Vern and Gladys without Ronnie noticing.

When she got back to Sabra, she was listening intently to what Doc was telling her.

'It won't be comfortable, but I'll try not to hurt you, OK?'

The girl nodded and glanced apprehensively at Tiel.

'Have you ever had a pelvic exam, Sabra?' she asked softly.

'Once.'

'Well, then, you know what to expect.' Tiel gave the girl's hand a quick squeeze. 'I'll be right over there if you—'

'No, stay here with me. Please.'

Tiel could tell by Sabra's grimace that she was in the throes of another pain. 'Doc?'

He was there in an instant, pressing his hands on the mound of her stomach. 'Sure wish he'd turn on his own.'

'I'm hoping for a girl,' Sabra told him on gasping breaths.

Doc smiled. 'Really.'

'Ronnie would like a girl too.'

'Daughters are great, all right.'

Tiel stole a glance at him. Did he have daughters? She'd taken him for a bachelor, a loner. Maybe because he looked like the Marlboro man. You never saw the Marlboro man with a wife and family in tow.

Tiel couldn't shake the feeling that she'd seen Doc somewhere before. His resemblance to the rugged models in the cigarette ads must be why he looked vaguely familiar.

When the pain passed, Doc placed his hands on the girl's raised knees. 'Try and relax as much as possible. And let me know if I'm hurting you, OK?'

'This might help.' For modesty's sake, Tiel spread the second sheet over the girl's knees.

Doc gave her an approving glance. 'Just relax, Sabra. It'll be over before you know it.'

'OK,' she replied timorously.

Tiel found herself holding her own breath. 'Breathe deeply, Sabra. It'll help you relax. You're doing great.'

But she wasn't. Doc's expression told her as much. He withdrew his hand from between the girl's thighs and, hiding his concern, bragged on how well she'd done. He took off the gloves and reached for the bottle of hand wash, rubbing it vigorously onto his hands and forearms.

'Is everything all right?'

It was Ronnie who had asked the question, but Doc addressed his answer to Sabra. 'You haven't dilated much.'

'What does that mean?'

'As hard and frequent as your pains are, your cervix should be dilated more than it is. The baby is trying to push its way out, but not all the parts of your body are ready for the birth.'

'What can you do?' Ronnie asked.

'I can't do anything, Ronnie, but you can. You can stop this foolishness and get Sabra to a facility where she'll receive proper obstetric care.'

'I already told you, no.'

'No,' Sabra repeated.

Before there could be any further argument, the telephone rang.

The unexpected, shrill sound startled everyone.

Donna was nearest to the ringing telephone. 'What should I do?' she asked.

'Nothing.'

'Ronnie, maybe you should let her answer it,' Tiel suggested. 'Don't you want to know what you're up against?'

He mulled it over for several seconds, then gave Donna the go-ahead to answer.

'Hello?' She listened for a moment, then said, 'Hi, Sheriff. No, he weren't drunk. Just like he told you, this kid here has got us held at gunpoint.'

Suddenly the front of the building was bathed in brilliant light. Everyone inside had been so focused on Sabra's condition that no one had heard the approach of the three squad cars, which had now flashed on their headlights.

Ronnie ducked behind a crisps display, yelling, 'Tell them to turn off those damn lights or I'm going to shoot somebody.'

Donna relayed the message. She paused to listen, then said, 'About eighteen, I'd guess. Calls hisself Ronnie.'

'Shut up!' Ronnie brandished the pistol at her. She screeched and dropped the receiver. The car lights went out.

Sabra moaned.

Doc said, 'Ronnie, listen to me.'

'No. Be quiet and let me think.'

The young man was flustered, but Doc persisted in a low, earnest voice. 'Stay here and see this thing through if you like. But the manly thing to do would be to let Sabra leave.'

'I won't go,' the girl said. 'Not without Ronnie.'

Tiel appealed to her. 'Think of your baby, Sabra.'

'I am thinking of our baby,' she sobbed. 'If my daddy gets his hands on the baby, I'll never see it again. I won't give it up. I won't give Ronnie up, either.'

Seeing that his patient was close to hysteria, Doc relented. 'OK, OK. What if a doctor were to come here?'

'You're a doctor,' Ronnie argued.

'Not the kind Sabra needs. I don't have any instruments. I've got nothing to give her to relieve the pain. This is going to be a difficult delivery, Ronnie. There could be serious complications. Are you willing to risk Sabra's life as well as the child's? You could lose one or both of them. Then, no matter how it pans out, it will all have been for nothing.'

The young man gnawed on Doc's words for a minute, then motioned Tiel towards the counter and the dangling telephone receiver. For several moments after Donna had dropped it, a man's voice could be heard, demanding to know what was going on. Now, it was silent.

'You do the talking,' Ronnie said to Tiel.

She came to her feet and wasted no time calling nine-one-one. As soon as the operator answered, she said, 'I need the sheriff to call me. Tell him to call the convenience store back.' She hung up before the operator could proceed with the routine drill.

Although she'd been expecting the telephone to ring, she jumped when it did. She answered it immediately. 'Sheriff?'

'Marty Montez.'

'Sheriff Montez, I've been appointed spokesperson. I'm one of the hostages.'

'Are you in immediate danger?'

'No,' she replied, believing it.

'Give me a run-down.'

She began with a brief and concise account of the robbery, starting with Ronnie's shooting out the security camera. 'It was interrupted when his accomplice went into labour.'

'Labour? You mean labour like having a baby?'

'Exactly like that, yes.'

After a pause, he said, 'Are these robbers by any chance a coupla high-school kids?'

'Yes.'

'What's he asking?' Ronnie demanded to know.

Tiel covered the receiver with her palm. 'He asked if Sabra was in pain and I answered.'

'Jee-sus,' the sheriff exclaimed in a near whistle. In a low voice he passed along to his deputies—or so Tiel assumed—that the hostage-takers were the kids 'outta Fort Worth'. Then to her, he asked, 'Is anybody hurt?'

'No. We're all unharmed.'

'Who-all's in there with you? How many hostages?'

'Four men and two women besides myself.'

'You're a smooth talker. You wouldn't by any chance be a Ms McCoy?'

She tried to hide her surprise from Ronnie, who was listening to her intently and closely monitoring her facial expressions. 'That's correct. No one has been wounded.'

'You are Ms McCoy, but you don't want 'em to know you're a TV reporter? I see. Your boss, guy name o' Gully, he's called my office twice, demanding we put out an APB for you. Said you started from Rojo Flats and was supposed to call him—'

'What's he saying?' Ronnie asked.

She interrupted the sheriff. 'It would be in everyone's best interest if you could provide us with a doctor. An OB if possible.'

'Be sure he knows that the baby is in a breech position,' Doc added.

Tiel relayed Doc's message. The sheriff asked who she was getting her information from. 'He goes by Doc.'

'You're kidding me,' he said. 'Doc's one of the hostages,' she heard him pass along. 'Doc says the Dendy girl needs a specialist, huh?'

'That's right, Sheriff. And as soon as possible.'

'If they surrender, we'll get her to a hospital pronto.'

'I'm afraid that's not a contingency.'

'Davison won't let her go?'

'No,' Tiel said. 'She refuses to leave.'

'What a mess,' he expelled on a heavy sigh. 'OK, I'll see what I can do.'

'Sheriff, I can't impress on you enough how badly this young woman is suffering. And . . .'

'Go ahead, Ms McCoy. What?'

'The situation is under control,' she said slowly. 'Please don't take any drastic measures. So far, no one has been injured.'

'And we'd all like to keep it that way.'

'I'm very glad to hear you say that. Please, get a doctor here as quickly as you can.'

'I'm on it. Here's the number of the phone I've got with me.'

She committed the number to memory. Montez wished her luck and hung up.

'He's working on getting a doctor here.'

'I like the sound of that,' Doc said.

'How soon before he gets here?'

Turning to Ronnie, she replied, 'As soon as possible. I'm going to be honest with you. He guessed your and Sabra's identity.'

'Oh hell,' the boy groaned. 'What else can go wrong?'

'**T**hey've been located!'

Russell Dendy nearly knocked down the FBI agent who happened to be standing in his path when the shout came from the adjacent room. He barrelled into the library of his home, which, since that morning, had been converted into a command post.

'Where? Where are they? Is Sabra all right?'

Special Agent William Calloway was in charge. He was a tall, thin, balding man who, if not for the pistol riding in the small of his back, looked more like a mortgage banker than a federal agent. He was calm and soft-spoken—most of the time. Russell Dendy had put Calloway's pleasant disposition to the test.

As Dendy stalked into the room blurting questions, Calloway signalled for him to pipe down and continued his telephone conversation.

Dendy impatiently punched a button on the telephone and a woman's voice filtered through the speaker. 'It's called Rojo Flats. Practically in the middle of nowhere, west-southwest of San Angelo.

They're armed. They tried to rob a convenience store. Now they're holding hostages inside the store.'

'Damn him!' Dendy ground his fist into his opposite palm. 'He's turned my daughter into a common criminal! And she couldn't understand why I objected to him?'

Calloway once again signalled him to keep his voice down. 'You said they're armed. Are there any casualties?'

'No, sir. But the girl is in labour.'

'Inside the store?'

'Affirmative.'

Dendy cursed lavishly. 'He's holding her against her will!'

The disembodied voice said, 'According to one of the hostages who spoke to the sheriff, the young woman refuses to leave.'

'He's brainwashed her,' Dendy declared.

The woman continued as though she hadn't heard him. 'One of the hostages apparently has some medical knowledge. He's seeing to her, but a doctor has been requested.'

Dendy thumped the top of his desk with his fist. 'I want Sabra the hell out of there, do you hear me?'

'We hear you, Mr Dendy,' Calloway said with diminishing patience.

'I don't care if you have to blast her out of there with dynamite.'

'Well, I care. According to the spokesperson, no one has been injured.'

'My daughter's in labour!'

'And we'll get her to a hospital as soon as possible. But I'm not going to do anything that will endanger the lives of those hostages, your daughter or Mr Davison.'

'Look, Calloway, if you're going to take a limp-wristed approach to this situation—'

'The approach I take is my call, not yours. Is that understood?'

From the start Calloway had doubted Dendy's allegation of a kidnapping. Instead he leaned heavily towards the more viable version: Sabra Dendy had run away from home with her boyfriend in order to escape her domineering father.

Russell Dendy wasn't accustomed to giving anyone else a vote in the way things were managed. His businesses weren't democracies, and neither was his family. Mrs Dendy had done nothing all day except weep and second her husband's answers to the agents' probing questions about their relationship with their daughter. Russ Dendy was practically spitting with fury. 'I'm on my way out there.'

'There's no room in our chopper for extra passengers,' the agent called to Dendy's retreating back.

'Then I'll take my Lear.'

He stormed from the room and began shouting orders.

Calloway disengaged the speaker phone and picked up the receiver, so he could hear the other agent more clearly. 'Guess you heard all that.'

'You've got your hands full, Calloway.'

'And then some. How're the locals out there?'

'Montez is a competent sheriff, but he's in way over his head and is smart enough to know it. He'll probably be glad to land the problem in our lap. He wants to avoid bloodshed.'

'Then he and I are on the same page. I think what we've got here is a couple of kids who've got themselves in a situation and can't find a way out. Do you know anything about the hostages?'

She gave him the breakdown by gender. 'One's been identified by Sheriff Montez as a local rancher. The cashier is a fixture at the convenience store. Everybody in Rojo Flats knows her. And that Ms McCoy who talked to Sheriff Montez?'

'What about her?'

'She's a reporter for a TV station in Dallas.'

'Tiel McCoy?'

'So you know her?'

He knew her and mentally formed an image: slender, with short blonde hair, light eyes. Blue, possibly green. She was on TV nearly every night. Calloway had also seen her at the scenes of crimes he'd investigated. He wasn't thrilled to hear that a broadcast journalist of her calibre was at the epicentre of this crisis. It was a compounding factor he could have done without.

'Great. A reporter is already on the scene.' He ran his hand round the back of his neck, where tension had begun to gather. It was going to be a long night.

The other agent asked, 'Gut instinct, Calloway. Did that boy kidnap the Dendy girl?'

Beneath his breath, Calloway muttered, 'I only wonder why it took her so long to run away.'

While they waited for the promised doctor to arrive, Doc gleaned a pair of scissors and a pair of shoelaces from the store's stock. He placed them to boil in a carafe usually used for water with which to mix instant hot drinks. He also took from the shelves sanitary napkins, adhesive tape and a box of plastic garbage bags.

Following that activity, the wait grew to be interminable. Everyone inside the store was aware of the increasing number of arriving emergency vehicles. They hadn't arrived running hot, but the absence of flashing lights and sirens made their presence even more ominous.

Tiel wondered if the back of the building was seeing as much activity as the front. Obviously that possibility occurred to Ronnie, too, because he asked Donna about a rear door.

'It's steel and bolted from the inside. It has a bar across it, and the hinges are on the inside, too.'

No one would be coming through the rear door silently.

That worry laid to rest, Ronnie divided his attention among Sabra, his hostages and the increasing movement outside, which was more than enough to keep him occupied. Tiel asked Ronnie if she could get into her satchel. 'My contacts are dry. I need my wetting solution.'

'OK. But I'm watching you. Don't think I'm not.'

She moved to the counter where Ronnie could see her digging into her satchel in search of the small vial of solution. She uncapped it and tilted her head back to apply the drops. 'Damn,' she cursed softly, holding a finger over her eye. She then removed her contact lens, dug around in her bag for another bottle of solution and proceeded to clean the lens in a small pool of solution in her palm.

Without turning to look at Gladys and Vern, she spoke to them in a whisper. 'Does your camera have batteries in it?'

Vern—bless him—was inspecting a loose cuticle on his left hand and looking about as conspiratorial as an altar boy. 'Yes, ma'am.'

Gladys added, 'It's all set to go. Get ready. We've got a distraction planned.'

'Wait—'

Before Tiel could finish, Vern went into a fit of coughing. Gladys leapt up, tossed their tote bag onto the counter within Tiel's reach, then started whacking her husband hard between his shoulder blades. 'Oh, Vern, not one of your strangling spells.'

Tiel popped in her contact and blinked it into place. Then, as everyone including Ronnie was watching the old man gasp and gurgle in an effort to regain his breath while Gladys smacked away as though beating a rug, she reached into the tote bag for the camera.

She flipped it on and punched the Record button. She then set it on a shelf, wedging it between cartons of cigarettes and praying it wouldn't be noticed.

Vern's coughs subsided. Gladys asked Ronnie's permission to get a bottle of water for him.

Tiel replaced the contact-lens cleaner and wetting solution in her bag and was about to withdraw her hand when she spotted her tiny audiocassette recorder. She hadn't intentionally brought it along. It was a tool of her trade, not a vacation item. But there it was, buried in the bottom of her bag.

She palmed the recording device and slipped it into the pocket of her trousers just as Sabra gave a sharp cry. Frantically, Ronnie looked around for Tiel. 'I'm coming,' she told him.

Giving the elderly thespians a thumbs up as she stepped round them, she rushed back to Sabra's side.

Doc looked worried. 'Her pains have slowed down somewhat, but when she has one it's acute. Where the hell is that doctor?'

Tiel blotted Sabra's sweating forehead with a pad of gauze she had moistened with cool drinking water. 'When he—or she—does get here, how effective can he be?'

'Let's just hope he has some experience with breech births. Or maybe he'll be able to convince Ronnie and Sabra that a C-section is mandatory.'

'And if neither is the case . . .'

'Maybe the baby will turn on its own. That happens.'

Tiel stroked the girl's head. Sabra appeared to be dozing. The final stages of labour hadn't even begun and already she was exhausted. 'It's good she can take these short naps.'

'Her body knows that later it'll need all the strength it can muster.'

'I wish she didn't have to suffer.'

'The doctor can give her an injection to relieve the pain. But the closer she gets to delivery, the greater the risk of giving her drugs.'

His fingers loosely encircled Sabra's wrist, as his thumb pressed her pulse point. 'I wish I had a blood-pressure cuff. And a foetoscope to monitor the foetal heartbeat.'

'Where did you get your medical training?'

'What really concerns me,' he said, ignoring her question, 'is whether or not he'll perform an episiotomy. It won't be pleasant, but if he doesn't, she could easily tear and that'll be even more unpleasant.'

'You're doing my nerves no good, Doc.'

He raised his head and looked across at her. 'I'm glad you're here.'

His look was intense, the eyes compelling, but she didn't look away. 'I'm not doing anything constructive.'

'Simply being with her is doing a lot. When she's having a pain, encourage her not to fight it. Tensing the muscles and tissue surrounding the uterus only increases the discomfort. The uterus was made to contract. She should let it go about its business.'

'Easy for you to say.'

'Easy for me to say,' he conceded with a wry smile. 'Breathe with her. Inhale through the nose, exhale through the mouth.'

'Those deep breaths will help me, too.'

'You're doing fine. She feels comfortable with you. You neutralise her shyness.'

'She admitted to being shy with you.'

'Understandable. She's very young.'

'She said you don't look like a doctor.'

'No, I don't suppose I do.'

'Are you?'

'Rancher.'

'You're a real cowboy then?'

'I breed horses, run a herd of beef cattle. I drive a pick-up truck. I guess that makes me a cowboy.'

'Then where'd you learn—'

The ringing of the telephone brought their private conversation to a halt and woke Sabra up. Ronnie snatched up the receiver. 'Hello? I'm Ronnie Davison. Where's the doctor?'

He paused to listen, and Tiel could tell by his expression that he was hearing something that distressed him. 'FBI? How come?' Then he blurted, 'But I didn't kidnap her, Mr Calloway! We were eloping. Yes, sir, she's my main concern too. No. She refuses to go to a hospital.'

He listened longer, then glanced at Sabra. 'OK. If the phone'll reach.' He stretched the cord as far as it would go. 'The FBI agent wants to talk to you.'

Doc said, 'It won't hurt her to stand up. In fact, it might do her good.'

He and Tiel supported Sabra beneath the arms and together assisted her to her feet. She baby-stepped far enough to take the extended receiver from Ronnie.

'Hello? No, sir. What Ronnie told you is true. I'm not leaving without him. Not even to go to the hospital. My daddy said he'll take away my baby, and he always does what he says.' She sniffed back tears. 'Of course I came with Ronnie voluntarily. I—' She caught her breath and gripped a handful of Doc's shirt.

He lifted her and carried her back to the makeshift birthing bed. Tiel knelt beside her and, as Doc had instructed, coaxed Sabra to relax, not to fight the contraction and to breathe.

Ronnie was speaking anxiously into the telephone. 'Listen here, Mr Calloway, Sabra can't talk any more. Where's the doctor we were promised?' He glanced through the plate glass. 'Yeah, I see him. You bet I'll let him in.'

Ronnie slammed down the receiver and dropped the phone back onto the counter. 'Cashier, wait until he's at the door before you unlock it. Then, as soon as he comes through, relock it.'

Donna waited until the doctor was pushing on the door before she flipped the switch. He came inside, and everyone in the store heard the metallic click when the door relocked.

Nervously the young doctor glanced over his shoulder at it before introducing himself. 'I'm, uh, Dr Cain. Scott.'

'Move over here.'

Dr Scott Cain was a handsome man of medium height and build, in his early to mid-thirties. Wide-eyed, he scanned the people huddled in a group in front of the counter. 'Never would've guessed I'd be called in on an emergency like this.'

Doc motioned him towards the girl. 'Is it OK?' Cain asked Ronnie, glancing fearfully at the pistol.

'Open up your bag.'

'Oh, sure.' He unlatched the black valise and held it open for Ronnie's inspection.

'OK, go ahead. Help her, please. She's in a bad way.'

'It would seem so,' the doctor remarked as a contraction seized Sabra and she moaned.

Doc was providing the doctor with pertinent information. 'She's seventeen. This is her first child. First pregnancy.' They took up positions near the girl, Doc on Sabra's right side, Dr Cain at her feet, Tiel on her left.

'How long has she been in labour?'

'Preliminary contractions started midafternoon. Her water broke about two hours ago. Pains escalated sharply after that, then for the last half-hour they've tapered off.'

'Hi, Sabra,' the doctor said to the girl.

'Hi.'

He placed his hands on her stomach and examined the mound with light squeezes.

'Breech, right?' Doc asked, seeking confirmation of his diagnosis.

'Right.'

'Do you think you can turn the foetus?'

'That's very tricky.'

'Do you have experience in breech births?'

'I've assisted.'

That wasn't the hoped-for answer. Doc asked, 'Did you bring a blood-pressure cuff?'

'In my bag.'

The doctor continued to examine Sabra by gently probing her abdomen. Doc extended the blood-pressure cuff to him, but he declined to take it. He was speaking to Sabra. 'Just relax, and everything will be all right.'

She glanced at Ronnie and smiled hopefully. 'How long before the baby comes, Dr Cain?'

'That's hard to say. Babies have a mind of their own. I would prefer taking you to the hospital while there's still time.'

'I can't leave on account of my father.'

'He's very worried about you, Sabra. In fact, he's outside. He told me to tell you—'

Her whole body jerked as though having a muscle spasm. 'Daddy's here?' Her voice was panicked. 'Ronnie?'

The news upset him as much as it had Sabra. 'How'd he get here?'

Tiel patted the girl's shoulder. 'It's OK. Don't think about your father now. Think about your baby. That's all you should be concerned with. Everything else will work out.'

Sabra began to cry.

Doc leaned towards the doctor and whispered angrily, 'Why'n hell did you tell her that? Couldn't that news have waited?'

Dr Cain looked confused. 'I thought she would be comforted to know that her father was here. They didn't have time to fill me in on all the details of the situation. I didn't know that information was going to upset her.'

Doc was so angry his thin lips barely moved when he spoke. But knowing that any outward display of anger would only make the situation worse, he remained focused on the business at hand. 'She hadn't dilated much when I examined her.'

The doctor nodded. 'How much? Was she dilated, I mean.'

'About eight, ten centimetres.'

'Hmm.'

'You son of a bitch.'

Doc's low growl brought Tiel's head up with a snap. Had she heard him correctly? Apparently so, because Dr Cain was regarding him with consternation.

What happened next was for ever after a blur in Tiel's memory.

Chapter 4

THE FBI VAN PARKED on the apron of concrete between the highway and the fuel pumps was equipped with high-tech paraphernalia used for deployment, surveillance and communication. It had arrived within minutes of Calloway's chopper from Fort Worth.

Dendy's private jet had flown to Odessa, where a charter helicopter had been standing by to whisk him to Rojo Flats. Upon his arrival, he had barged into the van, demanding to know exactly what the situation was and how Calloway planned to remedy it.

Dendy had made a general nuisance of himself, and Calloway had had all he could stomach of the millionaire even before Dendy began grilling him over the manoeuvre presently under way.

Every eye was on the television monitor, which was transmitting a live picture from a camera outside. They watched Cain enter the store, where he stood with his back to the door for a time before disappearing from view.

'Doc's no fool,' said Montez. 'You're asking for trouble, sending that rookie in there.'

'Thank you, Sheriff Montez,' Calloway said stiffly.

Then, as though Montez's statement had been prophetic, they heard gunshots. Two came a millisecond apart, one more several seconds later. Everyone inside the van began speaking at once.

The camera was showing them nothing. Calloway grabbed a headset so he could hear the communiqués between the men in position in front of the store.

'Were those gunshots?' Dendy asked. 'What's happening, Calloway? You said my daughter wouldn't be in any danger!'

Over his shoulder, Calloway shouted, 'Sit down and be quiet, Mr Dendy, or I'm going to have you removed from this van.'

Calloway left the overwrought father to his subordinates and turned back to the console.

Tiel had watched with disbelief as Dr Scott Cain yanked a pistol from an ankle holster and pointed it at Ronnie. 'FBI! Drop the weapon!'

Sabra had screamed.

Doc had continued to swear at Cain. 'All this time we've been waiting on a *doctor!*' he shouted. 'Instead we get you! What kind of stupid stunt is this?' The veins in Doc's neck had bulged with anger. 'That girl's in life-threatening trouble. Don't any of you federal bastards get it?'

Tiel had surged to her feet, begging, 'No, please no. Don't shoot.' She had feared she was about to see Ronnie Davison blown away right before her eyes.

'You're not a doctor?' the frantic young man had shrieked. 'They promised us a doctor. Sabra needs a doctor.'

'Drop your weapon, Davison! Now!'

'Ronnie, do as he says,' Tiel had implored.

'No, Ronnie, don't!' Sabra had sobbed. 'Daddy's out there.'

'Why don't you both put down your pistols.' Doc had regained some composure. 'We can all be reasonable, can't we?'

'No.' Ronnie, resolute, had clutched the pistol grip tighter. 'Mr Dendy will have me arrested. I'll never see Sabra again.'

'Maybe not,' Doc had argued. 'Maybe—'

'I'm giving you to the count of three to drop your weapon!' Cain had shouted, his voice cracking. He, too, it seemed, was cracking under pressure. 'One.'

'Why'd you trick us? My girlfriend is suffering. She needs a doctor.'

Tiel hadn't liked the way Ronnie's index finger was tensing round the trigger.

'Two.'

'I said no! I won't give her up to Mr Dendy.'

Just as Cain shouted 'Three' and fired his pistol, Tiel grabbed a can of chilli from the shelf nearest her and clouted him over the head with it.

He had dropped like a sack of cement. His shot went wide of his target, which had been Ronnie's chest, but it came within a hair's-breadth of Doc before striking the counter.

Reflexively Ronnie had fired his gun. The only damage that bullet did was to knock a chunk of plaster out of the far wall.

Donna had screamed, hit the floor and covered her head with her hands, then continued screaming.

In the resulting confusion, the Mexican men had surged forward, nearly trampling Vern and Gladys in their haste.

Tiel, realising that they intended to take the agent's pistol, had kicked it beneath a freezer chest out of reach.

'Get back! Get back!' Ronnie had shouted at them. He fired again for emphasis, but aimed well above their heads.

Now they all remained in a frozen tableau, waiting to see what happened next, who would be the first to move, to speak.

It turned out to be Doc. 'Do as he says,' he ordered the two Mexicans. He held up his left hand, palm out, signalling them to move back. His right hand was clamped over his left shoulder. Blood leaked through his fingers.

'You're shot!' Tiel exclaimed.

Ignoring her, he reasoned with the two Mexican men, who were obviously reluctant to comply. 'If you go charging through that door, you're liable to get a belly full of bullets.'

They understood only Doc's insistence that they remain where they were. They rebuked him in rapid-fire Spanish. However, the two did as Doc asked and skulked back to their original positions, muttering to each other and throwing hostile glares all around. Ronnie kept his pistol trained on them.

Donna was making more racket than Sabra, who was clenching her teeth to keep from crying out as a labour pain seized her. Doc ordered the cashier to stop making the godawful noise.

'I'm not gonna live to see morning,' she wailed.

'The way our luck's going, you probably will,' Gladys snapped. 'Now *shut up.*'

Donna's crying ceased instantly.

'Hang in there, sweetheart.' Tiel had resumed her place at Sabra's side and was holding her hand through the contraction.

'I knew . . .' Sabra paused to pant several times. 'I knew Daddy wouldn't leave it alone. I knew he would track us down.'

'Don't think about him now.'

'How is she?' Doc asked, joining them.

Tiel looked at his shoulder. 'Are you hurt?'

He shook his head. 'The bullet only grazed me. It stings, that's all.' Through the tear in his sleeve, he swabbed the wound with a gauze pad, then covered it with another and asked Tiel to cut off a strip of adhesive tape. While he held the square in place, she secured it with the tape.

'Thanks.'

'You're welcome.'

Up to this point no one had given any attention to the unconscious man. Ronnie approached, hitched his chin towards Cain. 'What about him?'

Tiel considered that a very good question. 'I'll probably get years in prison for doing that.'

Doc said to Ronnie, 'I recommend that you let me drag him outside, so his buddies out there will know he's alive.'

Ronnie apprehensively glanced towards the outside. 'No, no.' He looked over at Vern and Gladys. 'Find some duct tape,' Ronnie told them. 'Bind his hands and feet.'

'If you do that, you'll only be digging yourself in deeper, son,' Doc warned gently.

'I don't think I could get in any deeper.'

Ronnie's expression was sad, as though he was just now fully comprehending the enormity of his predicament. What might have seemed a romantic adventure when he and Sabra ran away had turned into an incident involving the FBI and gunplay. He was in serious trouble, and he was intelligent enough to know it.

The elderly couple stepped over the unconscious agent. Each took an ankle. It was an effort for them, but they were able to drag him away from Sabra, giving Doc and Tiel more room.

'They're going to lock me up for ever,' Ronnie continued. 'But I want Sabra to be safe. I want her old man's promise that he'll let her keep our baby.'

'Then let's end this here and now.'

'I can't, Doc. Not before getting that guarantee from Mr Dendy.'

Doc motioned down to Sabra, who was panting through another pain with Tiel. 'In the meantime—'

'Doc?' Tiel said, interrupting.

He turned to her abruptly. 'What?'

'I can see the baby.'

He knelt down between Sabra's raised knees. 'Thank God,' he said on a relieved laugh. 'The baby's turned, Sabra. I can see the head. A few minutes from now you'll have a baby.'

The girl laughed, sounding too young to be in the jam she was in. 'Is it going to be all right?'

'I think so.' Doc looked at Tiel. 'You'll help?'

'Tell me what to do.'

'Get a few more of those pads and spread them around her. Have one of the towels handy to wrap the baby in.' He had rolled up his shirtsleeves and was vigorously washing his hands and arms with Tiel's bottled cleanser. He then bathed them with vinegar. He passed the bottles to Tiel. 'Use both liberally. But quickly.'

In Cain's doctor's kit, Doc found a pair of gloves and pulled them on. 'At least he did something right,' he muttered. 'Get yourself a pair.'

She had just managed to get the gloves on when Sabra had another contraction. 'Don't bear down,' Doc instructed. 'I don't want you to tear.' He placed his right hand on the perineum for additional support to avoid tearing, while his left hand gently rested on the baby's head. 'You might move behind her,' he said to Tiel. 'Angle her up. Support her lower back.'

He coached Sabra through the pain, and when it was over, she relaxed against Tiel's support.

'Almost there, Sabra,' Doc told her in a gentle voice. 'You're doing fine. Great, in fact.'

Sabra jerked into a semi-sitting position, and grunted with the effort of expelling the baby. Tiel rubbed her lower back, wishing there was more she could do to relieve the girl's suffering.

'Is she all right?' The anxious father was ignored.

'Try not to push,' Doc reminded the girl. 'It'll come now without additional pressure. Good, good. The head's almost out.'

The contraction abated and Sabra's body collapsed with fatigue. She was crying. 'It hurts.'

'I know.' Doc spoke in a soothing voice, but unseen by Sabra, his face registered profound regret. She was bleeding profusely from tearing tissue. 'You're doing fine, Sabra,' he lied. 'Soon you'll have your baby.'

During the next contraction, almost before Tiel could assimilate the miracle she was witnessing, she watched the baby's head emerge. When she saw the newborn's face, its eyes wide open, she murmured, 'Oh my God,' and she meant it literally, like a prayer, because it was an awe-inspiring, almost spiritual phenomenon to behold.

But there the miracle stopped, because the baby's shoulders still could not clear the birth canal.

'What's happening?' Ronnie asked when Sabra screamed.

The telephone rang. Donna was nearest to it and answered. 'Hello?'

'I know it hurts, Sabra,' Doc said. 'The next two or three contractions should do it. OK?'

'I can't,' she sobbed. 'I can't.'

'This guy name o' Calloway wants to know who got shot,' Donna informed them. No one paid any attention to her.

Tiel began to pant along with Sabra as she watched Doc's hands moving round the baby's neck. Noticing her alarm, he said softly, 'Just checking to make sure the cord wasn't wrapped round it.'

Tiel heard Donna telling Calloway, 'Nope, he ain't dead, but he deserves to be and so does the damn fool that sent him in here.' She then slammed down the receiver.

'Here we go, here we go. Your baby's here, Sabra.' Sweat was running into Doc's eyebrows from his hairline, but he seemed unaware of it. 'That's it. That's the way.'

Her scream would haunt Tiel's dreams for many nights to come. More tissue was torn when the child's shoulders pushed through. A small incision under local anaesthetic would have spared her that agony, but there was no help for it.

The only blessing to come of it was the wriggling baby that slipped into Doc's waiting hands. 'It's a girl, Sabra. And she's a beauty. Ronnie, you have a baby daughter.'

Donna, Vern and Gladys cheered and applauded. Tiel sniffed back tears as Doc tilted the infant's head down to help clear her breathing passages since they had no aspirator. She began crying immediately. A wide grin of relief split his austere face.

Tiel wasn't allowed to marvel for long because Doc was passing the infant to her. The newborn was so slippery she feared dropping her. But she managed to cradle her and get a towel round her. 'Lay her on her mother's tummy.' Tiel did as Doc instructed.

Sabra stared at her bawling newborn with wonderment and asked in a fearful whisper, 'Is she all right?'

'Her lungs certainly seem to be,' Tiel said, laughing. She ran a quick inventory. 'All fingers and toes accounted for. Looks like her hair is going to be light like yours.'

'Ronnie, can you see her?' Sabra called to him.

'Yeah.' The boy was dividing his glance between her and the Mexicans, who seemed totally disenchanted by the wonders of birth. 'She's beautiful. Well, I mean she will be when she's all cleaned up. How're you?'

'Perfect,' Sabra replied.

But she wasn't. Blood had quickly saturated the pads beneath her. Doc tried to stanch it with sanitary napkins.

While Doc continued to work on Sabra, Tiel tried to distract her. 'What are you going to name your daughter?'

Sabra was inspecting the infant with blatant adoration and love. 'We decided on Katherine. I like the classic names.'

'So do I. And I think Katherine is going to suit her.'

Suddenly Sabra's face contorted with pain. 'What's happening?'

'Your uterus is contracting to expel the placenta,' Doc explained. 'Once it's out, we'll clean you up and then let you rest.'

To Tiel he said, 'Get one of those garbage sacks ready, please. I'll need to save this. It'll be examined later.'

She did as asked and again distracted Sabra by talking about the baby. In a short time, Doc had the afterbirth wrapped up and out of sight, but still tethered to the baby by the cord. Tiel wanted to ask why he hadn't cut it yet, but he was busy.

A good five minutes later, he peeled off the bloody gloves, picked up the blood-pressure cuff and wrapped it round Sabra's biceps. 'How're you doing?'

'Good,' she said, but her eye sockets were sunken and shadowed. Her smile was wan. 'How's Ronnie holding up?'

'You should talk him into ending this, Sabra,' Tiel said gently.

'I can't. Now that I've got Katherine, I can't risk my daddy placing her up for adoption.'

'He can't do that without your consent.'

'He can do anything.'

'What about your mother? Whose side is she on?'

'Daddy's, of course.'

Doc read the gauge and released the cuff. 'Try to get some rest. I'll be asking a favour of you later, so I'd like you to take a nap now if you can.'

Her eyes began to close. 'You were super cool, Doc.'

Tiel and Doc watched as her breathing became regular and her muscles relaxed. Tiel lifted Katherine off her mother's chest.

'What about the cord?' she asked Doc.

'I've been waiting until it was safe.'

The cord had stopped pulsing and was no longer ropy, but thin and flat. He tied it tightly in two places with shoelaces, leaving about an inch between. Tiel turned her head when he cut it.

She opened a box of pre-moistened towelettes. 'Do you think it's safe to use these on the baby?'

'I suppose. That's what they're for,' Doc replied.

Although Katherine put up little peeps of protest, Tiel sponged her with the wipes, which smelt pleasantly of baby powder. Having had no experience with newborns, she was nervous about the task. She also continued to monitor Sabra's gentle breathing.

'I applaud her courage,' she remarked. 'I also can't help but sympathise with them. From what I know of Russell Dendy, I'd have run away from him too.'

'You know him?'

'Only through the media. I wonder if he was instrumental in sending Cain in here?'

'Why'd you hit him over the head?'

'Referring to my attack on a federal agent?' she asked, making a grim joke of it. 'I was trying to prevent a disaster.'

'I commend your swift action and only wish I'd thought of it.'

'I had the advantage of standing behind him.' She wrapped Katherine in a fresh towel and held her against her chest for warmth. 'I suppose Agent Cain was only doing his duty. But I didn't want him to shoot Ronnie. And, just as earnestly, I didn't want Ronnie to shoot him. I acted on impulse.'

'And weren't you just a little pissed to discover that Cain wasn't a doctor?'

She looked at him and smiled conspiratorially. 'Don't tell.'

'I promise.'

'How'd you know? What gave him away?'

'Sabra's vitals weren't his first concern. For instance, he didn't take her blood pressure. He didn't seem to grasp the seriousness of her condition, so I began to suspect him and tested his knowledge. When the cervix is dilated to eight to ten centimetres, all systems are go. He flunked the test.'

'We both might get sentenced to years of hard labour.'

'Better that than letting him shoot Ronnie.'

She glanced down at the infant, who was now sleeping. 'How about the baby? Is she OK?'

'Let's take a look.'

Tiel laid Katherine on her lap. Doc folded back the towel and examined the tiny newborn, who wasn't even as long as his forearm. His hands looked large and masculine against her baby pinkness, but their touch was tender, especially when he taped the tied-off cord to her tummy.

'She's small,' he observed. 'A couple of weeks premature, I'd guess. She seems OK, though. Breathing all right. But she should be in a neonatal unit. It's important that we keep her warm. Try to keep her head covered.'

'All right.'

He was leaning close to Tiel. Close enough for her to distinguish each tiny line that radiated from the outer corners of his eyes. His eyes were greyish green, the lashes very black, darker than his medium-brown hair. His chin and jaw were showing stubble, which was attractive. Through the tear in his shirtsleeve, she noticed that blood had soaked through the makeshift bandage.

'Does your shoulder hurt?'

When he raised his head, they almost bumped noses. Their eyes were engaged for several seconds before he turned his head to check his shoulder wound. 'No. It's fine.' Hastily he added, 'Better put a diaper on her, then wrap her up again.'

Tiel ineptly diapered the baby while Doc checked on the new mother.

'Is all that blood . . .' Tiel purposefully left the question incomplete, afraid that Ronnie would overhear.

'Much more than there should be.' Doc kept his voice low for the same reason she had. 'It can't go on for long before we've got real problems. I wish I could've saved her this.'

'Don't blame yourself. Under the circumstances and given the conditions, you did amazingly well, Dr Stanwick.'

It was out before she could recall it. She hadn't intended for Doc to know that she recognised him. Not yet, anyway.

Although maybe her reporter's yen for provoking a response had goaded her into tossing out his name to see what his spontaneous, unrehearsed and therefore candid reaction would be.

His spontaneous, unrehearsed and candid reaction was telling. He looked at first astonished, then mystified, then irked. Finally, it was as though a shutter had been slammed shut over his eyes.

Tiel held his stare, her gaze virtually daring him to deny that he was Dr Bradley Stanwick. Or had been in his previous life.

The telephone rang again.

Ronnie reached for the phone. 'Mr Calloway? No, like the lady told you, he's not dead.'

Sabra had been roused by the ringing telephone. She asked to hold her baby. Tiel laid the infant in her arms. The new mother cooed over how sweet Katherine looked, how good she smelt.

Tiel stood up, physically exhausted, but mentally charged. She took stock of the situation. Gladys and Vern were sitting together quietly, holding hands. They looked tired but content.

Donna was hugging her bony chest with her skinny arms. The taller, leaner Mexican man was focused on Ronnie and the telephone. His friend was watching the FBI agent.

Vern had propped Agent Cain's back against the counter with his legs stretched out in front of him. His ankles were bound together with silver duct tape. His wrists were likewise secured behind his back. His head was bowed low over his chest, but every now and then he tried to lift it, and moaned.

'We've got him tied up,' Ronnie was telling Calloway over the telephone. 'We fired our guns almost at the same time, but the only one hit was Doc. No, he's OK.' Ronnie glanced at Doc, who nodded in agreement. 'Who's Ms McCoy?'

'Me,' Tiel said, stepping forward.

'How come?' Ronnie gave Tiel a quizzical once-over. 'OK, hold on.' As he extended the receiver to Tiel, he asked, 'Are you famous or something?'

'Not so you'd notice.' She took the receiver. 'Hello?'

The voice was government-issue—crisp and concise. 'Ms McCoy, FBI Special Agent Bill Calloway. Are you in a position to speak freely?'

'Yes.'

'What's the situation there?'

'Exactly as Ronnie described to you. Agent Cain caused a near disaster, but we were able to quell it.'

Taken aback, the senior agent was slow to respond. 'I beg your pardon?'

'I urge you to cooperate with Mr Davison from now on.'

'It's the Bureau's policy not to negotiate with hostage-takers.'

'These aren't terrorists,' she exclaimed. 'They're a couple of kids who are confused and scared and feel that they have exhausted all other options.'

Raised voices could be heard in the background. Calloway covered the mouthpiece to speak to someone else.

'Mr Dendy is very concerned about his daughter's welfare,' Calloway said when he came back on the line. 'Has Sabra delivered yet?'

'A baby girl. Both are . . . stable.' Tiel glanced at Doc, and he gave her a small nod. 'Assure Mr Dendy that his daughter is in no immediate danger.'

'Sheriff Montez informs me there's a local man in there with you who has some medical training.'

'That's right. He assisted Sabra through the labour and birth.'

Doc's eyes narrowed a fraction—the gunslinger about to draw.

'Sheriff Montez can't recall his name. Says he goes by Doc.'

'Correct.'

'You don't know his name?'

Tiel considered her options. She had been totally involved with the labour and delivery, but she wasn't entirely unaware of what had been happening outside. She'd heard the clap of helicopter rotors. Some would be police and medical choppers, but she would bet they also indicated the arrival of the media from Dallas—Fort Worth, Austin, Houston. Big stations. Network affiliates.

The active role she was playing in this unfolding story had automatically elevated its media-worthiness. She wasn't what she would term famous, but she was a flavour-enhancing ingredient to an already juicy story. Throw into that mix the involvement of Dr Bradley Stanwick, who three years ago had disappeared from the public eye shrouded in scandal, and you had a tasty potboiler that would cause a feeding frenzy among the press corps.

But Tiel wanted it to be *her* potboiler.

If she gave away Doc's identity now, she could kiss her exclusive goodbye. Everyone else would report it first. By the time she could produce her own account of events, the resurfacing of Dr Stanwick would be old news.

Gully would probably never forgive her for this decision, but, for the time being, she was going to keep this spicy titbit as her secret ingredient.

So she avoided giving Calloway a direct answer. 'Doc did an incredible job under very trying circumstances. Sabra trusts him.'

'I understand he was wounded during the exchange of gunfire.'

'A scratch, nothing more. All of us are all right, Mr Calloway,' she said impatiently.

'You're not being forced to say this?'

'Absolutely not. The last thing Ronnie wants is for someone to get hurt.'

'That's right,' the boy said. 'I just want to be able to walk out of here with Sabra and my baby, free to go our own way.'

Tiel conveyed his wish to Calloway, who said, 'Ms McCoy, you know I can't let that happen.'

'Mr Calloway, if you've had any interaction with Russell Dendy, then you can well understand why these two young people felt desperate enough to do what they've done.'

'I can't comment on that directly, but I understand your meaning.'

Apparently Dendy was within earshot. 'By all accounts the man is a tyrant,' Tiel continued. 'I don't know if you're aware of this, but he has pledged to forcibly separate these two and put the baby up for adoption. Ronnie and Sabra want only the liberty to decide their own future and that of their child. This is a family crisis, Mr Calloway, and that's how it should be handled. Perhaps Mr Dendy would consent to a mediator who could help them work through their differences and reach an agreement.'

'Ronnie Davison still has a lot to answer for, Ms McCoy. Armed robbery, for starters.'

'I'm sure Ronnie is willing to accept responsibility for his actions.'

'Let me talk to him.' Ronnie took the receiver from her. 'Listen, Mr Calloway, I'm not a criminal. Not until today, that is.' He looked down at Sabra where she lay with the newborn in her arms, and his face took on a pained expression. 'Talk to Sabra's dad, Mr Calloway. Persuade him to leave us alone. Then I'll release everybody. You've got one hour to get back to me.' He hung up abruptly.

Addressing his hostages, he said, 'OK, you all heard what I just said. I don't want to hurt anybody. I want all of us to walk out of here. So everybody just relax.' He glanced up at the wall clock. 'Sixty minutes, it could be over.'

'What if her old man don't agree to let y'all alone?' Donna asked. 'What're you gonna do to us?'

An uneasy silence descended over the group. All eyes turned to

Ronnie, but he stubbornly refused to acknowledge the unspoken question in their eyes.

Tiel crouched down beside Doc, who was attending to Sabra again. Her eyes were closed. Baby Katherine was sleeping in her mother's arms. 'How is she?'

'Too much bleeding. And her blood pressure's falling.' They were quiet for a moment, both looking at Sabra and disliking her paleness. 'I'm afraid of infection too,' he said. 'Dammit they both need to be hospitalised. What's that Calloway like?'

'All business, but he sounds reasonable. Dendy, on the other hand, is a raving maniac. I could hear him in the background issuing threats and ultimatums.' She glanced at Ronnie, who was dividing his attention between the parking lot and the Mexican duo, who were becoming steadily and increasingly edgy. 'He won't execute us, will he?'

Doc finished replacing the pads beneath Sabra, then leaned against the freezer chest. He wearily raked a hand through his hair. By city standards, it could have stood a trim. But somehow, on him, in this environment, the unkempt look was fitting.

'I don't know what he'll do. I don't think the boy has got it in him to line us up and shoot us, but there's no guarantee that he won't. In any event, talking about it won't affect the outcome.'

'Then what do you want to talk about?'

'Nothing.'

'Bullshit. You want to know how I recognised you.'

He merely looked at her, saying nothing. He'd built up quite an armour, but part of her job was piercing invisible armour.

'When I first saw you, I thought you looked familiar but couldn't place you. Then just before the delivery, it occurred to me who you were. I think the way you handled Sabra was the giveaway.'

'You've got a remarkable memory, Ms McCoy.'

'Tiel. You see, I covered your story.' She recited the call letters of the television station for which she worked.

He muttered an expletive. 'So you were among the hordes of reporters who made my life a living hell?'

'I'm good at my job.'

He snuffled a deprecating laugh. 'I'll bet you are. Do you like what you do?'

'Very much.'

'You enjoy preying on people who are already down, exposing their hardship to public scrutiny, making it impossible for them to pick up the pieces of their already shattered lives?'

'You blame the media for your difficulties?'

'In large part, yeah.'

'For instance?'

'For instance, the hospital buckled beneath the weight of bad publicity. Bad publicity generated by people like you.'

'You generated your own negative publicity, Dr Stanwick.'

Angrily, he turned his head away, and Tiel realised she had struck a chord.

Dr Bradley Stanwick had been an oncologist of renown, practising in one of the most progressive cancer-treatment centres in the world. Patients came from all over the globe, usually in a last-hope attempt to save themselves from dying. His clinic couldn't save them all, of course, but it had maintained an excellent track record of staving off the ravages of the disease and prolonging life, while also providing the patient a quality of life that made living longer worth while.

That's why it was such a cruel irony when Bradley Stanwick's young, beautiful, vivacious wife was stricken with inoperable pancreatic cancer.

Neither he nor his brilliant colleagues could retard its rapid spread. She opted for aggressive chemotherapy and radiation, but the side effects were almost as lethal as the disease. Her immune system weakened; she developed pneumonia. One by one her systems began to falter, then fail.

Not wishing her senses to be dulled by pain-relieving drugs, she declined them. However, during the last few days of her life, her suffering became so intense that she finally consented to a painkilling drug that she could self-administer through an IV.

All this Tiel learned through background research. Dr and Mrs Stanwick didn't become news until after her death.

Following her funeral, disgruntled in-laws began to make noises that perhaps their son-in-law had accelerated his wife's passing. Specifically, he had enabled her to kill herself by setting the dosage on the self-administering mechanism so high that she actually had succumbed to a lethal amount of narcotics. They alleged that her sizable inheritance was his enticement to speed things along.

From the start, Tiel had thought the allegations were nonsense. It was a foregone conclusion that Mrs Bradley's life expectancy was a matter of days. A man due to inherit a fortune could afford to wait until nature took its course. Besides, Dr Stanwick was affluent in his own right and she strongly doubted that he would risk his professional reputation even for his beloved wife's sake.

No evidence was found to substantiate the relatives' charge of criminal wrongdoing. There was no indication that Dr Stanwick had done anything to hasten his wife's death.

Nevertheless, the story didn't end there. During the weeks that investigators were interrogating Dr Stanwick, his colleagues, his staff, friends, family and former patients, every aspect of his life was extensively examined and debated. He lived beneath a shadow of suspicion.

The hospital where he practised soon found itself in the spotlight too. Rather than standing behind him, the administrators voted unanimously to revoke his privileges at the facility until he was cleared of all suspicion. No fool, Bradley Stanwick knew he would never be cleared of *all* suspicion. Once a seed of doubt is planted in the public's mind, it usually finds fertile ground and flourishes.

Perhaps the ultimate betrayal came from his partners at the clinic he had established. After working together for years, forging friendships as well as professional alliances, they asked him to resign.

He sold his share of the practice to his former partners, unloaded his stately home for a fraction of its value and left Dallas for parts unknown. If Tiel hadn't wound up in Rojo Flats, she probably would never have thought of him again.

She asked him now, 'Is Sabra the first patient you've treated since you left Dallas?'

'She isn't a patient, and I didn't treat her. This is an emergency situation, and I responded. Just as you did.'

'That's false modesty, Doc. None of us could have done what you did.'

'Ronnie, OK if I get a drink?' he suddenly called out.

'Sure. OK. The others could probably use some water too.'

Leaning forward, Doc took a six-pack of bottled water from the shelf. After taking two bottles for Tiel and himself, he passed the rest up to the boy, who then asked Donna to distribute them.

He drank almost half his bottle in one swallow. Tiel drank from her bottle, sighing after taking a long draught. 'Good idea. Trying to change the subject?'

'Look, Ms McCoy, you won't ever get an interview from me.'

'Prior to the . . . the episode, you lived a very active life. Don't you miss being at the centre of things?'

'No.'

'You don't get bored out here?'

'No.'

'Aren't you lonesome?'

He turned his head and readjusted his position so that his shoulders and torso were almost facing her. 'Sometimes.'

He was looking at her now, with probing intensity. Her tummy lifted weightlessly.

But then an uproar on the far side of the store brought her and Doc scrambling to their feet.

Chapter 5

TIEL HAD DUBBED the shorter, stockier Mexican man Juan. It was he who had caused the commotion. He was bending over Agent Cain, lavishly cursing him—at least she assumed he was cursing.

Cain was repeatedly screaming, 'What the hell?' and straining to free himself.

To everyone's dismay, Juan slapped a strip of duct tape over the FBI agent's mouth to shut him up. Meanwhile, Juan's taller companion let fly with a stream of Spanish that sounded both reproachful and confused by Juan's sudden attack on the agent.

Ronnie brandished his pistol, shouting, 'What's going on?

'He just jumped on him,' Gladys contributed. 'For no apparent reason. I don't trust him. Or his friend.'

'Why'd you jump him?' Ronnie asked the Mexican man.

Juan answered in Spanish, but Ronnie impatiently shook his head. 'I can't understand you. Just take that tape off his mouth.' He made himself understood by pantomiming peeling the tape off Cain.

The Mexican leaned down, pinched up a corner of the tape and ripped it off the agent's lips. He yelped in pain, then shouted, 'You son of a bitch!'

Doc, who'd returned his attention to Sabra, said, 'I need another packet of diapers.' Her bleeding had not abated. If anything, it had increased.

Tiel rushed back to Doc's side with a box of disposable diapers. She tore it open and he positioned one beneath Sabra's hips. 'What made you think of this?'

'She's bleeding through the napkins too fast. These diapers are lined with plastic.'

The exchange was spoken in an undertone. Neither wanted to panic the girl or further fluster Ronnie, who was watching the wall clock behind the counter.

Doc took Sabra's hand. 'You're still bleeding a little heavier than I'd like. Would you please reconsider going to the hospital?'

'No!'

He appealed to her. 'Listen to me a minute. I'm thinking not only of you and the baby, but of Ronnie too. The sooner he brings this to an end, the better it's going to be for him.'

'My daddy will kill him.'

'No, he won't. Not if you and Katherine are safe.'

Her eyes filled with tears. 'You don't understand. He's only pretending to want us safe. Last night when we told him about the baby, he threatened to kill it. That's how much he hates Ronnie, how much he hates our being together.'

She tilted her head down and rested her cheek against her newborn. The peach fuzz on the baby's small head blotted Sabra's tears from her cheeks. 'You won't change my mind about this. Until they let Ronnie and me walk out of here with Daddy's promise to leave us alone, I'm staying.'

Doc swiped his sweating forehead with the back of his hand and sighed. 'OK,' he said reluctantly. 'I'll do my best.'

'I don't doubt that.' Sabra winced. 'Is it really bad?'

'There's nothing I can do about the bleeding from the tear. But for the vaginal bleeding . . . Remember when I told you to rest because I might have to ask you to do something for me later?'

'Uh-huh.'

'Well, I'd like for you to nurse Katherine.'

The girl shot Tiel a stunned glance.

'The nursing will cause your uterus to contract and reduce the bleeding,' Doc explained. He smiled down at her. 'Ready to give it a try?'

'I guess so,' she replied, though she seemed unsure and embarrassed.

'I'll help you.' Tiel reached for the scissors, which had been wiped clean. 'Why don't I use these to clip the shoulder seams of your dress? That'll keep you from having to undress.'

'I'll let you ladies have some privacy. Uh, Ms, uh, Tiel?' Doc motioned her to stand, and they held a brief, private consultation. 'Do you know anything about this?'

'Nothing.'

'Well then, of the three of you, Katherine will be the most knowledgeable. Position her correctly and she'll act on instinct. At least I hope she will. A few minutes on each breast.'

'Right,' Tiel said with a brisk nod.

She knelt down beside Sabra and applied the scissors to the shoulder seams of her sundress. 'Now lower your bra strap and pull down the cup. Here, let me hold Katherine.'

When Sabra was ready, Tiel handed Katherine back to her. The moment the newborn felt Sabra's breast against her cheek, her mouth began rooting for the nipple. She found it, tried to latch on, couldn't. After several attempts, the baby began to wail.

Sabra sobbed in frustration. 'What am I doing wrong?'

'Nothing, sweetheart, nothing,' Tiel said soothingly. 'Katherine doesn't know how to be a baby any more than you know how to be a mom. Take a few deep breaths, then try again.'

A second attempt was no more successful. 'Know what? I think it's your position,' Tiel observed. 'If Doc supported your back it would enable you to cradle Katherine more comfortably.'

Doc was there in a blink. He knelt down behind the girl and helped ease her into a semi-sitting position. 'Now, just lean back against my chest. Comfortable?'

'Yes, I'm OK. Thanks.'

'Help her, Sabra,' Tiel instructed softly. With only a little manoeuvring and finessing, a tight suction was formed between breast and baby, and Katherine began to suck vigorously.

Sabra laughed with delight. As did Tiel.

'Had you decided ahead of time to breastfeed?' Tiel asked.

'Truthfully, I was so worried that somebody would find out about the pregnancy, that I didn't have much time to think about it. But I hear that nursing is better for the baby.'

'That's what I hear too.'

'You don't have kids?'

'No.'

'Are you married?'

It seemed that Sabra had forgotten Doc was there. Her back was to him, so to her he was like a piece of furniture. Tiel, however, was facing him and keenly aware that he was listening to every word. 'No. Single.'

'Have you ever been?'

After a hesitation, she replied, 'Years ago. For a short time.'

'What happened?'

'We, uh, went different directions.'

'Oh. Too bad.'

'Yes, it was.'

'How old were you?'

'Young.'

'How old are you now?'

Tiel laughed nervously. 'Older. Thirty-three last month.'

'You'd better hurry up and find someone else. If you want to have a family, I mean.'

'You sound like my mother.'

'Do you?'

'Do I what?'

'Want to have another husband and kids?'

'Someday. Maybe. I've been awfully busy establishing my career.'

'I can't imagine not wanting a family,' the girl said with a gentle smile for Katherine. 'That's all Ronnie and I talk about. We want to have a big house out in the country. With lots of kids.'

Unobtrusively, Doc signalled Tiel with his chin that it was time to switch sides. Tiel assisted Sabra, and soon Katherine was happily sucking away at the other breast.

Then the girl surprised them by angling her head back and asking, 'What about you, Doc? Are you married?'

'My wife died three years ago.'

Sabra's face fell. 'Oh, I'm so sorry. How'd she die? If you don't mind me asking.'

He told her about his wife's illness, making no mention of the conflict that followed her demise.

'Any kids?'

'Unfortunately no. We had just begun talking about starting our family when she got sick. Like Ms McCoy, she had a career. She was a microbiologist.'

'Wow, she must've been smart.'

'Brilliant, in fact.' He smiled, although Sabra couldn't see it. 'Much smarter than me.'

'You must've loved each other a whole lot.'

His smile gradually faded. What Sabra couldn't guess, but Tiel knew, was that during the investigation, it was disclosed that his wife had engaged in an extramarital affair. Bradley Stanwick knew of his wife's unfaithfulness, and generously assumed his share of the blame. His work schedule often kept him out late and away from home.

But the two were committed to making the marriage work. They were in counselling when her malignancy was diagnosed. Her illness had actually brought them closer together.

Tiel could see that, even after all this time, reminders of his wife's adultery still pained him.

When he became aware that Tiel was watching him, the wistfulness in his expression vanished. 'That's enough for now,' he said, speaking more brusquely than he probably intended.

'She's stopped sucking anyway,' Sabra said. 'I think she's gone to sleep.'

While Sabra was readjusting her clothing, Tiel took the baby and changed her. Doc eased the girl back into her original position, then checked the diaper he'd placed beneath her. 'Better. Thank God.'

Tiel cuddled the baby close and planted a soft kiss on the top of her head before returning her to her mother's arms.

The telephone rang. The hour was up.

Everybody snapped to attention.

Ronnie looked over at Sabra and tried to smile, but his lips couldn't hold the expression for long. 'Are you sure, Sabra?'

'Yes, Ronnie.' She spoke quietly but with resolve and dignity.

The boy lifted the receiver off the hook. 'Mr Calloway?' Then, after a momentary pause, he exclaimed, '*Dad!*'

'**W**ho's this?'

When the latest arrival was escorted into the FBI van, Calloway had ignored Russell Dendy's rude question and instead stood up to shake the man's hand. 'Mr Davison?'

'You've got to be kidding me.' Dendy had sneered with disgust. 'Who invited him?'

Calloway had pretended Dendy wasn't even there. 'I'm Special Agent Bill Calloway.'

'Cole Davison. Wish I could say it's a pleasure to meet you, Mr Calloway.'

Judging by his appearance, one would guess Davison to be a rancher. He wore faded Levi's and cowboy boots. Upon entering the van, he'd politely removed a straw cowboy hat. He had a stocky build and walked with a bow-legged gait.

He didn't ranch. He owned five fast-food franchises.

Calloway had welcomed him with a 'Thank you for coming so quickly, Mr Davison.'

'I'd've come whether you asked me to or not. I was on my way out the door when you called.'

Dendy, who'd been fuming in the background, had grabbed Davison by the shoulder and spun him round. He thrust his index finger into the other man's face. 'It's your fault my daughter is in the mess she's in. If anything happens to her, you're dead and so is your son—'

'Mr Dendy,' Calloway had interrupted sternly. 'One more word and you're out of here.'

The millionaire, ignoring Calloway's warning, had continued his harangue. 'Your kid,' he declared, 'seduced my daughter, got her preg- nant and then kidnapped her. I'm going to make it my life's mission that he never sees the light of day or breathes a breath of freedom. I'm going to make certain that he spends every second of his miserable life in prison.'

To Davison's credit, he had kept his cool. 'It appears to me you're partly to blame for all this, Mr Dendy. If you hadn't come down so hard on those kids they wouldn't've felt the need to run away. You know's well as I do that Ronnie didn't take your girl against her will. They love each other and ran away from you and your threats, is what I think.'

'I don't care what you think.'

'Well, I do,' Calloway said. 'I want to hear Mr Davison's take on the situation.'

'You can call me Cole.'

'All right, Cole. Anything you can tell us about your son and his frame of mind will be helpful.'

To which Dendy had said, 'How about some sharpshooters? A SWAT team? Now *that* would be helpful.'

'Using force would risk the lives of your daughter and her baby.'

'Baby?' Davison had exclaimed. 'It's come?'

'We understand she delivered a baby girl two hours ago,' Calloway had informed him. 'Both are reportedly doing OK. When was the last time you spoke to Ronnie?'

'Last night. He and Sabra were about to go over to the Dendys' house and tell her parents about the baby.'

'How long have you known about the pregnancy?'

'A few weeks.'

Dendy's face had turned beet red. 'And you didn't see fit to tell me?'

'No, sir, I didn't. My son confided in me. I couldn't betray his trust, although I urged him to tell you.' He had turned his back on Dendy and addressed the remainder of his remarks to Calloway. 'This evening, I found a note from Ronnie on my kitchen table. It said they'd come by hoping to catch me. They had run away together and were headed for Mexico. Said they'd let me know how to reach them when they got where they were going.'

'I'm surprised they would pay you a visit. Weren't they afraid you'd try and talk them into returning home?'

'Truth is, Mr Calloway, I told Ronnie if they ever needed my help, I was pleased to offer it.'

Dendy had attacked so quickly no one saw it coming, least of all Davison. Dendy landed on Davison's back with all his weight behind him. Davison would have fallen forwards, had not Calloway caught him and broken his fall. Sheriff Montez grabbed Dendy by the collar and hauled him backwards, slamming him into the opposite wall.

'There will be no more of that, Dendy. Do you understand me?' Calloway had shouted.

Dendy was red-faced and furious, but he nodded.

Calloway had then asked Davison if he was all right. Davison had picked his cowboy hat off the floor and dusted it off on his jeans. 'Never mind about me. I'm worried about those kids. The baby too.'

'Do you think Ronnie was coming to you for money?'

'Could be. I reckon they could've used some cash. Since I missed him today, I guess he decided to do this.' He'd gestured towards the store, his expression remorseful. 'My boy's not a thief. His mother and stepfather have done a good job with him. He's a good boy. I reckon he was feeling desperate to take care of Sabra and the baby.'

'He's taken care of her all right. He's ruined her life.'

Paying no attention to Dendy, Davison had asked Calloway, 'So what's the plan? Have you got a plan?'

Calloway had brought Ronnie Davison's father up to speed.

Checking his wristwatch, he'd added, 'Fifty-seven minutes ago, he gave us an hour to persuade Mr Dendy to leave them alone. They want his word that he won't give away their baby.'

'Give away the baby?' Davison had looked at Dendy with patent dismay. 'You threatened to give away their baby?' His disdainful expression spoke volumes. Shaking his head sadly, he'd turned back to Calloway. 'What can I do?'

'Understand, Mr Davison, that Ronnie will face criminal charges.'

'I reckon he knows that.'

'But the sooner he releases those hostages and surrenders, the better off he's going to be. So far no one's been hurt. Not seriously anyway. I'd like to keep it that way, for Ronnie's sake, as well as the others'.'

'He won't be hurt?'

'You have my word on that.'

'Tell me what to do.'

That conversation had resulted in Cole Davison placing a call to the store just as the deadline expired.

'Dad!' Ronnie exclaimed. 'Where're you calling from?'

Tiel and Doc moved forward and listened carefully to what Ronnie was saying into the telephone. Tiel imagined Ronnie was feeling shame and embarrassment, as any child experiences when caught red-handed by a parent he respects. Perhaps Mr Davison could impress upon his son the trouble he was in and influence him to end the standoff.

'No, Dad, Sabra's OK. You know I wouldn't've done anything to hurt her. Yeah, I know she should be in a hospital, but—'

'Tell him I'm not leaving you,' Sabra called to him.

'It's not just me, Dad. Sabra says she won't go.' As he listened, his eyes cut to Sabra and the baby. 'She seems to be doing OK too. Ms McCoy and Doc have been taking care of them. Yeah, I know it's serious.'

Tiel looked around at her fellow hostages. All, including the Mexicans, who didn't even understand the language, were still, silent and alert.

Ronnie was gripping the receiver so tightly his knuckles had turned white. His forehead was beaded with sweat. His fingers nervously flexed and contracted round the pistol grip.

'Dad, I love you,' he said. 'And I'm sorry if I've made you ashamed of me. But I can't give up. Not until Mr Dendy promises to let Sabra keep the baby.'

Whatever Ronnie was hearing made him shake his head and smile at

Sabra sadly. 'Then there's something you, Mr Dendy, the FBI and every-body else ought to know, Dad. We—Sabra and I—made a pact before we left Fort Worth.'

Tiel's chest constricted. 'Oh, no.'

'If Mr Dendy won't give up his control of our lives, our future, we don't want a future.'

'Ah Jesus.' Doc dragged his hand down his face.

Ronnie was looking at Sabra, who nodded her head solemnly. 'We won't live without each other. If they don't let us leave and go our own way, nobody leaves here alive.'

He hung up quickly. No one moved or said anything for several moments. Then, as though on cue, everyone began talking at once. Donna started to wail. Agent Cain kept up a litany of 'You'll never get away with this.' Vern professed his love for Gladys, while she begged Ronnie to think about his baby.

It was her statement that Ronnie addressed. 'My dad will take care of Katherine and raise her like his own. He won't let Mr Dendy get his hands on her.'

'We decided all this ahead of time,' Sabra said. 'Last night.'

Tiel knelt down beside Sabra. 'You can't mean it. Suicide isn't a way to win an argument. Think of your baby. She would never know you. Or Ronnie.'

'She would never know us anyway, if my daddy had his way.'

Tiel stood up and moved to stand beside Doc, who was making sim-ilarly urgent appeals to Ronnie. 'To take that many lives, Sabra's life, you'd only be validating Dendy's low opinion of you. Is that the legacy you want to leave your daughter?'

'We've thought about this for a long time,' Ronnie said. 'We gave Mr Dendy an opportunity to accept us, and he refused. This is the only way out for us. Sabra and I would rather die—'

'I don't think they're convinced.'

'Huh?' He looked at Tiel, who had interrupted him.

'I bet they think you're bluffing. They need to understand how seri-ous you are.'

'I've told them,' Ronnie said.

'But seeing is believing.'

'What are you suggesting?' This from Doc.

'There's media out there. Look, I'm a news reporter and I'm sure a camera crew from my station is among them. Let's get a cameraman in here to record you.' The boy was listening. She drove home her point. 'If Calloway could see you when you speak, see that Sabra is in total agreement, then I think he, your father and Mr Dendy would give more credence to what you're saying.'

Ronnie's lower lip was getting brutalised by his upper teeth. 'I don't know,' he said with uncertainty.

'Another thing,' Tiel argued, 'if Mr Dendy could see his granddaughter, he might back down. Up till now she's been just "the baby", a symbol of your rebellion against him. A video might make her real to him, cause him to rethink his position.'

He was struggling with indecision. 'Sabra, what do you think?'

'Maybe we should, Ronnie.' She glanced down at the child sleeping in her arms. 'What Doc said about the legacy we leave Katherine . . . If there's another way out of this, isn't it worth a try at least?'

Tiel held her breath. She was near enough to Doc to tell that he was as taut as a piano wire.

'OK,' Ronnie said tersely. 'One guy can come in. And you'd better tell them not to pull any tricks like they did with him,' he said, gesturing towards Cain.

Tiel exhaled shakily. 'Even if they tried, I wouldn't let them. Unless I recognise the cameraman, he doesn't come in, OK? I give you my word.' She turned to Cain. 'How can I contact Calloway?'

Chapter 6

TIEL WAS WASHING her chest with one of the baby wipes when she sensed movement behind her. She glanced round quickly, and it would be difficult to say who was the most discomfited, she or Doc. His eyes involuntarily dropped to her lilac lace brassiere. Tiel felt a warm blush rise out of it.

'Sorry,' he mumbled.

'I was a mess,' she explained, bringing her shoulder back round to conceal her front. Her blouse had been stiff with the dried sanguineous fluid it had absorbed when she first held the newborn against her chest. Doc had been conferring with Ronnie, so Tiel had taken the advantage of a moment's privacy to remove her blouse and wash. He'd returned before she expected him. 'I thought I should clean up before appearing on camera.'

She disposed of the wipe and pulled on a souvenir T-shirt she had taken from a rack.

'How is she? Any better?'

Doc nodded a hesitant affirmative, but his brow was furrowed with concern. 'She's lost a lot of blood, and needs to be sutured. Even though the bleeding has slackened, infection is a real concern.'

'What about the baby?' Tiel asked Doc.

'Heartbeat's strong. Lungs sound OK. But I'll feel a lot better when she's getting neonatal care from experts.'

'Maybe it won't be much longer. I have every confidence in the effectiveness of video. It will soon be over.'

'I hope so,' he said, giving mother and baby a worried glance.

'You did a terrific job, Doc. You're very good. Maybe you should have chosen obstetrics or paediatrics over oncology.'

'Maybe I should have,' he said grimly. 'I didn't have a very good success rate combatting cancer.'

'You had an excellent success rate. Far above the average.'

'Yeah, well . . .'

Yeah, well, I couldn't cure the one that really counted. My own wife. Tiel mentally finished the thought for him.

'What directed you towards oncology?'

At first it seemed he wasn't going to answer. Finally he said, 'My kid brother died of lymphoma when he was nine.'

'I'm sorry.'

'It was a long time ago.'

'How old were you?'

'Twelve, thirteen.'

'But his death had a lasting impact on you.'

'I remember how tough it was for my parents.'

So he'd lost two people he loved to an enemy he had failed to defeat, Tiel thought. 'You were powerless to save your brother or your wife,' she observed aloud. 'Is that why you quit?'

'You were there,' he said curtly. 'You know why I quit.'

'You were bitter.' Tiel knew that she was pressing her luck. If she probed too hard, too fast, he might clam up altogether. But she was willing to take the chance. 'Were you angry at your in-laws for making an unfounded allegation? Or at your associates for withdrawing their support?'

'I was angry at everybody. At everything. Goddamn cancer. My own inadequacy.'

'I see, so you banished yourself to this no-man's-land where you could *really* be useful.'

Her sarcasm wasn't lost on him. 'Look, I don't need you or anybody else analysing my decision. If I decided to become a rancher, or a ballet dancer, or a bum, it's no one else's business. And while we're on the topic of business,' he added in the same biting tone, 'this videotape idea of yours . . .'

'What about it?'

'Is it strictly for Ronnie and Sabra's benefit?'

'Of course.'

'But it'll also make one hell of a story for you.'

His soft and intuitive voice, along with his piercing eyes, made her guiltily aware of the audiocassette recorder in her trouser pocket. 'OK, yes,' she admitted uneasily, 'it'll make a great story. But I'm personally involved with these kids. I helped bring their child into the world, so my idea isn't completely selfish. I care a great deal what happens to Ronnie and Sabra and Katherine. I care what happens to all of us.'

After a significant pause, he said quietly, 'I believe that.'

His eyes were just as piercing as before, but the substance of this gaze was different. The heat of vexation that had suffused her gradually intensified into heat of another kind. For what seemed an endless time, they held each other's stare.

Finally, he said, 'You were terrific, you know. With Sabra. If I ever find myself in another emergency childbirth situation . . .'

'You know who to call for back-up. Partner.'

She stuck out her hand, and he took it. But he didn't shake it to confirm the partnership. He held it. Not so tightly that it was uncomfortable, but snugly enough to make it almost intimate.

'Do me one favour?' he asked softly.

Mutely, she nodded.

'I don't want to be on camera. Keep me out of it.'

'I'm sorry, Doc, I can't. You're already in it.'

'For us in here I am. I had no choice but to get involved. But I don't owe anybody out there a damn thing, especially entertainment at the expense of my privacy. Agreed?'

'I'll see what I can do.' Again, the secreted tape recorder felt very heavy in her pocket. 'I can't speak for the cameraman.'

He gave her a look that asked her not to insult his intelligence. 'Of course you can. You're calling the shots. Keep me out of it.' He emphasised each word.

Tiel wondered what he would do when he learned that the tape about to be recorded wouldn't be the only source of video available to her when she put her story together. He had already been recorded on video and didn't know it.

She would have to worry about that later, though. The telephone was ringing.

Calloway came to his feet when the van's side door opened. Sheriff Montez, whom Calloway had come to respect as a wise, savvy and intuitive lawman, entered first. He motioned inside a bandy-legged, potbellied, balding man who smelt like the pack of Camels that were visible in the breast pocket of his shirt.

'My name's Gully.'

'Special Agent Calloway.' As they shook hands, he added, 'Maybe we should talk outside. It's becoming crowded in here.'

Inside the van now were three FBI agents in addition to Calloway, Russell Dendy, Cole Davison, Sheriff Montez and the newcomer, who said, 'Then kick somebody else out, because I'm staying until Tiel is safe and sound.'

'You're the news assignments editor, is that correct?'

'Going on half a century. I rarely leave my post, Mr Calloway. That I did so tonight should give you some indication of how much I think of Tiel McCoy. You're Dendy, right?' Suddenly he turned to the Fort Worth millionaire.

Dendy didn't deign to reply to so brusque a greeting.

'Just so you know,' Gully told him, 'in my opinion, you're the cause of all this.' Leaving Dendy to smoulder in his wrath, Gully turned back to Calloway. 'Now, what is it Tiel's after? Whatever it is, she gets.'

'I've consented to her request of sending in a cameraman.'

'He's outside, geared up and raring to go.'

'First, I need to lay down some ground rules.'

Gully's eyes narrowed suspiciously. 'Such as?'

'This tape must serve our purposes too.'

Cole Davison stepped forward. 'What purposes?'

'I want a view of the store's interior.'

'What for?'

'This is a standoff, Mr Davison. Hostages are being held at gunpoint. I need to know who is where inside that store so I can respond accordingly.'

'That it?' Gully asked impatiently.

'That's it. I'll call Ms McCoy now.'

Gully motioned Calloway towards the telephone. 'Get after it. If you're waiting on me, you're backing up.' Calloway got through to Ronnie. 'This is Agent Calloway. Let me speak to Ms McCoy.' Within a second, the newswoman was on the line.

'Ms McCoy, your cameraman . . .'

'Kip,' Gully supplied.

'Kip is standing by.'

'Thank you, Mr Calloway.'

'I'm limiting this taping to five minutes. The clock starts as soon as the cameraman clears the door of the store.'

'I think that will be agreeable. Ronnie and Sabra should be able to get their message across in that amount of time.'

'I'm going to tell Kip to pan—'

'No, no,' she interrupted quickly. 'The baby's doing fine. I'll see to it that Kip gets close-ups of her.'

'You're saying not to tape the interior of the store?'

'That's right. She's beautiful. Sleeping just now.'

'I'm . . . uh . . .' Calloway wasn't sure what she was trying to communicate to him.

'What's she saying?' Gully wanted to know.

'She doesn't want us to video the store's interior.' Then: 'Ms McCoy, I'm going to put you on speaker.' He depressed the button.

'Tiel, it's Gully. How're you doing, kid?'

'Gully! You're here?'

'Can you believe it? Me, who never gets more than ten miles from the TV station, out here in jack-rabbit country. Mode of transportation was a helicopter. Noisiest goddamn contraption I've ever had the misfortune to fly in. How are you?'

'I'm all right.'

'You don't want Kip to pan the store's interior?'

'That's right.'

'OK. How about a wide shot?'

'That's very important, yes.'

'Got it. Wide shot, but nobody's aware of it. Pretend they're close-ups. Is that what you're saying?'

'I can always count on you, Gully. We'll be watching for Kip.' She hung up.

'You heard her,' Gully said, heading for the door of the van to instruct the photographer waiting outside. 'You'll get your interior shot, Mr Calloway, but for whatever reason, Tiel doesn't want everyone to know they're on camera.'

Tiel consulted her compact mirror, but she snapped it shut without primping. She reasoned that the more dishevelled she looked, the more impact the video would have. Swapping her stained blouse for the T-shirt was the only concession she made. If viewers saw her well coifed and well dressed, the video would lose some of its punch.

She wanted it to pack a wallop. Not only with home viewers, but with the TV station's powers that be. This opportunity had been handed to her, and she intended to capitalise on it. Her career would take a dramatic upward turn if she got the coveted hostess spot on *Nine Live*.

This story would be a boon to her chances of landing the job. It would be a huge story for several days. The TV station would benefit from her national exposure. She would be the darling of the newsroom, and her popularity would extend to the carpeted offices upstairs.

Eat your heart out, Linda Harper.

Ronnie interrupted her reverie. 'Ms McCoy? Is this him?'

The videographer materialised out of the shadows beyond the gasoline pumps. The camera was like an extension of his right arm. He was rarely seen without it. 'Yes, that's Kip.'

Mentally she rehearsed what she was going to say as an open. *This is Tiel McCoy, speaking to you from inside a convenience store in Rojo Flats, Texas, where a drama involving two Fort Worth teenagers has been unfolding. Earlier today Ronnie Davison and Sabra Dendy fled their high school in defiance of parental authority—and ultimately in defiance of the law. These two young people are now engaged in a standoff with the FBI and other law enforcement agencies. I am one of their hostages.*

Kip was at the door.

'How do I know he hasn't got a gun?' Ronnie asked nervously.

'I doubt he would know which end of a gun to point.'

Ronnie signalled Donna to activate the electronic lock. Kip pushed his way inside. The door relocked behind him. He jumped nervously when he heard the metallic click.

'Hi, Kip.'

'Tiel. You OK?'

'I'm fine. This is Ronnie Davison.'

'Hi. Where's the girl?' Kip asked.

'Lying down over there.'

He looked in Sabra's direction and hitched his chin in greeting. 'Hey.'

Katherine was asleep in her mother's arms. Tiel noted that Doc was sitting on the floor with his back to the freezer, where he could easily monitor Sabra but remain concealed.

'Better get started,' Kip said. 'That Calloway was hyper about this taking no more than five minutes.'

'I've got an intro to make first, then you can tape Ronnie's statement. We'll save Sabra and the baby for last.'

Kip handed Tiel the wireless microphone, then swung the camera up onto his shoulder and fitted the viewfinder against his eye socket. The light mounted on top of the camera came on. Tiel took up a preplanned position, where the majority of the store's interior could be seen behind her. 'Is this OK?'

'Fine by me. Sound level's OK. I'm rolling.'

'This is Tiel McCoy.' She made the brief opening remarks she had rehearsed, then signalled Ronnie forward.

He seemed reluctant to move into the bright light. 'How do I know they won't take a shot at me?'

'While you're on camera and posing no immediate threat? The FBI has enough of a PR problem without the public outcry that would create.'

Apparently he saw the logic in Tiel's argument. Moving into place, he cleared his throat. 'Tell me when to go.'

'You're on,' said Kip. 'Go.'

'I didn't kidnap Sabra Dendy,' he blurted. 'We ran away. Simple as that. It was wrong of me to rob this store. I admit that.' He went on to explain that they had been driven away by Mr Dendy's threat to separate them permanently from each other and their baby. 'Sabra and I want to get married and live together with Katherine as a family. That's all. Mr Dendy, if you won't let us live our own lives, we'll end them right here. Tonight.'

'Two minutes,' Kip whispered, reminding them of the time limit.

'Very good, Ronnie.' Tiel took the microphone from him and signalled Kip to follow her to where Sabra lay. Quickly he positioned himself above her for the best possible camera angle.

'Be sure you're getting the baby, too,' Sabra told him.

Ronnie had taken a typically masculine, aggressive approach. Sabra's statement was more eloquent, but chillingly resolute. Tears welled up in her eyes, but she didn't falter when she concluded with, 'It's impossible for you to understand how we feel, Daddy, because you don't know what it's like to love someone. You're willing to sacrifice me, and give up your granddaughter, just to have your way. That's sad. I don't hate you. I pity you.'

She ended just as Kip said, 'Time's up.' He turned off the camera and lowered it from his shoulder.

As he and Tiel picked their way back towards the door, he said, 'A guy named Joseph Marcus called the newsroom. Wanted to know if you were all right. Said he was worried sick about you.'

In the hours since her telephone conversation with him, she'd almost forgotten the wife-cheating, lying rat with whom she had planned to spend a romantic holiday.

'If he calls again, hang up on him.'

The unflappable photographer shrugged laconically. 'Whatever.' A pair of headlights flashed twice. 'That's my signal,' he explained. 'Gotta go. Take care, Tiel.'

He slipped through the door and Ronnie motioned Donna to lock it behind him.

Cain started laughing. 'You're a fool, Davison. You think that video means doodle-dee-squat? Calloway only saw a way to stall a little longer, get more manpower in here.'

'Be quiet!' Ronnie yelled.

He looked haggard. He had composed himself for the camera, but now his nerves were beginning to fray again. Fatigue, jangled nerves and a loaded handgun made for a lethal combination.

Tiel could strangle Cain for goading him. In her opinion, the FBI would be better off without Agent Cain. 'Ronnie, how about allowing us a bathroom break?' she suggested.

He thought it over. 'You ladies. One at a time. Not the men. If they have to go, they can do it out here.'

Donna excused herself first. Then Gladys. Tiel went last. While in the rest room, she rewound the audiotape in her pocket recorder and spot-checked it. Sabra's voice came through, muffled but distinct enough, talking about her father. She fast-forwarded, stopped it again, depressed the Play button and heard Doc's gritty baritone. '. . . at everybody. At everything. Goddamn cancer. My own inadequacy.'

Yes! She'd been afraid the tape had run out before that confidential conversation. He would be a fantastic guest to have on *Nine Live*. If she could persuade him to do it. She would just have to, that's all. Excited by the prospect, she replaced the recorder in her pocket, used the toilet and washed her face and hands.

Tiel rejoined Doc, whose gaze was fixed on the two Mexican men seated near the refrigerated cabinet. Tiel followed the direction of his thoughtful stare. 'I wonder about them,' he murmured.

'Juan and Two?'

'Pardon?'

'I nicknamed the short one Juan. The taller one—'

'Two. I get it.'

He turned away and resumed his spot near Sabra. Tiel looked at him quizzically as she sat down beside him. 'What about them?'

'I noticed them when they first came into the store. They were acting weird even then. I picked up this . . . I don't know . . . bad vibe.'

'Hmm.'

He chuckled with self-deprecation. 'I was leery of them, but never in a million years would I have looked twice at Ronnie Davison. Just goes to show how misleading first impressions can be.'

'Oh, I'm not so sure about that. I noticed you when you came into the store.'

Inquisitively, he arched an eyebrow.

The directness of his stare was both exciting and unsettling. It caused a fluttering in her tummy. 'You cast an imposing silhouette, Doc, especially with your hat on.'

'Oh. Yeah. I've always been tall for my age.'

It was meant as a joke, and it worked to the extent that Tiel was able to resume breathing.

Then he said, 'Thanks for honouring my request not to be on camera.'

A twinge of conscience was hard to ignore. She mumbled an appropriate response, then, eager to change the subject, gestured towards Sabra. 'Any change?'

'Bleeding's increased again. Not as bad as before. I should get her to nurse the baby again. It's been over an hour, but I hate to disturb her while she's sleeping.'

'They're probably already watching that video. Maybe she'll be in a hospital soon.'

'She's a trouper. But she's exhausted.'

'So is Ronnie. The longer something like this drags on, the more excitable everyone becomes. Nerves snap. Tempers flare.'

'Then guns.'

'Don't even say it.' She shuddered. 'For an instant there, I was afraid that Ronnie's concern about sharpshooters was valid. What if Calloway had bamboozled me? Agreeing to do the video could have been a set-up in which Kip, Gully and I were pawns.'

Adjusting himself into a more comfortable position, he asked, 'Who's this Gully?'

She described their working relationship. 'He's a real character. I'll bet he's giving them fits out there,' she said with a smile.

'And who's Joseph? Boyfriend?'

The unexpected question pulled the plug on her smile. She was about to tell him to mind his own business, but in view of the audio-cassette in her possession, she rethought her reaction.

A good way to win his confidence would be to confide in him.

'Joseph and I had several dates. Joseph was on his way to earning the designation of "boyfriend", but he failed to mention that he was another woman's husband. I made that discovery yesterday afternoon.'

'Hmm. Mad?'

'You betcha. Furious.'

'Regrets?'

'Over him? No. None at all. Over being such a gullible goose, yes.' She hammered her fist into her palm as though it were a judge's gavel. 'From now on, all future dates are required to tender no less than three notarised character references.'

'What about your ex?'

Doc had a real knack for instantly deflating her smiles with an abrupt and sobering question. 'What about him?'

'Is he a consideration?'

'No.'

He frowned doubtfully. 'You looked awfully funny when I mentioned him.'

Inwardly she was pleading with him not to put her through this. By the same token, telling the story would serve him right for being so nosy.

'John Malone. Great TV name, huh? With a face and a voice to go with it. We met through work and fell hopelessly in love. The first few months were bliss. Then shortly after we were married, he was hired by one of the networks to be a foreign correspondent. It was a fantastic opportunity for John, and I was totally in favour of it. I envisioned living in Paris or London or Rome. But his choice came down to either South America or Bosnia.'

Absently she picked at a loose thread on the hem of the T-shirt. 'Naturally, I urged him to take the safer choice—Rio. He wanted to be where the action was, where he would be guaranteed more air time. We argued about it. Virulently. Finally I said, "All right, John, fine. Go. Get yourself killed."'

Raising her head, she met Doc's eyes. 'And that's what he did.'

His expression remained impassive.

Tiel plunged on. 'He had gone into an area where journalists weren't supposed to go, and caught a sniper bullet. They shipped his body home. I buried him three months shy of our first wedding anniversary.'

After a time, Doc said, 'That's tough. I'm sorry.'

'Yes, well . . .'

They were silent for a long while. It was Tiel who finally spoke. 'What's it been like for you?'

'In regards to what?'

'Relationships.'

'Specifically . . .?'

'Come on, Doc. Don't play dumb,' she chided softly. 'I was candid with you.'

'Which was your choice.'

'Fair's fair. Share with me.'

'What do you want? Names and dates? Starting when, Ms McCoy? Does high school count, or should I begin with college?'

'How about since your wife died?'

'How about you mind your own business?'

'In light of your wife's affair, I think you'd find it difficult to trust another woman.'

His mouth compressed into a tight, angry line, indicating that she'd struck a tender nerve. 'You don't know anything about—'

But Tiel never learned from him what she didn't know anything about because he was interrupted by Donna's earsplitting scream.

Chapter 7

KIP'S VIDEOTAPE WAS playing simultaneously on two monitors in the van, with everyone inside clustered round to view them.

The images were poignant, heart-rending. The dialogue was disturbing. No new mother cradling her infant should be threatening to take her own life.

For several seconds after the tape ended, no one spoke. Finally Gully said out loud what everyone else was thinking. 'Guess that settles the question as to who's responsible for all this.'

Calloway held up his hand, discouraging any further comments on Russell Dendy's culpability. He turned to Cole Davison. 'What about Ronnie? How does he seem to you?'

'Exhausted. Scared.'

'High?'

'No, sir,' Davison replied briskly. 'He doesn't do drugs.'

'Did you see anything unusual that should alert us to an unstable state of mind?'

'My eighteen-year-old son is talking about killing himself, Mr Calloway. I think that sums up his state of mind.'

'You know him, Mr Davison. Do you think Ronnie is bluffing? Do you believe he would go through with it?'

The man wrestled with his answer. Then he lowered his head dejectedly. 'No, I don't think so. Truly, I don't. But—'

'But what? Has Ronnie ever shown suicidal tendencies?'

'Never.'

'A violent streak? Uncontrollable temper?'

'No,' he replied shortly. Nervously his eyes shifted from Calloway to the others, then back to the agent. 'Well, only one time. It was an isolated incident. And he was just a kid.'

Inwardly Calloway groaned. 'You'd better tell me about it.'

After a long, uneasy silence, Davison began. 'Ronnie was staying with me during his summer vacation. He was having trouble adjusting to the divorce. Anyway,' he said, shifting his feet self-consciously, 'he took a shine to this dog that lived a few blocks over. He told me her owner didn't always feed her, never bathed her. Stuff like that.

'I knew the owner. He was a mean ol' bastard, drunk most of the time, so I knew Ronnie was telling the truth. But it was none of our business. I told Ronnie to stay away from the dog.'

Dendy interrupted. 'Is this sad story going anywhere?'

Calloway shot him a look and came close to telling him to shut up before turning back to the other man. 'What happened, Cole?'

'One day Ronnie unchained the dog and brought her to our house. I told him to return her immediately. He started crying and refused to. Said he'd rather see her dead. I scolded him and went to get my keys, to drive the dog home.

'But when I came back, Ronnie was gone and so was the dog. Long story short, I searched for them all night. Had neighbours out looking for him, too. Early the next morning a rancher spotted him and the dog hiding behind his barn and called the sheriff.

'As we converged on the barn, I called out to Ronnie, telling him that it was time to take the dog back to her owner and go home.' He stopped speaking and stared at the brim of his hat. 'When we came round to the back of the barn, he was crying his heart out. He was patting the dog where it was lying right there beside him. Dead. He'd hit it on the head with a rock and killed it.'

The eyes he raised to Calloway were red with threatened tears. 'I asked my boy how he could have done such a horrible thing. He told me he'd done it because he loved the dog so much.'

Calloway curbed the unprofessional impulse to press the man's shoulder. Instead he said tersely, 'Thank you for the insight.'

'So he's a head case,' Dendy muttered. 'Like I said all along.'

Although Dendy's remark was unnecessarily cruel, Calloway couldn't entirely disagree with the connotation. This incident from Ronnie's childhood dangerously paralleled the present circumstances.

He turned to Gully. 'What about Ms McCoy? Did you see any signs that suggest she's under duress?'

'Not that I could tell. And I grilled Kip here real good.'

The FBI agent turned to the video cameraman. 'Everything was as they've told us? Nobody hurt?'

'No, sir. The FBI guy is tied up—taped, rather—but he's all right.' He glanced at Dendy apprehensively. 'But the girl?'

'Sabra? What about her?'

'There were a lot of bloody disposable diapers around.'

Dendy strangled on an anguished exclamation.

Calloway continued with Kip. 'Did you notice anything in your co-worker's manner or delivery that was out of the ordinary?'

'Tiel was same as always. Well, except for looking like hell.'

Finally the senior agent turned to Dendy, who was drinking from a silver pocket flask. 'Did you see or hear anything to suggest Sabra might be sending you a secret message?'

'How could I tell by seeing the tape only that one time?'

The fact that the tyrannical entrepreneur was uneasy and indirect with his answer was telling. Dendy finally had been confronted with the ugly truth: his mishandling of the original predicament had prompted Sabra and Ronnie to take desperate measures, which had gone terribly awry.

'Rewind it,' Calloway instructed the agent at the control panel. 'Let's watch the tape again. Anybody notice anything, call out.'

The tape began again. 'Tiel picked that spot so we could see the people behind her,' Gully remarked.

'That's the refrigerator where the door was shattered,' one of the agents said, pointing to a spot on the screen.

'Pause it there.' Leaning forward, Calloway focused not on the news-woman but on the group of people in the background. 'The woman leaning against the counter must be the cashier.'

Sheriff Montez said, 'That's Donna, all right. No mistaking that hairdo.'

'And that's Agent Cain, right, Kip?' Calloway pointed to a pair of legs, which he could see only from the knees down.

'Right. He's sitting with his back to the counter.'

'What about the other two men?'

'Mexican fellows. I heard them speaking in Spanish.'

'Oh Jeez.' Calloway sprang far forward in his chair so quickly the castors sent it rolling from beneath him.

'What?'

The other agents, responding to their superior's apparent alarm, crowded round him. 'This one.' Calloway tapped the screen. 'Tell me if he looks familiar. Can you bring him in any closer?'

The agent manning the controls isolated the Mexican man's face. The agents squinted at the grainy picture, then one of them snapped his head round and exclaimed, 'Oh, no!'

Davison jumped in. 'What's the matter?'

Calloway began issuing orders. 'Call the office. Get everyone mobilised. Put out an APB—Montez, round up all your deputies. Notify neighbouring counties as well. Tell them to start looking for an abandoned truck. Railroad car. Removal van.'

'Truck? Removal van? What the hell is going on?' Dendy had to shout to make himself heard above the confusion in the cramped van. 'What about my daughter?'

'Sabra, all of them, are in more danger than we thought.'

As though to underscore Calloway's distressing words, they heard the unmistakable crack of gunfire.

Donna's scream brought Tiel to her feet. 'What now?'

Ronnie was brandishing his pistol and shouting, 'Get back! Get back! I'll shoot you!'

Two, the taller of the Mexicans, had charged him. Ronnie had halted him at gunpoint. 'Where's the other one?' he shouted frantically.

Sabra screamed: 'No! No!'

Tiel whirled round in time to see Juan snatch Katherine from Sabra's arms. He clutched the newborn tightly against his chest. The infant began squalling, but Sabra was shrieking as only a mother whose child is in danger can shriek. She was struggling to stand, clawing at Juan's trouser legs, as though to climb them.

'Sabra!' Ronnie cried. 'What's wrong?'

'He has the baby! Give me my baby! Don't hurt her!'

Tiel lunged forward, but Juan thrust out his hand and the heel of it caught her in the sternum, forcing her back.

'Tell him to give her the baby!' Ronnie was clutching the pistol in both hands, aiming it directly at Two's chest. 'Tell your friend to give her the baby, or I'll kill you!'

Perhaps to see just how earnest Ronnie's threat was, Juan made the mistake of glancing towards the front of the store where the two were facing off.

Doc used that split second to make a lunge for him.

But the Mexican reacted instantly. He executed a practised uppercut that made a significant dent in Doc's belly. Doc bent in half at the waist, then collapsed to the floor in front of the freezer.

'Tell him to give her the baby!' Ronnie repeated in a shrill voice that splintered like thin ice.

Tiel was begging Juan not to harm Katherine. 'Don't hurt her. She's no threat to you. Give the baby to her mother. Please.'

Sabra was practically helpless. Nevertheless, maternal instinct propelled her to her feet. She was so weak she could barely stand. Swaying slightly, hands outstretched, she implored the man to return her baby to her.

Juan and Two were shouting back and forth to one another, trying to communicate above the other voices, including those of Vern and Gladys, who was cursing a blue streak. Donna was caterwauling. Agent Cain was shouting.

The gunshot rendered everyone speechless.

Tiel, who had been appealing to Juan, witnessed his grimace when the bullet struck. Reflexively, he grabbed his thigh. He would have dropped Katherine if Tiel hadn't been there to catch her. Holding the baby close, she spun round, wondering how Ronnie had managed to get off a shot so well placed that it had disabled Juan but hadn't endangered the baby.

But Ronnie still had his pistol trained on Two's chest and seemed as surprised as anyone that a gun had been fired.

Doc had been the marksman. He was lying on his back on the floor, a small revolver in his hand. Tiel recognised Agent Cain's weapon, the one she had kicked beneath the freezer and forgotten. Thank God Doc had remembered it.

He took advantage of the momentary silence. 'Gladys, get over here.' The old lady came scurrying over. 'Take the baby so Tiel can tend to Sabra. I'll take care of him,' he said, referring to Juan. 'Ronnie, relax. Everything's under control. No need to panic.'

'Is the baby OK?'

'She's fine.' Gladys carried the crying infant over to where Ronnie could see her for himself. 'She's mad as hell, and I can't say as I blame her.' Glaring back at Juan where he now sat on the floor gripping his bleeding thigh, she snarled with contempt.

Several jabs of Ronnie's pistol sent Two skulking back to his original spot. His expression was meaner and more agitated than before.

Doc placed Cain's revolver high on a grocery shelf, well out of Juan's reach, and knelt down to cut open his trouser leg with the scissors. 'You'll live,' he said laconically after assessing the damage and stuffing gauze pads into the wound. 'Lucky for you the bullet missed the femoral artery.'

Juan's eyes blazed with resentment.

'Doc?' Tiel had got Sabra to lie back down, but fresh blood was making the floor around her slick. The girl was ghastly pale.

'I know,' Doc said soberly, picking up on Tiel's unspoken alarm. 'Make her as comfortable as you can. I'll be right back.'

He had hurriedly bandaged Juan's wound and fashioned a tourniquet with another of the souvenir T-shirts. Evidently in excruciating pain, Juan was sweating profusely, and his straight, white teeth were clenched. But, to his credit, he didn't cry out when Doc unceremoniously and none too gently hoisted him to his feet and supported him as he hopped on one foot.

As they went past Cain, the agent addressed the gunshot man. 'You fool, you could've got us all killed. What were you—'

Quicker than a striking rattlesnake, Juan, using the foot of his injured leg, kicked Cain viciously in the head. Cain went silent and unconscious in the same instant.

Doc pushed Juan to the floor, propping him against the refrigerator, well away from his confederate. 'He's not going anywhere. But just to be safe, better bind his hands, Ronnie. His too,' he added, motioning towards Two.

Ronnie instructed Vern to tape the two men's hands and feet. He held the pistol on them while the old man went about the task.

The ringing telephone had gone unanswered and largely ignored. Tiel was working frantically to replace the blood-soaked diaper beneath Sabra, when the phone suddenly stopped ringing and she heard Ronnie shout, 'Not now, we're busy!' before slamming the receiver back into the cradle. Then he called, 'How's Sabra?'

Tiel addressed him over her shoulder. 'Not good.' She was vastly relieved to see Doc returning. 'What's going on?'

'Juan kicked Cain in the head. He's unconscious.'

'I never thought I'd be thanking that man for anything.'

'Vern is binding them. I'm glad they're . . . contained.'

She noticed the intensity in his face. 'They really had nothing to lose by trying to seize control of the situation.'

'True. But what did they have to gain?'

After thinking about it, she said, 'Nothing that I can see.'

'Nothing that you can *see*. That's what bothers me. There's more,' he continued in a lower voice. 'Men with rifles have taken up position outside. Probably a SWAT team.'

'Oh, no. Has Ronnie seen them?'

'I don't think so. That shot I fired must've got everyone thinking the worst. They might storm the building.'

The telephone rang again. 'Ronnie, answer it,' Doc called to him. 'Explain to them what happened.'

'Not until I know Sabra's all right.'

Although Tiel wasn't a medical expert by any means, Sabra's condition appeared critical to her. But, like Doc, she didn't want Ronnie any more frazzled than he already was.

'Where's Katherine?' the girl asked weakly.

Doc, who had done his best to stem the flow of fresh blood, peeled off his glove and smoothed her hair away from her forehead. 'Gladys is taking good care of her.'

'We're not going to get out of here, are we?' the girl asked.

'Don't say that, Sabra,' Tiel whispered fiercely, watching Doc's face as he read the blood-pressure gauge.

'Daddy's not going to give up. Neither am I. And neither is Ronnie.' She divided a glassy, hollow-eyed gaze between Tiel and Doc. 'Tell Ronnie to come over here. I want to talk to him. I don't want to wait any longer.'

Although she didn't specifically mention their suicide pact, her meaning was clear. Tiel's chest grew tight with despair. 'We can't let you do it, Sabra. You know it's not the answer.'

'Please help us. It's what we want.'

Then, against Sabra's will, her eyes closed. She was too weak to reopen them and lapsed into a doze.

Tiel looked across at Doc. 'It's bad, isn't it?'

'Very. Blood pressure's dropping. She's going to bleed out.'

'What are we going to do?'

Sternly staring into the girl's pale, still face, he thought on it a moment, then said, 'I'll tell you what I'm going to do.'

He stood up, retrieved the pistol from the shelf and approached Ronnie, who was waiting for an update on Sabra's condition.

The gunshots had plunged everyone in the van into near panic. Cole Davison had rushed outside, only to return moments later, yelling at Calloway because the SWAT team had been mobilised.

'You promised! You said Ronnie wouldn't get hurt.'

'Calm down, Mr Davison. I'm taking precautionary measures as I see fit.' Calloway held the telephone receiver to his ear, but thus far his call into the convenience store had gone unanswered. 'Can anybody see anything?'

'Movement,' one of the other agents hollered. Via a headset, he was communicating with another agent outside who was equipped with binoculars. 'Can't make out who's doing what.'

'Keep me posted.'

'Yes, sir. Are you going to tell the kid about Huerta?'

'Who's that?' Dendy wanted to know.

'Luis Huerta. One of our Ten Most Wanted.' To the other agent, Calloway replied, 'No, I'm not going to tell them. That might panic everyone, including Huerta. He's capable of just about anything.'

Ronnie answered the phone. 'Not now, we're busy!'

Calloway swore lavishly when the dial tone replaced Ronnie's frantic voice. He immediately redialled.

'One of the Mexicans in there is on the FBI's Ten Most Wanted list?' Cole Davison was increasingly distraught. 'What for?'

'He smuggles Mexican nationals across the border with promises of well-paying jobs, then sells them into slave labour. Last summer Huerta and two henchmen, realising they were about to be apprehended, abandoned the truck in the New Mexico desert and scattered like the cockroaches they are. All evaded capture.

'The van wasn't found for three days. Forty-five people—men, women and children—had been locked in from the outside. Huerta is wanted on forty-five counts of murder.

'For almost a year he's been holed up somewhere in Mexico. If he's resurfaced here, then I'm guessing that somewhere in the general vicinity there's a shipment of people waiting to be sold.'

Davison looked ready to heave his last meal. 'Who's the man with him?'

'One of his bodyguards, I'm sure. They're ruthless men. What puzzles me is why they haven't shot their way out before now.'

Dendy's chest rose and fell, emitting a gurgling sound like a sob. 'Listen, Calloway. I've been thinking.'

Even though Calloway kept the telephone receiver to his ear, he gave Russell Dendy his full attention. Dendy appeared on the brink of losing control of his emotions, no longer belligerent. 'I'm listening, Mr Dendy.'

'Tell Sabra she can keep the baby. I won't interfere. That videotape of my daughter . . .' He rubbed the back of his hand across leaking eyes.

'It got to me. Nothing else matters any more. I just want to see my daughter safely out of there.'

'That's my goal too, Mr Dendy,' Calloway assured him.

'Agree to any of the boy's terms.'

'I'll negotiate for him the best deal I can. But first, I've got to get him to talk to me.'

The telephone continued to ring.

Ronnie?'

The young man didn't realise that Doc was in possession of the pistol. Evidently, in all the confusion, Ronnie had forgotten about Cain's secreted weapon. Doc raised his hand, and, seeing the gun, the younger man flinched. Donna let out a squeal of fright.

Doc palmed the barrel and extended the grip towards Ronnie. 'That's how much faith I have in you to make the right decision.'

Looking terribly young, uncertain and vulnerable, Ronnie took the gun and stuffed it into the waistband of his jeans. 'You already know my decision, Doc.'

'Suicide? That's not a decision. That's a cop-out.'

'I don't want to talk about it. Sabra and I have made up our minds.'

'Answer the phone,' Doc encouraged in a calm, persuasive voice. 'Tell them what happened in here. They heard the shots. They don't know what's going on, but they're probably thinking the worst. Allay their fears, Ronnie. Otherwise, at any second a SWAT team may come barging in here.'

'What SWAT team? You're lying.'

'I saw men taking up positions while you were distracted by tying up those Mexican guys. The SWAT team is out there, itching for a signal from Calloway. Don't give him reason to activate them.'

Ronnie glanced nervously through the plate glass, but he could see nothing except the growing number of official vehicles.

'Let me answer the phone, Ronnie,' Tiel suggested, stepping forward to take advantage of his indecision. 'They could be calling to agree to your conditions.'

'OK,' he muttered, motioning her towards the telephone.

She counted it a blessing to stop the infernal ringing. 'It's Tiel,' she said, upon lifting the receiver.

'Ms McCoy, who fired those shots? What's going on in there?'

Calloway's brusqueness conveyed his concern. Not wanting to keep him in suspense, as succinctly as possible she explained how Cain's pistol had come to be fired. 'The situation is under control again. The two men who caused the fracas have been contained,' she said, using Doc's euphemistic terminology.

'You're referring to the two Mexican men?'

'That's correct.'

'And where is Agent Cain's pistol now?'

'Doc gave it to Ronnie. As a sign of trust.'

The FBI agent expelled a long breath. 'That's a hell of a lot of trust, Ms McCoy.'

'It was the right thing to do. You'd have to be here to understand.'

'Apparently,' he said drily.

While talking to Calloway, she'd been listening with one ear to Doc trying to persuade Ronnie to surrender. She heard him say, 'You're a father now. You're responsible for your family. Sabra's condition is critical, and there's nothing more I can do for her.'

Calloway asked, 'You don't feel in danger of him?'

'Not at all.'

'Are any of the hostages in danger?'

'Presently, no. I can't predict what will happen if those guys in body armour charge the place.'

'I don't intend to give that order.'

'Then why are they there?' He paused for a long moment, and Tiel got the distinct impression that he was withholding something. 'Mr Calloway, if there's something I should know—'

'We've had a change of heart.'

'You're giving up and going away?'

Calloway ignored her facetiousness. 'You'll be glad to learn that the videotape achieved what you hoped. Mr Dendy is ready to make concessions. He wants this to end peaceably and safely. As we all do. Do you think Ronnie'll go for total surrender?'

'He specified the conditions under which he would surrender, Mr Calloway.'

'Dendy will concede that this was a runaway and not a kidnapping. Of course the additional charges would stand.'

'And they must be allowed to keep their child.'

'Dendy said as much himself a few minutes ago. If Davison will agree to those terms, I guarantee that no force will be used.'

'I'll pass along the message and get back to you.'

'I'm standing by.'

She hung up. Everyone was listening intently.

'The kidnapping allegation has been dropped,' she told Ronnie, who was listening expectantly. 'You'll have to face other criminal charges. Mr Dendy has agreed to let Sabra keep the baby. If you agree to these terms and surrender, Mr Calloway gives you his personal guarantee that no force will be used.'

'It's a good deal, Ronnie,' Doc said. 'Take it.'

'No, don't.' Sabra had somehow managed to stand and was leaning heavily against the freezer chest in order to keep herself upright. Her eyes were sunken and her complexion was leeched of all colour. 'It's a trick, Ronnie. One of Daddy's tricks.'

Doc rushed over to lend her support. 'I don't think so, Sabra. Your dad responded to the video message you sent him.'

Gratefully she clung to Doc, but her dull eyes beseeched Ronnie. 'I won't leave until I know I can be with you for ever.'

'Sabra, what about your baby?' Tiel asked gently. 'Think of her.'

'Carry her out. Give her to someone who'll take care of her. No matter what happens to us—to Ronnie and me—it's important to me to know that Katherine is going to be all right.'

Tiel looked hopefully towards Doc for inspiration, but he seemed to feel as helpless as she.

'That's it then,' Ronnie stated firmly. 'That's what we'll do. We'll let you carry Katherine out. But we're not leaving until they let us go. Free and clear. No compromise.'

'They'll never agree to that,' Tiel said with desperation. 'That's an unreasonable demand.'

'You committed armed robbery,' Doc added. 'You'll have to account for that, Ronnie. Running away would solve nothing.'

Tiel glanced at Doc, wondering if he were listening to his own advice. The admonishment against running away could be applied to him and his circumstances three years ago. He didn't notice her glance, however, because his attention was on Ronnie.

'Sabra and I vowed that we would never be forced apart. No matter what. We meant it.'

'What about the others? Will you release them?'

He glanced beyond her at the other hostages. 'Not the two Mexicans. And not him,' he said of Agent Cain. He had regained consciousness but appeared incoherent. 'The old folks and her. They can go.'

When he pointed to Donna, she clasped her claw-like hands beneath her chin. 'Thank you, Lord.'

Gladys was still holding the sleeping infant in her arms, and Vern assisted her up off the floor. 'Before we go, I'm sure Sabra wants to tell Katherine goodbye,' he said.

The old lady carried the baby over to Sabra, where she was leaning heavily against Doc.

'Shall I notify Calloway of your decision?' Tiel asked Ronnie.

He was watching Sabra and his baby. 'Half an hour.'

'What?'

'That's the time limit I'm giving them to get back to me. If they won't let us leave in half an hour, we'll . . . we'll carry out our plan,' he said thickly.

'Ronnie, please.'

'That's it, Ms McCoy. You tell them.'

Calloway answered her call before the completion of the first ring. 'I'm coming out with the baby. Have medical personnel standing by. I'm bringing out three of the hostages with me.'

'What about the rest?'

'I'll tell you when I get there.'

She hung up on him.

As Tiel approached Sabra, the young woman was crying. 'Bye-bye, sweet Katherine. My beautiful baby girl; Mommie loves you. Very much.' She kissed Katherine's face several times, then turned her own into Doc's shirt and sobbed.

Tiel took the baby from Gladys, who'd been holding her because Sabra didn't have the strength. Tiel carried Katherine over to Ronnie. As the young man gazed at the baby, his eyes filled with tears.

'Thanks for all you've done,' he said to Tiel. 'I know Sabra liked having you around.'

Tiel's eyes appealed to him. 'I don't believe you'll do it, Ronnie. I refuse to believe you would—could—pull that trigger and end Sabra's life and yours.'

He chose not to respond and instead kissed the baby's forehead. 'Bye, Katherine. I love you.' Then he stepped behind the counter to release the electric door lock.

Tiel allowed the others to go ahead of her. Before stepping through the door, she glanced over her shoulder at Doc. He had eased Sabra back onto the floor, but he raised his head as though Tiel's gaze had beckoned him. Their eyes connected for only a millisecond, but, undeniably, it was a meaningful span of time and contact.

Then she slipped through the door and heard the bolt snap into place behind her.

From out of the darkness paramedics rushed forward. A man and woman wearing identical scrubs and lab coats materialised in front of Tiel. The woman reached for Katherine, but Tiel didn't relinquish her just yet. 'Who are you?'

'Dr Emily Garrett.' She introduced herself as chief of the neonatal unit at a Midland hospital. 'This is Dr Landry Giles, chief of obstetrics.'

Tiel said, 'Regardless of anything you've heard to the contrary, the parents do not wish to put the child up for adoption.'

Dr Garrett's expression was as guileless as Tiel could have hoped for. 'I understand completely. We'll be waiting for the mother's arrival.'

Tiel kissed the top of Katherine's head. She had a bond with this baby—she had witnessed her birth, her first breath, had heard her first cry. Even so, the depth of her emotion surprised her. 'Take good care of her.'

Dr Garrett took the baby and ran with her towards the waiting chopper, the blades of which were kicking up a fierce wind. Dr Giles had to shout to make himself heard above the racket.

'How's the mother?'

'Not good.' Tiel described Sabra's condition. 'Doc's most worried about loss of blood and infection. Sabra's increasingly weak. Her blood pressure is dropping, he said. Based on what I've told you, is there anything you can advise him to do?'

'Get her to the hospital.'

'We're working on it,' she said grimly.

The man approaching with a long and purposeful stride could only be Calloway. He was tall and slender, and exuded an air of authority. 'Bill Calloway,' he said, confirming his identity as soon as he joined her and Dr Giles. They shook hands.

Gully hobbled up to her in his bandy-legged run. 'Jesus, kid, if I don't die of a heart attack after tonight, I'll live for ever.'

She hugged him. 'You'll outlive us all.'

On the fringes of the growing group she noticed a stout man dressed in a white cowboy shirt with pearl buttons. Before she could introduce herself to him, he was rudely elbowed aside.

'Ms McCoy, I want to talk to you.'

She recognised Russell Dendy immediately.

'How's my daughter?'

'She's dying.' While the statement seemed unnecessarily harsh, Tiel was fresh out of compassion for the millionaire. Besides, if she were to make a dent in this stalemate, she must hit them hard.

Her blunt response to Dendy's question took him aback momentarily, which enabled Calloway to draw the other man forward. 'Cole Davison, Tiel McCoy.'

The resemblance between Ronnie and his father was unmistakable. 'How is he?' he asked anxiously.

'Resolute, Mr Davison. Those young people took an oath. Now that Katherine is safe, there's nothing to stop them from carrying out their suicide pact.' She used the words deliberately to emphasise the seriousness of the situation.

Calloway ran a hand through his thinning hair and watched the chopper with Dr Garrett and the newborn lift off. 'The hostages aren't at risk?' he asked.

'I don't believe so. Although there's no love lost between Ronnie and Agent Cain or the Mexican men.'

They exchanged an uneasy look all around, but before Tiel could ask what it portended, Calloway said, 'To summarise, Ronnie and Sabra are bartering with their own lives.'

'Exactly, Mr Calloway. I was sent to tell you that you have half an hour to get back to them.'

'With what?'

'Clemency, and freedom to go on their way.'

'You're a reasonable person, Ms McCoy. You know I can't make that kind of blanket deal with an alleged felon.'

Despair and defeat settled on her heavily. 'I'm only the messenger, Mr Calloway. I'm telling you what Ronnie told me. My gut feeling is that he means to do what he has said he will. Even if he's bluffing, Sabra is not.'

Calloway checked his wristwatch. 'Half an hour,' he said briskly. 'Not much time, and I've got some calls to make.' They turned in unison towards the van.

Gully was the first to notice that Tiel didn't fall into step with the rest of them. He turned and regarded her curiously. 'Tiel?'

She was walking backwards. 'I'm going back.'

'You aren't serious?' Gully's exclamation spoke for all of them.

They were looking at her with unmitigated dismay.

'I can't abandon Sabra.'

'But—'

She shook her head firmly, checking Gully's protest before it was out. Continuing to backtrack and widen the distance between them, she said. 'We'll be waiting for your decision, Mr Calloway.'

Chapter 8

TIEL STOOD FACING the door of the store for a full ninety seconds before she heard the bolt being released. As she re-entered, Ronnie eyed her warily.

'What did Calloway say?'

'He's thinking it over. He said he has to make some calls.'

'To who? What for?'

'I gather he doesn't have the authority to grant you clemency.'

Ronnie gnawed his lower lip which had already been so brutalised it was raw. 'OK. So why did you come back?'

'To let you know that Katherine is in excellent hands.' She told him about Dr Emily Garrett.

'Tell Sabra. She'll want to know that.'

The young mother's eyes were half closed. Her breathing was shallow. Tiel wasn't sure she was completely aware and listening, but after describing to her the neonatal specialist, Sabra whispered, 'Is she nice?'

'Very. When you meet her, you'll see.' Tiel glanced over at Doc, but he was taking Sabra's blood pressure, his eyebrows pulled together in the frown she'd come to recognise. 'There's another very nice doctor waiting to take care of you. His name is Dr Giles. You're not afraid to fly in helicopters, are you?'

'I did once. With my dad. It was OK.'

Sabra smiled, then her eyes closed.

By tacit agreement, Tiel and Doc retreated to their familiar posts. Seated on the floor with their backs propped against the freezer chest, watching the clock, it was the ideal moment for Doc to ask the question that Tiel expected from him.

'Why'd you come back?'

Even assuming that he would ask, she had no clear-cut answer.

Several moments elapsed. His jaw was dark with stubble, she noticed. His clothes, like hers, were grimy and bloodstained.

Blood was a cohesive agent, she realised. It wasn't necessarily the commingling of blood from two individuals that formed a bond between them. It could be anyone's shed blood that united people. Survivors shared a common ground. Their connection was rare and unique, and almost always unexplainable.

Tiel had taken so long to answer that Doc repeated his question. 'Why'd you come back?'

'For Sabra,' she replied. 'I was the only woman left. I thought she might need me. And . . .'

He raised his knees, propped his forearms on them and looked at her, waiting patiently for her to complete her thought.

'And I hate to start something and not finish it. I was here when it started, so I figured I should stick around until it's over.'

It wasn't quite as simple as that. Her reason for returning was more complex, but she was at a loss to explain her multilayered motivation to Doc when even to her it was unclear. Why wasn't she out there doing a live remote, taking advantage of the extraordinary insight she had on this story? Why wasn't she recording a voice track to couple with the dramatic images Kip was getting on video?

'What were you doing out here?'

Doc's question roused her from her musings. 'In Rojo Flats?' She laughed. 'I was on vacation.' She explained how she was en route to New Mexico when she heard of the so-called kidnapping on her car radio. 'I called Gully, who assigned me to interview Cole Davison. On my way to Hera I got lost. I stopped here to use the rest room and call Gully for directions.'

'That's who you were talking to when I came in?'

Tiel's gaze sharpened on him, her expression inquisitive.

He raised his shoulders in a slight shrug. 'I noticed you back there on the payphone when I came in.'

'You did? Oh.' Their eyes connected and held, and it was an effort for her to break that stare. 'Anyway, I concluded my call and was buying snacks for the road when . . . who should walk in but Ronnie and Sabra.'

'That's a story in itself.'

'I couldn't believe my good fortune.' She smiled wryly. 'Be careful what you wish for.'

'I am.' After a beat of five, he added quietly, 'Now.'

This time it was she who waited him out, giving him the opportunity either to expound on his thought or to let the subject drop.

'After I found out about Shari's affair, I wanted her to . . .'

'Suffer.'

'Yeah.' The long sigh he released around the word evinced his relief over finally getting the confession off his chest. Confidences wouldn't come easily to a man like him who had dealt in life-and-death situations on a daily basis. To have the courage and tenacity to battle such a seemingly omnipotent enemy as cancer, there was surely a fairly generous degree of the god complex in Bradley Stanwick's make-up. Vulnerability, any sign of weakness, was incompatible with that personality trait.

Tiel was flattered that he had revealed to her even a glimpse of this all-too-human aspect of himself.

'Her cancer wasn't punishment for her adultery,' she argued gently. 'It certainly wasn't your revenge.'

'I know. Rationally and reasonably I know that. But when she was going through the worst of it—and, believe me, it was sheer hell—I thought I had subconsciously wished it on her.'

'So now you're punishing yourself with this self-imposed banishment from your profession.'

He fired back, 'And you're not?'

'What?'

'Punishing yourself because your husband got killed? You're doing the work of two people to make up for the industry loss created when he died.'

'That's ridiculous.'

'Is it?'

'Yes. I work hard because I love it.'

'But you'll never be able to do enough, will you?'

An angry retort died on her lips. She had never examined the psychology behind her ambition. She had never *allowed* herself to examine it. But now that she'd been confronted with this hypothesis, she had to admit that it had merit. The ambition had always been there. But not to the degree of the last four years. She worked to the exclusion of everything else. It wasn't a matter of her career taking precedence over other areas of her life; it *was* her life. Was her mad, singular desire to succeed a self-inflicted penance for those few ill-chosen words spoken in the heat of anger?

They lapsed into silence, each lost in his or her own troubling thoughts, grappling with the personal demons they'd been forced to acknowledge.

'Where in New Mexico?'

'What?' Tiel turned to him. 'Oh, my destination? Angel Fire.'

'Heard of it. Never been there.'

'Mountain air and clear streams. Aspen trees. They'd be green now, not gold, but I hear it's beautiful.'

'You hear? You haven't been there either?'

She shook her head. 'A friend was lending me her condo for the week.'

'You'd be there by now, all tucked in. Too bad you placed that first call to Gully.'

'I don't know, Doc.' She glanced at Sabra, then looked at him. Closely. Taking in every nuance of his rugged face. Plumbing the depths of his eyes. 'I wouldn't have missed this for the world.'

The urge to touch him was almost irresistible. She did resist, but she didn't break eye contact. It lasted a long time, while her heart thudded hard and heavily against her ribs and her senses hummed with a keen, sweet awareness of him.

She actually jumped when the telephone rang.

Clumsily she scrambled to her feet, and so did Doc.

Ronnie grabbed the receiver. 'Mr Calloway?'

He listened for what seemed to Tiel an eternity. She wanted to take Doc's hand and hold on to it tightly, as people are wont to do when waiting to hear life-altering news.

Finally Ronnie turned to them and placed the earpiece against his chest. 'Calloway says he's got the district attorney of Tarrant County, and whatever this county is, plus a judge, himself and both sets of parents, agreed to meet and hammer this thing out. He says if I admit to wrongdoing and submit to counselling, maybe I'll get probation and not have to go to jail. Maybe.'

Tiel nearly collapsed with relief. 'That's great!'

'It's a good deal, Ronnie. Grab it,' Doc told him.

'Sabra, is that OK with you?'

When she didn't respond, Doc brushed past Tiel and knelt beside the girl.

'Oh God,' Ronnie cried. 'Is she dead?'

'She's unconscious but she's got to get help, son. And I mean fast.'

Tiel left Sabra in Doc's care and moved towards Ronnie. She was afraid that in his despair, he might yet turn the pistol on himself. 'Tell Calloway you agree to the terms. I'm going to cut the tape binding them,' she said, gesturing to Cain, Juan and Two. 'OK?'

Ronnie was transfixed by the sight of Doc lifting Sabra into his arms. Blood immediately saturated his clothes. 'Oh God, what've I done?'

'Save the regrets for later, Ronnie,' Doc said in a stern voice. 'Tell Calloway we're coming out.'

The dazed young man began mumbling into the mouthpiece. Tiel quickly retrieved the scissors they'd used earlier and knelt down beside Cain. She sawed through the tape round his ankles. 'What about my hands?' His tongue seemed thick.

'When you get outside.'

His eyes narrowed to slits. 'You're in deep trouble, lady.'

'Usually,' Tiel quipped, and moved to the Mexican men. Juan was enduring his leg wound stoically, but she could feel resentment emanating from him like heat from a furnace. Keeping as much distance as possible between him and herself, she cut the tape round his ankles.

She felt even more aversion for the one she'd nicknamed Two. His dark eyes roved over her with unconcealed malevolence and an intentionally demeaning, sexual suggestiveness that made her feel in even more need of a shower.

That chore completed, she said, 'Doc, go first,' and motioned him towards the door. 'Right, Ronnie?'

'Right, right. Get Sabra to someone who can help her, Doc.'

Tiel moved to the door and held it open for him. Sabra looked like a faded rag doll in his arms. She looked dead. Ronnie lovingly touched her hair, her cheek. When she didn't respond, he moaned.

'Hang in there, Ronnie, she's alive,' Doc assured him.

In a blink, he was gone, running across the parking lot carrying the unconscious girl.

'You next,' Ronnie said to Tiel.

She shook her head. 'I'm staying with you. We'll go out together.'

'You don't trust Calloway?' he asked in a voice made high and thin by fright.

'I don't trust *them*.' She hitched her head back towards the other three hostages. 'Let them go first.'

He contemplated that for an instant. 'OK. Cain. Go.'

The FBI agent skulked past them. Ronnie waited until he had been swallowed up by a crowd of paramedics and officials before he motioned Juan and Two towards the door. 'You next.'

After trying twice to escape, they now seemed reluctant to leave. 'Come on,' Tiel said, impatiently motioning them through the door. She was frantic to know how Sabra was faring.

Juan went first, limping noticeably. He hesitated on the threshold, his eyes darting to various points on the parking lot. Two, she noticed, was on Juan's heels, practically using the other man as a shield. They stepped through the door.

Suddenly the front of the store was seared with blinding light. The SWAT team, looking like black beetles, came scurrying from every conceivable hiding place.

Ronnie cursed and ducked behind the counter. Tiel screamed, but from outrage, not fear. She was too livid to be afraid.

Oddly, however, the tactical officers surrounded Juan and Two, ordering them to lie face down on the ground. Before Tiel could assimilate what had happened, it was over. The two men were shackled and dragged away by the SWAT team.

The lights went out as suddenly as they'd come on.

'Ronnie?' His name was bellowed through a bullhorn. 'Ms McCoy?' It was Calloway. 'Don't be alarmed. You've been in the company of some very dangerous men. We saw them on the videotape and recognised them. They're wanted by the authorities here and in Mexico. That's why they were so eager to escape. They're in our custody now. It's safe for you to come out.'

Far from being calmed by this information, Tiel was furious. How dare they not warn her of the potential danger!

With as much composure as she could muster, she said to Ronnie, 'You heard him. The SWAT team had nothing to do with you. Everything's OK. Let's go.'

He still looked afraid and uncertain. In any case, he didn't move from behind the counter.

God, please don't let me make a deadly mistake now, Tiel prayed.

'I think it would be best if you left the pistols here, don't you? Lay them there on the counter. Then you can walk out with your hands up, and they'll know that you're sincere in wanting to work things out.' He didn't move.

He looked tired, depleted, defeated. *Not defeated*, she corrected. If he looked upon this as a defeat, he might not leave. He might take what would seem to him the easier way out.

'You did an exceptionally brave thing, Ronnie,' she said conversationally. 'Standing up to Russell Dendy. The FBI. You and Sabra wanted someone to listen and play fair with you. And you've got them to do just that. That's quite an achievement. Set the guns down and let's go.'

He placed the two pistols on the counter, and as he wiped his damp palms on the legs of his jeans, Tiel exhaled the breath she'd been holding.

He licked his bruised lips. 'Go ahead. I'm right behind you.'

Nervously she turned towards the door, opened it and stepped through. The sky was no longer black, she noticed, but dark grey, so that the silhouettes of all the vehicles and people showed up against it. The air was already hot and dry. There was a light wind, carrying sand that abraded her skin as it blew across her.

She took a few steps before glancing back. Ronnie had his hand on the door, ready to push it open.

Ahead, waiting for her, she could make out Calloway. Mr Davison. Gully. Sheriff Montez.

And Doc. He was there. Standing a little apart from the others. Tall. Broad-shouldered. Hair lifting in the wind.

From the corner of her eye she saw the SWAT team herding Two into a van. The door was slammed closed and the van sped from the parking lot with a screech of tyres. Juan had been confined to a gurney, where paramedics were tending to him.

Tiel's glance had just moved past him when she did a double take. He began wrestling against the paramedic trying to insert an IV needle into the back of his hand. His mouth was moving, forming words, and she wondered why she found that puzzling.

Then she realised that he was shouting in English.

But he didn't speak English, she thought stupidly.

Furthermore, the words made no sense because he was yelling at the top of his lungs. 'He's got a rifle! There! Oh God, no!'

The words registered a split second before Juan sprang off the gurney. He launched himself into the man, his shoulder landing hard against the other's torso and knocking him to the ground.

But not before Russell Dendy got off a clean shot.

Tiel heard the shattering sound and spun round to see the door of the convenience store raining glass onto Ronnie's prone form. She didn't remember later crossing back to the entrance at a full-out run, or dropping to her hands and knees despite the glass.

She did recall hearing Juan shout—to save his life—'Martinez, Treasury agent, working undercover!'

The antiseptic the paramedic was dabbing onto her hands and knees made them sting. Tiel hadn't noticed the cuts at all until the paramedic began removing splinters of glass with tiny tweezers.

Seated on a gurney, she tried to see round the woman who was treating her. It was a chaotic scene. In the pale dawn, the lights of a dozen police and emergency vehicles created a dizzying kaleidoscope of flashing, coloured lights. Medical personnel, those who hadn't rushed to Ronnie's aid, were seeing to her, Treasury Agent Martinez and Cain.

The media had been denied access to the immediate area, but news helicopters buzzed overhead like brute insects. Parked on a ridge overlooking Rojo Flats was a convoy of television vans. The satellite dishes mounted on their roofs reflected the new sun.

Ordinarily she would be in her element in this kind of scene. But the customary rush of adrenaline just hadn't been there when she stared into the lens of the video camera to do her live report. She had shouted into her microphone as the CareFlight helicopter lifted off, bearing Ronnie Davison to the nearest emergency centre, where a trauma team was standing by to treat the gunshot wound in his chest. The fierce winds created by the whirling blades whipped sand into her eyes. It was the blowing sand to which she attributed her unprofessional tears.

As soon as she concluded her ad-libbed summary of the events of the past six hours, she listlessly passed the mike back to Kip, and consented to having her bleeding palms and knees examined.

'Tiel, you OK?' Gully came huffing up to her. 'The video looks great, kid. Best you've ever done. If this doesn't get you the *Nine Live* spot, then life ain't fair.'

'Have you heard anything about Ronnie's condition?'

'Not a thing.'

'Sabra?'

'Nothing. Not since the cowboy turned her over to that Dr Giles and they took her off in the chopper.'

'Speaking of Doc, is he around?'

Gully didn't hear her. He was shaking his head and muttering, 'Wish they had given me a crack at Dendy.'

'I assume he's under arrest.'

'The sheriff had three deputies haul his ass off to jail.'

Even though she had seen it with her own eyes, she still found it impossible to believe that Dendy had shot Ronnie Davison. She expressed her dismay to Gully. 'I don't understand how that could have happened.'

'Nobody was paying him any attention. He had put on a good show for Calloway. He led us to believe that he had seen the error of his ways, that all was forgiven, and that he only wanted Sabra to be safe. The lying bastard.'

Tiel's pent-up emotions boiled to the surface, and she began to cry. 'It's my fault, Gully. I promised Ronnie it would be safe for him to come out, that if he surrendered, he wouldn't be hurt.'

'That's what we all promised him, Ms McCoy.'

She turned towards the familiar voice, her tears drying instantly. 'I'm very put out with you, Agent Calloway.'

'As your colleague explained, I fell for Dendy's act of contrition. Nobody knew he had a rifle with him.'

'Not just that. You could have warned me about that Huerta character when I brought the baby out.'

'And if you'd known who he was, what would you have done?'

She didn't know, but somehow that seemed irrelevant. She asked, 'Did you know Martinez was a Treasury agent?'

Calloway looked chagrined. 'No. We assumed he was one of Huerta's henchmen.'

Remembering how the wounded, shackled man had flung himself at Dendy, she remarked, 'He did an awfully brave thing. Not only did he blow his cover, but he also risked his life. If any of the other officers had reacted more quickly . . .'

'I've thought of that,' Calloway admitted grimly. 'He'd like to talk to you.'

Calloway led her to another ambulance, apprising her along the way of Martinez's condition. 'The bullet went through his leg without nicking a bone or an artery. Twice tonight he got lucky.'

Martinez was hooked up to an IV and was also getting a transfusion of blood. But his eyes were clear. 'Ms McCoy.'

'Agent Martinez. You're very good at your job. You had us all fooled.'

He smiled, showing the very straight, white teeth she had noticed before. 'That's the goal of an undercover operative. Thank God Huerta was also fooled. I've been a member of his organisation since last summer. A truckload of people came across the border last night.'

'It was intercepted about an hour ago,' Calloway informed them. 'As usual, the conditions inside were deplorable. The people locked in were actually grateful for being taken into custody.'

'Huerta and I were on our way to make the sale to a wheat farmer up in Kansas. Huerta was to be arrested as soon as the transaction went down. We stopped here to get a snack.'

He shrugged, as though to say they knew the rest. 'I'm just glad that we'd left our weapons in the car. It was a twist of fate. If Huerta had been carrying, it would've got real ugly real soon.'

'Will you be in danger of reprisal?'

Again he flashed a smile. 'I'm trusting the department to make me disappear. If you ever see me again, you probably won't recognise me.'

'I see. One more question, why did you try and take the baby?'

'Huerta wanted to overpower Ronnie. I volunteered to distract everyone by grabbing the baby. Actually, I was afraid he'd do something to the child. That was the only way to protect her.'

Tiel shivered at the thought of what might have been. 'You seemed particularly hostile towards Cain.'

'He recognised me,' Martinez exclaimed. 'We'd worked a case together a couple of years ago. He didn't have the sense to keep his trap shut. Several times he nearly blew it for me. I had to shut him up.' Looking at Calloway, he added, 'I think he needs a refresher course at Quantico.'

Tiel hid her smile. 'We have you to thank for several acts of bravery, Mr Martinez. I'm sorry you got shot for your effort.'

'That guy—Doc—did what he had to do. If the situation had been reversed, I'd have done the same. I'd like to tell him I don't hold a grudge.'

Calloway said, 'He's already left.'

Hiding her disappointment and despite the cuts on her palm, Tiel shook Martinez's hand and wished him well, then was helped down out of the ambulance. As the ambulance pulled away, Gladys and Vern joined them.

Apparently they had returned to their RV, because they were wearing different clothes, smelt of soap and were looking as spry and alert as though they'd just returned from a two-week visit to a health spa. Tiel hugged them in turn.

'We couldn't leave without giving you our address and getting your promise to stay in touch.' Gladys handed her a slip of paper on which was written an address in Florida.

'I promise. Where are you headed from here?'

'Louisiana, to see our son and grandchildren,' Gladys replied. Then her demeanour changed. She blotted away the tears that suddenly appeared in her eyes. 'I just hope those two young people come through this. I'll be worried sick until I hear that they're all right.'

'So will I.' Tiel squeezed Gladys's small hand.

Vern said, 'We had to give our statements to the sheriff, then to the FBI agents. We told them you couldn't help hitting that Cain with the chilli on account of he was such an idiot.'

Gully snickered. Calloway tensed, but he let the criticism go without comment.

'Donna's hogging the TV cameras,' Gladys said with pique. 'To hear her tell it, she was a heroine.'

Vern reached into his tote bag, removed a small videocassette and pressed it into Tiel's hand. 'Don't forget this,' he whispered.

Actually, she had forgotten the camcorder tape.

Gladys said, 'We sneaked back into the store to get it.'

'Thank you. For everything.' Tiel got emotional again when they said their final farewell and headed for their RV.

Tiel turned to Calloway. 'I suppose you have some questions for me.'

In the van, Calloway plied her with coffee and breakfast burritos donated by the ladies' auxiliary of the First Baptist Church. It took an hour for him to get from her the information he required.

'I think that's it for now, Ms McCoy, although we'll probably have some follow-up questions.'

'I understand.'

'And it wouldn't surprise me if the respective DAs ask you to attend when we convene to discuss the charges against Ronnie Davison.'

'*If* you convene,' she said softly.

The FBI agent looked away, and Tiel realised he bore a large measure of guilt over what had happened. He hadn't noticed Dendy returning to the helicopter he had arrived in and retrieving a rifle from it. If the unthinkable happened and Ronnie died, Calloway would have much to account for.

'Have you received any update on Ronnie's condition?'

'No,' Calloway replied. 'All I know is that he was alive when they put him in the chopper. The baby is fine. Sabra is listed in poor condition, which is better than I had hoped for. She's received several units of blood. Her mother is with her.'

'I haven't seen Mr Cole Davison.'

'They let him accompany Ronnie in the helicopter.'

They were quiet for a moment, impervious to the activity of the other agents, who were busy with the 'mopping up'. Eventually Calloway signalled her out of her chair and escorted her outside, where the morning was now full blown.

'Goodbye, Mr Calloway.'

'Ms McCoy?' Having started to walk away, she turned back. Special Agent Calloway looked slightly ill at ease with what he was about to say. 'This was a terrible ordeal for you. But I'm glad we had someone in there as level-headed as you. You helped keep everyone sane and acted with remarkable composure.'

'I'm not remarkable, Mr Calloway. Bossy maybe,' she said with a wan smile. 'If it hadn't been for Doc—' She tilted her head inquisitively. 'Did he give you his statement?'

'Sheriff Montez took his.'

He motioned her towards the sheriff, whom she hadn't noticed leaning against the side of the van in the shade. He tipped his wide-brimmed hat and ambled towards her, but ignored her unspoken question about Doc.

'Our mayor has offered to put you up at the local motel.'

'Thank you, but I'm returning to Dallas.'

'Not right now you're not.' Gully had joined them, and with him was Kip. 'We're going back in the chopper to deliver this tape to the editor so she can start putting the piece together.'

'I'll go too, and send someone back for my car.'

He was shaking his head. 'Not enough room for more than two passengers, and I gotta get back. You take the mayor up on his kind offer. We'll send the chopper for you later, along with an intern to drive your car back to Dallas.'

She was too exhausted to put up a fight. They specified a time and place for her to meet the helicopter, and Sheriff Montez promised to have her there. Gully and Kip hustled off towards the chopper.

Calloway extended his hand. 'Good luck to you, Ms McCoy.'

'And to you.' She shook hands with him, but when he would have withdrawn, she detained him. 'You said you were glad it was me who was in there,' she said, nodding in the direction of the store. 'I'm glad it was you out here, Mr Calloway.'

The implied compliment seemed to embarrass him. 'Thank you,' he said briskly, then turned and re-entered the van.

Sheriff Montez retrieved her bags from her car and placed them in the back seat of his squad car.

It was a short trip to the motel. Six rooms were lined up along a covered breezeway that provided a hair's-breadth of shade.

'No need to check in. You're the only guest.' Montez slid from behind the steering wheel and came round to assist her out.

He had the room key and used it to open the door. The air conditioner had already been turned on. A vase of sunflowers and a basket filled with fresh fruit and baked goods had been placed on the room's one small table.

'You've all been very kind.'

'Not at all, Ms McCoy. Weren't for you, it could've gone a lot worse. None of us wanted Rojo Flats to be put on the map by something like a massacre.'

He touched the brim of his hat as he backed out, pulling the door closed behind him. 'Rest well. I'll be back for you later.'

Ordinarily the first thing Tiel did upon entering a room was switch on the television set. Whether or not she was actually watching, she was always tuned to a twenty-four-hour news station. Now, she moved past the TV set without even noticing it and carried her toiletry bag with her into the minuscule bathroom.

The shower was barely large enough to turn round in, but the water was hot and there was plenty of it. Standing beneath the steaming spray, she let it pound against her skull before shampooing. She used her hair dryer only long enough to blow out most of the water, then bent over the sink to brush her teeth.

All of which felt wonderful.

So why did she feel so lousy?

She had just filed the most important story of her career. *Nine Live* was as good as hers now. Gully had said so. She should be dancing on the ceiling. Instead her limbs felt as though they weighed a thousand pounds apiece. Where was the fizzy high she derived from a good news story? Her spirit was as flat as three-day-old champagne.

Sleep deprivation. That was it. Once she had napped for several hours, she would be right as rain. Her old self.

Back in the bedroom, she took a tank top and briefs from her suitcase and put them on, set her travel alarm clock, then turned down the bed. The sheets looked soft and inviting.

When she heard the knock, she took it for a ping in the air conditioner's mechanism. But when it was followed by a second, she moved to the door and pulled it open.

Chapter 9

HE STEPPED INSIDE, closed the door behind him, removed his sunglasses and hat and set them on the table. He smelt of sunshine and soap; he was freshly shaved. He had on clean but well-worn Levi's, a plain white shirt and cowboy boots.

If a team of mustangs had been pulling Tiel in the opposite direction, they couldn't have stopped her from throwing herself against him. Or maybe he reached for her. Afterwards, she didn't recall who moved first. And anyway, who initiated it was unimportant.

All that mattered was that he drew her into an all-encompassing embrace. Her body was flush with his, and they held each other tightly. He pressed her face into his chest to cushion the sobs that issued from her in short, noisy bursts.

'Did he die? Are you here to tell me that Ronnie is dead?'

'No, that's not why I'm here. I don't know any news about Ronnie.'

'I couldn't believe it, Doc. That horrible, deafening sound. Then to see him lying there, amidst all that glass and blood.'

'Shh.'

Comforting words were whispered across her hairline, along her temple. Then the words ceased, and only his breath, his lips, drifted over her brow, touching her damp eyelids. Tiel raised her head and looked at him through tearful eyes. Reaching up to touch his face, she made a small sound of want, which he echoed.

A heartbeat later, his lips were on hers. Insistent and hungry, they rubbed hers apart. Their tongues flirted, stroked, before his dominated. Tiel's hands met at the back of his neck. She threaded her fingers up through his hair and submitted to his kiss. His hands settled on her lower back and pulled her closer.

He kissed his way down her throat. She angled her head to one side, and he feathered her ear lobe with his breath, his tongue. Lifting her hair, he kissed her nape. The touch of his mouth there sent shivers of delight up her spine.

Then he carried her to the bed. It was only a distance of a few steps, but to Tiel it seemed to take for ever before she felt him stretched out alongside her.

He pushed his fingers into her hair and held it off her face. His eyes, practically liquid with desire, seemed to pour over her features. 'I don't know what you like.' His voice was raspy. Even more so than usual.

Her fingertip traced the shape of his eyebrow, followed the length of his straight, narrow nose, outlined his lips. 'I like you.'

'What do you want me to do?'

For one dreadful moment, she feared she would lapse into another crying jag. Emotion made her chest and throat tight, but she managed to contain it. 'Convince me I'm alive, Doc.'

He began by removing her tank top and lowering his mouth to her breasts. She began to feel increasingly restless and hot. Pressure gathered in the lower part of her body.

Suddenly he was off the bed. He undressed hastily. His chest had just the right amount of hair. His skin was taut. Muscles were well defined, but not grotesquely so. His belly was flat.

He stretched out on top of her, slid his arms beneath her back and hugged her to him.

And then he entered her.

'**D**oc?'

'Hmm.'

'Are you asleep? Is it all right if I ask you something?'

'Go ahead.'

'What are we doing?'

He opened only one eye to look at her. 'Do you want the scientific nomenclature, the polite phraseology or will twenty-first-century vernacular do?'

She frowned at his teasing. 'I meant—'

'I know what you meant.' The second eye came open, and he tilted his head on the pillow to look at her from a better angle. 'Just what you said earlier, Tiel. We're convincing each other that we're alive. It's not all that uncommon for people to want sex after any life-threatening experience. Or after a reminder of their mortality, a funeral for instance. Sex is the quintessential affirmation that you're alive.'

'Really? Well that's the most fantastic assertion of the survival instinct I've ever experienced.' He chuckled. But Tiel grew quiet, introspective. She blew softly against the chest hairs brushing her lips. 'Is that all it was?'

He placed his finger beneath her chin and lifted it until she was looking at him again. 'Anything between us would be complicated, Tiel.'

'Are you still in love with Shari?'

'I love the good memories of her. I also hate the painful ones. But, if you're suggesting that I'm fixated on her ghost, let me assure you that I'm not. My relationship with her—good, bad or indifferent—wouldn't prevent me from having another.'

'You'd marry again?'

'I'd want to. If I loved the woman, I would want to make a life together, and to me that means marriage.' After a moment, he asked, 'What about your memories of John Malone?'

'Like yours, bittersweet. We had almost a fairy-tale romance. Probably married too soon, aglow with passion, before we really knew one another. If he hadn't died, who knows? Career paths might eventually have led us in different and irreconcilable directions.'

'As it is, he'll remain in your memory as the martyred Prince Charming.'

'No, Doc. My memory isn't clinging to a flawless ghost either.'

'What about that Joseph?'

'That Joseph is married,' she reminded him.

'But if he weren't?'

She thought about Joseph Marcus a moment, then shook her head. 'We probably would have had a thing going for a while, and then it would have fizzled. He was a diversion. I can barely remember him.'

She levered herself up and combed her hands down his chest. 'You, on the other hand, I'll remember. You look exactly as I imagined you would.'

'You imagined me naked?'

'I confess.'

'When?'

'When you first came into the store, I think. In the back of my mind, I was thinking, "Whoa. He's yummy."'

'Why, thank you, ma'am,' he said. Smiling, he reached for a strand of her hair and rubbed it between his fingers. Gradually his smile relaxed, and when he spoke, his tone was more serious.

'We've been through a lot together, Tiel. A birth. A near death. Tense hours of not knowing how it was going to play out. Trauma like that does something to people. It binds them.'

His words echoed her earlier thoughts on the subject. But it wasn't very flattering that he ascribed their attraction solely to trauma, or that he could mitigate carnal desire with such a pragmatic, scientific explanation.

What if they'd met at a cocktail party last night? There would have been no sparks, no heat, and they wouldn't be in bed together now. Essentially that's what he was saying. If this meant nothing more to him than illustrating a psychological phenomenon, there was no sense in prolonging the inevitable goodbye.

Congratulations, Doc. You're my first—and probably last—one night-stand. She moved to get up, but he used her motion to pull her fully atop him.

'In spite of the danger to us—to everyone inside the store—I had incredibly vivid fantasies of this.'

She found enough voice to say, 'Of this?'

His hands smoothed down her back. 'Of you.'

He levered up his shoulders in order to kiss her. At first the kiss was slow, his tongue leisurely stroking her mouth while his hands continued sliding up and down her back from shoulders to thighs.

Then he was inside her again. Giving her more than intense pleasure. Giving her a sense of fulfilment and purpose that even her finest work had failed to provide.

Afterwards, Tiel was so totally relaxed, replete, that it felt as though she had melted and become a part of him. She couldn't distinguish her skin from his. She didn't want to. She fell asleep, her ear resting on his heart.

'Tiel? It's your alarm.'

She muttered grumpily and pushed her hands deeper into the warmth of his armpits.

'You've got to get up. The chopper's coming back for you, remember?'

She did. But she didn't want to. She wanted to stay exactly where she was for at least the next ten years. It would take her that long to catch up on the sleep she had lost last night. It would take her that long to get enough of Doc.

'Come on. Up.' He gave her butt an affectionate smack. 'Make yourself presentable before Sheriff Montez gets here.'

Groaning, she rolled off him. Round a huge yawn, she asked, 'How'd you know our arrangements?'

'He told me. That's how I knew where to find you.' She gave him a misty look and he said, 'Yes, he knew I wanted to know. Is that what you wanted to hear?'

'Yes.'

'He and I are buddies. Play poker occasionally. He knows my story, but he's good at keeping confidences.'

'Even from the FBI.'

'He asked if he could take my statement, and Calloway agreed. He had his hands full.' He threw his legs over the side of the bed. 'Mind if I use the bathroom first? I'll be quick.'

'Be my guest.'

In the process of bending down to pick up his boxers, he caught her with her hands far above her head, back arched, stretching lazily. 'Maybe I don't want you to get in that chopper.'

'Ask me not to and maybe I won't.'

'You would.'

'I have to,' she said ruefully.

'Yeah.' Sighing, he got up and went into the bathroom.

'Maybe,' Tiel whispered to herself, 'I could convince you to come with me.'

She removed a bra and panties set from her suitcase, put them on and was just about to step into a pair of slacks when she sensed Doc watching her.

She turned, ready with a suggestive smile and a saucy remark about peeping Toms. But his expression didn't invite either. In fact, he was practically bristling with rage.

Mystified, her lips parted to ask what the matter was when he held out his hand. Lying in his palm was the audio tape recorder. It had been in the pocket of her slacks, which she'd left along with her other dirty clothes in a pile on the toilet lid. He'd moved them, found the recorder.

Her expression must have been a dead giveaway of her guilt because with a vicious punch of his thumb, he depressed the Play button and his voice cut across the silence. '. . . *hospital buckled beneath the weight of bad publicity. Bad publicity generated by people like you.*' He stopped the tape and threw the recorder down onto the bed. 'Take it.' Looking scornfully at the tangled bedsheets, he added, 'You earned it.'

'Doc, listen. I—'

'You got what you were after. A good story.' Pushing her aside, he picked up his jeans and angrily thrust his legs into them.

'Will you stop with the righteous indignation and listen?'

He flung his hand towards the incriminating recorder. 'I've heard enough. Did you get everything? All the juicy details of my personal life?'

'I was doing my job.'

He buttoned his jeans and yanked his shirt off the floor.

'Nor is it my fault that you're a good story,' she shouted.

'I don't want to be a story. I never did.'

'Too bad, Doc. You are. You simply are. Once notorious, you're now a hero. You saved lives last night. Do you think that'll go unnoticed? Those kids and their parents are going to talk about "Doc". So are the other hostages. Any reporter worth his paycheque is going to be clamouring for the lowdown.'

He gestured towards the recorder again. 'But you've got them all beat, haven't you? I thought I was speaking confidentially. But you're going to use it, aren't you?'

'You're damn right I am!'

His jaw flexed with rage. He glared at her for several seconds, then marched towards the door.

Tiel barged after him, grabbed his arm and pulled him round. 'It could be the best thing that ever happened to you.'

He yanked his arm free of her grasp. 'I fail to see that.'

'It could force you to face up to the fact that you were wrong to run away. Last night, you told Ronnie he couldn't run away from his problems. But isn't that exactly what you did?

'You moved out here, refusing to accept that you're a gifted healer. That you could make a difference. That you *were* making a difference. For patients and families facing a death sentence, you were granting reprieves. God knows what you could do in the future.

'But because of your pride, and anger, and disillusionment with your colleagues, you abandoned it. If this story draws you back into the

limelight, if there's a chance it will motivate you to return to your practice, then I'll be damned before I'll apologise for it.'

He turned his back on her and opened the door.

'Doc?' she cried.

But all he said was, 'Your ride is here.'

Tiel's cubicle in the newsroom was a disaster area. She had received
hundreds of notes, cards and letters from colleagues and viewers, com-
plimenting her coverage of the Davison–Dendy story and commending
her for the heroic role she'd played in it.

As anticipated, she had been the centre of attention, and not only on
a local level. The compelling human element, the love story, the emergency birth of the baby and the dramatic dénouement had piqued the
interest of TV audiences all over the world.

She had been interviewed by reporters from global news operations.
National women's magazines were proposing articles on everything
from her secrets of success to the decor of her house. She was the unde-
clared Woman of the Week.

And she had never been more miserable.

She was making a futile stab at clearing off her desk when Gully
joined her. 'Hey, kid. Have I told you what a great job you did?'

'Thanks. It's nice to hear. But it's left me drained.'

'You look it. You're not your normal, hyperactive, supercharged self.
Is it Linda Harper? Are you sulking because she got the jump on you
and stole some of your thunder?'

'No.' She methodically ripped open another envelope and read the
congratulatory note inside. *I love your reports on the TV. You're my role
model. I want to be just like you when I grow up.*

Gully said, 'I can't believe you didn't recognise the Doc of standoff
fame as Dr Bradley Stanwick.'

'Hmm.'

Gully continued, in spite of her seeming lack of interest. 'Let me put
it another way. I *don't* believe it.' The change in Gully's tone of voice was
unmistakable, and there was no way to avoid addressing it. Slowly she
swivelled her chair round to face Gully.

He looked down at her for a long moment. 'I suppose you had your
reasons for protecting his identity.'

'He asked me to.'

'Oh.' He slapped his forehead with his palm. 'Of course! What's wrong with me? The subject of the story said, "I don't want to be on TV," so, naturally, you omitted an important element of the story.'

'It didn't cost your news operation anything, Gully.' She stood up and began tossing personal items into her bag in preparation of leaving. 'Linda got it. So what are you complaining about?'

'I'm just curious as to why my ace reporter wimped out.'

She spun round to confront him. 'Because it got . . .' She drew herself up, took a deep breath and ended on a softer note. 'Complicated.'

'Complicated.'

'Complicated.' She reached round him for her suit jacket, lifted it off the wall hook and pulled it on, avoiding his incisive eyes. 'I'm leaving.'

'So you're still going?' He fell into step behind her as she left the newsroom.

'I need the time away more than ever. You approved my request for days off.'

'I know,' he said querulously. 'But I've had second thoughts. I was thinking that you should produce a pilot *Nine Live* show. This cancer doctor-cum-cowboy would be a dynamite first guest. Get him to talk about the investigation into his wife's death. Then you could segue into his participation in the standoff. It'd be great! It'd be your ticket to the *Nine Live* hostess spot.'

'Don't hold your breath, Gully.' She pushed open the heavy exit door leading to the employee parking lot.

He followed her out. 'This is what you've worked for, Tiel. You'd better grab it, or it could still be snatched away from you. Postpone this trip until this is settled.'

'Uh-uh, Gully. I'm going.' She smiled. 'I'm tired of the dance, Gully. I'm weary of the constant jockeying for position. Management knows what I can do. They know my popularity with viewers is higher now than it's ever been.' She opened her car door and tossed her bag inside. 'They'll be hearing from my agent. I'm making *Nine Live* a condition of my contract. I don't get the show, they don't get a renewal. And I've received at least a hundred other offers this week to back up that mandate.'

She leaned forward and kissed his cheek. 'I love you, Gully. I love my work. But it's *work*; it's no longer my life.'

She made one stop on her way out of town—at a Dumpster behind a supermarket. She tossed two things into it. One was an audiocassette recording. The other was the two-hour videotape from Gladys and Vern's camcorder.

Tiel cursed the hopelessly snarled fishing line. 'Dammit!'

'They aren't biting?'

Thinking she was alone, she jumped, executing a quick turn at the same time. Her knees went weak at the sight of him. He was leaning nonchalantly against a tree trunk, his tall, lean form and cowboy garb in harmony with the rugged landscape.

'I didn't know you could fish,' he remarked.

'Obviously I can't.' She held out the tangled line and frowned. 'But since that's what one is supposed to do when there's a clear mountain stream running behind one's vacation condo . . . Doc, what are you doing here?'

'Good news about Ronnie, huh?'

Ronnie Davison had been upgraded from critical to good condition. If he continued to improve, he would be released to return home within a few days. 'Very good news. About Sabra too. I talked to her last night by phone. She and her mother are going to rear Katherine. Ronnie will have unlimited visitation, but they've decided to postpone getting married for a couple of years. Regardless of the outcome of his legal entanglements, they've agreed to wait and see if the relationship can stand the test of time.'

'Smart kids. If it's right, it'll happen.'

'That's their thinking.'

'Well, Dendy can be glad he won't be charged with murder.'

'No, but dozens of witnesses saw him attempt it. I hope they throw the book at him.'

'I second that motion. He nearly cost several lives.'

The conversation flagged after that. The silence was filled by the chirping of birds and the incessant gurgle of the stream.

Feeling silly holding the casting rod, Tiel laid it at her feet, but immediately wished she hadn't. Her hands suddenly seemed excessively large and conspicuous. She slid them into the rear pockets of her jeans, palms out. 'It's a beautiful place, isn't it?'

'Sure is.'

'When did you arrive?'

'About an hour ago.'

'Oh.'

Then, miserably, 'Doc, what are you doing here?'

'I came to thank you.'

She lowered her head and looked down at her feet. Her sneakers had sunk sole-deep into the mud of the creek bed. 'Don't. Thank me, I mean. I couldn't use the recording. I had a video, too. From Gladys's camcorder. The quality of the tape wasn't very good, but no other reporter in the world had it.'

She took a deep breath, glanced up at him, then back down. 'But you were on the tape. Recognisable. And I didn't want to exploit you after . . . after what happened in the motel. It was personal then. I couldn't exploit you without exploiting part of myself too. So I threw them away. No one ever saw or heard them.'

'Hmm. Well, that's not what I was thanking you for.'

Her head sprang up. 'Huh?'

'I saw your stories about the standoff, and they were outstanding. You deserve all the accolades you received. And I appreciate your keeping our private conversations private. You were right about the exposure. It was bound to happen with or without help from you. I see that now.'

For once in her life, she had nothing to say.

'But the reason I came to thank you is for making me take a hard look at myself. My life. How wasteful it's been. After Shari died and all that followed, I needed solitude, time and space to think things through, reassess. That used up . . . say six months. The rest of the time I've been doing exactly what you said, hiding. Punishing myself. Taking the coward's way out.'

The pressure building inside Tiel wasn't tension, it was emotion. Maybe love. OK, love. She wanted to go to him, hold him, but she wanted to hear what he had to say. Furthermore, he needed to say it.

'I'm going back. I spent the past week in Dallas talking to some doctors and researchers who are tired of having to go through umpteen committees and legal counsels to get approval of a new treatment when the patient is suffering and all other options have been exhausted. We'd like to take medicine out of the hands of lawyers and bureaucrats and return it to the doctors. So, we're forming a group, pooling our resources and specialities—' He looked hard at her. 'Are you crying?'

'The sun's in my eyes.'

'Oh. Well. That's what I came to tell you.'

Economically, efficiently, in as businesslike a manner as she could, she rubbed the tears from her eyes. 'You didn't have to travel all this way. You could have emailed me, or called.'

'That would have been cowardly too. I needed to say this in person, face to face.'

'How'd you know where to find me?'

'I went to the TV station. Talked to Gully, who also asked me to deliver a message.' A small bob of her head indicated that she was listening. 'He said, "Tell her I ain't dense. I just figured out the meaning of complicated." Does that make sense?'

She laughed. 'Yes.'

'Care to explain?'

'Maybe later. If you're staying.'

'If you don't mind my company.'

'I think I can tolerate it.'

He returned her wide smile, but his faltered, and his expression turned serious again. 'We're both pretty intense when it comes to our work, Tiel.'

'Which I believe is part of the attraction.'

'It won't be easy.'

'Nothing worthwhile is.'

'We don't know where it will lead.'

'But we know where we hope it will. We also know it will lead to nowhere if we don't give it a try.'

'I loved my wife, Tiel, and love can hurt.'

'Not being loved hurts worse. Maybe we can find a way to love each other without it hurting.'

'God, I want to touch you.'

'Doc,' she murmured. Then she laughed. 'Bradley? Brad? How do I call you?'

'A simple "Come here" will do for now.'

Then he closed the distance separating them.

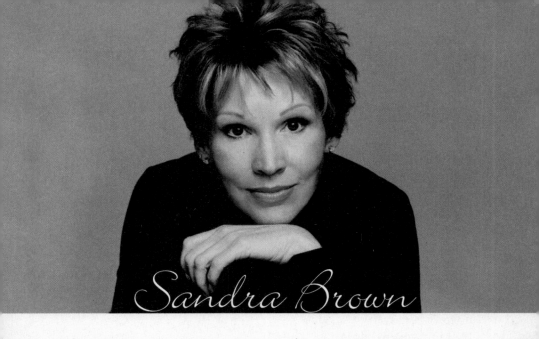

Sandra Brown

In 1979, Sandra Brown was working in television as a weather forecaster and features reporter when it all came to an abrupt and unexpected end. Undaunted, she grasped the challenge that her husband, Michael, then a television anchor man, set her: try your hand at writing. Sandra had, in fact, been longing to write a novel for years, and this was just the trigger she needed.

'It was scary then, and it's no less scary today,' she says, despite being a hugely successful novelist with a prolific output. She has had sixty-five books published, fifty of which have reached the *New York Times* best-seller list. Almost seventy million copies of her novels are currently in print and her work has been translated into thirty languages.

Back in the beginning, though, in response to her husband's challenge she went out and bought an armful of romantic fiction and exercise books, set up a typewriter on a card table, and began to write a romance. Since the successful publication of that first novel, she has been published under an assortment of pseudonyms and, in 1987, moved on from romances to mainstream fiction. She has never looked back. 'I think of my books now as suspense novels, usually with a love story incorporated,' she says. 'They take more plotting and character development. Each book is a stretch for me, and I try something interesting every time that males will like as well as women.'

A lifelong Texan, Sandra Brown met and married Michael, her college sweetheart, thirty-eight years ago. They have two children, Rachel and Ryan, now both adults, who were the inspiration behind their mother's first pen name: Rachel Ryan. Looking back to when she was a devoted parent and budding novelist,

Sandra says, 'At three thirty every afternoon I switched from writer to Mom, driving someone to ballet, someone else to soccer.' But she used that driving time to dream up new ideas, and once plotted an entire novel while on a school field trip.

Nowadays Sandra and her husband spend much of the year at their ranch in Arlington, Texas, along with their pet longhorn steers Boudreaux, Bowie and Bubba. The author admits that she found her earlier domestic life in the Texas suburbs quite bland, and she enjoys drawing her readers, many of whom might be in that same life situation, into a fantasy world of passion, intrigue and danger. 'I love being the bad guy, simply because I was always so responsible, so predictable growing up. I made straight A's and never got into any trouble . . . writing fiction is my chance to escape and become the sleaziest, scummiest role.'

Unexpected words, perhaps, from this glamorous woman who, as well as being a best-selling writer once worked as an actress and a model in Dallas. 'And I also wanted to be a dancer,' she muses, adding that success has changed her lifestyle but definitely not her personality or values. 'If I weren't a writer now, I think I'd probably be a floral designer.'

Anne Jenkins

FACT FILE

Birthplace: Waco, Texas.

Favourite childhood reading: Fairy tales, and books about imperilled heroes and heroines who live happily ever after!

Most influential book and why: *Magnificent Obsession* by Lloyd C. Douglas, because it touches on Christianity and is an unusual love story of self sacrifice and devotion.

Previous jobs: Several mini careers: live theatre, cosmetics manager, local television personality.

Pleasurable activities: Going to the movies, the theatre and travelling.

Healthy pursuits: Working out, biking, going to the beach.

Favourite music: Classic Rock, Country & Western, Musicals, Classical.

Claim to fame: 50 *New York Times* best sellers, including *Chill Factor* (2005), *White Hot* (2004), *Hello, Darkness* (2003), *The Crush* (2002), *Envy* (2001), *The Switch* (2000), *The Alibi* (1999), *Unspeakable* (1998), *and Fat Tuesday* (1997).

Relaxation: Spending time with my family, and my golden retrievers, Lucky and Chase.

Advice to aspiring writers: Practice, practice, practice.

Website: www.sandrabrown.com

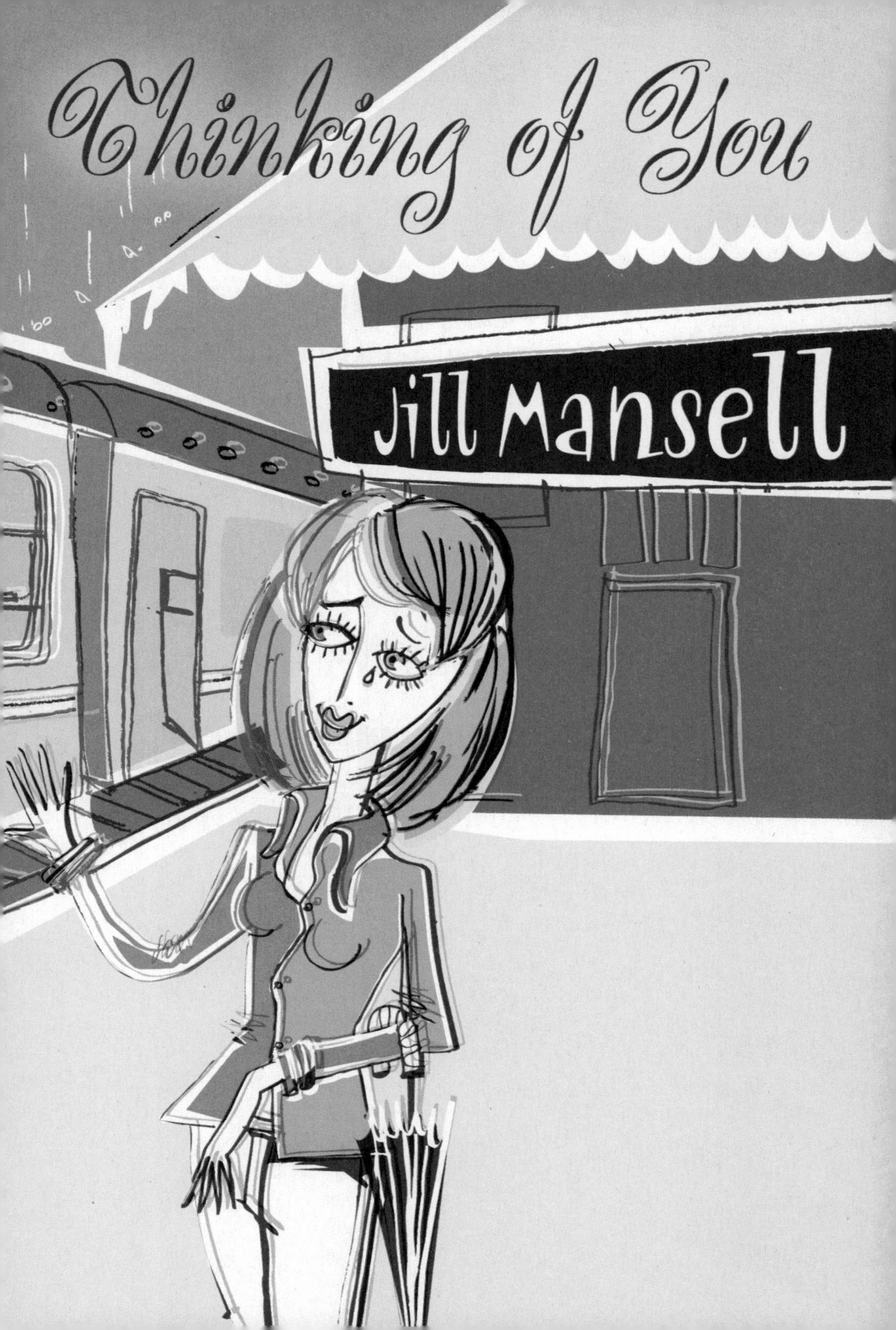
Thinking of You
Jill Mansell

When her beloved daughter Jem leaves home for university, single-mum Ginny is devastated. She may have gained control of the TV remote, and freedom from having to queue for the bathroom, but she hates the feeling of emptiness inside. The time has come to begin a new chapter in her life—but where to start?

Chapter 1

IF IT WAS SYMPATHY she was after, Ginny Holland might have known she'd come to the wrong place. Then again, it was early on a bright but blustery Saturday morning in October and her options were limited. And it was only over the road from her own house, which was handy.

'I can't describe how I feel.' She clenched a fist, pressed it to her breastbone and shook her head in frustration. 'It's just so . . . so . . .'

'I know exactly what it is. Bird's-nest syndrome,' said Carla.

Ginny pulled a face because it was so screamingly apparent that Carla didn't have children. 'Bird's-nest syndrome would be the name for the state of my hair. I have *empty*-nest syndrome. My nest is empty, my baby has flown away and I just feel all hollow inside like . . . like a cheap Easter egg.'

'Well, I think you're mad.' Carla was busy executing Olympic-level sit-ups, her bare feet tucked under the edge of the cream leather sofa, her hair swinging glossily to and fro. 'Jem's gone off to university. You're free again. You should be out there celebrating. Plus,' she added as an afterthought, 'Cadbury's Creme Eggs aren't hollow, they're full of goo.'

'Unlike you,' Ginny pointed out. 'You're heartless.'

'And you're thirty-eight, not seventy.' Having completed her five mil-lionth sit-up, Carla raised her legs in the air and without even pausing for breath began bicycling furiously. 'I'm a year older than you and look at me, I'm having a whale of a time! I'm in tip-top condition, men can't resist me and sex has never been better. I'm a woman in my prime,' she concluded. 'And so are you.'

Ginny knew her life wasn't really over, of course she did, but Jem's departure had nevertheless knocked her for six. She'd always been so happy and busy before now, so endlessly occupied, that this was a whole new experience for her. Nor did it help that it was happening as winter approached. Most of the jobs here in Portsilver were seasonal and she'd just spent the last six months being rushed off her feet working in a café down on the seafront. But the tourists had gone home now, Jem was in Bristol and Ginny was finding herself faced with way more spare time than she was used to. And as for Carla telling her she was a woman in her prime . . . well, she could end up being done under the Trade Descriptions Act.

Glancing at her reflection in Carla's glitzy over-the-top Venetian mirror, Ginny puffed away a section of overgrown fringe that was falling into her eyes. The aforementioned bird's-nest hair was long, blonde and wavy-with-a-definite-mind-of-its-own. Facewise, it wasn't as if she was a wrinkled old prune—if anything, Ginny knew she looked young for her age—but in glossy magazine world there was still plenty of room for improvement. It would be lovely to be as chic, groomed and effortlessly femme-fatalish as Carla but, let's face it, she simply couldn't be doing with making all that effort.

'You need to cheer yourself up.' Carla finished bicycling in the air, miraculously not even puce in the face. 'Have yourself an adventure.'

'I'm just saying, I miss Jem.' Ginny hated feeling like this. She tugged at a loose thread on her jumper sleeve. 'I really want to *see* her.'

'Fine. Go on then, if that's what you want to do. If you think Jem won't mind.' Rising gracefully to her feet and automatically checking her sleek, serum-fed hair in the Venetian mirror—yep, still perfect— Carla said, 'You've made a hole in that sleeve, by the way.'

Ginny didn't care; it was a manky old sweater anyway. More importantly, she'd got what she'd come for. 'Right, I will.'

'Will what?'

'Drive up to Bristol to see Jem. It's a great idea!'

'Now? Shouldn't you give her a ring first? She's eighteen,' said Carla. 'She could be getting up to any number of naughty things.'

To humour Carla, Ginny said, 'OK, I'll call her.' She made her way to the door. 'You have a lovely weekend and I'll see you tomorrow night when I get back.'

'I always have a lovely weekend.' Carla patted her flat brown stomach. 'I'm a woman in my prime, remember?'

'**M**um! I don't believe it—how fantastic that you're here!' Jem's face lit up as she launched herself like a missile into her mother's arms.

Oh yes, that was a good one. Or:

'Mummy, oh my God, this is the best surprise *ever* . . . you don't know how much I've *missed* you . . .'

Whoops, mustn't make herself cry. Deliberately banishing the happy scenarios her imagination had been busily conjuring up, Ginny blinked hard in order to concentrate on the road ahead. The journey from Portsilver in north Cornwall up to Bristol took three and a half hours and so far they were on schedule to arrive at one o'clock. Luckily, Bellamy enjoyed nothing more than a nice long ride in the car and was lolling contentedly across the back seat with his eyes shut and his tongue out. Every time Ginny said in her excited voice, 'Who are we going to see, Bellamy? Hey? We're going to see *Jem!*' he opened one eye and lazily wagged his tail.

If Ginny had owned one she'd have been wagging hers too.

It was three weeks since Jem had left home. Ginny had braced herself for the worst but hadn't braced nearly hard enough; the aching void where Jem had once been was a million times worse than she'd envisaged. Her daughter was the most important person in her life, it was as simple as that.

As she drove towards Bristol, Ginny scrolled through some of her happiest memories. Marrying Gavin Holland on her eighteenth birthday . . . well, it may have been a mistake, but how could she possibly regret it when between them they had produced Jem?

Holding Jem for the first time and sobbing uncontrollably because the rush of love was so much more overwhelming than she'd imagined. Then later, the first magical smile . . . the first day at school ('Mummy, don't leeeeave meeeee!') . . . and that look of blind panic on Jem's face after posting her letter to Father Christmas because what if he got her muddled up with the other Jemima in Miss Carter's class?

Oh yes, there were so many perfect moments. Ginny's smile broadened as each one in turn popped into her mind. She and Gavin had separated when Jem was nine and that had been sad, of course it was, but it truly hadn't been the end of the world. Gavin had always been a loving father and had never once let Jem down.

From that time on, Ginny and Jem had become truly inseparable, as close as any mother and daughter could be. It had always been the two of them against the world.

At that moment a wet nose touched Ginny's left arm and Bellamy, his head poked between the front seats, licked her elbow.

'Oh, sorry, sweetheart, I wasn't thinking.' Concentrating on the road ahead, Ginny gave his ears an apologetic rub. 'How could I forget you, hmm? The *three* of us against the world.'

The traffic on the motorway was light and by ten to one Ginny was on the outskirts of Bristol. Jem hadn't been keen on moving into the halls of residence. Instead, she'd decided on a flat-share in Clifton with two other students. This was where Ginny had helped her to unload her belongings from the car three weeks earlier, prior to the arrival of the other flatmates.

Now she was crossing the Downs heading for Whiteladies Road, before turning into Pembroke Road. Jem's flat was situated on the first floor of what had once been a four-storey Georgian house. Ginny waited until Bellamy had discreetly relieved himself against a tree in the front garden before ringing the doorbell. This was it, they were here and Jem was about to get the surprise of her—

'Yes?'

'Oh hi! You must be Rupert!' Ginny did her best not to gush in front of the flatmate Jem had told her about. 'Um . . . is Jem here?'

'No.' Rupert paused. 'And you are?'

'Oh, I'm her mum! And this is Bellamy, Jem's dog. How silly of me not to realise she might be out. I did ring a few times but her phone was switched off and I just thought she was having a long lie-in. Er, do you know where she is?'

Rupert, who was wearing a pair of white shorts and nothing else, was lean and tanned. He shivered as a blast of cold air hit him in the chest. 'She's working a lunchtime shift in the pub. Eleven till two.'

Lunchtime shift? Pub? Ginny checked her watch. 'Which pub?'

'No idea.' Rupert shrugged. 'She did say, but I wasn't paying attention. Somewhere in Clifton, I think.'

Since there were about a million pubs in Clifton, that was a big help. 'Well, could I come in and wait?'

He looked less than enthusiastic but said, 'Yeah, of course. It's a bit of a mess.'

Rupert wasn't joking. Upstairs in the living room there were dirty plates and empty cups all over the pale green carpet. An exotic-looking girl with short dark hair was sprawled on the sofa eating a bowl of CocoPops and watching a black and white film on television.

'Hello!' Ginny beamed at her. 'You must be Lucy.'

The girl blinked. 'No, I'm Caro.'

'Caro's my girlfriend.' Rupert indicated Ginny as he headed into the kitchen. 'This is Jem's mother, come to see her.'

Caro, through a mouthful of CocoPops, mumbled, 'Hi.'

'This is Bellamy.' Thank heavens for dogs, the ultimate ice-breakers.

'Right.' Caro nodded and licked her spoon.

Oh. Maybe not.

'So! Are you at uni too?' Nobody had offered her a seat so Ginny stayed standing.

'Yes.' Caro dumped her empty cereal bowl on the carpet, rose to her feet and headed for the kitchen.

Ginny, overhearing giggles and a muffled shriek of laughter, felt increasingly ill at ease. Moments later, Rupert stuck his head round the door. 'Would you like a cup of tea?'

'Oh, thank you, that would be lovely! White, please, one sugar.'

'Ah. Don't think we've got any sugar.'

Ginny said, 'No problem, I'll just have a glass of water instead.'

Rupert frowned. 'I think we've run out of water too.'

Was he serious? Or was this their way of getting rid of her?

'Unless you drink tap,' said Rupert.

Gosh, he was posh.

'Tap's fine,' said Ginny.

He grimaced. 'Rather you than me.'

'Just ignore him,' said a voice behind Ginny. 'Rupes only drinks gold-plated water. Hello, I'm Lucy. And I've seen the photos in Jem's room so I know you're her mum. Nice to meet you.'

Oh, now *this* was more like it. Lucy was tall and slender, black and beautiful. Better still, she was actually smiling. Ginny was overcome with gratitude. Within minutes, Lucy had cleared away armfuls of plates, chucked a slew of magazines behind the back of the sofa and installed Ginny in the best chair like the queen.

'Jem only got the job yesterday. Today's her first shift. Still, a bit of extra cash always comes in handy, doesn't it?' Lucy was chatty and friendly, the best kind of flatmate any mother could desire for her daughter.

Rupert and Caro stayed in the kitchen and played music, then Rupert emerged to iron a blue shirt rather badly in the corner of the living room where the ironing board was set up.

'I could do that for you,' Ginny offered, eager to make him like her.

Rupert looked amused. 'No, thanks, I can manage.'

'Jem's never been keen on ironing. I bet she's got a load that needs doing. Actually, while I'm here,' said Ginny, 'I could make a start on it.'

Jem's room was untidy but clean. Ginny's heart expanded as she drank in every familiar detail, the family photos on the cork board up on the wall, the clothes, books and CDs littering every surface. Unable to help herself, she quickly made the bed and hung all the scattered clothes in the wardrobe. This must be the new top Jem had bought in Oasis. Oops, and there was an oily mark on the leg of her favourite jeans—

The front door slammed and Ginny froze, realising that she was clutching her daughter's jeans like a stalker. Hastily flinging them back onto the bed, she burst out of the bedroom just as Bellamy began to bark. A split second later she reached the living room in time to see Jem and Bellamy greeting each other in a frenzy of ecstasy.

'I don't believe this! Mum, what are you *doing* here?' Jem looked up as Bellamy joyfully licked her face.

'Your mother's come all this way to see you,' Rupert drawled and Ginny intercepted the look he gave Jem.

Shocked, Jem said, 'Oh, *Mum.*'

'No, I haven't,' Ginny blurted out. 'Of course I haven't! We're on our way to Bath and I just thought it'd be fun to pop in and say hello.'

'Really? Well, that's great!' Letting go of Bellamy at last, Jem gave her mother a hug. Ginny in turn stroked her daughter's blonde, pink-streaked hair. It wasn't quite the reunion she had envisaged what with Rupert, Caro and Lucy looking on and her brain struggling to come up with an answer to the question Jem was about to ask, but at least she was here. It was better than nothing. She'd missed her so much.

'Bath?' Jem stepped back, holding her at arm's length and looking baffled. 'What are you doing going to Bath?'

Aaargh, I haven't the foggiest!

'Visiting a friend,' said Ginny. *Quick, think.*

'But you don't know anyone in Bath.'

I *know*, I *know!*

'Ah, that's where you're wrong,' Ginny said gaily. 'Ever heard me talking about Theresa Trott?'

Jem shook her head. 'No. Who's she?'

'We were at school together, darling. I got onto that Friends Reunited website, left my email address and in no time at all Theresa had emailed me. She's living in Bath now. When she invited me up to stay with her, I thought I couldn't drive past and not stop off here en route, that would be rude. So here we are!'

'I'm so glad.' Jem gave her another hug.

'Your mother was about to start ironing your clothes,' said Rupert, his mouth twitching with amusement.

Jem laughed. 'Oh, *Mum*.'

Deciding she hated him, Ginny looked Rupert in the eye and said, 'Hasn't your mum ever ironed anything for you?'

'No.' He shrugged. 'But that could be because she's dead.'

Damn, *damn*.

Dddddrrrringgg, went the doorbell.

'You may as well get that, Jem,' Rupert drawled. 'It's probably your father.'

Jem grinned and pulled a face at Rupert, then skipped downstairs to answer the door. She returned with a thin, dark-eyed boy in tow.

'Lucy, it's Davy Stokes.'

Lucy was in the process of pulling her grey sweater up over her head. Tugging down the green T-shirt beneath, she said, 'Hi, Davy. All right? I was just about to jump in the shower.'

'Sorry.' Davy, who had long dark hair, was clutching a book. 'It's just that I promised to lend you this so I thought I'd drop it round.'

'What is it? Oh right, John Donne's poems. Great, thanks.' Lucy took the book and flashed him a smile. 'That's really kind of you.'

Blushing, Davy said, 'You'll enjoy them. Um . . . I was wondering, there's a pub quiz on at the Bear this afternoon. I wondered if maybe you'd like to, um, come along with me.'

Rupert was smirking openly now. Ginny longed to throw something heavy at him.

'Thanks for the offer, Davy, but I can't make it. Me and Jem are off to a party. In fact we need to get our skates on or we're going to be late. We're all meeting up at three.'

Three o'clock? It was half past two already. Ginny wondered if Lucy was lying in order to spare Davy's feelings.

'OK. Well, maybe another time. Bye.' Davy glanced shyly around the room while simultaneously backing towards the door.

'Let me show you out,' said Rupert.

He returned moments later, grinning broadly. 'You've made a conquest there.'

'Don't make fun of him,' Lucy protested. 'Davy's all right.'

'Apart from the fact that he has no friends and still lives at home with his mum.'

'So, what's this party you've been invited to?' Ginny put on her bright and cheerful voice and looked at Jem, whom she'd driven for three and a half hours to see.

'It's Zelda's birthday. She's on our course,' Jem explained. 'We're starting off at this new cocktail bar on Park Street. I'd better get ready. What time do you have to be in Bath?'

'Oh, not right this minute. I can drop you off at the cocktail bar if you like.'

'Thanks, Mum, but there's no need. Lucy's driving and we're picking up a couple more friends on the way.'

'Jem?' Lucy's disembodied voice drifted through from Jem's bedroom. 'That black top you said I could borrow isn't here.'

'It is! It's on the floor next to the CD player.'

'The only thing on the floor is carpet.' Popping her head round the door, Lucy said, 'In fact all your clothes are missing.'

'I hung them up in the wardrobe,' Ginny said apologetically.

'Oh, Mum.' Jem shook her head. 'You'll be making my bed next.'

Lucy grinned. 'She's done that too.'

'Checking the sheets,' Rupert murmured audibly into Caro's ear.

'Well, I think we'd better leave you to it.' Realising that the girls had less than ten minutes in which to get ready and she was only in their way, Ginny clicked her fingers at Bellamy. She enveloped Jem in a hug and made sure it wasn't a needy one.

'What rotten timing,' said Jem. 'I've only seen you for two minutes and now you're rushing off again.'

Ginny managed a carefree smile. So much for her wonderful plan to spend the weekend with the person she loved more than anyone else in the world. 'I'll give you a ring in a few days. Bye, darling. Come on, Bellamy, say goodbye to Jem.'

Outside it was starting to rain. As she drove off, waving gaily at Jem on the doorstep, Ginny felt her throat begin to tighten. By the time she'd reached Whiteladies Road the sense of disappointment and desolation was all-encompassing and she no longer trusted herself to drive. Abruptly pulling over, willing the tears not to well up, Ginny took several deep breaths and gripped the steering wheel so hard it was a wonder it didn't snap in two. It's not *fair*, it's not *fair*, it's *just not*—

With a jolt she became aware that she was being watched. She turned and met the quizzical gaze of Davy Stokes. In the split second that followed, Ginny realised she'd pulled up at a bus stop, it was a bitterly cold rainy afternoon, and from the expression on Davy's face he thought she'd stopped to offer him a lift.

Oh, brilliant.

But it was too late to drive off. And at least she wasn't in floods of tears. Buzzing down the passenger window and reaching over, Ginny dredged *that* voice up again and said chirpily, 'Hello! You're getting terribly wet out there! Won't you let me give you a lift?'

'Is Henbury out of your way?'

Ginny had never heard of Henbury but after having driven two hundred miles up here and with the same again to look forward to on the return journey, what were a few more?

'No problem. You'll have to direct me, though. And don't worry if Bellamy licks your ear, he's just being friendly.'

'I like dogs. Hello, boy.' Having climbed into the car and fastened his seatbelt, Davy flicked his long dark hair out of his eyes and said, 'Did they talk about me after I'd gone?'

Ginny paused. 'No.'

He smiled briefly. 'Shouldn't pause. That means yes. Do they think I've got a crush on Lucy?'

'Um, possibly,' Ginny conceded with reluctance. 'Why? Don't you?'

'Of course I do. She's gorgeous. But I kind of realise nothing's ever going to come of it. I know I'm not her type.' Wistfully, Davy said, 'I had hoped to win her over with my deadpan wit, kind of like Paul Merton, y'know? Trouble is, every time I see Lucy my wit goes out of the window. I turn into a gormless dork instead.'

Ginny was touched by his frankness. 'Give yourself time,' she said.

'To be honest, she's out of my league anyway. You won't mention any of this, will you? Can it be just between us?' asked Davy. 'I've made enough of a berk of myself as it is.'

'I won't breathe a word.'

'Promise?'

'Promise. Shall I tell you something in return? I wasn't that taken with Rupert.'

'Rupert's a prat. Sorry, but he is. He looks down his nose at everyone. Carry straight on over this roundabout.'

'And you're still living at home, did somebody mention?'

'With my mother. Dad took off years ago. Mum didn't want me to move out,' said Davy, 'so I only applied to Bristol.'

Lucky, lucky mother. She'd asked her son not to move out so he hadn't. So simple, thought Ginny. Now why didn't I think of that?

'She might change her mind. Maybe Rupert will move out and you could take his place.' Ginny was only joking but wouldn't it be great if that happened?

'Except Rupert's hardly likely to move out,' said Davy, 'seeing as it's his flat.'

'Is it?' She hadn't realised that. 'I thought they were all tenants.'

Davy shook his head. 'Rupert's father bought the place for him to live in while he's here at university.'

'Oh. Well, that makes sense, I suppose. If you can afford it.'

'From what I hear, Rupert's father can afford anything he wants. Now take the next left. That's it, and ours is the one there with the blue door. That's brilliant. Thanks so much; maybe we'll see each other again some time.' Twisting round in the passenger seat, he said, 'Bye, Bellamy.'

'Good luck,' said Ginny. 'And you never know, things might work out better than you expect.'

Davy climbed out of the car. 'You mean tongue-tied good guy gets the girl in the end?' He gave a good-natured shrug. 'Maybe if this was a Richard Curtis film I'd stand a chance.'

Ginny watched him head into the house, the kind of modest, every-day three-bed end terrace that Rupert would undoubtedly sneer at.

'Time to go home, boy.' Patting Bellamy's rough head, Ginny said, 'So much for our weekend with Jem, eh? Sorry about that.'

Bellamy licked her hand as if to let her know that he had already forgiven her. Ginny gazed lovingly at him. 'Oh, sweetheart, thank goodness I've got you to keep me company. What would I do without you?'

Bellamy died three weeks later. The cancer that had spread so rapidly throughout his body proved to be untreatable. He was unable to walk, unable to eat, clearly in pain. The vet assured Ginny that putting Bellamy peacefully to sleep was the kindest thing she could do.

So she did it and felt more grief and anguish than she'd ever known before. Bellamy had been with them ever since Gavin had moved out. Someone had suggested getting a dog to cheer them up and that was it, a fortnight later Bellamy had arrived in their lives, so much better company than Gavin that Ginny wished she'd thought of it years ago. Gavin was unfaithful, a gifted liar and emotionally untrustworthy in every way. Bellamy wasn't, he was gentle, affectionate and utterly dependable. His needs were simple and his adoration unconditional.

And now Bellamy was gone.

This morning they had buried him in the back garden beneath the cherry tree. Jem had caught the train down last night and together they had sobbed their way through the emotional ceremony.

But Jem had lectures and tutorials back in Bristol that she couldn't afford to miss. Staying in Portsilver wasn't an option. Red-eyed and blotchy, she had reluctantly caught the lunchtime train back to Bristol.

Ginny was pretty blotchy herself. Set on distraction, she drove down into the centre of Portsilver and parked the car. At least in November it was physically possible to park your car in Portsilver. Right, now what little thing could she treat herself to? A gorgeous new lipstick perhaps? A sequinned scarf? Ooh, or how about a new squeaky toy for—

No, Bellamy's dead. Don't think about it, don't think about it.

Don't look at any other dogs as you walk down the street.

And *don't cry*.

In a few weeks it would be Christmas so how about making a start on some present buying instead?

Miraculously, Ginny began to feel better. Picking out stocking fillers for Jem, she chose a pale pink tooled leather belt and a notebook with a inlaid cover of mother-of-pearl.

This was something she had always enjoyed, buying silly bits and pieces. Having paid, Ginny left and made her way on down the street. Glancing across the road, she saw a woman she knew only as Vera and her heart began to thud in a panicky way. They weren't close friends but had got to know each other while taking their dogs for walks along Portsilver's main beach. Vera owned an elegant Afghan hound called Marcus, who was at this moment sitting patiently while his owner retied her headscarf. She was the chatty type. If Vera spotted her she would be bound to ask where Bellamy was.

Unable to face her today, Ginny ducked into the nearest shop. Inside, tables were decoratively strewn with china objets d'art, hand-crafted wooden animals and all manner of quirky gifts.

Quirky expensive gifts, Ginny discovered, picking up a small pewter-coloured peacock with a jewelled tail and turning it over in the palm of her hand. The price on the label gave her a bit of a shock—

blimey, you'd want real jewels for thirty-eight pounds. Then again, it wasn't her kind of thing but Jem might like it. Oh now, look at those cushions over there, she'd definitely love those.

Except Jem wasn't going to get the chance to love them because a surreptitious turning over of the price tags revealed the cushions to be seventy-five pounds each. Yeesh, this was a lovely shop but maybe not the place to come for cheap and cheerful stocking fillers.

Lurking by the table nearest the door, Ginny peered out to see if Vera was still there. Not that she disliked Vera, it wasn't that at all; she just knew that having to tell another dog lover that Bellamy was dead would be more than she could handle just now.

No, thankfully, the coast appeared to be clear. Glancing around the shop to double-check that there was nothing else she wanted to look at and might be able to afford—shouldn't think so for one second—Ginny became aware that she was the object of someone's attention. A black-haired man with piercing dark eyes, wearing jeans and a battered brown leather jacket with the collar turned up, was watching her. For a second their eyes locked and Ginny saw something unreadable in his gaze. Heavens, he was good-looking, almost *smoulderingly* intense.

And then it was over. He turned away with an infinitesimal shrug that indicated he'd lost interest. Brought back to earth with a thump, Ginny gave herself a mental telling off. As if someone who looked like a film star was likely to be bowled over by the sight of her, today of all days, with her puffy, post-funeral eyes and tangled hair.

Dream on, as Jem would say with typical teenage frankness. And quite right too. Oh well, at least she hadn't made an idiot of herself and tried smiling and batting her eyelashes at him in a come-hither fashion. Relieved on that score, Ginny turned away as the door was opened by another customer coming into the shop. She ducked past them and began heading swiftly in the direction of the car park. That was enough for one day; time to go home now and—

'I saw you.'

Ginny's heart almost leapt out of her body. A hand was on her arm and although she hadn't heard him speak before, she knew at once who it was. Who else could a voice like that belong to?

Whirling round to face him, she felt colour flood her cheeks. Crikey, up close he was even more staggeringly attractive. And clearly intelligent too, capable of seeing beyond her own currently less-than-alluring external appearance.

'I saw you,' he repeated.

He even smelt fantastic. Whatever that aftershave was, it was her favourite. Breathlessly, Ginny whispered, 'I saw you too.'

His gaze didn't falter. His hand was still on her arm. 'Shall we go?'

Go? Oh, good grief, was this really happening? It was like one of those arty black and white French films where two people meet and say very little to each other but do rather a lot.

'Go where?' Steady on now, he's still a complete stranger, you can't actually go back to his place, tear off his clothes and leap into bed with a man you've only just—

'Back to the shop.'

Ginny's imagination skidded to a halt in mid-fantasy. (He had a four-poster bed with cream silk drapes that stirred in the breeze drifting in through the open window—because in her fantasy it was a balmy after-noon in August.)

'Back to the shop?' Perhaps he owned it. Or lived above it. Oh God, he was reaching for her hand, this was *so romantic*.

'Come on, do yourself a favour and give up. You might be good,' he drawled, 'but you're not that good.'

What was *that* supposed to mean? Puzzled, Ginny watched him take hold of her hand, then turn it face up and, one by one, unfurl her fingers.

Her blood ran cold. The next second she let out a shriek of horror. 'Oh my God, I didn't even realise! How embarrassing! I can't believe I just walked out with it in my hand. Thank goodness you noticed! I'll take it straight back and explain . . .'

Ginny's voice trailed away as she realised that she was attempting to retrieve her hand and this man wasn't letting it go. Nor was he smiling at her absent-mindedness, her careless but innocent mistake.

'Now look,' said Ginny, flustered. 'I didn't do it on purpose!'

'I despise shoplifters. I hope they prosecute you,' the man said evenly.

'But I'm not a shoplifter! I've never stolen anything in my *life*. Oh God, I can't believe you even think that!' Hideously aware that people in the street were starting to take notice, Ginny turned and walked rapidly back to the shop still clutching the jewelled peacock and fight-ing back tears of shame.

Pushing open the door to the shop, she saw that there were a dozen or so customers wandering around, plus the woman who worked there. Hot on her heels—evidently ready to rugby-tackle her to the ground if she tried to escape—the man ushered her inside and up to the counter.

Ginny pushed the jewelled peacock into the woman's hands and gab-
bled, mortified, 'I'm so sorry, it was a complete accident, I didn't realise
I was still holding it when I left.'

'Sounds quite convincing, doesn't she?' The man raised an eyebrow.
'But I was watching her. I saw the way she was acting before she made
her getaway.'

Was this like being innocent of murder but finding yourself on death
row?

'Please don't say that.' The tears were back, pricking her eyelids.
Gulping for breath and aware that she was now truly the centre of
attention, Ginny clutched the edge of the counter. 'I'm an honest
person, I've never broken the law, I just wasn't *concentrating*.'

'Obviously not,' the man interjected. 'Otherwise you wouldn't have
got caught.'

'Oh, will you SHUT UP? I didn't mean to take it! As soon as I'd
realised it was in my hand, I would have brought it back,' Ginny
shouted. 'It was an *accident*.' Gazing in desperation at the saleswoman,
she pleaded, 'You believe me, don't you?'

The woman looked startled. 'Well, I . . .'

Gesturing towards the phone on the counter, the man said to the
saleswoman, 'Go on, call the police.'

'It was a mistake,' sobbed Ginny. 'My dog died yesterday. I only b-
buried him this morning.' As she said it, her knees buckled beneath
her. The tears flowed freely down her face as the saleswoman hastily
dragged a chair out from behind the counter. 'I'm sorry, I'm so sorry . . .
everything's just getting too much for me.' Sinking onto the chair,
Ginny buried her face in her hands and shook her head.

'She's in a bit of a state,' the saleswoman murmured anxiously.

'That's because she's been caught red-handed. Now she's trying every
trick in the book to get out of it.'

'Ah, but what if her dog's really died? It's awful when that happens.
And she looks terrible.'

'That's because she's guilty,' replied the man.

'You shouldn't be on your own, love. Is there anyone we can call?'

Pointedly the man said, 'Like the police.'

Shaking her head, Ginny muttered, 'No, no one. My daughter's not
here any more. She's gone. Just get it over and done with and call the
police. Go ahead, arrest me, I don't care any more.'

There was a long silence. Everyone was holding their breath.

Finally, the saleswoman said, 'I can't do it to her. Poor thing, how could I have her arrested?'

'Don't look at me. It's your shop.' The man sounded exasperated.

'Actually, it's not. The owner's gone to Penzance for the day and I'm just covering. But we've got this back.' The clink of the jewelled peacock's feet against the glass-topped counter reached Ginny's ears. 'So why don't we leave it at that?'

The man, clearly disappointed, breathed a sigh of resignation and said brusquely, 'Fine. I was just trying to help.'

The door clanged shut behind him. Ginny fumbled for a tissue and wiped her nose. Patting her on the arm, the saleswoman said kindly, 'It's all right, love. Let's just forget it ever happened, shall we?'

Chapter 2

'YOU'LL NEVER GUESS what I did last week.' Even as she said it, Ginny felt herself begin to blush.

'Hey, good for you.' Carla, tanned from her fortnight in Sardinia, gave a nod of approval. 'Welcome back to the real world and about time too. So where did you meet him?'

Honestly.

'I wasn't doing *that*,' Ginny protested. 'We're not all sex-crazed strumpets, you know.'

'Just as well. All the more men for me.' Amused, Carla said, 'So tell me what you were doing instead that was so much better than sex.'

'I didn't say it was better than sex.' Entirely unbidden, the image of that cream four-poster bed with its hangings billowing in the breeze danced once more through Ginny's mind, accompanied by the shadowy outline of a tall, half-dressed figure. 'It was horrible. I accidentally shoplifted something and got caught by this vile man who didn't believe I hadn't meant to do it. Don't laugh,' she protested as Carla's mouth began to flicker. 'It was one of the worst experiences of my whole life. I was almost *arrested*.'

'What were you trying to make off with anyway? Something good?'

Friends, who needs them? 'I wasn't trying to make off with anything. It was a miniature jewelled peacock. I didn't even like it.'

'Never shoplift stuff you don't like. What were you thinking of?'

'That's just it, I *wasn't* thinking. It was after we'd buried Bellamy. And then I'd taken Jem to the station. I thought a spot of shopping might cheer me up.' Ginny pulled a face. 'Now I daren't even go into a shop in case it happens again. At this rate it's going to be tinned carrots and cornflakes at Christmas.'

'You need to sort yourself out,' said Carla. 'Get your social life back on track, find yourself a new man. I mean it,' she insisted. 'Tinned carrots and a suspended sentence isn't the way forward.'

'I know, I know.' Ginny had heard all this fifty times before. 'But not until after Christmas, OK? Jem'll be back soon.'

'There, you see? You're doing it again. Putting your life on hold until Jem comes home.' Swivelling round on her chair, Carla peered accusingly up at Ginny's kitchen calendar. 'I bet you've been crossing off the days until the end of term.'

'As if I'd do that,' said Ginny.

As if she'd cross the days off on the kitchen calendar where Jem would see it when she got back; she wasn't that stupid. She was crossing them off on the secret calendar hidden under her bed.

'Anyway, enough about you. Let's talk some more about me,' said Carla. So far they were up to day eight of her eventful holiday in Sardinia. No man had been safe.

'Go on then, what happened after Russell went home?'

'*Thank you.*' Carla's eyes danced as she refilled their wineglasses. 'I thought you'd never ask. Well . . .'

Ginny smiled. Only nineteen more days and Jem would be back. She'd definitely drink to that.

It was the week after Christmas and Ginny was in the kitchen loading the dishwasher when Jem bellowed from the living room, 'Mum! GET IN HERE! *NOW!*'

In the living room she found Jem no longer draped across the sofa but catapulted bolt upright gazing at the TV screen. It was one of those daytime magazine-style programmes and the presenter was talking chirpily about singles clubs. Ginny, her heart sinking, said, 'Oh no, I'm not going to one of those, don't even try to persuade me—*Oh!*'

The camera had swung round to reveal the person standing next to the presenter.

'I'm so embarrassed,' groaned Jem. 'Tell me you had an affair and he's not my real father.'

Ginny, her hands covering her mouth, watched as the female presenter interviewed Gavin about the difference joining a singles club had made to his life. Gavin was beaming with pride and wearing one of his trademark multicoloured striped shirts—some might call them jazzy, Ginny called them eye-wateringly loud. In his jolly way he chatted with enthusiasm about the fun they all had together and the great network of friends he'd made since joining the club. 'I mean, I know I'm no Johnny Depp, but all I'm looking for is someone to share my life with, and I know the right woman has to be out there somewhere. That's not too much to ask, is it?'

'Uurrrgh, now he's flirting with the presenter!' Jem buried her face in a cushion. 'I can't watch!'

Excruciatingly, the presenter and Gavin ended up dancing together before Gavin swept her into a joky Hollywood embrace. Then that segment of the TV programme was over and singles clubs were replaced by a three-minute in-depth discussion on the subject of cystitis.

'I can't believe I'm related to him.' Finally daring to uncover her eyes again, Jem reached for her mobile and punched out her father's number. 'Dad? No, this *isn't* Keira Knightley, it's *me*. Yes, of course we've just seen it. I can't believe you didn't warn us first. What if all my friends were watching? Why do *I* have to be the one with the embarrassing dad?'

'It's his mission in life to make you cringe,' said Ginny.

Jem, having listened to her father speak, rolled her eyes at Ginny. 'He says he's feeling a bit peckish.'

'He's always feeling a bit peckish. That's why he has to wear big stripy shirts to cover his big fat stomach. Go on then,' Ginny sighed, 'tell him to come over.'

'Hear that?' said Jem into the phone. She broke into a grin. 'Dad says you're a star.'

'He doesn't know what we're eating yet.' Ginny wiped her wet hands on her jeans. 'Tell him it's salad.'

Gavin roared up the drive an hour later in his white, midlife crisis Porsche and they ate dinner together round the kitchen table. Jem's efforts to shame him, predictably enough, failed to have the desired effect.

'Where's the harm in it?' Breezily unrepentant, Gavin helped himself to another mountain of buttery mashed potato. 'I'm expanding my social life, having fun. I've met some smashing girls.'

Girls being the operative word. At times, Ginny found it hard to believe that she and Gavin had ever been married. These days he was forever announcing that yet again he had met the most gorgeous creature and that this time she was definitely The One. The girls invariably turned out to be in their twenties with short skirts, high heels and white-blonde hair extensions. These relationships weren't what you'd call a meeting of minds. They usually only lasted a few weeks.

'Aren't the women at this singles place a bit older than you're used to?' Ginny asked.

'So? Not a problem. Some of them have cracking daughters.' Gavin was unperturbed. 'You should try it yourself.'

'What? Chatting up fifty-something women then running off with their daughters?'

'The club. It'd do you the world of good. Jem's back at uni next week,' Gavin went on. 'Come along with me and I'll introduce you to everyone. It'd be fun.'

'Are you mad? I'm your ex-wife.' Ginny couldn't believe he was serious. 'It's not normal, you know, to take your ex-wife along to your singles club. Even if I did want to go, which I *don't*.'

Gavin shrugged. 'You've got to move with the times.'

'Dad, leave it, this is like when you try to persuade me to eat olives just because *you* love them. Mum's fine, she's not desperate like you.'

'I'm not desperate.' Gavin was outraged at this slur on his character.

'No, you're just a bit of a tart.' Reaching over, Jem gave his hand a reassuring pat. 'And that's not a criticism, it's the truth. But Mum isn't like that.' Turning to Ginny, she added, 'You never get lonely, do you?'

'Um . . . well . . .' Caught off guard by what had clearly been a rhetorical question, Ginny wondered if this might perhaps be the moment to confess that sometimes, if she was honest, she *did* get a bit—

'Thank *God*,' Jem continued with feeling. 'I mean, you wouldn't believe what some parents are like. There are some completely hopeless cases out there. Like Lizzie, one of the girls on my course; her mum and dad ring her up almost every day; they have no idea how embarrassing they are. And Davy's another one—his mother wouldn't even let him leave home and everyone takes the mickey out of him. I mean, doesn't she realise she's ruining his whole life?'

Poor Davy. Poor Davy's mother. Poor *her*. Feeling sick, Ginny drank some water. Part of her was relieved that Jem hadn't an inkling how utterly bereft she felt. The other part realised that, clearly, from now on she was never ever going to be able to admit it.

'She doesn't mean to,' Ginny protested on Davy's mother's behalf.

'Yes, but it's so . . . pathetic! And it means he doesn't fit in. It's like if a crowd of us go out for a drink we always pile back to somebody's rooms or flat afterwards for beer. But what can Davy do, invite everyone round to his mum's house? Imagine that! Sipping tea out of the best china and making polite conversation with somebody's *mother*.'

Ginny winced inwardly.

'Don't bother with him. Just leave him to get on with it.' Gavin, who was to political correctness what Mr Bean was to juggling, said, 'He sounds like a nancy boy, if you ask me.'

Ginny was balanced on a stepladder singing along to the radio at the top of her voice when she heard the distant sound of the front doorbell. It took a while to wipe her hands on a cloth, clamber off the ladder and gallop downstairs.

By the time she reached the hall, Carla was shouting through the letterbox, 'I know you're in there, I can hear all the horrible noise. Are you crying again? Come on, answer the door, I've come to cheer you up because that's the kind of lovely thoughtful person I am.'

Ginny opened the door, touched by her concern. 'That's really kind of you.'

'Plus I need to borrow your hair drier because mine's blown up.' Impressed, Carla said, 'Hey, you're not crying.'

'Well spotted.'

'You're wearing truly revolting dungarees.'

'Not much gets past you, Miss Marple.'

'And there's bright yellow stuff all over your face and hands.' Carla paused, considered the evidence and narrowed her eyes shrewdly. 'I conclude that you have been having a fight in a bath of custard.'

'You see? That's why the police never take a blind bit of notice when you try and interfere with their investigations.'

Carla grinned and followed her into the kitchen. 'What are you painting?'

'Spare bedroom.'

Carla raised her eyebrows. 'For any particular reason?'

'Oh, yes.'

'Am I allowed to ask why?'

Ginny made two mugs of tea and tore open a packet of caramel wafers. 'Because I've had enough of feeling sorry for myself. It's time to sort myself out and make things happen.'

'Good. But I don't quite see where decorating the house comes in.'

'Jem rang last night. She and Lucy were on their way out to a party. She sounded so happy,' said Ginny. 'They're having such fun together. Lucy got chatting to one of the boys from the rugby team and he invited her and Jem along to the match on Saturday.'

'Poor Jem, having to watch a game of rugby.' Carla shuddered and unwrapped a caramel wafer. 'I can't imagine anything more horrible.'

'But that's not the point. She's making more friends all the time. And before you know it, she'll be meeting *their* friends,' Ginny explained. 'So last night I decided that's what I should do too. Here's this lovely house with only me in it. So I'm going to advertise for—'

'A hunky rugby player of your very own! Gin, that's a fabulous idea!'

'Sorry to be so boring,' said Ginny, 'but I was thinking of a female. And preferably not the rugby-playing kind. Just someone nice and normal and single like me. Then we can do stuff together like Jem and Lucy do. I'll meet her friends, she'll meet mine, we can socialise as much as we want. And when we don't feel like going out we can relax in front of the TV, just crack open a bottle of wine and have a good gossip.'

Carla pretended to be hurt. Inwardly, she *felt* a bit hurt. 'You mean you're going to advertise for a new friend? But I thought I was your friend. I love cracking open bottles of wine! I'm great at gossip!'

'I know that. But you already have your life exactly the way you want it,' Ginny patiently pointed out.

'You'll like her better than you like me!' Carla clutched her hand to her chest. 'The two of you will talk about me behind my back. When I turn up on your doorstep, you'll say, "Actually, Carla, it's not really convenient right now."'

'Fine.' Ginny held up her paint-smeared palms. 'I give in. You can be my new lodger.'

Now Carla was genuinely horrified. 'You must be joking! I don't want to live with you! No, thanks, I like my own space.'

'Well, exactly. But I don't. I hate it,' Ginny said simply. 'I'm used to having someone else around the house. And as soon as I get this room redecorated I can go ahead and advertise.'

Carla rose to her feet and brushed wafer crumbs from her perfect black trousers. 'OK. If a lodger's what you want, then that's great. But I'm your best friend and don't you forget it. Can I borrow your hair drier now?'

It had been a busy night in the Royal Oak and Jem let herself into the flat expecting it to be empty. It was midnight and Rupert would be out at some trendy club somewhere. Lucy had already gone to Kerry and Dan's party. All Jem had to do was quickly change her clothes and re-spritz her hair and she would be on her way there too.

But when she pushed open the door to the living room, there was Rupert lying across the sofa watching TV and with an array of Chinese food in cartons spread out over the coffee table.

'Crikey, I thought you'd be out.'

Amused, Rupert mimicked her expression of surprise. 'Crikey, but I'm not. I'm here.'

'Why? Are you ill? Where's Caro?'

'Who knows? Who cares? We broke up.' He shrugged and reached for a dish of chicken sui mai.

'Oh, I didn't realise. I'm sorry.'

'So here I am, all alone, with more Chinese food than one person could ever eat. But now you're here too.' Patting the sofa, Rupert said, 'Sit down and help yourself. How was work this evening?'

Jem hesitated. He'd never asked her about work before. She suspected that Rupert was keen to have company and more upset about Caro than he was letting on.

'Um, actually I'm supposed to be meeting up with Lucy. At Kerry and Dan's party. Why don't you come along too?'

'Kerry the bossy hockey player? And carrot-top Dan the incredible hulk? I'd rather cut off my own feet. You don't really want to go there,' Rupert drawled. 'It's cold outside, it's starting to rain so you'd be drenched by the time you got there, and what would be the point?'

He *was* lonely, it was obvious. And speaking of cutting off your own feet, her new pointy pink cowboy boots were certainly killing hers. Jem hesitated, picturing the party she'd be missing. She was starving and the most anyone could hope for at Kerry and Dan's would be a dry French stick and a bucket of garlic dip. Whereas Rupert ordered take-aways from the smartest Chinese restaurant in Clifton.

'Maybe you're right.' Giving in to temptation, she sank down onto the sofa next to him.

Rupert grinned. 'I'm always right. Want a hand with those?'

Jem tugged off her left boot and heaved a sigh of relief as her toes unscrunched themselves. Having helped her pull off the right one, Rupert held up the boot and shook his head. 'You shouldn't wear these.'

'They're leather,' Jem told him. 'They'll stretch.'

'They'll still be horrible. How much did they cost?'

'They were a bargain. Twenty pounds reduced from seventy-five!'

'*Exactly*. Who in their right mind would want them?'

'*I* would,' Jem protested, looking at her boots and wondering if he was right.

Smiling at her expression, Rupert chucked them across the carpet. 'Enough boot talk. Have some wine. And help yourself to food.'

The king prawns in tempura were sublime. Greedily, Jem tried the scallops with chilli sauce. The white wine, too, was a cut above the kind of special-offer plonk she was used to. Closing her eyes and wriggling her toes, she said, 'You know what? I'd rather be here.'

'Of course you would. Staying in is the new going out.' Wielding chopsticks like a pro, Rupert fed her a mouthful of lemon chicken. 'Listen to the rain outside. We're here with everything we need.'

Swallowing the piece of chicken, Jem thought how much chattier Rupert was when it was just the two of them together. While he and Caro had been a couple, their attitude had always been . . . well, not stand-offish exactly, but distant. Now, taking a sip of wine, she realised he was showing definite signs of improvement. Wait until she told Lucy that super-posh Rupert might actually be human after all.

Actually, better text Lucy and tell her she was giving the party a miss.

By one they'd finished two bottles of wine. *Gangs of New York* wouldn't have been Jem's DVD of choice but the food more than compensated. When the film ended, Rupert said, 'Want to watch *The Office* next?'

'Ooh, yes.' Relaxed and pleasantly fuzzy, she beamed up at him. 'You know what? I'm really glad I stayed in.'

'All the best people do it. Unlike that rabble,' said Rupert of a group of noisy revellers making their way along the road outside. 'Listen to them, bunch of tossers.' Raising his voice, he repeated loudly, '*Tossers*.'

Jem giggled. 'I don't think they can hear you.'

Rupert leapt up from the sofa and crossed the room. Flinging open the sash window, he bellowed, 'Tossers!'

A chorus of shouting greeted this observation. Insults were flung up at him and a beer can made a tinny sound as it bounced off a wall.

'They tried to throw a beer can at me.' Casting around the living room, Rupert searched for something to throw in return.

Jem let out a shriek as he snatched up her boots and flung the first one out of the window. 'Not my boots!'

'Wankers,' yelled Rupert, hurling the second boot before she could stop him then slamming the window shut.

'Are you mad? Go and get them back! They're *my* boots.'

'Correction. They're horrible boots.' Amused, he reached out and grasped Jem's arms as she attempted to dart past him. 'And it's too late now, they've run off with them.'

'You bastard! How dare you?'

'Hey, sshh, they've served their purpose. I'll buy you a new pair.'

'That was the last pair in the shop!' Jem struggled to break free.

'And they were cheap and nasty. You deserve better than that. I'll buy you some decent boots.' Rupert was laughing now. 'OK, I'm sorry. I shouldn't have just grabbed them like that, but I've done you a favour. We'll go out tomorrow and find you a fabulous pair. That's a promise.'

Jem stared past him, lost for words. Her beautiful pointy pink cowboy boots, gone, just like that. Had they really been cheap and nasty?

'Come on.' Rupert tilted her face up to look at him. 'You know it makes sense.' His gaze softened as he stroked her cheek. 'God, you're a pretty little thing.'

Jem knew he was going to kiss her. As his mouth brushed against hers she felt a warmth spread through her body. Rupert's fingers slid through her hair then he drew her closer to him and kissed her properly.

It was great. Then he pulled away and cradled her face in his hands, his hazel eyes searching hers.

'What?' whispered Jem.

'Sorry, shouldn't have done that.' He smiled briefly.

Jem hesitated. Would it be too forward to suggest that he could do it again if he liked?

But Rupert was shaking his head now, looking regretful. 'Probably not the best idea.'

This was his flat, she was his tenant. Maybe he was right. Not hugely experienced sexually, one part of Jem was relieved that he wasn't employing all his seduction skills to inveigle her into his bedroom for a night of torrid passion. The other part of her wondered why not and felt, frankly, a bit miffed. Wasn't she attractive enough?

'Come on, let's watch *The Office*.' Rupert affectionately ruffled her hair before turning away to sort through the pile of DVDs.

And that was what they did. For the next hour, Jem sat next to him on the sofa gazing blindly at the TV, completely unable to concentrate on what was happening on screen. Her mind was in a whirl; all she could think about was that kiss, and the way Rupert had looked at her. Had the kiss put him off? Had she done it wrong?

Jem's heart broke into a gallop as Rupert moved, reaching forward for the remote control. He switched off the DVD and the TV, yawned widely and said, 'That's it. Time for bed.'

Was that some kind of code? Hardly daring to breathe, she watched him stand up, yawn again and stretch his shoulders. Turning briefly, he said, 'Night, then,' before heading for the door.

OK, not some kind of code after all.

'Night,' said Jem, confused and disappointed. All these months of sharing a flat with Rupert and she had honestly never thought of him in a romantic way, but that had been because he was so out of her league. Rupert's background, his gilded life and upper-class glamour set him apart from the rest of them. He and Caro moved in elevated circles, whizzing up to London at weekends, staying with friends in country houses and flying to Paris when the mood took them.

It was a different world.

He'd kissed her.

And now he'd gone to bed.

Let's face it, nothing was going to happen. She'd been naive to even think it might.

Jem had been in bed for ten minutes when the knock came on her bedroom door. Before she had time to reply, the door opened.

Rupert stood framed in the doorway, wearing shorts and nothing else. 'I can't stop thinking about you.'

'What?' It came out as a quivery whisper. Her pulse was going for some kind of world record.

'I can't sleep.' He tapped his head. 'You're in here. I've tried to get you out but you won't go.'

Moving towards her in the darkness, he went on, 'And I wondered if it was the same for you.'

Jem's tongue was stuck fast to the roof of her mouth. She couldn't say no, she couldn't say yes, she couldn't say anything at all.

'Room for one more in there?' Rupert tilted his head to one side.

Her fingers trembling, Jem reached for Barney Bear, the battered soft toy that had accompanied her to bed since she was five years old. Surreptitiously she dropped him down between the side of the bed and her chest of drawers, then lifted the duvet and pulled it back, moving over to make room for Rupert to join her.

'You're sure?' said Rupert as he slid into bed and took her in his arms.

'Yes,' Jem whispered. She'd never been more sure in her life.

At four o'clock, Rupert climbed out of bed and located his shorts.

Jem pushed herself up on one elbow. 'What are you doing?'

'Being discreet. Better if Lucy doesn't know about this.' Combing his fingers through his hair, he said, 'She might think three's a crowd, feel a bit of a gooseberry. Easier all round if you don't tell her.'

He had a point. This was Rupert's flat, she and Lucy were his tenants and it could cause awkwardness.

Except . . . did it mean what they'd just done was a one-off?

'Hey, don't look at me like that.' Having pulled on his shorts, Rupert bent over and kissed her. 'It'll be fun. Like having an affair without all the hassle of being married to other people. It's more exciting when no one else knows.'

Relieved, Jem wrapped her arms round his neck. 'You're right. It's easier if we don't tell Lucy. It'll feel a bit funny, though. We tell each other everything.'

Rupert grinned. 'Trust me, some secrets are better kept.'

Chapter 3

THE ADVERT HAD GONE into the classified sections of today's *Western Morning News* and the *Cornish Guardian*. Ginny had spent ages composing it, finally settling on: 'Cheerful divorcee, 38, has lovely room to let in spacious home in Portsilver. Would suit lady in similar circumstances. £60 pw inclusive.'

There, that sounded OK, didn't it? Friendly and upbeat? If she were looking for somewhere to live, she'd be tempted herself. Gazing with pride at the advert, Ginny felt a squiggle of excitement at the thought of the fun she and her new lodger would have, and—

Yeek, phone!

'Hello?' She put on her very best voice.

''Ello, love, you sound up for it. Fancy a shag?'

Oh God. Outraged, Ginny said in a high voice, 'No I do *not*,' and cut the connection. Her hands trembled. How completely *horrible*. Was this what was going to happen? Would she be harassed by perverts?

The phone rang again an hour later. This time Ginny braced herself and answered it with extreme caution.

'It's me. How's it going?'

Oh, the relief. Gavin. 'Nothing so far. Except some vile pervert.'

'What did you say to him?'

'I told him to fuck off.'

'Listen, let me know when anyone's coming round to look at the room. I should be there. It's not safe, inviting strangers into your home when you're on your own.'

Ginny relented. Gavin had offered before but she'd told him there was no need, seeing as she'd only be meeting women anyway. Now, though, she realised he was right. It was silly to take the risk.

'OK. If anyone *does* call.' Reluctantly, she said, 'Thanks.'

'No problem. I'm free this evening. You didn't, by the way.'

'Didn't what?'

'Tell me to fuck off.'

Ginny counted to ten. 'That was you? Thanks a lot.'

'Ah, but I got my point across. It might not be me next time.'

Gavin was annoying enough when he was wrong. When he was right he was insufferable. Ginny, who hated it when that happened, said, 'Fine then, but you can hide upstairs. I'm not having you sitting there like some minder while I'm talking to them.'

'You spoil all my fun,' Gavin protested.

The doorbell rang at seven o'clock on the dot, heralding the arrival of the first of the two potential tenants who had phoned that afternoon. More nervous than she let on—heavens, was this what it was like to go on a blind date?—Ginny shooed Gavin upstairs and took a steadying breath before opening the front door.

'Hello, love, I'm Monica. I've just been having a look at your window sills; you know they'd benefit from a quick going over with a dab of Cif. Brighten them up lovely, Cif would. Ooh, and those skirting boards could do with a dust.'

The trouble with blind dates was, it wasn't considered polite to take one look at the no-hoper in front of you and say, 'Sorry, this is never going to work out so why don't we just give up right now?'

Monica was short and squat, with permed grey hair and flicked-up spectacles. She looked like a short-sighted turtle. She also looked sixty-five years old. And she hadn't stopped talking yet.

'. . . that's what I do, love. Just dab a toothbrush in vinegar and scrub away like billy-o—those taps will come up like diamonds! Now, why don't we have a nice cup of tea and a good old chat before I take a look at my room, hm? Then we can start to get to know each other. Ooh, I say washing-up liquid from Marks and Spencer, bit extravagant, isn't it? Nice and weak, please, love, we can share the teabag. No sugar for me, I'm already sweet enough.'

Oh help, oh help, get me out of here.

'**S**he sounds perfect. When's she moving in?' As soon as the front door closed, Gavin came downstairs.

'Sshh, my ears hurt.'

'Want me to give them a polish with Brasso? That'll bring them up a treat.'

'What a nightmare.' Ginny shuddered. 'That was horrendous. I told her I had lots of other people interested in the room and that I'd let her know tomorrow.'

'You've only got one more to see. What if she's worse than her?'

Dumping the cups in the sink and thinking longingly of the wine in the fridge, Ginny said, 'There can't be anyone worse than Monica.'

'**H**i, come in, I'm Ginny.'

'Zeee.'

Ginny hesitated, wondering if the woman had a bumble bee trapped in her throat. 'Excuse me?'

'Zeee. That's my name. With three e's.' There was a note of challenge in the woman's voice, as if daring Ginny to query the wisdom of this. 'Zeee Porter. You shouldn't have a table there, you know. Not in the hallway like that. Bad feng shui.'

'Oh.' In that case, Ginny longed to tell her, *you* shouldn't have grubby blonde dreadlocks and you definitely shouldn't be wearing purple dungarees, because that's bad feng shui too.

Zeee Porter, she learned, was thirty-six and—incredibly for such a catch—still single. Currently the only man in her life was her spirit guide, Running Deer. During the summer months, Zeee surfed, worked as a henna tattooist and just, like, generally chilled out. The rest of the year she just, well, generally chilled out and waited for summer to come round again. Yes, she'd had a proper job once, in a vegan café in Aldershot, but being told what to do had done her head in.

'I just don't *need* that kind of hassle in my life.'

She evidently didn't need the hassle of shampoo or deodorant either. Ginny wondered if Running Deer wore a peg on his nose or if spirit guides weren't bothered by those kinds of earthly matters.

Ginny dutifully showed her the room she wouldn't be living in then said brightly, 'Well, I've got *lots* of other people to see, but I'll give you a ring tomorrow and let you know either way.'

'I haven't got a phone,' said Zeee. 'Phones are destroying the planet.'

'Oh.' Except for when Zeee had rung earlier to make the appointment, presumably.

'To be honest,' Zeee went on, 'I think we'll just leave it. No offence, but Running Deer's telling me he wouldn't be comfortable here.'

'Right.' Awash with relief, Ginny sent up a silent prayer of thanks to spirit guides everywhere. Hooray for Running Deer.

'**G**od, what a stink. Open the windows,' Gavin complained as he sloshed wine into two glasses up to the brim and handed one to Ginny. 'So that's it. You've seen both of them and neither fitted the bill. What happens now?'

'Re-advertise I suppose. Try again. Hope for better luck next time.' Ginny made headway into her much-needed glass of wine, more disappointed than she cared to let on by the events of this evening. She had been so looking forward to meeting someone lovely, the two of them hitting it off from the word go. Now she knew how naive she'd been and the sense of disappointment was crushing. What if she kept on advertising and no one suitable ever turned up?

By eight o'clock they had finished the bottle and Gavin was preparing to leave when the phone rang.

'Hi,' said a warm male voice, 'I'm calling about the house-share. Is it still going, or have you found someone now?'

It was more than a warm voice, it was a gorgeous voice, the kind that made you think the owner had to be gorgeous too. Wondering if maybe all might not be lost after all, Ginny said, 'No, it's still free.'

'Fantastic. Now it says here in the ad that you'd prefer a female . . .'

'Either. Really, I don't mind.'

'As long as it's someone you can get along with.' He definitely sounded as if he were smiling. 'I know, that's the important thing, isn't it? My name's Perry Kennedy by the way. And your house sounds just the kind of thing I'm after. How soon could I come round and take a look?'

Giddy with hope and three hastily downed glasses of wine, Ginny said recklessly, 'If you want to, you can come round now.'

Having expected so much, Ginny was relieved to see when she opened the front door that Perry Kennedy was six feet tall with wavy reddish-gold hair, sparkling green eyes and a dazzling smile.

'It's really good to meet you.' As he shook Ginny's hand he said, 'Hey, I love the way you've done the hall.'

Twenty minutes later they were sitting together in the kitchen chatting away as if they'd known each other for years. Perry's current flat was too small; it was driving him crazy. He was thirty-five, single but with a great crowd of friends in Portsilver and he loved socialising. A year ago he had moved down from London to Cornwall, selling his flat in Putney and ploughing the equity into a T-shirt printing business. His favourite food was Thai. He drove an old MG and he was *perfect*.

'Anyway, I'm taking up too much of your time. The room's great,' said Perry. 'And so are you. What shall I do, then? Leave my number and wonder if I'll ever hear from you again?'

Could she ask for anyone better? Ginny raced through everything she knew about him in her mind, searching for flaws and finding none. Perry was charming and brilliant company. OK, he wasn't a woman and they probably wouldn't spend a lot of time discussing nail polish, but other than that, were there any drawbacks at all?

'Or,' said Perry with a smile, 'do you think we might have a deal?'

Seeing no reason to prevaricate, Ginny threw caution to the wind. She beamed at Perry and said, 'We have a deal.'

He looked at her in delight. 'You don't know how much this means to me. The room's perfect. How soon would it be available?'

'Whenever you like.' Ginny watched him take out his wallet and count his way through a sheaf of twenty-pound notes.

'Would Saturday be all right?'

'Saturday? No problem.'

'Here, one month's deposit and the first month's rent in advance.' Perry pressed the notes into her hand and said, 'Before you change your mind. And you'll be wanting references of course. I'll bring them along on Saturday. Thanks so much for this.' He fixed Ginny with the kind of look that made her insides go wibbly. 'I'm so glad I met you tonight.'

'Me too.' She watched as he rose and reached for his car keys.

'I'd better get back. Saturday morning, OK? Elevenish, or is that too hideously early?'

Ginny shook her head. This was the start of her new life and as far as she was concerned Saturday couldn't come soon enough. 'No problem. Eleven o'clock's fine.'

The trouble with ex-husbands was you could always rely on them to notice things you'd much rather they didn't.

And, naturally, to take huge delight in pointing it out.

'Ha!' Gavin pointed a triumphant finger at her as he came down the stairs. 'You fancy him.'

'I do *not*.'

'Oh yes you do. I *heard* you.' Smirking, he launched into a wickedly accurate imitation of her, punctuated by slightly too loud laughter.

Why couldn't she have an ex-husband who lived five hundred miles away? Or in Australia? Australia would be good.

'He's moving in on Saturday.' Ginny was defiant. 'And I don't fancy him, OK? He just seems nice and we get on well together, that's all.'

'Hmm.' Gavin raised a playful eyebrow. 'Good-looking, is he?'

'Average,' said Ginny.

He grinned. 'This is going to be interesting.'

Interesting. She hoped so too.

By eleven o'clock on Saturday morning the house was all ready and, as if in celebration, the sun had come out. Perry Kennedy would be here soon. Ginny, working on not-sounding-as-if-she-fancied-him, had been practising her laugh as she tidied around the kitchen, making sure it didn't get too loud or high-pitched. Of course, once Perry had settled in and they became more used to each other, things would hopefully settle down and she'd stop feeling so—

Oh God, that sounded like him now! Flinging the J-cloth into the sink, Ginny wiped her hands on her jeans and fluffed up her hair. The throaty roar of a sports car outside died as the engine was switched off. She went to the front door and opened it.

'Hi, there.' Perry was already out of the car and waving at her.

'Hi!' Ginny watched as the passenger door opened to reveal a slender woman with a mass of long red-gold curls and pale freckled skin. She was staggeringly beautiful and wore a long black coat falling open to reveal a pale grey top and trousers beneath.

'This is Laurel.' Gavin ushered the woman towards Ginny. 'My sister.'

Oh, phew, of course she was. All that incredible red-gold hair—what a relief.

'Hi, Laurel, nice to meet you.'

Tonelessly, Laurel said, 'Hello.'

'Come on then, let's get this lot upstairs.' Already busy unloading the MG's tiny boot, Perry said, 'Laurel, you take these. I'll bring the rest of the bags.'

'Give some to me.' Keen to help, Ginny held out her arms.

Perry looked across at Laurel and said, 'See what I mean? Didn't I tell you how great she was?'

Ginny flushed with pleasure. She'd done the right thing.

Laurel nodded. 'You did.'

Once all the bags and cases had been taken up to the spare room, Ginny left them to it. In the kitchen she boiled the kettle and began making tea. After a couple of minutes, Perry rejoined her.

'Don't bother with tea.'

'No? Would you prefer coffee?'

He shook his head and produced the bottle he'd been concealing behind his back.

'Woo, champagne. On a Saturday morning!'

'The very best time to drink it. Quick, glasses,' said Perry as the cork rocketed out and bounced off the ceiling.

'Well, cheers.' Ginny clinked her glass against his; he'd only filled two of the three she'd set out. 'Isn't Laurel having any?'

'Laurel doesn't drink. Cheers. Here's to you.'

If Gavin were here now, he would tell her that replying 'Here's to both of us' would be flirty beyond belief. So Ginny didn't, she just smiled instead and took a demure sip of the champagne. As they heard the sound of furniture being moved around in the bedroom overhead she said, 'What's Laurel doing, doesn't she want to join us?'

'She's fine, best to leave her to get on with it.' Perry's eyes sparkled.

'She's just rearranging the room, getting her things unpacked.'

'Sorry?' Ginny thought she must have misheard. 'You said she was getting *her* things unpacked.'

Perry nodded. 'Yes.'

Her heart beginning to thump unpleasantly, Ginny said, 'But . . . why would she be unpacking her things? She isn't the one moving in. I've rented the room to *you*.'

Perry looked at her. 'God, I'm sorry, is that what you thought? No, no, the room's not for me. It's for Laurel.'

'But you were the one who came to see it! You said it was just what you were looking for!' Her voice rising—and not in an I-fancy-you way—Ginny said, 'You said it was perfect!'

He blinked, nonplussed. 'It *is* perfect. For Laurel.'

Frantically, Ginny ran back through everything he'd told her. 'No, *hang on*, you said your flat was too small . . .'

'It *is* too small. I mean, it's all right for me on my own,' Perry explained, 'but it's definitely a squash for two.'

Still in a state of shock, Ginny repeated, 'B-but I rented the room to *you*.'

'I know you did. That's right. I paid the deposit and I'll be paying the rent,' said Perry. 'No need to worry about that. I'll set up a direct debit. Really, everything's going to be fine.'

Fine? How *could* it be? Ginny's head was about to explode.

'You made me think it was you! You never once mentioned your sister. You *knew* I thought it was you.'

Perry spread his arms. 'Honestly, I didn't.'

'But the whole point of interviewing people when they come to look at the room is so that you can decide whether you want to share your house with them!'

'Is it?' Perry looked genuinely bewildered. 'I didn't realise.' He paused, then said eagerly, 'But it doesn't matter, because you won't have any problems with Laurel. As soon as I met you, I knew the two of you would get on brilliantly. You're just the kind of person Laurel needs.'

What? Ginny wanted to yell, this isn't about what somebody else needs, you idiot, it's about what *I* need.

'Oh, and I've brought the references.' Perry withdrew a couple of envelopes from his pocket. 'Laurel's honest, tidy, considerate—everything you could want in a housemate.'

This was all going so desperately, horribly wrong that Ginny was struggling to think straight. She wished Gavin could be here to back her up because right now she appeared to be the only one who thought there was anything amiss. Except if Gavin were here he'd be too busy laughing his socks off at the mess she'd managed to get herself into.

'Besides,' Perry went on, 'you did advertise for a female to share with. That was what you really wanted.'

'So why didn't Laurel come round to see the house herself?'

He sighed. 'Laurel was happy to carry on sleeping on my sofa. Finding somewhere else to live wasn't a priority as far as she was concerned. To be honest she's been a bit down lately. She broke up with her boyfriend last summer and things haven't been easy for her since then. She lost her job in London. Her ex-boyfriend met someone else and got engaged, which didn't help. Laurel was pretty fed up. I told her she should move out of the city and the next thing I knew, she'd turned up on my doorstep.' Perry paused, shrugged. 'Well, it was fine for a few days. It was great to see her again. Except she's decided she wants to stay in Portsilver now and my flat really isn't big enough for the two of us.'

'So move to a bigger flat.'

'Oh, Ginny, I'm sorry. I didn't mean to spring this on you. But when I met you, I just thought how fantastic you were, so chatty and bubbly, and I knew you'd be perfect for Laurel. Sharing a house with you is just what she needs to perk her up again.'

Ginny shook her head. 'The thing is, I—'

'Look, you'll have a great time with Laurel.' Perry gazed at her. 'And much as I'd like to be the one moving in here, that could never happen.'

'Why couldn't it?' Ginny rubbed her aching temples.

His eyes crinkled at the corners. 'Come on, you must know the answer to that one. You're gorgeous. How could I live in this house when I fancy the landlady rotten? That would be . . . impossible.'

Oh. So he *did* find her attractive.

'Sorry, was that a bit sudden?' Perry's smile was rueful. 'I'm usually a bit more subtle. But you did ask. If I'm honest, I've been sitting here wondering if you'd consider coming out to dinner with me next week. But who knows if I'll have the courage to ask you?' He pulled a wry face.

Ginny was lost for words. As she was floundering for a reply they both heard footsteps on the stairs. The next moment the door had swung open and Laurel entered the kitchen.

'I've unpacked.'

'Great.' Perry beamed at her.

Oh hell. Ginny took another gulp of champagne and found herself unable to meet Laurel's eye. If she was going to say something it had to be now, this minute. But how could she say it? How could she tell Laurel that she wasn't moving in after all, that she should get back upstairs and start repacking all her things?

'Is something wrong?' said Laurel. 'Perry? What's going on?'

Perry looked at Laurel and shrugged.

'Look, I'm sorry,' Ginny blurted out, 'but I didn't realise you were the one who'd be moving in. There's been a bit of a misunderstanding here. I thought your brother was the one looking for a room.'

Laurel frowned. 'No. He's already got his flat.'

'I know that *now*,' Ginny exclaimed, 'But he didn't mention it before.'

Laurel gazed steadily at her. 'So what are you saying?'

Oh God, what *was* she saying? It wasn't in her nature to deliberately hurt another person's feelings. If she didn't have Laurel, she'd have to go through the whole advertising-and-interviewing rigmarole all over again and who was to say she'd get anyone better next time round? Plus, Perry fancied her and was going to invite her out to dinner—

'Don't you want me here?' There were now tears glistening in Laurel's huge green eyes. 'Do I have to go?'

That was it. Shaking her head, Ginny said, 'No, no, of course you don't have to go. Everything's fine.'

Laurel smiled a watery smile. 'Thank you.'

Perry beamed with relief. 'Excellent.'

Instantly, Ginny felt better, no longer twisted with guilt. There, she'd done it. And she had a first date with Perry to look forward to, so everything *was* going to be fine. Forgetting what he'd told her earlier, she seized the champagne bottle and said gaily to Laurel, 'Let's celebrate!'

'I'm not allowed to drink.' Laurel shook her head. 'Because of my tablets.'

Tablets. Everything was going to be fine, Ginny reminded herself. Aloud she said sympathetically, 'Antibiotics?'

Laurel blinked. 'antidepressants.'

Oh.

'Right, I'd better get back to the shop.' Perry jumped up. 'I'll leave you two girls to get to know each other. Bye.'

Hastily, Ginny said, 'I'll just show you out,' and followed him to the front door.

'She's a lovely girl. You won't regret it.' Perry kept his voice low.

'Listen, if I manage to pluck up the courage to ask you out to dinner sometime soon, do you think you might say yes?' His smile was playful.

Ginny replied flirtatiously, 'I might.'

'Great. I'll give you a call. Just do me a favour, don't mention it to Laurel.'

'Why not?' Ginny was puzzled.

'Oh, it's just that she's been through a bit of a bad patch with men, you know? She's kind of anti-relationships right now. I told her you were divorced and she liked the idea of sharing a house with someone else in the same boat. If she knew we were meeting up with each other she might feel a bit odd-one-out.'

Ginny wondered if she really was doing the right thing here. Somehow, in the space of a morning, all her plans had been turned inside out. What had she let herself in for?

'Sshh, stop worrying.' Evidently capable of reading her thoughts—or more likely the panicky God-what-have-I-done look in her eyes—Perry raised his right index finger to his lips then smiled and tenderly pressed that same finger against her own mouth. 'You two'll have a great time.'

Brushing his finger like that against her lips had set off a deliciously zingy sensation in Ginny's knees. Crikey, if that was kissing by proxy she couldn't wait for the real thing.

'I really have to go.' Perry was glancing at his watch.

Ginny opened the front door and said, 'Bye then,' her mouth still tingling from the proxy kiss.

Everything *was* going to be fine.

'I think Perry got fed up with hearing me talk about it,' Laurel said tonelessly. 'Men aren't into that kind of thing, are they? Especially brothers. Every time I mentioned Kevin he'd try to change the subject. But I *have* to talk about Kevin,' she went on. 'I loved him so much, you see. *So* much. How can you forget someone who's broken your heart?'

'Well,' Ginny said uncertainly, 'er . . .'

'Although he's probably forgotten me.' Laurel wiped her eyes with a proper hanky. (Not even a tissue.) 'Because I just don't matter to him any more, do I? Kevin's moved on now, he met someone else in no time flat and loved her enough to ask her to marry him. I used to drive past his house, you know. One evening I saw them kissing on the front doorstep. I was so unhappy I thought I'd die. And you know what? She had fat ankles. Fat ankles, I swear! Really . . . *chubby*.'

Ginny did her best to look suitably shocked and sympathetic, but a terrible urge to yawn was creeping up her ribcage, threatening to make a bid for freedom the millisecond she relaxed the muscles in her jaw. For ninety minutes now she had been listening to the Story of Kevin. Ninety minutes was the length of an entire film. She could have watched *Anna Karenina* and been less depressed.

'I suppose I'm boring you,' Laurel said flatly.

'No, no.' Hastily Ginny shook her head.

'It's just that I thought we'd get married and have babies and be happy together for the rest of our lives, but he changed his mind and now I'm just left without *anything*. Why does life have to be so unfair?'

Oh dear, yet another unanswerable question. Slightly desperate by now, Ginny said, 'I don't know, but how about if you try to . . . um, stop thinking about him quite so much?'

Laurel gave her a pitying look, as if she'd just suggested switching off gravity. 'But I loved him so much. He was my whole world. He still *is*.'

Oh God.

Despite having promised to be in touch, Perry Kennedy hadn't called and Ginny was in need of some serious cheering up. Carla, who hadn't said as much yet but already wasn't sure she trusted Laurel's smooth-talking brother, made an executive decision and said, 'Right, I'm taking you out to lunch.'

Ginny looked up, surprised. 'When?'

'Today. Now. Unless you don't want to.'

'Are you kidding?' Ginny's eyes lit up. 'Of course I want to.'

Carla shrugged. 'Because if you'd rather stay at home and have a girly chat with your new best friend Laurel, I'd quite understand.'

'Shut up and take me out to lunch.'

Carla loved her job and was good at it. When potential clients contacted Portsilver Conservatories, she made an appointment to visit them in their homes and employed her own special no-pressure sales technique in order to persuade them that if they wanted the perfect conservatory, then her company was the one for them.

And in almost every case Carla succeeded. She travelled all over the southwest and often worked in the evenings and at weekends but that was a bonus too because it meant she could take other days off whenever she liked.

Like today, which she was determined was going to be a memorable one because the last few months hadn't been easy for her friend Ginny. She deserved a break. Personally, Carla suspected that this sudden crush on Perry was largely down to the fact that it had been a long time since Ginny had been so comprehensively targeted by an attractive man. From what she could gather, Perry Kennedy had made quite a play for her and she had been flattered by the attention. For Ginny's sake, Carla hoped she didn't end up getting hurt.

Ginny was enjoying herself already. Here they were whizzing along in Carla's sporty black Golf, the sun was out and she *wasn't* going to feel guilty about leaving Laurel at home. Three blissful Kevin-free hours stretched ahead. Maybe this was the answer to all her problems; she would simply have to become one of those ladies who lunched, every day of the week.

Well, maybe if she won the Lottery first.

'I wonder what he's doing now?' said Carla.

Instantly thinking of Perry, Ginny said, 'Who?'

'Kevin.'

'Don't. We mustn't make fun of her.'

'I'm not making fun. I'm really wondering. I'd love to meet him,' Carla said mischievously. 'Drag him into bed. See if he's worth all the hoo-ha . . . Look, here we are.' She indicated right and slowed down before turning into the driveway.

Ginny, reading the blue and gold sign, said, 'Penhaligon's.'

The restaurant was housed in a long, whitewashed and ivy-strewn sixteenth-century farmhouse with a grey slate roof and a bright red front door. A series of smartly renovated interlinked outbuildings extended from one end of the farmhouse, forming three sides of a rectangle round the central courtyard. As Carla parked the car, a black cat darted out of one of the outbuildings ahead of a middle-aged man who was carrying a small wooden cabinet. The man proceeded to load the cabinet into the back of a van. The cat, tail flicking ominously slowly, looked as if it might be about to launch itself at the man's legs.

'It's a restaurant and antiques centre,' explained Carla, fairly pointlessly as there was a sign saying so above the door.

Ginny was out of the car gazing up at the buildings. Sunlight bounced off the windows and the glossy tendrils of ivy swayed gently in the breeze. The smell of wonderfully garlicky cooking mingled with woodsmoke hung in the air. Animated chatter spilled out of the restaurant and from the antiques centre came the sound of Robbie Williams singing 'Angels'.

The black cat took a swipe at the man who was now closing the van doors. Darting out of the way, he said, 'Don't get stroppy, it's mine now.'

'Nnnaaarrh,' sneered the cat, before turning and stalking off.

'Bloody animal,' the man called after it.

'You've gone quiet.' Having watched him jump into the van and drive off, Carla gave Ginny a playful nudge. 'Cat got your tongue?'

And in a way it had. Well, maybe not the cat, but the sights and sounds and smells of Penhaligon's Restaurant and Antiques Centre. Captivated by the unexpected charm of it all, Ginny felt as if she was falling a little bit in love at first sight.

'One more drink,' Ginny urged, waggling the bottle of Fleurie at Carla. 'Go on, you can have another.'

'I mustn't, I'm driving.'

'Leave the car. We'll come and pick it up tomorrow morning. God, I *love* it here. Why can't all restaurants be like this?'

For a Tuesday lunchtime in February, Penhaligon's was impressively busy. The restaurant, with its deep red walls covered in prints and original paintings, was eclectically furnished with an assortment of antique furniture. The atmosphere was unstuffily friendly and the food divine. Having guzzled her starter of scallops in lemon sauce, Ginny was now finishing her smoked beef main course. Not to mention the best part of a bottle of wine.

'Go on then, you've twisted my arm,' said Carla.

One bottle became two. They talked nonstop for the next hour and watched through the window as the black cat stalked and intimidated visitors crossing the courtyard. A selection of music ranging from Frank Sinatra to Black Sabbath drifted across from the antiques centre and every so often they could hear the kitchen staff singing along.

'Coffee and a brandy, please,' Carla told the waitress when she came to take their order. 'Gin?'

Ginny nodded in agreement. 'Lovely.'

The waitress looked startled. 'Coffee and a gin?'

'Two coffees and brandies.' Carla was grinning. 'Her name's Gin.'

'Oh phew! I thought it sounded a bit weird! Just as well I checked.' The girl shook her head by way of apology. 'Sorry, my brain's had enough today. Busy busy.'

'Hey, Martha.' One of the men at the next table called over. 'On your own today, sweetheart? What happened to Simmy?'

'Simmy shimmied off to Thailand with three hours' notice—what more could we ask? So now we have to find a new waitress before my feet drop off. If you fancy the job, Ted, just say the word.'

Ted, who was in his sixties, said, 'I'd make a rubbish waitress, love. Don't have the legs for it. Table six are asking for their bill, by the way.'

'Thanks, Ted. Right, two coffees and two brandies. I'll bring them as soon as I can.'

Martha hurried off and Carla shared out the last of the second bottle of wine. She looked over at Ginny.

Ginny gazed back at her.

'What are you thinking?' Carla said finally.

'You know what I'm thinking.' A little spiral of excitement was corkscrewing its way up through Ginny's solar plexus. 'I could work here. I'd love to work here.'

'Are you sure? It's only February.'

'I don't care.' Working seasonally meant she was usually employed from April to October, but what the heck? Penhaligon's was calling her name. 'I've got a feeling about this place.' Counting off the reasons on her fingers she burbled excitedly, 'It's only . . . what, three miles from home? And no problems parking, *that's* a bonus. And the only reason I've never done proper waitressing before is because I didn't want to work evening shifts while Jem was at home, but now she's gone it doesn't matter!'

'And you'd be getting away from Laurel,' Carla pointed out drily.

'Oh God, that sounds terrible!'

'Terrible but true. You've gone and landed yourself with the world's most boring lodger and any sane person would get rid of her. But you're too soft to do that.'

This was only semi-true. OK, maybe she was soft—a *bit*—but there was also Perry to be factored into the equation. Ginny sensed that turfing his sister out into the street might not win her too many Brownie points in his eyes.

Knocking back her wine with a flourish, she said, 'Laurel or no Laurel, it makes no difference. If I want to be a waitress I *can* be a waitress. I think this place is great and I'd love to work here.'

'*Would* you?'

'Oh!' Ginny hadn't realised Martha was standing behind her with their drinks. Filled with resolve, she exclaimed, 'Well, yes, I would. Definitely!'

'Hey, excellent.' Martha's freckled face lit up. 'I'll tell Evie, shall I? She manages the restaurant. She'll be dead chuffed.'

The manageress click-clacked across the floor in double-quick time. She was in her mid-fifties, tall and as elegant as a racehorse, with tawny blonde hair fastened up in a chignon and beautifully applied make-up. Smiling broadly she held out her hand. 'Hi, I'm Evie Sutton. Lovely to meet you. When you've finished your lunch, would you like to come and have a chat with me in my office, or . . . ?'

'We're just drinking our coffee.' Indicating the spare chair at their table and feeling deliciously proactive, Ginny said, 'If you like we can talk about it now.'

Twenty minutes later she had the job. Four lunchtime and three evening shifts a week, starting as soon as she liked.

'Tomorrow, if you want,' said Evie as she handed her an application form. 'Just fill this in and bring it with you.'

'Perfect.' Ginny could hardly wait. 'Thank you so much, I know I'm going to love it here.'

'Oh you will, I can tell. And you've certainly made my day.' Evie's blue eyes danced. 'There's nothing more depressing than having to interview a bunch of no-hopers.'

Liking her more and more, Ginny said with feeling, 'Tell me about it.'

'We aren't going home yet. I want to see the antiques centre.' Buzzing with excitement and with her inhibitions loosened by alcohol, Ginny practically skipped across the sunny courtyard.

Inside the converted outbuildings, the stone walls were painted emerald green and an Aladdin's cave of well-lit paintings, mirrors, polished furniture and *objets d'art* greeted them. In the centre of the main room stood a magnificent jukebox currently playing Stevie Wonder's 'Superstition'. Further along, in one of the interlinked rooms to the right, they could see someone showing a couple of potential customers a walnut bureau.

'Look at this.' Ginny longingly ran her fingers over a bronze velvet chaise longue. Turning over the price tag she blanched and abruptly stopped envisaging it in her living room.

'Never mind that, look at *these*.' Twenty feet away, Carla held up a pair of heavy silver Georgian candlesticks. 'I love them!'

'Stop it.' Ginny's eyes danced as Carla attempted to stuff them into her cream leather handbag. '*Bad* girl. Put them back.'

'Damn bag's not big enough. No forward planning, that's my trouble. Ooh, now this is smaller.' Picking up an enamelled box, Carla playfully waggled it.

'Antlers!' Ginny let out a shriek of delight and rushed over to take a closer look. 'I've *always* wanted a pair of real antlers.'

'They wouldn't suit you. And you definitely couldn't slip those into your handbag.' As she said this, Carla's gaze slid past Ginny.

'And I'd rather you didn't try it.'

The moment she heard the voice behind her, Ginny knew. So did her skin, which came out in a shower of goosebumps, and her stomach, which reacted with a nauseous lurch of recognition.

'You can put that down too,' the voice continued, this time addressing Carla.

Taken aback by his tone, Carla put down the decorative enamelled box and said chippily, 'I wasn't going to steal it, you know. We were just having a bit of fun. It was a *joke*.'

'Good job you're not a stand-up comedian then. People might ask for their money back.'

'Well, you're full of charm, aren't you?' Her eyes flashing, Carla demanded, 'Is this how you treat all your customers?'

'Not at all.' His reply was cool. 'But you don't appear to *be* customers, do you? Call me old-fashioned but I'd class a customer as someone who pays for what she takes from a shop.'

Ginny closed her eyes. This was awful, just *awful*, and Carla was practically incandescent with—

'How dare you!' Carla shouted, marching towards the door. 'As if anyone in their right mind would even *want* to buy anything from your crappy shop. Come on, Gin, we're out of here. And don't worry, I won't ever be coming to this dump again.'

But *I* will, Ginny thought in a panic.

'Excellent.' Moving to one side, the man allowed Carla to stalk past him. 'Mission accomplished.'

'No, it isn't,' Ginny blurted out. 'Stop! Carla, come back, we're going to sort this out.'

'*Ha*. The only way we could sort this out is if I gored him to death with his own antlers.' Jabbing furiously at her phone, Carla said, 'Hello? Hello? Yes, I want a taxi *this minute* . . .'

'We came here for lunch.' Ginny turned in desperation to face the man. 'We had a lovely meal.'

'Did you pay for it?'

'Yes!'

'With your own credit card or with somebody else's?'

'Oh, for crying out loud, will you stop *accusing* me? We haven't—'

'Oh great, you're still here!' Evie appeared in the shop doorway, a bright smile on her face. 'I just came over to tell Finn all about you, but I see you've already met. Finn, did Ginny tell you the good news?'

'No, I didn't,' Ginny said hurriedly. 'You see, there's been a bit of a—'

'We don't have to advertise for a new waitress!' Evie turned to Finn. 'This is Ginny Holland and she's coming to work for us, isn't that—'

'No, she's not,' Finn said flatly. *Very* flatly.

'I'm coming to work for *you*,' said Ginny, looking at Evie and praying she'd believe her when the whole sorry story came tumbling out.

'Maybe you thought you were,' Finn countered, 'but Evie only runs the restaurant. My name's Finn Penhaligon and I own it, which means you *won't* be working here because I say so.'

Ginny felt as if her head was about to burst with the unfairness of it all. She'd *so* wanted to work here and it clearly wasn't going to happen now.

'It's him, isn't it?' Having worked out what was happening, Carla's lip curled with disgust. 'He's the one from that shop who made you cry.'

'I'd love to know what's going on here,' said Evie, bewildered.

'I'm sure he'll tell you. Sorry about the job.' Ginny swallowed hard. 'I'd have loved to work for you.' Following Carla to the door she checked she wasn't inadvertently holding some antique *objet* then opened her bag wide to demonstrate to Finn Penhaligon that there was nothing that belonged to him inside. Determined to retain at least a shred of dignity, she then met his gaze and said steadily, 'I know you think you're right, but you're wrong.'

'I know what I saw.' Unmoved by her declaration, Finn shrugged. 'You know what really gave you away? The way you looked at me when I stopped you outside that shop.'

The way she'd looked at him. In any other circumstances, Ginny might have laughed. He would never know it, but that hadn't been guilt flickering in her eyes.

It had been lust.

It was midnight, clouds were scudding past the moon and Ginny and Carla were on a mission under cover of darkness to retrieve Carla's car from the courtyard of Penhaligon's without being seen.

'What a *bastard*.' Carla was still seething about the treatment they had received earlier at the hands of Finn Penhaligon.

Ginny concentrated on the road ahead. 'I know.'

'You didn't tell me he was that good-looking.'

Ginny knew that too. She hadn't told Carla that she'd fantasised about Finn Penhaligon and didn't see the point in telling her now. 'Is this the turning? God, what if he's there? We should have worn balaclavas.'

'Balaclavas aren't my style. OK, here we go. Just pull up next to my car and I'll jump out. We'll be gone in—fuck, what's that on the wind-screen? If that sad git's given me a parking ticket . . .'

She was out of the car in a flash. As she wrenched the envelope out from under the windscreen wiper a dark shadow darted across the yard, miaowing loudly. For a couple of seconds the cat was caught in the beam of Ginny's headlights before it leapt forward again and disappeared from view. Oh brilliant, now it was probably under the car and if she tried to drive off she'd kill it.

Buzzing down her window, Ginny hissed, 'Where's the cat?'

'Don't know, but this is for you.' Carla handed her the envelope. 'No doubt a restraining order warning you not to go within five miles of him.'

Ripping open the envelope, Ginny said, 'Just see if that cat's under the car, will you?'

She was forced to switch on the interior light in order to read the note, which was from Evie. It was brief and to the point.

Dear Ginny,
   We need you! Sorry about today—Finn can be a stroppy bugger sometimes but he's all right really. I've spoken to him now and sorted everything out. I really hope you'll come and work here. Please give me a ring.

'What does it say?' Carla was peering through the open window. 'God, what's *that*?' As a door suddenly slammed across the yard, she jumped and whacked her head on the window frame. 'Ow, that *hurts*.'

'It's him.' Reading Evie's words was all very well but Ginny still had an overwhelming urge to stick her foot down and, tyres squealing, make a high-speed Steve McQueen-style getaway.

Except it wouldn't only be the tyres squealing if she ran over the damn cat. Stuck where she was, Ginny watched warily as Finn Penhaligon made his way across the courtyard. He was wearing a white shirt and dark trousers, and she didn't trust him an inch.

'On the bright side,' said Carla, 'he isn't carrying a gun.'

'Unless there's one in his pocket.' Ginny gave a nervous hiccup of laughter. 'Although I can't say he looks pleased to see us.'

'Damn, he's good-looking though.'

Carla hadn't said it loudly but noise evidently travelled across the otherwise empty courtyard.

'Thank you.' Gravely, Finn nodded at her then turned his attention to Ginny. 'Have you read Evie's note?'

'Yes.'

'And?'

'And she's right.' With a surge of reckless bravery Ginny said, 'You are a stroppy bugger.'

The look in his eyes told her he hadn't read the note himself, hadn't realised that this was what Evie had said about him. The next moment, to his credit, he smiled briefly.

'Well, maybe that's true. But I wouldn't necessarily call that a bad thing. What else did she say?'

'That she'd spoken to you and everything was sorted out.' Ginny still couldn't quite believe this was happening, that she was here, in the early hours of the morning, sitting in her car having this conversation. 'And she still wants me to come and work in the restaurant. Well, officially, I'd be working in the restaurant. Unofficially, of course, I'd be fiddling the bills, pocketing the tips and cloning people's credit cards.'

'I may have overreacted,' said Finn. 'When you're in this line of business, believe me, shoplifters are the bane of your life.'

Furiously, Carla hissed, 'Excuse me, she's *not* a—'

'OK, OK.' Finn held up his hands. 'Let's not get into all that again.' Addressing Ginny, he said evenly, 'Look, if you want the job, it's yours.'

Ginny could hear her pulse thud-thudding in her ears. Despite everything that had happened she did still want the job.

'What did Evie say to make you change your mind?'

His eyes glittered. 'Truthfully?'

'Truthfully.'

'I told her about the first time we met in that shop in Portsilver.' Finn paused. 'And Evie told me that she'd once walked out of a department store holding a Christian Dior mascara. She didn't realise until she'd reached her car, she took it back to the store and the saleswoman said not to worry, that she'd once left a shop carrying a toilet brush.'

Ginny looked at him. 'Is your cat under my car?'

He shook his head. 'No, she shot past me into the flat when I came out. So how about this job then? What shall I tell Evie?'

Revving the car's engine, Ginny said cheerily, 'Tell her I'll think it over.' Then, because it wasn't often she felt quite this in control, she flashed Finn Penhaligon a dazzling, up-yours smile. 'Bye!'

Chapter 4

GINNY'S HEART LIFTED when she heard Jem's voice; a phone call from her daughter always cheered her up.

'Hi, Mum, how's it all going? Are you and Laurel having a blast?'

If only. What was the opposite of a blast? A tired *phfft*, perhaps.

'We're fine!' Ginny was determined not to admit her catastrophic mistake to Jem. 'Laurel's settling in. How about you? Everything OK?'

'Better than OK.' Jem sounded on top form. 'I'm having such a great time, Mum.'

'Oh, darling, I'm so glad.' Impulsively, Ginny said, 'Listen, you haven't been home since Christmas. Why don't you come down this weekend? Dad would love to see—'

'Mum, I can't. My shifts at the pub, remember? I'm doing Saturday evening and Sunday lunchtime.'

Bloody pub.

'I hope you're not wearing yourself out,' said Ginny. 'I could send a bit more money if you want. Then you wouldn't have to work so hard.'

'I like working in the pub. Don't worry about me. And it's not long now until Easter, is it? I'll pop down then.'

'Pop? I thought you'd be back for the whole of the Easter break?'

'Well, that was the plan, obviously. But the landlord's already asked me to work through Easter. If I tell him I'll be away for a couple of weeks I might lose my job. Oh God, is it half nine already? I've got a tutorial at ten. Mum, I'll ring you again next week; you look after yourself and give my love to Dad. Have fun! Bye!'

Ginny missed Jem so much it hurt. She missed Bellamy dreadfully too. Instead of a life-enhancing new lodger-cum-friend she had Laurel. And instead of some form—*any* form—of love life she had a big empty void. Perry Kennedy, needless to say, had reneged on his promise to call and arrange a date for dinner, which made her feel not only unattractive but a complete fool to boot because she'd been gullible enough to believe he might.

In the kitchen, Radio Two was playing and Laurel was making bread.

'As soon as this bread's done I'm going to make a cherry and almond cake. Your favourite.'

'Right. Thanks, but you don't have to do that,' said Ginny.

'I want to. You deserve it. Oh, and Perry rang while you were in the shower. I told him how happy I was here.'

Perry had rung! Ginny's cheeks heated up at the mention of him.

Kneading away at the dough on the table, Laurel went on, 'He said could you give him a call when you've got a moment. Something to do with setting up the direct debit.'

'Right, thanks.' Did that mean he really wanted to talk to her about the direct debit? Casually, Ginny said, 'Well, I'd better be off. See you later.'

'Bye.' Laurel's clear green eyes abruptly filled with tears and her chin began to tremble.

Oh God, what now? Bewildered, Ginny hesitated in the doorway.

'Are you . . . will you be OK?'

'Yes, yes.' Floury hands flapping, Laurel wiped her eyes with her thin upper arms and nodded at the radio, now playing the Osmonds' 'Crazy Horses'. 'Sorry, it's this song. It just reminds me so much of Kevin.'

Climbing into the car, Ginny told herself she'd phone Perry in her own good time. No need to appear over-eager. She had lots to do today, *lots* to do, not least paying a visit to Penhaligon's to see Evie and discuss—

Oh, sod it.

The moment Ginny was round the corner and out of sight of the house she pulled up at the kerb and dug her mobile out of her bag.

'Hi there! How are you?' Perry sounded delighted to hear from her. 'How's everything going with Laurel?'

'Um, well . . .' Clutching the phone, Ginny cursed her inability to tell him the truth; it was all her parents' fault for drumming into her as a child the importance of being polite. 'Fine.'

'You see? Didn't I tell you it would be? And Laurel's so much happier now. You've done wonders with her.'

Ginny's mouth was dry with anticipation. 'Laurel said something about the direct debit?' Here was Perry's cue to laugh and reply, 'Hey, that was just an excuse to speak to you about our dinner date.'

Instead, he said, 'Actually, that was just an excuse to speak to you about Laurel's tablets. The thing is, she'd hate it if she thought I was checking up on her but it's important that she keeps taking them. I thought maybe you could subtly remind her next week about dropping the repeat prescription into the surgery, otherwise she'll run out.'

And become even more depressed. It didn't bear thinking about.

'Right.' Ginny bit her lip.

'Great.'

Disappointment flooded through her. 'Is that all?'

'Yes, I think so. Well, I'll leave you to get on . . .'

Buggering hell, that *was* all! The bastard! Sick to the back teeth of being polite—walked all over, more like—Ginny blurted out, 'To be honest, I don't think this is going to work. Maybe you should start looking for somewhere else for Laurel to—'

'Whoa.' Perry sounded alarmed. 'I can't believe you're saying this.'

Ginny couldn't quite believe it either, but she just had.

'Ginny, where are you now? We need to talk about this. Look, I know you don't want to go out to dinner with me but could we at least meet up for a quick drink? Are you busy today?'

Flummoxed, Ginny stammered, 'W-well no, I suppose not.'

'How about the Smugglers' Rest? Around one-ish?'

One-ish. That was two whole hours away. Trying not to sound too eager, Ginny said, 'One o'clock, the Smugglers' Rest. Fine.'

Perry was already there when she arrived, waiting at the bar. Hesitantly, he greeted her with a handshake—a *handshake*!—and said, 'It's good to see you again, you're looking . . . no, sorry, mustn't say that. What can I get you to drink?'

Ginny waited until they were seated opposite each other at a table by the window before uttering the question that had been rampaging through her mind for the last two hours.

'On the phone, why did you say you knew I didn't want to go out to dinner with you?'

Perry shrugged, glanced out of the window, looked uncomfortable. 'Because I could tell. Sorry, I really liked you and got carried away. Made a bit of an idiot of myself, I suppose. It was pretty obvious you weren't interested.' Clearing his throat, he took a drink. 'Look, this is embarrassing for me. Could we change the subject?'

'No.' Far too curious to leave it now, Ginny said, 'I don't know what I did to make you think that. I thought everything was fine. You asked me if I'd like to go out to dinner and I said yes.'

Perry shook his head. 'You said you might.'

'I *meant* yes.'

A glimmer of hope shone in his eyes. 'I thought you were just being polite, sparing my feelings.'

'Well, I wasn't,' said Ginny. 'I wondered why you hadn't called.'

Perry clasped his head in his hands. 'I'm such a prat. It's that fear-of-rejection thing. If I'm not five thousand per cent convinced that some-one's interested, I back off.'

'Well, you shouldn't.'

'Easier said than done.' Pausing then taking a deep breath, Perry said, 'OK, before I lose my nerve again, how about tomorrow night?'

'I'd love that.' Ginny found herself nodding to emphasise just how much she'd love it.

'Great. We'll go to Penhaligon's.'

Ah.

'Maybe not Penhaligon's. I'm seeing them this afternoon about a waitressing job.'

'Hey, good for you! They do fantastic food. OK, how about the Green Room on Tate Hill? I could meet you there at, say, eight o'clock?'

'Eight.' Ginny was happier than she'd imagined possible.

Perry grinned and took her hand, gave it a quick squeeze. 'You're incredible. No wonder Laurel's so happy living with you. She'd be dis-traught if she had to leave.'

Oh God, that was true. Her conscience pricking, Ginny reached for her spritzer and took an icy gulp.

'So what's she done?' said Perry. 'Is she untidy?'

'No.'

'Doesn't do her share of the housework?'

'No, it's not that.'

'Makes too much noise?'

Ginny squirmed. If anything, Laurel didn't make enough noise. She was quiet, thoughtful, considerate—technically, a model tenant with no annoying habits or antisocial tendencies.

'Does she use up all the hot water? Hog the TV remote?'

Laurel did none of these things. She just talked too much about Kevin, the man who had broken her heart.

'OK,' Ginny conceded. 'She can stay.'

Perry's look of relief said it all. 'Thank you. Really. God, I could . . . kiss you!' He glanced around the pub, which was filling up. 'Well, maybe not in here.'

'Chicken,' Ginny said playfully.

'Is that a challenge?' He rose to his feet and pulled her up to meet him. The next moment he was kissing her—kissing her *properly*—right there in the middle of the pub with everyone watching.

Crikey, not so chicken after all.

When Ginny arrived at Penhaligon's, Evie Sutton greeted her like a long-lost sister. It was three o'clock and lunchtime service was over. They sat together over a pot of coffee in the empty restaurant discussing the job, hours and wages, and Ginny filled in an application form.

'The shifts can be flexible, can't they? I mean, we're allowed to switch shifts if something crops up?' Apologetically, Ginny said, 'It's just that my daughter's away at university. If she decides to come home one weekend I'd hate to be working nonstop.' Not that Jem was showing much sign of coming down any time soon, but she lived in hope.

'No problem.' Evie nodded to show she understood. 'My three are all scattered around the country now, they've got their own lives. But when I can I grab the chance to see them . . .'

'Oh, I know. I miss Jem so much it's embarrassing!' Recognising a kindred spirit, Ginny said, 'In fact I've got a couple of photos in my purse.'

'Me too!' Delightedly, Evie fetched her handbag from the office and brought out photographs of her own children. As they pored over them together, Ginny wondered why someone more like Evie—or better still Evie herself—couldn't have replied to her ad for a lodger.

The phone rang in the office and Evie, in the middle of an anecdote about her younger son, went to answer it. Moments later the door of the restaurant opened and Finn Penhaligon strode in, raising an eyebrow when he saw Ginny sitting there. 'Oh. Hi.'

'Hello.' Ginny felt her mouth go dry; it was still hard to look at him without being reminded of a four-poster bed and ivory drapes billowing in the breeze. She really was going to have to knock that fantasy on the head, particularly seeing as she was the hussy who'd been kissed not two hours ago in front of a whole pub full of customers.

'Where's Evie?'

'In the office. I'm starting work here on Thursday, by the way. I'll be working four lunchtime and three evening shifts.' Ginny indicated the filled-in form in front of her and watched him pick it up.

'Right. Fine.' Scanning through it, he nodded then glanced at the photographs still on the table. 'Who's that?'

'My daughter. Jem.'

Finn studied the photograph. Finally, he said, 'What happened to her?'

'What? Oh, the hair! It's blonde, but she had the tips dyed pink.'

'No, I mean . . .' He frowned. 'Is this not the one who died?'

What?

'I don't know what you mean.' Bemused, Ginny said, 'Jem's my only daughter. She isn't dead!'

He shook his head. 'You said she was. In the shop that day. That's why the woman couldn't bring herself to call the police.'

'I swear to God I didn't say that! Why *would* I?'

'To play on our sympathy and get yourself off a shoplifting charge?'

'That's a wicked thing to say!'

'You were hysterical. You told us you'd buried your dog that morning.' He shrugged. 'Maybe that wasn't true either.'

'It *was* true. I loved my dog!'

'And then the woman asked who we could call and you said there was no one,' Finn persisted. 'You said your daughter wasn't here any more, that she was gone.'

The penny dropped. Mortified, Ginny realised that she had inadvertently misled them. 'She was, but I didn't mean she was dead. Jem's alive and well and living in Bristol.'

Finn surveyed her steadily. 'And there we were, feeling sorry for you.'

'You don't say. Well, excuse me if I didn't notice.'

'Anyway, you weren't arrested. So it did the trick.'

'Let me guess,' Ginny said heatedly. 'You don't have children. *Do you?*'

He surveyed her for a moment, then shook his head. 'No.'

'Well, that's pretty obvious, because if you did, you'd know that no decent parent would *ever* tell such a terrible lie to get out of *anything*. I would *die* for my daughter.'

'OK, OK. I'm sure you're right. Anyhow, can we put all that behind us?' Raising his hands, Finn said, 'We got off to a shaky start. But now you're going to be working for me, so it'll be a lot easier all round if we can just get along together. Don't you think?'

Still outraged but realising he was right, Ginny shook his outstretched hand and said, 'Yes, I do.'

'Good. Now if you'll excuse me, I need a word with Evie.'

He disappeared through to the office. Ginny drank her lukewarm coffee and sat back, idly twirling the ends of her hair. This was where she would be working, in this sunny, eclectically furnished restaurant with its beamed ceilings and burnished oak floor. The paintings on the crimson walls were a beguiling mix of old and modern, the velvet curtains at the windows were held back with fat satin ropes and on every table stood an unmatched bowl or vase containing spring flowers.

Waiting for Evie to return and having nothing else to do other than study her surroundings meant that only a few minutes had elapsed before Ginny spotted the scrunched-up note on the floor.

Bending down and retrieving it from its position halfway under table six, she briefly considered tearing it into teeny tiny shreds.

That would teach him.

But twenty pounds was twenty pounds and she couldn't bring herself to do it. Instead, reaching into her handbag and taking out her purse, Ginny swapped the crumpled twenty-pound note for two crisp tens and replaced them under table six.

Minutes later, Evie burst back into the restaurant, followed by Finn.

'Sorry to leave you all on your own! Finn kept me talking.'

I'll bet he did, thought Ginny, watching as Finn's dark eyes flickered in the direction of table six. When he saw the two ten-pound notes on the floor he almost—*almost*—smiled.

'Nice try,' said Ginny as their eyes met.

'What?' Evie clearly hadn't been in on the impromptu test.

Finn shook his head. 'Nothing. Right, I'll leave you to it. Looks like my New York dealer's arrived.'

A black car had pulled up outside the antiques centre. Ginny and Evie watched as Finn strode across the courtyard to greet the dealer.

'Yikes, it's a female. She won't stand a chance.' Evie looked sideways at Ginny. 'Did he just have another go at you?'

'He tried, but I'm getting used to him now. In fact I had a bit of a go back.' Proudly, Ginny said, 'He made one comment about Jem and I told him it was obvious he wasn't a father.'

'Ah. And what did he have to say about that?'

'Nothing. Well, he admitted he didn't have children.'

Evie sat back down opposite her. 'OK, seeing as you're going to be working here I'd better tell you. Finn was due to be married at Christmas. He and Tamsin had a baby last summer.'

'Oh God!' Covering her mouth in horror, Ginny gasped, 'Don't tell me the baby died!'

Evie shook her head. 'No, nobody died. Mae was born in July and she was the most beautiful thing you'd ever seen—well, with parents like that, what would you expect? Finn was completely besotted. He was just . . . lit up. He'd just bought this place and we were working night and day to finish the renovations and get the restaurant up and running. But he couldn't bear to tear himself away from Mae. She was always with him. You've never seen a happier man,' Evie said sadly. 'He was a born father.'

Ginny was utterly mystified. 'So what happened?'

'Oh God, it was awful. Finn was away one day at an auction in Wiltshire. I was here supervising the decorators in the restaurant when a taxi pulled up outside. This dark Italian-looking guy stepped out of the taxi and I went over to see what he wanted. He said he'd come to collect Tamsin and Mae. The next thing I knew, Tamsin came running out of the flat above the antiques centre carrying a load of bags. She gave me a letter to give to Finn. Well, by this time I was *shaking*. I said, "You can't take Mae away from Finn, he's her *father*." And this Italian-looking guy, who *was* Italian by the way, just laughed at me and said, "No, he isn't. I'm Mae's father." Then he looked at his watch and told Tamsin to get a move on, the helicopter was waiting.'

Ginny felt sick. What a terrible, terrible thing to happen. 'And was it true? About him being the father?'

'Oh, yes. Finn let me read the letter that night. Basically, Tamsin had met this Italian—Angelo Balboa, his name was—in a nightclub one night while Finn was away on a buying trip. They had an affair that carried on for a few weeks then ended when Angelo had to go away to Australia on business. When Tamsin found out she was pregnant it was a toss-up which of them might turn out to be the father. And when Mae was born—well, Finn and Angelo both have dark hair and dark eyes, so she could have got away with it.'

'So why didn't she?'

'Maybe the mention of the helicopter gave you a clue? Angelo Balboa is seriously wealthy. And Tamsin's always had a liking for the good things in life, especially good-looking zillionaires. I mean, Finn's done well for himself but he's not in the same league as Angelo. And I imagine this swayed Tamsin's judgment. In the letter she told Finn that she'd had a DNA test done, and that Mae wasn't his. Naturally, she'd then felt obliged to write to Angelo and let him know he had a daughter. And bingo, Angelo came up trumps! He did the honourable thing and announced that from now on, Tamsin and Mae were *his*.'

'What a nightmare. Poor Finn.' Now there was a sentiment Ginny had never envisaged herself feeling. 'What did he do?'

'What could he do? Apart from cancel the wedding and come to terms with the realisation that he wasn't a father after all.'

'God. And he hasn't seen them since?'

'Nope. They're in London with Angelo.'

'When did it happen?'

'October.'

October. And Mae had been born in July. So that meant Finn had had three whole months in which to bond with this living breathing baby, believing her to be his daughter and loving her more than life itself, before she'd been whisked away without even a chance to hold her in his arms one last time and say goodbye.

Imagining it, Ginny felt a lump form in her throat. She couldn't speak. How would she have felt if someone had tried to take Jem, as a baby, away from her?

'Maybe I shouldn't have told you.' Evie looked worried.

'No, you should.' Vigorously, Ginny shook her head. 'God, I've already put my foot in it once.' Another thought struck her. 'And it was only a few weeks after it happened that he saw me in the shop that first time. No wonder he wasn't in the sunniest of moods.'

'Now you know why Finn's got such a thing about honesty and trust.' Fiddling with the freesias in the vase in front of her, Evie said, 'Can't blame him, I suppose. Up until Tamsin left he'd always prided himself on being a great judge of character. It must come as a kick in the teeth when you realise you've got it so badly wrong about the woman you were planning to marry.'

Well, quite. Lots of people got it wrong when it came to choosing who to marry (mentioning no names . . . OK, *Gavin*). But what Tamsin had done was beyond belief.

When she arrived home at five o'clock, Ginny saw Gavin's Porsche parked outside the house. She winced slightly, because this meant he'd introduced himself to Laurel without her being there to act as a buffer.

She winced even more when, upon letting herself in through the front door, the first thing she heard was Gavin saying, '. . . I mean look at your shoes, they're *ugly*. You're never going to get wolf-whistled at in the street wearing shoes like that.'

Good old Gavin, as subtle and sympathetic as ever. Hastening into the living room, Ginny saw that Laurel was sitting bolt upright on a chair with a trapped-rabbit look in her eyes.

'Gavin, leave her alone.'

'Me? I haven't laid a finger on her. We're just having a friendly chat.' Gavin spread his hands. 'I popped over to see you and you weren't here so Laurel and I have been getting to know each other. And let me tell you, I've learned a *lot*.'

'He says I'm boring,' said Laurel, clasping her knees.

'*Gavin*.' Ginny shot him a fierce look. 'You can't go around saying things like that.'

'Yes, I can.' Unperturbed, he turned back to address Laurel. 'You *are* boring. You're never going to get over Kevin until you meet someone else to take your mind off him and you're never going to find someone else because all you do is talk about Kevin.'

'How long have you been here?' Ginny wondered if a good clip round the ear would do the trick.

'An hour. A whole hour, and believe me it's felt more like a week. I've been telling her, it's time to move on. Put the whole Kevin thing behind her.' Gavin made helpful, pushing-backwards gestures with his arms. 'And just move on. Which means getting out and socialising. You're not a bad-looking girl,' Gavin went on, sizing Laurel up like a racehorse. 'Nice face, decent figure. I don't much go for redheads myself but—'

'Good, because I don't go for men with double chins and receding hairlines.'

'Fair point.' Gavin wasn't offended. 'But I'm serious about you needing to get over this ex of yours.' He paused, looking thoughtful for a moment. 'In fact, I bet I know someone you'd hit it off with.'

Hurriedly, Laurel said, 'No, thanks!'

'See? Don't be so negative! I think the two of you would get along.'

'I'm not interested.'

Despite her misgivings, Ginny said, 'Who?'

'His name's Hamish. Lovely chap. Bit on the shy side, but a heart of gold. He's the sensitive type.' Gavin was warming to his theme. 'You know the kind. Writes poetry. Reads books.'

Ginny stared at him. 'How on earth do you know someone who writes poetry?'

'He's joined our club. It's a singles club,' Gavin explained to Laurel. 'Fabulous fun. We meet twice a week. What I could do is mention you to Hamish, put in a good word on your behalf, then when you turn up I'll introduce you to him and Bob's your uncle.'

'*No.*' Vehemently, Laurel shook her head. 'No way. Me, go to a singles club? Not in a million years.'

'So you'd rather be miserable for a million years.'

'I'm not going to a singles club,' Laurel repeated flatly.

'Leave her alone,' Ginny protested, but weakly because while Gavin might not be subtle, what he was saying made a lot of sense. It would be heavenly if Laurel were to meet a kindred spirit.

'You don't want to go on your own? Fine. Gin, how about the two of you coming along together?' Gavin the perennial salesman raised his eyebrows at Ginny, making an offer she couldn't refuse.

Maybe it would be worth it. 'Well . . .'

'Tomorrow night.'

'Oh.' Tomorrow was dinner-with-Perry night. 'I can't,' Ginny apologised. 'I'm busy.'

'Well, how about next week?'

'Excuse me, am I invisible?' Shaking back her hair, Laurel stood up and said impatiently, 'I told you I wasn't going and I meant it, so will you please stop trying to make me do something I don't want to do.'

Ginny met Perry the following night at the Green Room, the cliff-top restaurant on the outskirts of Portsilver. This time he didn't kiss her in front of everyone but the food was good, they talked nonstop and she still felt that spark of attraction every time she looked at him.

'Your ex sounds like a character.' Taking her free hand when she'd finished telling him about Laurel's run-in with Gavin, Perry idly stroked her fingers. 'How long have you two been divorced?'

'Nine years.' Ginny was finding it hard to concentrate; all of a sudden her hand had turned into an erogenous zone.

'Nine years. That's a long time. You must have had other relationships since then.'

'Well, yes.' Was he trying to find out whether she was a saucy trollop who bundled men into bed at every opportunity? 'Not many. Just . . . you know, a few.'

Perry raised a questioning eyebrow.

'OK, three,' said Ginny.

He smiled. 'That's good. Three's a nice ladylike number. I knew you were a lady.'

It was a compliment, but Ginny wasn't sure she deserved it. If she had been free of responsibilities her life, sex-wise, might have been far more eventful. But with Jem around, that kind of thing hadn't been a priority. Motherhood had come first and men had been a distraction she simply hadn't needed.

Perry carried on stroking her hand. 'It's more romantic when people take the time to get to know each other properly, isn't it? Too many people just go from one one-night stand to the next. And that just cheapens everything for me.' He gazed into Ginny's eyes. 'I'm so glad you're not like that.'

Bugger, thought Ginny. Just because she'd been like that in the past didn't mean she wanted to be like it now.

True to his word, when the meal was over, Perry kissed her in the car park then did the gentlemanly thing and helped her into her car— before Ginny could throw him over the bonnet and rip his shirt off, which was what she really wanted to do.

Oh well, it was flattering in its own way. If Perry thought she was a lady worthy of respect, that was . . . *nice*.

'You're gorgeous,' Perry murmured. Cradling her face between his warm hands he kissed her again, lingeringly, before pulling away.

See? That *was* nice. And a million times more romantic than being groped by some panting Neanderthal intent on getting inside your bra.

'I'll be in touch,' said Perry. 'Take care.'

He really likes me, thought Ginny, happiness bubbling up inside her as she drove out of the car park.

Wasn't that *great*?

It was Saturday evening and Penhaligon's was busy. Finn was there, greeting new arrivals, working the tables like a pro and attracting plenty of attention from the female diners. Watching him in action, Ginny saw the way they lit up and sparkled when he spoke to them, then chatted equally easily with the husbands of the married ones, ensuring they realised he wasn't a threat.

'Watching how it's done?' Evidently amused, Evie paused on her way to table six with two plates of mussels. 'Can't you just *feel* all those flirty female hormones in the air?' With a wink, she added, 'Good old Finn, he hasn't lost his touch.'

'I can see that.' As Finn crossed the room in order to answer the ringing phone, every female eye followed him.

'You'd better watch out. You could be next.'

Ginny grinned because the idea was so ludicrous. 'I don't think that's going to happen. He'd be too worried I might nick his wallet.'

Finn beckoned her over to the desk a few minutes later.

'Relative of yours?'

'What?' Ginny peered down at the diary where he'd written the name Holland for nine thirty.

'Table for two. I've just taken the booking. She didn't say so, but I thought it might be your daughter.'

Her heart leaping like a fish, Ginny wondered if it could be Jem. Had she come down to surprise her? And a table for two, did that mean she'd brought someone with her?

An hour later her foolish hopes were dashed as the door of the restaurant opened and Gavin walked in with a blonde who looked as if her lifetime ambition might be to appear on page three of the *Sun*.

Clearly struggling to match this vision with the photograph he'd seen of Jem, Finn said doubtfully, 'Is that your daughter?'

'If it was I'd tell her to get her roots done and wear a bra.' Awash with disappointment at having even thought it could be Jem, Ginny said, 'It's my ex with one of his lovely young things. At a guess I'd say he's probably not with her for her mind.'

'Now now.' Finn's mouth twitched. 'Never judge someone on first impressions. You of all people should know that.'

'Thought we'd surprise you,' Gavin said cheerfully when Ginny went over to hand them their menus. 'This is Cleo. Cleo, this is Gin.'

'Hiya!' Cleo actually had a sweet smile, but with her gauzy low-cut top and missing bra it wasn't likely that many men would notice.

'You did surprise me. When Finn said a girl had booked the table I thought it was Jem.'

Cleo giggled. 'That was me. Gavin asked me to call while he was in the shower.' She gazed around eagerly. 'I've never been to a restaurant like this before, I'm more of a burger girl myself.'

After their main course, Cleo tottered off on four-inch heels to the loo and Gavin beckoned Ginny over.

'Well? What do you think of her?'

'Nice enough. Pretty. Young.' Ginny shrugged helplessly; what did he expect her to say? 'Just don't marry her, OK?'

Gavin beamed; he never took offence. 'She's fun. Speaking of fun, how's the lodger? Still the life and soul of the party?'

'OK, OK.' Ginny acknowledged that if she was going to have a dig at his choice of girlfriend, it was only fair that he should be allowed to have a go in return about Laurel.

'So, Wednesday. Bring her along to our singles do.'

'Not that again. She won't go.'

'Ah, but it's up to you to persuade her.' Gavin looked pleased with himself. 'You'll have to tell Laurel that *you* want to go to the singles night, but that you're too shy to do it on your own. You beg her to go along with you for moral support. Brilliant or what?'

Transparent was the word that sprang to mind. Rather like Cleo's top. Ginny said, 'And you'll be there?'

'Of course I'll be there!'

'But what about Cleo?'

'Wednesday's her yoga night.' His eyes twinkled.

He was never going to change. When Gavin was eighty he'd be the scourge of the nursing homes; no still-sprightly widow would be safe.

'Everything OK?' Finn joined them.

'Wonderful, thanks. Great food.' Patting his stomach, Gavin said cheerily, 'I've just been persuading Ginny here to give the local singles club a try.'

The temptation to grab hold of Gavin's chair, wrench it backwards and tip him to the ground was huge. Would a bruised coccyx be painful enough? Did her ex-husband seriously not realise that she might prefer it if he didn't blurt out this kind of thing in front of her new boss? The new boss who was struggling to keep a straight face.

'I'm not interested in singles clubs!' Ginny felt herself going very red.

'Sorry, of course you're not.' Infuriatingly, Gavin winked and raised a finger to his lips, indicating that it was their little secret. 'Wednesday, eight o'clock. You'll love it. OK, sshh, Cleo's coming back.'

It was Wednesday night and they were actually here. Ginny couldn't quite believe it. Yesterday, she had discovered, was the anniversary of the day Laurel and Kevin had first met. As a result, Laurel had been inconsolable, gazing helplessly at a battered photo of her former love and mournfully wondering aloud, over and *over* again, why she was bothering to carry on because what was the point?

By the evening, Ginny couldn't have agreed more.

'Sorry, I know how boring this must be for you.' Laurel tugged the last tissue out of the box and wiped her eyes. 'I just miss Kev so much, you know? It's all right for you, you're completely over Gavin, you don't want him back. But I still want Kevin, more than *anything*.'

'I don't want Gavin back,' Ginny blurted out, 'but I'd like a man in my life. In fact, I'd love to try that singles club Gavin was talking about. Except . . . I couldn't go on my own.'

Laurel sniffed damply. 'You could. Gavin would be there.'

'Exactly! That's what makes it impossible. I wouldn't know anyone apart from my ex-husband!' Out of sheer desperation, Ginny pleaded, 'But if you'd come along with me, just once, you'd be doing me the biggest favour. Tomorrow night. Would you? Please?'

She didn't for a moment expect Laurel to say yes.

'All right then.'

Ginny gazed at her. 'Really?'

'If it's what you want, I'll do it,' Laurel said sadly. 'I'll hate it, of course, but if it makes up for me being a bit miserable sometimes.'

A *bit*?

Stunned, Ginny said, 'Well, thanks.'

Bugger, now that meant she had to go too.

The club was busy, which was a relief. The music didn't stop nor did an eerie saloon-bar silence fall as they walked in. But heads turned, they had definitely been noticed. Aware of dozens of pairs of eyes upon her, Ginny realised she was being subjected to the lightning appraisal afforded each newcomer. The other women were sizing up the competition, their collective gaze flicking over her hair, her face and her clothes. Gavin may have assured her that everyone was wonderfully friendly, but they weren't looking that thrilled to see her right now.

A quick glance around revealed that the women outnumbered the men in the club by about two to one, so their lack of enthusiasm was perhaps understandable. Ginny longed to run up to them and blurt out that it was OK, she wasn't here to snaffle their men.

But with Laurel at her side she could hardly do that.

Laurel said ruefully, 'Well? Seen anyone you like?'

'I think it might take more than twenty seconds.' Ginny briefly scanned the males on display wondering if there were, in fact, any she did like the look of. There was a wide-ranging choice—fat men, tall men, ones with hair and some without. Some were blessed in the looks department, while some . . . well, you could only hope they had sparkling personalities on their side.

But none, at first glance, made her heart beat faster. None of them was Perry-shaped.

However, there was one who was Gavin-shaped. Having spotted them he made his way over. Her eyes narrowing, Laurel muttered, 'He'd better not be rude to me.'

Which was a bit like hoping that a man-eating tiger wasn't going to take a bite out of your leg.

'Girls, girls, you made it! Excellent.' Gavin clapped Laurel on the back, almost flooring her. 'You're going to enjoy yourselves.'

'I won't. I'm only here because Ginny begged me to keep her company.' Tetchily, Laurel said, 'And don't call us girls. That's sexist.'

'Would you rather I called you a middle-aged misery?'

'Drinks,' Ginny cut in hastily. *Be nice*, she mouthed at her ex-husband.

'I am being nice,' Gavin retorted. 'She started it. I don't see what's so terrible about being called a girl. But anyway,' he added as Ginny shot him another fierce look, 'let's not bicker. We're all here to have fun, aren't we? Laurel, why don't I introduce you to a few of my friends . . .'

Wasting no time, he whisked Laurel off. Ginny approached the bar and ordered their drinks—an orange juice for Laurel and a vodka tonic for herself. In the mirror above the bar she could see Gavin introducing a reluctant Laurel to a mixed group of people. Craning her neck, Ginny wondered if one of them was Hamish, but since none of the men was wearing a kilt or brandishing a set of bagpipes, it wasn't possible to tell.

'Are you Gavin's ex-wife?'

Turning, Ginny saw an attractive brunette of her own age, wearing a cream trouser suit.

'That's right. I'm Ginny. Hi.' Shaking the proffered hand, Ginny said, 'How did you know?'

'Gavin told us you'd be coming along tonight. He said you were very pretty, like a young Goldie Hawn. Which didn't go down too well with the female contingent, I can tell you.' The woman smiled. 'I'm Bev.'

'Maybe I should have blacked out some of my teeth and stuck on a big wart.' Ginny pulled a face. 'Gavin did say everyone was friendly, but . . .'

'That's because everyone loves Gavin. He's our star performer. All the women want him and all the men want to be like him. But it doesn't work that way for us. And I know how it feels, believe me. The women aren't wild about me either.'

'Because they want to keep all the men here to themselves?'

'Not *these* men. They just can't bear the thought that one night George Clooney might walk in and they won't get first go at him.'

Entertained, Ginny said, 'And is that who you're waiting for too?'

'Well, I wouldn't say no. But I've actually got a bit of a crush on one of the men here.'

'Really?' Fascinated, Ginny scanned the room. Not that one, surely. Or him, or him. Definitely not *him* . . .

'It's Gavin,' said Bev.

'Blimey.'

'I know.' Bev tilted her head in rueful acknowledgment. 'It's hopeless. I'm forty! Maybe if I was ten years younger I'd stand a fighting chance, but I'm not. So I don't.'

'He might come to his senses one day and realise it's time to settle down with someone his own age.' Ginny said with feeling.

'But you can't see it happening?'

'To be honest, no. More chance of George Clooney walking in here.'

'Speaking of Mr Clooney,' Bev said in an undertone, 'here comes someone who looks . . . absolutely nothing like him.'

For the next ten minutes, Ginny chatted to Bev and an earnest bespectacled divorcé called Harold who was an accountant, forty-nine and very keen on growing his own vegetables. After that they were joined by Timothy, a thirty-four-year-old butcher by day and would-be Elvis impersonator by night.

Elvis with a lisp.

'You might not think I look much like him now,' Timothy said eagerly, 'but jutht wait till you thee me in my wig and make-up!'

Jim was next, a maths teacher whose wife had died three years ago. His interests were rock-climbing and playing badminton. 'But not at the same time!' With an ear-splitting guffaw, Jim clutched his sides. 'That would be dangerous!'

It was a relief when Gavin came over and reclaimed her.

'How's Laurel getting on?'

'Great guns. Hopeless with the men,' said Gavin. 'I warned her not to talk about Kevin but she couldn't help herself. Not the world's greatest chat-up line, telling men the reason you're not drinking is because you're on antidepressants because your boyfriend chucked you and you know you'll never get over him because he's the only man you ever loved. To be honest, they couldn't get away fast enough. Happily, I had the bright idea of introducing her to the three witches. Their husbands chucked them too,' he explained when Ginny looked blank. 'Bitter doesn't begin to describe them.'

'I thought this club was supposed to be friendly,' Ginny protested.

'Oh, come on, it's hilarious. And they're being friendly to Laurel. Look.' Gavin pointed them out, gathered around a table in the corner. Laurel was crying and talking and the three witches were nodding, evidently in agreement that Kevin was a bastard of the first order.

'So, no joy with Hamish. Which one is he, by the way?' Ginny peered around hopefully.

'Not here. Hasn't turned up tonight.'

That was that, then. After all the effort she'd put into dragging Laurel along. 'Brilliant. What a waste of an evening.'

'Hey, don't get niggly. He'll be here next week.'

'But we won't be. I'm not doing this again.' Ginny couldn't face another evening here; people were starting to dance and some of them were people who should never be allowed to dance outside the privacy of their own bedrooms. This wasn't her kind of place. She could be out with Perry now, having a lovely time . . .

Except that wasn't quite true, sadly. She couldn't be out with Perry because he hadn't phoned her all week. And out of practice with dating though she might be, even Ginny knew it wasn't cool to ring the man and demand to know why he hadn't rung you.

'You know, you might not have to come back.' Gavin turned her in the direction of the corner table. 'Look at Laurel.'

Ginny looked. Laurel was no longer crying. All four women were in hysterics, clutching each other and giggling like eighteen-year-olds.

'I didn't know she could laugh,' Ginny marvelled.

'She's joined the coven. You mark my words, she'll be back every week from now on.' Modestly, Gavin said, 'God, I'm brilliant.'

Was he? Could he actually have done something right? Deciding that he might have, Ginny gave him a grateful hug and was instantly aware of the waves of resentment being directed at her by all the single women in the room. Hastily she let go, stepping back and landing on somebody's foot.

'Ouch . . . thorry!' Wincing but putting on a brave face, Elvis Presley said, 'I wondered if I could perthuade you to danthe?'

'Of course she will,' Gavin said before Ginny could open her mouth.

The coven watched beadily as Timothy led her onto the dance floor. Ginny's heart sank as the music changed. Over in the corner the witches were sniggering.

Timothy, his mouth millimetres from her left ear as he steered her around, crooned happily along to 'Thuthpiciouth Mindth'.

They drove home at eleven o'clock. Encouraged by the fact that the three witches appeared to have taken Laurel under their wing, Ginny said brightly, 'Well? Not as terrible as you expected?'

Laurel looked shocked. 'What makes you think that? It was *worse*.'

'But you made friends with the wi— um, with those women, didn't you? I thought you were getting on really well with them.'

Laurel said flatly, 'They were awful.'

'I saw you laughing,' Ginny protested.

'It's called being polite. Sitting with them was awful, but marginally less awful than having to talk to the men.'

'So you didn't enjoy yourself.'

'Of course I didn't enjoy myself! Did *you*?'

'I thought it was . . . good.' Ginny gripped the steering wheel in order to lie with more conviction. 'I mean, it's always a bit scary going somewhere new for the first time, but maybe if you tried it again next week you might find yourself—'

'Oh, no.' Laurel shook her head with such determination that her long hair almost slapped Ginny across the face. 'I've done it once and that was enough. To be honest, I didn't realise you were this desperate to meet a new man.' In the orange glow of the street lamps, Laurel looked at Ginny as if she were a particularly slutty teenager and a severe disappointment to boot. 'I'm sorry, but if you really want to go to that place again, you'll just have to go by yourself.'

'He still hasn't rung,' said Ginny.

Carla was on her living-room floor doing sit-ups, her flat stomach sheeny with perspiration. 'Have you called him?'

'I can't.'

'So you're just going to wait?'

'What other choice do I have?'

Carla shrugged in mid sit-up. 'Call him.'

'No! The thing is, I don't understand it. He's so nice when I do see him. He really seems to like me.'

'Maybe he's seeing someone else,' Carla said.

This had crossed Ginny's mind. 'If he is, I wish he'd just tell me.'

Carla finished her two hundredth sit-up. Reaching for the phone on the coffee table, she said, 'What's his number?'

'Why?'

'Because you're my best friend and he's treating you like dirt.'

'He isn't really,' Ginny protested. 'That's the thing, when we're together he treats me like a princess.'

'Are you working on Friday night?'

'No. Why?'

'Just give me the number.'

Ginny was torn between stuffing her fingers in her ears—her own ears, not Carla's—and listening to Carla giving Perry a hard time.

'Is that Perry? Hi, my name's Carla James, I'm a friend of Ginny's.' Carla was in brisk, don't-mess-with-me mode, pacing the living room as she spoke into the phone. 'You remember Ginny, she's the one you haven't rung for the last week and a half.'

Ginny flinched and stuffed her fingers in her ears. Sadly it didn't block out what Carla was now saying.

'So I was wondering, do you have another girlfriend taking up all your free time? Or a wife perhaps?' Pause. 'Sure about that? OK, in that case, have you decided you don't want to see Ginny any more?' Pause. 'Well good, I'm glad to hear that, although I have to say I'm not sure you deserve her. If you were my boyfriend I'd have chucked you by now.' Pause. 'Oh, don't give me that. We're all *busy*. If you want to see someone you just have to make time. So how about tomorrow night?'

By this time squirming for England, Ginny was amazed she hadn't disappeared down *inside* the sofa. Jumping to her feet she escaped through to the kitchen.

By the time she'd finished noisily unloading the dishwasher, Carla came through to the kitchen looking pleased with herself.

'All sorted.'

'You bullied him into it,' Ginny wailed. 'That makes me feel *so* wanted and desirable.'

'Hey, you gave me his number. You wanted to see him again and now you're seeing him. More to the point,' Carla said crisply, 'so will I.'

'Why?'

'So I can check him out and give you my verdict. If I think he's giving you the runaround I'll tell you. Because you deserve better than to be mucked about by some smooth-talking bastard and I won't stand by and see you hurt.'

'You'll like him. You couldn't not like him,' said Ginny.

'Don't be so sure. So far he hasn't made the greatest impression. Anyway,' Carla took a bottle of Evian from the fridge and gulped half of it down in one go, 'you're both coming along to the Carson Hotel tomorrow night.'

The Carson was Portsilver's biggest hotel, reopening in grand style following a refurbishment that had taken eight months and cost many millions. It had been a coup for Carla, who had sold them the biggest conservatory her company had ever built. Ginny already knew no expense had been spared for tomorrow's bash. Hundreds of local businessmen had been invited, including Finn Penhaligon. It would be a spectacular night out.

It took Ginny, emerging from the restaurant kitchen, a couple of seconds to place the three women who had just arrived for lunch. Then it clicked. Eeurgh, the coven.

'I'm the duck, love. He's the crab.'

'Sorry.' Ginny hastily switched the plates she'd just put down. Behind her, she could feel the witches turning their attention in her direction.

'Ginny, over here.' Finn beckoned her over to the bar where they had congregated to order drinks. 'These ladies are saying they recognise you from somewhere.'

'It's Gavin's ex-wife, isn't it?' The head witch had an unpleasant gleam in her eye. 'You came along to our club last night, dumped your friend on us. We didn't get a chance to speak to you, which was a shame.' Turning to Finn, she explained, 'It's a singles club, we're very friendly. But some people don't like to waste time socialising with members of their own sex. Ginny here seemed far more interested in meeting the men.'

Ginny squirmed. On the other side of the bar, Finn's face was a picture. Of course it was; only last week she had been outraged by Gavin's suggestion that she might like to go along to the club.

'You didn't tell us you were going. What changed your mind?'

'I wanted Laurel to meet someone. I only went along to keep her company.'

The second witch smirked. 'But you didn't, did you? You abandoned her. And she told us you were desperate to meet a new man, that's the only reason she agreed to go with you.'

Ginny reached for the leather-bound menus and handed one to each of the witches. 'Well, don't worry. I won't be going back to the club.'

'Shame,' Finn drawled. 'Sounds like fun.'

'He's single.' Ginny eyed the coven who immediately perked up. 'If he thinks it's fun, why don't you persuade him to go along?'

Bingo. Clutching Finn's sleeve, the first witch exclaimed. 'Now that is an excellent idea.'

'Thanks for that.' Finn had waited until the restaurant was empty, the three witches having been the last to leave.

Revenge was sweet. Energetically clearing the tables, Ginny beamed at him. 'My pleasure. You'll have a lovely time.'

'I'd rather throw myself off a cliff. Not that there's anything wrong with singles clubs per se,' Finn said quickly. 'There's no shame in being on your own and wanting to change that.'

Ginny contemplated explaining all over again then decided against it. The more she protested, the more of a desperate Doris she sounded. Instead she nodded and said, 'I know.'

'Now, this isn't a date,' Finn announced when she returned from the kitchen to collect the tablecloths, 'it's a straight offer. I've been invited to the reopening of the Carson Hotel tomorrow evening and I can bring a guest. If you want to come along with me, you can.'

Talk about a turn-up for the books. Clutching the mound of table-cloths to her chest, Ginny said, 'You want me to go with you to a hotel? Aren't you worried I might steal a few bathrobes?'

Finn smiled. 'I'll just have to trust you to behave.'

'I might not be able to. Will there be lots of single men there?'

'I'd say it's a possibility. And while you're talking to them you can put in a good word for Penhaligon's.'

Ginny considered this. 'So I'd be allowed to plug your restaurant and chat up men at the same time?'

'Absolutely. As many as you like.'

Maybe he meant to be helpful but she couldn't help feeling patronised. Beaming at him, Ginny said, 'That's really kind of you, but no, thanks.'

'No?' Finn looked taken aback, rather like a do-gooder whose offer to have a lonely pensioner round for Christmas has been rejected.

'Actually, I'm already going along to the Carson do tomorrow night.

With my boyfriend.' Was it yukky to call someone your boyfriend when you were thirty-eight? Oh well. 'So I'll see you there.'

'Fine.' He looked amused. 'You can still plug the restaurant while you're there.'

'Of course I will.' As she swept past him with her armful of tablecloths, Ginny flashed him a jaunty smile. 'If I'm not too busy having fun.'

Chapter 5

'YOU LOOK NICE,' said Laurel.

Ginny was immediately overcome with guilt. Laurel was sitting on the sofa in her dressing gown, reading a novel with a depressing cover. The title of the book on her lap was *How Can I Live Without You?*

'Thanks.' She smoothed her lime-green silk dress over her hips and showed off the lilac shoes that matched her bag. 'These are a bit high, to be honest. I'll probably tip over and break an ankle. It's a shame you couldn't have come along too, but . . .'

'I know. Carla only had one spare ticket.' Laurel didn't seem too distraught. 'Don't worry, I thought I might ring Perry and invite him round.' Catching the flicker of alarm in Ginny's eyes, Laurel said, 'That's all right, isn't it?'

'Of course it is! Well, I'll just—' The phone in her bag was ringing. Praying it wouldn't be Perry, Ginny fished it out.

It wasn't, thank goodness. 'Jem! Hello, darling, how are you?' She waved, mouthed goodbye to Laurel and headed out to the hall.

'Great, Mum. I'm just calling to say don't ring me tomorrow morning because we're having a party tonight here at the flat and lots of people will probably end up staying over, so we'll all be asleep until midday.'

Ginny smiled, picturing the scene the morning after. The flat would be in a revolting state. 'OK, sweetheart, but don't forget to rope in all those overnighters to help with the clearing up.'

Jem laughed. 'No need for that. Rupert's already booked a team of cleaners to come and blitz the place tomorrow afternoon. It's one of the advantages of being rich—we don't have to do a thing.'

'That's good news, then. So you're all still getting on well together?' In the course of their conversations recently, Ginny had become increasingly alarmed at how often Rupert's name cropped up. But since Jem had never volunteered any information about any relationship with him, Ginny hadn't asked. Jem might regard it as prying, Ginny knew she wouldn't be able to pretend to be overjoyed.

'Everything's great.' Jem certainly sounded chirpy. 'We're busy doing all the food. Lucy and I are burning sausages and chopping onions . . .'

'And Rupert?' See? She couldn't help herself.

'Oh, he's a lazy bum. He's in the bath!'

What a surprise. But Jem was laughing, too happy to mind that Rupert was supercilious, selfish and not one of life's workers. Impulsively, Ginny said, 'Have you invited Davy to the party?'

'Mum, I'm beginning to think you've got a bit of a thing about Davy.' Jem giggled. 'You're always going on about him.'

That's because he's a nice boy, Ginny longed to say. Unlike some people I could mention. Aloud she said, 'Sorry.'

'To be honest, Davy and Rupert don't like each other much. So it was easier not to. Anyway,' Jem changed the subject, 'I haven't asked how things are with you. What are you up to this weekend? Anything nice?'

'Very nice, thanks.' Letting herself out of the house enabled Ginny to talk freely without being overheard by Laurel. 'In fact I'm off to a party myself tonight. The Carson Hotel's reopening at last, having a bit of a flashy do to celebrate. Carla invited me along with a friend.'

'Hey, Mum, brilliant. Who's the friend, one of Carla's toyboys?'

'Actually, he's someone I've been out with a couple of times.' Ginny said it casually, as if she'd been out with gazillions of men.

'Mum!' Jem, who knew she hadn't, was instantly agog. 'Who is he?'

'Just someone nice. Don't get excited.' It had been killing Ginny not to mention Perry before now but she didn't want Laurel to find out and Jem had never been one for discretion.

'Don't tell me not to get excited. I am excited! Is he handsome? Has Carla met him yet? This is so cool!'

Ginny crossed the road as Carla came out of her house. 'Yes, he's handsome. And Carla's about to meet him for the first time. In fact we're just off to the hotel now, so I'm going to say bye. Have a lovely time tonight, darling. Be good!'

Jem, sounding as if she was grinning, said, 'You too.'

'There he is.' Pride welled up as Ginny pointed across the room to where Perry was standing, smartly dressed (hooray) and (double hooray) handsomer than ever. When he spotted Ginny with Carla he broke into a smile that sent tingles of lust up and down Ginny's spine.

He joined them and she performed the introductions.

'It's good to meet you at last.' Perry shook Carla's hand.

'Hmm,' Carla said coolly. 'You may change your mind about that.'

Perry turned to Ginny. 'I reckoned she'd be scary and I was right.'

'Ginny's my friend. I'm looking out for her.' Carla's tone was crisp.

'Well, guess what? You don't need to.'

Her eyes flashed. 'When I start seeing a new man he's on the phone day and night. He can't keep away. We see each other all the time.'

'As long as they've done their homework and their mothers say they're allowed out,' Perry retorted.

'OK, stop it.' Ginny stepped between them—God, this was turning into *EastEnders*. 'No mud-slinging. I want you to be *nice* to each other.'

Perry shrugged. 'She started it.'

'What are you, a complete *wimp*?'

'Don't,' Ginny pleaded.

'Fine. I'm sorry. I'm sure he's wonderful.' Briskly, Carla nodded and glanced around the room. 'Well, I have to network. I'll leave you two to chat.' And she left them.

Alarmed, Ginny said, 'She isn't usually like that.'

'Don't worry, I know the type. Some women can dish it out but they can't take it. Look at her hair.' Perry's tone was disparaging. 'The outfit, the make-up. Hard as nails, desperate to prove herself. That's why she goes for younger men, so she can boss them around, be the one who calls the tune. But deep down? She's insecure.'

'Carla isn't insecure. She's—'

'Enough about Carla. You're here and that's all I care about.' Perry gazed deep into her eyes. 'We're going to have a good time tonight.'

Despite the tricky start, Ginny was glad to see him. Perry took two glasses of champagne from a waitress and they clinked them together.

'Here's to you. Looking fabulous.' He eyed her dress with appreciation. 'Now, tell me what you've been up to this week.'

So she told him about working at Penhaligon's and taking Laurel to the singles club, and about Laurel sitting at home in her dressing gown still depressed about Kevin.

'Think how much more depressed she'd be if she didn't have you.'

Glancing past her left ear, Perry said, 'We're being watched, by the way. Not one of your exes, is it?'

Ginny turned and saw Finn a distance away, talking to a luscious brunette but with his gaze flickering in their direction. 'That's my boss.'

Finn's attention was recaptured by the curvy brunette but Ginny, delighted he'd noticed them, found herself becoming more animated and moving closer to Perry, touching his arm as they talked. Later, when the situation arose, they would wander over and she would introduce Finn to Perry. Ooh, more drinks coming round, lovely.

Carla had spent the last hour circulating, greeting people she knew and introducing herself to those she didn't. The Carson Hotel was the only five-star hotel in Portsilver and its glittering reopening was a major event. Everyone was impressed by the Victorian-style conservatory, immaculately finished and commanding uninterrupted views over the ocean. Already she had been asked by three guests to supply quotes for extensions to their own homes or businesses.

So far, then, a successful evening. With one awkward exception.

On her way to the ladies' loos, Carla bumped into him. Without missing a beat, as smoothly as a conjuror executing a magic trick, Perry pushed open a door and drew her into an empty room.

'What?' Carla demanded fiercely.

'Has this ever happened to you before?'

Her eyes narrowed. 'You mean being kidnapped?'

'You know what I'm talking about.'

He was looking down at her, holding her by the shoulders against the wall. Carla swallowed and realised she was trembling.

'If you're trying to scare me . . .'

'No need,' Perry said with a smile. 'You're doing an excellent job of scaring yourself. So, ready to admit it now?'

Carla's mouth was bone dry. 'Ready to admit *what*?'

By way of reply he released one of her shoulders and laid the flat of his right hand over her sternum between the vee of her shirt and the base of her throat. Immediately—as if she needed reminding—Carla felt her heart thumping away, pounding as if she'd just run a marathon.

'Now, I'm no doctor,' Perry's tone was intimate, 'but I'd guess a hundred and twenty beats per minute.'

She was losing. He *knew*.

'That's what happens when you're trapped in a room with someone.'

'Except it was happening before, wasn't it? When Ginny first intro-duced us back there in the ballroom. I saw it happen.' Perry smiled again as he lightly brushed a forefinger over the frantically pulsating, all-too-visible vein in her neck.

This was terrible, a full-blown nightmare. Carla had always, *always* been able to hide her true feelings. It was a gift she prided herself on. Then again, had she ever experienced sensations as intense, as over-whelming as these before? The moment she'd clapped eyes on Perry Kennedy her body had reacted independently of her mind. She didn't believe in love at first sight but if she did . . . well, it would feel like this.

Except this man belonged to Ginny. And Ginny was her best friend. She *couldn't* allow herself to give in.

'It's the same for me,' Perry whispered. 'Exactly the same for me. You're the one, you're everything I ever wanted. Sorry, I know that sounds corny. But it's true.'

'Let go of me. This isn't going to happen. I don't want to see you again.' Light-headed and gulping for air, Carla tried to push him away.

'You will, you have to. Look, I don't want to hurt Ginny either, but I do need to see you again. Can we meet up tomorrow?'

'No.'

'I live in the flat above my shop. Twenty-five B, Harbour Street. Eight o'clock tomorrow evening suit you?'

Carla closed her eyes, pressed her trembling knees together. 'You're out of your mind. Ginny's my *friend*.'

'Eight o'clock it is then.'

'I'm going to tell her about this. I'm going to go out there right now and tell her what you're doing behind her back.'

'Eight o'clock,' said Perry.

This time Carla managed to free herself. Panting, she said, '*No*,' and stumbled out of the room.

'**H**ere he is.' Ginny was standing with Finn. Proudly she introduced Perry.

'Hi. Good to meet you.' Shaking Finn's hand, Perry said, 'Sorry to be so long. I got chatting to someone I know.'

Ginny said gaily, 'That's nothing. I've been chatting to lots of people I *don't* know, telling them why they should come to Penhaligon's! One couple are going to book a table for next week. They're looking for somewhere to hold their daughter's wedding reception.'

'Wedding receptions.' Perry shuddered. 'Sorry, my idea of hell. Kids running around screaming, babies crying . . . do you have children?'

'No.' Finn's jaw was taut.

'Sensible man. Don't go there. Can't see the attraction myself. Everyone tells you kids change your life . . . well, I don't want to change mine, thanks very much. Who needs all that grief?'

'Probably not the best thing to say,' murmured Ginny when Finn had excused himself and moved away to resume his conversation with the luscious brunette. 'His girlfriend had a baby last year. Finn assumed it was his, but it wasn't. She ended up leaving him and going off with the baby's father.'

'That's what I call a lucky escape. Oh, come on, don't look at me like that.' Perry grinned and slid his arm round her. 'Kids aren't my thing, that's all. And, trust me, there's nothing worse than a broody woman. I mean, look at Laurel. Half the reason she's taking this Kevin thing so badly is because she thinks she won't find another man before it's too late. Her hormones are in panic mode, flying around like headless chickens.' He gave her waist a squeeze. 'That's what I like about you.'

'What? That my hormones are flying around like headless chickens?'

'That they *aren't*.' Perry's green eyes glinted with amusement. 'You and Laurel are the same age but you've already got the whole breeding thing out of your system. Don't get me wrong, I think it's great that you have a daughter. I'm just not interested in having any myself.'

'You sound exactly like Carla.'

'God, don't tell me there's something we actually agree on. I'm not sure I'm happy about that.'

'Carla's all right.' Ginny so badly wanted the two of them to get along. 'Wait till you get to know her better.'

Perry pulled a face. 'I'd rather not.'

'Don't be mean. She's my best friend.'

'She's a viper. Anyway, why are we wasting time talking about her? I haven't even kissed you yet.'

Alarmed, Ginny squeaked, 'You can't do that in here!'

'I know. That's why I thought we'd take a walk around the grounds.'

It was ten past eight on Saturday evening. Ginny was out at work. Carla was standing in her kitchen. If she owned a pair of handcuffs she'd chain herself to the stove and swallow the key.

Oh God, this was unbearable. Last night she'd barely slept at all, her mind frenziedly replaying every second of the brief and fateful encounter with Perry Kennedy. And every minute of today had been filled with more of the same, because she couldn't stop thinking about him.

Twelve minutes past eight. She was winning so far. Meeting Perry mustn't happen, it just *mustn't*. He wasn't single, he was taken. More to the point, taken by Ginny.

Dry-mouthed, Carla looked again at her watch. Twelve and a half minutes past now. OK, maybe it was killing her but she only had another fifteen or twenty minutes to endure because surely if she hadn't turned up by eight thirty he would realise she wasn't coming.

Thirty minutes passed.

Forty minutes, then fifty. She was still here, she hadn't gone to Perry's flat. So why wasn't she feeling more relaxed?

At nine fifteen the doorbell shrilled and every nerve in Carla's body went into overdrive. This was why she hadn't felt more relaxed.

She opened the front door an inch, keeping the chain on, and hissed, 'Go away. I'm not going to do this.'

'At least let me in.' Perry was wearing a hat as an attempt at a disguise and spoke in an anguished whisper. 'I can't believe you made me come here. Laurel's just across the road, she could look out of the window at any moment and see me.'

Oh God, oh God. 'I can't let you in, I just can't.'

'Carla, I'm not leaving.' He clearly meant business. 'This is too important. We need to talk, you know we do.'

Carla trembled; she knew it too. But not here in her house, across the road from Ginny's.

'I'll come to your flat. You leave now. I'll follow in ten minutes.' Would she? Wouldn't she? She didn't even know herself.

'Promise,' Perry whispered.

'I promise.' Was that another lie? Maybe, maybe not.

'Ten minutes,' said Perry. 'I'll be waiting.'

'OK. Bye.' Carla closed the door.

She mustn't go, *she mustn't*.

She parked her car haphazardly at nine forty, too agitated and filled with self-loathing to even check her reflection in the rear-view mirror because that would mean having to look into her guilt-ridden eyes.

Hurrying along the narrow darkened street, Carla reminded herself that she knew barely anything about Perry Kennedy. When you met someone for the first time you could be wildly attracted by their out-ward appearance but they could have any number of unattractive char-acter traits that you had yet to discover.

OK, here it was, Perry's shop with its window full of printed T-shirts, and next to it the door leading up to his flat. Just an ordinary dark blue door with the 25B picked out in brass lettering that could do with a polish. See? She really didn't know him at all. Maybe a quick glance around Perry's flat would be enough to magically decimate any feelings she might have had for him. He might live in utter squalor, for instance. That would be enough to turn her stomach. Or he could have the walls plastered with posters of topless girls reclining on motorbikes.

Sick with excitement and shame, lust and fear, and hoping against hope that there would be *something* up there to put her off him, Carla rang the bell and prepared herself for Perry to answer the door.

She took a deep breath and waited.

And waited.

Rang the bell again.

Waited some more.

Nothing, oh God, he wasn't even here. Carla's heart began to clam-our as panic rose; how could he not be here now?

She couldn't ring the bell again—he wasn't in the flat and that was that. Or he was there and was determined not to come to the door. Or he *was* there but had knocked himself unconscious . . . Or he'd deliber-ately gone out.

Carla turned to leave. That was that then. Well, she should be glad that at least one of them had come to their senses and—

'Carla.'

She spun round, saw him standing there in the doorway and let out a strangled cry of relief. The next moment Perry, now minus his absurd hat, was wrapping her in his arms, frenziedly kissing her face and squeezing the air from her lungs.

'I thought you'd changed your mind,' Carla babbled helplessly.

'Never.'

'You didn't answer the door!'

'I wanted to see how long you'd keep trying. I needed to know if this means as much to you as it means to me.' He paused, gazing deep into her eyes. 'Does it?'

'You bastard, you know it does. Otherwise I wouldn't be here, would I? Ginny's my best friend, I *hate myself* . . .'

'Sshh, come on, let's get you inside.' He led her upstairs, and Carla knew that nothing about his flat, not even toenail clippings in the kitchen sink, could put her off him now. In her whole life she'd never felt like this before.

Their lovemaking was frantic, frenzied and heightened by guilt. Carla had never known sex like it—and in her time she'd known a lot of sex. But now, instead of a purely physical connection, her emotions were involved too. For the first time, Carla belatedly realised. The connection between Perry and herself was *there*, inescapable and so overwhelming she wanted to cry. This was what she'd been waiting for all her life and she hadn't even known it.

'What are we going to do?'

'Hmm?' Perry was snaking his hand along her thigh. 'I'll give you a clue . . . I may need a few minutes before we try it again.'

'I mean about Ginny.'

The hand stopped snaking. 'I don't know.'

'We have to tell her.'

'We can't.'

'We can. I'm an honest person,' said Carla. 'I don't lie to my friends.'

'Did you tell her you were meeting me this evening?'

'No, because I haven't spoken to her all day. I've deliberately kept my phone switched off. But I won't deceive her. If you want to be with me, you have to tell Ginny it's over.'

'Oh God.' Perry rubbed his face in despair. 'I *do* want to be with you. But . . . there's Laurel to consider. I'm not proud of this, but I charmed Ginny into taking my sister off my hands and the only way I could persuade her to let Laurel stay was by . . . well, I suppose you could call it emotional blackmail. But it worked. If I finish with Ginny, she'll chuck Laurel out, it's as simple as that.'

Carla recognised in a flash how alike she and Perry were; he had behaved ruthlessly towards Ginny and now she was equally prepared to be ruthless where Laurel was concerned.

'So? She's not five years old any more. She's a *grown-up*.'

Perry heaved a sigh. 'She's fragile. She's depressed and clingy, and I know I shouldn't have to feel responsible for her, but I can't help myself. Going to live with Ginny was perfect, but if Ginny won't keep her any more . . . well, Laurel will want to move back in here with me and I'll end up not being able to say no.'

Oh God, this was turning into a nightmare. Carla couldn't bear to think about the trouble this thing with Perry was going to cause. Life would have been so much simpler if they'd never met.

But they had, and now she wanted to make love to him again because one thing was for sure. Perry Kennedy had tipped her calm, ordered, super-efficient world off its axis and whatever else happened she knew she couldn't give him up.

It was midnight and Ginny, Evie and Finn were gathered round one of the tables having a drink to celebrate the end of a successful evening.

'Sorry I was late tonight, Finn,' Evie was saying. 'But my darling daughter rang me as I was about to leave the house. She's just moved into a new flat in Salisbury and they're throwing a house-warming party. So I'm going to be driving up there tomorrow morning!'

Ginny tried to suppress a stab of envy. Lucky Evie, off to see her daughter Philippa. She'd give anything for Jem to ring her up and say, 'Hey, Mum, we're having a party, you'll come along, won't you?'

God, she'd be there in a flash, like Superman fired out of a cannon. *And* she'd provide gorgeous food and do all the washing-up afterwards.

But there didn't appear to be any danger of that happening.

Lucky, *lucky* Evie.

'What's the flat like?' said Finn.

'Second floor, renovated Edwardian, two bedrooms. I can't wait to see it for myself. Ooh, you don't have a road atlas, do you?' Evie touched his arm. 'My neighbour borrowed mine and lost it.'

'There's one lying around somewhere. No idea where.' Finn frowned. 'I can look it up on the Internet if you like.'

'I know where your road atlas is.' Ginny jumped up. 'I saw it the other day.'

The atlas was in the second drawer down behind the bar, almost hidden beneath a pile of telephone directories. Feeling smug and efficient, Ginny produced it with a flourish, curtsied modestly and said, 'Thank you, thank you, it was nothing.'

'I love it when people do that.' Evie clapped her hands delightedly. 'I'll have to bring you back to my house to find all my long-lost bits and pieces. There's a blue sandal somewhere that's been missing for years.'

'What's that?' said Finn as something slipped out from between the pages and landed face down on the floor. Ginny bent to retrieve it.

It was a photograph. Ginny only looked at it for a split second but the image remained imprinted on her mind. She glanced over at Finn and handed it to him without a word. Evie, her eyes widening with glee, exclaimed, 'Finn, is it *rude*? Don't tell me it's a photo of you with some scantily clad girl!'

Ginny bit her lip and turned away, because in a manner of speaking it was. In the photograph Finn was sitting on a stone wall wearing jeans and a white T-shirt. It was a sunny, breezy day and the wind had blown a lock of dark hair across his forehead. The baby, clad only in a pink and white sundress, was beaming at Finn. And Finn was smiling back at her with a look of such love, joy and utter devotion on his face that anyone who saw the photograph would get a lump in their throat even if they didn't know the full story behind it.

'What *is* it? Show me,' Evie demanded, reaching for the photo in Finn's hand. Then she saw it and her expression abruptly changed. 'Oh.'

An awkward silence ensued before Finn took the photograph back from Evie and put it down on the table. Turning to Ginny, he said, 'You must be wondering what this is about. The baby is the daughter of an ex-girlfriend of mine. Well, ex-fiancée.'

Ginny wavered for a split second, then realised she couldn't tell him she already knew about Tamsin and Mae. Evie had related the story in confidence and the chances were that Finn wouldn't take kindly to discovering he'd been gossiped about behind his back.

'Right.' She braced herself; this was the kind of lying she found hardest to pull off. Assuming her I-know-nothing expression—a tricky balance between neither too wide-eyed nor too village-idiot—Ginny nodded and said innocently, 'So you were . . . um, engaged.'

Oh brilliant. *Mastermind* next. Then maybe a degree in astrophysics.

'I was.' Finn paused. 'I also thought Mae was my daughter. But it turned out she wasn't after all.'

'Oh! How awful.' Ginny put her hand to her mouth and shook her head in dismay. Act natural, *act natural*.

He nodded. 'It was. Tamsin got back together with Mae's father. They're living in London now. He's a very wealthy man.'

'Is . . . is he?'

'But then you already knew that.'

Whoosh went Ginny's face, faster than a Formula One car. Struggling to look as if she didn't have a clue what he was talking about, she raised her eyebrows and said, 'H-how would I know that?'

'Let me hazard a guess.' Finn glanced pointedly at Evie. 'Someone told you. Because I have to say, you're the world's most hopeless liar.'

'Yes, it was me.' Evie came clean.

'Thanks a lot,' said Finn.

'She wasn't gossiping about you,' Ginny put in hastily. 'She was just *explaining*. After that time I put my foot in it and said something awful about it being obvious you weren't a father. I felt terrible about that.'

'OK.' Picking up the photo once more, Finn said, 'So what do I do with this now? Throw it away, I suppose.'

'You can't.' Ginny snatched it away before he could crumple it in his fist. 'Not to a photograph like that.'

A flicker of something crossed his face. 'But it's based on a lie.'

'You're still not throwing it away.' To lighten the mood, she said, 'For one thing, it makes you look human.'

Finn said drily, 'Thank you again.'

'But it's true. Promise me you won't,' said Ginny.

He rolled his eyes but put the photograph in his shirt pocket.

'Right, I'm off.' Evie drained her glass and scooped up the road atlas. 'May I take this and bring it back on Monday?'

Ginny said enviously, 'Have fun tomorrow.'

'Oh, I will. I can't wait to see my baby again!' Too late, Evie realised what she'd said. 'Finn, me and my big mouth. I meant Philippa. I know she's grown up but she's still my baby to me.'

In a flurry of goodbyes, Evie left and Ginny finished her drink too before collecting her things together. As Finn showed her to the door, she said, 'I'm sorry about what happened with Tamsin and Mae. I can't imagine how that felt. You must have gone through hell.'

For a moment, Finn didn't reply. Then he nodded, his face turned away in enigmatic profile. 'I'd say that pretty much covers it. Mae was the centre of my world, the most important thing that had ever happened to me. One minute she was there and I would have died for her, literally. Then the next minute she's gone, and it turns out I was never even her father in the first place. I don't suppose I'll ever see her again. But she's alive and she's still the same child.' He paused. 'Just not *my* child any more.'

It was the most unbearably sad story. The lump was back in Ginny's throat. If Finn had been anyone else she would have thrown her arms around him. Instead, clutching her car keys and handbag, she said awkwardly, 'You'll meet someone else. The right person. And then you'll have a proper family of your own.'

'I thought I had a proper family last time. And look how well that turned out.' His dark eyes held hers for a second before he turned back to concentrate on the door handle. His tone dismissive, indicating that this conversation was now well and truly over, Finn said, 'I'm not sure I'd want to try again.'

Chapter 6

LAST WEEK, GINNY had been envious of Evie. Now she no longer needed to be because it was—*tra-laaa!*—her turn. Jem was coming home at last for Easter week.

'I swapped my shifts at the pub,' she told Ginny. 'Rupert's off to the South of France and Lucy's going back to Birmingham so I thought, Why stay here on my own when I can come and see you?'

Joyfully, Ginny said, 'That's *such* good news. I can't wait to see you again. And you'll be able to meet Laurel at last.'

'Not to mention Perry.' Jem sounded mischievous. 'I definitely want to meet him.'

'Yes, but you'll have to be discreet. Remember what I told you about Laurel.'

'I remember. Although I think it's pretty ridiculous, the two of you having to skulk around keeping it a secret.'

Ginny thought it was pretty ridiculous too, but at the same time she could see that Perry had a point. Not that they'd been doing much skulking around recently—he claimed to be so rushed off his feet at the moment they hadn't managed to meet up all week.

'I know, darling, but she's his sister and he's trying to spare her feelings. She's just been a bit depressed, that's all.'

'Well, tell her I'm great at cheering people up. I'll be down on Friday evening. Mum, you know how much I love you . . .?'

'Shameless child.' Ginny grinned, because this was a familiar grovel. 'Of course I'll pick you up from the station.'

'Yay. So you're free on Friday evening?'

'Absolutely.'

'In that case,' said Jem, 'why don't we have dinner at Penhaligon's to celebrate me being back? My treat!'

'Jem, you can't afford it.'

'Can't I? OK then, your treat! How about a table for three?'

'You, me and Dad? That's a nice idea.'

'Actually, I've already rung Dad—we're meeting up on the Saturday. I was thinking more you, me and Perry.' Sounding pleased with herself Jem said gaily, 'Clever, eh? This way I'll get to meet all your lovely new friends in one go!'

Just the sight of the peeling blue front door had a magical effect on Carla, drawing her towards it like a drug she was unable to resist. She'd been coming here for twelve days now and the magic was more powerful than ever. She rang the bell and Perry answered it. From then on they were cocooned in their own little world with trespassers prohibited and it was a feeling like no other she had ever known before. Total love. Total security. Total happiness.

Until Ginny found out.

Carla hated what she was doing but she couldn't stop doing it. Raising her hand to the bell she rang it quickly, twice. Waited breathlessly for the sound of Perry running down the stairs. Felt her heart quicken as the door began to open.

He grinned at her, ushered her speedily inside. 'Hello, you.'

Here came the feeling again. Sheer bliss. How could anyone give up something so utterly perfect?

After they'd made love Carla sprang her surprise.

'Tomorrow night we'll be doing this in a four-poster bed.'

'What?'

'I've booked us into Curnow Castle. Their best suite.' At an eye-watering £300 a night it had better be their best suite. 'You'll love it.'

'I won't, because I can't go. You'll have to cancel.'

'Why?'

He shrugged. 'I'm seeing Ginny tomorrow night. She wants me to meet her daughter.'

'Jem?'

Carla listened with growing dismay as Perry explained that Ginny had called him last night and invited him to join them at Penhaligon's. He had gently attempted to turn her down but evidently Jem was keen to meet him and . . . well, it had been an awkward situation.

'It means a lot to her,' Perry concluded reasonably. 'I couldn't let her down.'

'Because of Laurel.' Carla saw beyond the altruism in an instant. 'Because you need to keep the charade going. To keep Ginny happy.'

He spread his hands. 'Exactly. Not because I *want* to see her.'

'This is all wrong.' Vehemently Carla shook her head. 'Laurel's ruling your life, keeping *us* from being together.'

'Hey, hey,' Perry protested, 'we *are* together.'

'Are we? Hiding here in your flat like fugitives when we haven't even done anything wrong? I want us to be a proper couple!' Carla gazed at him in desperation. 'I love you. We can't carry on like this. It's not fair on any of us. And you're making a fool of Ginny. She's my *friend*,' her voice rose, 'and she doesn't *deserve* this.'

'I know. But we don't have any choice, not now at least. When the time's right I'll sort it all out.' Perry's tone was soothing, willing her to trust him. 'But not yet.'

'**S**ure she's not too heavy?' said Finn.

'Not too heavy.' As Ginny had been leaving the restaurant after a busy Friday lunchtime shift, Finn had pulled into the courtyard in the van. Back from a country house auction on Bodmin Moor, he'd proudly shown off the Victorian marble statue he had acquired. Since Tom, his assistant in the shop, was currently busy with a customer, Ginny had offered to help him lift it out of the van and into the shop.

Actually, marble was heavier than it looked. But today was Friday and Jem was coming home. Ginny was on such a high she was pretty sure she could lift the statue and the van single-handed, if required.

Luckily it wasn't.

'Got her?' Finn double-checked.

'Stop fussing. I'm stronger than I look.' Shaking her hair out of her eyes she grinned at him and wrapped her arms securely round the ankles of the female statue. Finn, at the other end, had his arms round the woman's bare chest. Together they moved backwards across the gravel, negotiated the doorway, manoeuvred the statue into an upright position . . . and breathed out.

'Well done.' Finn gazed at Ginny appraisingly. 'You *are* stronger than you look.'

'Just give me a telephone directory,' Ginny said modestly, 'and watch me rip it in half.' She ran her hand over the cool, silky-smooth marble of the statue's shoulder, thinking idly how nice it would look in her garden. 'How much are you going to be selling her for?'

'Three grand.'

Yikes, maybe not then. Perhaps B&Q did a cheaper version in fibre-glass.

'Good job you didn't tell me that before. I'd definitely have dropped her.'

'She's one expensive lady.' Finn gave the statue's bottom an apprecia-tive pat. 'And older than she looks.'

Ginny couldn't help wondering how it felt, having your bottom patted by Finn. Hastily she dismissed the thought, pulled herself together. 'No cellulite though. She's taken good care of herself. Or else gone under the knife, had a bit of a nip and tuck. You could call her Cher.' As Ginny said it, her phone began to ring and Carla's name flashed up on the screen. 'Speaking of women without cellulite . . . hello, you! Where have you *been*?'

'Just . . . busy.' Carla sounded more subdued than usual. 'Hi. Listen, I'm at home and I'd really like to see you. What are you doing?'

'Just finished work.' Intrigued, Ginny said, 'You sound mysterious. What's this about?'

'Can you come over now?'

'I've got some stuff to pick up in town first, but I can be there in about an hour. Jem's coming home!'

There was a momentary pause before Carla said, 'Is she?'

'I'm picking her up from the station at six thirty. I'm so excited I can't wait. And guess what? We're having dinner with Perry, the three of us!'

'Great.' Carla appeared to have other things on her mind. 'Um, so you'll be here in an hour?'

Ginny checked her watch. 'By four o'clock, I promise. I wish you'd tell me what this is about.'

'When I see you.'

Ginny put the phone back in her pocket. 'Carla's being mysterious.'

'You'd better get off, then. We'll see you tonight.'

'Eight o'clock.' Ginny beamed. 'I can't wait for you to meet Jem.'

'And she'll be meeting Perry as well. What if she doesn't like him?'

Was that a dig? Honestly, just because Perry had made one innocent, off-the-cuff remark about children and fatherhood. Couldn't he just be happy for her?

'She'll love him,' Ginny said firmly.

'**R**ight, I'm here. Tell me what's going on.' The moment Carla opened the front door, Ginny threw her arms round her. It wasn't until she'd been driving back from the shops that it had occurred to her that Carla might be ill. The moment this possibility had lodged itself in Ginny's brain she hadn't been able to think of anything else. And now Carla wasn't hugging her back, she was standing woodenly with—Ginny now saw—tears swimming in her eyes.

'Oh my God.' Ginny gazed at her in horror. Barely able to speak, she clutched Carla's hands tightly. 'Is it . . . is it cancer?'

Carla abruptly turned away, heading for the kitchen.

'It's not cancer.'

Oh.

'Well, *that's* a relief.' Following her, Ginny exhaled noisily and patted her heaving chest. Then, to be on the ultra-safe side, she said, 'So it's not any kind of illness?'

'Ginny, I'm not sick.' Carla turned to face her, and there was that weird edge to her voice again.

'Has someone died?'

Carla's perfectly symmetrical bob swung from side to side as she shook her head, but her lips stayed pressed together.

'Then you have to help me out here,' said Ginny, 'because I just don't know what this is about. I have no idea.'

'I know you don't,' said Carla.

'What's *that* supposed to mean? Why are you saying it like that?'

'Ginny, you mean the world to me. You're my best friend and I never wanted to hurt you.' Carla gripped the edge of the granite worktop behind her. 'It's Perry. He's seeing someone else.'

The kitchen was silent; it felt as if all the oxygen had been sucked out of the air. Carla couldn't bring herself to say the rest of it just yet. One bombshell at a time. This was hell, but it had to be done. Ginny was gazing at her, clearly lost for words and as shell-shocked as she had every right to be. God knows, she—oh, that *bloody* phone.

But when Carla looked at the bloody phone and saw who was calling, she knew she had to answer it.

'Hi, it's me. Listen, I'll be back by midnight at the latest,' said Perry. 'Wait for me at the flat.'

'Actually, I'm at home. Ginny's here. I've just told her.'

'*What?* You're not serious! About *us*?'

'Yes.' Well, near as dammit. She was about to.

'Jesus Christ, what have you done?' shouted Perry. 'I told you not to say anything!'

And where would that have got them? Evenly, Carla said, 'Well, I have.'

She switched off the phone. Ginny was staring at her, her eyes huge. 'Who was that?'

'I'm sorry.'

'Was it Perry? What's going on? OK, so you saw him with someone.' Ginny shook her head in bewilderment. 'But maybe you got it wrong, made a mistake.'

'I'm not wrong.'

'So he admitted it? You know he's definitely seeing someone else? What a *bastard*.' Her hands trembling, Ginny reached for a glass and ran cold water into it from the tap. 'When did you find out? Where did you see them? Damn, I really liked him too.' The glass clunked audibly against her teeth as she gulped down half the water in one go. 'Why can't anything ever go right for me? Do you know, I really thought we had something. And it turns out he's just another filthy rotten cheat after all. Oh no, poor *you*.'

'What? Why?' It was Carla's turn to be confused.

'Having to be the one to tell me. I bet you've been dreading it.'

Carla couldn't speak. The last few precious seconds of their friendship were ticking away. There was an unexploded bomb right here in the kitchen and any moment now she was going to press the detonator.

'So did you actually see her? What does she look like?'

Only a couple of seconds left now. Carla's mouth was so dry she could hardly speak. 'She looks . . . well, she looks like me.'

'Complete opposite of me then. I might have guessed.' Surveying her reflection in the window and running her fingers disparagingly through her tousled Goldie Hawn hair, Ginny said, 'Nature's way of telling you it's time you went to the hairdresser.' Then she patted her gently rounded stomach. 'And possibly had a go at a few sit-ups.'

'There's nothing wrong with you.' Carla couldn't bear to see her running herself down. Fiercely, she said, 'You're warm, funny, *beautiful* . . .'

'But not good enough for Perry, because he prefers someone who looks like *you*.'

Carla's finger had been hovering over the detonator button for what felt like hours. She didn't have to do this, she could carry on seeing Perry in secret. *No, she couldn't*. That would be deceitful.

Carla pressed the detonator. 'It's me.'

'What's you?'

'I'm the one he's been seeing. And I'm so *sorry*,' Carla blurted out. 'I hate myself, I can't believe this has happened. But it has. And you're my best friend,' she pleaded. 'I wouldn't hurt you for the world, but I've never felt like this about anyone before . . . I met Perry and it was just . . . well, like an earthquake or something. If I could have stopped it, I would. But I just *couldn't* . . .'

Ginny felt as if she was watching a film, one with a twist she hadn't been expecting. Carla's face was chalk-white, taut with strain. She had said what she'd clearly planned to say. She was like a stranger, or a character in *Doctor Who* peeling off her face to reveal the robot beneath. Because one thing was for sure, this was no longer the Carla she'd known and loved and trusted for the last fifteen years.

'You wouldn't hurt me for the world?' Ginny was privately amazed she could still speak. 'I'm your best *friend*?' Her voice rose. 'Well, that's fascinating. If this is how you treat your best friend, I'd hate to see what you do to your enemies.'

Carla flinched. 'I'm sorry.'

'Will you stop saying you're sorry? It doesn't mean anything! If you were really sorry, you'd never have started seeing Perry behind my back, would you? You would have said thanks but no thanks, like any normal friend, and walked away. It's called loyalty.' Ginny shook her head in disgust.

'I know and I *wanted* to do that. Believe me, I did. But I couldn't. I love him,' pleaded Carla. 'And he loves me. Sometimes these things just happen.' As she said it, they both heard the sound of a sports car screeching to a halt outside. A door slammed and footsteps raced up the path. The doorbell rang.

'Prince Charming, I presume. Riding to the rescue. How sweet.' Ginny's heart was hammering against her ribcage. 'How masterful. I suppose you've been sleeping with him.'

'Of course I've been sleeping with him.' Carla went to get the door. 'It's what normal couples do.'

The knife twisted in Ginny's stomach. With a jolt of pain, she realised Carla was right. All that so-called gentlemanly stuff about wanting to take things slowly and get to know her properly first hadn't been romantic after all. It had just been . . . bullshit.

And here he was, the bullshitter himself, bursting into the immaculate kitchen with a wild look in his eyes and his hair uncombed.

Suddenly he wasn't looking quite so irresistible any more.

Which, under the circumstances, was handy.

'I'm sorry. Ginny, I'm so sorry.'

Oh, for crying out loud, not that again.

'You're a wonderful person,' Perry went on, 'and I wouldn't hurt you for the world . . .'

'This is getting repetitive,' said Ginny.

'But I wouldn't, I swear to God. I never expected anything like this to happen. Neither of us did. But . . . it has.' Perry's hands fell to his sides, signalling defeat. 'It was a . . . a *coup de foudre*.'

'Right.' Ginny fantasised about seizing the heavy glass fruit bowl and hurling it at his head.

'It means love at first sight,' Perry added.

Patronising bastard. He thought she was gullible *and* dim.

'Actually, it doesn't,' said Ginny. 'It means struck by lightning.' Struck by lightning, struck by a heavy glass fruit bowl, she didn't mind which.

'You weren't supposed to find out like this but . . .'

'From the look of things you didn't want me to find out at all.' Leaving Carla out of it for now, Ginny concentrated all her attention on Perry. 'How long has it been going on?'

'Since that night at the Carson Hotel. We couldn't help ourselves. Took one look at each other and that was it. We just knew.'

'How lovely. Very romantic.'

'I'm sorry,' Perry said *again*. 'And I know this has come as a shock to you, but I hope we can still be friends.'

It was the pleading, let's-be-reasonable tone of voice he used that confirmed what Ginny had already suspected. Perry Kennedy had fooled her from the word go, manufacturing a relationship purely in order to offload his sister into her care. As if Laurel were a bin bag of old clothes and Ginny was his local branch of Oxfam.

And now, from the look of him, he was terrified she was going to give the bin bag back.

Interestingly, Ginny found she was able to separate out her emotions. Humiliation because she'd thought he liked her and he didn't. Anger because Jem was on her way home and today was supposed to be such a *happy* day. Humiliation again because the three of them were booked into Penhaligon's and she had boasted to Finn that Jem would love Perry to bits. And yet more anger because Perry had regarded her as a pushover.

Her stomach churning, Ginny realised that anger didn't begin to describe how she felt about Carla, her supposed friend. This was what hurt more than anything, because being betrayed by your best friend was a million times worse than being betrayed by a man.

Well, Carla and Perry were welcome to each other.

'So do you want to tell Laurel or shall I?'

Perry was looking nervous. 'Tell her what?'

'Oh, I think you know. You tricked me into taking your sister off your hands in the first place,' said Ginny. 'Well, I don't want her any more. You can have her back.'

He blinked rapidly. 'Ginny, you *can't*—'

'The three of you can live together. Won't that be fun?'

'But she's happy with you,' Perry pleaded.

'Not my problem. Believe me, I'll be happy when she's gone.'

'You wouldn't throw her out.'

'Wouldn't I? Watch me.' Ginny marched across the kitchen, pausing only to glance back in disgust at Carla. 'And I never want to speak to either of you again as long as I live.'

In two hours she had to pick up Jem from the station. As Ginny slipped back into her own house she prayed Laurel was out or asleep or upstairs listening to a Leonard Cohen CD.

No such luck. The second the front door clicked shut Laurel emerged from the kitchen.

'There you are! Now, does Jem like chocolate? Only I've made a lemon drizzle cake but if she'd prefer chocolate I can easily—*oh*.' Laurel looked concerned. 'What's happened?'

'Nothing. Nothing's happened. Lemon's fine. Or chocolate. Jem likes any kind of cake.'

'Only you look as if you've seen a ghost. Something's wrong.'

To tell her? Or not to tell her? Ginny was saved from making the decision by Laurel moving past her, opening the front door and peering out in search of whatever it was that might have caused the upset.

'That's Perry's car.' She pointed across the road. 'What's going on? Where's Perry?'

'OK.' Closing the door and leading her back into the kitchen, Ginny said, 'Would you be upset if I told you I've been . . . seeing Perry?'

Laurel looked astounded. 'You? And Perry? Seriously? But that's great! Why would I be upset?'

Exactly. Why would she have been?

'Sorry, Perry said you wouldn't like it. Anyway, I'm not seeing him any more. It's over now.'

'Oh phew, thank goodness for *that*.'

Ginny looked up. 'Why?'

'Because he's a *nightmare*.' Laurel rolled her eyes. 'For your sake, I'm so relieved it's over. I mean, don't get me wrong, I love him to bits but Perry's relationships always end in disaster. Where women are concerned he has the attention span of a gnat. One minute he's crazy about them, the next minute they're history. Oh God,' she covered her mouth in dismay, 'is that what he's just done to you?'

'No . . . no . . .' Ginny didn't have the heart to admit the real reason Perry had pretended to be keen on her. 'Well, kind of, I suppose. He's seeing someone else now.'

'Par for the course. You're well rid of him.' Laurel leaned forward, her forehead pleated with concern. 'Are you devastated?'

Devastated. Ginny tried and failed to summon up devastation.

'No. We only went out a few times. It wasn't serious.'

This clearly wasn't the answer Laurel wanted to hear. Or else she simply didn't believe her. 'You must be upset though. He's let you down. These things are bound to hurt.' Earnestly, she said, 'But I'm a good listener. You can talk about it as much as you want. It doesn't matter that he's my brother, you just let it all out, get everything off your chest, because I know there's nothing worse than feeling miserable and not being able to talk to someone about—'

'Actually, I don't do it that way.' Ginny had a brainwave. 'I find endlessly thinking and talking about a failed affair makes things worse. I prefer out of sight, out of mind. In fact, you could really help me if you want to. Make sure I *never* talk about Perry.'

'Of course I will! Don't you worry.' Laurel shook her head eagerly. 'I'll tell you the *moment* you mention his name.'

'And . . . and it might help if you try not to mention Kevin's name as well,' said Ginny. 'Because if you do, it'll only remind me of Perry and to be honest the less I'm reminded of him the quicker I'll forget he ever existed.' *Oh yes, brilliant.* Perry had his uses after all.

'Good point. OK, I'll do that. And don't worry, you've had a lucky escape. Think how much worse it would have been if the two of you had been together for as long as me and Kev—*oops*, sorry!' Laurel pulled an apologetic face. 'Nearly did it then!'

'But you stopped *yourself*. That's excellent.' Nodding encouragingly,

Ginny said, 'Just one thing before we start it properly. The reason Perry's car's outside is because he's seeing Carla now.'

'Carla? Your best friend?' Laurel's light green eyes widened in horror.

'Well, she *was* my best friend.'

'I don't believe it! You mean she stole him? What a *bitch*!'

'Thank you. I thought so too.'

'At least you know it won't last.' Laurel's tone was consoling.

'It might,' said Ginny. 'They're in love. Perry had a—'

'*Coup de foudre*?' Laurel gave an elegant snort of amusement. 'God, not another one.'

Overcome with curiosity, Ginny said, 'Why did you never tell me this about Perry before?'

'He's my brother and he's always been great to me. I'm not going to go around bad-mouthing him, am I? And I didn't know there was anything going on between the two of you.' Vigorously, she shook her head. 'If you'd mentioned it I could have warned you.'

'But Perry said—'

'OK, *stop*.' Laurel held up both hands like a traffic cop. 'Stop it *now*. See what you're doing? You're leading the conversation around to Perry again, obsessing about what happened! And it's my job to make sure you don't. So just clear him out of your mind. He isn't worth it.'

Ginny struggled to keep a straight face. She'd never imagined Laurel could be so bossy and forceful. Obediently, she said, 'Right.'

The day may have been tainted but it hadn't been ruined. The moment Jem jumped down from the train all thoughts of Perry and Carla flew out of Ginny's mind. For almost thirty seconds they just stood there wrapped round each other, hugging tightly. Jem, her baby, was home again and that was all that mattered.

Finally, grinning like idiots, they pulled away from each other.

'Oh, sweetheart, it's so good to see you again.' Her heart aching with love, Ginny said, 'You've had your hair cut.'

Jem reached out and gave Ginny's overgrown blonde hair a mischievous tug. 'You haven't.'

'And where are the sacks of washing? I thought it was in the student rules that you have to bring home a hundredweight of dirty clothes.'

'We've got a top of the range Bosch washer-dryer.'

'In that case I'll bring my washing to you. How's Lucy?'

'Fine.'

'Rupert?'

'He's fine too.'

'And Davy?'

'He's OK. Anyway, I'm here. Let's go. I can't wait to meet everyone.' Tucking her arm through Ginny's as they made their way down the station platform, she added with a complicit squeeze, 'Especially Perry.'

'I still can't believe it. What a bastard. How could he prefer her to you? And as for bloody Carla . . . I'm never going to speak to her again as long as I live. She's a complete *cow*.'

Ginny was touched by her vehemence. It was eight thirty, they were on their way to Penhaligon's and Jem was continuing to let off steam in the passenger seat. Since Laurel had banned them from discussing *that* subject in the house, Jem was now making up for lost time.

'From what Laurel says, it won't last long. Perry will dump her. I'll look forward to that.'

'And after it's over?' Jem was looking at her. 'What then? Don't tell me you'll be friends with Carla again.'

Ginny shook her head; her mind was made up on that score. 'That's not going to happen.'

'Good.' Jem sat back, satisfied.

'So what do you think of Laurel?' Ginny changed the subject.

'I like her! She's really nice. You said she was depressed but she seemed really cheerful to me.'

Ginny smiled to herself. This was true, the change in Laurel had been staggering. Who would have guessed that all Laurel needed to snap her out of her misery was another depressed person in the house? She was now positively revelling in her new-found role as chief cheerer-upper, even if Ginny wasn't mourning the loss of Perry quite as much as Laurel seemed to want to believe.

'And her cakes are out of this world,' Jem added cheerfully. 'That has to be a bonus.'

'It is.' Ginny nodded with relief because she might have told Perry she no longer wanted Laurel in the house but in her heart of hearts she'd known all along that she would never actually kick her out.

'So, hang on a minute, let's just get this straight. You thought Carla was a great friend and it turns out she's a complete witch.' Jem was now counting on her fingers. 'You believed Perry was perfect, the man you'd been waiting for all these years. And as far as you were concerned,

Laurel was depressed. You know, I think it's a good job I'm here,' she told Ginny. 'Because basically you're pretty hopeless. You've been wrong about everyone so far.'

Chapter 7

FINN EMERGED from his flat as Ginny was parking in the courtyard.

'Is that your boss? And you didn't tell me he was that good-looking either. For an older man,' said Jem.

'Sshh, keep your voice down.' But as he came over to greet them, Ginny suspected Finn had overheard.

'You must be Jem.' He smiled and shook her hand. 'We've heard a lot about you.'

'Ditto. You're the man who tried to have my mother arrested.'

'I hardly ever do that any more,' said Finn.

Jem gazed past him. 'I'm being hissed at.'

Ginny saw a large cat, her tail swishing, staring disdainfully down from the high, ivy-strewn courtyard wall.

'Her name's Myrtle. Not the world's friendliest cat,' said Finn. 'We think she's pregnant but nobody's been able to get near enough to find out for sure.'

'If she's this stroppy it's a miracle she got pregnant in the first place. I suppose it's like some women,' Jem went on pointedly. 'They don't look sex mad on the outside but deep down they're nothing but tarts.'

Finn threw a questioning glance at Ginny, who felt herself turning red. Oh brilliant, did he think Jem meant *her*?

'And if Myrtle's pregnant she shouldn't be climbing high walls. It's dangerous.' Moving past Finn, Jem held her arms up and made kissing noises. 'Come on, sweetie, let's get you down from there, shall we?'

Myrtle looked at Jem as if she was deranged before haughtily turning her back on everyone and springing like Spiderman from the top of the wall to the upper branches of the mulberry tree beyond it.

'Dr Dolittle, I presume.' Finn was amused by Jem's failure.

'I'm usually good with animals.' Disappointed, Jem watched as Myrtle elegantly picked her way along a branch before leaping across to the next tree. 'She doesn't look pregnant to me.'

Inside the restaurant, Finn looked around and said, 'No sign of Perry yet.'

'Just as well,' Jem retorted, 'if he doesn't want to end up being stuffed into a food processor.'

'He won't be joining us,' Ginny put in hurriedly.

Another raised eyebrow from Finn.

'Mum's been chucked. And guess who he's been seeing behind her back? Only her best friend,' said Jem.

'Who, *Carla*?' Finn looked startled.

'Could we change the subject?' said Ginny. 'My daughter's home and that's all I care about. We're here to celebrate.'

'And get the teeniest bit drunk.' Jem beamed at Finn, who was moving behind the bar. 'So we'll have a couple of glasses of house white to start with. Bucket-sized if you've got them.'

'That's not celebrating.' Taking a bottle of champagne from the fridge and removing the wire, Finn expertly uncorked it. 'Here, on the house.'

'Hey, I like this place!'

'Don't get used to it. Strictly a one-off.'

Jem's smile broadened as he filled their glasses and scrunched the bottle into a bucket of ice. 'You're nicer than I was expecting.'

His mouth twitched. 'You mean nicer *and* better looking?'

'Yes. Still single?'

'Jem!'

'Why?' said Finn.

Jem looked innocent. 'No reason. Just asking.'

After an hour, Ginny began to relax. Introducing Jem to Evie had been a joy, followed by Evie asking where Perry was and having to hear about what had happened, which wasn't. Then Evie had relayed the information to Martha who was even more outraged on Ginny's behalf. But after that it had got easier, helped along by the rest of the bottle of Moët and a generous serving of asparagus and artichokes, Jem's most favourite vegetables in the world.

'That was so gorgeous. I want to lick my plate,' Jem said longingly.

'Might be best not to. Finn'll turf you out.'

'So he runs the antiques centre by day and works in the restaurant in the evenings. Isn't that an awful lot of hours?'

'They're both his businesses. He wants them to do well. And the customers like having him around.'

Jem watched Finn chatting to a table of eight. 'But when does he get
time off?'

'When he needs it.' Suspicious of the direction her daughter's
thoughts were travelling in, Ginny changed the subject. 'Anyway, tell
me what's been happening in Bristol. You haven't mentioned boyfriends
for a while. Anyone exciting you want to tell me about?'

'Maybe the reason I haven't mentioned boyfriends is because I've
been working too hard as well.' But Jem's blue eyes were sparkling, her
tone playful. Relaxed by the champagne, she was clearly in the mood to
spill some beans tonight.

'Don't believe you.' Ginny waved her last spear of asparagus tantalis-
ingly over Jem's empty plate.

'We-ell, maybe there is someone.'

'And his name is . . .?'

Jem said, 'Do I get the asparagus?'

'Depends. Maybe. And his name is . . .?'

Wouldn't it be great if she were to say Davy.

'It's Rupert,' said Jem. And blushed.

Right. Bugger. Well, it wasn't really a huge surprise.

'Rupert? Gosh, that's a surprise! You two, a couple?'

'He's great,' Jem said eagerly, fencing the asparagus spear from
Ginny's fork and snaffling it before she could change her mind. 'Well,
you've met him, you already know how good-looking he is. We've been
seeing each other for the last few weeks.' Energetically, she chewed and
swallowed the asparagus. 'The thing is, though, we haven't told Lucy.
It's a bit awkward, you see, the three of us sharing the flat. Because we
all get on so well together, she might feel left out if she knew. So for
now it's our secret.'

Déjà vu. Déjà vu clanging away like a big old bell. Was it some kind
of inherited condition, Ginny wondered. Were she and Jem destined
only to meet men who didn't want their relationships made public?

Carefully, she said, 'Was that your idea or Rupert's?'

Jem considered this. 'Well, both really. I mean, Rupert said it. But it
just makes sense. I'd hate Lucy to feel like a gooseberry. *I'd* hate it if I
was the gooseberry.'

This was a fair point but Ginny couldn't help feeling uneasy.

'But you're happy?'

Jem beamed and took a gulp of champagne. 'Very happy.' Then she paused. 'I thought you'd be happy about it too.'

'Oh, sweetheart, I am. If you like him, that's . . . great. I suppose I was just thinking about this keeping-it-secret business because it's what Perry said to me. I don't want you to get hurt.'

'But that was completely different. Laurel is Perry's sister. To be honest, Mum, it was a dodgy excuse in the first place. You were a bit gullible. But Rupert's not like Perry, he's only doing it to spare Lucy's feelings. He's a nice person. And he's fun. Loads of girls at uni have a crush on him,' Jem concluded with pride. 'He could have anyone he wants. But he's chosen me.'

'That's because he has good taste.' Ginny reached across the table and gave Jem's hand a rub. Forcing herself to sound suitably enthusiastic she said, 'He's a lucky boy. And I can't wait to meet him again properly. The two of you could come down and stay for a weekend, how about that? Everyone enjoys a trip to the seaside, don't they?'

'Mum, Rupert isn't eight.' Jem rolled her eyes in amusement. 'What would we do, have picnics on the beach and build sandcastles?'

What was so terrible about a picnic on the beach? 'Well, no, but . . .'

'He's in the South of France now, staying in his dad's villa. I've seen photos of it,' said Jem. 'It's the most incredible place you've ever seen. His father's a billionaire!'

Was that the problem? Did Jem think her house wasn't glamorous enough to impress Rupert?

'Oh, well, then, that'll have to be my next move,' Ginny said lightly. 'Marry Rupert's father.'

Jem giggled. 'Don't be daft, you're far too old for him. He married his fifth wife last year, and she's twenty-two.'

Their main courses arrived and Ginny ordered a bottle of wine. The conversation turned away from Rupert and they chattered instead about clothes, shoes, Jem's customers at the pub and the rich American who had come to Penhaligon's last Wednesday and ended up offering Finn half a million dollars for his jukebox (*yes*, he'd been drunk).

Just after nine thirty the door opened and a family of six piled in. One of the girls spotted Jem and rushed over to their table.

'Jem Holland! You're back!'

Jem jumped to her feet and hugged Kaz Finnegan, her old school-friend. 'Kaz, so are you!'

'This is brilliant. Hi, Ginny! Someone told me you were working for dishy Finn. Lucky *you.*' Kaz looked at Jem. 'Now, listen, it's my birthday next Tuesday. Will you still be here then?'

Jem nodded. 'I'm back for a week.'

'Yay, so you can come to my birthday party. We've hired a marquee for the garden, and there's a band and everything. Loads of people invited.' Persuasively, Kaz said, 'And Niall's going to be there.'

Ginny smiled, because Jem and Kaz's older brother had had a teenage romance a couple of years ago and although the relationship had foundered when Niall had moved away to study for a degree in history at Manchester, she knew Jem still had a soft spot for him.

Ginny had a soft spot for him too, basically because he wasn't Rupert. 'Go,' she told Jem. 'You'll have a fantastic time. I'm working on Tuesday evening anyway.'

'With Finn Penhaligon.' Kaz's eyes sparkled. 'My mum has such a crush on him it's embarrassing. Is he fun to work for?'

At that moment, Finn walked past their table. 'He's a nightmare,' said Ginny. 'A complete slave-driver.'

Without slowing down Finn said, 'Some slaves need to be driven.'

By the time the pudding menus arrived Jem was sharing the last of the wine between their glasses. Dabbing at the drops she'd spilled on the tablecloth, she sat back and tilted her head to one side.

'What?' protested Ginny.

'We-ell, he's good-looking. And Kaz's mum fancies the pants off him.' Jem signalled with her eyebrows in Finn's direction. 'So what I'm wondering is, have you given it any thought at all?'

'No.' Ginny shook her head, hastily blanking out the mental image of that four-poster bed and those cream curtains billowing in the breeze while a semi-naked—'No, never, not at all, God *no.*'

'That's a lot of nos.'

It was. Too many. Ginny forced herself to stop shaking her head, which had acquired a momentum of its own. 'He's my *boss.*'

'That's a rubbish excuse. Lots of people fancy their bosses.'

'Look, we get on well together and that's enough of a miracle in itself, considering what happened the first time we met. But it's only been a few hours since I found out about Perry and Carla. I really don't think I'm cut out for this dating malarkey. I'd rather just . . . you know, live without the hassle.'

Jem looked disappointed. 'But I think he's nice. And I want you to be happy.'

Her heart swelling up like a giant marshmallow, Ginny reached across and clasped the hands of the daughter who meant the world to her. 'Oh, sweetheart, how can I not be happy? *You're back.*'

Early night for you,' Finn observed the following Tuesday. 'You'll be pleased.' For once all the diners had left in good time. By half past ten the restaurant was empty, leaving only Ginny and Finn to finish clearing up.

'Jem's gone out for the night. It's Kaz Finnegan's birthday do. Anyway, I've got that chef programme to watch,' said Ginny. 'The one about the French guy who bought the crumbling castle in Wales and turned it into a restaurant.'

'Damn, I missed it. Everyone's been telling me about that.'

'No problem, I recorded it.' Ginny, collecting cutlery to lay up a table for ten, said eagerly, 'I can lend you the DVD.'

Finn shook his head. 'It's OK, don't worry about it.' He turned his attention to counting the twenty-pound notes in the till.

Something about the way he said it aroused Ginny's curiosity.

'Don't you have a DVD player?'

Defensively, Finn replied, 'Yes, of course I do.'

'So why don't you want to borrow the DVD?'

He paused in the middle of cashing up, looked over at her for a moment. 'Because the DVD machine's still in its box.'

Mystified, Ginny frowned. 'OK, I know this is a pretty radical suggestion, but how about . . . ooh, let's see, taking it out of the box and connecting it up to the TV?'

Another lengthy pause. Finally he gave in, exhaled slowly. 'Because I tried that and I couldn't make it work.'

Oh, brilliant. Ginny did her best to keep a straight face. 'Right, so did you read the instruction manual?'

'Yes. But that just made everything worse, it kept going on about *scart* leads and . . . and *grinch* cables and stupid stuff that made *no* sense at all.' Finn shot her a warning look. 'And if you're laughing at me . . .'

'I'm not laughing.' Heroically, Ginny bit her lip but she was only human. 'OK, maybe smirking a bit.'

'It's not funny,' said Finn. 'It's embarrassing. I'm a *man.*'

'It's not as embarrassing as having to admit you're impotent.' Ginny said it without thinking, then hastily added, 'Not that I'm saying you *are* impotent, of course.'

'I'm not,' Finn said gravely.

'But you have to admit, it is *quite* funny.'

'We're not talking about impotence now, are we?'

Equally seriously Ginny shook her head. 'No, because impotence is never funny.' Good grief, was she really having this conversation?

'I can't set up DVD players.' Finn admitted defeat. 'Or video recorders. Or TVs, come to that. It's a recognised phobia,' he went on, 'of electrical leads and manuals that deliberately set out to confuse you.'

He was hating this; she was loving it. Ginny's mouth was twitching uncontrollably now. 'So, um, how do you usually deal with this?'

He looked slightly shamefaced. 'Get a man in.'

A man. Of course. Giddy with power, Ginny said, 'Would a woman do?'

This time she definitely detected a flicker of amusement. 'Would a woman do what?'

'Would you like me to set up your DVD player for you?'

He shrugged offhandedly. 'If you want.'

'Sorry. That's not good enough. Not nearly enough enthusiasm.'

Finn gave in gracefully, broke into a broad smile and pushed the till shut. 'OK, you win. Yes, please.'

They made it across the darkened courtyard without, for once, being ambushed by Myrtle. Upstairs in the flat, Finn brought out the DVD recorder, crammed haphazardly into its original packaging. The expression on his face as he handed it over made Ginny smile all over again.

It took her less than fifteen minutes to sort patiently through the spaghetti-like tangle of wires, plug them into the relevant sockets, set up the recorder and tune in the relevant channels.

'I don't know how you can do that.' Finn watched as she sat back on her heels and expertly keyed in instructions via the remote control.

'It's easy. Look, let me show you how to set it in advance.'

'Don't even try. I'll just press record when it's time to record something. That's as technical as I get.' Holding out a hand, he helped Ginny to her feet. 'But, thanks, I appreciate it. Now, do you have to rush off or can I ask you another favour?'

She breathed in the scent of his aftershave, experiencing a tremor as his warm hand clasped hers. 'You want me to fix your kettle?'

'The kettle's fine. I'll prove it to you. What I really want is for you to give me your honest opinion of this room.'

Ginny gazed around at the decor. 'I thought you'd never ask.'

It had, she learned, been Tamsin's idea to hire an outrageously trendy interior designer, lure him down from London and have him transform the flat while Finn had been away on a buying trip. Upon Finn's return, he had been confronted with aubergine-and-silver striped walls, a pistachio-green ceiling and a sixties-style, pop-arty aubergine-and-pistachio carpet. The lighting was futuristic, the sofas, sleek and uninviting, were upholstered in lime-green tweed.

Austin Powers would have thought it was shagtastic.

'You don't want to know the cost,' Finn said with a shudder.

'Did you tell her you hated it?'

'Couldn't. It was my birthday present. And Tamsin was so thrilled, I didn't have the heart to hurt her feelings.'

He must have loved Tamsin an awful lot. Whenever Gavin had bought her something horrific for her birthday Ginny had trained him to hand over the receipt at the same time. Then again, it wouldn't be quite so easy lugging an entire room back to the shop.

'So what happens now?'

'The whole lot has to go. I would have done it before but the restaurant had to take priority. It's been easier to just ignore it. But the other day I picked up some paint charts,' Finn went on firmly. 'And this time I won't be hiring a bloody designer.'

He made coffee with the non-broken kettle. Ginny sat down on the sleek, slippery sofa and spread the paint charts over the brushed aluminium—brushed *aluminium*!—coffee table. For the next hour they debated wall colours, curtains, furniture and accessories. Out with the new and achingly trendy, in with the unflashy and traditional. Ginny sketched out ideas and drew the room with cream curtains billowing gently at the open windows.

'Not blue curtains?' said Finn.

'No, too dark. Definitely cream.' Her mind was made up on that score; it might not be the bedroom but Ginny was adamant there would be cream curtains. And billowy ones at that. Oh, yes, they would billow if she had to smash all the windows herself.

'So how are you feeling about Perry now?'

Thanks for reminding me. 'Like an idiot.'

'Well, you shouldn't. He's the idiot.'

Acutely aware of Finn's proximity to her on the sofa—their shoulders were only millimetres apart—Ginny said, 'I'm out of practice when it comes to dating. I should have realised what his game was, but I didn't.

Maybe if I'd been out with more men I wouldn't have been so gullible.'

'Don't blame yourself. You're better off without someone like that. Carla would probably be better off without him too, but now she's being gullible.' Drily, he added, 'And look how much practice she's had.'

'You think I should feel sorry for her?' Ginny half smiled. 'I can't see that happening.'

'Maybe not. You just have to put it behind you and move on.'

'Is that what you did?' She felt brave enough to ask him now. 'After Tamsin left?'

Finn shrugged and this time his shoulder made contact with hers. 'It's the only thing to do.'

'But it's easier for some people than others. I wish I could go out, see someone I like the look of and . . . well, have a one-night stand, just for the hell of it. But I can't, because I'm not that kind of person and I never have been.'

'Never?'

'Never.' Recklessly Ginny said, 'If I told you how many men I'd slept with, you'd fall off the sofa laughing. Honestly, I'm pathetic.'

Finn raised an eyebrow. 'So you're saying you want to be like Carla?'

'God, no, nothing like that. Just . . . you know, once in a blue moon it'd be nice to think, Oh, sod it, why not?'

'Find someone you like the look of and just go for it?'

'Well, yes.' Ginny knew her cheeks were on fire. She couldn't believe she was having this conversation, and with Finn Penhaligon of all people. But her pent-up feelings were spilling out uncontrollably like molten lava. 'What are you doing?' she added, because he was now twisting round on the sofa, peering out of the window at something in the sky.

'Just checking if it's a blue moon.'

Her breath caught in her throat. This, subconsciously or otherwise, was exactly what she'd wanted to hear him say. Maybe it was pathetic, but after having her confidence dented—more like *smashed*—by Perry, she was ridiculously flattered to know that Finn Penhaligon would be prepared to have sex with her.

Except, terrifyingly, he appeared to have made his offer and was now awaiting her response to it.

Except, aaarrgh, what if it hadn't been an offer at all? Maybe he was a keen astronomer genuinely interested in discovering whether the moon tonight might actually be blue?

'Well?' Finn prompted, his dark eyes questioning.

Hopelessly unsure and petrified of making a twit of herself, Ginny said, 'Is it?'

'Take a look.' He gently turned her round to face the window. 'Tell me what you think.'

Her heart hammering against her ribcage, Ginny followed the line of Finn's pointing finger and saw the moon hanging low in the inky-black sky, partially obscured by the branches of a sycamore tree.

'So, does it look blue to you?' The words came out as a whisper, his warm breath circling her ear in such a way as to send Ginny's nervous system into a frenzy. But she still didn't know if this was all part of his seduction plan or simply an experienced astronomer asking a hopeless ignoramus an easy question.

'It looks . . . um, well . . . I think maybe it looks a *bit* blue.'

'Hmm.' He nodded thoughtfully. 'I think you could be right.'

'Yiawoooooow.'

'What's *that*?' Startled by the unearthly noise, faint but clearly audible, Ginny's eyes widened.

'Sounds like Myrtle, somewhere outside.'

'*Yiiaaarrrrlll.*'

'She's not happy. Oh God, what if she's been cornered by a fox?'

'Poor fox, he doesn't know what he's let himself in for. She'll rip him to shreds.'

'*Mwwwwaaaaaooowwwwww,*' Myrtle yowled, sounding more outraged than Ginny had ever heard her before.

'She's being attacked by something. I'll go and let her in.' Leaping up and slipping past Finn, she headed downstairs and opened the front door. 'Myrtle? Come on, sweetheart, it's OK, come inside.'

But although she heard another faint yowl, Myrtle didn't materialise out of the darkness and shoot past Ginny's ankles in a blur of indignant black fur. Finally, she closed the door and made her way back upstairs.

When she reached the landing she saw Finn standing at the far end of it, his hand resting on the handle of a half-open door that, if she'd got her bearings right, had to lead into the master bedroom. His dark eyes locked with hers for a moment, his expression unreadable. Then he held out his other hand and slowly beckoned her forward. His voice low and with a husky edge to it, he murmured, 'Come here.'

Oo-er. Tingling all over, torn between finding a missing cat and being drawn into Finn Penhaligon's bedroom, Ginny hesitated. Then again, what had Myrtle ever done for her? Maybe the time had come to be selfish for once. If Finn had decided that the moon was blue, who was she to argue?

Wandering in a dreamlike state towards him, she imagined herself unbuttoning Finn's white shirt, removing the leather belt that held up his black trousers, undoing the zip in a sensual manner. Oh Lord, she was disastrously out of practice, she hoped she didn't show herself up. Socks, for instance. Would he take his own socks off before the trousers came down? Surely he wouldn't expect *her* to deal with them. Heavens, she couldn't remember how socks got disposed of, she was going to make a complete fool of herself and—

'Take a look at this.' Finn noiselessly opened the bedroom door and drew her inside. As she held her breath the first thing Ginny realised was that she wasn't going to have to wrestle with sock etiquette after all.

Not with Finn either, come to that.

Another realisation was that as far as her long-cherished fantasy was concerned, she couldn't have got it more wrong if she'd tried. There was no four-poster, no cream hangings billowing gently in the breeze. The bed was king-sized and ultra-modern with a leather headboard and a heavy, expensive-looking dark blue suede bedspread.

Except it wasn't looking quite so expensive at the moment, what with all the gunk and slime smeared over the top-quality suede.

'Oh . . .' Ginny's hand flew to her mouth.

'*Yiaaaaaawwwwww,*' Myrtle yowled, furry paws extending and ribcage heaving as the next contraction gripped her body. As they watched, a silvery parcel emerged, slithering out of Myrtle and onto the bedspread only inches from the first blind mewling kitten. Twisting round, Myrtle used her sharp teeth to remove the covering membrane and bite her way—*euww*—through the umbilical cord.

'I didn't even realise she was in the flat,' Finn whispered.

'Oh *looook.*' Ginny tugged at his shirt sleeve as the first kitten, having staggered to its feet, promptly fell over the second. Struggling to get up again, it then slipped on a patch of slime and landed on its back. It lay there mewing piteously until Myrtle took pity on it and unceremoniously hauled it by the scruff of the neck over to her stomach.

'How do they know how to do that?' said Finn as the kitten, without a moment's hesitation, latched on and frantically began to feed.

'How did Myrtle know she had to bite through the cord?' Ginny shook her head in wonderment. 'I'm glad I didn't have to do that when Jem was born.'

Myrtle turned and blinked majestically, topaz eyes surveying her audience. For once she didn't snarl or hiss at them. 'Maybe now she's a mother she'll turn into a nicer cat.' Finn didn't sound too hopeful.

'Maybe she just has more important things on her mind right now, like bracing herself for the next contraction. How much did your bedspread cost, by the way?'

'Hundreds.' Finn paused. 'And hundreds. Tamsin chose it.'

Consolingly, Ginny said, 'It'll probably dry-clean.'

Since seduction was no longer on the menu—if it ever had been—they left Myrtle to the task in hand and headed back to the living room. Finn made more coffee and paced the kitchen while Ginny perched on a high stool at the counter and surfed the Internet on his laptop.

'Sit down,' she complained. 'You're making me jittery.'

'I am jittery. I feel like a prospective father.'

'Well, you aren't.' Ginny winced the moment she'd said it. What a thing to come out with. Luckily, typing 'cats giving birth' into Google diverted her attention.

Yikes, cats giving birth wasn't the straightforward procedure she'd imagined.

'What?' Observing her look of alarm, Finn plonked a mug of coffee in front of her.

'There's a whole list here of all the stuff you need when your cat goes into labour. A maternity bed.'

'Well, she's already helped herself to that,' Finn said drily. 'What else? Gas and air?'

'A heating pad,' Ginny read aloud. 'Clean cloths or towels. A weighing scale.'

'I've got bathroom scales.' Finn frowned.

'Sharp scissors,' said Ginny, pulling a face. 'Disinfectant. A small syringe. And dental floss.'

'Do I want to know why?'

'If the mother doesn't sever the umbilical cord, you have to do it yourself. You tie the dental floss round the cord before you cut it.'

'Interesting use of the word "you",' Finn observed. 'How about if we toss a coin?'

'I only fix DVD recorders.' Ginny held up her hands. 'Besides, she's your cat.'

He grimaced, then nodded at the computer screen. 'So is that it?'

'Not quite. Petroleum jelly.' Ginny read out the accompanying instruction. "'If the mother is having trouble giving birth you need to put some petroleum jelly on her to help ease the kitten out.'"

'Fine. I'll put some on her ears.'

'And we're going to need three tennis balls and a washed lettuce.'

'*What?*'

'Joking.' Ginny beamed.

'*Yaaaaiiioooooooow!*'

As they hurried back to the bedroom, Finn said, 'I don't think Myrtle found that joke funny.'

By three o'clock in the morning it was all over. Myrtle had given birth to a litter of four kittens and, thankfully, hadn't required the services of two incompetent human midwives.

Finn, busy making up the bed in the spare room, seeing as Myrtle had nabbed his own, came out and saw Ginny yawning and collecting together her jacket, bag and car keys.

'Are you off now? Drive carefully.'

Not *the* most romantic of sentiments but understandable, considering the circumstances. It crossed Ginny's mind that he might even have given her a goodbye kiss if she hadn't been yawning like a hippo.

'I will. Sorry, bit tired. See you tomorrow.'

'See you,' said Finn.

Was that a note of regret in his voice or was she imagining it?

Cattus interruptus, thought Ginny.

Damn.

Chapter 8

SAYING GOODBYE didn't get any easier. Jem was on her way back to Bristol and Ginny's throat was aching dreadfully with the effort of not making a public disgrace of herself.

To add insult to injury the train was on time. As it pulled into the station, there was a clap of thunder overhead and the first fat raindrops began to fall.

'Oh yuk.' Having painstakingly straightened her hair and keen to avoid it going stupid, Jem threw her arms around Ginny and gave her a kiss. 'Don't hang around out here, Mum, it's going to tip down.'

'I don't mind. Text me when you reach the flat, just so I know you've got back safely.'

'Yes, Mum, and I promise to eat plenty of fruit and vegetables and always wear a vest.'

'Don't make fun of me. It's my job to worry about you.'

'Well, you don't need to because I'm a big girl now.' Hauling her vast rucksack onto her shoulders, Jem moved towards the waiting train. With a grin she added, 'And you have to behave yourself too. No getting up to mischief while I'm not here to keep an eye on you.'

Without meaning to, Ginny's thoughts turned to Finn. Chance would be a fine thing. Since the arrival of the kittens there had been no more talk of blue moons. No flirtatious looks either, to the extent that she now wondered if she'd imagined them being there in the first place.

The heavens opened and with a squeal Jem leapt into her carriage. 'Bye, Mum! See you soon!'

'Bye, sweetheart.' Ginny blew a kiss as the train's doors slid shut and the ache in her throat gave way to tears. Thankfully the rain streaming down her cheeks disguised them and she kept a bright smile plastered to her face.

Jem blew extravagant kisses back, the train pulled out of the station and moments later she was gone.

Back to Bristol, back to Pembroke Road in Clifton, back to Rupert whom Ginny just *knew* wasn't right for her.

But Jem wasn't six years old any more, she couldn't simply forbid her to see him because, like skateboarding without a crash helmet, if she did, she'd only end up getting hurt. Jem had to be allowed to make her own mistakes. And, hopefully, learn from them.

Like the rest of us, Ginny reminded herself, thinking of Carla and Perry and the sorry mess that was her own non-existent love life.

Jem had texted Rupert on the train. He had flown back from Nice airport that morning. Letting herself into the flat she called out joyfully, 'Hi, honey, I'm home!'

'Hey.' He appeared in the hallway, impossibly tanned and clutching a bottle of lager. 'Honey, you shrunk your T-shirt.'

Jem gazed down at her front; the storm had followed her all the way from Cornwall and rain was bucketing down outside. Her cropped white T-shirt was now drenched and transparent, thanks to the long walk from the bus stop on Whiteladies Road.

'Don't try and cover yourself up. I like it.' Grinning, he gave her a cool beery kiss and trailed his hand down her chest.

'Is Lucy here?' Jem had to double-check.

'Not back yet. So, good time?'

'Great.' With an expert shoulder wiggle Jem released the straps of her wet rucksack and let it fall to the ground with a *thunk*. 'I went to a party, met up with loads of old friends.'

'Old friends, eh? Would that be old girlfriends or old boyfriends?'

'Both.' Entranced by the idea that Rupert might be jealous, Jem said, 'Actually, there was one old boyfriend there.'

Rupert raised a playful eyebrow. 'Should I be worried?'

'No. I don't fancy him any more.' It was the truth. Compared with Rupert, Niall had just seemed so . . . ordinary.

'Good.' And then Rupert was kissing her, and all thoughts of Niall Finnegan flew from her mind.

'What about Lucy?' breathed Jem as he led her by her wet T-shirt in the direction of his bedroom.

'Relax. She won't be home for hours.' As skilful as an ice dancer he manoeuvred her through the door, simultaneously unzipping her skirt and pulling the T-shirt off over her head.

'Anyway, what about you in the South of France?' Teasingly, Jem prodded his chest. 'Surrounded by beautiful girls in bikinis? You must have been chatted up.'

'Of course I was chatted up,' Rupert drawled. 'But all they're interested in is bagging themselves a guy with money. Not my idea of fun.' Gently he pushed Jem onto his double bed, gazed down at her and said, 'That's why I'm here now. Because you are definitely my idea of fun.'

Afterwards, Jem ran her fingers through her disastrous hair. 'I must look like a wet hedgehog.'

'You look gorgeous. Sexily dishevelled.'

'Sexily dishevelled. Is that flattering?'

'Now you're fishing. OK.' Gravely he surveyed her naked body. 'You have a great figure.' He ran an experimental hand up her shin. 'No stubble, always a bonus.'

Jem giggled. 'Cheek.'

'Ah, yes, glad you reminded me.' Skilfully flipping her onto her side,

Rupert carefully inspected her bottom. 'Excellent, no cellulite either.'

'Of course I don't have cellulite!'

'But you never know, it could arrive any day now. Does your mother have cellulite?'

'No, she does not!'

'Hey, I only asked. It's just that these things can be hereditary. We saw a few prime examples on the beaches last week, let me tell you. Like mother, like daughter, wibble-wobbling across the sand.'

'You're wicked,' said Jem.

'But you love me.' He flipped her back over, his hazel eyes glinting with intent.

Jem wouldn't admit it for the world but she was beginning to think she did actually love him. Let's face it, he was gorgeous. And they got on so well togeth—

'*Shit,*' hissed Rupert as the front door slammed.

Beneath him Jem froze. They heard the click-clack of high heels out in the hall, then Lucy called out, 'Where are you?'

'Fuck fuck *fuck*,' Rupert breathed. Eyes wide and brain racing, Jem glanced over at the wardrobe. Bulging with clothes, unread textbooks, tennis racquets and in-line skates, there wasn't room for a hamster let alone a fully grown eighteen-year-old.

A *naked* eighteen-year-old.

An hysterical giggle rose up in Jem's throat. Oh well, maybe it was fate. Sooner or later Lucy was going to find out about them anyway.

'Sshhh.' Rupert, who wasn't laughing, lifted himself off her in one swift movement. 'Hide under the bed.'

Was he joking? Clearly not.

'Rupert?' Lucy was knocking on the door now.

'Get down there,' hissed Rupert, rolling Jem to the edge of the mattress. Still grinning, she decided to humour him and dropped silently to the ground. Moments later, having hastily gathered up her discarded clothes, Rupert thrust them into her arms.

'Lucy? That you?' Yawning noisily, he called out, 'What time is it? I've been asleep.'

'You lazy bum, it's four o'clock! Where's Jem?'

'No idea. I don't think she's back yet.'

'She is. Her rucksack's on the floor.' The bedroom door was flung open and Jem saw Lucy's emerald-green high heels. 'You're not hiding her in here, are you?'

The bed creaked as Rupert sat up. 'If she's not in her room she must have gone out. Hang on, I'll get up. Why don't you make us some coffee?'

There was a pause. Jem held her breath. Then Lucy said, 'I've got a better idea. Why don't I wake you up properly?'

Jem frowned. What was *that* supposed to mean? She watched the shoes move towards the bed.

'Don't muck about, Luce. I've got a headache.'

'Now that's something I never thought I'd hear you say.' The bed-springs creaked again and one of Lucy's shoes disappeared from view; in disbelief, Jem realised that she was now sitting *on* the bed.

'Stop it,' said Rupert.

'Sorry.' Evidently unfazed, Lucy murmured, 'But I just don't think I can. Come on, what's the matter with you? Haven't you missed me?'

What? WHAT?

'Luce, will you—'

'Because I've missed you. Loads. In fact,' Lucy paused then said silkily, 'I'd say I missed you *this* much.'

Jem felt as if she'd been plunged into a vat of dry ice. Logically, she knew what was happening but her brain was refusing to make sense of it.

'OK, that's enough.' Rupert's tone was brusque. 'Game over.'

'What's the *matter* with you?' protested Lucy.

'Oh, I don't know,' Rupert drawled. 'Why don't you take a look under the bed and see if you can work it out?'

Jem couldn't believe he'd said it. Then again, Lucy hadn't given him much choice. She closed her eyes, bracing herself. When she opened her eyes again she saw Lucy, crouching down, staring at her.

'No. No.' Lucy shook her head. 'Tell me this is a joke.'

'I'll make the coffee myself,' said Rupert.

'You've been shagging both of us? You bastard!' shrieked Lucy.

'Be fair, you pretty much threw yourself at me. It was fun while it lasted.' He sounded bored. 'But now it's run its course.'

'You arrogant bastard! Get out of here,' Lucy screamed at him. 'I need to talk to Jem.'

'Fine by me.' Dragging on a pair of jeans, Rupert sauntered out of the bedroom.

'I don't believe this,' Lucy exploded. 'I just do not bloody believe it. He's been playing us for a couple of fools.'

Jem, emerging from beneath the bed, said, 'Could you look away while I get dressed?'

'Oh, for God's sake.' Impatiently, Lucy turned away. 'So this is what's been going on behind my back. Rupert must have thought it was hilarious.' She was fuming, shaking her head at the thought of it.

Hurriedly, Jem shook out her balled-up clothes and climbed into them, shuddering as the cold clamminess of the T-shirt hit her skin.

'Why didn't you say anything?' Lucy blurted out.

Stung by her tone, Jem shot back, 'Why didn't *you?*'

'Rupert didn't want you to feel left out.'

'That's what he said to me too.'

'Rupert lied to both of us. *Bastard*,' Lucy said vehemently.

'I heard that.' Rupert, leaning against the door, took a swig from another bottle of lager.

'Good.' Lucy swung round. 'And you can find yourself a couple of new flatmates. Because we are *out* of here.'

Jem looked at her in alarm.

'You're leaving? Fine. In fact, excellent.' Rupert shrugged, then in turn fixed his gaze on Jem. 'But you don't want to leave, do you? Lucy never meant anything to me, it was only ever a casual fling. But you and me . . . well, it's different. Something special.'

Jem's heart was racing; this was what she'd longed to hear for weeks.

'Forget it!' Incandescent with rage, Lucy yelled, 'We're both going!'

'You know, bitter and twisted really doesn't suit you.' Rupert raised an eyebrow. 'A woman scorned is never a pretty sight.'

'You make me sick,' bellowed Lucy.

Taking another swig of lager, Rupert smiled at Jem. 'You know why Lucy's so mad, don't you? She's upset because I prefer you.'

'You bastard!'

'Again? This is getting boring. Don't you have some packing to do?'

'Come on, Jem,' Lucy ordered. 'Let's go.'

'She's not your pet dog,' Rupert said coldly. 'She doesn't have to do what you say.' He turned to Jem. 'I don't want you to leave.'

'Jem!' snapped Lucy.

'I'm going to my room,' said Jem, 'to think.'

She sat on her bed and buried her face in her hands. Everything had been going so well, and now this. From next door came the crashings and bangings of drawers being yanked open and slammed shut as Lucy emptied them of her belongings. When her own door was pushed open she didn't look up.

'Don't go.' As Rupert spoke, the mobile in his jeans pocket beeped, signalling the arrival of a text. 'I want you to stay. It'll be just the two of us from now on. We can be a proper couple.'

Jem's chest was aching so much she felt as if she was literally being torn in two. Her instinct in the past had always been to side with a girl-friend against a boy. But this time was different; there was so much more at stake. Because, OK, Rupert *had* behaved badly but that was over now.

Far more important was how they felt about each other now that all the bad stuff was behind them. And she knew how she felt about Rupert. More to the point, she was realising how he felt about her.

CRASH went the wardrobe doors next door, followed by the furious jangle of coat hangers.

Rupert finished reading his text. 'My mate Olly's invited us to a party next weekend. Up in Scotland. Fancy that?'

'Is he the one with the castle?' said Jem.

'The one with the bloody enormous castle. Olly says we can hitch a lift up there in his uncle's helicopter if we want.'

Helicopter.

Castle.

She'd never been to Scotland before, not even on a train.

'Sorry,' Rupert continued. 'Jumping the gun. You might be about to call me a bastard and start emptying your wardrobe too.'

Jem looked up at him. Life without Lucy would be horrible.

But life without Rupert would be infinitely worse.

'I'm not.'

He broke into a wide smile. 'I'm glad.' His gaze softened as he put down his phone and the bottle of Pils. 'Very glad. Hey, you. Come here.'

He kissed her and Jem knew she'd made the right decision. They were a proper couple now. If this wasn't love, she didn't know what was.

There was a sharp knock at the bedroom door. Bracing herself, Jem peeled herself away from Rupert and went to answer it.

Lucy, her shoulders rigid, said, 'Well?'

'I'm staying.'

'With him?' Her mouth twisted into a pitying smile. 'Do you think he loves you? Because if you think that, you're even more stupid than—'

'Everything packed?' Rupert broke in coolly. 'Called the taxi yet? Tell you what, I'll even pay the fare. No hard feelings, sweetheart. It was a good contest but the best girl won.'

'You arrogant git.'

'Ah, but a generous arrogant git, you can't deny that.' Having pulled out his wallet, Rupert began counting out twenty-pound notes. 'Here you go, one month's deposit back and an extra twenty for the cab.'

'I feel sorry for the pair of you.' Lucy's eyes flashed as she uttered the words. The next moment she'd stalked out of the room.

'Obviously keener on me than she was letting on.' Rupert shrugged. '*And* a bad loser.'

'Don't.' Jem felt a pang of guilt. 'She's my friend.'

'Not any more she isn't.' Sliding his arms round her waist he winked and said, 'You're all mine now.'

'**S**hould have thought of this years ago,' said Finn. 'Inviting women to come up and see my kittens. Beats etchings any day.'

'That's because etchings are boring,' Ginny told him, 'and kittens are unbelievably cute. The only problem is, the women are going to be so bowled over by them, they won't take a blind bit of notice of you.'

Finn nodded gravely. 'Story of my life.'

'As if. I bet you've spent your whole life fighting them off.'

Finn uncorked a bottle of wine and poured out two glasses. As he put one down next to her, he raised a playful eyebrow. 'So does that mean you think I'm moderately attractive to the opposite sex?'

Luckily, Ginny had the distraction of a kitten on her lap. The kitten promptly obliged by letting out a stream of wee that missed her skirt by an inch. By the time she'd mopped up the puddle and returned the per-petrator to Myrtle, the need to reply had passed. Instead she raised her wineglass and said brightly, 'Here's to toilet training. Cheers.'

'To toilet training.' Finn paused. 'Not the most glamorous toast I've ever heard.'

'Sorry. I'm not in a glamorous mood.' Ginny, who had spent the evening putting on a determinedly brave face, shook her head.

'Is it about Perry?'

'God, *no*.'

'Jem then,' Finn guessed.

She nodded. 'Yes.'

'You're missing her.'

'Missing her and worrying about her. She's got herself involved with a boy I don't trust an inch.' Ginny could recall this afternoon's breezy phone call from Jem practically word for word. Evidently, she and Rupert were a proper couple now, Lucy had moved out to give them some space and everything was fantastic. When Ginny had said worriedly, 'Lucy's gone? Won't you miss her?' Jem had laughed and said blithely, 'Mum, why would I miss her when I've got Rupert? Everything's cool!'

'She's only eighteen. It probably won't last.' Finn was doing his best to reassure her.

'Yes, but what if it does? They're living together.' Ginny shuddered as she said it. 'And he's not a nice person. Too much money, too little . . . heart. He thinks he's God's gift.'

'Good-looking, then?'

'Very.'

'Is that why you don't trust him?'

She nodded. 'That and his personality.'

'Then she'll see through him,' said Finn. 'Jem's not stupid.'

'I didn't think I was stupid either,' Ginny retorted, 'and look at what happened to me.'

'Well, that's over now. Ready for another one?'

For a split second she thought he meant another man. But no, he was only taking her empty glass.

'It's just so hard, having to sit back and do nothing. I know I have to let her make her own mistakes but I'm her mother.' Taking the refilled glass, Ginny said, 'It's like standing by while a surgeon operates on your daughter, knowing he's incompetent and doing it all wrong.'

'Hey.' Finn patted the empty space next to him on the sofa. 'They're young. Give them a couple of weeks and it could all be over.'

Ginny left the squirming kittens in the cat basket and joined him. The shirt he was wearing was her favourite, cobalt blue cotton and as soft as peach skin. Well, it *looked* as soft as peach skin; she hadn't actually touched it. Nor was she about to tell him it was her favourite.

'I hope you're right about that. She's smitten at the moment. He's whisking her up to a castle in Scotland this weekend. In a helicopter, for God's sake.'

Drily, Finn said, 'Sounds familiar.'

'Oh bugger. Sorry.' Too late, Ginny remembered how Tamsin had made her exit from Portsilver, whisked away by her wealthy Italian lover in a helicopter. She clutched Finn's arm. 'I'm really sorry, I didn't mean to remind you.'

Ha, the material of his shirt *was* as soft as peach skin.

He smiled slightly. 'I hadn't actually forgotten.'

'Wine's gone to my head. I was too wound up to eat earlier.' Ginny patted her empty stomach by way of explanation. 'Now I'll have to get a cab home.'

'My fault for opening the bottle.'

'Or mine for coming up to see your etchings. I mean kittens.'

'Hey, you're here now. You've seen the kittens and the bottle's open. We may as well finish it.'

Myrtle and the kittens fell asleep. For the next forty minutes they drank wine, ate crisps and discussed the restaurant. Evie had been chatted up earlier by an estate agent who had done his best to persuade her to give him her phone number.

'I don't know why she wouldn't.' Finn frowned. 'He seemed like a nice enough chap.'

'Too nice.' Ginny did her best to explain why Evie hadn't been tempted. 'Verging on oily. That man was a super-smooth operator. Yuk.'

'He was handsome though, wasn't he?'

'Way too handsome. You wouldn't want to get involved with some-one like that, not in a million years.' Ginny dabbed at the crisp crumbs speckling her top and licked her fingers, then washed down the salti-ness with more wine.

'I don't want to get involved with him,' said Finn.

She gave him a nudge. 'I meant no woman with an ounce of brain would want to. Good-looking men are nothing but trouble.'

'First Rupert, now the guy from table six. They're good-looking so you automatically don't trust them.' Finn paused. 'Isn't that prejudiced?'

'Absolutely. But it's also common sense. OK-looking men are OK, but really handsome men are a nightmare. Number one rule, don't touch them with a barge pole.'

'I see.' Raking his fingers through his hair, Finn said thoughtfully, 'Would you say I was good-looking?'

'What?' She sat back, as if he'd asked her to calculate a tricky alge-braic equation. Actually, an algebraic equation would have been easier.

'I'm interested. When I look in a mirror I just see me, the same me I've always been,' said Finn. 'Dark hair, straight not curly. Grey eyes. Scar on left temple from some kid at school hitting me with a discus. Nose got broken once playing rugby, but still in one piece. Jaw, gener-ally in need of a shave. That's it, that's all I see.' He gazed at Ginny. 'But I have been told I'm a good-looking bloke. So I just wondered what your opinion was. Do you think I am?'

If he had the guts to ask, Ginny decided, then she had the guts to answer. Glad of the insulation provided by several glasses of wine she said, 'OK, first things first, you really shouldn't have allowed your nose to go off and play rugby. And second, of course you're good-looking.'

Finn tilted his head a fraction, still doubtful. 'Really?'

Did he seriously have no idea? Ginny nodded and said, 'Really.' Then, because he clearly needed the reassurance, she added, '*Very*.'

Finn studied his wineglass for a couple of seconds, but she began to suspect that he was struggling to keep a straight face. 'So you're saying it doesn't matter how nice a person I might be, or how much I might like you, you wouldn't be interested in me because of the way I look.'

Oh, for heaven's sake, he'd been taking the mickey all along. If she'd been sober, Ginny realised, she would be all of a fluster now. But by a stroke of luck she wasn't, so she shrugged and said cheerfully, 'Correct.'

'That's discrimination.'

'Don't feel too sorry for yourself. Plenty of women out there who wouldn't turn you down.'

'But I'm not talking about other women. I'm talking about you. You're saying you wouldn't consider a relationship with someone like me, purely because of my external appearance.'

Ginny didn't know whether to nod or shake her head. 'Yes . . . I mean no . . . I mean, that's *right*.'

'But that would be unfair. You'd be dismissing me without giving me a chance. So technically I could take you to court,' Finn said idly. 'I could sue you for unfair dismissal.'

Ginny took another glug of wine. 'Fine. So sue me.'

There was a glimmer of amusement in his eyes. 'I'd rather try to persuade you to change your mind.'

'That's bordering on smooth talk. If you carry on like that you'll end up like Evie's estate agent.'

'Sorry. Fate worse than death. So you're saying men like me are useless when it comes to long-term investments. We're only good for meaningless flings, have I got this right?'

'Pretty much.' Ginny shrugged in agreement.

'And you were saying only last week how you wished you could have a meaningless fling.'

OK, now there was no getting away from it. He was definitely suggesting what she thought he was suggesting. Her mouth drier than ever, Ginny said, 'Was I?'

'Oh, yes. You were.' There was a note of playful challenge in his voice. 'And I'm just saying, if you still feel the same way, I wouldn't object.'

'That's very generous of you.' Ginny paused. 'But where would I find a good-looking man to have a meaningless fling with at this time of night?'

Finn laughed. Then he leaned towards her. 'Close your eyes.'

Yeeeeeek.

'Why?' As if she didn't know.

'Will you stop arguing and just do it?'

He wanted to. And he was gorgeous. What's more, she'd fantasised about this happening for months.

Casting all doubt aside, Ginny stopped arguing and just did it.

How could you regret an experience like that? God, how could anyone?

It was one o'clock in the morning when Ginny slid out of bed. The sex had been glorious, like losing her virginity all over again. Actually, that was a stupid comparison; tonight had been a million times better than her first time. But it was also, now, undeniably tinged with awkwardness because she had to keep reminding herself that she and Finn weren't in a relationship, that this *was* only a meaningless fling. So instead of the two of them lying in each other's arms, whispering and laughing together and, well, making plans to see each other again, she had to pretend to be a modern, no-strings kind of girl who'd had a great time but now needed to get home, put it behind her and get on with her busy, single-girl life.

Like Carla.

Finn raised himself up on one elbow. 'Going to the bathroom?'

In the darkness she could just make out the glitter of his eyes. If she could see him, did that mean he could see her? Hastily holding in her stomach and reaching for her shirt, Ginny said, 'No. Home.'

'Why?'

She was filled with sadness. 'Because it's time to go.'

'You don't have to,' said Finn.

He was being polite, saying the gentlemanly thing. The last thing he wanted was for her to leap back into bed with a squeal of delight, crying, 'OK then, I'll stay!' As far as men like Finn were concerned, their worst nightmare was finding themselves trapped with someone clingy and overkeen.

'Thanks, but I'd rather get home.' Dressing at the speed of light, Ginny shot him a casual, unclingy smile. 'We've had a nice time, haven't we? But now it's over. Time to leave. No need to get up,' she added as he made a move to push aside the bedclothes. 'I'll see myself out.'

Stepping into her shoes and hastily smoothing down her hair, Ginny bent and gave him a quick careless kiss on the cheek. 'Thank you, that was fun. Bye.'

After a pause, Finn said, 'Bye.'

And that was it. Easy.

If Carla could see her now she'd be so proud.

Dan the Van rattled into the courtyard in his mud-spattered green van at midday. Ginny, poking her head through the kitchen door, called out, 'It's all right, he's here. I'll go and fetch them.'

Dan had blotted his copybook this morning, forgetting the raspberries when he'd arrived earlier with the rest of the fruit and veg. As Ginny made her way out of the restaurant, he leapt out of the van looking harassed and burbling apologies. 'I'm so sorry, I can't think how it happened, I could swear I ticked everything on the list, this has *never* happened to me before . . .'

'Dan, it's fine.' Ginny attempted to calm him down; normally shy and retiring, Dan was the world's most conscientious delivery man. 'You're here now and it's only twelve o'clock. Really, it doesn't matter a bit.'

'I feel terrible though. Do you think I should apologise to Finn?'

'There's no need, he doesn't even know about it. Hello, beautiful,' cooed Ginny as Dan's dog whimpered a greeting from the passenger seat of the van. As sweet-natured and shy as Dan, Stiller was a lanky, tousled, slightly unhygienic mongrel with a curly tail.

'OK, if you're sure.' Unloading the tray of raspberries and evidently still racked with guilt, Dan thrust them into her arms.

As Ginny took the tray, they both heard a car coming up the driveway. 'Sounds like our first customers arriving. I'll take these through to the kitchen.'

'Don't forget to tell chef I'm sorry.'

'Dan, stop apologising, it really doesn't—'

'Hello? Excuse me? Where would I find Finn?'

Ginny turned to look at the owner of the voice, which sounded as if it had been dipped in golden syrup. The girl was tall and probably in her late twenties with glossy, almost waist-length brown hair and silver-grey eyes. She was wearing a black T-shirt and narrow white jeans with—

'Finn Penhaligon,' the girl elaborated, clearly wondering if Ginny understood English. Pointing first to the antiques centre then to the restaurant and enunciating slowly she said, 'Is he here?'

Resisting the urge to enunciate back, Ginny said, 'I think he's in the antiques centre.'

'Thank you.' The girl opened the rear door of her black car and leaned into it, scooping out a baby in a scarlet sundress. She hoisted the baby onto her hip and began to make her way towards the honeysuckle-strewn entrance of the shop. Then, abruptly stopping, she thought for a moment before turning back to Ginny. 'Actually, could you do me a favour? I'll wait out here and you take her in.'

Ginny froze, because the baby had twisted round to look at her and there was no longer any question of who Finn's visitors were. 'Sorry?'

'Take her in, tell Finn there's someone here to see him. Yes,' Tamsin nodded, pleased with herself, 'that's a much better plan.'

'I can't do that.'

'Of course you can. Don't worry, she won't cry. Just give the raspberries to him.' Tamsin nodded at Dan the Van, who was so stunned he immediately took the raspberries from Ginny. 'There, you see? Not too difficult! And now you take Mae. This is important; I want Finn to see her before he sees me. *There* you are.'

Ginny wanted to shout, 'I can't do this, I slept with Finn last night!' But it was too late, Tamsin had already plonked Mae into her arms.

'I'll take the raspberries in.' Dan the Van scurried off.

'And I'll stay here.' Tamsin, her silvery eyes sparkling with anticipation, gave Ginny a gentle push in the direction of the shop. 'Don't worry, he's going to love it. Off you go!'

But I'm not going to love it, Ginny thought. I *slept* with Finn last night. She shook her head and said, 'I'm sorry, I really can't, it's not—'

'Oh, for heaven's sake, what is the big deal here? One little favour, that's all I'm asking!' Stepping away and raising her eyebrows in disbelief, Tamsin said, 'What possible difference can it make to *you*?'

Inside the antiques centre a dozen or so potential customers were browsing, the warm air was heavy with the scent of old, cared-for wood and beeswax polish, and 'Unchained Melody' was playing on the jukebox. Ginny saw Finn standing with his back to her, chatting to a couple of Japanese tourists who had just bought a Georgian writing chest.

She waited for him to finish the conversation. Mae gazed around the

Aladdin's cave with interest and spotted a life-size enamelled parrot. Entranced by the bright colours she pointed and exclaimed, 'Birdie!'

'I know,' whispered Ginny, her heart hammering wildly. 'Clever girl.'

'BIRDIE!'

Finn smiled and turned to see who was making all the noise. When he spotted Ginny his smile broadened. Then his gaze shifted and the expression on his face changed as he recognised the baby in her arms. The smile fell away, and in the split second that followed Ginny glimpsed shock, anguish and joy.

It was heartbreaking to imagine the pain he must have gone through.

'Birdiebirdie,' babbled Mae, pointing at the ceiling and beaming over at Finn.

He excused himself from the Japanese couple and came over, his jaw taut. 'What's going on?'

'Tamsin's outside. She asked me to do this. I didn't want to,' said Ginny, 'but she insisted. Here, I need to get back to the restaurant.' She handed Mae to him. Unperturbed by all the pass-the-parcelling, the little girl reached out with both hands and spread her fingers like tiny starfish against the sides of Finn's face. Maybe subconsciously she recognised him as having been a previous fixture in her life, because her smile was so dazzling, a lump rose in Ginny's throat.

For several seconds, oblivious to his surroundings, Finn stood there holding Mae in his arms. This was the baby he had witnessed being born and fallen in love with at first sight, the baby that had changed his world for ever. For four months she had been his daughter, until the day in October last year when she had vanished from his life—had been summarily removed from it by Tamsin—and he had learned that she wasn't his daughter after all.

But love, as Finn had discovered to his cost, wasn't as fickle as a DNA test. His feelings for Mae hadn't dissipated. He hadn't stopped grieving for the loss of the child who had made his life complete.

Making his way out into the sunshine, Finn saw Tamsin waiting for him. 'What's this about?'

'Hello, Finn.' Tamsin smiled, though there was a note of tension in her voice. 'I thought you might like to see Mae again.'

'Boobooboo,' burbled Mae, delightedly waving her arms.

'And?' Finn said steadily.

'And?' Tears welled in Tamsin's silvery eyes. 'Oh, Finn, I suppose I was kind of wondering if you might like to see me again too.'

'I can't believe she's turned up!' Evie was agog, peering through the restaurant window, torn between indignation and glee. 'The nerve of that girl. What do you suppose she's doing here? Damn, *why* did I never take up lip-reading?'

'Come away from the window.' Ginny didn't have any idea what was going on either, but she knew she felt sick.

'I can't, it's not physically possible. Oh God, look at Mae, she's so gorgeous. I can't believe how much she's *grown*.'

'Evie, they'll see you.'

'Ha, you're joking, they wouldn't notice if we ran out there naked and did the Macarena.'

Ginny flushed. Last night Finn had seen her naked. She'd seen him naked too.

'Tamsin's crying,' Evie announced with relish. 'She's wiping her eyes. Have we got any binoculars?'

'No, but we've got a table of eight arriving any minute, so maybe we should—'

'Damn, they're going!'

'Tamsin and the baby?' Unable to help herself, Ginny rushed up and hovered behind Evie, keen to see them getting back into the car. No such luck. When she peered over Evie's shoulder, she saw all three of them disappearing through the front door that led up to Finn's flat.

'Some people are so thoughtless.' Evie heaved a sigh of frustration. 'No consideration for others. Wouldn't you just love to know what's going on? I'm telling you, I'd give my right arm for a listening device.'

'What's going on?' Finn looked at the woman he'd once loved. Tamsin even managed to look beautiful when she was crying.

'Oh, Finn, you don't know how hard this has been for me. I made the biggest mistake of my life when I left you.' Biting her lip, Tamsin said tremulously, 'I've been such an idiot. Believe me, if I could turn back the clock, I would. I wish I'd never met Angelo.'

'He's the father of your child.'

'I know, I *know* that, but I'm trying to say I wish Mae was yours. I made one mistake.' Tamsin held up a French-manicured index finger for emphasis. '*One*. You were away and along came Angelo. He made a fuss of me, flattered me. It was a moment of madness. I slept with him. He wanted me to dump you and become his girlfriend but I told him I couldn't because I loved you. Of course I felt guilty, but it was just a one-off with Angelo and I learned a valuable lesson. I told myself that as long as you didn't know about it, we'd be OK.'

'And then you found out you were pregnant.' Finn spoke without emotion.

'Yes.' Fresh tears were now rolling down Tamsin's tanned cheeks. 'But I refused to even consider the possibility that it could be Angelo's. I just so desperately wanted you to be the father.'

Finn looked over at Mae, who had fallen asleep on the sofa. 'But I wasn't.'

'I know, I know. And you loved her so much.' Tamsin wiped her eyes with the back of her hand. 'I thought I could handle not knowing for sure, but once she was here I just couldn't. It was the guilt, I suppose. I just had to know the truth.' She paused, swallowed. 'That's when I had the test done. And then the results came through. Oh God, that was the worst day of my life. I knew I had to tell Angelo. He had a right to know. I'm sorry, this is so difficult . . .'

'So you told him,' Finn supplied. When Tamsin and Mae had disappeared, she had left him a letter but this was the first time he'd heard the explanation from her own mouth.

'I did. And he decided he wanted us to be together. He convinced me that I'd be doing the right thing and I was in such a state by then that I couldn't say no. Angelo's a forceful character; he organised everything and I just went along with it.' Tamsin shook her head. 'I hardly knew what was happening. It was all a blur.'

Finn looked at her. 'And now?'

'Oh, Finn, I was wrong. It's over between me and Angelo. The only person he cares about is himself. He liked the idea of having a daughter to show off, but ask Angelo to look after Mae for an hour and you'd think I was telling him to chop off his own legs. We had a day nanny and a night nanny. Materially we had everything. But I knew I didn't love Angelo. And I don't think he loves Mae.'

'And now you've left him.' Finn's tone was even. 'You've brought Mae down here. But you still haven't told me why.'

'Oh, Finn, I made the worst mistake in the world and I'm sorrier than I can ever say, but I never stopped loving you. And I know how much I must have hurt you, but we were happy together before, weren't we? You, me and Mae were a proper family. So I suppose what I'm saying is, do you think there's any chance—for Mae's sake if not mine—that you could ever forgive me and we could be happy again?'

Chapter 9

LUNCHTIME IN THE RESTAURANT had been an ordeal for Ginny, what with Evie's endless speculations and the nest of snakes squirming away in her stomach. Finally the last diners were despatched, the dining room was in a state of readiness for this evening's influx and Ginny was able to leave.

Finn emerged from his flat as she was about to unlock the car. At the sight of him heading towards her, the snakes went into frenzied wriggly overdrive. Ironically, too, the shock of this new situation with Tamsin was far greater than when she'd found out about Carla and Perry, which just went to show how much less Perry had meant to her than she'd imagined at the time. Last night with Finn had been in a completely different league, Ginny realised.

When he reached her, Ginny saw the signs of strain in his face. His hands were pushed into the pockets of his trousers and his shoulders were tense. Fixing a troubled gaze on her, he came straight to the point.

'Ginny, sorry about this but there's something we need to discuss. Obviously, Tamsin's turned up. Not what I was expecting, but there it is. And there are issues to sort out.' Finn paused, clearly hating every second of having to explain to her. 'Now, last night was great, really it was, and I don't want you to feel . . . well, pushed aside or ignored, but now that Tamsin's here it's a bit of an awkward—'

'Look, it's fine.' Ginny blurted the words out, unable to bear his discomfort for another second. He was being a gentleman again, doing his best to let her down gently, making sure she understood the situation. 'You don't have to say anything. I completely understand. It's not as if we're in a relationship,' she went on. 'It was one night, it was what we both wanted at the time, but it didn't *mean* anything.'

Finn looked slightly taken aback at the vehemence of her tone, startled but at the same time visibly relieved. 'Right. Well, um, absolutely. So long as you're sure you're OK about it. We'll just . . . carry on as normal.'

'Completely as normal. As if it never happened.' Ginny nodded firmly, because it was so clearly what he needed to hear. Then, unable to contain herself a moment longer, she said, 'But are you all right? Am I allowed to ask what's going on? What are they doing here?'

Finn hesitated. 'It's difficult to explain. I can't really—'

'Oh God, she's coming out,' Ginny yelped. Her heart leaping with fresh guilt, she yanked open the car door. 'I'll leave you to it.'

But she was stopped by Tamsin hurrying over to them waving one arm to attract Ginny's attention. 'Hello,' she called out, making her way across the courtyard. 'Don't rush off!'

But I *want* to rush off, thought Ginny, panicking that Tamsin might somehow have discovered it was her who had spent time last night in Finn's bed. Had she found a stray blonde hair on the pillow perhaps, and carried out a quick DNA test? Or spotted a pair of knickers and immediately deduced that there was only one woman around here frumpy enough to wear sensible black size 14s from M&S? No, it couldn't be that, she'd definitely been wearing pants when she'd left the flat.

'Can I ask you something?' Tamsin, who was surely a size 8 La Perla thong girl herself, reached the car and touched Ginny's arm.

No!

'Yes.' Cautiously, Ginny nodded, praying she wasn't about to be asked if she could just give that DNA sample now.

'It's just that you were so good with Mae earlier, and Finn and I *really* need some quality time together.' Tamsin's smile was complicit, her tone confiding. 'So I wondered if you'd be an angel and baby-sit for a few hours this evening.'

'Um . . .' Caught off guard, Ginny faltered. It was a terrible idea.

'We'll pay you, of course. Whatever the going rate is.' Tamsin gestured airily, signalling that she hadn't the least idea what the going rate might be. 'Sorry, I'm used to live-in staff, I'm going to have to learn all this new stuff! But don't worry, Finn will sort you out.'

Actually, he gave me a pretty good sorting out last night. Ginny wondered what would happen if she said this aloud. Instead she shook her head and said, 'Sorry, I can't do it. I'm busy tonight.'

'Really?' Tamsin looked shocked, as if Ginny had just turned down the offer of a week on Necker Island with George Clooney. 'Are you sure? Isn't it something you could cancel?'

'No, it isn't.' Ginny didn't have anything on this evening but she was buggered if she was going to baby-sit.

'It doesn't matter,' Finn cut in impatiently. 'We don't need a baby sitter. We're not going anywhere.'

Tamsin said, 'Oh, but—'

'I haven't seen Mae for eight months.' He shook his head firmly. 'Why would I want to leave her here with someone else?'

Especially with *me*, thought Ginny.

The last time Carla had seen Tess Whelan she had felt incredibly sorry for her. It had been four weeks ago and Tess, then nine months pregnant, was lumbering around her house like an exhausted elephant. As she'd made a pot of tea and flicked through the colour brochures of conservatories, she had been massaging her aching back, complaining good-naturedly about not being able to paint her toenails and giving Carla . . . well, far too much information, frankly, about practising contractions, piles and the need to visit the loo every twenty minutes.

What's more, Tess had been wearing a hideous T-shirt stretched over her grotesquely swollen belly and elastic-waisted trousers. She might have been pretty once but now she just looked knackered. Carla, feigning sympathy, but inwardly repulsed, hadn't been able to get out of the house fast enough.

She hadn't been much looking forward to coming back again either. If Tess Whelan had been a wreck before giving birth, God only knew what she'd look like now with a wailing, puking baby in tow.

'Hi there! Lovely to see you again. Come on through.'

Carla's jaw dropped open at the sight of Tess. Her blonde hair was shining, her face glowed and she was wearing size ten jeans and a lacy pink cropped vest.

'Good grief, what happened to your stomach?'

Tess grinned and patted her flat abdomen. 'I know, isn't it great? Like a miracle. All thanks to breastfeeding, my health visitor tells me. And I'm eating like a horse but somehow everything just snapped back into place. Come on through and meet Alfie.'

Carla was stunned. 'So how's it going?' she asked as she followed Tess through to the living room.

'Fantastic. So much easier than I'd been expecting. You hear all these nightmare stories about having babies, don't you? But Alfie's so good, he's an absolute angel. I've never been happier.' Tess paused then said, 'To be honest, I was never the maternal type. But my husband was so keen I kind of felt obliged to go through with it. And now Alfie's here, I can't imagine life without him. He makes my life complete.'

That's how I feel about Perry, Carla thought smugly.

'And here he is!' Tess's face lit up with love and pride as she presented her son for inspection.

Carla gazed down at the baby, awake but silent, lying on a squashy blue and white beanbag. Alfie was wearing a tiny white T-shirt and a nappy. His dark eyes were watchful, his hair grew tuftily on top of his head, and his miniature fingers clenched and unclenched as he steadily returned Carla's stare.

Oh God.

Oh God . . .

'Are you all right?' said Tess anxiously.

'Fine,' Carla croaked. 'Fine.' Then she said the four words she'd never said before in her life and had certainly never envisaged herself saying. 'Um . . . can I hold him?'

It was extraordinary, an epiphany, beyond anything she'd ever experienced before. Tess bent down and picked up Alfie then tenderly kissed him before handing him over. Carla took him in her arms and felt as if . . . oh God, as if her life could at last become truly complete.

Not with Alfie obviously. He belonged to Tess. But with a baby of her own. Hers and Perry's. How could she ever have imagined she didn't want a child? Well, she clearly hadn't met the right man before now.

Cradling Alfie, Carla bent her head and inhaled the blissful baby smell of him, an indescribable mixture of milk and warmth and newness. When his tiny starfish hand closed around one of her own fingers, Carla wanted to explode with happiness.

This, *this* was what she wanted.

'**Y**ou what?' Perry started to laugh.

'I want a baby.' It was like finding God, as pure and as simple as that. Carla had barely been able to concentrate earlier on closing the deal for the Whelans' new conservatory but somehow she'd managed it. Turning up at Perry's shop afterwards, she had persuaded him to come for a walk with her along the beach.

'This is a joke, right?' He stopped and tilted his head to one side.

'It's not a joke.'

'But you hate kids. You told me that. You said you'd never wanted children of your own.'

'I know I did. But I was wrong.' Carla couldn't contain her happiness, her certainty. 'My body *told* me I didn't want them, because I hadn't met the right man. But now I have.' She reached for Perry's hand, which had slipped out of hers. 'And I want one more than anything, with you. We'll be even *happier*—'

'Hello? Earth to Carla? What makes you think I want children? I can't stand bloody kids. I was delighted when you told me you didn't want any yourself. As far as I was concerned, it was the icing on the cake.'

'But I've changed my mind,' Carla said urgently, 'and so will you. Perry, this is so *right*. We love each other. It'll be perfect.'

'I promise you it won't.'

Adrenaline was racing through her body. It was a blow, but she was a star saleswoman; she could win him round. Men often panicked at the prospect of fatherhood but they succumbed in the end.

'If you hated the idea that much, you'd have had a vasectomy.' Carla's tone was almost playful.

'Jesus. If there's one thing worse than babies, it's the thought of some quack advancing on my tackle with a scalpel.' Grimly, Perry shook his head. 'I've heard enough horror stories to put me off that idea for life. Anyway, if you were so sure you didn't want kids, why didn't you get yourself sterilised years ago?'

Carla was triumphant. 'Because *obviously* my brain was telling me that one day I might change my mind! And it was right!'

Perry's smile was long gone. He gazed past her, out to sea, his left hand rubbing his chin. Looking hungrily at him, at the golden bristles on his jaw and the glossy red-gold of his hair, Carla envisaged the baby they would have. She *would* be able to change his mind, this was a deal she could definitely close. Men just needed a bit of gentle persuasion sometimes, that was all.

'When did this happen?' Perry spoke abruptly as seagulls wheeled overhead and waves slid up the beach.

'Today. This afternoon. I went to this house and saw—'

'So you've still got your coil in?'

Carla nodded, smiling slightly. Never one to hang around once her mind was made up, she'd already phoned her doctor and made an appointment for tomorrow morning to have it removed. She was thirty-nine after all, with no time to lose.

Perry looked at her, long and hard. Then he broke into a smile. 'What are you trying to do to me?'

'Nothing horrible, I promise. Just show you how much I love you.' Carla wound her arms round his waist, held him tightly. 'It's the right thing to do, I promise you. You won't regret it.'

'**F**inn, what's going on?' Evie demanded when Finn appeared in the restaurant on Friday lunchtime.

'Me? I've spent the morning selling antiques.'

'Don't give me that. You know what I'm talking about.' Evie, who wasn't in awe of Finn, asked the questions no one else dared to ask. Ginny, polishing glasses behind the bar, watched the look of annoyance on his face.

'It's none of your business what's going on.'

'But are you *crazy*? Tamsin messed up your life last year and now she's back. Does that mean you're going to let her do it all over again?'

It was early; none of the diners had arrived yet. Finn, clearly not in the sunniest of moods, squared up to Evie. 'I don't have to explain myself to you. I'm an adult capable of making my own decisions.'

'And trust me, you're making a bad one,' she shot back.

'Don't tell me how to live my life.'

'Why not?' Evie retorted. 'Someone has to try to knock some sense into you. And God knows, everyone else can see that what you're doing is wrong.' Gesturing towards Ginny, she said, 'Can't we?'

Hastily Ginny said, 'I don't want to get involved.'

'But you *should*.' Evie was adamant, on a complete roll now. 'We all work together! We're friends, aren't we? That's what friends are for. Bloody hell, if I said I was having an affair with a seventeen-year-old boy who'd asked me to marry him and wanted me to lend him a hundred grand to pay off his gambling debts, would you two stand back and let me do it?'

'Right now? Like a shot,' said Finn.

'See? And now you're angry with me.' Changing tack, Evie said, 'But you shouldn't be, because we're only saying all this because we care about you.'

Less of the *we*, Ginny thought in alarm.

'I know you love Mae,' Evie went on, 'but I don't believe you still love Tamsin. And that's no basis for a relationship. OK, Tamsin's a beautiful girl. She's sexy, I appreciate that. But fancying a glass of milk doesn't mean you have to buy the cow. If it's sex you're after, there are plenty of women around here who'd be only too happy to hop into your bed. I promise you, Finn, all you have to do is click your fingers and they'll be queuing up for a quick—*urk*.'

'Oooh!' Appearing in the restaurant doorway with Mae in her arms, Tamsin surveyed them with amusement. 'All of a sudden there's an awkward silence. Should my ears be burning?' Then, as her gaze settled on Ginny, her smile broadened. 'Except if they were, they couldn't possibly be redder than your face.'

Ginny wished she could sink down through the floor.

'We were talking about work,' Finn said. 'Did you want something?'

'Just came to say goodbye.'

This pronouncement caused Evie's eyebrows to shoot up into her hairline, and Ginny's hopes to rise in similar fashion. Tamsin, swaying over to Finn, said cheerfully, 'We're off into Portsilver to buy Mae some new clothes and have a play on the beach. Back by three, OK?' She proffered Mae for a kiss. 'Say bye bye.'

Beaming, Mae gave Finn a kiss on the cheek and said, 'Ghaaaa.'

Finn stroked her silky dark hair. 'Ghaaaa to you too. Have fun.'

'Look at them.' Clearly revelling in the sight of Finn and Mae together, Tamsin said with pride, 'She's crazy about him!'

Ginny swallowed disappointment and thought, Me too.

To make up for the hour she'd taken off to go to the doctor's surgery, Carla had been forced to work until eight. Now she click-clacked her way down Hudson Street and stopped outside Perry's front door. Ringing the doorbell, she experienced a thrill of anticipation.

And there were his footsteps on the stairs . . .

She was taken aback when the door opened to reveal Ally the dim Goth who worked in Perry's shop.

'Hi, Perry's expecting me.'

Ally blinked at her through a curtain of dyed-black hair. 'Yeah, he said you might drop round. Come on up then.'

It wasn't until they reached the living room that Carla realised there was definitely something not quite right going on here. For a start there were disgusting incense candles smouldering in holders on the window sill. And there was a small mountain of assorted carrier bags stuffed with God knows what piled up on the sofa.

More to the point, there was no sign of Perry.

'Where is he?'

'Hmm? Oh, gone away.' Peering round the room, Ally said vaguely, 'Hang on, it's around here somewhere.'

'Gone *away*?' Carla's stomach did a swallow dive. 'Where?'

'No idea, he didn't say. Just told me he needed a break and put me in charge of the shop. Bloody long hours but he said I could move in here while he's gone so that makes up for it. Ah, here it is.' She found the envelope she'd been searching for and handed it to Carla.

How could Perry have gone away? In the space of . . . what? Eleven hours? He'd been fine when she'd left here this morning. Carla ripped open the envelope.

> Carla,
> I loved you but you've scared me. I don't want kids now and I never will. I'm going away for a while to think things through. Don't bother trying to phone me—I won't pick up. I thought you were my ideal woman but now it's all spoilt.
> Sorry, not much good at this. In future I'd better stick to women who've had hysterectomies!
> Best, Perry

Carla crumpled the letter in her fist and squeezed until her knuckles clicked. Best, Perry. *Best, Perry.* Yesterday he'd loved her but now it was over, in the past, switched off like a tap.

'Everything all right?'

'Fine. Couldn't be better.' Carla shoved the scrunched-up note into her bag and wondered if there was an extra-sharp knife in the kitchen drawer. Half of her wanted to slash her wrists but the other half—actually by far the bigger half—wanted to slash Perry's.

And maybe slice off another treasured appendage while she was about it.

'**S**even pints of Blackthorn, four white wines and five Bacardi Breezers.' Having shoved his way through the crowd to the bar, Spiderman added in a friendly fashion, 'You all right?'

Jem looked up. Oh yes, she was just tickety-boo. The beer pumps were playing up tonight and best bitter was splattered across the front of her white shirt. But Spiderman was the first member of the fancy dress crew to say anything remotely friendly to her tonight, so she forced herself to smile.

'Great, thanks. Dry white?'

Spiderman, aka Darren, said triumphantly, 'I'd prefer wet.'

Hilarious. When it came to razor-sharp ripostes, Darren was no Jonathan Ross. Then again, at least he'd been invited to Alex and Karen's party tonight, which was more than she had been. Jem got on with the business in hand, flipping the tops off the Breezers. All week she'd been hearing people chatting excitedly between lectures and tutorials about

Alex and Karen's fancy dress party, deciding what they were going to wear. Everyone was going apart from her and Rupert, who had announced that he'd rather sieve his intestines through a colander.

Jem began pouring the Blackthorn into pint glasses, the familiar sense of abandonment nestling in her stomach. Earlier this evening Rupert had made love to her and she'd felt wonderful, special. Then afterwards he had showered and changed and driven up to Cheltenham for the stag do of an old schoolfriend's brother, absently kissing her goodbye and telling her he'd be back sometime tomorrow.

There was a burst of laughter from the crowd a short distance from the bar. Involuntarily glancing up from the cider pump, Jem saw Davy and Lucy dressed as a pair of New York gangsters in sharp suits and fedoras. Once upon a time Davy had been the ignored one, the geeky outsider. Now, unbelievably, Lucy had moved in with him and was busy dragging him by the scruff of his neck out of his shell. They were living with Davy's mother—how sad was that?—yet, weirdly, appeared to be having a good time.

Neither of them had so much as glanced in her direction. She might as well be invisible for all the attention anyone else was paying her. Ugh, and now cider was dripping onto her jeans.

'Last orders,' bellowed the landlord, clanging the bell.

Jem finished lining up the wines, the ciders and the Breezers. She totted up the bill and took Spiderman's credit card, ready to slot it into the machine.

'So you'll be finishing soon,' Darren said bouncily, his mask pushed up to his forehead and his manner jovial.

'As soon as everyone's gone.'

'Are you coming along to the party, then?'

Was it Jem's imagination or did the pub suddenly go a few decibels quieter? Either Clint Eastwood had just walked in or Spiderman had said the Wrong Thing.

She shook her head. 'Um, no.'

Darren was oblivious to his faux pas. 'Why not?'

Because nobody wants me there. Everyone hates me, haven't you noticed? Jem didn't say this out loud. She pushed the credit card reader across the bar and said, 'Just put your PIN in, please.'

'But that's daft if you're not doing anything else! Hey, Alex.' Darren turned and grabbed Alex by the shoulder. 'I've just been telling Jem, she should come along to the party, yeah?'

Jem felt hot and sick. Alex was looking embarrassed now while the rest of them were nudging each other and smirking.

'Er . . . the thing is, it's fancy dress,' Alex mumbled.

'And I have to get home,' Jem blurted out, hideously aware of Davy and Lucy watching from a safe distance as the scene was played out for their entertainment. 'But . . . um, thanks anyway.'

Ceris Morgan, whom Jem had never much liked and who she knew for a fact fancied Rupert, was dressed as a French maid. Unable to resist joining in, she adjusted her saucily low-cut top and said in a singsong voice, 'We wouldn't be rich enough. Jem isn't interested in parties thrown by boring old *ordinary* people any more. She's got Rupert.'

'**S**ix pints of Blackthorn, four white wine spritzers, three Bloody Marys and two Bacardi Breezers,' said Alex, flushed with triumph at having made it back to the pub.

It was Sunday lunchtime and the bedraggled survivors of last night's party, still in fancy dress, were all set to carry on. By the sound of things it had been a resounding success. At least Davy and Lucy weren't here, which would only have made things more stressful.

Sadly, Ceris was.

'Ooh, what a night. You missed out big-time.' Ceris lit a Silk Cut and blew smoke across the bar. 'You really should have come along to the . . . oops, I forgot! You weren't invited!'

Flushing, Alex the peacemaker said hastily, 'It's not that Jem wasn't invited. She just didn't have anything to wear.'

'Oh, I don't know.' Ceris smirked. 'She could have come as a two-faced bitch, that wouldn't have needed any dressing up.'

Splooooooosh went the fountain of soda water as Jem's finger squeezed the trigger on the mixer gun. Heavens, how had that happened?

'Aaaarrrgh!' Ceris let out a screech as piercing as nails down a blackboard, her maid's uniform instantly drenched. Now that she'd started, Jem discovered she didn't want to stop. Ceris was a spiteful bully who revelled in belittling others and deserved to be taken down a peg or two. And how better to do it than with a drenching? Feeling empowered and better already, Jem carried on aiming the gun at Ceris until every inch of her was dripping with bubbly, ice-cold soda water.

'Put the gun down.' The pub landlord's big hands closed over Jem's, prising her away from her new favourite toy.

'You complete bitch!' Spitting with rage and shaking soda water out of her hair, Ceris bellowed, 'My dad's a lawyer, he's going to sue you!'

'No, he isn't.' The landlord fixed Ceris with a look of weary distaste. 'You're loud and you're drunk.' Then he turned to Jem. 'And you're fired.'

The whole pub was by this time agog.

'Great,' said Jem, wiping her wet hands on a bar towel. 'I've always wanted to go out with a splash.'

Who cared anyway? There were a million other pubs in Bristol. Although she was beginning to wonder if she wanted to do bar work any more, what with the way it messed up her social life. As Jem trudged back to the flat it occurred to her that she could always take out another loan and just enjoy herself instead. Then she and Rupert would be able to see more of each other. Wasn't that a better idea? Loads of people did it and didn't waste time worrying about being in debt. You just paid off what you owed at some stage in the distant future when it was more convenient. When you thought about it, a bigger loan made so much more sense.

Turning into Pembroke Road, Jem's heart leapt at the sight of Rupert's car parked outside the flat. Oh, thank God, he was home. Her pace quickened. Rupert would roar with laughter when she told him what had happened and he'd tell her she'd done exactly the right thing. Best of all he would put his arms around her and make her feel loved, which was exactly what she needed.

Jem ran up the steps, fitted her key into the lock and pushed open the front door.

'Rupert!' She could hear the shower running in the bathroom. Just the thought of Rupert naked, lathering his tanned body with shower gel, produced a fizz of adrenaline and brought a smile to Jem's face. She kicked off one boot and stealthily tested the door handle in case Rupert had changed the habit of a lifetime and locked it. No, he hadn't. She levered off the second boot and peeled off her less than alluring purple socks. She'd never had sex in a shower before.

But Rupert had.

It seemed, in fact, he was doing it right now.

Jem froze on the threshold of the overheated bathroom as she saw too many arms and legs through the misted-up frosted glass of the shower cubicle. Intermixed with the roar of the water, she now heard groans and murmured words uttered by a female. Next, even worse, came Rupert's voice going, 'Oh yes . . . oh yes . . .'

Oh no. Please no. Don't let this be real.

But they were getting louder now and body parts—a tanned buttock here, a splayed hand there—were pressing up against the glass. Before anything more conclusive could happen, Jem raced over to the basin and turned the hot tap on full blast.

It did the trick, like hurling a bucket of water over a couple of fighting dogs. Now she knew the true meaning of 'cooling their ardour'.

'Fuck it,' yelled Rupert as the water in the shower ran from steaming hot to stone cold in two seconds flat.

'*Waaaah*,' screeched a female voice, frantically scrabbling to slide open the shower door. 'Turn it off, turn it off!'

Jem grabbed the navy towels hung over the brass rail and bundled them into her arms. Moving back to the door she whipped out the key in the lock on the bathroom side and waited for Rupert and his companion to emerge from the cubicle.

'WAAAAAHHH.' Having stumbled out and seen Jem standing there in the doorway, Caro let out an ear-splitting scream and stepped back, cannoning clumsily into Rupert.

Caro.

'Oh, for fuck's sake.' Rupert looked over at Jem and exhaled. 'You're supposed to be at work.'

'Sorry to spoil your afternoon.' The words were spilling out of Jem's mouth automatically. 'I thought I'd come home early and surprise you. And guess what? I did.' She turned to Caro. 'Did Rupert tell you we're together now?'

'No.' Caro smiled slightly. 'He just said he'd been shagging you.'

Caro had always had an intimidating, supercilious air about her.

'OK,' said Jem.

'I'm sorry.' Moving towards her, Rupert held out a hand for the towels.

Jem took another step back. This was turning into quite some afternoon. 'Actually, I don't think you are. But never mind.' Her tone conversational, she added, 'You will be.'

Still clutching the collection of towels, she slammed the door shut and used the key to lock it.

From inside the bathroom, Rupert shouted, 'Jem, don't be stupid.'

'I'm not. I've *been* stupid, but I'm over that now.'

Was her plan too harsh? No, of course it wasn't.

Ten minutes later she banged on the bathroom door and sang out, 'Right, I'm off. Don't you two catch cold now. Bye!'

Chapter 10

'JEM?' WHEN GINNY OPENED the front door at ten o'clock that night she thought she was hallucinating.

'Oh, Mum.' Jem's face was white, stained with tears, a picture of grief as she stumbled into Ginny's arms.

'Sweetheart, what's going on? What's happened?'

Please don't let her be pregnant.

'Is it Rupert?' she said gently some time later when Jem had reached the messy, sniffing, over-the-worst-of-it phase.

'Y-yes.' Jem nodded, then miserably shook her head. 'W-well, no. He's only part of it.'

'OK, sweetheart, you're here now. Whatever it is, we'll sort it out.'

Jem wiped her eyes on the sleeve of her sweatshirt. 'No need. I've already sorted it out.'

Had she murdered him? 'What do you mean?'

'It's all over. I'm not going back. Not ever.'

Something about the flat tone of Jem's voice caused the hairs on the back of Ginny's neck to prickle in alarm.

'Jem, you have to tell me what happened.' Would she turn in her own daughter? Call the police? Or would she protect her, lie for her, whisk her off to Argentina for a life on the run from the authorities?

Yes, Ginny knew this was what she'd do. Nobody deserved to go to prison for murdering Rupert.

'Oh, Mum, it's all been so horrible. Rupert's been seeing someone else. I caught him with her today. It's Caro, his old girlfriend. You met her that time you called in.'

'I remember.' Ginny hadn't liked Caro either. 'What did you do?'

Jem told her. When it became apparent that she hadn't left the two of them dead, Ginny hugged her harder than ever. 'Oh, darling, everything's going to be fine. How will he get out of the bathroom?'

'Through the window I suppose. He'll have to climb down the drainpipe naked and ring someone else's doorbell to be let back in.' She paused and wiped her nose. 'Shame not to catch it on a camcorder.'

Even the feeblest of jokes was surely a good sign. Ginny stroked Jem's hair and handed her a clean tissue. 'You just wait, when you get back all your friends will rally round and—oh Jem, don't cry, when they hear what you did they'll love you for it.'

'They won't' Sobbing again, Jem rocked with misery against her.

'They will!'

'They won't because I'm not going back. Because I don't have any f-friends, Mum. Everyone hates me . . . they *do* . . .'

'Oh, now that's not true! What about Lucy?'

'Hates me. She was seeing Rupert as well. When he chose me, she moved out.'

Oh Lord. So much she hadn't known. So much Jem had been keeping from her. Determined not to give up, Ginny said, 'Well, there's Davy.'

'Ha, he hates me too. And he's best friends with Lucy now. That's where she moved to when she left the flat.' Pulling her messy face away from Ginny's shoulder, Jem said, 'I don't have anywhere to live any more. I lost my job in the pub today. And on Friday my course tutor called me into his office and gave me this big long lecture on how disappointed he is with me. He thinks I'm going to fail my exams. And he's right, I am going to fail them, so what's the point of taking them? I was so worried about it yesterday,' Jem raced on, 'I didn't know what to do, but now that everything else has happened I don't have to worry any more. Because I've made up my mind, I'm not going back.'

'Sweetheart, you can't—'

'Mum, I *can*.' Nodding vigorously, Jem clutched Ginny's arms. 'I gave university a try and it didn't work out. So that's it. I've decided. I'm going to move back in with you.'

'**E**xcuse me? I don't want to be a nuisance.' The elderly female customer on table four tentatively touched Ginny's arm as she passed. 'But, um, do you think I could have my credit card back?'

Oh God.

'What are you looking for?' Finn found her two minutes later, rifling through a pile of menus and the sheaf of credit card slips.

'Mrs Black's credit card. I've lost it.'

'First rule of stealing credit cards,' Finn observed. 'Try not to let the rightful owner see who stole it.'

'What did I *do* with the damn thing?' In desperation Ginny peered into the bowl of white roses on the bar.

'Panic over.' Having opened the till, Finn held up the missing Visa card. 'In with the tenners.'

Ginny fanned herself vigorously. 'Sorry, brain's gone AWOL.'

'I'd already noticed.'

Damn, so he'd spotted her earlier, trying to serve puddings to the party on table eleven waiting for their starters.

'They didn't mind.' Defensively, she said, 'They laughed about it.'

'I know they did. It's not a criticism. I'm just saying you're a bit distracted.'

'A lot distracted.'

'Anything you want to talk about?'

'Yes please.' Ginny nodded, grateful for the offer. Her brain was in such a muddle she badly needed an impartial opinion from someone she could trust.

'Look, it's ten past two. Can you hang in there until three? When everyone's gone we'll have a proper chat, OK?'

'I don't know what to do,' Ginny concluded an hour later. They were sitting at one of the tables by the window, drinking espressos. She had told Finn everything. 'I was so devastated when Jem left home . . . in one way this is a dream come true. I can't think of anything nicer than having her home with me again. But I want what's best for Jem and I'm not sure that's it. I don't want to force her to go back, but what if she leaves and regrets it for the rest of her life?'

Finn, having paused for a moment, resumed stirring sugar into his coffee. 'She can take a degree when she's eighty-five. There's no age limit.'

'I know, I know there isn't. But she'd like to do it now, if only everything else hadn't gone wrong. She's always been so happy and popular. Losing her friends has knocked her for six and she just feels so alone. It breaks my heart, it really does.' Through the window Ginny saw Tamsin emerge from the flat with Mae on her hip.

'OK, this is only my opinion but Jem's almost finished her first year. Exams are coming up and it seems a shame not to take them,' said Finn. 'Then she's got the summer break to decide what to do.'

Ginny experienced a rush of gratitude. 'That's what I think too.'

Glancing across the courtyard as Tamsin and Mae disappeared inside the antiques centre, Finn continued, 'And after that, it's up to her. She can find another flat to share, make new friends, carry on with the course. Or stay down here with you. Or she might decide to try something completely different, take some time out and go travelling. Like Dan did.' He pointed through the window at the green-painted van trundling over the gravel. 'He spent two years going round the world after finishing his PhD.'

'Dan has a PhD? In what?'

'Astrophysics.'

Blimey. Ginny watched as Dan, lugging crates of fruit and veg out of the back of the van, loped off in the direction of the kitchen. She'd never known that about him. And he'd ended up as a delivery driver, so what did that tell you about astrophysics?

'Did you go to university?'

Amused, Finn shook his head. 'Too busy working for a firm of auctioneers, learning about antiques before setting up my own business.'

Ginny sighed. And he'd ended up doing all right for himself. 'I still don't know what to do about Jem.'

'What does her dad say?'

Tuh, Ginny had phoned Gavin this morning and he'd been no use either. 'That it's up to Jem.'

'Cheer up. Everything'll sort itself out.' Finn's gaze softened, distracting her with the kind of thoughts she didn't allow herself to think any more. 'Give her a few days to work things through.'

'That's the other thing Gavin said. I just wish—'

'AAAARRRRGH!' The ear-splitting scream jolted both of them; in a split second Finn was out of his seat. Through the window Ginny saw Tamsin racing across the gravel in her tiny skirt and spindly high heels, to where Mae was sitting behind Dan's van being cautiously investigated by Stiller.

'Get away from her, you *beast*,' Tamsin yelled as Stiller interestedly sniffed Mae's face. Swooping down like a bony eagle, she scooped Mae up into her arms. Stiller, disappointed at having lost his new playmate, waggled his tail and licked hopefully at Mae's dangling feet.

'UGH! NO! *Filthy* animal! Are you out of your *mind*?' Tamsin roared as Dan rounded the corner of the restaurant. 'Letting a dog run loose to attack an innocent *baby*?'

Poor Dan turned white with horror, searching for signs of blood.

Finn was out of the door now with Ginny inches behind him. 'OK, calm down, nobody's been attacked.'

'But they could have been,' screeched Tamsin, long hair swinging as she inspected Mae for signs of injury. 'That monster could have done anything!'

Dan stammered, 'Oh God, I'm so sorry, I had no *idea* . . .'

'Dan, it's all right.' Finn took control of the situation, gesturing with his palms down that Dan wasn't to get upset. 'What I want to know is how Mae came to be on her own out here.' He looked at Tamsin, who immediately tightened her grip on Mae and went on the defensive.

'Oh, so this is my fault, is it? I put my daughter down for two seconds because she didn't want to be carried. All I did was say hi to Tom and ask how things were going. The next moment I looked down and Mae had crawled out of the shop. In two *seconds*,' Tamsin declared vehemently, holding her thumb and forefinger half an inch apart for added emphasis. 'You know how fast she can scoot along when she wants to.'

'I do,' Finn nodded. 'But not fast enough to get away if a car had driven into the courtyard.'

Tamsin's voice grew shriller. 'I was listening out for cars! My God, do you think I want my baby to be run over? If I'd heard an engine I'd have been there. But to let a dog loose is just . . . irresponsible.'

Poor Stiller, alarmed by all the shouting, had by this time backed away and pressed himself against Dan's corduroy trouser legs. Blissfully unaware of the kerfuffle she had caused, Mae clapped her hands together and burbled, 'Dogga-dogga-bleuwwwww.'

'OK, let's calm down.' Finn was clearly keen to avoid a slanging match. 'Mae's fine, nothing happened.'

'Nothing *happened*? God, she reeks! Smell her,' Tamsin ordered. 'That bloody dog slobbered all over my baby—and it's not even a pedigree!'

Dan and Stiller were by now both quivering with shame. Rushing to their defence Ginny said, 'Tamsin, Stiller's the sweetest, gentlest dog you could ever meet. I promise you, he wouldn't hurt anyone. Mae would never come to any harm with him.' Her tone was placating, meant to make Tamsin feel better, but Tamsin was by this time beyond reassurance.

'No harm? Are you serious? A stinking filthy dog crawling with germs licks my daughter's face and you think that's *safe*?' Her eyes wide, she said hysterically, 'My God, and I thought you were a competent mother! If that's how you feel I won't be asking you to baby-sit again.'

Excellent, thought Ginny, because I wouldn't do it anyway.

And by the way, Finn deserves *so* much better than you.

The excitement among the crowd was palpable, fans buzzing with growing anticipation as the hands of the clock moved towards seven thirty. It wasn't often that a genuine A-list Hollywood celebrity came to Bristol to sign copies of their autobiography, but Marcus McBride was on his way. Now forty, he had been a true star for almost twenty years, something of a hellraiser early on in his career, but talented and dedicated enough to get away with it. With his dark, unconventional looks, undoubted intelligence and quirky sense of humour, women all over the world had fallen for Marcus McBride's charms. The opportunity to buy his just-published book, have it signed by Marcus himself and actually get to shake his hand had been just too good to pass up.

'Look, I bet that's him!' Lucy pointed up at the grey sky and hundreds of pairs of eyes followed the direction of her arm as the faint winking lights of a helicopter appeared in the distance.

'It's starting to rain.' Davy pulled a face as a raindrop splashed into his left eye. 'You know, we could always forge his signature, pretend we met him and just go for a drink instead.'

But he said it good-naturedly, knowing it wasn't an option. Lucy was looking forward to seeing Marcus McBride. And his mother would have his guts for garters.

'Poor Rhona, missing out on all this.' Lucy was still watching as the helicopter grew larger. 'She'd have loved it.'

Davy smiled, because his mum had never made any secret of her crush on Marcus McBride. When she'd heard he was coming down to do a book-signing in Bristol she had been beside herself with excitement. It was just a shame she wasn't able to come down to the shopping centre herself.

The helicopter landed somewhere behind the complex and everyone in the hundreds-long queue began mentally preparing themselves. Lucy checked her camera for the umpteenth time. 'I'll take loads of photos,' she had told Rhona, 'of Marcus and Davy together when he signs the book.'

'Bless you.' Rhona had smiled, touched by her thoughtfulness.

'Your collar's crooked,' Lucy told Davy now, busily straightening it. 'There, that's better.'

'I'm sure it'll make all the difference. Along with this.' Davy ruefully ruffled his new haircut, still unused to it. Lucy had dragged him along to a trendy salon, standing behind him like a prison warder until she was completely satisfied with the short, spiky cut the stylist had teased out of his previously long, straggly, and determinedly unstylish hair.

'Stop moaning, it looks great.'

'Get a move on,' the man behind them murmured impatiently. 'The queue's moving.'

It was, but with several hundred people ahead of them Davy wasn't holding his breath. Marcus McBride hadn't even made his entrance into the bookshop yet.

'Look at him, that's the kind of man I could go for.' Now they'd shuffled along a bit, Lucy was able to drool over a huge promotional poster of Marcus in the shop window. 'I wonder what he'd do if I kissed him?'

'Nothing,' said Davy. 'It's only a poster.'

'*You*.' Lucy dug him in the ribs. 'I'm going to miss you when I move out of your mum's.' Tilting her head to one side she said, 'Remember when you had that big crush on me? Whatever happened to that?'

'I don't know. Just kind of evaporated.'

'And now you don't fancy me any more. At *all*.' She pulled a tragic face. 'It's not very flattering, you know.'

'Sorry.' Davy grinned. 'Don't take it personally.'

'But you were besotted with me.'

Davy shrugged. He was glad his inconvenient crush on Lucy had subsided of its own accord, to be replaced by an easy camaraderie. Because he was no longer hopelessly tongue-tied in her presence they were able to banter together like . . . well, best friends.

He inhaled a blast of the peppermint chewing gum being noisily chewed by the man behind them. Lucy had picked up a sheaf of details from a flat-letting agency on the way home this afternoon. He would miss her too.

Aloud Davy said, 'You don't have to go.'

She slipped an arm through his, gave it a grateful squeeze. 'I know I don't have to. But I should. Your mum's fantastic and I love her to bits, but I can't stay on for ever. The whole point of leaving home and being a student is so you can live like a student and do studenty things.'

'Making a mess, having all your friends round, getting drunk, sleeping with people your parents wouldn't approve of,' said Davy.

'Arguing about who finished the milk and put the empty carton back in the fridge.'

'Sorry, I forgot that one.'

'Wondering where the terrible smell's coming from, then finally discovering an open tin of tuna under the living-room sofa.'

'That old classic.' Davy shook his head sympathetically. 'I can see why you miss it so much.'

'There are good bits too. Like borrowing your flatmate's clothes,' Lucy pointed out. 'And sharing each other's make-up.'

They fell silent for a couple of seconds, both thinking.

'I wonder what's happened to Jem?' Lucy spoke at last. 'No one's seen her all week.'

Davy knew how hurt Lucy had been when the whole Jem and Rupert thing had come out, with Jem choosing to stay with Rupert rather than siding with her best friend.

'Maybe she's ill.' But they'd both heard about the mixer-gun incident and Jem's instant dismissal from the pub. 'I could give her a quick ring,' he suggested. 'Check she's all right.'

But Lucy was already shaking her head. 'Don't bother. She's got Rupert to look after her.' Pressing her lips together she said, 'Anyway, let's not talk about them. Let's talk about whether this damn queue is ever going to move . . .'

At that moment, almost as if she had caused it to happen, a whoop of excitement went up inside the shop, indicating that Marcus McBride had made his entrance. Flashbulbs went off like fireworks, people were jumping up and down to get a better view and applause broke out.

Over the course of the next thirty minutes the queue edged forward, into the back of the store at last. Shop assistants demonstrated how to hold open their already-bought copies of Marcus McBride's autobiography at the title page, ready for his pen to make its illegible squiggle. As they neared the front of the queue and the desk at which he was sitting, they saw him for the first time. Flanked by burly minders and uniformed security staff with hi-tech earpieces, Marcus was squiggling away and flashing his famous smile with production-line regularity. Anyone who'd hoped to stand and chat for a minute or two was firmly moved along. Nothing was allowed to interrupt the flow.

More minty fumes indicated the arrival of a fresh piece of chewing gum in the mouth of the man behind them, ensuring he had nice breath for his fleeting encounter with Hollywood royalty.

Almost there now. Marcus McBride was wearing a tight pink T-shirt, black jeans and blue cowboy boots because he'd reached the level of film stardom that meant you could throw on whatever you liked and not be laughed at. Which must be nice, Davy thought with feeling, as the overweight woman in front of him readied herself for her turn.

'Got it open to the right page? Right, off you go,' ordered the strict sergeant-major type in charge at the head of the queue. The woman tottered up to the desk, said breathlessly, 'You're my favourite actor!' and held out her book.

Smile, squiggle, smile, all over.

'Next,' barked the sergeant major as Lucy readied herself to take the all-important photo.

'Hurry *up*,' the man behind Davy hissed, blasting him with mint.

Davy moved forward, held out his book and self-consciously half turned so that the camera wouldn't just get a shot of his back. He felt rather than saw the signature being scrawled on the title page of the book he was still holding and, glancing behind Lucy, noted that the man behind her was fidgeting in an agitated fashion with something in his trouser pocket.

Flash went Lucy's camera, temporarily blinding Davy. He hoped he hadn't had a gormless expression on his face. In the split second that followed, Davy glimpsed another flash, of metal this time. Blinking, he realised that Mint Man had pulled a knife from his pocket and was now gripping it tightly in his right hand, keeping it hidden from view beneath his jacket. The sergeant major was making urgent sweeping movements with his arms. It was Mint Man's turn next.

'No!' yelled Davy, realising that no one else had spotted the knife.

Mint Man shot him a look of wild-eyed fury and launched himself at the desk. Davy, who had always loathed rugby at school, flung himself at Mint Man and tackled him to the ground. God, it hurt. All the air was punched from his lungs and Mint Man was now roaring like an enraged bull elephant. Dazedly Davy became aware that he was being crushed beneath a scrum of bouncers and security guards. Next moment he felt himself being hauled to his feet. He could hear screams of panic all around him, interspersed with barked orders from security and loud staccato cursing from Mint Man.

Someone yelled, 'Oh God, he's been stabbed,' and Davy stumbled towards Lucy, feeling sick at the thought that the knife had gone into the madman on the ground. Then he saw the look of terror in Lucy's eyes and heard her gasp, 'Oh, Davy, oh my God, *someone call an ambulance* . . .'

'**H**e's been arrested and taken down to the police station. Long psychiatric history, it turns out.' The sergeant-major type, who was actually Marcus McBride's PR manager, brought Davy and Lucy up-to-date in one of the offices behind the shop. 'Apparently, Princess Margaret told him to do it.'

'This was my best shirt.' Davy stuck his finger through the slash in the bloodstained blue and green striped cotton and looked mournful.

'I'm sure we can come to some arrangement.'

'There.' The doctor finished applying the last of the skin sutures and peeled off his surgical gloves. 'You'll live.'

'I'll call it my duelling scar.' Davy inspected the cleaned-up knife wound inflicted by Mint Man's panicky response to being brought down. At twenty centimetres long it had bled profusely and looked spectacular but was actually far less painful than it appeared, which he didn't mind at all. If it had been a stabbing injury rather than a shallow slice across his chest, on the other hand . . . well, the thought of it was enough to make him feel a bit queasy.

The door to the office opened then and Marcus McBride walked in, exuding charisma.

'Hey, kid. You did good.' He shook Davy's hand and this time his smile was genuine. 'You're a hero.'

Embarrassed, Davy said, 'I'm not really the heroic type.'

Outside, they had to have their picture taken by a clamour of photographers. Davy, wearing his bloodstained shirt, stood awkwardly while Marcus McBride rested his arm across his shoulders. Still in a daze, Davy told the waiting journalists his name. They wanted to see the wound across his chest. When they asked him how he felt, he said, 'Like a Page Three girl,' and everyone laughed.

Five minutes later the press were despatched. Marcus said, 'Seriously, you did great. I don't know how to thank you. I'd offer you a signed copy of my book, but . . .'

'We've already got one.' Lucy held up the carrier bag containing the copy Davy had flung aside before tackling Mint Man to the ground. Luckily it didn't have blood on it.

'We'll sort something out.' The sergeant major consulted his watch. 'Now, is your car here or do you need transport home?'

'We caught the bus,' said Davy.

'No problem. I'll organise a car.' Taking out his mobile phone, the sergeant major began rattling out orders.

An idea had come into Davy's mind; he plucked up the courage to voice it. 'Actually,' Davy looked at Marcus, 'you know you said you didn't know how to thank me?'

'Yes.'

'Well, my mum would love to meet you. She couldn't be here tonight but she's only ten minutes away.'

'Sorry, son.' Having concluded his call, the sergeant-major said firmly, 'Can't do anything now, we're behind schedule as it is. Some other time, OK?'

Deflated, Davy said, 'Oh. OK.'

Rhona finished the washing-up and took a cup of tea through to the living room. She switched on the TV and semi-watched a programme about a woman so addicted to shopping for new clothes that she was on the verge of being declared bankrupt.

At least that was something that she was never going to suffer from. Even observing the woman on TV as she rushed through Marks & Spencer grabbing armfuls of dresses off the rails made Rhona feel jittery and nervous.

Oh well, never mind about that. It was a shame she hadn't been able to go down to the shopping centre this evening but she couldn't help the way she was. Maybe in time the panicky sensations would subside of their own accord. And at least Davy and Lucy were down there getting a book signed for her, so she wasn't completely missing out . . .

When the doorbell rang some time later, Rhona padded out to the hall. She opened the front door and looked at Marcus McBride.

For several seconds she carried on looking at him, as if he were a crossword clue she couldn't quite work out. Because it couldn't *really* be Marcus McBride.

'Rhona?'

'Yes.' How incredible, she could still speak. Well, just about.

'Hi, I'm Marcus.' The visitor on the doorstep took her hand and gravely shook it.

'How . . . how, how . . . I mean, how . . .?'

'Davy happened to mention that you'd like to meet me. And I said great, because I wanted to meet you too.'

Rhona wondered if she had fallen asleep in front of the TV and was in fact having a dream. Then again, her dreams had never been as good as this. Unsticking her tongue from the roof of her mouth, she said, 'Davy?'

'Your son?' Marcus broke into a smile. 'That's why I'm here. I want to tell you, he did a very brave thing tonight. I'm very grateful to him.'

'*My* son did a brave thing?' Rhona closed her eyes for a moment;

when she opened them again Marcus McBride was still there, waiting on her doorstep and looking incredibly *real*. 'Um . . . where is Davy?'

'Over there in the car. With Lucy. Look, I can't stay long, my PR guy's giving me a hard time. But when Davy said you'd like a visit, how could I refuse? He's fine, by the way.'

'Fine? What d'you mean, fine? Why wouldn't he be fine?'

And, surreally, Marcus McBride explained what had happened at the book-signing. Rhona's stomach clenched with horror and disbelief and she ran down the path to the waiting car. Wrenching open the rear door she shouted, 'Davy, how *could* you? You might have been killed! Oh my God, look at your *shirt* . . .'

Lucy used up the rest of the film in her camera taking photos of Rhona and Marcus McBride. Finally Marcus gave Rhona a kiss on the cheek.

'Now I really have to go. Thanks again.' He shook Davy's hand and said, 'You take care of yourself.'

'Bye,' said Davy.

The car pulled away. Rhona clapped her hand to her chest and said, 'I can't let you out of my sight for two minutes.'

Davy rolled his eyes. 'Mum, there's no need to fuss. *I'm OK.*'

'**O**h!' Expecting the postman and getting Finn instead came as some- thing of a shock. Probably for Finn too, thought Ginny, clutching the front edges of her dressing gown together and praying her hair wasn't too scarily bed-heady.

'Sorry. I was on my way into Portsilver and I wondered if you'd seen today's paper.'

'It's eight o'clock. I haven't seen the kettle yet. Why?' Ginny reached out for the newspaper he was holding but Finn hesitated.

'Your daughter's friends in Bristol, Lucy and Davy. What's Davy's surname?'

Ginny searched her brain. 'Um . . . Stokes.'

Finn looked relieved. 'It is the right one then.' He handed over the folded newspaper and added, 'Bit of excitement up in Bristol. I thought it might give Jem the excuse she needs to ring her friends.'

The doorbell had evidently woken Jem too. Appearing on the stairs behind Ginny, she said evenly, 'I haven't got any friends in Bristol.'

'No? Oh, well, then,' Finn retrieved the paper once more, 'you won't be interested in seeing this.'

Jem nodded at the newspaper. 'What's Davy done?'

'If he's not your friend, why would you care?'

'Oh, for heaven's sake, give it to me!' Bursting with curiosity, Ginny snatched the folded paper. 'I want to know!'

Finn said with amusement, 'Don't show Jem.'

Ginny's jaw dropped as she found the piece. 'Oh, good grief.'

'OK,' grumbled Jem, peering over her shoulder. 'I want to know too.'

Finn left them to it. Together Jem and Ginny devoured the article.

'Thank goodness he's all right,' said Ginny. 'He could have been killed.'

'Mm.'

'Sweetheart, Finn's right. You should give Davy a ring.'

'I can't.' Clearly emotional, Jem failed to control her wobbling lower lip. 'There's no point.'

'There's every point. You can congratulate him!'

'I might not get the chance,' Jem said miserably. 'He'd probably just put the phone down.'

It was no good; Ginny did her best to reassure her but Jem was adamant, convinced that any attempt at contact with Davy or Lucy would be met with a snub.

Her unhappiness was so apparent, Ginny thought her own heart would break.

Twenty-six hours later and Ginny's forehead was taut with concentration. It had been seven months since she'd last made the journey up the M5 to Bristol and that time she hadn't needed to pay attention to the first bit of the return journey because Davy had been sitting next to her in the passenger seat instructing her when to turn left and right.

Now she was on her own, attempting to retrace the route through Henbury on memory alone, and it wasn't an easy task. Had they turned right at the Old Crow pub or gone straight over the roundabout? When they'd reached the junction past the petrol station, had they turned left? Oh God, this was hopeless; at this rate come midnight she'd still be driving round in circles.

It took a while—OK, another forty minutes of being lost—but finally Ginny turned into a street she dimly recognised. This was it, she was sure. And the one thing she did remember was the tidy, pocket-sized front garden and the royal-blue front door. Trundling along in second gear like a kerb crawler, she passed brown doors, red doors, white doors, green doors . . .

Ooh, there it was. At last.

Would Davy even be in?

And would Jem ever speak to her again when she found out what she'd done?

Oh well, Finn had given her the day off work and she'd driven all the way up to Bristol for a reason. It would be silly to turn round and go home now.

The front door was opened by an anxious-looking woman who clearly didn't welcome the interruption. Glancing at her watch, then up at Ginny, she said distractedly, 'Yes?'

'Hi. Is Davy here?'

'Sorry, he's out. Are you another journalist?'

Ginny took a deep breath. 'No, I'm Jem Holland's mum.'

'Oh, thank goodness! Come on in, Davy's about to be on the radio.'

Not thank goodness she was Jem's mum, Ginny realised as Davy's mother bundled her into the house, but thank goodness she didn't have to miss hearing her son being interviewed.

Together they sat in the kitchen and listened to the old-fashioned wireless on the kitchen table. After fifteen minutes it was all over.

'Phew, sorry about that. I'm Rhona,' said Davy's mother. 'Davy's never been on the radio before.' Overcome with emotion she wiped the corners of her eyes with a tissue. 'Was that presenter having a bit of a dig, d'you think?'

Ginny knew at once what she meant. To begin with it had all been about what a hero Davy was, but towards the end of the interview the presenter had said slyly, 'And I gather you still live at home with your mother, which seems extraordinary to me. Does that not set you apart from your fellow students?'

Davy, of course, had roundly denied it but the interviewer had been unconvinced. 'You have to admit, though, it's an unusual situation. Most young people starting university can't wait to grasp their independence. Did your mother not want you to move out, did she put pressure on you to stay, or was it your own decision? Are you a bit of a mummy's boy at heart?'

Now, with the radio turned off, Ginny wondered what she was supposed to say. She shrugged. 'Honestly? Yes, I suppose he was having a dig. But who cares what he thinks? If Davy wants to stay at home, that's his choice.'

Rhona nodded slowly, lost in thought. Then she looked over at Ginny. 'It was you who gave Davy a lift home once from Clifton, wasn't it? He told me you live in Cornwall. So you're up here visiting your daughter?'

'No. Jem's at home in Cornwall. She's broken up with her horrible boyfriend.'

'Rupert.' Rhona's lip curled. 'I've heard all about him.'

'Jem's eighteen. She made a big mistake. And now she wants to give up university, come back home and live with me.'

'How wonderful. But you don't seem that thrilled. Don't you want her back?'

Rhona clearly didn't understand. Ginny exhaled and twisted the bracelet on her wrist. 'Of course I do, more than anything. But I want what's right for Jem, not what's right for me.'

'Oh God,' said Rhona. 'You're so brave.'

Ginny shrugged. 'I don't feel it.'

They sat in silence for a while. Finally Rhona announced, 'I had a brain haemorrhage, you know, four years ago. In British Home Stores.'

'You did?' Ginny was startled. 'I didn't know that.'

'No? Well, I don't suppose you would. Davy doesn't feel it's anyone else's business why he chooses to stay at home. But that's the reason, even though I was one of the lucky ones. Made a good recovery.' Rhona tapped her left leg. 'Apart from a bit of a limp. But it frightened the living daylights out of me, I can tell you. I've been terrified of it happening again and not having anyone around to help me. I get panicky in shops too, which isn't ideal. That's why Davy and Lucy were the ones queuing up to see Marcus McBride. Because I couldn't face it myself.'

'I'm not surprised,' exclaimed Ginny. 'Oh, please,' she added as Rhona's eyes filled with tears. 'You mustn't blame yourself for what happened to Davy.'

'I don't.' Rhona fished up her sleeve for a tissue. 'It's not that. I love having Davy at home with me, but it's not fair on him, is it? I'm not an invalid, after all. And he's a young lad with his own life to live.'

Ginny nodded in agreement. 'He is.'

'I can't do it yet.' Rhona swallowed. 'But I'll do it soon. I know it's nearly time to let him go.'

'It doesn't mean he's going to stop loving you,' said Ginny.

Rhona managed a watery smile. 'He'd better not.'

Davy arrived home fifteen minutes later. Rhona, greeting him at the door, hugged him hard and exclaimed, 'You were brilliant on the radio. I was so proud! It sounded just like you!'

Then she murmured something Ginny couldn't make out and sent him ahead into the kitchen where she was waiting for him.

'Hello, Davy.'

'Hello, Mrs Holland.'

Mrs Holland. So polite. Ginny said, 'You're looking . . . smart.'

He rubbed a hand self-consciously over his head. 'Lucy made me have my hair cut.'

'It suits you.'

'Thanks.' He paused. 'Is Jem all right?'

Would Jem ever forgive her for being an interfering mother?

'No.' Ginny shook her head, a lump springing into her throat. 'No, Davy, she's not.'

It was five o'clock on Saturday afternoon and Jem was alone in the house, having spent the day with her father. Poor Dad, he'd done his best to cheer her up and probably thought he'd succeeded, but lovely though it was to see him again she'd been glad to get back to the sanctuary of her old bedroom, released from the pressure of smiling and pretending to be fine.

Mum was still working at the restaurant, Laurel had gone shopping in Newquay and it was a relief to be on her own, although watching *Moulin Rouge* on DVD probably hadn't been the best idea she'd ever had. Sprawled on the bed with a tin of Laurel's home-made biscuits, Jem's eyes brimmed at the thought of poor gorgeous Ewan MacGregor and the heartbreak in store for him when Nicole Kidman finally died in his arms. Why couldn't she be adored by someone as wonderful as Ewan, who would never have had sex in the shower with an old girl-friend behind Nicole's back? How could she have been so stupid as to be taken in by Rupert's pseudo charms? Why, *why* hadn't she marched out of the flat with Lucy? She must have been out of her mind.

Tears slid down Jem's cheeks and dripped off her chin as she gazed blindly at the TV screen. Nicole was looking stunning while elegantly coughing up blood when the doorbell rang. Without enthusiasm Jem hauled herself off the bed and padded downstairs.

Lucy was on the doorstep.

Dumbstruck, Jem gazed at her. Past Lucy, perched on the front wall, was Davy wearing an extremely green shirt.

Jem's heart was pounding; she was hideously aware of her swollen, froggy eyes. At last she said, 'What are you doing here?'

'Oh, Jem, look at the state of you. Why do you think we're here?' For a second it seemed as if Lucy might burst into tears as well. Holding out her arms and shaking her head she said, 'We've come to take you back with us.'

'Really?' Jem's bottom lip began to tremble.

'Really.'

'Oh, Luce, I'm sorry. So sorry for everything.'

'I know. Come here.'

They hugged and laughed and cried a bit on the doorstep. Then Davy, ambling up the path, said, 'I'm not really a huggy person,' and gave Jem's shoulder an awkward pat instead.

'I can't believe you came all the way to Cornwall.' Overwhelmed, Jem said, 'How did you know this address? Did you catch the train?'

Lucy's dark eyes shone. 'Your mum came to see us.'

'My *mum*? When?' Did Ginny have a tardis she didn't know about?

'Today,' said Davy.

'But she's working at the restaurant, they've got a wedding . . . oh . . .'

Lucy said gravely, 'She lied.'

'She's just gone to the shop to pick up some food. We're staying for the night. You can invite us in if you like.' Davy rested his hand lightly on his chest. 'It's not doing my terrible knife injury any good, you know, standing out here.'

'Oh God, of course, come in!'

'He's having you on.' Lucy rolled her eyes. 'It's nothing more than a scratch. I could have done better with one of my fingernails.'

'I want to hear all about it,' said Jem as she ushered them inside.

The change in Jem was unbelievable, heartwarming. Jem, hugging her, had said, 'Mum, I can't believe you did this. Everything's sorted out now. I'm so happy.'

'She just couldn't bear the thought of having you back here with her,' said Lucy. 'She was desperate.'

Ginny smiled at them, because every maternal fibre of her being longed to hold on to Jem for ever, keeping her safe from harm at home. They were young, they couldn't begin to understand that making it possible for her daughter to leave again was one of the most grown-up things she'd ever done.

But this time, she knew, Jem would be happy. For the last few weeks of term all three would be staying with Rhona in Henbury. Davy was moving into the tiny bedroom that had been Lucy's, and Lucy and Jem were taking over his old room. Together, they were going to put all their energy into revising for their exams and, hopefully, Jem would be able to put in enough work to pass. Then, after the summer break, Lucy and Jem would get a flat-share together.

All in all it was a happy ending. But arriving back in Portsilver at midnight, after driving the three of them back to Bristol, had been a depressing experience for Ginny. Laurel was upstairs asleep and the house had seemed unbearably quiet. She had gone to bed feeling empty, lonely and bereft all over again, unable to stop herself thinking, *what about me? Where's my happy ending?*

Chapter 11

'STOP OGLING the boss.'

Ginny jumped, unaware that Evie had emerged from the restaurant kitchen. 'I wasn't!'

'Yes, you were.' Evie's eyes danced. 'Mind you, I can't say I blame you. Gorgeous shoulders. Spectacular bum.'

'Sshh.' Did Evie have to be quite so loud? Finn was only twenty feet away, showing out the last diners of the afternoon. And now he was closing the door, turning to see what all the shushing was about.

'What's going on?'

'Nothing.' Evie, who had no shame, said, 'We were just admiring your body.'

'*You* were,' said Ginny, glasses clinking as she indignantly gathered them up.

'Fine, I was admiring. You were ogling.'

'I wasn't, I was thinking about Jem.' Keen to change the subject, Ginny said, 'She phoned this morning to tell me her tutor's really pleased with all the work she's put in over the last couple of weeks. He thinks she might scrape through her exams after all.'

'That's great news.' Evie knew how worried she'd been about Jem. 'But I still know an ogle when I see one. I have an eye for these things.'

Life, Ginny thought, would be so much easier if only she could get over this hopeless, pointless, *ridiculous* crush.

As if to hammer the point home, the front door opened and Tamsin burst into the restaurant with Mae on her hip.

'I'm in love.' Tamsin's eyes were shining.

Which was the kind of announcement that might have got Ginny's hopes up, except that in her free hand Tamsin was waving some kind of glossy brochure. Rushing over to Finn, she gave him a don't-smudge-my-lipstick kiss and said, 'Darling, you have to see it. Six bedrooms, sea views, Clive Christian kitchen and an ensuite bathroom to die for. It's the house of our dreams, a proper family home. I told the agent we'd meet him there at five o'clock.'

'Six bedrooms.' Finn studied the brochure in alarm. 'Jesus, have you seen how much they're asking for it?'

'That's only a guide price, we can make an offer.' Eagerly pointing to the photos, Tamsin said, 'Look at the snooker room. And that garden!' She turned her bewitching smile on him. 'And six bedrooms isn't so many. After all, we don't want Mae to be an only child.'

Ginny felt a bit sick but there was no escaping their domestic bliss. Tamsin insisted on showing her and Evie the brochure, cooing delightedly over every detail of the house and explaining how unsuitable the flat was now that Mae was walking.

'We have to get it. It's just perfect.' Swishing back her long hair, Tamsin gave Ginny a sympathetic look. 'I bet you'd love to live in a house like this?'

Ginny wondered what Tamsin would do if she said, 'Yes, but only if I could live in it with Finn.'

Obviously she didn't say it. Heavens, what was the matter with her today? Half an hour ago she'd been quietly ogling Finn from a distance. (Wouldn't Evie be delighted to know she'd been right?) And now here she was, fantasising about making smart remarks to her rival.

Except Tamsin wasn't a rival, was she? Tamsin was having a proper grown-up relationship with Finn, rather than a sad, fantasy one.

Dutifully, Ginny said, 'It looks wonderful.'

'Dadadablaaa,' sang Mae, clapping her hands at Finn.

'You want to go to Daddy? Here, you take her. She weighs a ton.' Having passed Mae over to him, Tamsin gazed raptly at the two of them, then back at the photograph of the house. 'How could any child not be happy, growing up in a place like this?'

Driving home from the restaurant, Ginny resolved to get a grip, put the whole Finn thing behind her and get on with her life. Make the most of what she had, which was a *lot*. Healthy happy daughter. A job she enjoyed. A nice house. And there were so many other things to take pleasure in too, like art, books, walking on the beach, listening to music . . .

Feeling more positive already, Ginny buzzed down the car windows and made a conscious decision to find joy in those small things in life that it was only too easy to overlook, like the sunshine warming her face and those delicious little white clouds dotting the sky. Cornwall was beautiful. David Gray was singing on the radio and she loved David Gray. Turning up the volume, Ginny was tempted to sing along, but that might spoil it; the last thing David needed was her caterwauling mucking up his beautiful heartfelt vocals. She'd just listen instead and think of other miraculous things like the crumbly deliciousness of Laurel's lemon drizzle cake, the incomparable sight of dolphins frolicking in the sea off Portsilver Point, the smell of hot tarmac . . .

Oh, yes, hot tarmac, one of the all-time greats. Ginny slowed to a halt and beamed at the middle-aged man holding the STOP/GO lollipop sign currently directing her to STOP.

'Lovely day,' Ginny called over to the lollipop man, who was wrinkled and leathery from long years in the sun.

'Too nice to be working.' He beamed back at her, evidently a cheery soul. Well, why wouldn't he be, able to enjoy the smell of fresh tarmac all day long? With a flourish he swivelled the lollipop sign round to GO and Ginny gave him a little wave as she set off, breathing in deeply in order not to miss a single lungful of the hot, tarry deliciousness.

All too soon the moment was past, the joy behind her. Sniffing the air, desperate for one last hit and not finding it, Ginny was bereft. Half a mile further down the road and unable to bear it a second longer, she pulled into a driveway and rapidly reversed the car. It was no good; you couldn't open a bag of Maltesers and only eat one, could you? Exactly. And if she wanted to go back and experience the smell of tar again . . . well, was there anything wrong with that? It was one of life's harmless pleasures, for heaven's sake. What's more, it was free.

The lollipop man looked surprised when he saw her. As luck would have it, Ginny again found herself up against the STOP sign.

'Are you stalking me?' He winked at her. 'Look, I'd love to meet up with you for a drink but my old lady would have my guts for garters.'

Ginny grinned, 'guts for garters' always conjured up a wonderfully bizarre image in her mind. Then she got on with the serious business of inhaling the tar fumes which were, if such a thing was possible, even more irresistible this time.

'Forget something, did you?' Lollipop man nodded genially. 'Bad as my old lady, she'd forget her head if it wasn't screwed on.'

Jolly banter over, he swivelled the lollipop and waved Ginny through for the second time. She breathed in the addictive scent of the tar as she passed it being spread like sticky jam on the other side of the road.

Moments later the elusive sense of familiarity finally clicked into place in her brain and Ginny realised when she had last been enthralled by the smell, so long ago now that it simply hadn't registered before.

It was when she'd been . . . Oh no, no, surely not . . .

Somehow, on autopilot, Ginny managed to park the car at only a slightly wonky angle in the town's central car park. When she climbed out, her legs almost gave way. OK, collapsing in a heap would just waste time and be an embarrassment. Girding herself, she clutched her handbag and headed for the shops.

At the threshold of Boots she stopped. The assistants knew her here; what would they think if they saw her come in and buy a . . . no, she'd have to go somewhere else.

There was a small pharmacy in St Aldam's Square that she'd never visited before. Having done the deed, Ginny emerged and hurried away, checking left and right as she went, making sure there was no one around who might recognise her and demand to know what was in her bag.

The public lavatories weren't ideal but getting home wasn't an option; that would take fifteen minutes and she had to know *now*. And they were at least very nice public lavatories, scrupulously clean and freshly painted, with bright hanging baskets of flowers outside.

Locking herself in the far cubicle, Ginny trembled as she unwrapped the packet and read the instructions. She peed on the stick and closed her eyes, waiting for the chemicals to do their thing. Outside the cubicle she could hear a mother trying to persuade her young daughter to wash her hands.

'Come on, Megan, be a good girl, don't splash.'

Time was up. Ginny opened her eyes and looked at the stick thing.

Oh God.

Oh *God*.

Ginny gazed blankly at the grey door of her cubicle and heard

Megan's mother say with resignation, 'Oh, you silly girl, *look* what you've done now. *That's* not very clever, is it?'

You're telling me, thought Ginny.

Gavin didn't mind having his bottom pinched. In fact he positively welcomed it. He just hadn't been expecting it to happen as he threaded his way along a crowded street in Padstow.

'Hello, stranger!' He threw out his arms and gave Bev a kiss, delighted to see her. 'I was hoping it'd be someone young, female and dazzlingly gorgeous.'

Bev, her smile lopsided, said, 'Oh, well, one out of three isn't bad.'

'Don't give me that. You wouldn't want to be twenty-one again. And for an older woman you're looking great.' Gavin admired her shiny dark hair, scarlet dress and voluptuous figure.

'And you still haven't signed up for those How to be a Diplomat evening classes.'

He beamed. 'I'm set in my ways. There's no hope for me. Anyway, fancy bumping into you here. We've missed you at the club.'

Bev shrugged. 'I gave up waiting for George Clooney to join. Anyway, you're looking well.' She admired Gavin's suit. 'Who'd have thought you could look so smart? I almost didn't recognise you without one of your lairy shirts on.'

'Business. Long boring meeting with a short boring client. How about you?'

'Much more fun. A very unboring meeting with a rather exciting new friend.' Bev's eyes sparkled as she moved back to the table she'd been sitting at when she'd jumped up to surprise him.

'Excellent. Can I meet her?'

'Very funny. It's a male friend.' Indicating with pride the empty beer bottle on the table next to her almost finished glass of wine, Bev said, 'But you're more than welcome to stay and say hello. He's just gone inside to buy the next round.'

'So you've found someone you like at last.' It was pretty obvious from the way her whole face was lit up that she was smitten.

'I know! Can you believe it? I stopped going to the club and told myself that from now on, if it was going to happen, it'd happen.' Bev clicked her fingers and beamed at him. 'And bam, a few weeks down the line, it did happen. Guess how we met!'

'You took a job as a stripper.'

'Gavin, you philistine, how did I ever fancy you? I was weeding my front garden! On my hands and knees with my big bum in the air, pulling up dandelions.'

Gavin the Philistine wisely kept his thoughts to himself. But it was undeniably an enticing mental image.

'When this guy who was walking past stopped at my gate.'

Of course he did, thought Gavin the Philistine.

'He was lost,' Bev went on. 'He asked me for directions to Lancaster Road.'

Oh yes, classic manoeuvre.

'And somehow we just clicked.' Bev clicked her fingers to demonstrate. 'It was incredible, we just carried on talking and didn't stop, there was this incredible . . . *chemistry*.'

Total pro.

'After about an hour he asked me if I'd like to meet him for a drink that evening. And that was it. I said yes, of course. We went out and had the most amazing time. It was as if we'd known each other for ever,' Bev said dreamily. 'At last, I'd found my perfect man. He's so kind and such a gentleman, so interested in *me*. It's almost too good to be true. This is only our third date but I've just got this *feeling* about Perry, I really think this could be—'

'Whoa,' Gavin abruptly halted her. 'What did you say?'

'It's only our third date. We met last Sunday.'

'Never mind that. Is his name Perry Kennedy?'

'Oh my God, yes it *is*! Do you know him?'

Up until that moment Gavin had simply recognised Bev's new chap as a fellow womaniser, a man after his own heart and where was the harm in that? Now, like plunging into the sea in diving boots, it struck him that there *was* harm in it. He hoped he wasn't as bad as Perry Kennedy. He'd never deliberately set out to deceive a woman.

Bev, her smile wavering, said, 'Why are you looking at me like that?'

'I know him. He's bad news. A fake.' Since there was no kind way to say it, Gavin didn't waste time wondering how to soften the blow. 'He went out with Ginny, duped her, played her for a fool. She found out he was shagging her best friend. And it turned out he's done it a thousand times before.'

Poor old Bev, the smile had well and truly melted from her face. Shock radiated from her. And any minute now, Perry would emerge from the bar with their drinks.

'I hate him for what he did to Ginny,' Gavin went on. 'He broke her heart'—OK, bit of an exaggeration—'and he'll break yours too.'

God, he hoped she wasn't about to burst into tears.

But Bev was made of sterner stuff. She exhaled slowly, sat back in her chair and said, 'Story of my life. I suppose I should be used to it by now. If something seems too good to be true, it probably is. And there was me, thinking my luck had changed.' She exhaled. 'Thinking I was irresistible.'

'Sweetheart, you are.' For an older woman anyway, Gavin allowed. 'All the more reason not to get involved with a bastard like that. Trust me, he's all pain and no gain. You need to cut and run.'

Bev glanced down at her shoes. 'Easier said than done in these heels.'

She was wearing red strappy four-inch stilettos adorned with butterflies, the shoes of a woman out to impress the new man in her life. Quite sexy, actually.

Gavin said, 'You could always take them off.'

'Oh God, why does this have to happen to me?' Bev glanced over her shoulder to see if Perry was on his way out.

'It doesn't only happen to you. Men like him need teaching a lesson.'

'Pot.' Her tone was dry. 'Kettle.'

'Ouch. That's me put in my place.' Gavin's eyes crinkled at the corners. 'I'd better get off, leave you to it.'

'Where are you going?'

'To get something to eat. Why?'

She shrugged. 'Could you do with some company?'

'Only if you promise not to keep nagging me about my terrible ways.'

Bev slipped her feet out of her stilettos, stood up and drained her glass of wine. 'And you aren't allowed to keep saying you could quite fancy me if only I wasn't so old. Just for once, try and be nice to me, OK? I'm a woman in crisis.'

Gavin winked and said, 'My favourite kind.'

The queue at the bar had been ridiculous. Having finally been served, Perry emerged with a drink in each hand. Bev was nowhere to be seen.

The table at which he and Bev had been sitting was now occupied by a family of four. Approaching them, Perry learned that it had been free when they'd got here.

He scanned the rest of the drinkers gathered outside. No one else was wearing a red dress. Had Bev gone inside to the loo and somehow managed to slip past him unnoticed?

Yet more waiting. She didn't return. Feeling increasingly foolish, Perry finally approached the group of office workers at the table behind the one now occupied by the family of four. 'Um . . . excuse me, did any of you notice what happened to the lady who was sitting over there? Dark hair, red dress . . .'

'She pulled.' A freckled, tufty-haired boy grinned at his friends.

'What do you mean?' Perry's shoulders stiffened.

'She was sitting there on her own. Then this guy walked past. The next moment she jumped up and launched herself at him. Pinched his bum and everything. They were all over each other.'

'They talked for a bit,' the girl at his side elaborated, 'then walked off together down the road.'

'She just went off with him?' Perry blinked in disbelief. 'What did he look like?'

'Forties. A bit overweight. Losing his hair at the front. Not exactly Pierce Brosnan.' The girl shrugged then said thoughtfully, 'He had a nice smile though. And sparkly eyes. He looked quite . . . fun.'

The boy sniggered. 'She obviously thought he was fun.'

Perry was in a state of disbelief. Bev had abandoned him for another man who wasn't even that good-looking. Gone off with him just like that, without so much as a goodbye.

How could she?

He'd never been so humiliated in his life.

Bev was smiling to herself.

'What?' said Gavin.

'I've just realised something.' She turned onto her side to face him. 'I bet I'm the oldest person you've ever slept with.'

'By a mile. But you know what? It wasn't as scary as I thought.'

'Cheek!' Bev hooked one of her bare legs over his.

'It's a compliment. Seriously.' In return Gavin pulled her against him. 'You know a lot of tricks.'

'Years of practice. Almost as many as you. And a man in his forties is past his sexual peak. Whereas I,' she trailed the tips of her fingernails in tantalising circles along his inner thigh, 'am a woman in my prime.'

'Past my peak? Now that's a slur I'm going to have to disprove.' He rolled her over, intent on making his point, but Bev wriggled away before he could pin her down.

'No time now. It's eight o'clock. I have to be at work by nine.'

This was frustrating but true. Neither of them had expected last night to end the way it had. Following dinner in Padstow, Gavin had invited Bev back to his house in Portsilver for a nightcap. At first they had talked about Perry Kennedy. Then they'd stopped talking about him because that was just depressing, and had moved on to other subjects instead. It was at this point that Gavin had realised how refreshing it was to be able to hold a flirtatious conversation with someone who had a brain, intellectual curiosity and a quick wit. Bev was terrific company, she made him laugh and she didn't look blank when he mentioned Nixon and Watergate. She knew who Siouxie Sioux was. She remembered a world before mobile phones.

OK, not everything they'd discussed had been intellectual.

After that, the rest had just happened. He'd been making coffee in the kitchen and Bev had been spooning sugar into his cup. His hand had accidentally brushed against hers and she'd jumped, spilling sugar all over the work surface. Amused, Gavin had said, 'Do I really have that effect on you?'

'Yes,' said Bev. 'You do.'

'When we were outside that wine bar you said you used to fancy me. Was that a joke?'

She shook her head. 'No, it was the truth.'

The next thing he knew, Gavin had found himself kissing Bev. Sugar crystals had scrunched underfoot as they'd clung to each other. The coffee had been abandoned, the spilled sugar was still there. Last night had been a revelation, all the better for being so unexpected. Sex with Bev was a joy.

A repeat performance would have been nice but she was out of bed now, hurriedly dressing in order to shoot home and shower and change before heading off to work.

In no time at all she was ready to leave. Gavin realised he didn't want her to go. When she gave him a goodbye kiss, he said, 'What are you doing tonight?'

'Me? Nothing. Watching *Last of the Summer Wine*. Polishing my zimmer frame. Looking through my Thora Hird scrapbook.' Bev shrugged. 'How about you?'

'Well, if you could bear to give *Last of the Summer Wine* a miss, I could demonstrate that I'm not past my sexual peak.'

Bev's eyes danced as she kissed him on the nose. 'I suppose I could always record it.'

The postman had delivered a hat trick of envelopes together with a small recorded-delivery parcel addressed to Laurel. Ginny carried them through to the kitchen and opened the first envelope.

Electricity bill, fabulous.

The second was water rates, great.

The third was a bank statement. Quickly skimming through the statement revealed that her balance was less than it should have been. Checking through more carefully, Ginny saw what was missing.

'Laurel?'

Laurel appeared in the doorway. 'Yes?'

'Your rent hasn't gone through yet. Could you have a word with Perry, see what's happened?'

'Oh.' Laurel shifted awkwardly, not meeting her gaze. 'Um . . . he can't afford to pay it any more.'

'Excuse me?'

'Sorry. I meant to tell you.' Laurel's tone was defensive; she'd clearly known for a while.

'So who is going to be paying it?'

'I don't know.'

Ginny shook her head in disbelief. 'Look, I have bills to pay.' The words came out clipped and irritated. 'Jem isn't working any more so I'm having to help her too. You can't expect me to say oh well, never mind, maybe we'll have a lucky night at the Bingo. If Perry's not paying your rent any more, you'll have to pay it yourself.'

With her pale green eyes, Laurel had never looked more like Ophelia. 'But I don't have any money.'

The knicker elastic of Ginny's patience finally snapped. 'Then you'll just have to do what normal people do and get yourself a job!'

Laurel flinched as if she'd been slapped. 'I can't.'

'You *can*,' Ginny shot back, 'you just don't *want* to. And I'm sorry, but if you don't pay your rent you aren't staying here. Because you aren't the only one with problems, OK? Things are pretty crap for me as well right now, but somehow I have to get on with it, because that's life.'

Laurel welled up. She glanced at the small parcel on the kitchen table.

'That's yours. It came just now.' Ginny eyed it jealously; how come Laurel got sent a parcel while all she got was stinking rotten bills?

'Thanks.'

'Open it, then.'

Miserably Laurel did as she was told. Her chin began to wobble as the wrappings came off.

Ginny's eyes widened. 'Somebody's sent you a Gucci watch!'

'No.'

'You mean you bought it for yourself?' Bloody hell, how much did a Gucci watch cost?

'If you must know,' Laurel blurted out defensively, 'I bought it for Kevin's birthday. I thought it would make him love me again. He's *always* wanted a Gucci watch.' She unfolded the accompanying note, scanned the few lines and crumpled it in her hand. 'But not from me. I can't believe he sent it back. Oh God, why can't I ever get *anything* right?'

Ginny's own hormones were jangling. 'Look, I thought you'd stopped all this. It's crazy, Laurel. Kevin's never going to love you again. He's never going to come back. It's over and you have to accept that.' Before Laurel could start sobbing she added hastily, 'And look on the bright side. You can take the watch back to the shop and get a refund.'

And pay your rent with it, hopefully.

'I can't.' Laurel sniffed and gazed mournfully down at the watch. 'I bought the watch three weeks ago. They only give you your money back if you return it within fourteen days.' Tears were once more sliding down Laurel's colourless cheeks. 'I just don't know what to do any more.'

'Don't you?' It was knicker-snapping time again. With an embryo in her stomach and bills strewn across the kitchen table, Ginny felt the elastic go *twaannggg*. Her voice spiralling, she yelped, 'Seriously, *don't* you? Because I can tell you. You have to forget Kevin and stop feeling so sorry for yourself. You need to sort out your life and start acting like an *adult*. And if you want to carry on living in this house you have to get out there and find yourself a *job*.'

Ginny took a deep breath. Crikey, had she really just said all that? From the way Laurel stifled a horrified sob, ricocheted off the doorway and stumbled out of the kitchen, it rather seemed as if she had.

Upstairs in Jem's bedroom, Ginny sat in front of the computer scrolling through images of embryos in the womb. Her own, she discovered, had by now developed fingers and toes and a face of sorts—albeit with huge alien eyes and low-slung ears. It also had a sense of smell (how could they *tell*?), a pituitary gland in its brain and a tiny heart pumping away in its chest.

Oh God, she really was having a baby. One reckless moment and this was the life-changing result, how could she have been so—

'Um, hello?' A cautious tap was followed by Laurel pushing open the bedroom door. Ginny pounced on the mouse and fired frantically at the page-closer like a demented person on a rifle range, finally managing to clear the screen a millisecond before Laurel came into the room.

Prickling with adrenaline she said, '*What?*'

Laurel flinched. 'Sorry. Um, I'm just going out to the chemist to pick up my prescription. I wondered if there was anything you wanted while I was there.'

Well, let's see, how about some nipple cream and a box of breast pads, a thousand packs of nappies and some Farley's rusks? Oh God, actually she quite fancied a couple of Farley's rusks . . .

'No, thanks.'

'Oh. OK.' Pause. 'I'm really sorry about . . . you know, the rent.'

Ginny steeled herself; Laurel knew she was a soft touch. Well, not this time. Stiffly she replied, 'So you keep saying.'

Her ploy evidently thwarted, Laurel's face fell. 'Anyway, I'll be back in half an hour.' She twisted the doorknob this way and that. 'And I'm going to sort everything out. I promise.'

Talk about emotional blackmail. Ginny refused to give in. Turning back to the computer she said, 'Good.'

Three hours later there was still no sign of Laurel. Ginny unloaded the washing from the tumble drier and carried the basket of dry clothes upstairs. It was unlike Laurel to be gone for so long but it hadn't been an ordinary day; maybe she'd gone into town to visit the Job Centre.

By the time she'd finished sorting out the clothes, Laurel still hadn't returned. Her conscience beginning to prick, Ginny let herself into Laurel's bedroom in search of a clue as to where she might have gone.

The sunshine-yellow room was incredibly neat. Apart from the handbag on the bed, nothing was out of place. Laurel's handbag. Ginny frowned at the sight of it; surely when you left the house to go to the shops you took your handbag with you? Picking up the bag she discovered Laurel's purse and credit cards were inside it..

That was a bit weird, wasn't it?

Her heart beating a little faster, Ginny pulled open the drawers of the chest next to Laurel's bed. The first drawer contained underwear, ironed and folded. The second held tights and petticoats, again arranged as pristinely as if they were part of a shop display.

The bottom drawer contained several framed photographs of Kevin (who was *so* not worth all this angst and grief), the box containing the Gucci watch, an old navy man-sized lambswool sweater with holes in both elbows and a pale grey leather-bound diary.

Ginny swallowed. Should she? Shouldn't she? This was Laurel's private diary and she really shouldn't read it. Moving over to the bedroom window, Ginny peered out; nothing would make her happier than to see Laurel making her way down the street, heading home. Then she could put the diary back where she'd found it.

But the road was empty; there was still no sign of Laurel in her long dress and droopy cardigan. She'd been gone for more than three hours. Without her handbag.

Feeling increasingly uneasy, Ginny opened the diary, flicking through dozens of densely written pages until she reached the most recent entry.

There were splodgy teardrops on the paper. Laurel had written:

> *Kevin sent back the watch with a letter telling me not to contact him again. Ginny found out about the rent not being paid and went mad. I know she doesn't want me here any more. She said if I don't get a job I'll have to move out, but how can I get a job when I feel like this? She doesn't understand. No one does.*
>
> *It's pointless. I can't carry on like this. I hate the person I've become. I know what I have to do and now's the time to do it.*
>
> *Goodbye Kevin, I loved you so much. Enjoy your life. And don't worry, I won't be bothering you again.*

Her heart clattering against her ribcage, Ginny re-read the words. There was no mistaking Laurel's intention. She could be dead already, floating in the sea or lying in a battered heap at the foot of the cliffs. Or she could have gone to the chemist to collect her prescription for antidepressants and be taking them right now, grimly swallowing every last tablet in the bottle . . .

God, how could she have shouted at someone who'd been prescribed antidepressants? And what had been Laurel's last words to her before miserably leaving the house? 'I'm going to sort everything out. I promise.'

Shakily, Ginny realised that she might as well have handed over the loaded gun herself. Laurel had come to her expecting understanding, and had got yelled at by an over-hormonal harpy instead.

Ginny stood up, hyperventilating and feeling sicker than ever.

She knew what she had to do now.

Ner-ner-ner-ner-ner-ner-ner.

Come *on*.

Ner-ner-ner-ner-ner.

Oh please, *please* don't do this now. Just start, damn you.

Ginny wiped a slick of perspiration from her upper lip and frenziedly pumped the accelerator, her stomach clenching as the rate of the
ner-ners decreased.

Ner . . . ner . . . ner . . . ner . . .

Click.

Bastard car. Ginny thumped the steering wheel in despair.

A knock on the driver's window made her jump. Her heart plum-
meted when she saw who was standing next to the car.

'I've got a charger if you want to borrow it.'

'What?' The unexpectedness of the encounter had caused Ginny's
brain to go temporarily blank.

'Your battery's flat,' said Carla. 'You left your headlights on last night.'

'What?' Ginny stared at the switch on the dash and realised it was
true. 'You mean you *saw* my headlights were on and you did *nothing*?'

Carla stiffened. 'You said you never wanted to speak to me again. I
only came over here now because you look a bit agitated.'

A *bit* agitated? 'Oh fine. So if you'd seen me being run over by a bus
last night you'd have left me lying in the road? Thanks a lot. You *knew*
I'd have a flat battery today but you just . . . just . . .' Ginny bashed the
steering wheel again, unable to look at Carla with her swingy geometric
bob, pink power suit and flawless make-up.

'Look, I said I'd lend you my charger.'

'That's no good, that'll take hours. I need the car *now*.'

'OK, if it's that urgent I'll give you a lift. Where are you going?'

'I DON'T KNOW.' Ginny let out a bellow of panicky despair. 'That's
the thing. I don't *know* where I'm going, I just know I've got to try to
find her before . . . . oh God, before it's too l-late . . .'

'Right, get out of the car.' Carla snatched the keys from the ignition,
hauled Ginny out onto the pavement and said briskly, 'We'll go in mine
and it doesn't matter how long it takes. Is she in Bristol?'

'What?' Ginny found herself being propelled across the road and into
Carla's car. 'Why would she be in Bristol?'

Carla looked at her. 'Is this not Jem we're talking about?'

'No, no. It's Laurel.' Shaking her head, Ginny spilled out what had
happened this morning.

Carla, having listened in silence, said, 'Shouldn't you phone the police?'

'I did! But Laurel hadn't written "I am going to kill myself" so they just said wait and see if she turns up. You can't report an adult as missing until they've been gone for twenty-four hours. It's all right for them,' Ginny said frustratedly, 'but how do they think I feel? It's all my fault.'

'Don't blame yourself. If it's any comfort,' said Carla, 'I'd have pushed her off a cliff months ago. So where to?'

Helplessly Ginny said, 'Anywhere. Everywhere. The chemist, I suppose. The doctor's surgery. We could drive up to the cliffs. Or try the beach, ask the lifeguards if they've seen her. She was wearing her brown dress when she left the house.'

'Long thin female, long red hair, long brown dress.'

'And I suppose we should check with Perry. She could be with him.' Ginny felt sick at the thought of explaining to Perry what had happened if Laurel wasn't there. Carla could do that.

'He's not living in Portsilver any more. And he's changed his number.' Carla paused then said bluntly, 'It's over between me and Perry. I haven't seen him for weeks.'

'You're kidding.' For a second Ginny forgot about Laurel. 'Why, what happened?'

'It's just over, that's all. I'll tell you later.' Keeping her gaze fixed on the road ahead, Carla said, 'For now let's just find Laurel.'

They didn't find her. The four hours she had been missing became five, and five stretched into six. No one had seen Laurel anywhere, she hadn't been to the pharmacy to collect her pills and there had been no sightings of her either along the cliff top or on the beach.

'Well, that's good news,' said Carla, attempting to cheer Ginny up. 'At least they haven't pulled any bodies out of the sea.'

But this was no consolation. Laurel was still missing and in a desperately vulnerable state. Having left a message on the kitchen table for Laurel to call her mobile the minute she got back, Ginny nevertheless punched in her home number for the hundredth time and listened to it ringing in an empty house.

'Where next?'

'Sadler's Cove, we haven't tried there yet.'

'Right,' Carla announced an hour later, 'that's enough. I could have carried on longer, but not in these shoes.'

Her impeccable black leather high heels were dusty and scuffed from scrambling down the narrow stony path to Sadler's Cove. Clouds had obliterated the sun and everyone was now leaving the beach for the day. Hollow with fear, it occurred to Ginny that when they arrived back at the house, there could be sombre-faced police officers on the doorstep waiting to break the worst possible news.

But when they finally reached home there was no police car outside. Instead, mystifyingly, Ginny gazed at the battered green van parked behind her own broken-down car and said, 'That's Dan.'

Carla raised an eyebrow. 'New boyfriend?'

'Hardly. Dan the Van, he delivers to the restaurant. What's he doing here?' Even as she was scrambling out of the car Ginny could see the van was empty. Was Dan here visiting one of her neighbours?

'Oooh, you gave me a fright!' Laurel clutched her bony chest as the kitchen door crashed open. 'What's the matter? You look as if you've seen a ghost!'

Wild-eyed and panting, Ginny surveyed the scene. Laurel and Dan the Van were sitting cosily together at the kitchen table, drinking tea and making inroads into the orange drizzle cake Laurel had baked yesterday. Like a small boy, Dan guiltily brushed cake crumbs from his wispy beard and attempted to stand up.

'Sit *down*,' Ginny barked, causing him to hurriedly resume his seat. Turning back to Laurel she said, 'For God's sake, where have you *been*?'

Laurel looked alarmed. 'Out. Why?' Then her expression changed as she saw Carla in the doorway. 'What's *she* doing here?'

'I'm sorry.' Dan the Van was clearly terrified. 'Maybe I should go—'

'No, you will not,' Ginny and Laurel chorused.

'I'll tell you what I'm doing here.' Carla, her eyes flashing, advanced into the kitchen. 'I've been helping Ginny to look for you. Or, more accurately, to help her look for your dead body. Oh, yes,' she went on as Laurel blanched, 'we've spent most of the day trawling the clifftops and beaches while we searched for your corpse. We called the police and spoke to the lifeguards and I've had to cancel three important appointments with clients, so God knows how much money you've cost me. It's just a shame you never learned to *read*.' Reaching across the table she snatched up the note Ginny had left and shook it in Laurel's horrified face. 'Because Ginny's been frantic with worry, and all you had to do was pick up the phone and tell her YOU WEREN'T DEAD.'

Ginny raked her fingers through her hair. 'OK, let's all calm down.'

'Why would you think I was dead?' Laurel was perplexed.

Carla glared at her. 'Because you wrote all that stuff in your diary about how you were going to end it all.'

'*What?* You mean you went up to my room and actually read my diary?' Laurel's voice rose. 'My *private* diary? Well, thanks a *lot!*'

'You selfish ungrateful *dimwit!*' Carla shot back. 'You should be thankful Ginny bothered because I'm telling you now, if you lived in my house I'd—'

'Stop this, stop it.' Ginny held up her hands like a football referee because too much was happening at once and all this shouting wasn't getting them anywhere. To Laurel she said, 'I'm sorry I looked in your diary but you said you were only going out for half an hour. You were upset. You didn't even take your handbag with you. Once I saw what you'd written, I was worried sick. That's why I left the note asking you to call me as soon as you got home.'

'We only got back twenty minutes ago. I did ring you, but your phone was busy. I would have called again, but we were talking about . . . things. And then you burst in through the door like a tornado.'

Mortified, Dan said, 'It's all my fault.'

'No, it isn't. I just jumped to the wrong conclusion.' Desperate for a cup of tea, Ginny filled the kettle and gestured for Carla to sit down. 'Anyway, panic over. You can tell us what you've been doing. How did you meet Dan?'

Laurel looked blank. 'Who's Dan?'

This was surreal. Surely Dan didn't have an identical twin brother. Ginny said, 'Dan, help me out here. Am I going mad?'

He shrugged, embarrassed. 'Everyone calls me Dan the Van because of my job. But it's just a joke. My real name's Hamish.'

Over cups of tea and crumbly slices of orange drizzle cake, Ginny and Carla heard the whole story. Having taken Ginny's outburst to heart and realised that the time had indeed come to get her act together, Laurel had left the house in order to pick up her repeat prescription, pondering her future en route. The queue at the chemist had been epic, practically trailing out of the shop, so she'd wandered down the road for a bit.

There was a bit of a queue in the bakery too, but this time Laurel waited in line. When it was her turn, she plucked up the courage to tentatively ask the baker if by any chance they had a vacancy for a part-time cake-maker.

Scornfully the baker informed Laurel that making bread and cakes involved getting up at three o'clock in the morning and finishing at six in the evening. It was hard physical work, their particular speciality here was lardy cake and no, they didn't have any vacancies anyway.

Humiliated by his rudeness, Laurel hurried out of the shop. Behind her she heard a man protest mildly, 'That was uncalled for.'

She was on her way back to the chemist when someone tapped her on the shoulder. Turning, she saw the man who had been standing behind her in the queue.

'Don't let Bert upset you. His wife walked out on him last week.'

'I'm not surprised.' Her sympathiser was on the scruffy side, lanky and tall, but he had gentle eyes and a kind face.

'Look . . . um, I don't know if you'd be interested, but there's a woman in St Austell who sells cakes at the farmers' market. I happen to know she's looking for help.'

St Austell was miles away, right down on the south coast of Cornwall. Tempted to say no outright, Laurel nevertheless found herself hesitating, reluctant to end the conversation. If anything, this man seemed almost shyer than she was.

'Would she bite my head off?'

He smiled and his whole face lit up. 'Her name's Emily Sparrow. Can you imagine anyone called Emily Sparrow biting anyone's head off?'

'You lost your place in the queue.' Laurel realised he'd left the bakery empty-handed.

'Hey, their pasties aren't that great. There's another shop a bit further down the road. Do you have a pen on you?'

Laurel indicated her bagless state; all she'd come out with was her house key and the doctor's prescription in her cardigan pocket.

'Me neither. Never mind, I've got one in the van.'

He had a nice voice too, reassuringly gentle and well spoken. Laurel found herself walking with him to the next shop, where he bought three pasties. Then they made their way back to his parked van and he explained that he'd been out on his delivery round since seven o'clock. She jumped when he opened the van's passenger door and a big hairy dog scrambled out.

'Don't worry about Stiller, he's a softy. We always have a break around now. Are you hungry?'

'Actually, I am.' Laurel hadn't realised until now how enticing the hot pasties smelt. 'Did you buy that one for me?'

'I did. Although if you don't want it I'm sure it wouldn't go to waste. I'm Hamish, by the way.'

Hamish? Hamish! Good grief, surely not the Hamish who wrote poetry and who'd failed to turn up at the singles club that night all those months ago. The one Ginny's ex-husband had insisted would be perfect for her.

The three of them entered the park, where benches were dotted around, and Hamish shared the pasties out.

As soon as the first mouthful of pasty had been swallowed, Laurel heard herself asking, 'Do you know someone called Gavin Holland?'

Hamish looked astonished. Then nodded. 'Yes. Why do you ask?'

All of a sudden Laurel felt extraordinarily brave. She looked directly at him and said, 'You stood me up.'

He stared at her. 'I did? Oh God, you mean that time at the club? I lost my nerve at the last minute, chickened out. You mean . . . ?'

She smiled and nodded, no longer afraid. 'My name's Laurel.'

It had all become more extraordinary after that; it was as if several protective outer layers had fallen away, leaving them able to discuss anything and everything without embarrassment. There was a connection between them that Laurel had never experienced before, not even with . . . no, she wasn't even going to *think* about Kevin. Before she knew what was happening, they were back at the van and Hamish was writing down the name and address of the woman in St Austell who ran a cake stall at the farmers' market. Then he looked at Laurel and said shyly, 'If you're free, I'm on my way back there now.'

And that had been that. Together the three of them had driven down to St Austell and Hamish had introduced her to Emily Sparrow who, as promised, wasn't shouty at all. He offered to pick up the supply of cakes Laurel made each Tuesday while he was on his rounds, so they could be sold at the Wednesday market. It was all so simple and straightforward that tears of relief had sprung into her eyes. OK, it wasn't a full-time job, but it was a start.

To celebrate, they had taken Stiller for a long walk on the beach. The conversation didn't falter once. When Laurel asked Hamish if Gavin had described her as boring, Hamish was perfectly honest. 'Yes, he did, but have you seen his girlfriends? Giggly airheads in miniskirts.'

After three hours on the beach they had driven back to Hamish's cottage and dropped off an exhausted Stiller. When Laurel had rubbed his ears and said goodbye, Stiller had gazed up at her with such a look of pleading in his liquid brown eyes that she'd found herself saying, 'Don't worry, boy, I'll see you again soon.' Then, realising how presumptuous that sounded, had glanced at Hamish to see if he'd noticed.

'I hope so,' Hamish had said.

'**W**ait till Gavin hears about this.' Having watched from the window as Hamish gallantly helped Laurel into the van's passenger seat, Ginny rejoined Carla at the kitchen table. 'He's going to be unbearable.'

'No change there then.' Carla's smile was tentative. 'Just kidding. How is he?'

'Same as ever. Gavin's never going to change.' Pausing, Ginny dabbed up cake crumbs with her finger and popped them into her mouth. 'So, how about you?'

This was what they'd both been waiting for. Carla braced herself.

'It was the biggest mistake of my life, the worst thing I ever did. And I'm sorry.' Abruptly her eyes filled. 'Oh, Gin, I'm so sorry. And I've missed you so much. Can you ever forgive me?'

Carla, who never cried, now had tears running down her cheeks. Quite suddenly, what would have been unthinkable twenty-four hours ago became the natural, the *only* thing to do. Plus, Ginny realised, if Lucy had been able to forgive Jem, then she could do the same with Carla. Some men simply weren't worth losing a best friend over.

And Perry Kennedy was no loss to either of them.

'It's forgotten,' said Ginny, and Carla threw her arms round her.

'Thank you, thank you . . . oh God, it's just been so *awful* without you. It's like when someone dies and you keep picking up the phone to ring them, then realising you can't do it any more. You wouldn't believe how many times I did that.'

'Me too.' There was a lump in Ginny's throat now; the last few weeks hadn't exactly been uneventful. 'So tell me what happened with you and Perry. Did you chuck him or did he go off with someone else?'

'Neither. I told him I wanted a baby and that was it. He took off.'

The word 'baby' gave Ginny a bit of a jolt. Recovering herself, she said incredulously, 'What on earth made you tell him that?'

'Because it was true.'

'*What?*'

'I wanted a baby.'

Ginny shook her head. 'Is this a joke?'

'No! All my hormones exploded at once. It happened just like *that*,'

Carla clicked her fingers, 'and took me over. Like being abducted by aliens. I couldn't think of anything else. I couldn't even *sleep*, I was so busy thinking about it.'

'So you told Perry you wanted a baby, and . . .?'

'He panicked. I wasn't safe any more. When I went round to his flat the next day, he was gone.' Her smile crooked, Carla said, 'You must be glad.'

'For all our sakes. How do you feel now? Do you still want a baby?'

'I don't know. Sometimes I think I do and other times I wonder if I'm mad. It comes and goes in waves,' Carla admitted. 'The nappy thing could be a problem.' Ever fastidious, Carla wrinkled her nose.

'Nappies are the pits.'

'And what happens when you want to go out at night and enjoy yourself? Babies can be such a *tie*.'

'They can. It's a shame you can't leave them at home, put them in the baby equivalent of kennels.'

'Exactly! I was *thinking* that! Oh, you.' Realising she was being made fun of, Carla jumped up and gave Ginny another hug. 'I'm so glad we're OK again. We should be celebrating! Is there wine in the fridge?'

'Sorry. We've got orange juice.' Lovely fruity *orangey* orange juice . . .

'No wine at all? That's terrible! Never mind, I've got some.' Closing the fridge, Carla said, 'I'll zip home, bring back a couple of bottles and we'll have a lovely catching-up session. You can tell me what's been going on with you.'

You're kidding.'

'No,' said Ginny.

'Oh my *God*.' Carla was so stunned she almost slopped red wine over her pink skirt. 'What are you going to *do*?'

'Ah well. That I don't know.' Ginny clutched her almost empty pint glass of orange juice. 'It's all a bit of a mess. There I was, worried sick that Jem might get pregnant. And instead it's happened to me.'

'Maybe subconsciously you did it on purpose,' Carla offered. 'You know, you missed Jem so much that you wanted another baby to replace her.'

'I did *not* do it on purpose. And we weren't irresponsible either.' Ginny shook her head in frustration; she'd been through that night in her mind a thousand times. 'We used something, OK? The bloody thing just didn't bloody work.'

'So. Are you keeping it?' Carla was ever practical.

Ginny, who wasn't, said, 'I can't get rid of it.'

'You'll have to tell Finn.'

'I definitely can't do that!'

'But he should know!' said Carla.

'As far as Finn's concerned, it was a one-night stand that meant nothing. God,' Ginny's face reddened at the memory, 'he was practically doing me a favour. He's got Mae and Tamsin now. This is the last thing he needs.' Realising that Carla was gazing at her with an odd look on her face, she said defensively, 'What are you thinking?'

'You've got a baby in there!' Dreamily Carla pointed at her stomach. 'An actual real baby! When it's born I'll be able to hold it as much as I want. And play with it, and talk to it and . . . and *everything*.'

'Ye . . . es.'

'But don't you see how fantastic that is?' Triumphantly Carla said, 'Now I don't have to worry any more about having one of my own!'

Chapter 12

IT WAS A FLIMSY excuse but the best he'd been able to come up with at short notice. Finn felt like a teenager as he drove to Ginny's house and it wasn't a sensation he was comfortable with.

Having to work alongside her in the restaurant wasn't helping; his feelings for Ginny were flatly refusing to go away. It was killing him, not knowing if she felt anything for him in return. And now he'd made up his mind; he *needed* to know if there was any chance at all of some kind of future for them.

He pulled up outside Ginny's house, aware that it was a risky thing to do. The situation he now found himself in with Tamsin was impossible; he knew he didn't love her. Except there was Mae, who he *did* love, to consider as well.

Shit, what a nightmare. But he was here now and he was going to tell Ginny the truth. Just like spotting a rare antique in an auction, you could maintain a poker face and apparent indifference for so long, but once the bidding started, sooner or later it became necessary to declare an interest. After that it was up to her; she could laugh in his face and tell him to get lost. Or she could say yes.

Either way, at least the agony of not knowing would be over.

Right, here goes. Finn switched off the car's engine and reached for the cardigan on the passenger seat. His stomach was clenched, his mouth dry and he was about to make the riskiest bid of his life.

He rang the bell and watched through the distorted glass as a blur of pink approached. Recognising Ginny's dressing gown, he pictured her naked beneath it before hastily banishing the image from his mind.

Then the door opened and—*Jesus*.

'Hey, Finn. Good to see you!'

Completely wrong-footed, Finn found himself succumbing to Gavin Holland's enthusiastic handshake. As if mistaking Gavin for Ginny wasn't terrifying enough, he was now forced to make conversation with a man wearing a lace-trimmed pink dressing gown that failed to conceal his hairy chest.

'Excuse the outfit. I've just had a shower.' Gavin, evidently unconcerned, said cheerfully, 'So what brings you here?'

Thank God he had his flimsy excuse. Finn held up the pale green angora cardigan and tried not to look at Gavin's bare feet. 'Er . . . Ginny left this behind this afternoon. I was just passing and thought she might need it. Is she, um, around?'

'Upstairs, having a bath. We're going out to dinner tonight.'

We? Hoping he'd misunderstood, Finn said casually, 'With that girl you brought to the restaurant that time? What was her name? Cleo?'

'No, no. Long gone, that one. My bimbo days are over now. I've seen the error of my ways.'

'Oh.' Ginny was upstairs in the bath and the ex-husband with whom she'd always remained friendly was wearing her pink dressing gown and announcing that he'd seen the error of his ways. And they were on their way out to dinner together. What was there to misunderstand? Swallowing that kicked-in-the-teeth feeling and marvelling that he could sound so normal, Finn said, 'Ginny didn't mention any of this.'

'Typical woman, she's not sure it'll last. I've blotted my copybook too many times before for her liking. But I'm working on proving her wrong. It's taken me a while to come to my senses but this time it's for good, I just know it is.' Gavin paused, his eyes sparkling. Those pretty young creatures are all very well, but sometimes the more mature woman just has . . . you know, that edge.' He broke into a grin. 'And if she heard me calling her a more mature woman she'd rip my head off!'

'Right. That's great,' he lied. 'I'm pleased for . . . both of you.' And then he left before he ripped Gavin's undeserving head off himself.

Ginny emerged shivering from the bathroom wrapped in a towel.

'When I said you could use my shower I didn't mean you could use all the hot water. That bath was *lukewarm*.'

'Sorry.' Gavin, whose boiler had broken down, appeared at the foot of the stairs. 'Anyway, how do I look?'

She softened, because the change in Gavin in the last couple of weeks had been a revelation. Whether or not it would last was anybody's guess—personally, Ginny was giving it two months, max—but he was certainly making an effort for Bev. 'Very handsome. In an overweight, thinning-on-top kind of way.'

'Charming. There are times I wonder why I divorced you. Then I remember.'

'I divorced you,' Ginny retorted. 'Hot-water hogger. But I like your shirt.'

Pleased, Gavin adjusted the cuffs of the smart, dark blue shirt he'd bought specially for tonight. It was the most ungarish one he'd ever owned. 'Bev said blue was my colour.'

'Bev said this, Bev said that,' Ginny teased, because he was at that besotted stage where he liked to include her name in every conversation. 'Who was that at the door earlier?'

Gavin was now busy admiring his smartened-up appearance in the hall mirror. 'Hmm? Oh, just Finn. He dropped off the cardigan you left at work. Hadn't you better get ready? Bev's going to be here soon.'

Following a business meeting in Exeter, Bev was coming straight to the house before the three of them went out to dinner together. Ginny said, 'Are you sure I won't feel like a gooseberry?'

'Of course you won't. We'll have a great time.'

'No lovey-doveyness then. You have to promise.'

'My hands shall remain above the table at all times.' Gavin waggled them to illustrate. 'Mind you, can't make any promises about other body parts.'

Ginny headed for her bedroom, combing her fingers through her wet hair but not before flicking a playful V sign at Gavin in the hall below. He was in love—again—and it wasn't his fault she was jealous.

She *would* enjoy the evening once she got her happy head on; it was just the mention of Finn that had knocked her off kilter. Sitting at a table for three was fine in its own way, but if her life could have been different, how much lovelier it would be to have someone of her own and be part of a table for four.

Carla, sipping ice-cold Moët, watched as Lawrence deftly worked his magic on her hair. Still desperate to make up for her previous transgressions, she had done her utmost to persuade Ginny to come along to Lawrence's for the cut of a lifetime, her treat.

But Ginny, blinking her fringe out of her eyes and too impatient—as ever—to wait for an appointment, had taken the kitchen scissors up to the bathroom and performed her usual snip-and-hack job. Annoyingly, her hair had looked fine afterwards.

'See?' Ginny had executed a happy twirl, showing off her habitual no-style style. 'Look how much money I've just saved you!'

Carla had given up. What Ginny didn't know—couldn't begin to understand—was that coming here to Lawrence's was about so much more than just perfect hair. His tiny one-man salon was possibly her favourite place in the world, rose-pink and womb-like, and Lawrence himself was a psychiatrist, therapist and counsellor rolled into one. You could tell him anything and he wouldn't be shocked. He loved to talk but never gossiped. Once upon a time he'd been married with children; now, in his early fifties, he was gay and happily ensconced with a policeman called Bob. Lawrence was funny and wise, adored by everyone and a magical stylist. *And* he served champagne. Oh yes, Ginny definitely didn't know what she was missing.

'You're better off without him, darling,' he said now. 'Men like that? Professional heartbreakers, take it from me. And if you'd had a baby, what kind of a father would he have been?'

'I know that now. I was just so overwhelmed with the idea of it.' Carla took another sip of champagne. 'I wanted a baby; it didn't occur to me that he wouldn't feel the same way.'

'Lots of men don't. After our first two, Linda wanted a third and I wasn't so keen.' Wagging his scissors at Carla in the mirror, Lawrence shook his head and said ruefully, 'I tell you, never argue with a woman whose hormones are raging, because you'll never win.'

Carla knew he had three children, all grown up now, to whom he was extremely close. 'So how did she get you to change your mind?'

'Fait accompli. She came off the pill without telling me.'

'But how did she know you wouldn't leave her?'

'I loved my kids. Linda knew that once I was used to the idea I'd be fine. And of course she was right. Anyone ready for a top-up?' Lawrence added another inch to Carla's glass and refilled the one in front of the girl having her lowlights baked under the heat lamp.

Pleasantly relaxed by the champagne, Carla grinned across at Lawrence's other client. 'So announcing that I'd made an appointment to have my coil whipped out probably wasn't my cleverest move.'

The other girl and Lawrence looked at each other in horror and gasped, then burst out laughing.

'But I thought he'd be pleased!' said Carla.

'Such a novice.' Lawrence patted her shoulder fondly. 'Next time, subterfuge. Remember, you're the woman. You call the shots.'

'Unless it's condoms.' Carla pulled a face. 'Not much you can do about them.'

'Yes, there is.' The other girl winked. 'That's easy. You just have to be discreet.'

Carla snorted; this was why she *loved* coming here. 'Come on! You mean slip it off halfway through and hope he won't notice?'

'When I wanted another baby my fiancé said it was too soon. Same as you did.' The girl pointed at Lawrence. 'But my hormones were all over the place and I *knew* I wanted another one. So I took this really fine needle and stuck it through every condom in the box.' She grinned. 'All twenty-four of them.'

Carla clapped her hands in delight; she'd *never* have thought of that. 'And he couldn't tell?'

'I didn't use a knitting needle. Just a tiny weeny one from a hotel sewing kit. And then you smooth over the hole in the wrapper with your finger so it's hardly visible.'

'Did it work?' Carla was enthralled.

The girl waved her free hand and said airily, 'Well, things changed. You know how it is. But hey, it could have worked.'

It could. Carla marvelled at such subterfuge; it was reassuring to know she wasn't the only one seized by that desperate, primeval urge to procreate. And this girl had a child but hadn't let herself go, which she also approved of. Her figure was fantastic and she was wearing casual but definitely expensive clothes.

'Right, that's you done.' Lawrence laid down his scissors. 'Now, just give me ten minutes to deal with these lowlights and I'll be back to do the blow-dry. There's a piece in here you'll love,' he went on, handing Carla a glossy magazine. 'Irish woman gives up her baby for adoption, twenty years later the daughter traces her but the mother's only got days left to live—it'll break your heart.'

Lawrence led his other client over to the sink and began removing the dozens of foil wrappings from her head while Carla buried herself in the story. It *was* a tear-jerker, so much so that she barely noticed the ringing of the girl's mobile phone. God, imagine realising you were dying of cancer and not knowing if you'd get the chance to meet your long-lost daughter again before you pegged it, then hearing the doorbell go one day and looking up from your sickbed to see—

'Oh, *hi*, so you got my text! How have *you* been?' The girl's tone was flirtatious; she wasn't speaking to her maiden aunt.

'Of course I'm fine. Everything's great, I just thought we could meet up, seeing as I'll be in London for the weekend anyway.'

This was someone she was definitely keen on. Carla read on.

'Absolutely. It's a date.' The girl was triumphant. 'I knew you'd want to. Now, shall I bring Mae? Ha, thought not! No, no problem, I'll leave her here. God knows, I deserve a couple of days off. What would you like me to wear?' She paused then gurgled with laughter at his reply. 'Why am I not surprised to hear you say that?'

Carla frowned. Had the girl just said Mae? And if she had, why did the name ring a faint but somehow significant bell?

Mae, Mae . . .

Carla froze, placing it at last.

Bloody hell. *Mae*.

It had been an eventful morning so far, what with saying goodbye to Laurel and now this. Ginny drummed her fingers on the steering wheel and inhaled the smell of fresh-cut grass while the drivers of the two cars yelled at each other and pointed increasingly dramatically at their dented wings. Nobody had been hurt, it was only a minor accident but they were blocking the road and now she was going to be late for work.

Who'd have thought it? Laurel had actually gone, moved in with Dan the . . . no, not Dan the Van; she had to get used to calling him Hamish now. It just went to show, though, didn't it? As Gavin's granny had always said, there was a lid for every pot. And Hamish was Laurel's lid. They were perfect together, besotted with each other and so well suited that it didn't even seem strange that after so short a time they were going to be living together in Dan the—Hamish's tiny farm cottage.

A horn hooted behind Ginny as another driver grew impatient. A door slammed and a woman shouted, 'Oi! Shift those cars out of the way!'

The two men ignored her and carried on arguing. Ginny heard the tap-tap of irritated high heels. Next moment a woman peered into her car and said, 'I'm not waiting here for the next hour, watching these two slug it out. If you give me a hand, we can bounce that Renault out of the way.'

Ginny had seen cars being bounced before; it was a strenuous business. She looked at the woman and said, 'Sorry, I can't. I'm pregnant.'

Gosh, it felt funny saying the words aloud to a stranger.

Bloody hell, I'm having a *baby*.

'Oh.' The woman looked disappointed.

'Hang on.' Ginny opened her door, clambered out and approached the arguing men. 'Hi, we need to get past. If you won't move your cars, we'll have to shift them ourselves. But I'm a little bit pregnant so I'd rather you did it.'

The younger of the two men, shaven-headed and awash with tattoos, turned and looked her up and down. Finally, he heaved a sigh of resignation. 'You sound just like my missus when she's trying to get out of the washing-up.'

Ginny was just pulling into Penhaligon's courtyard when her phone rang. She parked and flipped open her mobile. Carla.

'Hi there, I've only got time for a quickie.'

'That's what got you into trouble in the first place.'

'I'm late for work!'

'Never mind that.' Carla sounded gleeful. 'I've just found out a couple of things you might like to hear.'

'What kind of things?' Hurriedly Ginny leapt out of the car; the restaurant was fully booked this lunchtime.

'OK, number one. I think I know how you got pregnant.'

'Carla, I did biology at school, I *know* how it happened.'

'Will you listen to me? Tamsin was desperate for another kid straight after she'd had Mae. I'm guessing it was because she wasn't sure Mae was Finn's and wanted one that definitely was.'

'What? *What?*' Flummoxed, Ginny stopped racing across the gravel.

'But Finn *didn't* want another one, which was a pain,' Carla machine-gunned on. 'So Tamsin sabotaged his condom supply, punctured every last one of them. Except then the Italian-billionaire thing started up again and she left for London. But she forgot to tell Finn what she'd done.'

Ginny frowned as the door of the restaurant opened. 'Carla, is this what happened *in a dream*?'

'No! It's real! And she's gone shopping this afternoon so the coast's clear if you want to check it out.'

Finn was standing in the doorway with Mae in one arm and a handful of folders in the other. 'Ginny, you're late.'

'Sorry, sorry, two cars crashed in front of me and the road was blocked.'

'But Gin, that's not all, you'll never guess what else I—'

'Come on, there are customers waiting in the shop *and* I'm supposed to be phone-bidding at Sotheby's.'

'Brrraaa brrraaaaa!' Mae waved her hands in the air like a demented bidder.

'I have to go,' Ginny muttered into the phone.

'No! You can't! Wait until you—'

'Get the sack?' Aware of Finn's pointed gaze, Ginny said hastily, 'I'll call you later,' and cut Carla off in mid-squawk.

'Are you OK?' Finn touched her arm as she rushed past him.

Oh God, why did he have to touch her? 'Of course! Why wouldn't I be?'

'You look a bit pale.'

'I'm fine.'

Bloody hell, was that how it had happened? Really?

It was no good, she had to find out if Carla was right. Lunch in the restaurant had gone on for what felt like weeks. At three thirty Ginny lurked outside the entrance to the antiques centre peering through the crack in the door until she saw that Finn was occupied with a couple of potential customers.

He paused and looked up when she rushed in.

'Sorry, I brought something over for Myrtle and the kittens. I didn't realise you were busy . . . doesn't matter . . .'

'You could just leave it by the front door,' said Finn. 'I'll take it up later.'

Nooooooo. Ginny clutched the clingfilm-wrapped parcel of smoked salmon trimmings she had cadged from the kitchen.

'Or,' Finn added as an afterthought, 'you can take it up yourself if you wanted to see them.'

Yesssssss. Beaming with relief, Ginny said, 'Thanks, I'll do that. Just for five minutes.'

But first things first. Once up the stairs she turned left along the landing and made directly for the master bedroom.

Oh God, this was mad. The outcome was the same, whether or not Tamsin had sabotaged the condoms. But the compulsion to know the truth had her in its grip. Panting, Ginny headed for the chest of drawers on Finn's side of the bed and slid open the uppermost drawer. There was the box, right at the back, lying on its side with some of the packets spilling out amidst a jumble of old belts, pens, swimming goggles and sunglasses. Scooping up a handful of packets she realised it was too dark here in the bedroom to examine them properly and too risky to turn on the light. Closing the drawer she hurried through to the living room, ignoring the excited squeaks of the kittens. OK, over by the big window would be best. Ginny held the first one up to the light, her hands trembling as she ran the tips of her fingers over the plastic-coated foil. God, her heart was racing so hard it was impossible to—

'OW!' She let out a shriek as without warning something heavy landed on her shoulder. The condom packet flew out of her grasp and Ginny spun round in alarm. Bloody Myrtle, what a fright. Disentangling Myrtle's claws from her white lycra top, she plonked the cat down and bent to retrieve the dropped condom.

Bugger, what were the odds? Ginny gazed in dismay at the packet, clearly visible but unreachable, in a deep gap between polished oak floorboards. You could fling five hundred condoms up in the air and not one of them would fall into one of the gaps between floorboards. And she couldn't leave it there; that would be just too bizarre.

OK, think, think. Stuffing the rest of the condoms into her bra, Ginny raced into the kitchen and yanked open the cutlery drawer. A knife? A fork? Grabbing one of each, she returned to the living room and fell to her knees in front of the window. The knife was useless, the fork no better. Damn, why did these packets have to be so slippy? It was like trying to hook out a strand of overcooked spaghetti, and the more often it slid back down into the gap, the more her hands shook and the sweatier her palms became. OK, deep calming breaths and try again, and this time—

'Ginny, what are you *doing*?'

Ginny froze, knife and fork in hand. Slowly, very slowly, she looked over her shoulder. Finn had a point; what *was* she doing?

'Eating wood lice for lunch?' Finn suggested.

'Um . . . um . . .' It was no good; he was crossing the room now.

Finn paused with his hands on his hips, gazing down. Reaching out and taking the fork from Ginny's grasp, he bent and deftly hooked out the condom packet in one go.

Typical.

'Right. Thanks.' Ginny snatched it up and said, 'Sorry about that! It just . . . well, Myrtle ambushed me and I jumped a mile . . . it just flew out of my pocket, and of course I couldn't *leave* it there . . .'

Finn frowned. 'It flew out of your pocket?'

'Yes!'

'Your jeans pocket?'

Bugger, nothing else she was wearing *had* pockets. As she cast about in desperation, Finn raised a hand signalling that he'd be back in a moment. Returning from the master bedroom an uncomfortable thirty seconds later, he said, 'How strange, I could have sworn I had a box of condoms in my bedside drawer. But the box is empty. They've all gone.'

Ginny's mouth was as dry as sand. OK, here was her chance to come clean, to explain everything, to tell Finn that she was pregnant . . .

'What's that crackly sound?' Finn was listening intently.

Super-aware of the rapid rise and fall of her ribcage, Ginny said, 'I can't hear it.' She tried to stop breathing completely.

'Kind of plasticky and crackly.' Finn's gaze was now fixed on her chest. 'One side of you has gone a funny shape.'

Ginny looked down. Her right breast was smooth and normal. The left one resembled a Christmas stocking. It looked as if . . . well, almost as if she'd stuffed a handful of wrapped condoms into her bra. Slowly she reached into the V-neck of the thin lycra top, scooped out the offending packets and handed them over. 'I'm sorry.'

Finn gave her an odd look; frankly she couldn't blame him. 'I don't get it. Can't you buy your own? Or ask Gavin to do it?'

It was definitely, definitely time to tell him now. Flustered and searching for a way to begin, Ginny said, 'Look, I can explain, there's a reason for . . . for . . .'

'Carry on,' Finn prompted when her voice trailed away.

But it was no good; from where she was standing, Ginny had seen the car pull into the courtyard. She shook her head. 'Tamsin's back.'

He heaved a sigh, glanced down at the condoms in his hand. 'I'd better put these back in the drawer.'

Ginny braced herself; she'd endured this much humiliation, what harm could a bit more do? Clearing her throat as Finn turned away, she said, 'Could I have one?'

He stopped. 'Excuse me?'

You heard. 'Could you just . . . lend me a condom? OK, not *lend*,' Ginny hurriedly amended as his eyebrows shot up.

'Sure one's enough?' There was a definite sarcastic edge to his voice.

What the hell. 'Better make it two.' Oh God, what kind of a conversation was this to be having with the father of your unborn child?

Without another word Finn dropped two condoms into her outstretched hand before heading through to the bedroom. He re-emerged as Tamsin ran up the stairs. Having jammed the two condoms into her jeans pocket—so snug that nothing short of a nuclear explosion would dislodge them—Ginny said hastily, 'Hi, you've had your hair done! It looks great!'

'I know.' Tamsin smugly shook back her glossy-as-a-mirror, conker-brown locks. 'What are you doing here?'

Well, I *was* about to tell Finn that I'm having his baby.

Which would probably have captured Tamsin's attention but Ginny couldn't quite bring herself to say it. 'I brought some salmon trimmings up for Myrtle.'

Not that stroppy, lethal-clawed Myrtle deserved them.

'What, *those*?' Tamsin eyed the still unopened, cling-wrapped parcel on the window ledge.

'And I needed to discuss next week's shifts with Finn.'

'Thrilling.' Losing interest, Tamsin waved her armful of glossy carrier bags at Finn. 'Darling, wait until you see what I've bought, I've had *such* a lovely time! Where's Mae?'

'Martha's taken her out in the pushchair for a couple of hours. We've been pretty busy today.'

If Finn meant to make Tamsin feel guilty, it whizzed over her head.

'Great, maybe she'd like to baby-sit this weekend. My friend Zoe's invited me up to stay for a couple of days.' Her hair swinging some more, Tamsin dumped the carriers on the floor and began rummaging through them. 'And I got you a fab shirt . . . hang on, it's in here somewhere.'

Ginny made her excuses and left before Tamsin could find the fab shirt and make Finn try it on.

'**A**bout bloody time too.' Carla was out of her house a nanosecond after Ginny arrived home.

In the sunny kitchen each of them held a wrapped condom up to the window.

'Three holes,' Carla pronounced.

'Four in this one.' The needle marks were practically invisible to the naked eye but you could just feel them if you ran your fingertips over the plasticised foil. No wonder Finn hadn't noticed.

'So that's it. Now you know.'

'Tamsin got me pregnant.' Ginny pulled a face. 'Sounds like the kind of headline you'd read in the *News of the World*, all about turkey basters and lesbians.'

'*Anyway*,' said Carla, 'you haven't heard the other thing yet. She's going up to London this weekend.'

'I know. To see her friend Zoe. I was there when she told Finn.'

'Hmm. I was there when she arranged it.' A knowing smile played around Carla's perfectly lipsticked mouth. 'And I'm telling you now. If that was a girl she was speaking to on the phone, I'm a banana.'

It was another hectic night in the restaurant. Ginny hadn't meant to say it this evening but she was being sorely provoked. Finn had spent the last two hours being decidedly offhand and shooting her filthy looks from a distance. It was both disconcerting and hurtful. When her pen ran out and she went through to the office to pick up another, he stopped her in the corridor on her way back.

'Sorry, we don't keep extra supplies of condoms in this office.' If his mood had been better it could have sounded light-hearted, even playful. But it wasn't, so it didn't.

'My pen ran out.' Ginny held up the new one. 'The old one's in the bin if you want to check. And I've already said sorry about earlier.' Deep breath. 'Look, I still need to talk to you about the . . . um, condoms.'

Finn's jaw was set. 'No need. But as far as I'm concerned you're making a massive mistake.'

'Am I?' Whatever he meant, it was clearly unflattering. Fury bubbled up and Ginny blurted out, 'Well, maybe I'm not the only one. Because I'd double-check who Tamsin's seeing this weekend if I were you.'

Yeek, she'd said it. Well, Finn *should* know.

He stood there, motionless. 'What?'

'You heard.' Ginny instantly wished she'd kept her mouth shut.

What was that expression, shoot the messenger? Finn was certainly looking as if he'd like to shoot her.

'What makes you say that?'

'Don't ask me. Ask Tamsin.'

Without another word Finn turned and left. God, what a mess, what an absolute balls-up. Shaking, Ginny realised that now he would accuse Tamsin of seeing someone else. Tamsin, in turn, would deny it and heatedly demand to know who was spreading these lies. And then what? Without any concrete evidence, it was Tamsin's word against hers . . .

It was too horrible a prospect to even contemplate. There was only one thing to do. Ginny braced herself, clutched her brand-new pen and went back to work.

Tamsin had just had a bath and was wrapped in a turquoise robe, painting her toenails shell-pink. When Finn entered the living room she looked up and smiled. 'Hi, darling. Mae's asleep. What are you doing back so early?'

She was beautiful. Any man would lust after Tamsin. If what Ginny had said was true, it would be the best news he'd heard in months.

'I've been working too hard. Time for a break,' said Finn. 'We're going up to London together this weekend. I've booked us into a suite at the Soho.'

For a second there was silence.

'Oh Finn, I'd have loved that.' Tamsin was filled with regret. 'But I can't. I promised Zoe I'd stay with her. The thing is—and this is top secret—she's just had a facelift and looks a complete fright. I'm just going along to cheer her up and take her mind off the fact that she looks like Frankenstein's ugly sister.'

'Right.' Finn held her gaze, the confident unwavering gaze of a woman who could lie about the paternity of her child and not let it trouble her.

'But some other time,' Tamsin beamed up at him. 'Definitely. In fact how about next weekend? Then we can—what are you *doing*?'

'Borrowing your phone. That's all right, isn't it?' Finn scooped up the tiny mobile that Tamsin never let out of her sight and began deftly scrolling through the list of names. 'Ah, here we go . . .'

'That's *my* phone!' Tamsin leapt up in a panic as he held it to his ear. 'Look, you can't just—'

'Zoe? Hi, this is Finn Penhaligon. How are you? Now, listen, this is just a preliminary call, but I'm ringing round Tamsin's friends to see who might be able to make it along to a surprise party for her at the Connaught this Saturday evening.' He paused, listened, then said, 'Well, that's great news,' before handing the mobile over to Tamsin. 'Here, you can speak to her now. Zoe's thrilled. She says she'd love to come.'

Ginny jumped a mile and almost dropped the sticky toffee puddings she was carrying through from the kitchen when Tamsin burst into the restaurant. She was wearing jeans and a white T-shirt and had a face like thunder as she stood in the centre of the noisy, crowded room beadily eyeing each table in turn. Evie, raising her eyebrows at Ginny, approached Tamsin and said, 'Are you looking for someone?'

'I'm seeing who's here.' The words came rattling out like marbles. 'Finn wouldn't tell me, but it has to be someone in this restaurant.' Tamsin continued to scan the diners before turning to blurt out, 'You won't *believe* what they've just done to me, some petty, spiteful . . . jealous . . .' Her voice trailed away as her gaze came to rest on Ginny. Slowly, incredulously, Tamsin drawled, 'Or maybe you would believe it. Look at your face! You know exactly what I'm talking about, don't you? Who told Finn?'

Ginny stared back. OK, this was now officially a nightmare. Licking dry lips, she said, 'I did.'

'You! *How?* My God, I might have guessed. You interfering bitch.' Tamsin's voice rose and her features narrowed. 'Let me guess, you were jealous because I had Finn and you don't have a man of your own. You can't bear to see other people happy so you have to stir up trouble by poisoning their minds!'

Close, thought Ginny. I'm jealous because you have Finn and you don't deserve him. You're cheating on him, which is something I'd *never* do. God, look at everyone *watching* us.

Levelly she said, 'I didn't lie.'

'You've probably got a crush on him.' Tamsin's upper lip curled.

'Right, that's enough.' Evie ushered Tamsin towards the door. 'You're upset, let me take you back to—'

'No!' bellowed Tamsin, wrenching free. She grabbed a carafe of white wine from the nearest table, spun round and hurled the contents straight at Ginny. 'You bitch, you've ruined my life!'

Everyone in the restaurant gasped. For the second time in three minutes Ginny almost dropped the sticky toffee puddings. Then, blinking wine out of her eyes, she saw that they'd been caught in the onslaught too, which meant they couldn't be served to paying customers. Oh well, waste not, want not . . .

'Aaarrrgh!' Tamsin, who clearly hadn't been expecting a mere waitress to retaliate, let out a shriek and leapt back. She gazed in disbelief at the brown sludgy gunk sliding slowly down the front of her white shirt and jeans.

'It's not your day, is it?' said Ginny. 'First your life is ruined, now your outfit.'

Incandescent but unable to escape Evie's iron grip, Tamsin stamped her feet and let out another ear-splitting howl of rage. At various tables people began to whisper and giggle.

The husband of the couple who had ordered the sticky toffee puddings looked at Ginny and said tentatively, 'Were those ours?'

Ginny's knees were trembling but she managed to keep her voice steady. 'I'm so sorry. And there aren't any more left. But I can really recommend the chocolate torte.'

By some miracle she managed to drive home without ending up in a ditch. It was only nine o'clock, which had Carla running across the road shouting, 'Oh my God, what happened?'

Ginny was incapable of sitting down. Revved up and hyperventilating, she paced around the kitchen. Finally she finished relaying the showdown in the restaurant and shook her head. 'That's it, I've lost my job. I'm going to move to Scarborough.'

'Sit down. Calm down. So he *still* doesn't know you're pregnant.' Banging kitchen cupboard doors open and shut, Carla said, 'Bloody hell, I'm trying to get you something to drink here and all I can find is hot chocolate.' She took down the tin and gave it a shake. 'Have you even been to Scarborough?'

'We went there on holiday once when Jem was a baby. It has a nice spa thingy. And it's a long way from here.' Ginny's stomach lurched as the phone burst into life. Oh, God, this couldn't be good for the baby.

'Don't answer it if you don't want to,' said Carla.

But caller ID showed that it was Jem.

'Yay, Mum, you're there! You'll never guess what!'

Even when she was having a crisis, hearing Jem's voice cheered her up. Glad of the distraction, Ginny said, 'What won't I guess?'

'Marcus McBride's got a beach house in Miami. He's just emailed

Davy and said if we want a holiday in July, we're welcome to use it. And it's, like, the coolest house on the planet!'

'Gosh.' Ginny wondered how much the plane tickets would cost.

'*And* he's taking care of the flights,' Jem went on excitedly. 'Isn't that amazing? We won't get to see him—he's going to be away filming in Australia while we're there—but when Davy said there'd be three of us, he was fine. He even said the more the merrier and why didn't Davy's mum go along too?'

'And is she?'

'No! Rhona said it was our trip and she'd stay at home. Which is serious progress, because her and Davy have never been apart before. That's OK with you then, is it? If I go to Miami in July?'

'Of course it is, sweetheart.'

'I'd better get off now. Everyone's going to be so jealous when they hear about it! So, everything all right with you, Mum?'

'Yes, yes, fine. Bye, darling.'

'That's someone else you're going to have to tell before the baby actually pops out.' Carla was nothing if not full of useful advice.

'I know. Don't nag.' Ginny put down the mug of hot chocolate which was vile and lumpy.

'It feels like we're waiting for the world to end. You'd think somebody would have phoned by now, even if it's just to tell you you're sacked.'

'If Tamsin phones, it'll be to tell me I'm dead.' A kind of hysteria struck Ginny. 'She could call the police, have me done for assault with a deadly pudding. Oh God, what if she hasn't been cheating on Finn? What if I made a—'

Drrrrrrrinnnggg. The sound of the doorbell caused both of them to jump off their chairs.

'This really isn't good for me.' Ginny pressed a hand to her chest.

'I'll go and see who it is.'

'No.' Shaking her head, Ginny said, 'This is my mess. It's up to me to sort it out.'

Her heart went into overdrive when she saw Finn, who clearly wasn't in the mood to waste time.

'Can I come in?' Already over the threshold before Ginny could reply, he stopped dead when he saw Carla. Brusquely, he said, 'Could you leave us?'

'No, I couldn't.'

'Carla.' Ginny tilted her head helpfully towards the door. 'Please.'

'Please what?'

'Go home.'

'Spoilsport,' Carla muttered as she left.

'I'm not sorry about the sticky toffee pudding, so don't expect me to apologise for that. And I'm leaving the restaurant, which saves you having to sack me.' The words came tumbling out; until that moment Ginny hadn't even known she was going to say them.

'I wasn't planning to sack you,' said Finn. 'You don't have to leave.'

Ha, he didn't know the half of it.

'I'm still going to.' Her fingernails dug into her clenched palms. She was; it was the only way. Far better that he didn't discover the truth.

'It's all over, by the way. They've left.' Finn's expression betrayed the way he felt. 'Tamsin and Mae.'

'I'm sorry.' This time Ginny meant it. He must be devastated.

'It had to happen.' Finn shrugged. 'Getting back together with Tamsin was never going to work. I wanted it to, because of Mae. But it's no way to live. Tamsin wasn't the one who left Angelo, by the way, before she arrived back down here. He chucked her. It all came out tonight. She's been angling to get back with him for weeks. And was just about to, if she had her way.' Surveying Ginny, he added, 'She still doesn't know how you found out.'

There was no reason not to tell him now. 'Carla was at the hairdressers. She overheard Tamsin arranging it on the phone this morning.'

'Carla. I might have guessed. Anyway, it's over. They've gone. I don't imagine I'll be seeing them again.'

How he must be feeling beneath the calm exterior didn't bear thinking about. Feeling horribly responsible, Ginny said, 'But you could if you wanted to.'

Finn shook his head. 'It's over, dead and buried. As far as I'm concerned it was over between Tamsin and me long ago.' He paused. 'And Mae isn't mine. I know that now. Saying goodbye hurt like hell, but it's not like last year. This time it's been kind of inevitable.'

'Really?' Well, that was a relief.

'Really. If I'm honest I was looking for a way out. And for Mae's sake it's better that it happens sooner rather than later. So that's it. All over.' Finn shoved his hands into his pockets. 'Life doesn't always turn out the way you expect, does it? You think you're in control, but you're not.

It's like getting on a plane to Venice, then getting off and finding yourself in Helsinki.'

Ginny's stomach was in knots.

Tell him you're pregnant.

I can't, I can't do it.

Just *tell* him.

I really can't. God, news like that, tonight of all nights, could finish him off for good.

Aloud, she said, 'Gavin and I went to Venice for our honeymoon. Maybe I should have gone to Helsinki instead.'

It was meant as a flippant remark to make him smile, but clearly Finn wasn't in the mood. Almost angrily he said, 'And did you think that at the time?'

Ginny was taken aback by his vehemence. 'No, of course not. I knew what Gavin was like, but I was young and stupid. I thought I could change him.'

'And now?'

She shrugged. 'Now I'm old and stupid. But this time he tells me he's changed.'

'Do you believe him?'

Did a leopard ever really change his spots? Who knew? But when you saw Gavin and Bev together they certainly seemed happy. 'I'm a romantic,' said Ginny. 'I want to believe it.'

'Right.' Abruptly Finn said, 'Well, good luck.'

'Thanks.' That was it, then. Resignation accepted. she wasn't going back to work.

'Bye.' He turned and left the house, closing the front door without so much as a backward glance.

God, what a night. Ginny rubbed her face, then her hair. Too traumatised for tears, she picked up the phone to dial Carla's number.

The next moment, the doorbell rang again. Speak of the devil. Padding down the hall, Ginny pulled open the door and—

'You're mad. I can't believe you're being so gullible.'

'What?'

'Gavin.' The look Finn gave her was fierce. 'He's going to break your heart.'

Mystified Ginny said, 'Not *my* heart. What are you talking about?'

Finn was visibly taken aback. 'So you're not seeing Gavin?'

'Bloody hell, *no*! We've been divorced for nine years. I went out to dinner last night with him and his new girlfriend. Her name's Bev and she's lovely.' Ginny realised she was babbling. 'And she's as old as me!'

'I thought you and Gavin were back together.' Frowning, Finn said, 'When I dropped your cardigan off, Gavin was wearing your dressing gown.'

'His boiler broke down.' Gavin would think it was hilarious, Ginny realised, to answer the door in a girly dressing gown. 'I said he could use my shower, that's all. God, if I ever thought of getting back with Gavin I'd have myself certified.'

'Sorry. I can't believe I got it wrong.' Finn shook his head, his expression unreadable. 'So . . . um, will it work out, d'you think, with this Bev?'

'Truly? I shouldn't think so for a minute. Bev's great, like I said. But Gavin's never going to change. This is a novelty for him. Personally I give it a couple more weeks.' It was a pretty irrelevant conversation but Ginny pressed on anyway. 'And deep down, I think Bev does too. She said something last night about if it doesn't work out, at least she'll have got Gavin out of her system.'

There was a long pause. Finally Finn said, 'Not necessarily.'

'Why not?'

He shrugged. 'Doesn't always work that way.'

'Well, they're adults.' Ginny felt herself getting hot, unnerved by the intensity of Finn's gaze. 'Why are you looking at me like that?'

'Probably because I slept with you and didn't get you out of my system.'

Ginny's knees almost buckled. 'Wh-what?'

'Sorry. Being honest. You did ask.' Finn raked his fingers through his hair. 'And I know you only wanted a one-night thing, but I haven't been able to forget it. At all. Obviously, I couldn't say anything before, and maybe I shouldn't be saying it now.' He swallowed and Ginny heard the emotion in his voice. 'But it's been a hell of a day and I needed you to know how I feel about you. If I'm honest it's how I've felt the whole time Tamsin's been back.'

Ginny was speechless. Finally, she stammered, 'M-me too.'

It was Finn's turn to look stunned. 'Really?'

'Oh, yes. *God*, yes. Really.'

He kissed her and she'd never felt so alive nor so terrified. Pulling away, Ginny said, 'There's something else I have to tell you. I didn't mean it to happen.'

'Didn't mean what?'

Her courage failed. 'I can't tell you.'

Yes, you can. You must.

No, I can't, can't, *can't.*

'OK,' said Finn. 'Is it good or bad?'

'I don't know.'

'I love you. Does that help at all?'

Tears sprang into Ginny's eyes. 'I'm pregnant.'

Finn was motionless. 'You are?'

'Yes.' She saw the look on his face, realised what he was wondering and burst out, 'It's yours, I swear. I haven't slept with anyone else—not for years. I'm sorry!'

To her relief Finn relaxed visibly, half smiling. 'No need to apologise. I'm glad you haven't slept with anyone else.' Glancing at her stomach he added, 'Is everything OK?'

'With the baby? Oh, yes. I've had a scan.'

'Were you ever going to tell me?'

'No. I thought I'd move to Scarborough.' Ginny was still in a daze of happiness. 'Until this afternoon you had a family.'

Finn pulled her into his arms. 'I had a child who wasn't mine and a girlfriend I didn't love.' His gaze softened. 'Even worse, I was *in* love with someone who worked for me, but couldn't tell her because she was back with her ex-husband . . . hang on, so what was all that with the condoms?'

At last, a question she could answer. The two she and Carla had examined earlier were still in the fruit bowl on the kitchen table. Reaching over and fishing them out, Ginny said, 'Tamsin wanted another baby last year but you weren't so keen. So she stuck a needle through every packet in the box.'

'Good job the vicar didn't call round this evening.' Finn raised an eyebrow at the fruit bowl, then ran his fingers over the packet in his hand. 'Just as well it didn't work.'

'Except it did. Right result,' said Ginny, 'wrong womb.'

'Are you kidding? Tamsin finally did something that turned out well.' Pushing her wayward hair back from her face, Finn said, 'This could be the happiest day of my life. In fact, I think we should celebrate.'

Ginny trembled with pleasure as he kissed her again, then regretfully pulled away. 'I should phone Carla. She'll be wondering what's going on.'

'Carla's a grown up.' Finn surveyed her with amusement. 'I'm sure she can hazard a guess.'

'But she hates not knowing things. It drives her insane. Plus,' said Ginny, 'she'll come over and start hammering on the front door.'

Her mobile was still lying on the kitchen table. Picking it up and locating Carla's number, Finn rang it.

Carla snatched it up on the first ring. 'This is killing me! You're either shagging him or having the most almighty row.'

'Well done,' said Finn. 'Your first guess was correct.'

'Waaaah!' Carla squealed.

'Thanks. We think so too. So we'd appreciate it if you didn't come rushing over here because Ginny and I are going upstairs now.'

Ginny, seizing the phone, added happily, 'And we may be gone for some time.'

The next morning it was necessary to make another phone call, this time to Jem.

'Hi, darling, how are you?'

'Great, Mum. Did you get the photos I emailed you?'

'I did.' Ginny smiled, because Jem's happiness was infectious and the photos of her with Davy and Lucy attempting to rollerskate had been hilarious. 'Listen, there's something I have to tell you. It might come as a bit of a shock.'

Jem's tone changed at once. 'Oh God, are you ill?' Fearfully, she said, 'Is it serious?'

'Heavens no, I'm not ill!' Looking over at Finn, squeezing his hand for moral support and feeling him squeeze hers in return, Ginny said, 'Sweetheart, I'm pregnant.'

Silence. Finally Jem said soberly, 'Oh, Mum. I don't know what to say. I suppose it's Perry Kennedy's?'

'Good grief, no, it's not his!'

'Mother!' Stunned, Jem let out a shriek of outrage. 'Excuse me, but do you even *remember* that big lecture you gave me before I left home to start university? And now you're telling me you've gone and got yourself pregnant? How many men have you been sleeping with? And do you have the *faintest* idea who's the father?'

Jem was screeching like a parrot. Aware that Finn was able to hear everything, and that he was finding her daughter's reaction hugely amusing, Ginny offered him the phone.

'Oh, no.' Finn grinned and held up his hands. 'This time I'm leaving it all up to you.'

Chapter 13

SUMMER WAS OVER, autumn had arrived and red-gold leaves bowled along the station platform, threatening to get on the line and cause untold havoc with the train schedule. Ginny's mind flew back to this time last year, when she would have given anything for that to happen. Then she blinked hard, because although mentally she might be more able to accept it this time round, hormonally any excuse for a well-up and she was off.

Luckily, distraction was at hand.

'Stop it,' said Jem.

'Stop what?' Gavin looked innocent, which was never a good sign.

'Ogling that girl over there.'

'I wasn't.'

'Dad, you were. And the one who works in the ticket office.' Jem looked at Ginny. 'You were chatting her up. We both saw you.'

'It's called being friendly,' Gavin protested. 'Can't you lot *ever* give me the benefit of the doubt?'

After twenty years? Frankly, no. Ginny rolled her eyes and felt sorry for Bev. Their relationship had lasted four months, which was longer than anyone in their right mind would have predicted.

'The train's due in five minutes.' Jem was gabbling into her phone, excited to be on her way back to Bristol. 'I've got three bottles of wine in my case, and two of Laurel's cakes. Are we having pasta tonight?'

Ginny watched her, suffused with love and pride. Still deeply tanned after the three-week holiday in Miami, Jem was every inch the confident, vivacious nineteen-year-old looking forward to her second year of university. And she had plenty to look forward to, not least sharing a three-bed flat in Kingsdown with her two best friends. Poor Rhona, it hadn't been easy, but she'd finally accepted that the time had come for Davy to leave home and—

'Ginny, is that you?'

Swinging round, Ginny came face to face with a large, florid woman in a too-tight tweed coat who clearly knew her from somewhere.

'My goodness it is!' The woman let out a cry of delight. 'How amazing! How *are* you?'

Always a nightmare. Ginny hated it when this happened. Pretend you recognise them and attempt to bluff it out, or admit defeat and hurt their feelings?

'I'm *fine*! Gosh, fancy bumping into you here!' Since it was already too late to come clean, Ginny submitted to being enveloped in scratchy tweed and kissed on both cheeks.

'I'm just catching the train home! I've been visiting my aunt in Tintagel. It's so good to see you again . . . you haven't changed a bit!'

You have, thought Ginny, frantically attempting to peel back the years and picture the woman as she might have looked. To make matters worse, Jem had now finished her phone call and was making her way over.

'My daughter's catching the train too.'

'Your daughter? Well I never!' Beaming at Jem, the woman said, 'And what's your name?'

'I'm Jem.' Jem turned expectantly to Ginny. 'Mum? Who's this?'

Bugger, *bugger*. Ginny said, 'Darling, this is . . . ooh, excuse me . . .' Pressing her hand to her mouth she failed to stifle a tickly cough, then another one, then another . . .

'Lovely to meet you, Jem. And I'm Theresa Trott. Your mum and I were at school together, ooh, *many* moons ago!'

Jem said brightly, 'Oh! Friends Reunited.'

'Well.' Theresa looked bemused. 'I suppose we are.'

Ginny cringed, wishing her daughter didn't have the memory of an elephant when it came to names.

'No, I mean the website. You're the one who contacted Mum last year.' Jem was delighted to have made the connection. 'She drove up to Bath to meet you.'

'That was someone else,' Ginny said hurriedly.

'No it wasn't! It was Theresa Trott!'

By this time thoroughly bewildered, Theresa said, 'But I don't live in Bath, I live in Ealing.'

'What's going on?' Gavin joined in.

'Dad, do something with Mum. She's lost her marbles.'

'OK, I'm sorry.' Ginny held up her hands. 'I lied.'

Startled but determined to carry on as if nothing had happened,

Theresa shook Gavin's hand and said, 'So you're Ginny's husband, how nice to meet—oh, I say!' Her eyes widened as Ginny's voluminous white jacket parted to reveal the unmistakable bump beneath.

'Bloody hell!' Gavin stared at it too. Indignantly, he said, 'Where did that come from? It sure as hell isn't mine.'

He thought he was so funny. At that moment something snuffly brushed against Ginny's left ankle. Relieved, she turned and scooped the little dog up into her arms and said, 'Rescue me.'

Finn rose to the occasion like a true pro. Back from taking Rocky for a discreet pee on a patch of grass outside the station, he fixed Theresa Trott with a winning smile. 'Shall I explain? Gavin is Ginny's ex-husband. I'm her future husband and the baby's mine. The dog is ours as well. His name is Rocky. The baby's due in January and Ginny's marrying me soon after that.'

'He's going to be my stepfather.' Jem grinned, sliding her arm through Finn's.

'How lovely.' Dumbfounded but clearly entranced by Finn, Theresa said brightly, 'Well, congratulations. And there's me, never been married at all!'

Ginny shot Gavin a warning look, daring him to announce that this could be because she was fat, frizzy-haired and wearing a coat that made her look seventy.

'Ah,' said Finn, 'but you never know when the right one's going to come along. It could happen at any time.'

See? Ginny glowed with love and pride; that was the difference between Gavin and Finn. She'd definitely made the right choice this time.

Theresa, her chins quivering with gratitude, beamed up at Finn. 'That's what Mummy and Daddy keep telling me.' She blinked eagerly. 'So how did you and Ginny meet?'

As the baby kicked inside her, Ginny heard the train approaching in the distance.

'Actually, I caught her shoplifting,' said Finn.

Jill Mansell lives with her partner, Cino, and children Lydia and Cory in Bristol and is a full-time writer. Actually, that last part is not completely true, Jill tells me as we chat on the telephone. She watches TV, eats fruit gums, admires the rugby players training on the sports field behind her house, and spends hours browsing ('another word for research') on the internet. Only when she has run out of all possible displacement activity does she put her feet up on the sofa, turn down the TV, take out her fountain pen and A4 notepad and start to write. However unorthodox this régime may be, it certainly seems to work for Jill, who is currently writing her twentieth novel.

Jill Mansell

I asked her about her life before she became a writer. 'For eighteen years I worked as an elecro-encephalographic technician at the Burden Neurological Hospital in Bristol and I absolutely loved it—once I learned how to say it! It was a very varied job and I was dealing with everything from migraines to epilepsy and brain tumours. The only drawback was the money, or rather the lack of it, and that's why I started writing. I joined a local evening class in creative writing, thinking I would try to write the kind of book I like reading and, after a couple of rejections, I finally found an agent and a publisher. For a couple of years after the first books were published, I still worked at the hospital. That was such a bizarre juxtaposition, being half-and-half, doing the exciting but not very glamorous job and then getting into the world of publishing. One minute I would have a patient trying to strangle me and the next I'd be meeting my editor for a gourmet lunch!'

Has Jill ever found it difficult to come up with a plotline? 'Not yet, thank God. I write feel-good fiction. I don't like writing miserable, gloomy stuff. And I get my ideas from everywhere and anywhere—I eavesdrop a lot, and watch far too much daytime TV. The problems pages in magazines and newspapers are another terrific source. For *Thinking of You*, the seed was sown by my daughter Lydia's first-ever sleepover. She was twelve at the time and happily skipped off to her friend's house for the afternoon and night. But I found myself sitting on my own, watching all the telly programmes we usually watched together and feeling miserable. Suddenly it hit me that in six years' time she would be leaving home to go off to university and it was then that I thought: What must it be like for a single parent when your only child leaves home? What do you do then? I've already told Lydia, who's now fourteen, that she can never, ever go!'

With an initial idea brewing, how does Jill begin a novel? 'I go through my book of babies' names. All my characters' names have to go well together. That's what I find so hard about reading the Harry Potter stories—Harry, Hermione, Hagrid, Hogwarts. All those H's! I like my characters to have names that begin with different letters. Once I have those, the people quickly become real and I search through the telephone directory for surnames and the Yellow Pages for interesting jobs. After that they are off and away.'

So for *Thinking of You* did she always plan to write a parallel love story for single-mum Ginny and her daughter, Jem? 'No, I didn't really. It just happened and then I encouraged it. It was interesting because Ginny is thirty-eight years old and yet she makes exactly the same mistakes as her eighteen-year-old daughter. It just goes to show that being a grown-up doesn't stop you making the wrong decisions!'

When Jill first introduces the hero, Finn Penhaligon, into *Thinking of You*, he catches Ginny accidentally shoplifting. Obviously, I had to ask Jill if she had herself ever suffered from a similiar 'senior moment'? 'God, yes. I have night-mares about it. I once walked out of Marks and Spencer's with two great big fluffy dressing gowns over my arm. I'd completely forgotten about them. Luckily, I quickly realised and rushed back into the store. It can happen so easily when you've lots on your mind, and I'm a very absent-minded person.

'I write feel-good fiction. I don't like writing miserable, gloomy stuff.'

'Oh, and I have to tell you about a funny thing that happened to me the other day,' Jill continues, her bubbly, vibrant personality fizzing down the tele-phone line. 'I was browsing—I mean, researching—on the internet and found a quiz all about me. It was for my novel *Good at Games*, which I wrote about ten years ago. I decided to take the quiz and I scored six out of ten! "Nice try but could do better" was the verdict. It did make me laugh.'

Finally, I asked Jill what she thought the best thing was about being a writer. 'Freedom and flexibility, which is fantastic when you have children. I can also sit at home with my slippers on, which means my shoes never wear out!'

Jane Eastgate

susan duncan

salvation creek

'It seems ridiculous to worry about the future. I don't even know if I have one. The truth is, none of us do. If you can look at that simple fact from the right angle, it is empowering. I finally stop hedging my bets. In a peculiar way, what I've arrived at is faith. Not the religious kind, but the sort that comes from inside yourself.'

Susan Duncan

PROLOGUE

THERE IS A HOUSE on a high, rough hill that overlooks the tawny green waters of Lovett Bay. It is pale yellow, with three chimneys and a red tiled roof splattered with lichen. An elegant verandah, with stately columns and polished wooden floors, stretches from end to end, and on a still, summer evening it is quite magical to dine there, watching the light fade and birds fly home.

The house is reached by a steep, winding stairway that begins at the shore and seems to meander on and on to nowhere. Sometimes, if it is early enough in the morning, or late enough in the afternoon, swamp wallabies pause on the pathway and stare with big, uncertain eyes before suddenly taking fright and thumping off into the bush. In summer, the path is flecked with mint-coloured moss, the same shade of green as the blotches on the smooth trunks of the spotted gums that form a towering canopy in front of the sky. The climb is steep and yet if you take it slowly and pause to look at Lovett Bay, there is no need to feel tired or breathless.

Many boats are moored in the bay, soome big and immaculately maintained, with tall masts that seagulls or cormorants cling to, scanning the waters for their next feed. Others are the dreams, perhaps broken, of people who have seen beauty in an old wreck and who plan, one day, to restore it to former glory. Many of these wrecks have sat for years and I have never seen anyone go near them. Sometimes, the Water Police do a tour of the bay in one of their orange and white motorboats and, from time to time, one or two of the rottenest vessels are towed somewhere else or taken out to sea and sunk.

It is more than six years now since I first started trekking up these steps, and when I reach the fork in the pathway near the top I still can't decide which way is preferable. The right fork is steep and leads to a vast, spongy lawn, which isolates the house, like an emerald lake, from the muted, scraggy bush. The other pathway is a gentle ascent but it veers slightly away from the house and leads to an old wooden work-shed that lacks even a hint of the grandeur of the main house.

The house is called Tarrangaua, which is an Aboriginal word mean-ing, I am told, 'high, rough hill'. But I cannot find the word in any Aboriginal dictionary. The woman who named the house was a famous Australian poet, Dorothea Mackellar. She died in 1968, so I cannot ask her how the name came about. It is certainly grand, and so was she.

She would arrive in a chauffeur-driven yellow Rolls-Royce at Church Point, where her caretaker would wait for her with the launch. Lovett Bay, you see, is accessible only by boat—unless you want to walk five kilometres along the escarpment, then down into the valleys of the Ku-ring-gai Chase National Park. It is a sensational walk, which takes about an hour and a half, but it is tough in parts, with steep rocky tracks where you can easily lose your footing. In contrast, the boat trip is five minutes of pure pleasure as you cut past McCarrs Creek, then Elvina Bay, and finally swing west into Lovett, with the wind blowing in your face and the snap of salt air in your lungs.

At the time the house was built for Dorothea Mackellar in 1925, she was wealthy, single, forty years old and already involved in a love affair with the brandy bottle. But I knew nothing of all this when I first made my way past the house and into Lovett Bay. I was a messy, jangly forty-eight-year-old struggling to find a place to belong. I'd watched two of the most important people in my life slide slowly and painfully into death and the horror of it stubbed out hope, blotted out my idea of where I fitted in. I'd been spinning in a career for more years than I cared to remember, where the days had become a blur of office politics and pressures, where I felt only a rising sense of detachment. I had no idea what I was looking for to give my life new purpose, only that when I found this intangible *something*, I would be able to still the restless-ness. Begin again.

As I bumped across the water in a leaky tin dinghy to see a property for sale in Lovett Bay, I did not know that the journey had begun. That Tarrangaua, the pale yellow house on the high, rough hill, would hold the key to it all.

1

ONE MORNING, for no reason at all, I cannot find the strength to get out of bed. It's midwinter in Melbourne. Trees are naked under a dirty brown sky. The alarm clock went off an hour ago. The thought of throwing back the covers and putting my feet on the floor fills me with terror. I lie there, squeezing my eyes shut. Descending slowly into a deep, dark hole that I welcome. When I look at the clock again, two hours have evaporated. I reach for the phone and call the doctor.

'I can't make the decision to get out of bed.'

'Stay there, then. Stay there for as long as you want. You're ill.'

I put the phone back in its cradle, look around an anonymous mustard bedroom in my rented house. Mirrored closet doors reflect a haggard old woman. I turn away and face the window, counting on my fingers. Eighteen. Eighteen months since my brother, John, and my husband, Paul, died. For a second only, I squint into the future. The vacant spaces are unbearable.

The crying starts in silence. Tears wetting the pillow, dampening the collar of my pyjamas. Through the day it builds, until swollen eyes reduce the world to a narrow slit and my dog, Sweetie, climbs on the bed for the first time in her life to press her warm, black body close. When the maelstrom ends two days later, nothing has changed. My brother is still dead. And so is my husband.

My brother battled cancer for five years. They say a heart attack killed him. But it was exhaustion. I sat, the night before he died, on a white chair on white carpet in his white bedroom. He lay on a white bed under white sheets, so thin, frail and white himself, he barely existed. He breathed in quick little sips, the tumours in his lungs wider than his arms. They squeaked like an old flywire door when you rubbed them. As I'd done in the past to relieve a smidgen of his pain. On this night, he moved a finger. No rub. Thank you. Nearly dead.

'Shall I hold your hand?'

The finger again. No.

So I sat, truly frightened for the first time. As stupid as I know this is, my brother had been ill for so long I thought he would just stay ill. I refused to accept that he would die. Not the handsome, blond, blue-eyed big brother who built a billycart so his irritating little sister could be dragged along behind when he went out double-dink riding with his friend. Not the brother who got his girlfriends to make his sister's clothes because he thought her mother had lousy ideas about what suited her. Not the brother she had loved without question all her life. Larrikin, gambler, beautiful dresser, generous spirit, comfort and support. Not her big, invincible brother.

As a child, John was wise and compassionate. Almost five years older than me, he steadied the impact of rocky episodes in my parents' marriage. Sometimes, at the height of their disappointment with each other, they would turn to us children standing white-faced and trembling and demand that we choose between them.

'Choose no one,' my brother would whisper in my ear, his arm protectively round my shoulders.

'But I want Mummy.'

'Choose no one and they will have to stay together.'

My brother recognised early the power of emotion. Once, my mother hit him. I can still smell that cold, damp morning when my father's belt came out and she wrapped it round John's legs as he marched barefoot down the path in front of the hydrangeas.

'You are *not* going to school without your shoes!' she snapped.

'I told you. I can't find them!'

'Get back inside and have another look!'

'No!'

Whip. A red streak on white legs. My mother sitting abruptly on the concrete pathway. Crying with shock and remorse.

John squatted beside her and pulled her head to his chicken chest. Holding her until she calmed. 'Please, Mum. Don't hit me again. It upsets you too much.' He'd always been unbeatable.

My husband's illness, like my brother's, came out of nowhere. Paul's sneezing woke me at about 2 a.m.

'Get a tissue, for heaven's sake.'

The sneezing continued. Seriously cranky, I turned on the light. His eyes were open but unseeing. Please, God, please. Not both my boys.

He was still breathing when they lifted him into the ambulance, the seizures settling into a steady pattern. I climbed into the seat beside the driver, who was a calm young woman with an open face.

'This is going to sound bizarre,' I babbled. 'Two Sundays ago, Paul dreamed his friend, Terry, who is dead, landed in a plane and tried to convince Paul to join him on a trip. Exactly a week later, Paul dreamed that his mother, who died before Terry, was asking him to follow her.'

The driver said nothing.

'I guess what I want to know . . . Is my husband dying back there?'

'It doesn't look good,' she said, gently.

A few hours later, when the drugs kicked in and the seizures finally abated, when life and understanding filled Paul's eyes again, one of the doctors asked him a question: 'Who is the Queen of Australia?'

'I suppose you mean that bloody Elizabeth,' he grumbled.

I laughed with relief. This was the Paul I knew so well. Irreverent. Pig-headed. Caustic. Unswervingly true to the political heritage of his Irish ancestors. Thank you, God. I owe you.

Days later, after tests and then more tests, the tidy neurosurgeon with thinning hair pulled the flimsy curtain round Paul's hospital bed. 'There's a tumour at the front of your brain. It's the size of a small apple.'

Paul smiled. As though he'd known all along. I thought I might faint.

'You can operate, can't you?' I asked.

'We'll have to. The tumour is putting pressure on the brain.'

'Well, it could be all right, couldn't it?'

'We won't know until we've done a biopsy.'

Three days later the worst possible news. Glioblastoma. A quick growing, aggressive son-of-a-bitch that could not be stopped. A death sentence. I didn't owe God at all.

The tumour gobbled everything. His brilliant intellect. Laconic humour. Razor-sharp wit. Once a voracious reader, he would lie in bed, book in hand, but he seldom turned the page. I stopped by the hospice every morning on my way to work as the editor of a national women's magazine. On my way home, I called in to see my brother, then drove another two suburbs to visit Paul again. To sit alongside his bed until he drifted into sleep. Which meant getting home late. Wondering when to fit in a load of washing. When to clean the house. Whether it was selfish and irresponsible to steal an hour for a hot bath. Whether I could find enough strength and energy for the day ahead. There was not enough time. Ever. Nothing done properly.

Occasionally, Paul would suddenly become lucid again, in a way that made me think—hope—that the experts were wrong: 'What's on the cover of the magazine this week?' Halfway through my answer, he'd drift off again into a strange world where thoughts were tangled and friends, many long dead, flickered in and out of his mind: 'Must look up Don in Hong Kong next time.'

'Yes, great idea.' Don had succumbed to alcoholism a decade earlier.

My brother died as the sun came up on a Wednesday morning. His flame-haired, sharp-tongued wife, Jan, whom we call Dolly, steadfastly by his side as she had been throughout their lives together. I set aside Saturday morning to write his eulogy, so when the phone rang I flew into a rage at the interruption.

'What!'

'It's the hospice. Can you come and see Paul?'

I wanted to scream 'No!' Wanted to yell at everyone to leave me alone, to give me a break, just a tiny break, so I could write my brother's life in a way that did him justice.

'What's the matter?'

'Well, he's had a bit of a fall. Can you get here? He's asking for you.'

In his room with its views across monochrome Melbourne suburbs, Paul lay on a mattress on the floor. Another, empty mattress had been placed next to him. So I knew he was dying. The empty mattress was for me. A nurse had told me that when death approached, a second bed appeared for families to lie close and hold tightly for the last time.

I crawled onto the mattress beside him and cradled his head in my arms. 'I love you more than anyone in the world,' I whispered.

He lifted his hand with its beautiful long fingers and pointed to where his heart was fading away. 'More,' he said. He smiled wonderfully.

The fall, I discovered, had been caused by a heart attack. And that's what killed him. Not the tumour at all. So we had two funerals in a week. My brother's in Melbourne. Paul's in Sydney, his home town.

A few days after Paul's funeral, when it was Monday again, I zipped on my work face, climbed into my high heels and returned to my office to sit behind my desk. I locked loss in a hollow space and, fortified with my good old Melbourne public-school upbringing, which hammered home the maxim that the best way to get over a problem is to get on with it, I goose-stepped onwards.

Until the day I couldn't get out of bed.

I have been lying under the quilt in my manky cotton pyjamas for five days. I suppose I must have fed the dog and I have a vague memory of the phone ringing. I also recall opening a can of tomato soup, which is what my mother gave me when I was a little girl and my tummy felt bad.

On the sixth day I finally get up, walk the dog, shower, dress, turn the key in the ignition and swing carefully into peak-hour traffic. I pick up coffee from the corner shop. Hang my coat behind the office door. I sit behind my huge, ugly desk and wish every celebrity to hell, every whining bad-luck story to the same place.

Colleagues look enquiringly at me. 'Better?' they ask.

I smile. 'Yup. Virus or something. Fill me in.'

Covers to choose. Stories to chase. Staff to manage. Crying often, but pretending it's over a reader's heartbreaking story. I alone know I don't really give a stuff about the readers any more.

Sometimes, when the cover lines won't gel, I daydream about being dead. Escaping the whole shit bundle of grief in a single bound.

But then I hear my brother's words: 'All those people who kill themselves and I lie here fighting to live another minute.'

Paul's words: 'Live for the quicksilver moments of happiness. Recognise and absorb them. They are rare and precious.'

I have long given up the search for happiness, though. What I want now is peace. No stress. No responsibility. Work, a career, the media— it is all a silly game, anyway, when death is inevitable.

During those awful first months after the boys died, a routine begins with my stepdaughter Suzi. We meet on Friday nights for dinner in a pub in St Kilda. Suzi, big-eyed and skinny in her fashionably frayed charity-shop clothes. Suzi, who was there when her father died. Who sat with him each afternoon. Who loved him unconditionally. Which was the only way with Paul. She listens and listens and is the only one who lets me drop the façade of coping.

We never alter the routine. I order the same main course every week. So does Suzi. Lamb for me, steak for her. And the same wine. Death has snatched away any illusion of control and only dogged routine gives me a semblance of stability.

Black-clad waiters take our orders and give us respite from our everyday world. When Suzi and I cry, as we often do, they look the other way, or bring a glass of water and no words. Or a sinful pastry. The kindness of strangers. It is overwhelming.

One night, when it is nearly midnight, wine blots out my last vestige of emotional reserve.

'You know, you're a gift, Suzi. A gift in my life. If I'd had a child I would have wished for you.'

She shrugs as though it's no big deal. 'You have me,' she says.

And for a moment I feel as though I belong somewhere. But I back away from the impulse to make Suzi an anchor. Anchors, if they do not come from within yourself, can die on you. Or move on. Or turn out to be just plain unreliable.

There are moments, though, when my breath comes in short gasps and a single word or sound, such as my brother's name or an ambulance siren, can trigger waves of panic that make me want to vomit.

I discover quickly that there is no such thing as an ordinary moment any more. Too many ordinary moments have ended in disaster. Like going to bed one nondescript night and waking up to a husband with a brain tumour. Like listening to my brother's light cough and then getting a phone call to say it's a rare kind of cancer. I begin to assume the worst outcomes from the most trivial events. If Suzi is late for our dinner, it's a crash, not heavy traffic. If the phone rings late at night, it's a death, not a friend touching base.

At the office, I sometimes find myself sitting and staring at nothing, playing little mind games. I ask myself: if I die tomorrow, who will miss me? Will there be any regrets? Answering the regrets part is easy. I've danced at the White House with tall, handsome soldiers in crisp dress uniform. Driven around Somalia with men carrying machine guns perched on the roof of the car. I've jumped ice floes in Newfoundland to photograph helpless baby harp seals being clubbed to death. I've wandered through Imelda Marcos's vast, stuffed closets in Malacanang Palace, in the Philippines, counting her shoes and fur coats. Spent an afternoon with a sober Richard Burton in his movie-set trailer, lulled by his seductive voice and charmed by his earthy humour. Heaps of assignments, miles of travel, mostly at someone else's expense. An interesting, privileged, capricious journalist's life.

No. No regrets. I'll die without feeling there is still much to do. But the other question, the one about who will miss me, I find difficult to confront. Because no one will, not for long anyway. Transitory lives like mine touch many surfaces but rarely leave a mark. So when an old skin cancer on my top lip returns, I merely shrug.

'How much of the lip will go?' I ask the doctor.

'Nearly all of it.'

He reaches for my hand but I move it away, pretend I don't see his gesture of compassion. 'That's OK. I'm OK with that. It's not like I'm a young girl with her life ahead of her.'

But what I mean is that if death is the final outcome of life, what does it matter whether you have a top lip or not?

'I can book you into a hospital or you can have it done at the clinic,' he says. 'If we do it at the clinic, I'll do the lip reconstruction myself. In hospital, you can use a plastic surgeon of your choice. Do you want to think about—?'

'The clinic will be fine. Thanks.'

That night I call in, as I do at least twice a week, to have dinner with my brother's wife, Dolly. She cooks, I eat. She's chopping onions when I mention that I need to have a little surgery on my lip.

'I'll drive you to the clinic,' she says.

'Nah, I'll take a cab. It's no big deal.'

She looks at me sharply. Then changes the subject. 'They call us the Black Widows, you know,' she says. 'Sounds a bit glamorous, doesn't it?'

We are both flippant about death in those early days after the boys are buried. Flippant in a way that shocks some friends, but allows us to publicly acknowledge their absence without being shattered by it.

'Jesus, Dolly. Remember Paul's funeral? Remember dear old Keith, coming up to us? "Don't stand too close," you said. "We're on a roll!"'

Dolly laughs, throws the onions into a frying pan and wipes tears from her eyes. Onion tears? We fill our glasses with more wine.

'The poor bastard took off like a rabbit.'

Dolly brings our plates to the table. Huge steaks with a mushroom and onion sauce, mashed potato and a fresh green salad with lots of chopped parsley, the same as her mother makes.

'So do you want me to drive you to the clinic on Monday?' she asks again, sitting down to eat. Wine flows again.

'No, thanks. It's easier to grab a cab.'

Dolly looks at me hard. Torn between respect and concern.

'I'll be fine. Prefer to go alone.'

'Should we open another bottle?' she asks.

The following Monday, I call a cab to take me to the clinic. I arrive on schedule to find a yellow room full of anxious, mostly middle-aged people. There will be a long wait, the receptionist tells me. One by one, as names are called, people disappear and return a while later with red-rimmed eyes and bandages over ears, arms, noses, foreheads. They look like casualties of war as they sit and wait for pathology results.

Then it's my turn. I lie in a chair like a dentist's.

The knife cut feels like a gentle tug and most of my top lip is flicked into a shiny, kidney-shaped stainless-steel dish. Wads of bandages are pressed hard on the wound and the tinny scent of blood fills the room. After a while, when the blood flow eases and the pathology results confirm all the cancerous skin has been cut away, the specialist begins to rebuild my lip, taking flesh from inside my mouth and pulling it forward to drag it up over the missing bit. He hums through his work.

Then he leans across me, and it is the first time I've felt a body closely since I crawled onto the mattress beside my dying husband. It is strange: I can lose a lip, deny pain, smell my own blood and remain detached, yet the casual touch of another human being almost brings me undone.

After eight hours, I leave the clinic with a brick of bandage balanced on a tender new lip like some kind of primitive tribal decoration. I am told to avoid hot food, drink through a straw, stay quiet.

At the house, my mother waits with every kind of liquid food lined up on the kitchen worktop. I'd tried to stop her coming from her home at the foot of the Blue Mountains, but seeing her face is unexpectedly comforting. She hands me a drink with a straw and sends me to bed.

I am supposed to spend a week convalescing, but two days later I drive to the office. I look bizarre, but work offers routine and I grab it like a lifeline. At home, there's too much time to think. There is a tight band of pain round my chest, though, and I wonder if I am on the edge of a heart attack or just slowly going mad. I do not care much, either way.

Suzi senses my detachment from my own welfare and insists on making an appointment with a shrink. I keep the date, although I am ashamed that Suzi thinks I need psychiatric help. Shrinks, I think as I sit in the dimly lit office, are for wimps.

'So tell me why you're here,' she says.

'Well, my brother and husband died within three days of each other. About nineteen months ago. And I still feel a bit sad sometimes. So I need some tools. To cope with grief. Give me the tools. I'll do the rest.'

She looks at me over her glasses, that kind and clever shrink, and suggests I start right back at the beginning, before the boys were even ill. By the third session, there is very little she doesn't know.

She explains that most people feel guilty for being the one still living. She teaches me to focus on the great times, not the moments I let slip past unnoticed. She brings me to understand that grief goes on for a long time, perhaps for ever, but it's possible to live with it. Not for it.

Then, one day not long after she says it is time for me to move on from her, I reach the real turning point. Tired of the stress, I decide that I hate my job and that a fat salary can't paper over the cracks any more.

I can't remember the last time I sat in the bath with a glass of white wine and sang my lungs out. I can't remember the last time I woke up and looked at the day ahead with enthusiasm.

The concept of jumping from a career into nothing is frightening. All my life I've never leapt until I had somewhere to land. Always the job, then the life. That's how I've lived. Now I am turning all that around. Life first. How utterly terrifying. Because by taking the life option I am once again opening myself to being vulnerable. But I understand the victory in realising that hurting is one way of knowing you are alive.

I join the ranks of the unemployed a little less than two years after the boys die, selling the monster white house with its lacy gazebo overlooking the Nepean River in NSW where Paul and I based ourselves.

Earlier in the year I bought an apartment in Melbourne as an investment. It will provide an adequate rental income, and I have enough money to live on, if I'm careful, for the rest of my life. My plan now is to search for a new, cheap house, in a new town, where I plan to make new friends and take up a worthy cause. I am going to reinvent myself and leave loss packed in a tightly shut corner of my mind.

I have just three months before the new owners take possession of the big white house. I begin the search for a new home immediately. The company car is back with the company. I now have a high-slung, big-wheeled, grunty secondhand ute that can claw through creek beds and scale mountains. Its name is Fearless Fred. My dog, Sweetie, too old to jump, puts her front paws on the edge of the truck tray and I heave her in. With a sniff and a scratch, she settles down next to the icebox as though she's been a ute dog all her life.

'Forward ho, huh, old girl?' I say, slamming the tailgate.

That lovely, placid Rottweiler and I travel through towns too small to support a local bakery. Towns where the only restaurant is a laminated annexe off the rusty, local service station. In bigger towns, where there are coffee shops and at least one chemist, fresh fruit gets piled into the icebox and I drift along, apple in hand, assuming my new home will suddenly appear to me in a flash of recognition.

After trudging around a few properties described glowingly in real-estate advertisements, I break the property description code. 'Charming country cottage' means an ant-infested ruin with a sagging verandah.

'Acreage with beautiful views' means the soil is so poor you couldn't grow a weed. No photo of the house is just plain scary. Don't go there.

'Why are these people selling?' I ask one agent after another.

There is a tragic sameness to the answers: 'Couldn't make a go of it.'

It forces me, eventually, to think beyond the romantic notion of plunging into a new environment. Who will be my friends in this town where I know no one? Who will I talk to? What will I fill my days with?

Pulling the plug on one life and launching another is, I am beginning to understand, fraught with risk. But I struggle on. I see mudbrick houses, pole houses, log houses, iron houses, stone houses and even a house with a thatched roof and a herb garden that nearly seduces me. But it is in a cold, cold valley where the sun lingers only for an hour or two through winter, and I know that eventually it will be depressing, not quaint. On all these forays, Sweetie, loyal, patient, soft-eyed and trusting, never strays from my side. She is the best dog.

The journey leads me to my cousin Jayne in Wangaratta, where she and her husband, Edward, and her father, my Uncle Frank, grow luscious peaches and nectarines. Sweetie and I arrive late on a hot summer night, so I park the ute under a row of peach trees near the house and sleep there soundly. In the very early morning, Jayne, one month older than me, peers into the back, wondering what on earth has pitched up in her orchard. Some itinerant picker looking for work, she thinks.

'It's you!' she shrieks.

'Yeah. Got here late last night.'

'Why didn't you knock, you silly old cow?'

'Used to sleeping out now. I quite like it. It's sort of liberating.'

'You've gone daft. Well, you better get up and come in. We're having breakfast and we're busy. It's picking time.' She marches off to the house. Turns back with a grin. 'And don't pinch any fruit off the trees!'

The branches around me bend with plump, golden peaches. I stretch and snap one off, pressing my nose to furry skin that smells like a lazy summer. I bite into it and juice trickles down my chin. When it's finished, I pick another.

I'm not sure when I realise that the tight band squeezing my chest isn't there any more. Perhaps it is on the second, absurdly magical, moonlit night at Jayne's home, when I sit on the porch in a tattered chair sipping a frigidly cold beer with my Uncle Frank. In the distance, peach trees—their lush, musky scent drifting on the warm night air—stretch like ghostly armies towards the magnificent Victorian Alps.

'How'd you cope, Frank, when Belle died?' I ask him. Frank's beautiful, busy wife was barely middle-aged when her car smashed into a tree.

'Didn't do so good at first. I'd have a few drinks, and that'd help for a minute. But after a while, booze just made it worse. Found that out.'

'What? So you stopped drinking?'

'Yeah, which wasn't that easy. Plays dirty tricks on you, your noodle. If you don't watch it. Always wants to push you down the wrong road. One drink, I'd think. It'll help. But it didn't.'

'Frank?'

'Yes, love?'

'I can't seem to settle. Can't find my feet somehow.'

'Yeah. It's a bugger that. But you'll come good.'

We sit silently and my mind fills with memories of the boys. Instead of shutting them down, I let them swirl and take shape. How lucky I am to have known two such wonderful men. Odd, to call my husband wonderful, though. In reality, we fought and often went our separate ways. He was difficult, fascinating, volatile, infuriating, vibrant and never, ever dull. A blue-eyed bull of a man with tight, curly blond hair who always had a dream that only he thought was possible. But somehow, through even the worst times, we never lost sight of the fact that we cared for each other.

After nearly a week trawling the area with real-estate agents, Sweetie and I make our way back to the white elephant on the Nepean River. The new owners of the house are due to move in and I have to move on. Desperate for somewhere to land while I search for the dream house, I decide to make the Melbourne apartment a temporary base. Temporary because I need the income from the rent if I am to avoid dipping into capital. From the apartment I will search, once again, for a piece of earth where I will plant a lemon tree and a herb garden. The lemon tree is for my father. To him, a house didn't become a home until there was a lemon tree. A herb garden fills me with contentment, though. All those flavours. All that healing. The thrill of picking and eating what you have grown. It is the most basic instinct.

Back at the sold house, the slow, sorry business of reducing two lives to one begins. It is crammed with the confetti of our irregular lives. Acres of books, out-of-date clothes, thousands of unedited photographs. Choosing what to keep is an awful process.

Every so often, a stack of Paul's old notebooks, filled with his spidery writing, turns up. I read them at first, to feel close to him, but soon it is as though I am opening someone's mail, prying into a private part of a life. I put the notebooks aside.

At his clothes closet, I open and close the door quickly. The clothes seem to wait for Paul to fill them, and for a blinding moment I think he might walk out of the shower with a towel round his waist, saying, as he always did, 'Baby, where's my . . .?' In the end, I pack the clothes and take them with me. I do not really understand why.

The removal men arrive with a semitrailer big enough to live in. Eighteen years of memories are crammed into the long, dark space and the past is closed down. Fearless Fred is loaded to bursting point with Sweetie and my old Burmese cat, Banana, plus brooms, mops, pot plants and suitcases. The house is clean and empty. My mother stands in the driveway. She looks abandoned. She moved from Melbourne to the foot of the Blue Mountains in 1989, to be near me when her relationship with my brother's wife failed to thrive. Now her son is dead and her daughter on the move. Paul's death changed both our lives.

I climb behind the wheel and swing onto the stinking hot bitumen. It will be the early hours of the morning before I put the key in the lock in Melbourne. No matter where it might lead, I've made the leap. No job to give structure to the days. No one to take into account. There's only me. Essentially, I can do what I damn well please. I thought it would feel like freedom but it feels more like entering a dark tunnel. It is just three months since I left the office behind.

The apartment is one of two in a sombre, 1930s liver-brick building in a trendy suburb. It is in perfect order. Luxurious. But it feels like a genteel prison. Because there is nowhere to go each morning after I've showered and dressed. After a month, the gloomy green pittosporums that block the afternoon sun in the courtyard garden are depressing, so I dig them out. When the courtyard is planned and planted, which doesn't take long because it is small and I have plenty of time, I decide to paint the bedroom walls. I discover old fireplaces concealed behind Gyprock walls in nearly every room. Time to get practical! I will have a fire in the bedroom and another in the sitting room, to keep me warm when winter comes. I am being constructive! By the time I organise a builder to install bookcases on either side of both fireplaces, I have filled in three months. Busy! Busy! Busy!

Now what? Back to perusing the real-estate ads in the Saturday paper, making appointments and wandering the countryside.

Retiring is not easy. Even if you hate what your work has come to mean to you, as I have, it still provides a daily goal. Now there is nothing to focus on except myself. Which I thought would be a relief. Only it isn't. The blunt reality is that I am forty-four years old, overweight, with a self-image that's shot to hell.

My Friday-night dinners with my stepdaughter Suzi continue, and sometimes, on a Sunday afternoon, I join her, her partner and friends at a gig in a pub somewhere, listening to music that seems to come from another planet. I end up drinking too much and getting home when most people are leaving for work. I am too old for this, I realise, and it makes me feel seedy. There has to be more.

How much of our self-image is tied up with what we do, and when we cease to do it we wonder if we have anything left to offer, personally or professionally? Five phone calls trying to become a volunteer worker result in rejection. I don't consider finding another partner. If my mind drifts in that direction for a moment, I yank it back: 'Too fat, too old, too independent . . . too hard!' Too scared is probably closer to the truth. After eighteen years in a rigorously faithful relationship, the idea of sex with anyone else is terrifying.

Then one morning the cat leaps out of his basket next to the heater and drops dead. He lies in a heap and the sight wrecks me. After sitting next to him for an hour or two on the floor, the grief of the past few years eventually settles back into its closed niche and I call my brother's friend James to ask in a thick voice if I can dig a hole somewhere on his property. There's no room in my little courtyard, and anyway, Banana always preferred wide-open spaces.

'Plenty of land here,' he says. 'We'll find a top spot for him.'

'Thanks. I'll be there this afternoon.'

All I can think as I drive along, glancing at the little body lying stiff-legged in his basket, is that it's another bloody death. Another empty compartment. I begin to wonder if I attract it.

Not long after the move to Melbourne, the phone rings at about 10 p.m. It's Pat, a friend of my mother's. 'Your mother is in intensive care,' she explains in a quiet and calm voice. 'Heart attack. An ambulance took her off about an hour ago.'

I ask no questions. Just drive all night to Sydney.

I have always had an uneasy relationship with my mother. We love each other, of course, but sometimes I want to throttle her. And she, me.

I wonder if her ambition for her only daughter was blighted early. I was born with a lazy eye, a strawberry mark down my face and not enough chin, so a glamorous marriage was out of the question. An operation fixed the lazy eye and the strawberry mark faded in a few months. But it was not enough to transform me into *pretty*.

There was also the problem of my disposition. As a teenager, I was a judgmental little prig. And what I hated, above all, was alcohol. This made life a bit strained, considering my parents bought a country pub after my father retired from his job in the public service at Bonegilla migrant camp, near the Albury–Wodonga border.

Twelve hours later, when I reach the hospital, the receptionist cannot find my mother listed in intensive care. I think for a suffocating moment that she must be dead.

'Ah, here she is. Ward C, Room 14.'

Relief pounds through my body. 'Is that the cardiac ward?'

'Oh, no. It's where they put people with problems they can't identify.'

A roaring red rage consumes me, driven by my mother's selfishness and my own stupidity. Not getting enough attention? Fake an illness. I should have known. When I find her room, she is sitting up in bed, perky and pink, eating chocolates.

'You seem well for a woman who had a heart attack yesterday,' I remark.

She looks me in the eye without a tremor of unease. 'I've had three more this morning. Two mild, one big.'

She is so convincing that for a second I believe her. But her pale blue nightie falls neatly from its embroidered yoke. No tubes or wires there. She is snappy, alert and healthy. Then my anger at being manipulated deflates. She is my mother. The loss of my brother, her adored only son, made her mad with grief. Perhaps this is her way of focusing on a situation that hurts her less. I turn and walk out.

A few years later my mother confesses her heart attack had, in fact, been haemorrhoids.

'Why did you tell everyone it was a heart attack?'

She's dismissive. 'Nobody mentions haemorrhoids!'

'So did you get your haemorrhoids fixed?'

'I couldn't talk about them. I told you that!'

'But I could have been killed driving all night. With no sleep.'

'Rubbish! I didn't get a proper night's sleep for years after you and your brother were born.'

I give up. My mother is who she is. In a way, her weakness has become my strength. I never expect sympathy, do not seek coddling. I learned very early that to look for sympathy from my mother was to invite a ticking off. 'Pull yourself together,' she'd say. 'Don't make a fool of yourself. Not in public.' Another era. A different generation. Mostly, she is just as tough with herself in a real crisis. When she is in her early eighties and falls, breaking a wrist, she shrugs off the discomfort and manages on her own at home. And when she flies headfirst down some stone steps not long after her wrist heals, she laughs at the absurdity of her large breasts finally being useful. 'Might've broken a few ribs if they hadn't cushioned the fall,' she jokes. Sometimes, it's impossible not to feel proud of her.

A phone call comes midmorning in early August as I'm wandering the Melbourne apartment looking for something to polish.

'It's Fleury's birthday. Come to Pittwater for the weekend.'

'Stewart! How are you? What are you up to?'

Stewart and my husband were great friends and I tagged along until the friendship became mine as well.

'Good. I'm good. Can you make it?' he asks. 'July the 23rd.'

I hesitate.

'Be great if you could help with the cooking. And Sophia needs a lift.'

The clinchers. I'm needed. Can't say no to all that. Especially the cooking. I love it. Passionately.

'You're going to be the surprise guests,' Stewart adds. 'You and Sophia.'

Part of me wants to stay safely at home. Another part says get a life. 'Great. I'll be there. Get Sophia to call me.'

I have not met Sophia yet, know her only as Stewart's and Fleury's friend who writes a column for a Melbourne newspaper. She is a Buddhist, lots of fun, apparently, and very clever.

That night, I undress for bed. Look in the mirror. The sight is shocking. Being a fat boss is fine. Being a single, unemployed, overweight woman in her mid-forties makes me want to hide in a closet. I'll have to get a new shirt, one of those big flowing things, to hide the rolls.

Sophia and I meet on a cold morning two weeks later. She parks her ancient orange Volvo off-street, behind the apartment.

'We won't get there before dark,' I say, anxious about our late departure.

Sophia is dismissive. 'Of course we will. We'll be in Sydney by lunchtime at the latest.'

'It's an eleven-hour drive! It's nearly nine o'clock now!'

'You weren't planning to do the trip in *one day*, were you?' Sophia, rugged up in a navy cashmere sweater, orange trousers, a windcheater, her white hair springing in all directions, looks terrified.

'I always do it in one day.'

'It's not safe to drive for more than six hours in a day, even with ten-minute breaks every two hours.' Her tone is schoolteacherish.

'OK, we can stop somewhere if you're tired. But if we both feel OK, we'll go on. Yeah?'

Air drizzles out of her in relief.

We begin our drive under a leaden sky, feeling each other out. She is bright and funny, well read and articulate. We discover we were born in the same hospital in a small country town on the border of Victoria and New South Wales. Our parents might even have known each other.

'Heard your brother died. And your husband.'

'Yeah.'

'My mother and sister, too. Six months between them. Nursed them both. How're you doing?'

'Good, yeah, really good,' I lie. 'Don't understand this dying shit though. I mean, what's the point of it all?'

'The Buddhists understand it. Only ones who do.'

'What's their take on it?'

'Well, years ago, when I was in my hippie phase, my dad died. I was in Kathmandu when I got the news. I was completely devastated. I wanted to know why. Why him? Why at that particular time? Why ever? I went to see a monk at a monastery. Know what he said?'

I shake my head.

'Everything that is born must die.'

Everything that is born must die. So simple. Inevitable. Accept it.

'Once you understand that, you should try to look for the gift in the death of your husband and brother.'

'Are you mad? What kind of gift is it to have half your family die?'

Sophia smiles smugly and doesn't answer. As we drive, the sky drifts from black to grey to hot blue.

'So what was the gift *you* got out of the death of your mother and sister?' I am aggressive with her. I want to put her on the spot.

'Oh, that's easy,' she says. 'I learned anything can happen to anyone at any time and you must live each day the best way you can.'

'Do good, do you mean?'

'Oh yeah. But be the best person you can, too. You know, nothing gives wisdom faster than a good attitude to death.'

By midafternoon we cross the long, straight bridge that spans the Murrumbidgee River and the lush river flats where fat cattle graze in the thin, sharp winter light. We know, by now, that we will be lifelong friends. An hour later we cross the Yass River into a wide main street speckled with solid old buildings. I itch to continue. So near. Just three or four hours, tops. But Sophia is firm. She won't push the limits.

'There'll be a lu-verly motel here.' She grins. 'We'll find the cheapest. All we're gonna do is sleep there. They're all the same in the dark.'

I give in. We check into a tired motel and dump our bags on the worn brown carpet. Then we go out to dinner at a Chinese restaurant. Two beers each. The food is sugary with a sticky coating on the beef.

'What's the plan tomorrow?' Sophia asks.

'Get up and go. But we've gotta find a present for Fleury. What about flowers? Heaps of them. From the wholesale markets. We drive past them on the way into Sydney.'

'Fill the house with them.'

'Look great for the party.'

We beam at each other.

Back at the motel, Sophia climbs into her pyjamas and mumbles some prayers, doing a series of prostrations on the worn carpet. Soon she slides under the orange chenille covers, flicks off her light and falls asleep.

I sit in bed, wide-eyed, with a book. The sheets are clean but the bedspread smells of other people. I try to read in a little pool of weak fluorescent light but I can't concentrate on the words. My head spins with recipes for possible party dishes. Lots of people. Keep it simple. One dish lunch. Plenty of nibbles and a huge dessert. Think about the practical. Put off the personal. *Busy. Busy. Busy.* I turn off my light.

In the morning, the cold makes our noses dribble. Cold water on the windscreen cracks and melts the frost. I start the engine, switch on the heater, silently urging it to kick in quickly. Our breath erupts in clouds.

Sophia belts up carefully, indicates with a slight incline of her head that she is ready to move. I slide into gear and pull out of the motel.

'I'm not sure, but I reckon we'll miss the market. Closes around eight and I don't think we'll get there until after nine,' I say.

'Let's give it a go anyway.'

We make our way through folding blue hills along a highway edged with twisted silver gums. The road hums an endless single note. It's nearly 10 a.m. when we veer off the highway to go to the Flemington markets, where there's acres of cold, concrete emptiness except for one bloke with a few buckets of pink tulips. We scoot over to him. Sophia, a seasoned negotiator from years of travelling in India and Nepal, tries to get him to throw in a bucket to hold the flowers but he won't do it.

'Bastard,' she mutters, not used to defeat.

'Very un-Buddhist of you.'

She grins.

We lay armloads of tulips, deliciously pink and feminine and still in tight buds, gently on the back seat. I turn off the heating. Don't want them to burst open before we get there.

Sophia grabs the street directory and gets us back onto the highway without mishap. Stewart rings when we're twenty minutes from the centre of Sydney. I pass the mobile to Sophia and he gives her an address and directions.

When we reach Stewart's office in Surry Hills, he is waiting outside in his car with his dog, Gus, beside him in the front passenger seat.

We wave madly and stick our heads out of the car windows, yelling happily. 'We're here! Gidday.'

'Follow me,' he shouts, pulling in front of us.

Everywhere I look I see places where Paul and I once ate or drank. When we drive past his favourite pub I half expect him to step a little unsteadily out of the doorway, his face moony with contentment. Paul always loved a jar with his mates. Every Friday afternoon he held court in a corner of the bar. He charmed, entertained and provoked. His mind moved like mercury but not much held his interest for long.

We met in New York when I was twenty-six and he was thirty-nine. At least, that's what he told me. Three years later, when he was still having a thirty-ninth birthday, I tackled him. He cheerfully explained that like W. C. Fields he intended to remain thirty-nine for ever. He must have been forty-two when we met and I wonder, now, if he wasn't already disappointed with the way his life had turned out. Everything came so easily to him when he was young that when his luck dried up, as it always does for a while, he couldn't handle it. Or maybe, like me, he'd reached the age when the seedy side of journalism wore out his hubris.

The door of his favourite old pub stays shut as we drive past, though, and we claw through the clogged city to sort out the jumbled lanes of the Harbour Bridge and then cruise through suburbia.

Stewart is covered in dog hair when he gets out of the car in the vast open-air car park of the supermarket in Mona Vale. He tolerates a hug and shouts at Gus to *shut up* at the same time. Gus keeps barking.

Sophia looks sideways at Stewart, smiles. 'Helloooo, Stewart.' She kisses his cheek and the three of us—greyer, fatter, slower and less sparkling than we remember ourselves—go shopping.

'Does Fleury know we're here?' Sophia asks.

'Nope,' Stewart says. 'It's still a surprise.'

'When's she coming to Pittwater?'

The party is a Saturday lunch. It is Thursday.

'Tomorrow night.'

'But the surprise will be ruined! Can't you make her stay in town until Saturday lunchtime?'

'No one makes Fleury do anything.'

When we've filled three trolleys with everything from fillets of beef to chicken wings, Stewart pays the bill. We load the shopping into his dog-hair encrusted car and follow him to Church Point.

We scoot past million-dollar houses, a few rackety old holiday shacks from the fifties that haven't succumbed to property developers, and a couple of swanky marinas. Where the sea tickles the roadside, a few mangroves cling to muddy flats, and, further on, little dinghies bob up and down on lazy waves. It is a sparkling, summery, seaside day and the gloom of Melbourne fades into a shadowy memory.

Just past a bucolic general store, ferry wharf and a motel and restaurant that look as though they've seen more halcyon days, Stewart turns into Mitchell's Marina, where he keeps a boat, because the only way to get where we're going is across the water. There's a chaotic collection of long, slender yachts loaded with tackle, glamorous motor cruisers, and bare-boned runabouts with outboard motors. Halfway along the jetty, Stewart's bright yellow commuter boat is already loaded with six cases of wine, delivered earlier and left unattended.

'Don't you worry stuff will get stolen?' I ask.

'Stuff gets knocked off from time to time but everyone knows who's done it and the word goes around,' he says.

As commuter boats go, the *Yellow Peril*, as I'm later told it's nicknamed, is a Rolls-Royce. Padded seats. A canopy for shelter from the rain. A steering wheel instead of a tiller. But to me it looks small and bouncy.

Gus jumps aboard without being told to and scrambles into the front passenger seat. Stewart follows. We hand him bag after bag of shopping. Then our baggage. Then the flowers. Sophia and I fossick for a seat. We are clumsy and flat-footed in the confined, unsteady space.

'So *this* is Pittwater,' I say.

'Yep. It's been home to smugglers, convicts, fishermen, farmers, layabouts, entrepreneurs, brothel owners, artists, writers and, until the last few years when real-estate prices surged, the odd bloke who was doing it a bit hard,' Stewart says.

Sophia shuts her eyes, raises her face to the sun. A closed smile creeps into her lips.

'They reckon if you stay two years, you never leave,' Stewart adds.

'That's a long time to take to settle in.'

'Ah, don't be seduced by the sea and sun. Living here full time takes stamina.'

Stewart turns the key and the engine kicks into life with a cough. We cruise sedately through a maze of boats rolling gently on their moorings. We're moving at a snail's pace, which I assume is Stewart's way of giving us a guided tour.

'Nah. You can't speed through the moored boats,' he explains when I thank him. 'It's against the law. Too many kids and a few blokes have gone overboard when they've been hit by a big wake.'

At the end of the go-slow zone, where the waterway opens up, Stewart pushes forward the throttle. Tulips scatter everywhere. Sophia and I lunge to grab them, rocking the boat dangerously.

'Slow down, Stewart!' Sophia shouts.

He doesn't hear her and we look at each other and laugh, falling back into our seats and letting a few tulips become offerings to the sea.

We pass a lovely white wooden cottage at the water's edge, another that is built on pylons. Just beyond a plain grey boathouse there's a wind-beaten finger of land Stewart tells us is called Woody Point.

'This is Towlers Bay,' he yells, swinging past a shallow water marker at Woody Point. 'We're nearly there.'

An eclectic mix of houses with jetties and boat sheds beads the coastline on the southern side of the bay. Some are grand, with acres of glass, some simple, with fibro walls and sagging decks. The northern side is thick with rugged bushland, and near the escarpment ochre rocks with almost human features hang precariously. There's a beautiful, sheltered, quarter-moon beach and, behind it, dense, dark rain-forest trees loom out of a damp gully. Stewart's house is located towards the end of Towlers Bay, where a freshwater creek runs from the escarpment to the tidal flats. There's a shelf, or drop-off, and the water changes from the blue of the deep to sandy turquoise. It's like a tropical paradise.

When Stewart pulls into his dock, Gus dashes past Sophia and me, knocking us sideways. He leaps off the boat before it's stopped moving.

'What do you want us to do?' Sophia asks.

'Jump off,' Stewart says.

Sophia and I look at each other. OK, we nod. We can do that.

Stewart holds the boat firmly against the pontoon as we scramble off. He passes me a rope. 'Hold this. Don't let it go.'

He and Sophia unload the shopping carefully. Soon the pontoon looks like a garbage dump. There are boxes and bags everywhere. I glance along the weathered grey planks of the jetty to steps that climb to a brown timber house above us with a deck covered in a rampant vine.

'How do we get the shopping up there?'

'We carry it,' Stewart replies.

'Oh.'

There are six cases of wine, forty or so shopping bags. Luggage. For a moment my holiday spirit falters. Five trips at least. Each.

Stewart takes the rope and secures the boat. He lifts two cases of wine and sets off. Sophia sighs and gathers two thick handfuls of shopping bags. I look for the ice cream, milk, butter and cream—and follow the leader. At the top of the stairs, hot and sweating, I strip off my sweater.

'You stay here,' I tell Sophia, who is in the kitchen, swilling a glass of water. 'We need someone to unpack the shopping as we bring it up.'

She has an arm that is weak from a car accident some years ago. I have always been as strong as an ox, healthy as a buffalo.

It takes four trips to clear the dock. By then the fridge is full to bursting point and most of the non-perishables are stacked in the laundry. We're pretty pleased with ourselves and to celebrate we crack open some icy-cold beers, then sit on the deck and absorb the view. Darkness falls in quickly, quietly. The evening is clear, the stars luminous. Later, a huge, almost full moon creeps silently above the horizon, coating the bay in a pale, shivery light. The night is filled with good friends and good wine, and dinner is one of Stewart's famously hot curries. For a long while, I put aside loss.

Friday is a frenzy of preparation. We can't find any instructions on how to poach the glistening, giant salmon that Stewart bought at the Sydney fish market, so we decide to throw in about six bottles of white wine with a few bay leaves, some onions, carrots and celery, and put the lid on top. Basic French cooking rites.

We slather a whole fillet of beef in crushed garlic and sit it on a bed of thyme to rest overnight. By the afternoon, most of the work is done and we mooch around feeling clever and competent.

Stewart is in the shower when the phone rings, and he yells to us to pick it up.

'Hi, Fleury!' I gush, without thinking. Oh shit.

Sophia looks at me. Speechless. Stewart, wrapped in a towel, takes the phone. Game over.

Fleury arrives late Friday afternoon to our cries of 'surprise', even though it isn't any more, and we crowd round the table for dinner. We sit down to bowls of thick minestrone with grated parmesan, with lots of sourdough bread to mop our bowls. We wash down camembert and quince paste with red wine, and rehash old times. We toast absent friends and family, wiping tears, more aware than ever that we, too, are creeping closer to the finishing line, and fall into bed.

In the early hours of Saturday morning, low clouds drift in bringing drizzling rain. By the time we gather round the breakfast table, the damp, grey weather looks entrenched.

'It *will* clear,' Stewart insists, used to getting his own way.

But by noon the drizzle has developed into steady rain and there's no way it's going to fine up. Tables are moved inside, the fire lit, food planned to be hot instead of room temperature.

Guests arrive on the local pink water taxi and trickle up to the house under umbrellas, smelling of damp wool and wet leather shoes. So I don't see his face until he walks into the sitting room. He is, to me, quite beautiful and I am drawn to him. It is an impulse without reason.

There are crises in the kitchen. The salmon poacher is too big for the stove and I can't get the liquid to reach boiling point. The frying pan is too small to sear the beef before putting it in the oven. It feels like chaos, which in a kitchen makes me want to cry. When I look around, everyone is having a great time. They don't care that the sauce béarnaise for the beef is curdled or worry that the salmon will give everyone food poisoning. After a couple of glasses of wine, neither do I.

At one stage I become drunkenly fixated on something Sophia said on the drive to Sydney. I seek her out.

'Got a question. Remember you said I should look for the gift?'

Sophia hasn't a clue what I'm talking about.

'You know, the gift. The gift in death. The gift the boys left.'

'Oh yeah, yeah, yeah.'

'Well, I thought about that a lot. I think I know.'

'Yeah?'

'It's learning to live in the moment, right? Not to let life thunder past while you fight change? Right? I've worked it out.'

She pats me and wanders off.

The next day the party splits up. Sophia leaves for the airport, and nearly everyone else heads back to town.

'Back to bloody Melbourne,' I whinge. 'Cold feet and dark days.'

The sun has returned to Pittwater and the world is a sparkling blue.

'Why don't you stay on for a while?' Fleury asks.

'Nah, got to get back.'

'What for?'

I stop and think. Nothing urgent. Only the dog. But she's in good hands with the next-door neighbours. They adore Sweetie.

'Yeah, could stay on, then. If it suits you.'

'Great! Enjoy. That's what Pittwater is all about.'

'Just until the weather turns.'

I expect that to be the following day. But I'm still here two weeks later when, one night when I am alone at the house, the phone rings.

'Would you like to have dinner?' he asks.

'When?'

'Tonight?'

'Sure. But I don't know how to use local transport. If you can find your way back here from Church Point, I'll cook.'

And when, a few bottles of wine later, on a deck dappled by the shadows of the bush, he says, 'Let's go to bed,' I nod easily.

It is no big deal, after all, to cast aside inhibition when desire drowns the rational mind. One night, I think. It can't hurt.

But it opens a floodgate and the harm is done. It isn't the sex. It is the light, cool touch of skin on skin, the whispered words late into the night. It is understanding that some little corner of yourself you'd thought long dead has merely been lying in wait.

When he gets up to return to the city not long before dawn turns the bay into a pool of shining light, I feel reborn and Pittwater seduces me. After two intense weeks, I return to Melbourne to pack. I plan to lease out my apartment and rent a house on Pittwater. I tell myself it is because I have fallen in love with the sea and the sun. I tell myself that perhaps I have found a place where I can settle. Everything I tell myself is true. But it is also true that this fling, this affair, or whatever it is, makes it easy to jump quickly from the old, drab life to the new. Easy to discount the difficulties of Pittwater living. Easy to be reckless.

2

THE APARTMENT in Melbourne is packed away into a garage in less than two weeks. A real-estate agent quickly finds a tenant. Fleury offers the Towlers Bay house as a temporary base and Sweetie is delivered into my mother's care while I search for a property to rent.

Moving to Pittwater is like waking up one morning to find yourself on a new planet. It is a place where the rhythm of the sun and tide set schedules. Wake at dawn. Kayak at high tide. Eat when you're hungry. Sleep when it's dark. There are no cars, no streetlights, no crowds.

Here, the back yard is the rugged bush and soaring escarpments of the Ku-ring-gai Chase National Park. The front yard is the bay, where stingrays glide along the sandy bottom and armies of soldier crabs, blue as the sky with purple striped legs, march across the tidal flats.

As I knew it would, the affair continues. Hormones I'd forgotten existed suddenly leap into gear, and the whole dissolute business is kicked along by a sense of the illicit. Because he is, of course, married.

It's easy, at first, to shove that thought into the dark recesses of my mind. I have never met his wife. I tell myself I am not hurting anyone. I am clear that this is a fling and will wear itself out in a very short time.

After all those years of work, the years of grief, the years of feeling lost, suddenly I am catapulted into a world where the only responsibility is pleasure. There are no commitments, no expectations, no demands.

The lover and I discover we have similar backgrounds. He grew up in a country pub. So did I. He worked as a journalist around the world. Me too. We wonder why our paths never crossed. And then we realise we did meet once, in New York, at a journalists' bar. Why didn't we click then? 'The time just wasn't right,' we agree, blithely ignoring the fact that he is married and the time is still decidedly not right.

I know, from the first, that this is not a man you would want for ever. But when he says, one day, that we are in a relationship, not an affair, I stop thinking about ending it and slide easily into the role of mistress. For a while, it gives me the illusion of belonging somewhere. But there is never contentment, only gut-gnawing anxiety because he does not come home to me each night and he is mercurial and women are drawn to him. I cannot be sure he always turns away from their invitations. Yet I am blind and deaf to all hints that he is a compulsive womaniser, a man who can never be faithful, not even to his mistress.

On days when I don't race to the city to meet him, I take long walks through the Ku-ring-gai Chase National Park, my mind spinning in never-ending loops. Will he call today? Will I see him tomorrow? Is it over already and I don't know it? I stride, hatless under the sun, willing myself to be slim and fit.

Sometimes, when he lightly refers to a cyclonic week at home, firecrackers of hope explode brightly and I think, Oh, the marriage must be coming to an end. But it isn't. And anyway, if hazy dreams of a future together even nibble at the edge of my mind, all I can see are the faces of children. So I settle for crumbs and tell myself each crumb is worth more than a whole cake with anyone else. But, really, it isn't.

I walk so long and often, my weight loss is dramatic, and friends look confused when I say hello. I preen. I like the new persona. Old clothes are flung into the charity bin at Church Point and my new wardrobe is fresh and sexy. I book a regular leg wax, change the colour of my hair and do not understand that I am reinventing myself until much later. My confidence blossoms.

'How did you do it?' people gush.

I do not, cannot, mention the lover. So I talk about my exercise regime. I do not say that tears often mingle with sweat as I tramp through the bush. Because up high on the escarpment where the world is pure, I see clearly that the affair can never offer anything of value. Beneath the snatches of time together are lies, a duplicity I never dreamed I could embrace, and a deepening distaste for the person I am becoming.

I walk to ancient sacred sites, where Aborigines once used flat sandstone outcrops for their rock engravings of fish, whales, emus, goannas and wallabies. It is like stepping into my own private, ancient art gallery, where the walls are textured by needle bush, tea tree and dwarf apples; where the silver trunks of young scribbly gums glitter starkly against the bright blue sky. Where the sky, its own ever-changing canvas, provides a dome for a gallery of subtle, timeless beauty.

On a day of misty rain, the achy smell of damp, charred black trees, the remnants of the 1994 bushfires, ignites pangs of undefined yearning so intense I double over. Up here on the escarpment, where my lies to myself sit like lead in my mind, I know the affair is wrecking me. It will leave me altered and stunted, like the burned-out stumps around me.

By Christmas, I still haven't found a house to rent. And it's summer, the high season, when rents soar and houses that lie vacant most of the year suddenly roar to life. I cannot abuse hospitality any longer. The lover, anyway, has always refused to commute here and I am afraid our meetings in the city will eventually be discovered. I need a place of my own.

In Sydney I look for a house to share with a long-time friend, Pia, who is recently divorced, and my husband's youngest daughter, Lulu, who's in her twenties. When we find a house with three levels (one each), we cautiously move in.

To our surprise, we three women have a grand time living together and evolve into a peculiar sort of family unit. Pia and I wave Lulu to work then sit down to breakfast. She tells me how to keep white clothes white and I tell her how to grow hydrangeas from cuttings. We throw lots of boozy dinner parties. Lulu puts up with both of us but watches a lot of television after dinner in her own sitting room.

At weekends Pia and I join an old friend, Tony, a wonderfully wicked theatrical and literary agent, at his shack at Little Gairie Beach, in the Royal National Park. The shack, a relic from the Depression, is less than basic. No running water. No electricity. The loo is a plastic bucket under a toilet seat in an outdoor cupboard. It is Tony's job to dig a hole somewhere to empty the bucket but sometimes he puts it off for too long. I learn to pee behind trees or grab a shovel and head into the hills.

Whenever we take off, I load a Thermos of soup, cooked legs of lamb, jars of gravy and mint sauce, kilos of sausages and large cakes, into a huge backpack so heavy it takes two people to lift it onto my back.

'This is Susan, our packhorse,' Tony says, making introductions to the shack community. Tony, in his late fifties, is a sixty-ciggies-a-day man, so he can't carry much of a load. And he loves a drink. Although you would never know to look at him. His excesses leave no visible marks. He is slim. Handsome, too, in the way that turns people's heads.

Pia carries her share but has a bad back to protect. I relish my own strength and tell people with pride that I am *strong as an ox, healthy as a buffalo*. I lug our three days' worth of supplies a couple of kilometres from the car park along a goat track cut into the side of the cliff.

When we arrive at the shack, Tony always immediately lights the old kerosene fridge, which takes about six hours to work up a decent chill. Then he shoves ice trays in the freezer so he'll have cubes for his late morning gin and tonic ('with lime, dear, not lemon, if you don't mind'), and assembles the bar (rum, gin, whisky, wine).

His shack, with its 1950s kerosene heater and ragged linoleum floor, is like the tatty holiday shacks of my childhood where the roof leaked and you ran riot, and if anything got damaged no one yelled.

At Little Gairie Beach, Pia and I sleep in bunk beds in an alcove separated from the living room by long strands of beads. Tony sleeps on a divan in the kitchen-cum-sitting room. Every night he coughs in violent, racking spasms. In the mornings, we urge him to quit smoking.

'Why?'

'Because you cough all night!'

'What rot!' he says.

In less than a year, the landlord turfs us out of our three-level home because she wants to move in. So we set off again, this time to a big white house on a main road that overlooks a park. Here, there are no places to escape from each other. For me, the move is disturbing, almost disorientating. A reminder that I have no roots. No place where I belong. I'm still floating aimlessly and it's scarier than ever.

The affair has long passed the point of being thrilling. Putting yourself last in the queue for attention creates anger and resentment. Yet every time I feel I can no longer continue, the dark spectre of loneliness smothers my shaky shreds of courage and I stay on and on. I begin going out with other men but it feels like an even bigger duplicity and I badly hurt an old friend whom I allow to misinterpret the time we spend together. To blur the edges of a useless, careless life, I party harder.

When I'm offered a job two years after my bid at 'retirement', I grab it like it will save me. The work is the stuff of dreams. Travel editor for a national women's magazine. I sail on the luxurious *Queen Elizabeth 2*; I snorkel among the teeming coral reefs of Fiji with the son of Jacques Cousteau; I sleep on the ground at Palm Valley in Finke Gorge National Park and wake drenched with dew to find a kangaroo staring at me. It is a privileged job and lifestyle but I move through it all like a sleepwalker. Some inner core is wearing out and I know it.

Driving to the office towards the end of spring, looking at the people in the traffic with phones crammed to their ears, I wonder what the hell I think I'm doing. I am back on the treadmill.

I quiz myself: 'If I could do whatever I want, what would it be?'

The answer rockets back: 'Return to Pittwater.'

The idea swirls and eddies. There are many reasons *not* to go there, all practical. There's the commute to work by ferry and car. And boats! What do I know about boats? If I buy one, how will it be to set off alone across dark waters when I come home late at night? There's the relentless schlepping of the groceries. Shop to car to dock to boat to dock to house. At the end of a day when you are tired before you begin, it wears down even the most dedicated offshore residents. And there is the lover, who would find it inconvenient. But our Sydney lease is due for renewal and we are wondering whether to go our separate ways. After two years, we have begun to grate on each other at odd moments.

When I get to the office, semi-dazed people are girding for another day of going through the motions. Or that's how I see it this morning. My contact book lies neatly on the desk. I idly flick the pages until I reach the Rs. The number for the Pittwater real-estate agent is still there, written in red ink more than two years earlier. I punch in the numbers. The phone is picked up by an agent I've never met.

'Do you know the area?' she asks.

'Yes. A little. I once spent a bit of time at Towlers Bay.'

'So you know the houses are all water access, that you have to take a ferry or use a boat?'

'Yeah.'

'I have to ask. Most people have no idea how life is lived here.'

'That's OK. So what have you got?'

'A fabulous house came on the market this morning. Sounds like it could be what you're looking for.'

I don't get excited. 'Waterfront?'

'Yep. Deep waterfront.'

'Where?'

'Scotland Island.'

'Oh.'

Deep waterfront is good: it means boat access during the lowest tides. But I don't want to live on Scotland Island. When I looked at houses there on my first attempt at Pittwater living, it seemed as crowded as suburbia. I decided that great views couldn't compensate and I was looking more for comfort than a community. But that was two years ago.

'Just come and look,' says the agent. 'If you don't like it, don't take it!'

I put down the phone, collect my bag, return to the car and drive immediately to Pittwater, leaving work untouched, telling no one where I have gone. Forty-five minutes later, I stand in the scrappy little Church Point real-estate office, still not quite sure what I am doing.

'I'm Susan. Come to see the house on Scotland Island.'

The real-estate agent flaps around making phone calls, checking the timing is OK with the owners, grabbing the file on the house.

'Keys?' I suggest, trying to be helpful.

'No. Don't need keys.'

'Doesn't the place lock up?'

'Oh yeah, but people around here don't bother. If anything goes missing, nearly everyone knows where it is and who's borrowed it.'

She calls the pink water taxi while I check out properties for sale on the notice board, then we head off.

'That's the house. Over there,' she says from the end of the Church Point ferry wharf.

It's a pleasant, low-slung wooden house that seems to overhang the shoreline. So far, so good. The water taxi drops us at a jetty that leads straight to the front door. Level access, easy schlepping, a prize on Pittwater. It's the beginning of the seduction.

'Does the water wash inside at high tide?' I ask, not altogether joking.

The agent grins. 'You might want to roll up your rugs during a *king* tide.'

The house has the feel of a sprawling boat shed. It is shacky and casual but properly built. The kitchen is part of a long, T-shaped room that includes a dining, sitting and entrance area. There's a study space with views to Church Point. The main bedroom, once a separate boat shed, is connected to the house by a back porch and French doors open onto the front deck. The house faces west, so there is afternoon sun. A plus in winter. A negative in summer. It will broil. But there are double doors everywhere so it opens up to let the sea breezes flow through. A positive. There are angles and corners and an upstairs bedroom that is like a ship's cabin, high above the sea.

We settle on a date for me to move in, two weeks later.

'You won't regret it,' says the agent.

Friends shake their heads in concern, convinced I have been both reckless and stupid. That I will live to regret this latest, mad whim.

They do not see, perhaps, the courage it takes to walk away and embrace change. And yet without change, without taking risks, where is growth to come from? At this stage of my life, the growth I want has nothing to do with the material. I want to know about the mind and spirit now. I want to understand why some people wake up joyful each day and others struggle out of bed. Why do some people die too young? Why does success fall at someone's feet while others slog and get nowhere? Are there heroes—or are we all flawed? Is it luck? Is it timing? My friends might shake their heads but at least I am having a go. I guess I am finally taking responsibility for my own happiness and not looking for it through anyone else.

Dismantling my city life is easy. A huge garage sale. By Sunday night, the rental house is empty except for Sweetie, a few pieces of furniture such as the bed, and stuff that evokes cherished memories.

Pia and Lulu have already moved to separate inner-city apartments. They say Scotland Island is too far and too hard. But I suspect they think I've lost the plot good and proper this time.

Moving day is bright and sunny but I feel like shit. Can't rev up energy or enthusiasm. I am aware I've frittered away the opportunities for so many new starts. It's hard to believe this move is going to be any different. The view is just better.

Everything that is small enough is packed into cardboard boxes. Instant necessities are packed into two clothes baskets to take in the car. The rest will go in a truck with the removalists. I have become expert at moving. In the back yard, Sweetie lingers in her kennel.

'Come on, old girl. Time to get up.'

Her pretty head is resting on her front paws, and she doesn't raise it when she lifts her eyes to look at me. I kneel and ruffle her fur.

'Come on, Sweetie. It's moving day. Let's go.'

She looks away and groans. She is thirteen years old and, according to the vet, four years past her use-by date. I have a sickly feeling that this is the end. Her once-glossy black fur is faded into brown and grey and everything that is born must die. Right? Yeah. Bloody damn right.

When the removalists arrive they help me put her in the car to take to the vet, who explains she has a tumour that's ruptured her spleen.

'Is there anything we can do?'

'Well, she'll probably live a couple more days but all we can do is dose her with painkillers. That's about it.'

'What would you do if it was your dog?'

'I'd put her down.'

I crouch on the floor with my faithful old dog, cradling her head in my lap, stroking her gently. She knows what is ahead, in the way animals always do, and struggles briefly when the needle goes into her thigh. But she doesn't take her eyes off me.

'Oh, Sweetie. What a great dog. What a good dog.'

And she is dead. Closed down and gone.

I have nowhere to bury her, no nearby friend with a farm.

'She's not going on any bloody garbage dump,' I tell the vet.

'She can be cremated, if you like. Her ashes will come back here for you to pick up.'

I nod because I cannot speak and the vet lifts Sweetie and she is gone. I make a vow to bury the box when I find a home where I will spend the rest of my life. Until then, the box will come with me. No matter how many times I move.

I write out a cheque and leave, anger quickly pushing aside grief. Another bloody loss. Everything that is born must die. The line spins in my head and I hate the truth of it.

At the house, the removal van is loaded, the boys waiting for directions. The lover calls as we set off. I don't mention Sweetie. Fake breeziness. This is not a man who likes to share the downside.

'When can I see this fabulous house?'

Never! 'Whenever you like.'

And the one piece of baggage I should have dumped before all else slides effortlessly along with me.

Three young men and a dog wait at Cargo Wharf, where any large-scale loading or unloading takes place in this part of Pittwater. Two are obviously brothers: small-boned, sinewy, tanned. It's the tail end of spring but they wear shorts, scruffy T-shirts and bare feet. The third man is taller, bulkier, with tightly curled black hair and a winter pallor. He is dressed in jeans and a checked flannel shirt and has socks and boots on his feet. I suss already that he is newly a local.

The dog is a beautiful, glossy black labrador in his prime. Focus on the job, I quickly tell myself.

Cargo Wharf, a little beyond Church Point ferry wharf, is wide enough for a couple of trucks side by side so I drive right to the edge of the wharf. Wind down the window. 'Gidday.'

The boys straggle to their feet. Smiles everywhere. Jump off their rusted old barge onto solid ground.

'Yeah. You'd be Susan, then?'

'Yeah. Going to Scotland Island. Mottles' old house.'

'Oh, right. George's place. Know where you mean, now. Anyway, I'm Andrew. This is my brother Chris. And he's Paul.'

'No sign of the truck?'

'No. Not yet.'

'Don't know where they've got to. I left about half an hour after them.' I figure they're pushing the number of hours to do the job as high as they can. 'So you put everything on this barge?'

'Uh-huh.'

It's long and flat. Cracked with random holes in the deck. There are no side rails. Nothing to stop everything falling off.

'Ah, how does all the stuff stay on?'

Andrew grins. 'Don't worry, we haven't lost anything yet.' He looks at his watch. 'Those blokes know where to come, don't they?'

'Yeah, I gave them all the landmarks. Drew a map.'

'Bit worried about the tide, that's all. If it gets much later, by the time we load and get there, it'll be low tide. Makes the job a lot harder.'

'How much leeway have we got?'

'From now? About half an hour.'

'Even if they're later, we'll still be able to unload, right?'

'Yeah. But it means a lot of lifting. Much trickier.'

Shit. It's nearly lunchtime. Where are those blokes?

Half an hour later they casually roll onto Cargo Wharf, hands filled with sandwiches. Passively aggressive. They throw open the doors of the truck and settle to eat, and watch the Pittwater boys do the work.

Andrew shrugs. Jumps lightly into the truck. Starts work. Polite. No drama. The city men are shamed, look sheepish. Bolt their food and pitch in. Hard to hold on to the upper hand when there's no contest.

Sofas, a couple of armchairs, a couple of tables, dining-room chairs, sideboard, coffee table and two beds. Four lamps. Paintings. Books. Clothes. Kitchen equipment and crockery. Minimum of bed linen and towels. Tubs of Iceberg roses and herbs. That's it. No dog. No kennel. Slam the door shut on that one. No tears, please.

It all gets piled onto the barge. My belongings are layered and braced against each other. Nothing is tied.

'Can I get a lift to the house with you guys?'

'Yeah, sure. Climb on.'

'Where's the engine? How do you steer this thing?'

Andrew points at a battered old tinny, which is what aluminium dinghies are called in this part of the world. It's tied alongside and he jumps into it. 'The tinny does the steering by pushing the barge.'

He yanks the engine cord. After a couple of coughs it kicks into life. We pull slowly away from the wharf. That tiny little tinny carefully pilots us to Scotland Island. We ride the wakes from passing boats and not a stick of furniture moves.

'Can there be a better way to travel?'

Paul laughs. 'I haven't lived here too long,' he says, 'but I don't think I'll ever leave.'

We dock about five feet from the front door.

'If we'd caught the tide at exactly the right time, we'd just slide stuff off the barge onto the deck and into the house,' Andrew says.

The drop from the jetty and deck to the barge is now about two feet. Doesn't sound like much, but when you're lifting heavy furniture from an unstable base, any advantage counts.

'What a bugger.'

He smiles. 'It's not too bad. Would have been worse in another hour.'

Doesn't anyone whinge around here?

The empty house smells of wood and floor polish. And the sea. Dust motes frolic in shards of sunlight. Nothing is locked. I throw open all the doors and look up McCarrs Creek, across to Elvina Bay. Water traffic buzzes by. Tinnies. Cabin cruisers. A beautiful wooden rowing boat with a man in a wide-brimmed hat. And silent yachts under sail.

A tight little band of anxiety loosens round my chest. It's too beautiful, too bloody exquisite not to feel a touch of joy. Sweetie would have loved it. Bad timing, old girl. But when is death ever good timing?

When the last few boxes and a bed are carried up the steps from the end of the jetty, I say, 'I've put cold beers in the fridge. How about it?'

'That'd go down OK.'

The boys sit on the jetty. Legs hanging over. Feet above the water. The bay picks up the pink of a sunset sky and life feels soft.

'So you boys do this all the time?'

'Nope.' They all say it at once.

Andrew and Chris like to sail. 'See that black boat over there?' Andrew asks. 'I'm restoring it.' Sunlight fills his face. 'Then I'm going to sail it. Maybe around the world one day.' Chris has the same dream.

'Moving business is a way to get the money together.'

Paul is qualified to skipper a water taxi, a ferry and a charter yacht. 'Not sure what I really want to do yet. I'm looking around. Testing a few things. So what brought *you* here?' he adds.

'Felt like a change.'

'Helluva change.'

'Yeah, well, sometimes you need a helluva change.'

'If you last two years here, you hang on for life,' Andrew says.

'That's the golden rule, is it? I've heard someone say that before.'

'I move people in, I move people out. Some hate it from day one, can't cop boats, weather, rough days. Others settle here so easily, it'd take a bomb to shift them.' Andrew finishes his beer. Gets up.

'Another beer?'

'No, thanks. Gotta get going.'

'Can you pick the ones who will last?'

'Mostly.'

'I'm here for the long term. That's the plan.'

Chris stands alongside his brother. 'You never know how it's gonna go. Wait and see,' he says.

Paul hesitates over another beer, then declines. He'll be stranded or have to take the ferry from Bells Wharf if he stays on.

I watch them walk down the jetty. The boys untie and cast off. Chris pushes the barge away from the jetty with a foot, then leaps for the deck. No chance he will miss. He stands as though there's an invisible yarn knitting water, barge and man into a single unit.

It's dark enough to turn on lights in the house. But I hesitate. Don't want to disrupt the outside light. The softness. The rosy satin smoothness of a day that doesn't seem quite as terrible as it was earlier.

I leave the bedroom doors open on my first night in the little boat-shed bedroom alongside the main house, the floor only inches higher than the water when the tide is in. From my bed, I see stars in a black sky. And a few lights. There's a wondrous peace but I cannot sleep. What am I looking for? I ask myself. What can I do to ensure this change is different from all the others? Only just before dawn, I fall asleep.

Sharp knocking wakes me. It's a blinding blue day.

'Susan, is it?'

I lift my head and look at a cheery, open face, blonde hair hanging to her shoulders, a couple of kids leaning on either side of her, gathered into her skirt. They are standing on the deck outside my bedroom, beaming politely, not quite leaning into the bedroom, but almost.

'They told you that this is a public thoroughfare, didn't they?'

'No.' I struggle to get a grip on consciousness. I am in bed. Having a conversation with a total stranger. Who knows my name.

'It's the only way to get to the ferry at Bells Wharf from our house. Well, see ya, then. Thanks a lot.'

I fall back on the pillows. So, the whole of Scotland Island can, if it wants, wander past my bedroom doors—French doors, mostly glass. Jeez. Bugger. Typical bloody Pittwater. There's always a twist.

Get up. Open a can of Coke. Begin unpacking.

Lunchtime and I'm still in pyjamas. Everything is in place. Have discovered a huge cupboard big enough to turn into an office. Fabulous shelving, like a boat. Maybe I'll start a new project. Write a book.

I set up the ironing board where I can look at the passing parade of boats. I feel invisible, as you do when you are inside and everyone else is outside. But occasionally someone waves from his tinny as he passes. I return the salute and feel a bit like a fish in an aquarium.

A man rows closer and closer. When he reaches the deck that embraces the front and sides of the house, about eight feet from where I'm ironing, he waves and I open the window.

'Heard you'd moved in.' His hat is askew. Grey hair flowing. I know him from dinner parties at Towlers Bay.

'Yeah. Yesterday. How you doing?'

'Saw you ironing.' He holds the edge of the deck to stop the boat from drifting away. He looks comfortable. As though it's the most natural thing in the world to pull up in a rowing boat and talk to a woman through a window while she's doing her ironing in her pyjamas.

'Want a cup of tea?'

'Lovely. Got a biscuit to go with it?'

He stays in the boat and I pass him tea and toast. The day is sunny and warm. He pulls off his hat and closes his eyes, raising his face to the sun. So many people do that here. As though it's life-giving. And we talk for a while, about sea eagles and fishing, and the day feels full.

How to describe my first Monday morning as a commuting resident of Scotland Island? Picking around the crumpled shoreline in air tangy with brine. Hills green and feathered with mist. The serenity of a soughing sea. Waiting in the crooked wooden shelter shed at the end of Bells Wharf for the ferry. Watching the fuzzy dawn world sharpen with the rising light. It is a caress of the senses. It feels like a prayer.

Within a week, my routine is established. Rise at 6.15 a.m., make tea, shower, dress and walk to Bells Wharf to catch the older of the two ferries, the *Curlew*, on her 6.50 a.m. run. At high tide, when water slops over the goat track that leads from the house to Bells Wharf, I put on rubber boots. Eventually, I learn to leave a pair of office shoes in the car.

There's a dog gate at the start of the jetty. I am told it must be firmly closed at all times. 'Dogs love ferries,' someone explains. 'Ride 'em all day if they can. It's a bugger, though, if they jump off in one of the bays. Means you've gotta go and pick 'em up after work.'

It is amazing, at first, to see that Lenny, the early-morning ferry driver, is greeted like a close family member by commuters, although he never says much. Some mornings, if a regular is missing, Lenny looks up the stairway that climbs in terraces nearly to the top of the island. If Bob or Bill or Maude is in sight, he holds the ferry. An extra moment or two on the water, the same kind of moment that on the road makes drivers foam at the mouth, costs nothing here.

Lenny has been at the helm of the old *Curlew*—a beautiful navy-and-white wooden ferry built in the 1920s—for the past thirty years. He's a little bloke in his late sixties with big, work-cracked hands, and he moves around the vessel as though he is part of the deck. If you need him earlier than the scheduled first run, you let him know and he's there. Doesn't matter whether it's still the dead of night.

Many friendships, which begin easily here anyway, are initiated on the ferry. Overriding the casual friendliness, though, is a cast-iron respect for privacy. Gossip, the kind that picks away until it creates a sore, is an absolute no-no. Live and let live prevails here.

When the sun shines and we passengers sit in the open air on the rear deck, a simple 'Good morning' turns into an exchange of local information. For me, on those early trips, it is about garbage-collection days, how to get newspapers delivered, where to find someone to clean the roof and gutters—essential when you gather water from the rain run-off for your tanks.

The ferry ride takes about five minutes, and at Church Point commuters scatter in all directions. Some catch a connecting bus to the city, some car pool. Some walk to the public car park and drive to work, which is what I do. Church Point is like a town square in an old village.

Just to arrive here is to be enfolded in the warmth of a vibrant community, to feel as though you belong somewhere.

There are a few tables with bench seats, a scattering of shade trees and a bottle shop. There's also a restaurant and takeaway food bar, post office and convenience store, where most of us pick up the newspapers and the milk. A notice board flutters with announcements for everything from home help to dock sales (no garages here!). Significant community events are chalked up on a nearby blackboard—events such as the Scotland Island Fair and the ANZAC Day ceremony.

As the weather warms up, the evening crowd lingers at the Point until the last ferry at 7.25 p.m. There are kids, dogs, youngies and oldies gathered together in chaotic cheer because the twilight is just too damn gorgeous to rush through. Kids strip off to their undies and leap into the water. Excited, bright-eyed dogs chase sticks or balls. Everyone's wet. Everyone's feeling fine. There's a rare kind of freedom. The kind that comes from feeling secure in your environment.

Over the next weeks my spirit soars when I drive round the last bend from Mona Vale to Church Point. Past the old boat sheds, little beaches and mangroves. When the water is high, dinghies bob on their moorings; at low tide, they lean in the sand. There's a constant, reliable simplicity to this physical world. Lushness comes from the musky smell of the sea and early-morning mists. From evenings when the sun drops behind the hills of Elvina Bay and night fans out under a hailstorm of stars. From sudden squalls with lightning flashes that fire up the bays, from pounding rain so thick you can't see through it.

And when an Antarctic wind occasionally races in from the Pole, it whips the sea so hard that, for a while, it can't be trusted. The water taxi cancels services; tinnies can sink. Here, where there are no streetlights, the moon's pale, silvery glow silently guides late-night commuter boats safely round moorings and illuminates dusky bays.

Commuter traffic, mostly banged-up open tinnies, beats past my window. Elegant cruising yachts glide past under sail. Cargo boats loaded with building materials churn along. Always a new sight, new action, a new event that engages you. Makes you wonder what is going on. Which in turn helps you to feel part of a bigger picture.

But friends are cautionary. Nodding their heads, shaking their fingers. 'The novelty will wear off.'

'Maybe.'

But you have to have a go, don't you?

It is impossible to resist entertaining prodigiously in the first euphoric flush of this return to Pittwater. I host lunches and dinners outside on the deck. The tide comes and goes. The wine flows recklessly.

I want everyone—the naggers and the pessimistic—to see what they're missing by holding safely to their suburban lives. I also want to share the whole, amazing experience of offshore living.

Naturally, not everyone agrees that I have found nirvana. Some friends feel stranded on the island, made anxious by the giant moat that separates them from their familiar shackles. But it is that moat that gives me the sense of being separated from a pressured world.

Cooking becomes an even greater passion here. Why dredge through traffic to trendy restaurants when you can sit and eat on a sunstruck deck, splashing hot feet in cool water, a glass of wine in your hand? Surrounded by a languid, instead of a rushing, world.

On a good day, when the water is smooth and the tide's right, a couple of quacking penguins might cavort in front of us, bringing a smile to even the most harassed city faces. Sometimes, a kookaburra snatches a chicken fillet from a plate without disturbing the salad. It is a performance so precise we clap and do not begrudge him the food.

We rely on tank water on Scotland Island, which means that if you are not frugal and there's no rain for a long time, you run out. I hate being short of anything, so I install my own idiosyncratic systems to use as little water as possible and still stay within the boundaries of hygiene. Showers are three minutes long and there's an egg timer in the bathroom that rings when the time is up. Women may pee in the loo but it's only flushed every five pees unless it's urgent. Boys go to the far end of the deck round the corner of the house and pee in the water. Clothes washing is done in one big load once a week. Vegetable washing water is recycled to water the pot plants. Guests get into the swing of it with good humour. Or they don't bother coming back.

In summer, when there is rarely any wind at dawn, the kayakers go out, gliding soundlessly through the water. Some kayaks are wooden and sanded and varnished to an elegant toffee glow. Most are multicoloured, vibrant slashes on glassy water. Boats on their moorings sit almost still just before the sun rises, and the light is gentle enough to make even neglected vessels, festooned with grunge, look loved.

When the rain falls heavily, long plastic raincoats, jackets and waterproof overalls, known by sailors as *wet-weather gear*, are hauled off hooks and pulled over working clothes. High heels are carried in shopping bags, briefcases wrapped in garbage bags. Little kids waddle under a bulk of plastic, shoulders hunched, dragging reluctant feet, their backpacks drooping. Why would they want to leave this freedom for a sardine-tinned classroom? No matter what the weather?

In a big wind, tree tops bow and rain blows in horizontal sheets. The water taxis raft up to their houseboat base and hunker down. No one goes out unless there's absolutely no choice. There are horror stories, rarely told but never forgotten, that linger in the lore of the area. The huge motor cruiser blindly crunching over a little tinny in the murky twilight and killing the driver. A toddler slipping silently overboard in a fierce storm, his father jumping in to save him and both drowning.

Like any paradise, you cannot take it too lightly.

Summer is consuming. There's always a party. A weekend sail. A time to jump in someone's boat to find a secluded little beach for a swim and a picnic. On Pittwater, parties blow in on the evening breeze when a neighbour comes home with a boatload of freshly caught fish and, as he passes, yells that dinner is at his house. Bring your own booze.

In the lead-up to Christmas, the island pops with exploding champagne corks. There's the sound of laughter, of people congregating. Smoke rises from barbecues, with the spicy smell of sausages cooking.

Blokes and their dogs suddenly start appearing at the water's edge, throwing sticks, balls, anything to get their pups to swim further and further, faster and faster.

'You in training or something?' I ask different folks from time to time.

'Yeah, mate.'

And because it's said with such wryness, I don't think to ask what for.

About a month before Christmas, when Marie, my next-door neighbour, and her two boys take a twilight swim, the family dog, a desert-red kelpie with yellow eyes called Mabo, paddles after a tennis ball as though his life depends on it.

'Mabo in training too?' I ask when I wander onto the deck to say hello, a sarong round my waist, no shoes and a stained old T-shirt.

'Nah. He's too old to race,' Marie says.

'Race?'

'Yeah.'

'What race?'

'The dog race.'

'What dog race?'

Marie turns to look at me, her lovely blue eyes wide with surprise. 'You don't know about the dog race?'

'Nope.'

'Ah well,' she says, wading out of the shallows to join me on the deck, 'it's a rare cultural event here. Every Christmas Eve we all gather at the Point for the Scotland Island Dog Race. Anyone can enter; he or she just has to pay the entry fee of a long-neck bottle of beer and a can of dog food. Winner takes all. The race starts around six o'clock but we usually get there an hour or so earlier for a few drinks. It's a festive kind of time. Just about the whole of Pittwater turns up.'

'So where do the dogs race to and from?'

'From Scotland Island, just near Bells Wharf, to Church Point.'

'How's it organised?'

'Well, I wouldn't say it's *organised*. It sort of falls into place. Like most stuff on Pittwater.'

'What are the rules?' I ask.

'Rules? Well, I don't know about *rules*. First dog on the beach wins. That's about it.'

The toddler, Oliver, has fallen asleep on Marie's lap, Matthew, just old enough to be in his first year of school, goes inside to watch television.

'How do you do it all?' I ask. 'How do you do the schlepping, the boats, the life, *and* little kids?'

'There's no choice so you don't think about it.'

'Your little bloke's a terror on the jetty, though.'

'Yeah, thinks it's a personal racetrack.'

She laughs, but I've seen her white-faced with fear when he's suddenly dashed along the jetty in a fit of sheer devilment. I have also seen Marie dock and tie her boat in a body-bending gale with Oliver strapped to her back, Matthew ordered to sit still in his life jacket until she gives the word to move. The boat surges, dives, bangs and teeters. The pontoon churns. She braces with legs astride, the kid on her back weighing her down. Then when boat and dock rise in unison, she grabs Matthew's hand and shouts *Now!* They leap. It is a terrifying but regular event, one that young mothers all over Pittwater think of little note.

'Ever get you down? Wear you out?'

'Nah. Love it. Kids grow up fast here, but the right way. They learn about swimming, fishing, boats and exploring before shopping malls and video games.'

After Marie's gone home with the boys, I call my mother, who is coming soon for her regular two-week stay with me at Christmas.

'Do you want to bring Wally?' I ask.

Wally, her big, amiable, slobbery Rottweiler who prefers to lean on people than stand on his own four paws, loves a swim, even in winter.

'Is there somewhere you can put him?' she asks.

'Oh, yeah. He'll be fine. Still likes a swim, does he?' I ask, innocently.

'Mad about it. He's in the river every chance he gets.'

Right! We have our own entrant in the dog race.

'Are you entering Gus?' I ask Stewart a week or so before Christmas.

'Nah. He's too old.'

'Do you think your girls would like to swim with my mother's dog?'

I have learned that owners either swim with their dogs or kayak or row alongside. No boats with engines are allowed.

'Sure,' he says. 'I'll ask them.'

When my brother, John, was alive, Christmas was an event. We all trooped to Melbourne every second year for a sumptuous feast, which he planned with the precision of a major military campaign. John had a passion for food, and he had always been adventurous with it. He loved oysters at an age when most of us retched at the sight of them.

On school holidays at my grandparents' home, we'd be sent off to the dam (to get us out of the way) to catch yabbies by dangling a piece of raw meat from a string. When our buckets overflowed, one of us would run back to the house to fetch our mother. She'd light a campfire on the bank of the dam and boil a billy until steam filled the air. Then she'd grab those snapping, angry crustaceans behind the neck so they couldn't bite her, and chuck them in the hot water. When the yabbies turned from muddy brown to raging red, she tipped out the water and showed my brother how to rip off their tails and suck out the meat in noisy slurps. They'd eat their way through a bucket load, then start again.

I remember my mother sitting on the cracked clay dam bank, hair bright blonde in the sun, teeth flashing white, with my brother crouched next to her. Both of them golden, somehow, and incredibly beautiful. I watched their abandoned gluttony enviously but couldn't bring myself to taste even a morsel of the muddy white flesh.

I wouldn't even eat fish when my father, trying to make amends after losing heavily at the racetrack, would come home with deep fried flake and vinegar-soaked chips. My mother and brother loved fish, a rare treat in those landlocked days when we lived at Bonegilla migrant camp, where Dad worked after he quit the army and before he bought the pub. At heart, my father and I preferred rissoles. He'd eat them for breakfast, lunch and dinner, and if my mother didn't make them regularly enough, he'd shuffle into the kitchen and make them himself.

'Got to loathe the smell of them,' my mother told me years later. 'It's all he ever wanted to eat. Rissoles . . . and mushrooms.'

My father was passionate about mushrooms. Every autumn, the whole family trekked through soggy paddocks in cheek-whipping winds, picking everything from tiny, shiny white buttons to field mushrooms the size of dinner plates. When the car was so crammed with boxes that the only place my brother and I could sit was on each side of my mother's lap, we drove home to peel, clean, cook and bottle. I was always terrified a poisonous mushie or two must surely have found their way into the bottles, so I'd beg my father not to eat them, and when he just smiled and loaded up his plate, I watched and waited for him to suddenly retch and gag, to go purple and then die. I was an adult before I felt safe eating mushrooms.

One Christmas, my mother experimented with the stuffing for the Christmas bird, adding a can of chopped water chestnuts, crystallised ginger and plenty of orange rind to the mix. My father and I looked at each other and pushed it aside. We didn't like surprises in our food.

Mum made that ritzy stuffing the first Christmas after the pub was sold and my parents moved us into the wastelands of outer Melbourne suburbia. Our new house was a spit from where my mother was raised.

'Used to be cherry orchards here,' she told me soon after we moved in. 'My sisters and I would steal in at night and eat them until we turned purple. Then we'd go home and face a belting.'

And she looked wistfully across the jam-packed houses from the window of her split-level home—the best she and my father could manage financially. Not exactly her retirement dream of a grand house with a sweeping staircase. But the split level gave her four steps and she contented herself with those.

'You'll just have to sweep down *slowly* in your gowns,' she told me. 'Make the most of it.'

For whom? For what? I asked myself. It was *her* dream of grandeur, not mine. My parents were better off than many, with enough to see them through to the end of their lives, but only if they were careful and lived with constraint. There weren't enough resources after the pub was sold for my mother's legendary wild flings (flying lessons when she turned forty) and her lavish entertaining. Anyway, by then Dad had a rotting liver from too many brandy heart-starters for breakfast, and lungs choking with nicotine.

You've got to do what you enjoy, I thought at the time, because there's no telling how it's going to end up. But I forgot all that as the years marched on. By the time my parents relocated to suburbia, my brother had ditched law for the racetrack and turned into a charming but wild larrikin. Every now and again, a debt collector would knock at the door and my father would pay up. Debt, to my father, was the greatest of all shames. Thank God he lived long enough to see my brother triumph.

I'd dropped out of university for a career in journalism instead of focusing on making a successful marriage. I was never going to turn into the powerful beauty my mother had been in her youth. She'd been a knockout, apparently. Her waist a man's hand span, her eyes bluer than sapphires.

'Engaged twenty-two times,' she told me as I grew taller and taller, all legs with a rather large nose she referred to as my *peckin' thing*.

Looking back, the move to the brick vanilla, as we called the new house, was not one of the glossier times of my mother's life. That first Christmas, when we struggled to embrace the barren confines of suburbia after being sprawling country kids all our lives, was a shocker. It felt hotter than an oven indoors so we set the table on the concrete slab we called the patio, on the shady side of the house. We'd all thought it would be a relief to be together for a quiet family Christmas instead of dishing up roast turkey and ham for a hundred guests at the pub. But as we sat there with the hose running over our feet to cool us down, without a crowd, it didn't feel like Christmas.

After that year, my brother, in his early twenties, took over the Christmas celebrations. And as his fortunes improved, the event grew.

After he married Dolly, they became extravaganzas. In their big sitting room, sofas and armchairs were shoved against the walls to make way for thirty feet of trestle tables. Plastic garbage cans were filled with ice and loaded with enough beer and wine to sustain thirty or so guests through a five-hour lunch and a late supper of leftover turkey and ham sandwiches. When we were tipsy enough, we sang Christmas carols, then turned up the music and danced until we ran out of puff.

But my brother is dead. And Christmas since his death has been more of an ordeal than a celebration. However, this first Pittwater

Christmas, I am determined to revive the Duncan family tradition. I want it to be a grand time for the fourteen people who will gather around the table on the deck at about noon. My goal is to restore, if I can, a little of the old *joie*.

I begin making the pudding only a week before Christmas Day. Which is a bit scary because it's a three-day process. First, double the recipe. Then candy the orange and lemon peel and soak the raisins, sultanas, dates and currants in four times the suggested amount of brandy, letting the fruit sit for a couple of days. Stir every time you go past the bowl and make a wish. Invite everyone who passes to stir and make a wish. Watch them succumb to the sweet, dizzying brandy fragrance. See them close their eyes, breathe deep and hold their breath. Then wish.

When I finally cook the pudding mixture about three days before we're due to eat it, I'm anchored to the house for the next six hours, topping up the water in the pot. It's a broiling job but easily bearable. When the heat feels overpowering and sweat rolls down the valley in my back, I walk out of the door and fall into the sea. Nice life, huh?

In that final week of Christmas frenzy, I pick up my mother and Wally. The evening before Christmas Eve, my mother polishes silver cutlery at the dining table while I make jugs of brandy sauce and assemble the dry ingredients for the turkey stuffing. This year I'm trying ground hazelnuts and grated orange and lemon peel in sourdough breadcrumbs. There's more of her in me than I like to think, sometimes.

The fridge is bursting with smoked salmon, smoked trout, ham and turkey, all the sauces and as much booze as we can fit in. The rest will go into iceboxes in the morning.

First thing on Christmas Eve, I make up the bed in the top bedroom—the captain's cabin for Pia, my old housemate from Sydney. She's due around lunchtime. I've convinced her to get here in time for the dog race. The house gets a final dust and mop, and just as I put on the kettle, Bomber and Bea, two recent friends, wave from their barge. I rush out on the deck.

'Come on in. Just put the kettle on.'

Bomber and Bea run a mooring service from an emerald and white working boat called the *Trump*. Bea sticks her head out of the cabin when I call. Marley, their highly strung black kelpie, streaks up and down the deck, barking her head off.

'Can't come in. Too busy,' she yells. 'Shut up, Marley!'

'See you at the dog race?'

'Shut up, Marley! Yeah. See ya. Shut up, you brainless bloody dog!'

When I try to pin down details about entering the dog race, though, people look at me blankly.

'I told you. The race just happens,' Marie says when I call her for more information. 'Everyone knows it's on Christmas Eve, and if you want to be in it, get to the Point with your dog around five o'clock.'

Right!

Wally's been in full training with Stewart's and Fleury's daughters, and he looks as sleek as a seal. My stepdaughter Lulu arrives midafternoon with Bella, her border collie, and we decide Bella should enter the race too. She's the kind of dog who loves swimming even more than running. Drops twigs in your lap all day, mutely begging you to throw them. Which gets a bit wearing after a couple of hours. For us, not her. I've never seen that dog tire.

'The team's looking pretty good,' I announce happily. 'Might just have to have a small bet on them both.' And for a moment, I am overwhelmed with memories of my gorgeous gambling brother.

In her corner, my mother is suddenly still, her face turning grey.

'John would have loved a day like today,' I say, to let her know I understand what she's feeling.

And she nods, because she cannot speak.

At 5 p.m. Stewart swings past in his boat and picks us up, dogs and all. He drops us at Church Point and goes back to collect his own team.

There's already a crowd at The Point. Women in sarongs and bikini tops, kids either naked or wearing swimsuits, men in shorts. Everyone's holding a glass of beer or wine. And there are dogs everywhere. But there's no sign of a race headquarters, a place to sign up.

'What's the drill?' I ask over and over again.

People shrug and smile. 'Relax. Have a beer. It'll happen.'

As the race time gets closer, a fleet of tinnies and one or two posher commuter boats (they're fibreglass instead of aluminium) gather offshore like a ragtag navy. Excitement fills the air. Someone starts a book on the race, odds are chalked up. Diesel, a lanky black dog, is favourite.

The story of how the race originated is murky. The most reliable source says that when there were two ferry services competing hotly for local business, both drivers had a dog. In a heated argument one evening, one driver threw down the gauntlet: 'My dog could wear lead boots and still beat your bloody mutt.' Or words to that effect.

The ferry captains agreed to a dog race from Scotland Island to

Church Point. When locals heard about it, everyone with a dog that could swim naturally wanted to be in the race, which has now been going for about thirty years. But that's open to debate, too.

When we're all primed with enough drinks, and before the sun gets too low, an anonymous voice yells for everyone to get their dogs on Bomber's barge, the *Trump*, or into their own boats to be shipped to the starting point. Which is Matty's barge. Unnamed, it floats a little offshore from Bells Wharf.

'Wally! Bella! We're off,' I call.

Both dogs happily jump onto the *Trump*, and soon they're on Matty's barge, ready for the race start. There are three fights before the gun is fired. To break them up, owners shove their dogs overboard and then haul them out of the water again.

When the starting shot rings out, every dog jumps and starts swimming—except Wally. He stands and looks around.

'Swim, Wally, swim!' I shout, urging him on.

He wags his stumpy tail and doesn't move. In the end, I push him off the barge and he sinks. For a moment I think I've killed him. Then he rises, paddling happily. I jump back on the *Trump*. Then turn to watch Wally's progress. He's still paddling happily. In a circle. Going nowhere.

'Think that dog needs rescuing,' Bomber says after a while. 'We'll get him in the boat.'

Meanwhile, Bella is swimming magnificently with Stewart's daughters kayaking behind her. So once Wally's been delivered back to the *Trump*, we head to Church Point to see the end. Bella is brilliant. Coming third. We're all there to cheer her madly.

'That's not Bella,' Lulu says flatly. She points out to sea. '*That's* Bella.'

Bella, the girls tell us later, followed a floating stick. She came in second last. With the stick, though. Which was a triumph of sorts.

After the race, Lulu grabs Bella and returns to Sydney for Christmas with her father's side of the family. Pia, Wally and I hitch a lift on a boat and return to Scotland Island, where my mother waits at the end of the jetty for news of Wally's epic swim.

'Well, how did my Wally do? Did he win?'

Pia and I look at each other and crack up.

On Christmas Day, we set up an icebox at the end of the jetty and fill it with champagne. The table is set in front of the French doors. Pia lays out smoked salmon and smoked trout. She readies a metal bucket for the prawns that Marty and Witch, my brother-in-law and his partner, are bringing, and sets the sauce alongside. The turkey is in the oven, the potatoes are almost done, and the ham was baked first thing in the morning. It does, indeed, look like a feast. *Saluté, my brother John!*

Pia's dad arrives in a water taxi with his brother and sister-in-law visiting from Belgium. We hand them champagne as they get off the boat and their faces suddenly fill with excitement.

Friends roll in. By the time we've had a few glasses of champagne and finished the seafood, a high, fine layer of cloud has filtered the sun and the wind has dropped to a tickle. It's a perfect day for sitting on the deck wearing reindeer hats, in full view of a passing world that waves and shouts 'Merry Christmas' and 'You all look ridiculous'.

After the pudding, Pia's uncle sings 'The First Nöel' in French, his beautiful tenor voice drifting across the silken water, and we join in the chorus in English.

'*C'est magnifique*,' he says, waving his arm at the surroundings. He slips his arm round his wife's waist and then says formally to me: 'Thank you. This is a Christmas to be memorable.'

3

As SUMMER ROLLS into autumn and the days become shorter, the evenings crisp, I am lying in my room, doors open to the water. It is about 3 a.m. and I am awake. I still don't have a home to call my own, and often on sleepless nights I roll over and silently ask the boys to help. To tell me where to go, what to do.

It is the weekend, and Pia is asleep upstairs in the captain's cabin. We've got a team coming for Sunday lunch and I'm fretting because I can't sleep. Exhaustion is becoming a constant condition.

Music filters through to me, the tinny electronic kind of music you hear from musical Christmas cards or mobile phones. I ignore it for a while, but then I realise it is coming from the kitchen. I get up and walk along the back porch, the music getting louder all the time. When I go into the kitchen, it seems to be coming from the cupboards under the sink. I lean down and search for the source. But my heart is racing.

When my husband died and I went back to our Nepean home to sell it, the microwave, at various and very odd times, would suddenly erupt into the same kind of music. When I mentioned this rather strange phenomenon to my mother's friend Pat, who looked after the house when Paul and I travelled, she kindly refrained from saying I'd gone nuts. But one night when Pat and I were sitting down to dinner, the microwave burst forth with a loud rendition of 'Danny Boy', Paul's favourite song. Pat ransacked the kitchen trying to figure out where it was coming from. Neither of us could really believe the microwave was singing! We never did find any other source. But that microwave played on and off until I sold the house and moved to Melbourne.

As weird as this sounds, I will not apologise for believing then (and now) that it was a message from Paul. Trouble is, you never know what this kind of message means. Did playing 'Danny Boy' mean that Paul approved of selling the house? Or that he wanted me to stay put?

Now weird stuff is happening again. Pia comes downstairs.

'What in God's name is that awful music?' she asks. 'Turn it off, it's the middle of the bloody night.'

'I can't find where it's coming from.'

As suddenly as it started, the music stops.

'It's coming from in there somewhere,' she says, indicating a mess of kitchen gadgets, from garlic crushers to serving spoons. 'I'll sort it out in the morning.'

We both go back to bed. The music starts once more.

'I'm not bloody getting up again,' she calls.

And before long the music stops.

I lie awake, looking out at the night sky, clear and starry. A green satellite-shaped object appears and I wait for it to move on. A plane, I think, or a reflection of some kind. But it doesn't move. It hovers there. I think about waking Pia again but decide not to. I know what it is all about. I just have to wait to see what it brings. Thank you, boys. They are looking after me. I know it.

Bizarre? Delusional maybe? But not to me at this time. Slowly, without quite understanding it, I begin searching for a house to buy.

It is late, about 10 p.m. I wait at Church Point for a water taxi to take me home after a tedious, nitpicking day at the office. The nights are hardening as winter encroaches. Cold bites deep. There are no red and green water-taxi lights in the distance, so I go to check the ads in the real-estate display window next to the ferry wharf office.

In the top left-hand corner, there's a rather bad photograph I haven't noticed before, though it looks like it's been there a while, of a green tin house with an oddly shaped window. It is in Lovett Bay. I assume it is on what I think of as the right side (north-facing), because I know Lovett Bay quite well. The only house I've seen for sale (on the wrong side, south-facing) is a rackety old fibro shack with a sinking pontoon and falling-down awnings.

The house in the photograph is all hard edges, corrugated iron, small windows and built like a fortress. Not my style at all. But the image niggles me on the trip home. I will never be able to explain why, but I call the real-estate agent the next day and arrange to see it midweek. When Wednesday rolls around, the new real-estate agent motors up to the Scotland Island house in a flaking tinny. The boat belongs to her assistant. This agent, all bouffant blonde and crisp creases, doesn't live offshore and sits in the boat with a frozen, tense expression.

'Gidday. Great day,' says the assistant, a barefoot Scotland Islander. 'Let's go,' she adds, revving the motor.

We motor past Trincomalee, a lovely old white weatherboard home that dominates the point between Elvina and Lovett, then begin to veer towards what I consider is the wrong side of Lovett Bay.

I look at the agent aghast. 'We're not going to that awful old fibro shack, are we? I haven't got the slightest interest in that.'

The women nod. The assistant gets earnest. 'It's not awful. Just take a look. It has the most enormous potential.'

Potential. I hate that word. Especially when used by real-estate agents.

'We're nearly there. Take a look at it anyway. Go on,' she insists.

The ferry wharf supports the usual wooden shack but this one is crammed with rank, overflowing wheelie bins. It's a pigsty kind of welcome. We pick past the rubbish. Inside the shed every mariner businessman's calling card is pinned to the walls: SUZUKI MOTORS SERVICED, TREE LOPPING, LEARN FRENCH AT HOME.

A red flag is tucked into the supporting beams.

'Hang the flag and the ferry stops,' the assistant explains.

'It's not on the regular route?'

She shakes her head. 'No.'

The raucous shrieks of cockatoos in the trees above are deafening. An engraved sandstone sign declares LOVETT BAY 1895. Huge sandstone boulders topple into a crescent-shaped beach where the sand is almost red. I look up the hill to where a ragged sandstone track climbs mysteriously through the bush.

'What's up there?'

'Another house.'

And no more is said.

We walk past dinghies racked in lines. An old wooden surfboard.

'That's called the Taj Mahal.' The head agent points at the mustard-yellow house, blocky, with lots of glass, looming behind the boat shed.

'Why the Taj Mahal?'

'Ken's palace for his bride.'

I visualise a handsome young man consumed with a grand passion.

A tall, skinny bloke with dreadlocks, huge bare feet, tanned hands and ceramic blue eyes is scraping clean a yacht, bottom-heavy with sea creatures. He stops scraping to let us past and smiles shyly. I trip on the tram track that launches the boat. Quick tanned hands hold me up.

'Jesus. Thanks. Are you Ken?'

'No. No.'

There's a whiff of something foreign in his words. He points inside the shed, beyond iron, cable, wood and glue. Ken, grey-haired, wiry, around sixty years old, is hunched into a telephone, drumming up business. So much for my notion of a young, lovestruck Adonis.

I decide I hate this part of Lovett Bay. It feels foreign and uninviting. Isolated and brooding. Then I see the house. Blinds hang brokenly. Dejection and depression enshroud it like an invisible cloud. Green summer mould clings to railings and shaded woodwork. Under the house there's a junk heap. Planks of wood, old windows, pots, pans, paint tins, chain, ropes, a clothes line, the water heater.

It's a dump yard, I want to say. But I ask: 'Who owns this place?'

'Gordon Andrews.' An expectant wait.

'Should that mean something?' I'm a little arrogant because I don't want the house. There's power, isn't there, when you do not desire something?

We follow the path made from wooden sleepers hammered into the ground, supported by wooden pegs. Thick, plaited boat rope is looped on handrails. With the words *enormous potential* tolling painfully, I stomp up the final steps to the front door. Glass. No privacy.

'He designed the first decimal currency.'

'Huh?'

'Gordon Andrews.'

The assistant fluffs with ambition. The house is rectangular, with two bedrooms at the far end. Sliding glass doors from the sitting room lead to a boxy deck that overlooks the bay. There is a kitchen, a bathroom and a back deck where three stumps carved into gruesome faces surround an old-fashioned wood-burning brick barbecue.

'The bedroom walls could be easily removed,' enthuses the assistant. 'See, they're more like partitions than walls. If you built new rooms under the house, this could turn into a really big living room.'

I have fallen through a time warp and landed in the sixties. A built-in green sofa, bright red tractor-seat stools, cubed shelving. Masks leer and jeer from walls. Floor sanding ends raggedly at the entrance to the bedroom, revealed behind a calico curtain.

'Why's he selling?'

'He's about eighty-five.'

'Right.' I look at my watch. Time to go. I begin walking back to the boat, not even glancing behind me. 'Looks newly built,' I say.

'Yeah, in 1994. Gordon was the first to get going after the bushfires wrecked this side of Lovett Bay. Nothing left standing.'

'So he was about eighty years old when he started over?'

'Musta been.'

Shame floods my face in red splashes. 'Courageous old bloke.'

'Cranky, more likely.'

But I understand now. Floor sanding that reaches as far as his energy. The home-grown masks replacing a lifetime's collection of art. The shoestring decor thumping with style. His own. Inimitable.

I make an offer and shock myself. I have no idea why I've done it. I don't want the house. But the offer is low, much lower than Gordon wants. So I assume it will be rejected. I put the house out of my mind on the ride back to Scotland Island.

'Let's keep looking,' I say. 'A house with a deep waterfront. Winter sun. Lots of it.'

When I get home, I ring the lover and tell him I have made an offer on a house. I want his support and approval, perhaps because my father always told me not to worry about the big decisions: 'Your husband will make those,' he used to say as I grew up. Ideas like that have a way of sticking to the walls of your mind. Even though I had waved the flag of liberation from the day I turned the first page of Kate Millett's *Sexual Politics*, I was still seeking approval.

But the lover flits around my questions, noncommittal.

My hurt turns into anger. 'I'm about to spend a lot of money and you can't even give me an opinion!'

'Gotta go. The other phone is ringing.'

I wonder why I even mentioned the house. I don't intend to buy it. To get his attention? Probably. I can relax, though. Gordon will never accept the price. But as a group of us sail in the evening, my thoughts keep going back to it. I start to see where I can make changes and mentally calculate what they will cost. Maybe, just maybe, it has possibilities.

There isn't much wind at twilight, and it's a long, slow sail. I've left a pot roast of beef braised in red wine in the oven. By the time we pack the boat away we are two hours later than planned, and I joke about *boeuf brûlée*, but the smell as we walk up the jetty is delicious.

Later, as talk drifts into the late hours, I slip off to bed. I feel too tired to think. It's an aching tiredness and my bones feel too heavy for my muscles and my head is thick and muddled.

When the phone rings at seven thirty the next morning, I am shaky from too little sleep and too much red wine. For a moment, ludicrous hope blooms that it is the lover finally offering support. I pick up the phone. I will be late for work. But what does that matter on a morning when I feel the stitching is unravelling anyway?

'He said yes.'

'Who?'

'Gordon! The house you looked at yesterday. It's yours!'

'Oh shit.'

'It's a great deal.'

'Oh shit.'

But I do not withdraw. I let the deal go ahead. I want a home base. Tiredness clamps like a vice on every part of my body. For more mornings than I care to think about, I have woken feeling as though I need to sleep for another six hours. It's a creeping exhaustion that builds through the day. Sometimes, I put it down to partying hard and a dysfunctional relationship. At other times I blame getting older. I tell myself I'll snap out of it once I have a house to call my own.

'When does he want to settle?' I ask the agent.

'Will a month be OK?'

'Yeah. Sure.'

One more time, I think. I can pack one more time.

I crawl back into bed and sleep for another six hours. This time, when the phone wakes me, I am calm.

'Hello.'

I drill energy into my voice. Zip on the rubber suit of the happy mistress. Gay. *Toujours gai.* 'Hi.'

'Any news about the house?' the lover asks.

'Yeah. The deal's done. The price was too good to walk away from.'

'What d'ya pay?'

The phone crackles with easy intimacy. I have already hurled yesterday's lack of support into a chasm. I give him the figure.

'Let me check it out before you sign anything.'

And I slide easily into the illusion of being cared for.

He cuts off the call before I realise the conversation is dead. Always, always, he leaves only emptiness. There's never even the most ordinary, implicit kind of support couples take for granted. Ordinary. When had the state of *ordinary* become so damn desirable?

Gordon Andrews invites me for coffee a couple of weeks after contracts are exchanged. His voice on the phone is firm and youthful. 'Few things I need to explain,' he says. We set a time for Saturday. I plan to take the ferry to get a grip on the transport system.

It's mid-April. Autumn and, to me, the most beautiful season on Pittwater. Nights are clean and cool, dawns break pink as a rosy-breasted galah. It is dark now, when I leave to catch the morning ferry, so I carry a torch. The easy old goat track was mostly washed away during a big summer storm and I have to pick my way over submerged rocks. It is the day's first challenge and I have begun to think of the easy access to the Lovett Bay ferry wharf with relief.

On the Saturday morning I'm due to meet Gordon, the usual cheery faces peer through the bedroom window.

'Hiya, Susan.'

The team from the house round the bend is off shopping. I lift a hand but not my head. Another hour in bed. Soaking tiredness. I vow to drink less, walk more, eat better, when I move house. Begin again. Again.

I look at the long, skinny stick of my arm. My skin hangs loosely and is ageing into fine, gathered wrinkles. New, funny white spots, two or three, resist a tan. Are these age spots? As I lie in bed, depression slips on like a second skin. There is no excitement about buying this house. I feel too tired even for that.

Gordon expects me at 11 a.m. for coffee. I slouch around until I miss the ferry and have to call a water taxi. To give myself a boost, I search for omens. The day is sunny. Good. Water taxi prompt. Good. High tide. Good. Annette driving the water taxi. Good.

'Bought old Gordo's place, have you?' she asks. Annette is soft-hearted, sunny-tempered with gentle eyes and a lovely smile.

'Yup. Tell me about Gordon. What's he like?'

'Wait and see.'

'I'll need you to get me home again,' I say when she drops me at the Lovett Bay ferry wharf. I feel suddenly stranded and unsure.

'Call me. Not much on so far. Shouldn't be a wait.'

She pulls away as I climb the yellow steps with the white safety stripes. The rubbish is gone, the wheelie bins are closed and clean. Another omen. 'Give up on the bloody omens,' I chastise myself.

It is quiet and still as I walk along the waterfront to see my new home. The boat shed is closed and deserted. I realise I have no idea where I am. I do not know where on the vast Australian coastline Lovett Bay bites in. I have no idea if the sinister-looking red escarpments that rise on both sides of the bay have names. I am clueless. Have I, I wonder as I climb the steps, made the most expensive mistake of my life?

Scotland Island is a large, ebullient community where the population is mostly full time and not made up of weekenders. There is always company if you want it. This little corner of Lovett Bay, as far as I can see, has four houses, one on either side of me and another hut, Japanese-looking, behind Gordon's house. It's not exactly a bustling village. Who will I find for company? Who will go past my door and call in? This is not a thoroughfare. This is a dead end.

Gordon's front door is shut with a white curtain pulled across it. *Closed!* it screams. *Go back!*

I knock. Then call. And call again: 'Hello? Helloo-oo?'

A grunt. Movement. The curtain swishes back and Gordon peers suspiciously from behind metal-framed glasses before he opens the door. I expect frailty. But he is sexy. He's tanned, and wears a bold silver necklace, a bright white, stretch T-shirt, blue jeans faded to perfection. His arms are heavily muscled and he looks strong.

'Come in.'

He stands aside and lets me in to the main room, where his macabre masks dominate the walls, casting a manic pall.

Gordon notes my fascination. 'They're for sale.'

'Uh, they're great. Really. But I'm going to have to unload stuff to fit in here. Can't take on any more.'

He lets it lie and leads the way through the house. We step into an enclosed front deck that's surrounded by a spiked picket fence so high it shuts out the water view if you're sitting down. At the eastern end there are green plastic boxes growing parsley, mint, coriander and Thai basil. Gordon is a cook, as it turns out.

He points me to a lovely hand-hewn wooden bench and takes the canvas chair for himself. We settle at a slightly unstable, weathered grey table, handmade from a slice of a tree trunk.

'Did you build all this?'

He ignores me. 'I've got a couple of requests,' he begins formally.

'Sure.'

'My son likes the rug. Can I take it?'

I haven't even noticed it, so I spin round and check out the floor. The rug seems to be a piece of manufactured carpet: Berber.

'Sure, take it. That's OK.'

'And the curtains. He can use those too.'

Made from flecked calico that Gordon has sewn himself.

'Fine.' I loathe curtains anyway and wonder why he needs them here.

I look back at Gordon, wondering what's coming next, and I have a niggling sense of déjà vu. Then I remember. A bad-tempered old bastard disembarking from a water taxi in the weeks before Christmas. He'd staggered with his shopping bags and I'd reached to help him. Trying to take them to pass to him when he was solidly on the ferry wharf steps. 'Get away,' he ordered, his elbow pushing me aside.

I'd held my hands up in mock surrender and let him be. Shocked. It was Annette's shift driving the water taxi. 'What's his problem?'

She laughed. 'That's just Gordon.'

Today, though, he's polite. He is on a mission to sell me his furniture and as many works of art as possible. There isn't much space, it turns out, in his retirement home in a nearby suburb.

'Coffee?'

'Yes. Lovely.'

He pushes himself up, moves into the kitchen unsteadily. There is, after all, a frailty that cannot be disguised under the Jimmy Dean clothes.

Alone, I look at his stifled view of Lovett Bay. Gordon has created a textured, layered site. The shining green water is used as a backdrop for wispy conifers, spindly acacias, prostrate grevilleas and sapling gums, self-sown after the bushfires. Hue upon hue of peaceful green. The greenery is beautiful but I love to look at water and want to see more of it. A couple of saplings might have to go.

My mobile phone blurts, breaking the peace.

'How's it going?'

The lover. On a Saturday. Historic.

'Great! It's going to be fantastic.' I oversell, rushing for impact, waiting for the phone to go dead before I finish. But he hangs on the line.

'It's a lot of money . . . maybe too much?'

I hold back a surge of red anger. Advice after the event. And what does he know about this area anyway? 'Maybe. But who gives a rat's? Anyway, locals always think strangers are wood ducks.'

He laughs. 'What's a wood duck?'

'Someone who pays too much.'

'OK. I'll call ya.' And he is gone.

Gordon returns with a pot of dense black coffee. We sip it.

'Just a couple of other things,' he says. 'The shelving in the sitting room. It's an original design. I'd like to take it.'

I wander inside, holding my demitasse. The shelving is a series of boxes, all different sizes, and crammed with sentimental treasures. Stuff that only has meaning to him.

'Take it.' I am tired again. I want to go home and lie down.

But he hasn't finished. 'The table is for sale.' A stiff, knotted finger points at an exquisite blond-wood table.

'Gordon, I love the table. You built it, did you? But I have one.' My own battered table has a history, moments snagged in my mind by a burn, a stain, a mark. I will not trade it in for a part of Gordon's history. 'Perhaps,' I say, 'you could leave a very small piece of *you* here. Nothing much. An old, signed postcard. A small piece of art.'

He looks at me silently for a moment, then nods, changes tack. 'Are you frightened of snakes?' he asks.

'Snakes? Oh, snakes are OK.'

But it's a lie. In fact, snakes terrify me. Send me into hyperventilating panic. Growing up in Bonegilla migrant camp, I saw a lot. Red-bellied blacks, mostly. As a child I quickly learned that screaming *Snake!* would instantly snap a parent out of inattention. I overused the technique, of course. Once, baled up by a swaying black snake, eyes glittering, tongue flicking, I screamed and screamed and no one came.

My father finally walked over. Tired of the racket. I stood rigid. It was the first and only time I saw my father, a huge, towering, shuffling man, run. He grabbed a spade, flew in and whacked the snake's head off.

We lived in Block 23, then, in a corrugated-iron house among many others. My father was in charge of supplies for the thousands of post-war immigrants from Latvia, Estonia, Lithuania—names that sounded thrilling and exotic to my young ears.

'A big one, ja, that snake?' said Nicky, running to help my father. A woolly bear of a man from Yugoslavia, he gathered me up and stilled my tears and fear. Nicky looked after our garden and often earned extra income by baby-sitting my brother and me. We would laugh and dance and sing. Long before my parents returned from their party, I would collapse and sleep exhausted on Nicky's lap. My mother told me years later that his wife and children had been killed in the war. It explained the silent tears that sometimes ran down his cracked cheeks; tears of laughter, I'd thought, when they'd been pure grief.

I loved Nicky. All day, before the routine of school stole my freedom, he'd trundle me to and fro in his wheelbarrow. To be with him, I'd jiggle my cot to the bedroom window when I was supposed to be down for an afternoon nap, strip off my clothes and climb out. I would run helter-skelter in search of Nicky, grazing shins, elbows and chin.

'Mrs Duncan, here is your daughter. But we don't know where her clothes are,' was a common lament.

In that tight migrant community I was safe, even if I didn't always find Nicky. We moved when I was nine years old, to a country town near Melbourne, where my parents bought the pub.

My fear of snakes stems from those early country days, but I don't want to tell Gordon I loathe them, so I lie.

'Glad you like 'em,' Gordon says.

He beckons and I follow, this time going out the back where he's a built a simple, raised brick barbecue. He lifts the tin lid. Coiled thickly, a diamond python sleeps.

'Lives here,' Gordon says. 'That's Siphon Python. Wouldn't like to have him moved along.'

'Of course not.'

Gordon gazes fondly at the black snake with creamy dots that form diamonds along its sides. 'Quite beautiful, aren't they?'

'Tell me about your work, Gordon.' I barely restrain myself from running back inside.

Gordon, who was labelled a dope at school, was actually brilliant. He became one of Australia's leading industrial designers. His most widely recognised achievement, though, was to design a new currency for Australia when we shifted from an imperial to a decimal system in 1966. His notes were bold and colourful, full of Australian imagery. They were reproduced on tea towels, money boxes, key rings and posters. And not a single royalty went into his bank account.

By the time we sit down and talk on his deck, he is riddled with bitterness. Bitter that he never received the financial recognition he felt he deserved. Bitter about losing his original house in the 1994 fires. Bitter most of all, I suspect, about the dastardly business of growing old.

What saves him from being just another disappointed, twisted old man is his sense of the absurd. Around the barbecue, permanently fixed, the three sawn logs have been transformed into rude, larrikin faces with lolling tongues. Gordon's permanent guests. A perfect social solution. Over the next few weeks I learn that he feuded with almost everyone at some time. There's a bright red rooster painted on a mustard door leading to the bathroom. It brings life to a dead spot in the house. Chooks are great company. Was this his dinner guest each night?

What he struggles to show me that morning are the hours of work in every single detail of the house. But I failed to understand that until much later, when I thoughtlessly ripped out so much of his heart.

Two weeks after coffee with Gordon, the same boys, Andrew, Chris and Paul, the same barge of five months ago, arrive to help me move house. Again.

The boys know what to do so I don't have to be there. Don't want to be there. My mood is pessimistic. If I look at my past form, there is no reason to expect life here to be any different. I want to change badly. I want to get fit and healthy, find my old energy. But I've tried so many times now, and I've fallen back into old patterns. Can I begin the slow, hard grind of change again? Can I do it alone? Can location help?

My last night on Scotland Island, I sleep less than I am awake, covered by a blanket of wet sea mist that seeps under doors and through gaps in the wooden walls. This time, the move is timed for a 2 p.m. high tide. I plan to meet the boys at the new house in the late afternoon.

When I leave for work at 6.30 a.m., an early freezing westerly scoots down McCarrs Creek to bang at the doors, blowing hard. I put on an old grey tweed coat that I joke will outlive me. But the cold is on the inside as well. I feel ill. I don't know why. I blame it on apprehension. I hope the wind drops by the time the barge arrives.

Gordon has locked the house and the boys call me, stranded. Already on my way home, I divert to the retirement village to pick up the keys. I suspect it is a final gesture of defiance from Gordon, but when I walk into the reception area, past stooped old women glued to walking frames, my anger dissolves. 'This will be the end of him,' I think.

In fact, Gordon has reached the end. Less than two years later, he is dead, but not before I invite him back to see how I've changed his house. He is gracious enough to say: 'It's what I would have done if I'd had the money.' I think, in his shoes, I might have cried.

The water taxi drops me at the ferry wharf. Everything is unloaded and the garden looks like a refugee camp. Inside the house, there's a moss green wall with a huge, empty white space left by Gordon's shelves. It makes the house feel like it's been abandoned and looted.

The boys bring in the furniture and stand holding it, wondering where it should go. Sofas are too big, the table too long.

They see my distress and make suggestions. 'Angle the sofas like this. They'll fit,' Paul says.

They rush around, lifting, adjusting, until I have a room that functions. Table, chairs, sofas, coffee table. Anything that won't squeeze into this tiny space is stacked under the house in Gordon's old workshop.

'This is a bloody disaster,' I moan.

The boys console me. 'Look at this.' Paul leads me onto the front deck and points through to a cleft in the hills on the other side of the bay. 'What a view of the waterfall. Magical.'

I see the rocks, but if there is water it can only be a trickle.

'And what about this?' Pulling me to the back deck and into a little trellised space where Gordon has built a bench. 'You get winter sun here. What a place to lie and look at the bush!'

I lie on the bench. It is Gordon's length and a few inches too short for me. Paul shrugs his shoulders and gives up.

Another bloody brilliant mistake. The biggest yet.

'Gotta go before the tide's too low to get the barge out,' Andrew says.

'OK, guys. Thanks a lot. For everything.'

They give me a hug and a kiss. 'It'll be right. You'll be right.'

When they've gone, I reach for wine. Drink myself into a crying jag. When the bottle is nearly empty, I wander onto the front deck. The moon is high behind the house, lighting the bay, turning the mangroves along the shore into writhing bogeymen. It's low tide and there's a huge new beach where I'm used to seeing water. I remember too late the real-estate agent trick of only showing Pittwater properties at high tide.

Around midnight, I wander down the steps to the water. It's a still, cold night. The air is tangy, seagrass flops limply in dark patches. My forty-ninth birthday is looming. Not much to show for it. Have I found my place finally? I look up at my house. I can always sell. But the thought of another move is crushing, and somewhere in that swell of self-pity I decide to give this everything I've got. And I think of Sweetie, her box of ashes. It's time to lay her to rest, no matter what my future holds.

In the morning, before the sun is up, I wake with a thumping headache and vow, again, to go on a health kick. I make tea and toast, and take it onto the deck to wait for the dawn. It arrives in a blood-red rush, turning the escarpment a fiery orange and bringing the bay to life. As if on cue, birds begin racketing around and a school of tiny fish speeds past in a froth of water, followed by bigger, jumping fish that rise and plop loudly. Five kookaburras join me, one by one, and eye my toast greedily. The littlest one is tousled, like he was late getting up and didn't have time to brush his hair.

'Scruff Bucket. That's your name.'

He is the last to fly away. I go inside intending to shower and unpack but instead return to bed. There's no need to hurry. It's Saturday. When I wake it is nearly noon.

I squeeze in a lunch at Towlers Bay, drinking too much, as usual.

At some blurry point, Stewart leans across the table to me: 'You're turning into a drunk, you know.'

His words shock me into sobriety. 'Stewart, I have often seen you in the same state but I would never say anything like that to you.'

The entire table is silent. Watching. Waiting.

'I apologise,' he says.

And chatter fires up as though someone's pulled the cord of an outboard motor.

But I *know* I'm drinking too much. And it scares me. As a kid, I hated alcohol. Watching my father negotiate life through a lurching haze put me off it for years. Somewhere along the line I forgot all those fears and joined the drinking crowd. But a drunk? Me? All I'm doing is blurring the edges of a rather useless life, aren't I?

On Sunday morning I have a ferocious hangover. Again. I vow to cut back on booze. Again. Not that it's a problem. It's a healthy move. Right?

A week later, dusk rolls in from the east. It is mid-May and the air turns thin with cold as soon as the sun drops. The lover finally finds the time to come to Pittwater. But he leaves after a quick house tour. Now, it's too early to sleep, too late to make something of the next few hours.

I vow to eat a proper dinner. My body, when I run my hands down it, is papery thin. Outside it begins to rain heavily, banging on the tin roof like a thousand drumsticks. There are no leaks. The house is solid.

The next morning, the waterfall across the bay is frothing white and magnificent. It roars and I find myself busting with joy at the sight of it. I reach for the phone and dial a local builder to make an appointment. I am glad I am here. I just have to extend the house and it will be fine.

Two weeks later, I feel a lump in my right breast.

4

'CAN'T FEEL ANYTHING,' a local doctor tells me the next day, when I stop by his office to get it checked out.

'Great.'

Yippee, is what I'm thinking. But he insists on a mammogram and I go confidently round the corner to the clinic. The mammograms go directly to the doctor and I forget to ring to make another appointment.

The receptionist calls me two days later. 'When would you like to come in?'

'How about next week? I've got a lot on right now.'

'Can you make it any sooner? How about tomorrow?' she suggests, and a worm of fear wriggles uncomfortably in my stomach.

The next day I return to the same little office while the doctor reads the diagnosis. I am detached. Tough. He hands me a referral to a specialist, tells me to call him if I can't get a quick appointment.

'Do you understand what you have to do?'

'I know all about it,' I say. 'My husband died of a brain tumour, my brother died from thymoma.'

He is silent.

I pay the bill and walk to the car, where I sit and cry. I cannot help believing that I've done this to myself, that I'm being punished for my sins. But I still have a sliver of hope. Maybe it is benign, not malignant. I dial Fleury and ask her to find the best breast cancer specialist in Sydney.

'Who needs one?'

'Me.'

'Ah shit.'

I refuse her offer of comfort, refuse to go to town to stay with her. I want to be at home. So much for happy dreams and good omens. I am a moron. All the old feelings of anger and despair come surging in. The more I turn to the lover for support, the more he withdraws.

'Of course I'll support you,' he says. But he doesn't return my phone calls. He is called away suddenly during lunch. I believe the excuses. Cannot grasp that nearly three intense years can mean nothing to him.

'Most men would walk away,' I say, testing his resolve.

'I wouldn't like to think I'm that kind of man.'

But he is, of course.

I do not fear death, I realise. I fear being ill and in pain. On my first visit to the specialist, to schedule the biopsy, I set the rules.

'I watched my brother go through chemotherapy so I don't want chemo. If things are that bad, I'd rather buy a ticket to Tuscany and sit out death with great food, good wine and Dean Martin belting out "Volare" on a bad sound system. OK?'

'Deal,' said the specialist, an affable, grey-haired man used to women placing their lives in the bowl of his hands.

A week later, a soft-voiced technician, overflowing with kindness, stabs me with a long, thick needle at the edge of my nipple. It hurts like hell and tears fill my eyes but I do not flinch.

Then the wait in the specialist's office, high above the outside world, in a room where the windows do not open, the air is recycled. Ahead of me are two other women who look like hunted animals. One of them is weeping silently. I pull a novel out of my handbag and tune out.

I jump when my name is called and follow the specialist into his office. Benign? Malignant? One word, life. One word, death.

I sit still and silent, my back ramrod straight. 'So do I buy a ticket to Tuscany?' I ask when the silence begins to feel smothering.

He opens the folder, pulls out some papers clipped together. Looks at them. Takes a breath. Does not look at me.

'Yep. It's Tuscany,' he says.

Someone lets off a thousand tiny birds in my stomach, all beating wildly to escape.

'Thought it might be like that.'

'I won't be able to save the breast.'

Already it is an anonymous appendage. Not *your* breast. *The* breast.

'Oh well. I've got two.'

I am appalled at my own words. Am I becoming my mother? A woman who makes light of catastrophe? And then, instantly: So what? I will be dead long before I fully develop her most irritating traits.

'The tumour is directly underneath the nipple.'

Tumour. I absorb the word. Miss bits of what he's saying. Hear only that my right breast is scheduled for the trash can. I wonder if that is where it actually goes, tossed out like a piece of steak that's gone bad.

'Do you understand what I'm saying?' the specialist asks, then adds, 'We also have to take out most of the lymph nodes under your right arm, to see whether any are affected.'

'Oh yes. Quite. Don't worry. I understand. I've been through all this before. First with my brother, then my husband. I know the routine.'

As I speak, I see doors stretching down an endless corridor like a long line of piano keys, slamming in my face.

House plans? Slam.

Holiday plans? Slam.

Work plans? Slam.

Get a dog? Slam.

Life? Slam.

In a wave of nausea, I confront my own mortality and wipe out, in an instant, the human instinct to look ahead. The waiting begins.

'We won't know how far it's gone until after the operation.'

'Can you take a shot? Guess?'

'No. But I think you've had the tumour a long time.'

'What's the worst-case scenario?'

'It's progressed to the bone marrow.'

'What happens then?'

'For most people, it's chemo.'

'What's the success rate?'

'Varied.'

'I told you. Chemo is not on.'

'Let's worry about that if the time comes. We won't know until after surgery, until we see if it's progressed to the lymph nodes.'

This is the moment, I believe, that I shut down. I do not ask any critical questions. My chances of survival? What kind of breast cancer? I do not want to know. Detail equals pessimism. No more questions, Susan. You are in control. You will take on the fight. You will win. Statistics don't apply to you.

A silent mantra begins: I am strong and my body is strong. I am strong and my body is strong. With the first flicker of doubt, slip into the mantra, over and over again.

I go through the process of scheduling surgery like a sleepwalker, feeling detached. The specialist's secretary avoids my eyes, and deals matter-of-factly with the details.

Seven to ten days in hospital.

Fine.

Is there anyone at home to look after me after surgery?

No.

Whom should they call in the event of an emergency?

My mother? No. A distantly located cousin? No. Work colleagues? No. The lover? NO! Fleury, I finally decide. Good, strong, loyal, smart, a wonderful, dear, funny, completely non-judgmental friend.

I walk out of the specialist's office, buy a bottle of French champagne and meet Pia at a hairdresser's in Darlinghurst. We laugh and joke our way through a cut, streaks and the wine. I am manic and a little crazy and Donald, the hairdresser, looks at us warily.

'What's going on, girls?' he asks.

'It's OK, Donald, nothing serious. Little trip to the hospital ahead.'

It is late in the afternoon and Donald lets his little Jack Russell terrier, Lucy, come into the main part of the salon from her bed downstairs. Lucy is outrageous, cheeky, full of herself, a shocking flirt. I watch her and I do not think about cancer.

'Where did you get Lucy?'

Donald gives me a card with the breeder's name. I put it in my handbag with the receipt for the hairdressing bill and forget about it.

Pia and I stumble out of the salon into a cold, windy June night.

'Will you be OK? Do you want to stay in town?' she asks.

'No. I want to get home.'

'What about dinner somewhere? You need company.'

'Don't be a dope. I'm fine.'

I laugh and smile, wave goodbye. As I slam the car door behind me, though, I cave in, suddenly limp. The effort of *toujours gai, toujours brave* is exhausting.

I go home, not out to dinner as I once would have done. I do not want to be around friends. I want the peace of Lovett Bay. I want the sound of the waterfall to put me to sleep. I want to wake up and watch the early-morning sun turn the escarpment a burning orange. It is the physical world I crave. Already Lovett Bay has become my sanctuary.

I sleep that night in fits and starts. My mind flutters, screams, races. All the old clichés spin through my head: Regrets? Finest moments? Worst moments? And the big one: What the hell is it all about?

Find the strength within, I tell myself. I recite my mantra: *I am strong and my body is strong.* Again and again until it puts me to sleep.

Next morning, on the way to work, it is raining and I get wet racing from the water taxi to the car, but I don't care. The traffic is bad but it doesn't irk. I press the button for the elevator just once, even though it takes a long time to arrive. Already, my view of the world has changed. Don't sweat the small stuff.

I stride down the long corridors of the office. In Lego cubicles along the western wall, voices rise and fall on telephones. Stories bought and sold, pictures bargained for, souls for hire to the highest bidder.

All day I sit in my cell and go through the motions, harbouring my little secret. *Toujours gai.*

As I pull on my coat to leave at 5.30 p.m. I stick my head into the editor's office. 'I'll be needing a bit of personal time.'

'Why?' Not when.

'I'm having a breast lopped off.'

My voice wobbles. Which makes me furious. I turn to leave but she jumps up, grabs my arm, leading me to a seat.

'What's going on?'

The compassion in her tone nearly brings me undone.

'Breast cancer. Have to have a breast removed. Just take a few days. Shouldn't be away for long.'

'What's the prognosis?'

'Don't know. Won't know until after surgery.'

'Are you frightened?'

'Oh, no. It's much easier to deal with your own mortality than to face losing people you love.'

But it's a lie. They are both devastating.

Two weeks later, I check into hospital. A little thin, nervy man takes my details across a reception counter and then leads me to my room.

'It's a wonderful room,' he says. 'Light, comfortable. Views. But you have to share it until we can get you a private room. In a couple of days.'

It is like being shown a hotel room but there's no mini bar, no fridge and check-out time isn't negotiable. The view directly across the road is of the hospice. I see it immediately and try never to look at it again. I am *not* going there. That is *not* my future.

The day I arrive I stay in my street clothes for as long as possible, sitting and reading a book in the recliner chair by the bed. Nurses come and go, blood samples are taken, vital signs recorded. Allergies noted.

'Hi, I'm Maggie. You can get changed now.' A nurse is holding one of those white cotton robes with ties at the back. 'Put this on and get into bed. I'll be back in a minute.'

I want to shout that it's the middle of the day and nobody goes to bed at this time unless they're sick. And I don't feel sick. Tired, but not sick.

So far the second bed has remained empty. 'Who's going into the other bed?' I ask the nurse when she returns.

'Woman with a brain tumour.'

'What stage?' A question I do not dare to ask of my own condition.

'Not good.'

Maggie rolls up the rubber blood-pressure bag, cool fingers lightly find the pulse in my wrist. She counts the seconds on her watch. Then she pats my arm, tells me she'll be back with an injection shortly. Pethidine. The happy drug. Something to look forward to.

While I wait for nirvana, my room-mate is wheeled in, white-faced and frail. As soon as the nurses leave, her husband, daughter and son creep in, form a human chain round the bed. The daughter begins a prayer.

I don't want to be here. This grief and love is private. For what they are doing is saying farewell.

Surgery is scheduled for 2 p.m. The pethidine shot calms me, and by the time I am moved to the operating theatre I feel everyone is my new best friend. I engage the nurses in disjointed conversation.

Then the countdown. A whack on my hand, find the vein, a jab. The sickening smell of anaesthetic, spotlights overhead.

'Count backwards from ten.' Voices are friendly, as though we've known each other for years.

I make it to seven and blackness descends.

I am angry when a woman's voice cuts through my world of peace, calling my name. I want her to go away. Shut up.

'Susan. Wake up. Can you hear me? Susan!'

I open my eyes and they are already filled with tears. I cannot understand my grief. The oxygen mask is heavy on my face.

'Good girl. That's it. Slow breath. Relax.'

I feel like a child, defenceless. A young face swims into focus.

'What's your name?'

'Susan.'

'Where do you live?'

'Lovett Bay.'

'OK. We're just going to leave you here for a while, until the anaesthetic wears off. Then we'll take you to your room, OK?'

I wake up when I am being dragged gently onto the bed in my room. There are tubes in my hand, tubes in my chest, tubes filled with rainbow coloured fluids.

'Press this for pain.' A little black cylinder is squeezed into my hand and my thumb placed on a red button. Press for escape. 'Don't worry, you can't overdose. It's self-regulating.'

There is hardly any pain but I press it all night, every time I wake. A small reprieve from the moment I will have to look down at my chest, note the new body formation.

After a few days, hospital begins to feel like a safe haven. No need to think about being different yet. Everyone around me is branded in some way. There is no way of knowing how far the cancer has progressed until after surgery and pathology on the lymph nodes removed from under the arm, so waiting for the pathology results is terrible.

After two days I ask the surgeon when he visits for the daily check-up if there are any results.

He is snappish. 'If I had news I'd tell you.'

I want to scream at him. Slap him. I have a right to ask!

He checks the tubing running from under the skin where my breast once was; he feels the bones. I ask him how his day has gone.

'Operated on a twenty-one year old this morning. Twenty-one!'

Slap. Perspective in a flash.

On the fourth day, I do not ask. But when he sits by the bed and sandwiches my hand in his, I can hardly breathe.

'One lymph node affected,' he says. 'And only the smallest trace measurable. Nothing really. A minute trace.'

'What does that mean?' At last I can ask.

'Not the best-case scenario. But the second-best-case scenario.'

His words send me into a giddy spin of euphoria. Normal, I think, life can be normal again. Wind back the clock. A second chance.

The surgeon snatches back control. 'Of course there is no way of knowing what is ahead. All it takes is for one little cell to get through the lymph system to metastasise. There are no guarantees. Getting through the first two years without a recurrence is a start, but we don't give you the all-clear until you've been cancer-free for five years.'

'All-clear?'

'Well, there's never a complete all-clear. We never know what's ahead, do we?' He stands, takes my hand. 'So go home and enjoy life.'

The words sound ominous. I am on a slippery dip, hurtling towards hope only moments before plunging into despair. Which I disguise with a public mask of good cheer. *Toujours gai.*

The lover visits once. Quickly, in the early morning, on his way to the airport, which gives him an excuse to rush or he'll miss the plane. His face, usually a featureless mask, registers shock when he sees me reach for a glass of water with the arm that no longer segues into a breast. My movement is slow and painful. Crippled. It is the moment, I think, when he finally understands that everything has changed. It is the moment I understand that the affair is over. It takes a while longer to accept it.

Eight days after surgery, I beg to be allowed out. The surgeon wants me to stay another two days. We compromise on one more day.

Witch, my brother-in-law's beautiful, voluptuous partner, takes me home, driving through a Saturday-morning world that is pristine, sharp, vibrant. The great big black hat of doom has lifted at least a little. There is time, who knows how long, to begin again. Another chance. Don't blow it. Not this time. Because it's my last chance.

Kay, a friend and colleague, insists on coming to stay for my first week at home after surgery. She bustles in, loaded with fresh fish and vegetables, all sorts of herbs, crusty bread. A feast after brown paper hospital fare. We settle into a cosy daily routine of late breakfasts and early dinners. Each afternoon, we both take a book to our bedrooms. I read until Kay calls dinner is ready and we sit down to a beautifully set table, candles lit, as though we are celebrating. After what feels like a lifetime of drinking wine with food, I reach for a glass of water. It's hard to be sociable without the crutch.

On her last day, Kay makes tortilla the traditional way she learned when she lived in Spain. It is golden and fragrant with garlic, rich with potatoes and eggs. It is the most delicious dish I have ever eaten.

It feels abso-bloody-lutely sensational to be out of the airless cocoon of the hospital. Most days the phone rings regularly. Concerned friends, great friends. Their support means so much.

I wear a little woollen prosthesis that I slip into the empty cup of my bra for the first three months after surgery, until the long, livid scar has healed. It's a pink-satin-covered lump and I hate it. I have already asked the surgeon if I might have the second breast removed. He thinks I am frightened of a recurrence. But it is the thought of a fake body part that is repulsive. He tells me to wait a while. But I am determined.

Once you've had cancer it creeps around your mind like a whispery guilty conscience. What is this lump? What is this ache? Minor physical discomforts are filled with threat. Is it back? I have rejected chemo but the pressure is on. Memories of my brother lying in hospital, a drip drizzling a poisonous chemical cocktail through collapsing veins, surges into my mind every time I am pushed by one friend or another to have this drastic treatment.

My case, though, is so different from my brother's. The surgeon has told me I am a borderline case. No lymph nodes contaminated means no chemo. Minuscule contamination? Up to me to make the decision. He also says he thinks a five-year course of tamoxifen, two little pills a day to suppress my body's oestrogen, will suffice.

But a work colleague, high-powered and persuasive, will not drop the case for chemo: 'Just go and talk to the oncologist.' She has done the research, like a good journalist, and she insists I write down a name and phone number. After two fraught days, I make the appointment.

In the oncologist's waiting room, wonderful paintings hang on the walls, fresh flowers grace coffee tables and lifestyle magazines are piled high. When a door opens, a round-faced woman with dark brown hair and a cheery smile calls my name. She indicates a seat beside her desk, and pulls a file towards her, opening it to a letter from the surgeon. She gives the impression she's reading it for the first time, and perhaps she is.

'What would you do?' I ask her.

She sighs and leans back in her chair. 'I would have the treatment.'

'Why? I'm told I'm a borderline case.'

'Because you have two types of cancer cells. One a greater risk than the other.'

I do not ask any more questions. I agree to the treatment and make an appointment for a couple of days after my forty-ninth birthday. I'm expecting to have lunch with the lover. He's never forgotten a birthday.

That night I call Sophia, seeking courage. No, seeking more than courage. I want her to tell me I am taking the best course. Because I feel like I am spinning in a whirlpool of rage and confusion. There are no straightforward answers. Will chemo guarantee I beat cancer? No. Is tamoxifen enough? There is no way of knowing. Can I be sure a little cluster of cells isn't already mutating somewhere else in my body? No.

'My sense of security is gone,' I tell Sophia on the phone.

'Well, that's not a bad way to live,' she says.

'Next you're going to tell me it's another bloody gift!'

She laughs her big, fat, gorgeous belly laugh. 'Ah, darlin'. That's exactly what it is. Only fools think they're promised more than the moment they're in. And the only absolute cure for life is death.'

The lover dumps me formally at my birthday lunch. A lunch he does not confirm until the last minute.

'Are we having lunch or not?' he asks.

Why don't I just terminate the call, press a tiny button and zoom him into space for ever? 'Yeah. Sure. Where?'

We make a time and place and my phone goes dead. Low battery.

I wear my uniform of jeans, loose shirt. I want to be interesting and sexual, revel in my last white-napkin lunch before beginning chemo. But I feel I have passed my use-by date. I cannot even conjure up a smile. *Toujours gai* is gone for ever. Soon I will be bald, without eyebrows and eyelashes, stamped as a person who now belongs to a different club.

The restaurant is beautiful, white tablecloths, perfectly tweaked table napkins, glittering glass. I let the waiter fill my glass with wine and feel a sudden thrill at being careless of my physical well-being. I drink it recklessly, and within a few minutes I am quite drunk. It feels wonderful. Like days of old. The second glass is gulped and it is enough to make me throw caution to the wind.

The lover reaches beside his chair and puts a shopping bag in front of me. 'Happy birthday.'

When I open it I find two books, one about the destruction of love, another about dogs.

'Trying to tell me something?' I ask.

Another gulp, another empty glass. Because I know he is. And yet I cannot believe this is the official moment. It is my birthday, for God's sake. I have just lost a breast. I am about to begin chemo. How hard is it to give me one frivolous day to sustain me through the next few months?

He shifts in his chair, trying to make himself taller by straightening his back. The expression on his face is almost neutral but not quite. There is a hint of power. He looks like an actor about to break into the defining soliloquy of the play.

'All my relationships eventually come to an end,' he says.

And I cannot remember anything else. I turn to reach for the wine and knock over the ice bucket. Waiters rush over to fix the mess.

But I do not make a scene. I have never made scenes. I do not cry. I try for a line that is light (my mother again!) but come up with one that I am ashamed of to this day: 'I gave it everything I had. I guess it wasn't enough.' Jesus, where were the violins?

I see his jaw jut a little more. Power. Control. And I fall off the shaky edge of what I thought was love into hate and anger. Such a fine line.

When the waiter comes by with a fresh glass and bottle, I ask for the dessert menu. This time the lover is shocked and cannot fake neutrality. Was I supposed to get up and leave? Break down?

I slowly swallow every last mouthful of dessert. He can bloody well wait. I am seriously drunk, with an irresistible desire to get even drunker. The lover gets more and more aloof but never impatient. The performance of the damned has him riveted.

I look at him after what seems like only minutes and notice city lights with rain halos. Outside it is now dark and wet. I am deliciously, almost paralytically drunk. At some point I hazily remember that my mother, here for my birthday party, is waiting for me in a nearby restaurant where she is lunching with friends.

I stagger to my feet, thanking him for lunch politely, like someone I don't know well, and leave. Just before I reach the door onto the street, I turn and ask him to call the restaurant where my mother waits. 'Tell them to get my mother to stand outside. I'll be there in a moment.'

He nods. He is anxious to be away now. I suspect he has another date. Drinks with the new mistress. Poor cow.

I stagger the two blocks to my mother and then make her drive us to Church Point. Which is a pig of a thing to do. At home, she rarely drives further than her local shopping centre.

She accelerates/brakes all the way home through rain and wind, never letting the speedo jump beyond forty kilometres while I fill the car with great big bellowing howls. She thinks I am going to tell her I have not long to live and she is silent.

The Point shimmers in the wet. Tinnies joggle and clunk in the faint swell, tied side by side like Turkish slippers. The rain strobes through streetlights and textures the night, heavy enough to frost the water.

People in wet-weather gear huddle under shelter, beers in their hands, unworried by the rain. I scan the hooded faces. Who will help? Boxes to unload and an arm still tender where the lymph nodes have been removed, a chest where the scar is still a ruby slash. And my mother, nearly eighty, shaking from exhaustion and fear for her daughter.

'Matty,' I scream from the car, 'can you look after my mother?'

Matty is the man you call for any job too big to do yourself—rubbish removal, sandstone paving, bobcat work. 'Matty's boys', as they are known, hover around him, a ragged collection. The core is Big Jack, the muscle, Scotty, the doer, and Bob, the fisherman.

'Yeah, mate,' he says. He takes a last lung-busting drag on his smoke, sculls the dregs of beer from the bottle. With the style of the ritziest doorman, he ushers my mother into the Church Point world: 'C'mon on then, mate,' he says, holding out a work-stained hand.

My mother feathers up like a happy chook, smiles flirtatiously. It's the kind of attention she loves. Matty glides her down the jetty as though she's a fragile, ancient duchess.

Matty's boys, almost synchronised, finish their beers and come over to me like unsteady soldier crabs. Without a word, they take the boxes of wine and the shopping, and in minutes the water taxi is ready for take-off.

'Will you be all right, mate, at the other end?' Matty asks.

He has seen my swollen face. No questions, though, that might intrude. The Pittwater way.

'Yeah. Thanks, Matty. Owe you a beer.'

He picks his way back to the bottle shop. His boys close in around him halfway up the jetty, like a dark cloud.

The rain has stopped and the water is a black satin sheet. I watch the fantail of the water taxi's wake and a sliver of relief slips in. After the dozen or so half-hearted attempts to end the affair over the years, he has finally severed the cord. He loves me. He loves me not. It's a big fat not.

The wine and shopping are piled onto Ken's dock and I leave it all there. I'll deal with it in the morning. If it rains again, too bad. I'll get every guest at my birthday party—a quickly thrown-together celebration—to carry a couple of bottles on their arrival.

That night, even my mother's snoring does not wake me. But the relief is turning back into anger. And, ever so cunningly, I slip away from the fear of cancer into the rage of the wronged.

The next morning there are questions in my mother's narrowed eyes as we sit over tea and toast at the kitchen table. I have the post-binge blues, a drilling headache. Get through today. Tomorrow will be better. But tomorrow is the party. A final fling before treatment. I curse the stupid impulse. And the next day? Chemo.

'I had an affair, you know.' As though saying it out loud will somehow give it substance. 'He ended it. Yesterday.'

'Oh, is that all it was,' she says lightly. 'I thought it was about something serious, you know, like dying or something.' She adds a casual aside: 'Anyway, men don't like mutilation.'

I scrabble for her meaning. Is she saying they are weak and can't cope with illness? Or that I am no longer desirable in any way?

She gets up and goes to her suitcase to get me my birthday present. It's a lace and satin teddy. Fragile, feminine, sexy. The style of top that will hang flatly and therefore emphasise where there is no longer any breast. I say thank you and wrap it up again. Now I know where I get my appalling ability to choose the wrong gifts.

Six days later, I wander around the corridors of Royal North Shore Hospital, searching for the right room for chemo treatment.

'It's an omen,' I tell Pia when I call her on the mobile, panicked, lost. 'I'm not meant to have this treatment.'

'Why don't you ask someone for directions?' Pragmatic as ever.

'Yeah, OK. I'll do that.'

'Do you want me to drive over and come with you?'

Of course I do. I'm looking for comfort. But there are no fairy godmothers. No magic wands. None that work, anyway.

'Nah. I'll be OK.'

At the main desk I query a harassed receptionist. She directs me. At another desk, another receptionist hands me forms to complete.

There's an illusion of normality in the chemo ward. A tea room, with sandwiches and biscuits. Even cake. I eat insatiably. And then a chubby-faced nurse calls my name.

I step from earth to a strange new planet where people sit around grey-faced and silent in large vinyl armchairs that hiss with every wriggle. Violently coloured drips hang from steel poles. Thin wires of life? Or delaying death a little longer?

'Do I really need to do this?'

The nurse looks at me. There is compassion and patience. How many times has she heard the same question? Unfair to ask. Impossible not to.

'No one is forcing you to do this. Take a while. Think about it.'

'Would you have it, if you were me?'

She looks at my chart. 'Yes,' she says.

And I let go. I hold out my hand, palm facing the floor, and she slips the needle into the big vein just below my wrist. When the drip is flowing smoothly, the nurse walks away. I sit there, trapped, committed.

I've chosen a chair at the back of the room, where the outside world is a distant smudge. To one side, almost behind me, there is a stretcher with an old, wispy-haired man lying on it, with grey skin stretched tight across his cheekbones. He is stick-thin under his everyday clothes. Except for a tight, swollen tummy that points straight up. The old man groans. Not loudly. More in anguish than pain.

I watch the clock through blurry eyes, willing the two hours to fly past. Hurry up, drips, hurry up! Fluorescent red. Clear saline. But they don't hurry and I cannot move until the needle is pulled from my hand. I cannot even scream. In death's counting house, we are all polite.

When I walk out of that first session filled with my new, toxic blood I feel like a bug-eyed alien. In my pocket is a little bottle of pills. For post-treatment nausea.

'Drink lots of water,' the nurse told me. 'All day. Flush it out.'

'How much water?'

'As much as you can stand. At night, too, if you can.'

I walk to the car park, focus inwardly to assess any differences. Dizziness? Illness? Lightness? All I feel, though, is disconnected. I check my hair in the rearview mirror. Still firmly attached. I have been told I can expect it to start falling out before the second treatment. I dread losing eyelashes more than being bald.

My mind fizzes silently. I do not want to be this person filled with stomach-churning fear and leaden despair. For a moment, I yearn for *toujours gai*. But it is *toujours gai*, I suspect, that's caused my problems.

I stay with Pia that first night, in her apartment in the city. When I finally sleep, it is to wake up drenched in sweat. The sheets are sodden. I feel like I'm on fire, or in a sauna. I have no idea what is happening. I shower, crawl back to bed. I don't need a sheet or blanket. And it is a cold, July night.

By morning, the night is a distant memory and I feel almost normal. I shower, dress and go to work. By the end of the day, though, I am mush. I want to go home. My home. I call Pia and tell her not to expect me.

At Mona Vale I pull in to the fruit market. Carrots. Apples. Celery. Garlic. Anything to restore what chemo has zapped. The woman working the cash register watches as I reach into my bag for cash. The little needle spot on my hand is purple now, with bruising.

'Chemo?' she asks.

'Yes?' I turn the word into a question.

'I had it ten years ago. You'll be right.'

I want to kiss her. She's had it and survived. I will too.

That night, I look at the anti-nausea pills and reject them again. I do not feel ill. On the bedside table I line up a jug of water, a glass, a stack of books. The arsenal, as I come to call it.

At 3 a.m. with a full moon blasting through the bedroom window, I sit bolt upright. Before I can get up, I have vomited all over the floor. I should have taken the pills. I am too exhausted to move and leave the vomit there. Drink some water and go back to sleep.

At work the next day, I cannot get warm, cannot think straight. I thought I understood the meaning of 'bone tired', but I didn't. Not until now. But I refuse to give in. I keep going to work. It's the contact with other people that allows me to check whether my mind is spiralling into a kind of madness or whether I'm still seeing the world rationally.

A week after my first treatment, I'm back in the waiting room with the beautiful paintings. Then it's my turn.

'Feel all right after treatment?' the oncologist asks.

'Yep.' I forget to tell her about the sauna sweat on the first night.

'Any nausea?'

'Oh, yeah. Threw up on the second night.'

She looks shocked. 'That shouldn't happen. Did you take the pills?'

'No.'

'Why not? You're supposed to take the pills for the first three nights after treatment.'

'I thought you only took them if you felt sick. I didn't feel sick until I threw up.' I've never been good at understanding instructions.

She sighs. 'Take them next time, OK?'

She gives me a referral to a nearby blood-testing clinic. Tells me to arrange a test one week before my next treatment, which is scheduled in three weeks, to make sure I've remade enough white blood cells to replace the ones that have been nuked.

The vein in my left arm is in for a pounding. My right arm is off limits for even a blood-pressure test. Lymphoedema is the big bogeyman.

Swelling that will not retreat, leaving one limb much bigger than its partner. Without the full quota of lymph nodes, my arm is no longer as efficient at cleaning out bacteria. An infection of any kind is a danger—from a knife-cut while peeling potatoes to a mosquito bite.

It takes a few scares until I accept that a small tube of antiseptic is my new constant companion. But I instantly reject babying my right arm. Not practical in an environment where everything is carried in and out.

During the second treatment, I endure but do not cry, although I hate the thin, dead smell of chemo in that room where we sit strung up to chemicals so deadly that, when the old boy's pee bottle spills, men arrive in white boiler suits and contamination masks to clean up.

After that second treatment, I behave quite bizarrely when I leave the clinic. I arrive back at Church Point almost euphoric. As I wait for the water taxi I invite almost total strangers (no one who lives in this part of the Pittwater community is a *total* stranger) home to dinner. I know I am worn out, but invitations come tumbling out of my mouth. Perhaps it's desperation, to be around people who talk about kids and cooking and boats and fishing . . . and holiday plans. As I am dropped off at Ken's dock at the Lovett Bay boat shed, I add up the number of people who have said yes. About eight, I think. Easy.

There is a man on the pontoon. Middle-aged, with dark, wavy hair and eyes so brown they seem black. He's helping one of the boat-shed boys carry a mast.

'Do you need another pair of hands?' I ask. 'I'm *really* strong.'

'We'll be right,' says the stranger.

When the mast is laid on the jetty, the stranger stands and looks across the bay. Shoulders hunched. Bright white T-shirt ringing his neck under a navy windcheater. Worn working boots below his jeans.

'Hello,' I add.

'Uh-huh.' His face is weary but deeply tanned.

'I'm Susan. I bought Gordon's place.'

'I know.'

'Oh.'

Silence. Then he remembers the normal protocol. 'Oh, I'm Bob.'

'Do you live around here?'

'Yeah.' He spins and points up the winding sandstone path to the pale yellow house with the graceful columns. Says nothing.

'Oh, so that's your house. I've wondered who lives there,' I say.

And then it registers. His wife is ill. Cancer. I'd heard about it. But wallowing in my own fog, I'd pushed the information to one side.

'Come and have dinner tonight,' I babble.

'I don't know,' he says. 'My wife . . .'

'Yeah, I know. Cancer. Me too.' I hold out my hand for him to see the little patch of cotton wool.

'Then you understand,' he replies. 'But I'll ask her. Let you know.'

He moves off along the jetty, one shoulder lower than the other, walking crookedly. Head bent low.

'Seven o'clock, if you can make it,' I call out.

He stops and turns, head hunkered deep into his shoulders like a turtle. 'Might be too late for her, she gets tired. Thanks, anyway.'

'How about six?'

'I'll ask her.'

'OK.'

I watch him walk towards the pathway that climbs to his house.

About half an hour later, the phone rings.

'Thanks, but we won't come to dinner,' Bob says. 'Barbara's a bit tired.'

'OK.' Intrusive. I've been intrusive and pushy. Feel I've overstepped some fragile line. I back off.

'She says lunch would be good sometime,' he adds.

'Oh! That's terrific. When would you like to come? This Saturday?'

'I'll talk to Barbara and let you know.'

I put the phone down, vaguely exasperated. I'm used to instant results and Bob, I think, is hard to get a lot of words out of.

Some nights, the moon is so bright through the bedroom window I have no need of a light. Not even to read a book. I plunge into master food writer Stephanie Alexander's odyssey into southwest France. Reading about food is endlessly reassuring. There's a predictable outcome, a vicarious pleasure and no one is ever threatened. Her mouthwatering account of making a traditional peasant dish called *Poule avec sa mique* (chicken with a dumpling) is inspiring. First, you bone a chicken and make a rich stock from the bones, then the flesh is stuffed with a blend of tarragon, chopped ham, pork mince and breadcrumbs. The stuffed bird is then wrapped in muslin and poached—along with a large, tasty, juicy dumpling—in the stock heavily laden with vegetables. I read it over and over for a while, tempted by its complexities. I vow to make it one day. Which becomes a tiny rub on a steamy window to take a tentative glimpse at a future.

In the cool hours before dawn, as I sip endless glasses of water, the idea of spending a whole day cooking a 'simple' meal is incredibly tempting. So much easier than the racking business of sitting at an office desk. My concentration at work, after the second treatment, is scatty. I cannot stop my mind from shooting off in a thousand different directions. Easier by far, I decide, to follow the directions in a recipe than to try to fill a glaring white page with words. So it isn't that hard when I step into one of the grey-carpeted cubicles one morning and withdraw (again) from my career. I have heard, anyway, that they're looking for a replacement for me.

I sit in the straight-backed chair opposite the business manager (the boss is on holiday) and take control. It's wonderful, the freedom of having nothing to lose.

'I've heard you're looking for a replacement for me,' I tell her flatly.

She swallows and looks at the file—my file—on her desk.

'Where did you hear that?' she asks.

'All over town. I even know who's been offered my job. I can't work out, though, whether you're lining someone up to replace me now—or because you think I'm going to drop off the twig shortly?'

'Oh,' is all she can manage. My bluntness has shocked her.

'It's OK,' I say, relenting. 'Let's just be adults, admit what's going on and come to some kind of arrangement.'

Her face stains with red but she smiles. 'That'd be wonderful.'

By lunchtime, I finish my goodbyes, climb into my car and vacate my parking space for the last time. If I didn't feel so absolutely wrecked with tiredness, I would have sung out loud. What matters now is living. Not existing. My only goal now is to get well and survive.

And to make *Poule avec sa mique*.

A few days after quitting my job, the phone rings in the middle of a silent morning and I jump with fright.

'Hello?'

'It's Bob.'

'Hello. How are you? How's Barbara?'

'She's . . . ah . . . lunch. We can make lunch on Friday. She'd love it.'

'Great. It will just be us. No one else.'

'That's good.'

'Is there anything that she can't eat?'

'No. Anything is fine,' he says.

The phone goes down abruptly. Not a great talker, this Bob. His reticence is disorientating. A whole bunch of polite little asides go unuttered, like I've been cut off midstream. But there's no bullshit.

I put the phone back in the cradle and rub my prickling head. Hair drifts down in a sunbeam of light and lands on the floor like snipped threads. *My* hair. This morning, the pillow looked like a moulting dog's bed. Soon I'll be bald. *Hat* gets added to the shopping list. Make an appointment to get my hair trimmed—that's the hair that's holding on.

At the hairdresser's, Simon, who would rather be an actor, is kind. He reaches for clippers in his industrial grey salon next to the chicken shop in Mona Vale and starts at the back, perhaps to ease the shock. I bury my head in a book until he tells me I have to look up so he can level the sides. It's a close-cropped shave that reveals the shape of my head in detail. I expect to be horrified, but I like it.

'I reckon you've got a couple of weeks before it all falls out,' he says. 'Sorry.'

I feel a swell of loyalty to him. So many are appalled by the merest whiff of illness.

I cruise Mona Vale searching for a hat, but it's winter and stocks of summer hats are nonexistent. The takeaway food shops layer the smell of deep-fried chicken heavily in the air. Along with the exhaust fumes of idling cars waiting for someone to pull out of too few parking spaces, the atmosphere is rank. My stomach flip-flops. A burning taste of chemicals rises up and my legs suddenly feel like balloons filled with concrete. I drag myself into a coffee shop to sit for a while. To adjust to the unfamiliar sensation of weakness. It's not just unpleasant, it's downright scary. I close my eyes for a moment.

'Would you like to see a menu?'

The waitress wears a T-shirt that fails to meet the top of her jeans. Her tanned stomach is flat. A silver ring winks from her navel. It's impossible to look anywhere else.

'Coffee. Flat white. That will do.'

The waitress flicks the menu away cheerfully. My eyes clang shut again.

Coffee arrives with a deliberately loud clunk. They are not used to seeing people doze at café tables in Mona Vale and they find it disturbing. I drink up quickly and leave.

Outside, the hat search begins again but I hesitate to try on the few I find. When a saleswoman insists I try on a hat that costs more than a week's grocery budget, I turn on her. Angry.

'My hair,' I explain forcefully, 'is falling out. I will leave a great handful of it in your hat if I try it on.'

She backs off. Silent. But I have noticed the recoil in her eyes at what she suddenly realises is not a punk haircut but a sign of illness.

Two shops further along, I pick up a white cotton summer hat with a small brim that I can pull low. It costs twenty dollars, wraps into a small ball, washes easily and will keep off the sun. I pull it on, pay and leave.

Over the next few weeks, as I lose more hair until I am completely bald, I encounter great compassion from most people. Men stand to give me a seat on the bus, old women pat me on the arm in silent sympathy as they pass, salesgirls lift heavy items into my supermarket trolley. It is a deep, enveloping kindness that is completely new to me. Occasionally, though, I see retreat in the eyes of strangers, as though to come near might risk infection. It is fear of their own mortality that they cannot face, not my bald head, grey face and dark-circled eyes.

Back at Church Point, the water taxi nudges into the ferry wharf and I pass over the shopping bags. It's low tide. The step into the taxi is a long way down. A month ago I could have jumped in, balancing easily. Now I hesitate. Weakness. Bob is driving (is everyone called Bob?) and without a word he puts out a hand. I grab it and step down safely.

'How you doing?'

'Great.'

'Yeah. I can see. Got someone at the other end?'

'Just drop me at Ken's dock. It'll work out.'

He cruises from the Point towards Lovett Bay. The landscape slips by. Spotted gums like sentries, blue water sliding into deep green in the bay. Coastlines like broken honeycomb. White cockatoos. Always white cockatoos. Sulphur-crested, big, loud, incredibly clumsy. Wonderful. Fine salt spray dusts my face, soothing and cool. My heart lifts as urban life gets further away. *I am strong and my body is strong.*

When we reach Ken's dock, Water-taxi Bob passes out the grocery bags and asks again if I'll be OK.

'I'll help you get them to the house,' he offers.

'It's good exercise. Keeps me fit,' I reply. I grab a handful of bags and head off. *I am strong and my body is strong.*

Ken is in the boat shed when I walk past with my new haircut. He pulls off his breathing mask. 'Gunna join a rock band, are you?'

'I'll be bald soon anyway.'

Ken looks stricken. 'Jeez, mate. What's going on?'

'Bit of treatment, Ken. Nothing to worry about.'

He asks no more questions. 'Boys! Help Susan with the shopping!'

The boys leap to grab bags. In minutes, everything is piled at the front door and they scamper back to the boat shed, barefoot, even in winter.

By four thirty, the groceries are packed away and the sun is a sinking orb. The bay shimmers like a copper tray. From the deck I can see the boys, showered, wet-haired, squeaky clean, still barefoot. When the sun drops behind the hill that rises from the cleavage of Lovett and Elvina bays and a sudden chill unfurls, sinking the temperature three or four degrees, the bay slides from copper into a still, silver slate. The boys leap into their tinnies and, with a roar, head off to wherever home is.

For Veit, the tall young man with the shy smile, dreadlocks and ceramic blue eyes who stopped me from falling the very first day I came to look at Gordon's house, home is his sixty-foot, steel-hulled, half-finished boat moored in the middle of the bay. Summer or winter, he lives on her. She has no name yet. Veit is waiting until he meets a woman who will share his itinerant life. He will name it for her.

Everyone has a dream on Pittwater. To catch the biggest fish. Sail the fastest race. Return a wrecked old boat to former glory. Maybe just to kayak under a moon so big and bright it turns night into day. Dreams that cost almost nothing except effort and are therefore possible.

There is a classlessness among the permanent population here, one that the weekenders do not entirely understand. Weekenders roar in to eat and drink and barely wet a toe, even in the heat of a summer day. For them, and I do not mean to sound smug, the only social infrastructure of note is trade. Plumbers, electricians or marine specialists: the essentials of boat-access-only living. The rushing weekenders who successfully manage to straddle both Pittwater and urban life tend to be the people who love boats. Not in a way that makes sense to most of us—that is, to climb on board, go for a gentle row, paddle, sail or chug, have a picnic and return to the mooring—but deeply and passionately. Anything that floats will do. A little putt-putt, a launch, a sailing dinghy. And if it is a wooden boat, ah well, that is truly the stuff of dreams. Prized and cherished, these boats are scraped, painted and polished, and glisten on their moorings or sailing on the water.

Ken has a wooden sailing boat called *Sylphine* with a voluptuous, spreading hull, which he treats like a Fabergé egg, but the most coveted boat hereabouts is *Perceverance*, the perfect Pittwater wooden launch, owned by Perce, a gorgeous, beautifully mannered shipwright.

All boats are known by their names or their class. When you wait for the ferry, you wait for the *Curlew* or the *Amelia K*. Or when a working barge goes past, it is the *Trump* or the *Laurel Mae*. Rarely 'Bomber's' or 'Toby and Dave's barge'.

I knew Toby years before coming to Pittwater, when he sold advertising for magazines and newspapers and dined in five-star restaurants at his employer's expense. His shirts were always eye-piercingly white, his trouser creases sharp enough to cut cakes, his hair regularly trimmed. He still worked in the media when I found him, one day, at Church Point, having a Friday evening beer before catching the ferry home.

'Toby?' I asked, hesitantly. 'What on earth are you doing here?'

'Bought a little place on Scotland Island. Live here.'

'Really?' So Mr Urbane had an offshore bolt hole. How little we really know about what goes on in people's minds, I thought.

One day I heard he'd bought a partnership in a boat. A barge, the *Laurel Mae*. And he intended to run it as a business.

'Do you know what you're doing, Toby?' I asked him one evening when I'm passing through the Point and he's having a beer.

'Oh, yeah. As much as you ever know what you're doing.'

About a month later, I find Toby on the deck of the *Laurel Mae* at Cargo Wharf. Arms muscled and tanned. Faded grey singlet and navy shorts accordioned at the crotch, socks the same colour as the clay at the wharf. A new man. His own man.

'Don't miss your office desk, then?'

Toby grins. 'Not a lot, mate.'

Cargo Wharf, where the *Laurel Mae* is tied up, is the industrial estate of Pittwater. Huge bags of sand are lined up to be lifted by crane from land to water, along with bundles of wood, pipe, tin, and other landscaping and building supplies.

Twice a week the reeking garbage truck is driven onto a long flat barge from Cargo Wharf and ferried round the bays and Scotland Island. Garbage, which is piled in bins at public ferry wharves, is tossed into the truck's gawping black hole, where it is crunched and munched and swallowed whole. Bagged garbage is picked up from private docks by a couple of lean young blokes who splash around, mobile phones to their ears, on a long, flat barge. One Sunday when I'm on the way to Church Point in the water taxi, I see the two boys quietly sailing around in an exquisite little wooden boat. It looks antique and delicate and it's been sanded and painted to perfection. When I catch the boys clearing the garbage at Lovett Bay a few weeks later, I ask them about the boat.

'Bit of a passion, mate,' they say. 'Old wooden boats. Yeah, bit of a passion. Found her rotting and did her up. Saved her. Pretty bloody beautiful, isn't she?'

To pass the time, I think about ideas to transform my house. Maybe wide sliding doors from the bedroom onto a new, vast deck, so in summer I can push my bed outside. Live in the physical world, if by then that is the only way. If I am bedridden.

It's a dreadful word, and I rear back from it. I will not be spending days in bed, inside or out. *I am strong and my body is strong.*

I stride inside and grab a pencil and a piece of paper. Draw, erase, draw again. But then the fear of illness trickles in once more. I throw the pencil down. Stop it, I shout silently. You cannot afford the luxury of ambivalence. To let your guard down is reckless!

I reach for cook books, flick through pages searching for ways to make the baby leg of lamb for Bob and Barbara's lunch irresistible to a woman whose taste buds must be fickle and dulled. Hazy ideas float through my mind as I skim recipes. Where would a fireplace go? What about the kitchen? I settle on a recipe for the lamb at the same time as I vow to call the builder. Bugger it. If I'm going to die, I'm going to die in comfort!

On a glorious Pittwater night my friend Michael, who took over the lease on the Scotland Island house, paddles over by moonlight. I am in bed but not asleep when he sticks his head round the door.

'Come on, get up,' he says. 'This is too good to miss.'

He is new to Pittwater, I think a little crankily, as I follow him outside in my pyjamas. But he is right. The night is spectacular. The escarpments shimmering with silver, the night sky undercoated with the softest pink. The whole bay shining and, right through the middle like a silver stairway, light accordions out to sea.

We manoeuvre the kayak past the mangroves to the point where Salvation Creek, which runs down from the national park, joins Lovett Bay. It is a beautiful creek in a damp gully where life and growth is rampant. In the first days of moving to Lovett Bay, I wandered at low tide to find out for myself what lurked at the end of the shoreline. As I stepped into the gloom of a rain forest, thousands of insects hurtled in the light and shadow. Palms as tiny as cocktail umbrellas sprouted wildly, delicate maidenhair ferns cascaded and forests of fungi filled the air with a stewy smell. Moss, thicker than carpet, softened sharp-edged rocks, and after scrambling over huge, slippery boulders for a while, I found a waterfall. Later I was told that this is the creek that never dries up, even in the most severe drought. The name, Salvation, is fitting.

At low tide, the creek trickles onto the sand flats; at high tide, it is still too shallow for any boat bigger than a tinny. So there is never any boat traffic here. As we paddle along, the silence is lyrical and we do not speak as we turn and glide smoothly back to the house.

'Thanks,' I say.

My friend nods and keeps paddling his way home.

Friday morning is quite beautiful. Sunny, crisp, vibrant. I stroll to the fringe of the night's high tide. A big one, spilling a foot or so over the sea wall. It is not long past the time when the sun swathes the bay in an orange glow, when the tree tops look like they are burning. About four or five early-morning kayakers glide past as usual, their paddles dipping into the dark satin water.

The boats on their moorings hover over their reflections like conjoined twins. Sea eagles who nest high in the rocky escarpment on the Elvina side of Lovett Bay, swoop and soar. Is it a mating ritual? Or is the day, for them also, too exquisite not to feel a surge of joyful energy?

Midmorning, I call the builder on his mobile. 'Think I'll go ahead after all,' I tell him.

'Right,' he replies.

'When can you come over for a chat?'

'I'll call you Monday with a time. Does that suit you?'

'Yeah, great.'

There's a long pause.

'How are you doing?' he asks tentatively.

'Who knows?'

'Right,' he says quickly.

After I put down the phone, I wander into the kitchen to get lunch going. The lamb goes into a heavy cast-iron pot. I squeeze a bulb of garlic until it breaks up and chuck the pieces in with the lamb. I drizzle balsamic vinegar over the top so it collects in a glossy brown pond in the base, chuck around plenty of salt and pepper. The lid goes on and the whole lot is shoved into the oven to cook on a low heat for about three hours. At the end of that time, the lamb will emerge with a caramelised skin and flaking, moist meat infused with the nutty flavour of roasted garlic and the sharp sweetness of vinegar.

There are little new potatoes, green beans, baby carrots and a salad of bitter leaves—bitter greens are good for the liver. Barbara's liver is under assault from chemotherapy and so is mine. Every little bit helps.

I do not know what to expect of Barbara. Have never caught even a fleeting glimpse of her. She and Bob live high above the ramshackle waterfront neighbourhood and the path from their house to their dock does not pass my home.

When the lunch is organised, I wander onto the deck where the table is set. The day is warm enough for a T-shirt, but the light is thin, brittle, watery. It is undeniably still winter.

Bob and Barbara appear from the front of the boat shed about fifteen minutes early, walking slowly, Bob's arm round Barbara's waist. There is an intense intimacy about the two of them. A grimy little grub of envy is born and quickly slain. I turn into the house and pull the door behind me gently. But I have seen that Barbara stops often to catch her breath. By the time they reach the front door, they are perfectly punctual.

'I'm Barbara.' She holds out a long, slim hand and smiles, looking directly at me. Her face is pale, her hair golden with coppery highlights. Her eyes, the colour of curaçao, are the kind that can be said to sparkle.

'Come on in. It's really lovely to meet you,' I say.

Bob is dressed up. A T-shirt with a collar. He plonks a couple of bottles of wine on the counter, a red and white, both very good. Barbara eases herself carefully onto the sofa.

I rush around, filling in the empty spaces with action. Opening the white wine, peering into the oven. 'Can you pour the wine please, Bob?' Then I fall back on the old journo's technique of asking questions to settle my nerves and their shyness: 'So! How long have you two lived here?'

Bob begins to answer. A pair of king parrots, red and emerald green, male and female, take up positions on the rail outside, like an audience in fancy dress. He struggles for the right words.

'How long ago did you come here?' I prompt.

'That first glimpse? January the 28th, 1993. We didn't move here until later, though.'

'You remember the exact day!'

'Oh, yes.'

Barbara slides smoothly in. 'We were bushwalking, Bob and I, along a section of the North Lovett Bay fire trail. Trying to find the public wharf. The trail had become indistinct and eroded, with archways of evil lantana ready to spike unwary bushwalkers, so we decided to retrace our steps.' As they turned, she explains, they looked down to the water, velvety and green. Barely visible through swathes of pink-flowering lantana and dense bush, Barbara saw the rear of a large old home. 'It was the roof I saw at first. Old terracotta tiles covered with lichen. And three chimneys. I felt, I confess, a hint of mystery.'

'Go on,' I interrupt. 'I've just got to get lunch ready.'

'Don't worry. The story can wait until we're all sitting down.'

'Will you carve?' I ask Bob.

'Love to,' Bob replies.

When we're all sitting down at the table on the deck, Bob lays slices of lamb out on a plate carefully as if he were arranging flowers. Adds vegetables, passes it to Barbara. All small portions. Like a child's. He does the same for me, but the portions are larger. When his own plate is ready, he sits down, raises his glass.

'To new neighbours,' I toast.

'I can drink to that,' Bob says.

We all clink glasses and it feels oddly festive.

'Watch out for Scruff Bucket, the kookaburra,' I say to Barbara. 'He's partial to lamb and the bloody magpies will eat the nose off your face.'

Barbara moves the food around her plate. Not eating much.

'So go on with your story,' I say. 'You've just seen the roof.'

'Oh, yes, that's right. Well. I looked at the building and said to Bob, what a lovely-looking old house.' She spears a little meat. Chews it.

'What did Bob say?' I butt in.

Bob looks up from his food. 'Damp in winter. Faces south. Escarpment to the rear. Cold. No way.'

'So you were looking for a place to buy as you walked?' I ask.

'Uh-huh,' Barbara says. 'We'd lived in Mount Eliza in Victoria for most of our lives. Bob wanted a change. I did too. Our family had grown up and they didn't need us any more, and we felt it was time to lead our own lives. But we weren't looking for anything offshore. And Bob was right about the house that day. With the escarpment hard up against the back of the building, it had to be cold and damp.'

So they retraced their steps, she says, without even a backward glance and never thought about the house again.

'In September 1993, we rented a house at Newport on the northern beaches and started searching for a home around Pittwater in earnest,' she continues. 'We wanted a home to use essentially as a base for travelling. Which we'd been promising ourselves we'd do for years. After a

Salvation Creek | 407

couple of months we'd found nothing in our price range and we were getting desperate. So Bob and I decided to contact a local offshore real-estate agent to see what was available in boat-access-only homes.'

On a balmy afternoon in November 1993, Barbara looked at eight properties on Scotland Island and the western foreshores of Pittwater.

'There were a couple of possibles on the south side of Lovett Bay,' she says. 'But nothing came close to the house of our dreams.'

Late in the afternoon, Barbara climbed into the real-estate agent's boat to go home. There were brochures on the floor and she picked them up, glancing at one picture of a rather beautiful house with a long, columned verandah. The house was called Tarrangaua. Built, according to the leaflet, for Dorothea Mackellar, an icon of Australian poetry who wrote 'My Country', a poem that sums up every Australian's nostalgia for a wild, untamed landscape.

'I wanted to see the house. Just out of curiosity. It was way beyond our price range. But it would be an interesting end to the day.'

Barbara walked slowly up the sandstone steps, about eighty or so, she estimated, then paused. The beauty of the house and the environment was almost shocking. The view across Lovett Bay was simply spectacular. Then she turned and faced the house.

'Time seemed to stand still,' she says.

We have stopped eating, Bob and I. Barbara's food lies barely touched.

'Then I stepped forward and opened the front doors. They swung into a long sitting room with polished wooden floors and beams in the ceiling. I felt that glow of reaching one's place. Do you know what I mean? When you walk into a space and feel warmth and serenity?'

'As though you've found where you belong?' I suggest.

'Exactly!' she says, smiling. 'Perhaps that's how you felt when you bought this house?'

'That's another story,' I say. 'Let's finish this one first.'

She laughs a little and sips her water.

'When Bob returned from a business trip the following evening, I told him I had found a dream. I thought he would dismiss it immediately. But he was curious, I think. So he came with me to see it.'

Bob climbed the steps behind his wife, pausing every now and then to look across Lovett Bay. Neither of them said much, not even when they reached Tarrangaua. Barbara let Bob enter the house first to wander alone for a while. When she followed him inside, she found him standing in a small room at the eastern end of the house.

'I could see that, like me, he felt comfortable.' Barbara says.

He looked through the armies of spotted gums, some of them shedding their salmon-pink bark to reveal smooth, lime-green trunks. Then he turned to his wife and slipped an arm round her shoulders. 'I always thought Shangri-La would be to be able to sit in your office and look out of your window at your boat,' he said to her.

'There was a faraway look in his eyes,' Barbara says. 'I knew then that he loved the house—because of the atmosphere it created. There was order, but also wildness. Simplicity, but with an overriding formality. But I didn't know how we could find a way to buy it.'

When she voiced her misgivings, Bob just smiled. 'Let me worry about that,' he told her. And the business of buying the *house on the high, rough hill* began.

The story seems finished. The sun, by now, is hard on my back, like a warm blanket, but it shines in Barbara's eyes. I am about to go inside to get her a hat but she continues talking and I sink back into my seat.

'There were two quite strange coincidences before we took possession of the house,' she says. 'First, we realised that it was the lovely old home we had seen from the rear on our bushwalk the previous January. Second, the contract of sale was to have been exchanged in late December but we had a daughter's wedding in Melbourne, so we asked if the date of exchange could take place on January the 28th, 1994. I didn't realise the significance of the date until a couple of years later when I was throwing out some old diaries. I discovered that I'd noted the bushwalk on January the 28th, 1993. So we took possession of this wonderful old house a year to the day from that first glimpse.'

Barbara looks around the table at us. The story, it seems, is now ended. But we are all silent for a little longer.

'Are you happy, living there? Was it the right move?' I ask her.

'These have been the best years of my life,' she says.

And because her life is visibly running out, there is nothing more to say. Bob reaches for her hand and holds it tightly. She smiles at him in a way that closes other people out, and gently withdraws her hand.

Lunch drifts along again and we exchange information about ourselves. Bob is fifty-six years old, they have four children, love sailing, and Barbara is passionate about bush regeneration, which is why she hates that *evil* lantana. Bush regeneration is big in Pittwater, she tells me. It means clearing out introduced and often invasive species and giving the original Australian bush a chance to regrow.

'It's a skill even enthusiastic bush regenerators don't always understand,' she says. 'The Australian bush is so fragile, so easily trashed.
People rush in and get it all wrong and do more damage than good.'

'Actually, Barbara, I don't know much about native plants.'

She smiles wryly, then looks me straight in the eye. 'Why don't you
learn about them? This is the best place in the world to start.'

I shrug, noncommittal. To me, the Australian bush can be lacklustre,
even downright unfriendly. It's full of scratchy plants that spike and
lacerate and it's always dry and crackly with dead branches. There's not
much that's lush and inviting about it at all.

'I like walking in the bush, Barbara, as long as I'm on a track, and I
love the smell after it's rained. Sort of new and lung-cleansing. But I like
a garden to have flowers, and trees that change colour with the seasons.
I like the bush to stay in the bush.'

I break off because I see her smiling and there's a dreamy look in her
eyes. 'Places can change people,' she says, 'weave a kind of magic.'

'Perhaps,' I reply.

At the end of lunch, when it's too cold to sit on the deck any longer,
Bob and Barbara get up to go home.

She turns at the door and asks: 'Are you enjoying living here?'

'Oh, yes, I love it.'

'We knew Gordon, you know. Not well, but enough.'

'Gordon was the first to build after the fire,' Bob says.

'Yes. Tough old bloke. He's going to hate me soon, though. I'm going
to extend the house.'

'Are you?' Barbara asks, surprised.

'If I'm going to die, I'm going to die in comfort.'

Barbara laughs. 'Oh, you'll be all right.'

And she says it with what seems like prescience, so it gives me comfort. I remember then, living with the boys when they were dying.
Remember the importance of talking to them about the future. Taking
away, even for a few minutes, the heavy tread of death.

'Tell me, do you know anything about Dorothea Mackellar?' I ask,
trying to change the subject.

Barbara smiles. 'A little,' she replies.

'I'd like to find out more about her.'

'Come for a cup of tea tomorrow.'

To be honest, I don't *really* care much about a poet who's been dead
for thirty years. But I agree because I like Barbara's company.

5

THE MORNING AFTER LUNCH with Bob and Barbara, I feel too tired to vacuum, and gardening is out, because every time I bend over the world swims dizzily for about three minutes and I'm overwhelmed by a desire to throw up. I decide to clean out a couple of handbags. In one, I find the card with the name and phone number of the Jack Russell breeder that Donald the hairdresser gave me. On a whim, I call her.

'I've got a real little darling pup,' she enthuses, 'gorgeous, so gorgeous a friend wanted her immediately.'

'Oh, so your friend wants her?'

'Oh, no! She already has three dogs. She'd take her, though, if she didn't already have three dogs. And her sister. She's gorgeous too.'

'Your friend has a sister?'

'No, the puppy has a sister. There's two of them. The last of the litter. Don't know what I'll do if I can't find homes for both of them.'

There's a big sigh on the other end of the phone. Visions of lethal injections, glue factories, everything horrendous, flash through my mind.

'I suppose I could take both of them.'

'Oh, luv, I'd give you a discount if you did. Fifty dollars off each.'

Great. Only half the national debt. But I am in *live for the moment* mode. The breeder talks incessantly. A few words sink in. *Worms, raw eggs, house-training*. But I am not concentrating. I am trying to understand why I think taking on two little puppies seems like a good idea when I hardly have the energy to walk to the water taxi.

'Are you there, luv? Did you get the address?' she asks nervously.

'Oh, yeah. Right. For the cheque. Run that past me again?'

'The puppies will be on the plane from Canberra next Monday. I'll let you know the flight details. They're house-trained, too.'

'Fantastic.'

'Well, nearly. And they come to the call of PUPPPPIEEEES!'

An ear-splitting squawk reverberates down the line and, muttering a quick goodbye, I hang up. Sisters, I think. Sisters.

There is a quirk in my personality that makes me take on double what is feasible. The trait filters through every aspect of living. My husband always said that when I cooked I made enough to feed the Russian army. I'm not sure where the impulse comes from. Was it growing up in the country where one minute there was bounty, the next nothing? But I haven't gone hungry since I lived in London when I was barely twenty-one. Perhaps I'm just no good at working out quantities.

The idea of the puppies is hugely cheering when my diary is littered with gruesome appointments. Blood tests. Chemo dates. Naturopath consultations. Lymphatic massage. When your life is on the line, you grab every remotely rational sliver of help—or do I mean *hope*?

For the first time in my life, instead of taking my body blithely for granted, I am aware of every tiny function. Watching my own body so closely makes me, in turn, study everything that grows. Trees, flowers, animals. And by studying what makes them thrive, a subtle logic begins to prevail in the way I look after myself. Drink alcohol? Pay the price. Eat rubbish? Pay the price. Do everything right? Enjoy the well-being.

It's about three hours until I'm due to have tea with Barbara, so I check out the fridge to see what's there to make a cake. Eggs? Yes. Butter? Yes. Lemons? Yes. OK, so it's a lemon cake. One of those quick ones you whiz up in the food processor. It fills the house with a fragrance that sets the mouth salivating. When it's cooked, I turn it out onto a plate and coat it with lemon syrup with a big slug of gin added. Bugger our livers, I think, and with that thought comes the understanding that it will always be a struggle to do only what it is good for the body. And it is better, perhaps, to aim for balance.

That late winter afternoon, I climb the sandstone steps to Tarrangaua for the first time. Carrying a bloody huge cake after doubling the recipe. Overdone it again. Oh, well, Barbara can freeze it. Pull it out when people call in. As they do, when you are ill.

The steps are steep and uneven. Dizziness swoops in. I have to stop and put the plate down and then sit. From out of nowhere, my skin prickles with a mass of burning pins and needles. I whip off my hat to cool my body and wonder what is happening to me. When the world stops spinning, I get up and tackle the climb once more.

Barbara waits on the verandah, sitting in a cane armchair. From the top of the steps, a little way from the house, she looks like a photograph of a woman from a long-gone era, fragile, delicate, with the ghostly pallor of early black-and-white pictures.

'How are you?' I shout from the lawn.

Barbara waves, indicating that I should use the front door steps to reach the verandah, which stretches the length of the house. I plonk the cake on the table and sink into another cane chair.

'Bit of a hike up here. How do you do it?' I ask.

'Keeps you fit,' she replies, looking at the cake.

'What about after a few drinks?'

'Did you notice the turn? The corner? Near the top? That's known as Barb's Rest. Bob and I were at the Point one Friday evening. It was summer and hot and thirsty weather. We had a few drinks to cool down, and then a few more. I made it home as far as the turn, where I quietly sat down and decided it was the perfect spot for a bit of a nap.'

We laugh.

'This is a place where, if you are not careful, drinking becomes a way of life,' she adds.

'My dear, I am—or was—a journalist. Drinking *is* a way of life.'

She looks at me without smiling. 'Not much gets done if you drink a lot.' Don't waste time, she is saying. Not when we know it is finite.

On the round wooden table in front of her there is a stack of books and old magazines.

'There's a bit of a mystery about Dorothea,' she says, leaning forward, businesslike, moving folders around. She pushes the cake aside as though she doesn't quite know what to do with it.

'Lemon cake,' I say to help her out. 'Thought you could freeze leftovers. Pull it out when you need it.'

'Thank you. Looks delicious.' She gets up and goes towards the kitchen, calling to Bob. 'Susan's brought a cake.' She pauses, looks down at the cake. 'All of it is here to stay.'

Bob comes to the kitchen door that leads to where we're sitting, nods to me and looks at the cake. 'Big cake. Cup of tea?'

'Oh, yes. Lovely. Thank you. With milk. No sugar.'

He disappears.

I turn to Barbara: 'Mystery?'

Bob rematerialises from the kitchen. Two plates each bearing a slice of cake. Half the size I would cut.

Barbara says nothing for a minute or two. A document on the table, bound in plastic, catches my eye and I pull it out. It is titled *Search for Solitude*, subtitled *Dorothea Mackellar and her Lovett Bay retreat*.

'What's this?' I ask.

Bob returns carrying flowery bone-china mugs filled with steaming tea. He puts a cup in front of each of us without a word and then goes.

'Bob's working. On a design for a new kiln.' Barbara sips her tea, breaks off tiny bits of cake and eats delicately.

I shovel cake down my throat in large lumps.

'It's a project I have begun,' Barbara explains about the yellow folder. 'And one I hope you might finish.'

I want to ask her what she means. But I know what she means. And to ask would be rude. She does not want me to pretend I do not understand what she is saying.

My friend Sophia, the Buddhist, taught me that truth is easier to handle than lies.

'I may die soon,' I said to her one day. I expected her to tell me it was rubbish, to pull myself together.

'Yes,' she said simply. 'You could die soon.'

For a moment, I was furious with her. She was supposed to prop me up emotionally, wasn't she? Then I loved her for her answer. She was the first, in a long line of doctors, friends, family and colleagues, who actually articulated the word *die*. It was a relief, and with her I didn't ever have to pretend everything was fine when it was just plain hideous.

So I wait silently for Barbara to go on, to unveil the mystery.

'That's the research I've done so far,' she says finally, pointing at the document in my hands. 'Read it, and tell me what you think.'

'What's the mystery?' I ask again.

'Come back to me when you've read that. Then we'll talk.'

'OK. By the way, I'm getting a new puppy—well, two new puppies. They arrive on Monday.'

'Now there's trouble,' she says.

I walk down the sandstone steps clutching her research, not convinced, I must admit, that there could be anything too interesting in the life of a long-dead spinster poet. And how much trouble, I ask myself crossly, can two little puppies be?

That night I check out the bookshelves for anything to do with raising and training dogs. There's nothing. I begin to wonder if I should cancel the puppies. Can't look after myself properly at the moment. How can I cope with energetic young pups? Then the image, quick as a flash, of soft, warm bodies. Cold, wet noses. Unfettered exuberance. Companions. Love. Two little beings that are my own. So I don't cancel.

I go to bed early feeling exhausted. The phone rings when it is cold and dark. It's the breeder with the arrival time for the puppies. Ready for pick-up at two thirty the following day. I cut the conversation short. Too tired to be polite.

Then suddenly a toe-tingling heat, pins and needles again, rises like a surging surf and swamps me. I throw off the quilt. Unbutton my pyjamas. Sweat rolls down my back. I fight the urge to vomit. Then, in moments, I'm back to a teeth-chattering cold. I haul the bedclothes back on, then another flush explodes. Fast and furious.

I phone the oncologist in the morning. 'What's going on? I keep feeling like I'm going to explode with heat. The next minute, I'm freezing.'

'Hot flushes. You're in menopause.' She is happy. Chemo has done its job. The oestrogen has leached out of my body.

'Is there anything I can do?'

'Nope. Hormone replacement is not for you. So hang in with the flushes, OK? Just hang in,' she says.

'Yeah. But this feels like the last straw.'

'I know you don't think so now, but you'll get used to them and they'll start to lose their intensity in a couple of years. Roll with them.'

I hang up in despair.

Within a week, the last shreds of my ability to concentrate evaporate. Any close-fitting clothing makes me feel like someone is suffocating me. I stand at bank tellers' windows and see wariness in their faces when I suddenly break into a drowning sweat. Chemo left me with very little control over my body. Now I have even less. Panic attacks hit me anywhere, but for some reason mostly in supermarket parking lots.

The flushes surge in at around twenty minute intervals. I spend a lot of time putting clothes on and then taking them off. Sometimes the desire to strip off is almost overwhelming, even in the middle of a busy street. Anything to cool down before I explode. It's a new hell. And I hate it. But I will not—I abso-bloody-lutely will not—give in. One gift cancer has given me is the knowledge that life, in just about any form, is precious. I doubt I will ever be careless of it again.

I call the water taxi when it's time to pick up the puppies.

'Off to another treatment?' asks Water-taxi Bob.

'Nope. Picking up two Jack Russell puppies. From the airport.'

'Yours?'

'Yep.'

'Now there's trouble,' he says, laughing.

I wonder briefly why everyone keeps mentioning the word 'trouble'. Puppies can't be too hard to handle, can they?

It's been nearly two months since I drove through crowded city streets. People honk and shake their heads in mock despair when I fail to accelerate fast enough for them. Everyone around me seems to be going at frantic speed. Lovett Bay has changed my pace.

I hear yapping from the moment I step out of the car at the cargo terminal of Sydney airport. Two sets of high-pitched yelps, constant, ear-piercing, furious. The clerk is pathetically grateful to hand them over and wishes me a fervent 'Good luck'.

I load them into the back of the car and open the cage door. The first puppy to poke out a velvety little nose I call Vita. The second, shyer but bigger, with the gentlest face and roundest brown eyes, I call Dolce. I know it is corny but I don't care. Sweet life, gentle life. That's my goal.

I lift them out of the cage, each small enough to fit in one hand, two warm, frightened little puppies that lean against my chest as hard as they can. Their hearts race and they smell like fresh bread. I inhale deeply and it drowns out the smell of chemo that comes up from my lungs with every breath.

Vita's face is tan. Matching hindquarters lead into a tan tail. The rest of her is starry white. Dolce's face is also tan but with a little black through it. She has a white blaze and fluffy mutton-chop whiskers. Her tail is tan but the tip looks like it's been dipped in white paint. When it wags it's like a frantic flag of surrender. Her confidence is shaky. I hold her harder. Soothe her. Vita is looking around, scoping the landscape.

I put them back in the cage for the drive home. They are quiet. *Good puppies.* I pull into the supermarket car park and lock them in the car. After a quick scoot around the aisles, stuffing the trolley with dog food, collars and leads, and doggy treats, I tiptoe back to the car. Listening for a racket caused by two frightened puppies. All quiet. *Good puppies.*

Annette swings the pink water taxi in to dock, churning the water like a flamenco dancer's frilly skirt. I load the puppies on first.

'Who are these?'

'My new family.'

'Oh . . .' She goes quiet. A cold wet nose pushes through the bars to get closer to her fingers. 'They are . . .' she says. 'They are . . .'

'Heaven!'

'Yep. That's the word.' But she leaves me with the feeling she was going to say something else.

The puppies are frantic when the throttle moves forward. I try to soothe them but Dolce throws up. I feel for her. I get seasick too.

At the Lovett Bay ferry wharf, Annette hands up the smelly cage. 'Happy families,' she says, screwing up her nose.

Later in the afternoon, I put collars and leads on the puppies and take them up the hill to visit Barbara. Her wide smile erases the tiredness from her face, and she scoops them onto her lap.

'I haven't had time to read your document yet,' I explain.

We sit on the verandah in the late-afternoon light. Great swaths of towering eucalypts, back-lit by the setting sun, roll like moss down the hillside. Near the house, the feathery foliage of wattle trees bleaches to gold and a border of agapanthus defines the edge of the lawn.

'Read it when you're ready,' Barbara replies.

Bob, again, brings slightly underfilled mugs of hot tea and slightly undersized slices of lemon cake, then disappears. The tea has the same earthy smell that came from my grandmother's kitchen when tea was routinely brewed strong and black on a wood-burning stove. Bob's tea always makes me think of my granny, whose name was Henrietta. She was a superstitious old girl who believed she had second sight. She passed on her I-told-you-so kind of magic to my mother, who wielded it indiscriminately. As a result, my childhood was hostage to superstition. Never put new shoes on the table (bad luck). No carnations or lilies in the house (death in the family). Never cut your fingernails on a Sunday or Friday (more bad luck). Never give away a knife without getting a coin for it (cuts a friendship). And on and on.

'Old Etty died,' my mother would tell me. 'Saw it coming. Picture fell off the wall last week.'

One day I plucked up enough courage to ask her why, if she'd foreseen a calamitous event, she hadn't done anything to stop it.

'You can't intervene in the natural course of life,' she replied.

'Then what's the point of having second sight?'

I got a pat on the hand and a sad little shake of the head, as if to say that one day I would understand. Maybe she had a point. Musical microwaves, little green satellites, my obsessive search for omens . . . I wonder, though, whether omens were a device I conjured up to allow me to take actions I knew were wrong. Cross two creeks in one day bearing the lover's name? The gods must be smiling on the relationship.

I have not seen the lover since my dreadful birthday lunch, nearly two months ago, nor had a phone call from him to see how I'm doing.

Sometimes I try to conjure his face, but it is already blurred in my memory. All that anguish and pain and I cannot even recall the way the pieces of his face fit together.

Barbara passes me a pamphlet covered in crude, ugly drawings of a fat little creature with a pointy head and eight legs.

'What's this?' I ask.

'Now you've got a couple of dogs, you'd better find out about ticks.'

My face must have gone even whiter than usual. 'Ticks?'

She points at the drawings. 'That's the life cycle of ticks. The ones that can kill a dog are the fully grown ones, the paralysis ticks.'

'What do you mean, kill? They don't really kill a dog, do they?'

'Oh, yes, they do.'

The puppies are dozing peacefully on Barbara's lap. I can't bear the thought of anything happening to them. I take Dolce from Barbara and tuck her under my chin, snuggling into her fur.

'So much for paradise, huh, little puppy? We're going to have to learn about these ticks then, aren't we?' I have fallen into the habit of talking to the puppies in a way that non-animal-lovers find borderline mad.

'Take the pamphlet with you. I've got another one,' Barbara says. 'And stay and have dinner.'

I don't need any persuading. The idea of going home to a cold, empty house isn't half as tempting as staying in Tarrangaua.

She goes into the kitchen to tell Bob I'll be joining them for dinner. We sit down to carrots, beans, courgettes, pumpkin, potato and cauliflower and a piece of golden, crumbed chicken. When I cut into the meat, it oozes thick rivers of butter and garlic.

'This is yummy. Thank you.'

Bob grins and raises his glass as if he's going to make a toast but he doesn't say anything.

'How are you getting on with the neighbours?' Barbara asks.

'Great,' I say. 'Well, I've seen more of Ken than anyone else because I walk past the boat shed all the time. But I've met Jack and his partner, Brigitte, and their two gorgeous boys. No one seems to live in the house at the end. I've never seen anyone there.'

'They're weekenders, but they don't get here very often.'

'So, tell me what summer is like. Do you see many snakes?' I ask.

'Yeah,' Bob says, 'but they're usually more afraid of you than you are of them. And the pythons, you know they're harmless, don't you?'

'Gordon showed me his python. Sleeps in the barbecue.'

'Syphon?'

'Yeah, that's the name. I steer clear of him.'

'He won't hurt you.'

'You're better off letting him hang around,' Barbara says. 'They eat the rats and mice and they don't let other snakes—poisonous ones, like red-bellied blacks and brown snakes—move into their territory. At least, that's the theory.'

'Yeah, well . . . I let him have his space.'

When I look up from eating, I see the puppies have climbed onto the sofa, where they're asleep.

'God, sorry. Look at the puppies.'

I jump up to move them to the floor, but in unison Bob and Barbara tell me not to worry. 'They're fine. Let them be.'

They're rock-bottom exhausted. And Barbara looks worn out. So as soon as we've finished eating, I get up to go. As I push back my chair, Barbara claps her hands quickly and loudly, and a giant, hairy black spider falls from the ceiling.

I scream. Feel like I'll faint.

Barbara laughs, unaware that I'm dizzy with fright. 'It's a toy,' she says. 'Don't worry. It's a toy.'

But my heart beats wildly. I don't feel strong enough for this kind of joke. Bob must see it written on my face. He takes Barbara's arm and says once is enough with the spider joke for me. The shock has sent me into a huge flush. Sweat erupts from every pore.

I hook up bleary-eyed puppies to their leashes and borrow a torch. On the way down the steps I imagine boojums lurking in every dark corner, giant ticks on every illuminated blade of grass. I duck and weave to avoid touching overhanging boughs and jump in the shower immediately I get home, pulling the puppies in with me. If they have a tick it is going to be either scrubbed off or drowned.

The puppies stand wet and shivering. For them, the day has turned sour. I dry them off and make up their bed in the corner of the bathroom. I add a hot-water bottle. Next, I spread newspaper all over the floor. A precaution only. They're partially house-trained. Right?

The next morning I walk into a bathroom that looks like a shit storm. With a stomach already tender, I quickly close the door and retreat to the kitchen. Put on the kettle. Not ready to cope yet. But the puppies are awake and alert. The yapping begins. To quieten them, I let them into the sitting room, where they both piddle instantly. It is the beginning of chaos, a chaos that escalates daily. About the best that can be said for it is that it takes my mind off cancer and the ex-lover.

Over the next few weeks I test the breeder's notion that the dogs are trained to come to the call of 'Puppies!'. They do. But only when they want to. They quickly become known around the bays as the 'terrierists', two tiny, shiny white streakers who think they've landed in the best back yard in the world. At first, people are patient. And I have no idea when the puppies take off at dawn (when the first yapping begins and I let them out so I can return to bed) that they are wreaking havoc over kilometres of land—private and national park. All I know is that they run off and return a couple of hours later, happy and tired and ready for a snooze. I assume, as little puppies, they will hang around the neighbourhood. They are on the rampage, though. And the mad, yapping hunt begins from the moment I let them out. But no one says a word to me. Everyone knows I am being treated for breast cancer. No one wants to add to the burden. And no one knows what to do.

As if the rampaging isn't bad enough, things are even worse on the nights I go out. Leaving them locked inside. Dolce and Vita begin an incessant, high-pitched yap that carries up the hill and over the bay. It has the same effect as fingernails scratching a blackboard. My neighbourhood is fracturing. Windows are being slammed shut, televisions turned up, and partners start to argue about how to handle the problem. I, of course, know nothing of this. The yapping starts only after I leave home. And it stops when the puppies hear the water taxi return.

One morning, Bob calls. 'Ah, well, it's um, it's, well, the puppies,' he begins. 'Debbie's rung me.'

Debbie's from Frog Hollow, the dark, misty bay east of Lovett where there are also only five houses.

'What's Debbie's problem?' I ask Bob.

'Ah, well, they're chasing . . .um . . . the dogs, well, they're chasing wallabies,' he finally blurts out.

'Why didn't Debbie call me?' And yet, as I ask the question, I realise I barely know her.

'She called Barbara and Barbara thought I should tell you,' he says. 'Because we've thought of a way to help.'

'Is it serious, then? Are people angry, or just Debbie?' I ask.

Bob's reply is slow, the words carefully chosen. 'Nobody is angry; they are concerned,' he says. 'People live here because they love the wildlife and the bush. They don't want to see it harmed.'

'What harm?' I ask with iron in both syllables.

'The puppies are causing a lot of trouble, chasing wallabies and brush turkeys. It's better to face the problem now before it gets too big.'

'But they're puppies; they're not big enough to hurt wallabies. And birds can fly away. This is just hysterical stuff, isn't it? I bet Debbie doesn't like dogs!' I fume.

'It's not only Debbie,' Bob says. 'Brigitte's unhappy. Maureen around in Towlers has seen them running wild. She worries about the wildlife.'

'But they're so little. They can't be causing much trouble,' I insist.

'There's two of them. Which means they're a pack. And packs, eventually, do damage.'

Bob says he'll come down in the late morning to work out a plan and suggests I take them out on their leashes for the next few days.

'What you need,' Bob says when he arrives later, 'is a dog run.'

'No way! I am not going to cage these puppies. I cannot, I just cannot do it to them. I'd rather take them with me wherever I go.'

I hand Bob a cup of tea and he drains it quickly. He focuses on the tea leaves, staring any place but at me.

'I'll put in the dog run anyway. We'll see what happens,' he says firmly.

We are silent for a while. I am inwardly raging, convinced it is more a political exercise to keep dogs out of the area than any real threat. I do not even think to say thank you, to appreciate he is trying to help.

'Er, there's been another problem,' Bob says, still not looking at me. 'When you go out, they yap. They never let up. Doesn't matter if it's day or night. Apparently you can hear them in Elvina Bay.'

'Do you hear them? Up at Tarrangaua?' I ask.

'I have heard them. It's pretty terrible. Sorry to be the one with all the bad news. But their yapping is the kind that drives you nuts.'

'Like I said, I'll take them with me when I leave the house. That will fix both problems.'

Bob builds the dog run in the back yard that afternoon. But I won't use it. Every morning, I put the puppies on their leashes and take them for a walk. They are anxious and resentful at having their freedom curtailed and so am I. But the word goes around. I am trying to train them. The unspoken, unspecified pressure eases.

Hot on the heels of the puppy problems, I have a routine blood test and my white blood cell count is so low that my third treatment has to be postponed. The result makes me feel like I'm fading away. Since chemo started, I've tried to deny the weakness and dizziness, but the reality is that most days I am crying tired. I am stick-thin and I have no energy. The dreaded hot flushes wake me at twenty- to thirty-minute intervals nearly all night. But I tell myself every day, over and over, that *I am strong and my body is strong* until I believe it, despite evidence to the contrary.

The blood-test news knocks me flat, though. It's firm, scientific evidence of a frailty I refuse to acknowledge.

I make an appointment to see a Chinese herbalist recommended by one of the naturopaths I am seeing. In his North Sydney office he tells me my pulse is very weak, not the pulse checked in Western medicine, another, deeper pulse, which explains why I feel quite shockingly frail. He hands me seven brown paper bags, each containing his mixture of dried brown bits and shell grit—well, that's what it looks like—with instructions to boil up one bag's worth every morning. I must drink one cup of fluid at the beginning and end of every day. It's a five-year plan and I must not miss a day. I know that's impossible. If I miss a day, does that mean all is for nothing?

The bill is around $180, and I need a follow-up appointment in seven days. The costs are not reclaimable from medical insurance. Memories of the boys and the search for miracle cures come flooding back. Desperate people do desperate things.

Every morning, I tip the contents of a brown paper bag into a saucepan and simmer it for half an hour, filling the house with a smell like decaying mushrooms. Then I strain half the concoction into a cup and drink it down quickly. It tastes foul. The other half of the brew is to have with dinner. Breakfast consists of lecithin, Missing Link, ascorbic acid, fish oil, flax seed oil, and on and on, all tipped into a blender with soy milk, a banana and maple syrup. That's followed by a handful or two of vitamins from what looks like a personal apothecary lined up on the kitchen worktop. My entire life is focused on taking care of myself.

There is no doubt, though, that my body is highly toxic. One night, when the puppies still slept in the bathroom, in their early days of house-training, I got up to go to the loo. I didn't want to wake the puppies so I went outside to pee on the grass at the back of the house. Two days later I noticed a dead patch in the midst of the green. I couldn't figure it out. Then I remembered. My pee was so toxic I killed the grass.

When Fleury calls a couple of days after the blood-test results, I burst into tears on the phone. 'I feel as though it's one thing after another. I never seem to be able to recoup before the next onslaught.'

Before I can even put up a protest, she arranges for Sophia to come and spend time with me. The pretence they devise is that Sophia needs quiet time to work on her book about the Lama Yeshe. Lovett Bay is ideal, they insist. I let them think I believe them.

Within a day, Sophia is running the household like she's been here for ever. She walks the puppies. I sleep as long as I wish. We eat lunch and I go back to sleep. When I shop for supplies, I come home and there is Sophia, waiting at the old wooden ferry wharf, Walkman to her ear, gyrating in a dance all her own among the wheelie bins and over-flowing garbage. When the water taxi gets close enough to drown out her music, she turns and smiles. She reaches for the shopping.

While I am out, the laundry mysteriously appears clean in my cup-board. The floors gleam, appliances on the kitchen worktop suddenly sparkle. When I try to thank her, she asks, 'What for?' She tells me I am teaching her so much in this funny little corrugated-iron shack.

'Yeah? Like what?'

'Silence. I am learning about silence.'

We are sitting on a sofa each, sipping tea, midmorning.

'This is not a quiet place,' I say. 'Those bloody cockatoos—'

'A different kind of silence,' she cuts in. 'How many houses do you walk into where there is the background babble of a television or a radio? The silence in this house lets you hear life.'

'Oh, get over it.'

'No, I mean it. And there are huge swags of time. Empty. Waiting for you to fill them. No distractions. That's a gift.'

Sophia gives me peace. And has the grace to tell me it is a gift I've given her. And she listens and listens and listens. Where have I gone wrong, I want to know, so that my lover left me? What did I do?

'It's over, Susan,' Sophia tells me one cold night. 'Let it go.'

Under her careful prompting, I find a way to let go of the bitterness and anger. I learn to loosen the iron grip of self-pity. On days when I succumb, Sophia always finds a story to tell me of others with no upside in their lives. It is never a lecture; it is a way of building a set of balances in my head. Feel bad? Fine. But remember, it could be worse.

Halfway through Sophia's visit, I ring a friend and ask if I can borrow her boat to learn to drive. She is a weekender, one of the people who come to Pittwater to 'lunch'. Her instinct is to say no. I can almost hear the word. But she can't bring herself to be mean-spirited when she knows I am ill, so she says yes.

I worry that Sophia misses her morning papers. Part of her job as a columnist is to keep up with the news. So if I learn to drive a boat, we can motor over each morning, the two of us, to get the papers and perhaps a cup of coffee and rejoin, for a short time, the *crowd*.

The boat key is under the pot plant alongside the house keys. Weekenders lock their homes. I put the key in the ignition and the boat starts. We untie and set off. Easy.

'Nothing to it,' I yell over the engine.

After months of waiting for ferries or calling water taxis, which are expensive, the instant freedom of a boat is fantastic. Brimming with confidence, I push the throttle forward, as I have seen Annette do on the water taxi, and the boat points heavenwards before settling back down on the water.

'Jesus!' Sophia shrieks. Her hands grip the dash in front of her.

I laugh. Terrified and jubilant. Why did I think this was going to be so hard? 'How about fish and chips at Palm Beach?' I yell.

Sophia can't hear so I throttle back. Suddenly. And we both almost crack our chins on the dash as the boat comes to a sudden stop.

'What did you say?' Sophia tries not to show her nervousness.

'I was thinking about fish and chips at Palm Beach but maybe we should skip it. Do it another day.'

The heady freedom is suddenly dulled by the realisation that I am dangerously ignorant about boats. There might not be roads but there are rules, and I haven't a clue what they are.

When we see the *Curlew*, all blue and white and matronly, cutting through the water towards us, I panic. Sophia's laugh has an edge of hysteria. I stall the boat trying to rev it to get out of the way. The ferry pulls round us. Horst, who's driving, scowls.

'Shall we still try for the papers?' I ask weakly.

Sophia looks at me sternly. 'Are you mad? We barely missed a ferry!'

'Right.'

The engine comes to life again with the first turn of the key and we motor home sedately. By the time we reach the dock, we've both had it.

I look at the ropes. Look at the cleats on the pontoon. Look at Sophia. 'How do you tie up a boat?' I ask. I've untied one heaps of times. But never tied one up. Boat owners do that.

'Dunno,' she says. She steps off the boat carefully. When she is reunited with solid ground, she turns. 'Boats,' she says, taking a deep breath and tucking her chin into her ample bosom, 'are unnatural. I am going to the house to put on the kettle and have a whisky.'

I secure the boat using shoelace knots with big bows. It looks weird but it should hold even if a sudden, tricky winds erupts from nowhere.

The next day, when I wander out onto the deck to make sure the boat is still there, the tide is out. The boat is aground, heeling awkwardly to one side.

'Ask Ken if it's OK, or whether we've done some awful damage,' I say to Sophia when she joins me.

She disappears inside the boat shed, emerging moments later with Ken. She points and waves her arms around. I can tell she's giving him an account of our first solo voyage. His body shakes with laughter.

'He says not to worry,' Sophia reports on her return. 'There's no damage. But we shouldn't leave it there too long.'

'How long is too long?'

'Too long is when it starts to do a bit of damage,' she explains.

'Oh. Right.'

Over the next couple of days, the weather starts to pick up and the wind whistles into the bay. Sophia decides to weed the rear garden and I take a book to read in the shelter of the back porch while she works.

She quits weeding at four in the afternoon and goes inside for a shower. A couple of minutes after the water is turned on, a loud scream comes from the bathroom.

'What's the matter?' I call, panicked.

'Ticks. Ticks. Bloody ticks all over me. Ah!'

'Get in the shower and wash them off.'

'They're under my skin. There's bloody hundreds of them.'

'Can I come in? Can I have a look?'

The bathroom door slides back. Sophia stands there in her underwear, both legs covered in tiny red welts with a black spot in each of them.

'Hang on.' I rush for Barbara's pamphlet and flick through it. 'They're seed ticks,' I announce.

'I don't care whether it's a seed tick or a cattle tick. What do we do?'

'Well, I don't know. Hang on, I'll ring Barbara.'

When I get off the phone, Sophia is still muttering under the shower.

'Barbara says get a razor and shave them off,' I yell out to her. 'Then slap on some antiseptic. There's a razor in the cupboard.'

A couple of days later, when the welts have subsided a little, we've just about forgotten the fear and idiocy of our maiden voyage.

'Feel up to another go in the boat?' I ask.

Sophia looks at me with a frown.

'Just a little excursion,' I plead. 'To the Church Point store. For a newspaper and coffee and perhaps pastries?'

She sighs and grabs her jacket. 'Let's go then,' she says.

It takes about ten minutes to untangle the knots. Sophia waits inside the boat, eyebrows raised. When we are finally untied, I jump on board. The breeze is quite brisk, the water a little choppy. But it's a fine day. I turn the key in the ignition. Three times. The engine screeches but fails to catch. I look up and notice that land is a good swim away.

'Who'd have thought wind could move us so fast?' I say, nervously.

'It might be an idea, next time, to start the engine *before* we cast off,' Sophia says drily.

'Yeah.'

We begin to giggle uncontrollably.

A minute or two later we hear Ken's voice. 'Give it some choke,' he shouts from his jetty. 'It's the lever above the throttle. Lift it up.'

Looking down, I see a little flap of plastic. I lift it. Turn the key. Once. Twice. The engine gargles into a full-bellied roar.

'We're off!' I announce happily.

We cruise sedately and the water becomes a highway to anywhere. A thrilling sense of absolute freedom rises up. Panic doesn't set in until Church Point looms. The two ferries, one docked and one sounding the final bell for passengers, are tied on either side of the wharf. In between them, people are coming and going in tinnies at what seems to me to be reckless speeds. Sophia is rigid, her face stony.

I decide to aim for the pontoon at the rear of the Church Point store. There's a large deck where day trippers and some locals read newspapers over a cup of coffee. As we chug in, I can't help feeling that everyone is watching, pointing and shaking his or her head.

Until you've been steering a boat for a while, it's impossible to judge speed and distance. It's not like a car when you hit the brakes and it stops. You need to come in fast enough so you still have control if there's a wind, slow enough so you don't crash. But I've misjudged badly and we're going much too fast about ten feet from the pontoon.

'I'm gunna jump off and tie up,' I tell Sophia, who looks stricken at being left on board alone. I pull the throttle into neutral, kill the engine and leap. 'Ah shit!' I say in frustration.

'What? What?' Sophia asks.

'Forgot the rope!'

The boat quietly churns forward under the deck, coming exquisitely to rest between two leaning pylons. 'Chuck me the rope,' I tell her.

She spins blindly. 'Where's the bloody rope?'

'It's on the bow. You'll have to reach through the front to get it.'

I leap up the steps to kneel on the restaurant's deck. Sophia passes me the rope and I pull the boat around, sliding it into deeper water. When we are lying alongside the pontoon, tied quite neatly with more shoelace bows, there is scattered applause from the coffee drinkers.

Sophia steps off with as much dignity as she can muster, and we go inside to order enough food to keep us busy for an hour. Neither of us wants to climb back into the boat too quickly.

When our coffee arrives, Sophia finds her voice. 'It might be an idea, to grab the rope *before* you leap off the boat,' she says tightly.

We settle into our normal silence, flicking pages. We sit there long enough for the tide to turn. Warmed by the sun. Filled with food.

'Ready to hit the track?'

Sophia looks around. There is no other way home that doesn't involve a long swim or the expense of a water taxi. She sighs long and loud. 'Let's go,' she says.

We both get on the boat and I start the engine. It ticks over first go. I untie, coiling the ropes neatly. Then I reverse slowly out of the space.

'Think I'm getting the hang of this,' I say.

Sophia does not respond, does not even look in my direction. Her eyes seem to be closed and I'm not sure she's breathing.

When we're clear of the wharf, the deck and any traffic, I slowly ease the boat forward, pointing home. Sophia's eyes open. A good sign.

The wind has dropped. We make it to the entrance of Lovett Bay. At the pontoon, I grab a rope and jump off, tying up neatly. Then I look up and see the boat drifting away.

'Jesus.'

The rope is tied firmly to the dock. It's just not tied to the boat. Sophia looks ready to explode but she is still close enough to throw the rope to. She catches it and holds tightly while I pull the boat in.

'Had enough of this for a while,' I say.

'I'll say.'

At the weekend, my friend comes and collects her boat.

'How did it go?'

'Great. Yeah. Really great.'

Sophia, good Buddhist that she is, says not a word.

A few days later, as night spills in, I sit at the old wooden kitchen table already dressed in my pyjamas. A new blood test has revealed that my cells have built up and tomorrow is third chemo treatment day, two weeks overdue. Sophia is coming with me to sit in that awful grey room full of grey faces. I'm so grateful. It is terrible place to be alone.

At the kitchen sink, Sophia washes lettuce for a salad.

'You wash each leaf so tenderly,' I observe. 'I just chuck 'em all into the salad spinner, swizzle them around, spin, and there you go.'

Her way of answering is to tell a story about Lama Yeshe. One day, a woman whose turn it was to cook, Sophia says, was washing a big bunch of spinach roughly and hastily. Lama Yeshe saw her carelessness and came to take over her work. He washed each leaf with infinite care. The young woman got the message.

'I learned that if you do a job, do it as though it is the most important job in the world,' Sophia explains. The satisfaction, she adds, is immense. And there is no boredom because you are thinking about the task, giving it your best.

Much later into the treatment, when even sweeping the floor is unthinkable, I long to be able to do all the old physical chores I'd once resented. Cleaning. Weeding. Ironing. I suddenly see them as a privilege of the fit and healthy.

When Sophia finally leaves, it is like losing a sister. The house feels as though the vibrancy has gone out of it. But she's already stayed longer than she should have. At home, as well as writing her weekly column, she visits people in nursing homes, and works for the Jewish Library, where she helps Holocaust survivors write their memoirs. She is useful.

Sophia tells the neighbours what I might need, arranges for Veit, from the boat shed, to call in regularly. She tells him to use the washing machine, which gives him his excuse to knock on the door. To me, she says he needs somewhere to do his laundry and how perfect it would be if he could use my washing machine. No debts. No one a martyr. We become friends, Veit and I. I cook for him often, which means I bother to eat. I'm sure Sophia knew that would happen, too.

After she leaves I have no one to baby-sit the puppies, so I ask my friend Michael, who took over my lease on the Scotland Island house, if I can drop them at his jetty when I go out. They'll be safely confined to the island, where most of the dogs roam happily.

'Fine. As long as they don't cause any problems,' he says.

I load them onto the water taxi and drop them off on the way to Church Point and swing past on the way home to collect them. It seems a perfect solution. And they love it! They wait expectantly every morning for the big trip to the fun park.

One midweek evening I pick them up just before dark and the phone is ringing as I walk up the steps to the house.

'Hello?' I say, short of breath.

'Uh, Susan, it's Lewis. From the Island.'

'Hey, Lewis, how are you?' Lewis is an electrician who has a wonderful spaniel called Billy.

'Ah, good, mate, yeah, good. Um, it's about the puppies.'

My heart sinks. 'Yes?'

'They got into the house, into the cupboard with the dog food. Finished it off. Don't mind 'em eating the food, but don't want 'em tracking through the house when we're not there.'

'Sure. Quite understand. I'll keep them home in future.'

At the weekend, Michael rings to tell me there're complaints coming in from all over the Island. The puppies have been on the rampage. Chasing cats, chooks, other dogs, anything that moves. Uncatchable, always running just out of reach.

'Sorry, love, but you can't drop them here any more,' Michael says. 'I want to relax when I get here, not be bombarded by upset neighbours.'

'Absolutely. Quite understand.'

Over the next few weeks I realise my only remaining recourse is to take the puppies everywhere with me. Make the car a second home. But they are not good travellers and throw up as soon as we start winding along McCarrs Creek road. Then they trek vomit from one end of the car to the other. I fence off the car seats and put a disposable covering on the carpet in the back of the station wagon I bought after I sold Fearless Fred when Sweetie died. As soon as I leave the car, the puppies rip through the barrier easily and plunge into the groceries stacked on the seats. I arrive home with half-eaten mince, chops and chicken. So I try packing groceries into storage boxes, but without the groceries to keep them busy the puppies yap incessantly. The parking attendant beneath the surgery of my naturopath asks me to find somewhere else to park. Their yapping penetrates the walls of the shopping centre and drives shoppers to despair.

I am close to despair myself. The physical effort of taking them everywhere, pee stops, cleaning up poo from sidewalks, worrying about them locked in the car on sunny days, is too much. The dreaded dog run begins to look more and more attractive.

One morning I shower and wander out onto the deck in my dressing gown. The lawn is covered in fluffy white balls. It looks like it's been snowing. I wonder where it's all come from.

Back inside, I reach for my clothes. Jeans, knickers, bra, T-shirt, little satin-covered fake tit . . . no little satin-covered fake tit anywhere. The image of pure white balls of fluff scattered on the lawn begins to make sense. It's all that's left of my prosthesis.

'*Puppiiiiiies!*' I scream.

They roar up to me, tails wagging, happily anticipating treats.

'You little bastards,' I yell.

Hurt and confused, they walk away, tails curled under their tummies.

The puppies' escapade forces me to go in to the city to buy a proper prosthesis. An excursion I've been avoiding for a couple of months.

The little silicone blob I am fitted for is soft and pink and looks like a jellyfish. When I lie down during the day, it shoots up defiantly while my other breast swells softly over the side of my rib cage. I give it a name. Tom Tit. Sometimes, I forget to wear it. Forget I need it. Because I have stopped looking in mirrors.

During one of my regular teas with Barbara, I tell her about the problems with the puppies in the car parks. I try to make it sound funny but she sees through the humour to the frazzled woman underneath.

The next day Bob calls: 'We've got a courtyard at the back of the house where the puppies can stay while you're out.'

It feels like someone has just lifted a concrete hat off my head. 'Thank you, Bob. Thank you.'

One evening when I'm struggling with the shopping, Jack from up the hill grabs the bags from me. 'Leave your shopping at the ferry wharf in future,' he tells me. 'I'll carry it up to the house for you.' Help seems to come from every direction and the weight of coping alone lifts.

When I have my final chemo treatment, a week after the scheduled time because my white blood cells are slow off the mark again, it is nearly four months since it began. I celebrate with Bob and Barbara at Tarrangaua with a cup of tea and a slice of cake. The partying has slowed down to almost nothing and it feels good.

Around the same time as chemo finishes, the builders call to say they're ready to come and discuss plans for the extension on the house.

I know exactly what I want. A simple house where the outside is allowed to be part of the inside.

I feel a stirring of precious energy, so precious I can't afford to waste it. So when the ex-lover eventually calls—who knows why?—I let the answering machine pick up his message. I do not return the call.

One night, with the doggies tucked in bed beside me—in a weak moment I lifted them onto the bed for a quick cuddle and they immediately assumed ownership of the entire area—I start to read Barbara's document. It is her research into Dorothea Mackellar's life and the history of Tarrangaua. Towards the end, she writes this extraordinary tale:

> About a year and a half after we moved in, I looked out of the window of my study, which had once been Dorothea's bedroom, and saw the strangest sight. There was a woman, wearing a longish dark dress and a huge sun hat, walking quite sadly, it seemed to me, with her head down. Her steps were slow and tentative, as she headed towards the steep slope leading to the water's edge. She disappeared for a moment, then came back into view, but I still could not see her face. And then she followed an old sandstone pathway, narrow and rarely used, to the waters of Frog Hollow.
>
> I tried to think who she might be. I thought briefly of the neighbours but dismissed the idea. I felt she had stepped out of another era. Her ankle-length dress fell in thick, heavy drapes in that old-fashioned russet brown that was so popular after the First World War. And her hat was large, straw and similar to the style seen in photographs of people in the 1930s. It was a mystery to me.
>
> I didn't mention this 'sighting' to Bob. I felt silly and melodramatic. Because I felt from the first moment the figure appeared that she was a ghost. The ghost of Dorothea.
>
> Bob would have told me to have a cup of tea and a rest. So I said nothing. But I sat and waited, hoping she would return. She didn't return that day and I have never seen her since.

'You're the first person I've told about that ghost,' Barbara says when I call in to see her the next afternoon. She is in her nightwear. As she mostly is, these days. 'I've always wanted to follow up seeing that ghostly woman with someone who knew Dorothea,' she adds. 'I need to know if this apparition had any resemblance to her. Could it have been her ghost or was it someone passing in fancy dress? That, you see, is the mystery I would like to solve.'

I've baked scones and we tuck into them. 'There must be someone around who remembers her,' I say, talking with a mouth full.

Outside the sky is black. An icy westerly wind builds. Our ears tune in to the sounds outside: the rushing whoosh and, suddenly, the rain.

'What about the old-timers around here? Why don't we try to find a couple of them? Take a cattle prod to their memories,' I suggest.

'Not that simple,' Barbara says. 'Pittwater is a funny place. People come here full of enthusiasm. But many don't stay. After a while, it gets too hard. Two years sorts most people out.'

'So the removalists told me,' I say. 'But there must be someone.'

Bob walks in from his workshed, smelling of wood shavings. Cold air hangs off him. 'Figured it all out?' he asks, moving in front of the fire.

'We're trying to work out who would have known Dorothea,' Barbara explains. 'She died in 1968, and she didn't come here for the last eleven years of her life. So we're looking for people who were adults, or at least old enough to have accurate memories, about forty-five years ago.'

'That can't be too hard,' I say. 'I'll start asking around.'

Bob and Barbara exchange a smile. Barbara has searched for six years without success. But a gritty kernel of determination settles inside me.

'Bit of a challenge for me. Fill in some time,' I say flippantly.

Bob moves from the fire. 'Got a bit more to do. Then I'll come in.'

I get up. 'Come on, puppies,' I say, 'let's attack all those steps. I want to get home before dark.'

'There's an old pathway,' Barbara says, 'that runs from Bob's shed to the back of your house. It's overgrown but Bob will clear it. Easier than going up and down the steps.'

'I've never noticed it. How long's it been there?'

'Years. Once, a doctor owned the house directly behind you. Where the old chimney still stands. According to local legend, he was in love with Dorothea and used the path to visit her. Locals call it Lover's Lane.'

'Did Dorothea return the affection?'

'Not according to legend.'

'Then we should rename it. How about Barb's Lane?'

Barbara smiles and, for a moment, weariness falls from her eyes. 'Oh, Lover's Lane will do. I think it will have its day again, that lane.'

It seems an odd response but I let it go.

Bob and I walk out together. I pile on clothes—scarf, sweater, jacket.

'Put this on.' Bob hands me a bright yellow slicker.

I grab the puppies, open the back door and peer out. It's dark enough to be late evening. Light from Bob's shed shines like a beacon.

'So what goes on in that mysterious shed of yours?'

'Bit of this. Bit of that. Come and have a look.'

He grabs a puppy, stuffs her down his shirt. It's Vita and she squirms with delight, licks his face. I do the same with Dolce, who is less entranced. We run for the shed, a dark brown weatherboard building about ten metres from the house.

'So this is where you come to escape.'

I say it lightly but Bob is serious.

'Come out here to think,' he says. His eyes are black. Shoulders hunched. He struggles to find words.

I cringe at my thoughtlessness. What he is dealing with, Barbara's illness, is inescapable. But I cannot talk about illness and death right now. Too many of my own fears.

Bob goes straight to the workbench in front of the window. He is silent and lets me poke around. It's a shabby, spider-web-encrusted shed with grimy windows. Machinery is everywhere—sanders, grinders, saws. Nails, screws, nuts and bolts scattered like shiny confetti. Hammers and screwdrivers, all sizes, and dusty containers full of treasures. Everywhere, the underlying smells of paint and turpentine.

'Has anyone ever done a biography of Dorothea?' I ask, picking up the biggest screwdriver I've ever seen.

He hands me Vita and leaves the shed. Wordless. I'm not sure what to do. Wait? Go? After a minute or two, the back door bangs shut. A shadow streaks through the rain.

'Here,' Bob says, pushing a book in a wet plastic shopping bag towards me. 'This is the only book we've found about her life.'

In the bag there's a faded paperback with a drawing of a coquettish-looking young woman on the cover. *My Heart, My Country*, by Adrienne Howley. I turn to the back cover to read the blurb.

'Who was Adrienne Howley?' I ask.

'She nursed Dorothea for the last eleven years of her life in a hospital in Randwick,' Bob says.

'Is she still alive?'

'I don't know. Good place to start, though. With your search.'

That night I call Sophia in Melbourne. 'Bob needs to talk about death and dying. I don't think I can help him,' I tell her.

'Why not? You know more about it than most people.'

I hesitate. 'It's too close to home. I thought *you* might call him, talk to him. You're good at all that stuff,' I say.

'Ah, come on. That won't work. You're right there!'

'But what if I say the wrong thing? Make it worse? Barbara's fading. Bob says chemo is not a cure. It's just giving her more time.'

'Does Barbara talk about her health?'

'Not in any way that admits any possibility that she won't survive.'

'How does he handle that?'

'Life goes on as usual. They're getting the painters in soon, to paint the house. I want to help them both but I don't know what to do.'

'Be there for the family. They will be so busy supporting her, they will need support themselves,' Sophia suggests.

'What about finding little goals? Not tiring, unachievable goals. Just interesting events that can be brought to her door.'

'Go on.' I hear Sophia settling into the deep chair by her phone.

'Well, she's fascinated by Dorothea Mackellar. There's a biography written by a woman called Adrienne Howley. If she's still alive, I think Barbara would like to meet her. Thought I might try to find her.'

'Hang on a sec.'

The phone clunks and footsteps echo. After a few minutes, Sophia settles back into her chair.

'Hmm, I thought so. Adrienne Howley. She's a nun, a Buddhist nun.'

It feels like cymbals clashing, drums rolling, crowds cheering, the universe reeling—all at once. Fate? Coincidence? What does it matter?

'I don't know where she is right now, but I'll make a few calls and let you know,' Sophia says.

It takes a week for Sophia to find Adrienne Howley's phone number. In another twist of fate, it turns out she lives just north of Newcastle, only three hours' drive from Lovett Bay. A manageable day's round trip.

'She's written a book you should read,' Sophia tells me. 'It's called *The Naked Buddha*. It's a simple explanation of the life and teachings of Buddha. It's very good.'

'How did a nurse in an old people's nursing home end up writing a biography of Dorothea Mackellar and a book explaining Buddhism?'

'Give her a call and find out. And get her organised to meet Barbara.'

'You don't think it will be too much for her? She's pretty fragile.'

'Ask her. But do it before you ring Adrienne.'

It's difficult, when you feel weak and ill, to find the energy to talk to a stranger. Perhaps Barbara has other, more pressing chores.

Bob is in the shed when I walk up to tell him about Adrienne. It still looks like a madman's hardware sale. In the daylight, I can see broken furniture stacked in a corner. There's a loft, too, which is used as storage for huge bags stuffed with sails for his boat, he tells me.

'That's my boat down there. *Larrikin*.' He points out of the window.

'The one with her backside sticking out of the water?'

Bob's not fond of my description. 'She's a racing boat. Built to be light and take the weight of people in the rear.'

'I see,' I say, looking around. 'I have never really asked what you do.'

'I fix problems.'

'What kind of problems?'

'Engineering problems.'

'And?'

'And what?'

I give up. 'Now, listen. I've found the writer—well, Sophia's found her, the woman who wrote Mackellar's biography.'

Bob looks shocked. 'Already?'

'Actually, it took longer than we thought. She's a Buddhist nun.'

'*Nun!*'

'Buddhist nun.' I can barely speak. Laughter set to explode. 'So do you think Barbara would like to meet her?'

'She's inside. In bed. Today's not a good day for her.'

'Well, can you ask her at some stage? Today if possible?' My old journalistic habits have kicked in. I'm anxious to nail down the story.

He drops a metal tube and walks towards the house. I'm left standing.

'Come on!' he calls impatiently.

Barbara is asleep in the end bedroom, so we tiptoe to the kitchen for a cup of tea. Bob reaches inside the fridge and pulls out two plates—one with an orange and almond cake, another with a lemon cake.

'There're a few scones here, too,' he says, his eyes smiling.

'Overdoing the cooking thing, aren't I?'

'I design and build kilns,' he says, as if there'd never been a break in the conversation in the workshed.

'Is that why Barbara loves pottery? Why there's so much in the house?'

'Brick kilns,' he says. 'Not pottery kilns.'

'Oh. Have you built many?'

'Yeah.'

Silence. Not comfortable. We both turn with relief when Barbara opens the kitchen door, looking so tired I feel like holding her up. But she smiles, takes a cup of tea and, when Bob asks, says yes, it would be wonderful if Adrienne Howley could visit.

Bob sees me out through the back door.

'There're a couple of points I forgot to mention,' I tell him.

He stops, which I gather is a signal to continue.

'Adrienne is in her seventies.'

He shrugs. 'I can drive her up the hill in the ute.'

'She's also blind.'

I don't know why, but I never doubted for a moment that an elderly, blind, Buddhist nun wouldn't hesitate to climb into a total stranger's car, drive for three hours, then climb on a boat, and clamber up more than eighty steps to sit and talk to a woman dying of cancer about a poet who'd died more than thirty years ago.

6

I AM EXPECTING an answering machine, which is usually what you get when you're in a hurry to contact someone. But Adrienne Howley picks up the phone on the second ring. Fate again? After burbling a slightly chaotic explanation of why I'm calling, I hear a long sigh from the other end of the line.

'Tarrangaua,' she almost whispers. 'Oh, I'd love to come. I've always wanted to go back there and I never thought it would happen. Thank you, thank you for asking me.'

And it's as simple as that. All she has to do is arrange for her cat to spend a couple of nights with her local vet while she is away.

I had begun this for Barbara, thinking in some idiotic way that when someone is dying she deserves to have every wish fulfilled. But it was giving me a large dose of happiness, too. I'd done the same thing for what we all knew would be my husband's last Christmas. I'd rushed around trying to find everyone's dream gift, which, for his daughter Lulu, was a border collie puppy. At the time I thought it was madness but Lulu adored that dog, Bella. She put a new structure in Lulu's life when the framework centred on her father collapsed. It was worth it.

Of course, the one wish that really mattered to Barbara was impossible to arrange.

There is a large sign announcing Lorn Learning Centre on the front verandah that I *think* belongs to Adrienne's house. There's nothing about Buddhism. But a woman appears wearing the deep maroon robes of a Tibetan nun. Can't be too many Tibetan nuns in Newcastle, I think.

'Adrienne?' My voice is overloud in the still, tree-lined street.

She nods.

'I'm Susan.' I walk up to her and put out my hand, which is unseen.

She is small but not frail. Except for her skin, which is paper-thin. Her eyes are bright blue. Although she is well into her seventies and cannot see, she moves quickly and gracefully.

'Come in. I have tea and biscuits, if you like. Or juice, or iced tea.'

'If you don't mind, we'll get going.' I am anxious to move on. To get back before dark.

On the highway, a light rain blows in random waves. Oncoming cars, headlights on full beam, loom out of the grey weather like giant insects.

I want Adrienne to be the source of all wisdom on this trip, to show me the path to contentment. I want to ask her all the questions under the sun and have her give me answers that will guide me for the rest of my life. And yet I should know by now that I have to find them myself.

Adrienne does not play that game as we sit enveloped in the car. Instead, she tells me about being diagnosed with cancer and sailing around the world with a mad sea captain, waiting to die. Five years later she realised that her imminent death was taking a long time, so she abandoned ship and returned to Australia, where she eventually studied Buddhism.

When I ask her why Buddhism, she says with unexpected vehemence, 'Because nothing in my life ever made any sense. I wanted to try to make sense of it all. The meaning of life, if you don't mind the cliché.'

We talk in short bursts on that drive, taking turns in an odd little mental soft-shoe shuffle that, as trust grows, leads us closer and closer to telling the truth about ourselves.

Her laugh is loud and packed with irony when I ask whether she has found the meaning of life. 'What I have found is the ability to live life in a way that is useful. And that has made some sense of it all.'

When she tells me she works in palliative care, I wonder again at the hand of fate. If Barbara wants to talk about death, Adrienne will know how to handle it.

For a while we are silent, just swooshing through the rain. Every so often I glance across at Adrienne. I want to ask her a question, but do not know how to begin.

'Is there a way,' I finally ask, 'to learn to make only the right decisions?' I am, of course, thinking about the ex-lover.

'Ah,' she says, a smile playing around her mouth. 'What is right? What is wrong? When it's all added up at the end, how do we know?'

She is silent then, for so long that I stumble into an oversimplified explanation of my enquiry because I feel I cannot mention the ex-lover. 'Am I doing the right thing by Barbara by trying to give her little goals, moments to look forward to? Am I making it easier or harder for her?'

'What is your motive?'

'To create hope.'

'That is a good motive.'

'I get a surge of hope and confidence when people include me in future plans,' I explain. 'If they believe I have a future, perhaps I do.'

'Do *you* believe you have one?' Adrienne asks.

'Some days I do, some days I don't. Sometimes, I think feeling hope is a kind of emotional torture because, of course, all it takes is a single badly chosen word or some thoughtless remark to shatter it.'

'That's because,' Adrienne said, 'you are trying to find hope in the words and actions of other people. You must have it yourself.'

By the time we reach Church Point, the rain has stopped. I call Bob and he arrives in his boat. Adrienne steps into the tinny like a teenager. We set off for Tarrangaua at a slow and easy pace.

'You'll be staying with me,' I tell Adrienne. 'I hope that's OK. Barbara gets tired really quickly.'

She nods, then we are all silent. Adrienne is entranced. She breathes in the sea air as though it is a delicate perfume. She turns her face to the stern to catch the gentle drift of sea spray, and closes her eyes.

When we reach the pontoon, Adrienne climbs the ramp as though she's been doing it all her life and waits onshore while we tie up the boat. The rain starts to fall lightly again, so I thank Bob, grab Adrienne's arm and lead her to my house.

'We'll have dinner at home tonight and then go up to Tarrangaua tomorrow morning. Is that OK?'

'Of course, dear.'

'I've got steaks for dinner,' I say, 'but if you're a vegetarian I can cook up a frittata.'

'If I were cooking for myself, I would eat vegetarian, but Buddhists must eat whatever is put in front of them—and I love beef!'

Adrienne and I make our way to Tarrangaua around eleven the next morning. Adrienne moves slowly but firmly, never stumbling.

The sky is blue and the bay even bluer. It is high tide and there's just enough swell to send corkscrews of light shimmering from one shore to the other. Everything smells new and fresh after the rain and the earth underfoot is soft. Halfway up the steps, the cockatoos go berserk, flapping around a towering spotted gum like an army of mad archangels.

'There's a goanna trying to get up the tree,' I tell Adrienne, 'and the birds aren't happy about it.'

'Probably a nest somewhere,' she replies.

The goanna, its black and pale green body blending neatly into the colours of the tree trunk, whips its tail back and forth but is no match for the cockatoos. There are eight of them and they dive-bomb the giant lizard until it climbs down the tree to the ground, defeated. The birds fall silent and watch the goanna lumber off into the scrub, each bright yellow crest clenched in a tight curl like a question mark. After a few moments, they fly off calmly. The threat is over. We resume our climb.

At the top of the winding stairway, where the workshed looms, Adrienne stands still. I will never forget the rapture on her face.

'This was the place she loved best. This is where she always longed to be,' Adrienne says. She means, of course, Dorothea Mackellar.

Bob is at the door. He explains that Barbara is not well enough to get up today. Does Adrienne mind talking to her in the bedroom?

Barbara sits up in bed in her large, dimly lit bedroom. She is glowing pink from her shower. She looks incredibly young and carefree and her eyes are filled with anticipation.

Adrienne and I sit on two chairs culled from the dining room and Barbara straightens her carefully prepared list of questions. I've brought a tape recorder and we press the button.

'Is the house different?' Barbara asks Adrienne. 'How did you find it when you arrived at the front door?'

Adrienne pulls her chair closer to Barbara. 'It felt a little ghostly, I suppose, at first. I felt perhaps she was saying, "Oh, you're back again."'

'Did you come here very often?'

'I never came here with Miss Mackellar, although I visited the house a couple of times with her permission. She was in hospital at the time.'

'How did you find it then?'

'It was beautiful.'

'There is very little mention of this house, Tarrangaua, anywhere.'

'This was her private place. Here she was out of the public eye altogether. She loved the isolation and was passionate about the bush.'

'There is a nearby pathway known as Lover's Lane. Do you think there was anyone around here in whom she had a romantic interest?'

'No, I don't think so,' Adrienne replies, after a moment. 'She had friends who came up from Sydney occasionally. But Dorothea was a very private person and she would be circumspect about anything like that. She had strong feelings about what constituted good behaviour.'

'Did she have much of a sense of humour?'

'Yes, and a quick wit that could be very cutting if anyone tried to put anything over her or take advantage of her. Can I ask why you're so interested in Miss Mackellar?' Adrienne asks. 'Your questions go far beyond what I thought you'd want to talk about.'

'I guess my interest was spurred along by the bushfires when the house, and virtually the history of it, could have burned to the ground. I wanted a record of what had been here and I realised I had to find out more about Dorothea Mackellar. You are the only direct link we have found to her. How long did you know her?'

'Eleven and a half years, twelve hours a day, six days a week, and she loved to talk. On a good day she never stopped talking.'

'She loved language, I suppose.'

'There would be certain words that would always affect her. Just the names of some colours would bring tears to her eyes. She thought that "The Colour of Light" was her best poem.'

'She never married and never had any children. Do you think she felt her life had been wasted in any way?'

'No, I think she was quite satisfied. She had done what she could and left something behind her that was worth while. But there was sadness. At times. She could not mention her brother Keith, who was killed in the Boer War, without tears spilling. Right to the very end.'

Barbara puts her notebook aside, slipping her pen inside the pages. 'I have only one more question. What did she wear, do you remember? Were her clothes dark or light? Did she wear hats?'

Adrienne thinks for a while before answering. 'She liked softly coloured clothes, as I recall. Yes. And some bright florals. She always wore a bright floral housecoat indoors. I'm not sure about hats. By the time I knew her, she didn't go out much.'

Barbara lies back on her pillow and I leave the room. Disappointed for her. Dorothea looked nothing like her ghost. There is no more mystery, except to wonder whom it was who passed by so whimsically.

Adrienne stays with Barbara and the two of them talk. Not about Dorothea, Adrienne tells me later. About family, love, dreams and hopes.

By mid-November, after the wild spring winds have scattered the last of the bright yellow wattle, chemo is almost a month behind me. Barbara is fading slowly but fighting every step of the way.

I have a boat, now. One of Bob's, which I've named *Tin Can*. I ask him if I can buy it after Barbara tells me he is planning to design and build a smaller boat to whiz to and from Church Point.

'Only if you give it a test run first,' he says.

'Could you give me a couple of lessons, too?'

'Yeah. But there's not much to driving a boat. Five-year-olds can do it.'

The first time we go out, we motor slowly because I know that's the best way from my forays with Sophia, but when we hit the open part of the bay, he tells me to push the throttle forward. We race along, and I think I'm doing brilliantly until I look at Bob's wincing face.

'What's wrong?' I shout.

'You're breaking my bloody balls!' he shouts back.

'Oh God, sorry.'

I yank the throttle back and he nearly goes through the windscreen.

'Sorry.' Oops. Forgot that little lesson with Sophia.

He breathes again. White-faced. 'There's a middle speed, you know. There's not just slow and flat out.' He reaches for the throttle and moves it until we're rocking along nicely. 'Right. Now turn back to Lovett Bay.'

I swing the wheel sharply and almost shoot Bob out of his seat. He bumps his head hard against the side window.

'Oh God, I'm so sorry.'

He gets back his balance and looks at me. 'You are the worst learner I've ever experienced. A shocker.'

And we laugh because we both know it's true and Bob's face is transformed. The lines of weariness soften, the tight band of restraint around his mouth relaxes. He looks years younger.

'What you need is practice,' he says. 'Every day. On your own.'

Nearly a month after my last chemo treatment, the new editor at a magazine I once edited has offered me part-time work and I decide to take it on. I am worried about being home all day with nothing to think about except my health. And I've committed to house renovations. I need the extra money. The plan is to spend three nights a week staying with Pia. Bob and Barbara will look after the puppies and I will return home every Thursday night for a three-day weekend.

My head is still bald but no one seems to care. I try, for a day or two, to wind a scarf round it. Then I stop. I am who I am. And right now, that means bald. There will be no more bending to be someone I am not. Not for a job, a man, a friend or even a life. Somehow, during the last few months, I have finally grown into my skin. The influence of environment or the threat of mortality? Probably a bit of both.

But I have no idea how to handle life beyond chemo. Do I march on as though cancer never invaded my life? Am I cured? The truth is, no one ever gives you the all-clear so the threat of a recurrence means a sense of being constantly on the edge of a precipice. Physically, I just thought I'd quickly feel OK and bounce back to normal. I wasn't prepared for the tiredness to continue and even escalate for the first few months after the end of chemo. And my concentration is still shot. Two-minute spans are about the limit.

Every day, hot flushes pound in and out with their attendant waves of nausea, and they make interviewing people hell. Nearly everyone is kind and understanding. People do their best to help me out. A cold drink, a box of tissues to mop the sweat, a fan turned directly onto my face.

Glenn Close, the American actress, is particularly kind when I interview her in Queensland on the set of the mini-series *South Pacific*.

'If I break into a sweat,' I tell her, 'please don't worry. I had my last chemo treatment a month ago and my body is still adjusting.'

She looks at me closely, a slight woman with flawless skin and clear grey eyes, exuding health, sexuality and intelligence. 'Come inside where it's cooler,' she says. 'Tell me how we can make you as comfortable as possible.'

No fuss. Just cuts to the practical. She lets me bumble around my questions, never loses patience when I repeat one or two and makes me feel like a member of her family. But coming home from that assignment, with my right arm encased in a tight elastic bandage to prevent lymphoedema, which is sometimes triggered by long flights, I know I've done a poor job. My mind is like a quagmire.

I have lost, too, the journalistic instinct for the headline quote—the sensational sentence that catapults a bland interview into hot gossip. Cancer, which threatened my well-being, makes me suddenly protective of other people's welfare. So I self-edit and soften indiscreet words that I know would cause a furore in print. It is a form of professional suicide, but I can't live any other way now.

On a personal level, every simple decision seems to have major ramifications. What kind of takeaway food might do me harm? Will colouring my hair—when it regrows—increase the risk of cancer? What is good for me? What will hurt me? The cancerous growth has been removed so, *technically*, I am not sick any more. Only I am sick from chemo. And I am caught between wanting to push myself harder and being terrified that it might hurt me. It's a bastard not knowing *why* you've had a disease because it means you have no idea what to do in future to prevent it happening again.

One night, Pia returns late to her apartment with a group of friends in tow, and the music plays until 3 a.m. I cry from sheer weariness and cannot get up the next morning. But if it isn't the noise of a party disturbing me, it is the sound of drug deals taking place in the lane alongside the building, the guttural scream of buses climbing the hill outside the front windows. City noise is like the constant hammering of a headache.

At Pittwater, my tired mind winds down just by sitting for a few moments and watching light play on water. Colours are always changing. Silver dawns, fiery sunsets, hard, flat noons when the sun sucks the colour from the trees, lush late afternoons when greens turn deeper and deeper. The bay is its own kaleidoscope. Silver, turquoise, lime, blue, gold, orange. The smells, too. The dank, briny scent of low tide when the sand lies exposed and wet. The dusty, roasted smell of eucalypts in the heat of a forty-degree day. The sugary fragrance of wattles.

Then there's the wind. Each one has a personality. A southerly is clean and cool, a northerly clingy and damp. In summer, a hot, parched westerly brings the fear of bushfires until a frisky sea breeze forces it back the way it came. Sometimes the wind whisks the water until it is lacy with whitecaps and it is pleasant simply to sit and listen to the sounds changing with the weather. The song of casuarinas, the taffeta rustle of cabbage palms, the agonised creaking of spotted gums. And occasionally, the snap and crash of a huge branch falling to the ground. It is impossible to disengage from the physical world and I am reminded, over and over, that control is an illusion.

I manage to stagger around the office for three months in what seem like smaller and smaller circles. Then, as the first wispy new fluffs of hair blossom into a full, curly thatch of an entirely new colour—black when I'd been red—I understand I can no longer go on. It is not just the exhaustion. It is the wrenching sadness I feel every time I walk into a tall, dark building, leaving behind the sky and the light of day.

I miss the feel of the breeze on my face. I miss the puppies and their uninhibited joy. I miss the easy, quiet pace of a community that has become a family. Every moment locked away in an artificial environment feels wasted. If my time is to be cut short, then every moment must be as good as it gets. So I resign from my work. Again. I have done it so often now, it holds no fear for me. This time, it does not feel as though I am leaping into nothing, but as though I am grabbing what is most important to me at this stage of my life.

It seems ridiculous to worry about the future. I don't even know if I have one. The truth is, none of us do. If you can look at that simple fact from the right angle, it is empowering. I finally stop hedging my bets. In a peculiar way, what I've arrived at is *faith*. Not the religious kind, but the sort that comes from inside yourself.

I slip back into the harmony of Lovett Bay life instantly and time, which I once filled with work, frantic partying or the lover, slows to a manageable pace. There is time to daydream, time to clean the grungy corners of windows and take pleasure in it, time to talk to Barbara.

I decide to get my growing hair coloured and go back to the hairdresser who was so kind when it was falling out.

'Turn it auburn,' I tell him. 'A good, rich, red-brown colour.'

Four hours later, I emerge fuchsia pink. 'You could guide the ferry in at midnight with your hair,' Bob says when he sees it.

I return to the hairdresser. 'Make it blonde.'

A week later, a friend comes to lunch. 'Interesting shade of green in your hair. Looks good with the purple streaks. Going punk?' she asks.

Back to the hairdresser. 'Plain white will do.'

I return from the washbasin and look in the mirror. My hair is canary yellow.

In the mirror I see Col, who owns the wonderful poultry supply shop Caotic Chook next to the hairdresser's. He's in shock.

A few minutes later his wife, Cher, rushes in with a glass of red wine. 'Col thought you might need this,' she says.

Back in Lovett Bay, the boys in the boat shed see me coming and money changes hands. 'You let me down, Susan,' says Veit.

'What do you mean?'

'I tipped black this time. I lost the bet.'

My loyalty to the hairdresser finally ends. I get a number two clip and begin again. *Au naturel.*

Brigitte rushes in one morning on her way to catch the ferry. 'Susan! Susan!' she says. Always the double-barrelled monicker. 'Do you think you could possibly cook for the Elvina Bay Fire Shed dinner this month?'

'Sure. When is it and how many people?'

'Friday night. There's usually about thirty people.'

'Thirty!'

'Yeah. But you only have to do one course. There's always a dessert competition and four or five people make cakes or pies, or something.'

'Is there a budget?'

'Well, spend as little as possible. The idea is to raise money for the fire brigade. So you're OK? You'll do it?' She's rushed and rushing.

'Yeah. But how? Do I cook here or there?'

'Cook everything here and we'll all help to carry it. I can do rice, if you need it. Let me know.'

And she is gone.

On Thursday, when the builders come by via water taxi to discuss plans, I am knee-deep in osso buco. My biggest saucepans are scattered all over the kitchen worktops and the smell of garlic and lemon fills the air. I slap cups of tea and slices of lemon cake in front of them and leave them to look around and measure on their own.

Late on Friday afternoon, Bob comes to help load the boat: one large cast-iron pot and three enormous stainless-steel pots. They weigh a ton each. Bob carries them uncomplainingly but I can see faint lines of disapproval round his mouth. I've overcatered. We both know it. I hand over a garbage bag filled with washed lettuce and a large bottle of salad dressing. Then another garbage bag filled with cooked penne I plan to warm in hot water for a minute or two before serving.

'Is there anyone meeting us at the other end?' Bob asks.

'No. I don't think so.'

He sighs. 'Well, at least it's high tide. We can take the boat right in to the sea wall to unload. Means it's not quite so far to carry everything.'

He starts the boat and we chug out of Lovett Bay and round the bend into Elvina Bay. The fire shed is on the south side of the bay. There's a small group of people gathered out front, who turn as we approach and wander down to the boat.

'Hi. I'm Lisa.'

'Hi. I'm Alan.'

'He's Roy,' says Lisa, pointing at her husband, a quiet, shy bloke.

They grab saucepans and bags and I follow them empty-handed.

From six o'clock onwards, tinnies glide in slowly and men, women, young kids and toddlers stroll, race or stumble towards the fire shed.

When the crowd looks big, Roy drives the bright, shiny fire engine with its tank and hoses outside onto the grass, just in case we need shelter. He is laconic, with a dry sense of humour, and makes us all laugh.

Lisa, who is clearly a phenomenal cook and an even better organiser, directs the boys to set up serving tables, haul out piles of mismatched plates and cutlery. She slams a load of homemade sausage rolls into the oven to feed the kids. People pay seven dollars and get a ticket for dinner, kids run riot and entertain themselves, and it's a great night out. Bottles of wine are opened and glasses filled and there's a quiet exchange of local information. Who needs hoses for a fire pump? Should there be a fire shed Christmas dinner this year as well as a kids' musical concert? How's the season looking for bushfires?

When everyone's eaten and the desserts have been judged, Lisa looks around. 'Bit left over, isn't there?'

'Nearly all the salad has gone, though,' I say in defence.

'Hmm. Well, I'd say it's a perfect result. There's a fire shed meeting on Monday night and this will feed everyone.'

She grins and so do I, and we begin loading leftovers into plastic containers to freeze. When it's time to leave, she thanks me, and so does everyone else. And they say wonderful things about the food and I feel as though I have been useful.

The boys in the boat shed, always friendly and cheerful even on the dankest mornings, are my daily entertainment. Each day I watch big, tired yachts, with peeling paint and a whole marine environment attached to their hulls, get transformed into confidently beautiful vessels. At the risk of sounding sentimental, I feel that Lovett Bay is having the same effect on me. Layers of emotional baggage are being sifted so I can edit out the lousy episodes and store the finer moments. The last shreds of grief about the boys, the anger with the lover? Tossed out and drowned. I don't know if I would have done this in the course of time or whether being ill hastened the process. Whatever the answer, whenever I make a wish (on a falling star, on the first cherry of the season, on any number of rites instilled by my mother), it is always the same. *Give me health and I will take care of the happiness myself.*

Much later, when I have nestled into the unhurried tempo of a life that revolves round weather and whim instead of deadlines and schedules, I learn my Little Gairie Beach shack buddy, Tony, is seriously ill.

'Come and stay,' I tell him when I visit him in hospital where he's having chemo and radiation therapy for oesophageal cancer. 'Come to Lovett Bay and let me feed you up. We'll pretend we're at the shack.'

'Your house,' he says to me with a raised eyebrow, 'is exactly the same as the shack except it has running water. I,' he adds like a politician delivering a speech, 'reminded you about the best parts of your childhood at *my* shack and you went off and found a shack of your own.'

And I realise he is right. When my brother and I were still at primary school, rare family holidays usually meant a trip to Phillip Island, where we stayed in a wobbly shack built from bits of wood nailed to a frame. The shack belonged to my grandfather's sister and her husband, Auntie Mert and Uncle Albert, who created wonderful designs out of shells set in concrete and and panelled the side and front fence. Before they fixed up the shack and sold it at a profit, the roof was tin and the kitchen had a single kerosene burner in one corner. When it rained, every bucket, bowl, dish and cup was put into action to catch the leaks. There was a dunny out the back and a cold-water shower outside. Swimming was supposed to keep you clean; the shower was just to rinse off the salt water. At night we lit hurricane lamps because there was no electricity and the house was filled with the permanent pong of kerosene mingled with the smell of the sea. Come to think of it, they were the same smells that wafted through Tony's Little Gairie Beach shack. Perhaps that's why I instantly loved it there.

Just after sunset each night at that funny little shell house, we'd wrap ourselves up in coats and scarves and rush across the road to the beach to watch the penguins. There were hundreds of these shy little black and white birds that looked like they were surfing in on the waves to attend a formal dinner party. They'd hit the beach and waddle up to their burrows in the sand dunes. After the penguin parade (as it is still called, although I understand there are now reserved seats and tourist buses at the site), we'd scamper home to a dinner of bread, butter, raspberry jam and cream. There may have been a sausage or a chop as well, of course, but all I remember is the richness of the butter and cream. The thick, soft slices of fresh white bread. And the wonder of ruby-red raspberry jam made by the farmer's wife down the road.

In Auntie Mert's and Uncle Albert's shack, no one ever told us to pick up our clothes, wash our hands or say our prayers. My father didn't drink much because it was a fair distance to the pub, and my mother relaxed and came shell-hunting with us. We valued cowries above all, with their exotic leopard spots, and put them to our ears to hear the sea.

'Here, Possie,' my brother would say, 'listen hard. Can you hear mermaids singing?'

I sniffed because I was just starting to question Santa Claus and fairy tales and I thought my brother was setting me up. But I heard their song, so when he grabbed my hand and pulled me along to the rockpools at low tide I followed happily.

'What are we looking for?'

'Sea horses!'

I imagined great beasts with fins and gills and hoofs shaped like fish tails, so I wasn't prepared for the delicate little creature he pointed out.

'It's too small to be a horse,' I grumped, disappointed.

'But in the water, it has the strength of ten horses,' he said. 'And look! Starfish!'

I leaned closer and saw a teaming saltwater city. Tiny fish, shells with worms peeking out, crabs, and those magical seahorses and starfish.

'It's a fairyland,' my brother told me.

And for a while, I believed in fairy tales all over again.

That shack was paradise and Tony, also a country kid, probably had one just like it in his childhood too. Perhaps that's why he fell in love with the crumbling hut at Little Gairie Beach.

In his hospital bed, Tony plucks the edges of his sheet, mulling over my offer of a bed and home care.

'So come home with me. Please. I'd love it,' I say.

He hesitates a second longer. 'Yes,' he says finally, and for a moment he grins in that naughty little boy way he had before his illness.

For the first day or two at Lovett Bay I let him rest in bed, but he cannot settle his mind, worrying about his business, the people who depend on him and, of course, his health. Because I think it may divert him if only for a moment or two, I suggest he watched events unfold at the boat shed. 'You'll be constantly entertained,' I promise.

It happens to be the day Ken's wooden sailing boat, *Sylphine*, the one he sails in the Woody Point races, is to go back in the water after a long time in the slip. Toby and Dave are there on their barge, the *Laurel Mae*, to drop the boat gently into the water. It all goes according to plan. Except it lands in the water upside-down, sinking so quickly the boat-shed blokes don't have time to turn it upright. It goes straight to the bottom. Which gives everyone such a shock, they just stand and look for a full minute or so. Then it's bedlam. Ken races in and gets into a wet suit. He and one of the boys, who's already in a wet suit, dive deep, come up for air, discuss options, dive again, and so on, until there's a plan. Eventually, the boat is brought up and righted, no damage done.

By the end of the whole event, Tony has tears running down his cheeks from laughing silently, too sore in his chest and throat to make a sound. 'This is a good place for me to be right now,' he whispers, adding, 'What do you think they'll come up with for an encore?'

He dies in hospital two months later. His wake is held at Little Gairie Beach and we all trek there to bid him goodbye. It's a still, perfectly bright day and the sea is flat as a sheet of glass. As we gather on the rocks at the seashore to toast Tony's colourful life, his sister puts down her glass of wine to say a few words. Out of nothing and nowhere, a wave rushes in, snatches the wine and roars back out to sea. It is behaviour so quintessentially Tony, we all gasp.

'He may be dead,' someone says, 'but he isn't gone!'

Out of the blue, Bob rings and suggests a walk.

'Where to?' I ask, not quite understanding why he's asking me along.

'What about up to Flagstaff?'

'Where on earth is that?'

'I'll show you.'

We set off in the late morning. Bob is dressed defensively in long sleeves, trousers tucked into socks, a hat and boots. I wear a short-sleeved T-shirt and long trousers.

'I should have told you to wear long sleeves,' Bob says as we walk alongside the creek, heading west. 'The bush can get prickly.'

I shrug. I am feeling well and strong, as I always do until I try to do any physical work. I'm not sure why, but I can never remember I am still recovering until I hit a wall of exhaustion.

Just past the last house and near the mouth of the estuary, there's a thicket of short, stubby, baby cabbage palms, with thorns that rip deep into your skin if you brush past too close. We bend almost double and clamber through a natural tunnel between the plants, trying not to touch them, but it's impossible. When we emerge into less dense scrub on the other side, there are pinpricks of blood on both my arms.

'I hope you know the way. Looks like nothing but scrub to me,' I say.

'This is an old walk, quite famous once, and there's a path here. We just have to find it,' Bob replies.

The walk, Bob explains, was built in 1895, when it was part of a grand scheme to make this area of Pittwater a fabulous national park on the same scale as Yellowstone National Park in the United States.

'Bit of a hike to get here from Sydney. It's a wonder they bothered.'

'People came for the wild flowers. The land was thick with them in spring. Quite beautiful.'

The bush is lush after heavy spring rains and the undergrowth is thick and ferocious. Prickly Moses cuts my cheeks. Why, I wonder silently, am I enjoying this so much? And the answer rockets back: because I'm in the bush and I love it and it's a challenge.

Bob climbs steadily towards the escarpment. The track is barely defined or non-existent.

'How do you know where we're going?' I ask.

Bob doesn't answer and we trudge on.

'See this,' Bob says, kneeling to brush away dead leaves and dirt. He reveals three perfect, man-made sandstone steps. 'This is the old path. We're going the right way.'

We climb through bush that changes from dense rain forest to rocky escarpment. We go past xanthorrhoeas with grassy skirts and long spikes, Christmas bush ready to break into masses of delicate red and yellow star-shaped flowers, pale mauve grevilleas, deep purple hardenbergia and, at our feet, cheery blue-faced daisies called brachycome. Barbara, I realise, has been subtly teaching me to recognise the plants of Lovett Bay, nudging me towards a greater understanding of the bush.

'How much further?' I ask Bob. Sweat is rolling down my face, the back of my T-shirt is stuck to my skin.

'Not far. A couple more turns and we're there.'

Nearer the summit, the vegetation changes dramatically. The soil is sandy and loose and stands of gnarled old banksias grip the side of the hill, blazing with orange and yellow flower cones. Small steps are chipped into a couple of rocky outcrops, then the track veers left. Ahead, there's a long, shadowy sandstone cave with a wooden table and bench seat. It smells musty, like an old wardrobe that hasn't been opened for years.

'God. How long has this been here?' I ask.

Stupid question. Millions of years probably. But the table and seat? Ten years or maybe one hundred years? I want to sit and absorb the cave but Bob seems uneasy, pacing in one spot, unable to sit down.

'Let's get to the top,' he says. 'It's not far at all, a few more steps.'

We move through lots more prickly Moses. By now, both my arms are badly scratched and bleeding. I think about lymphoedema, wonder briefly if I'll have to give up bushwalks. But that's no way to live. I just have to remember to bring antiseptic ointment at all times.

We emerge at the top of the escarpment where the wind is strong and cool. The landscape tumbles roughly below. Boats sit on the water like giant seagulls, and jetties finger their way along the shorelines. Scotland Island floats alone. Where we stand, there's an old iron and wooden seat. Eventually, I sit on it and stare all the way to the Pacific Ocean.

I realise that Bob is still nervy. 'Are you ever going to sit?' I ask.

'Barbara is getting worse,' he replies.

'That's what happens, Bob. You can't change that. Short of a miracle, there will be more bad days than good from now on.'

He turns away, but not before I see tears in his eyes. His shoulders are hunched up and his arms hang rigidly by his sides, fists clenched.

'But what can I do?' he asks. 'What should I do?'

I realise then that the reason we've walked to this place high on a hill is to talk about Barbara. He understands I am aware of what lies ahead for him. He wants to know what to expect, how to care for the woman he loves and whom he's been married to for thirty-five years.

'I don't know what's right or wrong,' I tell him. 'I only know what I failed to do when I had the chance. I can tell you that your own life has to be put on hold. Barbara comes first. Everything now is about her welfare and conjuring up every bit of happiness possible.'

'But she wants to go on with painting the house,' Bob says, frustration exploding in every word. 'I think it's madness. The house will be a mess, the fumes will knock her around.'

'It's what she wants. You can both stay with me until the fumes fade.'

He looks at me incredulously. 'Why would you do that?'

'Why did you and Barbara care for the puppies, help me every day?'

He sits, at last, on the seat, tension oozing out of him in long, flat ribbons. 'Barbara hates the idea of hospital. She wants to stay home.'

'That's fine while she's still able to get up and walk around,' I respond.

'But one day she won't be able to get out of bed at all. And you'll need help to care for her properly.'

'I have the help,' he replies. 'Our children will come, when it's time. One of them is a nurse.'

'When Sophia cared for her mother and sister, she brought in the equipment she knew they would need long before it was required, so that when the critical moment came, they didn't have to wait.'

'Equipment?'

'The wheelchair. The bedpan.'

'Yeah. I guess it has to come to that.'

We linger in silence on the big rock where a flag flew on special days one hundred years ago. The guy-rope anchors and the central cavity for the flagpole are still there—the reason the lookout is called Flagstaff.

Bob stands up, ready to head home. 'Not many people remember this pathway,' he says, closing the subject on death.

The house painting goes ahead in a frenzy of drop sheets, ladders and singing painters wearing splattered overalls. 'They're Italian,' Bob says, as though that automatically explains the singing.

Bob and Barbara move into my still unrenovated house, for a short stay—just while their bedroom is being worked on. For me, it is a wonderful time. Every night there is a team to cook for, which gives me a central purpose. Every day Barbara rests and Bob disappears to his workshed, unless I am out and Barbara is alone. Then he sits on the sofa closest to where Barbara rests, sketching ideas.

Bob, it turns out, can do almost anything. Build houses. Design boats. Fix engines. Even repair appliances. He is an engineer with a licence to do electrical and plumbing work. He fixes a leak I didn't even know I had in the bathroom. Gets the extractor fan working over the stove. I see his mind whirring constantly. When he's tongue-tied, I realise it's because his words can't keep pace with his thoughts. When he is silent, he is observing, assessing, storing information, thinking. He is not frightened of the kind of responsibility that means making hard decisions. He does not need applause to make him feel big. He is, I understand one day, one of the few grown-ups I have ever met.

I am often gone for part of the day, seeing one doctor or another, trying to rebuild my strength and, to be honest, seeking constant reassurance that the cancer has not returned. I usually come home in the afternoon, crash for a couple of hours, then brew my evil-tasting concoctions. Do they help? I don't know.

On the first Tuesday morning of Bob and Barbara's stay, I leave home early for an appointment. My mobile phone rings when I am halfway to the city.

'Barbara can't get out of bed,' Bob says. 'What should I do?'

Without asking any questions, I turn the car round and head home. When the water taxi drops me off, I race up Ken's jetty and run up the steps to the house. At home, Barbara lies in bed, happy and smiling. For a moment, I can't understand the panic. She is pale, but looks relaxed.

'I'll get up in a minute,' she says.

Bob grabs my elbow and takes me outside. 'She's been saying that since eight o'clock this morning. If she could get up, she would. Today's the day for another chemo treatment.' Barbara would never skip those.

Bob goes up the hill to his house to call her doctor. Then he rings me. 'They say get an ambulance and get her to hospital.'

'How do we do that?'

'I'll take care of it. You stay with Barbara.'

When you live in water-access-only areas, the Water Police become your water ambulance. They are based in McCarrs Creek, only minutes away. The police call an ambulance, and when everyone is assembled at the police office at the marina, the police and the ambulance staff both come over in the police launch to fetch the patient.

The police arrive with the ambulance attendants and their gear. A stretcher is placed alongside the bed and Barbara is gently moved onto it.

'I'm not bedridden, you know,' she says emphatically. But her eyes are filled with tears and all we can do is hold her hand and nod.

They carry her down the steps, those lovely young men with open faces and strong bodies, and place her in the boat so gently that Barbara feels no pain. Then they cast off, with Bob on board, and move slowly across the water. I gather the puppies and go inside.

Memories of my husband and brother, of the nightmare rushes to hospital, of seizures, of surgery, yammer in my mind. I don't want to go through it all again, the drawn-out wait for death, the grief that grinds through every day even while a loved one is still alive. Grief that leaves you without the strength to feel, for a little while after they die, anything but relief. And when the relief fades and the final reality of death seeps in, you're left with huge waves of pure, lonely grief and it's all you can do to keep standing.

I call in to see Barbara in hospital with a huge bunch of hydrangeas. They give the barren hospital room a lift but it is a bleak place. Hard to bear when the elegant verandah of Tarrangaua beckons with its views of a teeming outside world.

'I want to be at home,' Barbara says.

'I'd want to be home, too,' I reply, holding her hand for a moment.

There are three other people in the room, wheezing and coughing. Better by far to hear the music of the bush and the water.

'Can you cope if Barbara comes home?' I ask Bob after I return to Lovett Bay that evening. 'It's a huge job. Relentless.'

'We'll manage,' he says. And he quietly explains that he's been ready for this situation since long before our chat on Flagstaff. He will care for her while she can still get out of bed. As her health breaks down even further, their children will be called on. First Kelly, an experienced intensive-care nurse. When two people are no longer enough, Meg, an engineer, will come. 'Three of us can handle it,' Bob says.

'Four,' I say. 'Let me help where I can.'

As soon as Barbara returns home, the community kicks in gently. Debbie from Frog Hollow brings Thursday-night desserts. Ann from Little Lovett Bay comes to read on Wednesday evenings. I call in for chats, loaded with cakes or a stew or a frittata. Veit, from the boat shed, carries the food up the steps and occasionally stays to eat some of it. As each week unfolds, there are new dramas and problems, but mostly Barbara's transition from being unwell to invalid is smooth and dignified.

One day, despite Barbara's ravaging illness, one of the neighbours calls in to see her to try to put pressure on me to get rid of the puppies, which I still don't have completely under control.

I rage when Barbara tells me what's happened. My rage is with the neighbour, for her selfishness when Barbara is so ill. But I also feel threatened. My puppies are my anchors, part of the reason I get up, go walking, and remember to eat. They are my family.

Not long afterwards, the puppies flush a dying wallaby out of the bush onto the sand flats, where it collapses. The puppies circle it, yipping hysterically, trying to get at its throat. Up the hill, Brigitte, who is pregnant, is watching through binoculars and crying even more hysterically. Her two little boys are distraught.

'Jesus, what's going on?' I ask.

Pia is staying for a few days and we go onto the deck to take a look.

'Oh shit,' I say.

I rush out and grab Veit from the boat shed, telling Pia to get up to Brigitte's house to shake her out of her hysteria.

Veit and I run for the wallaby and grab a puppy each.

'Wait here while I lock the puppies inside,' I tell him.

When I return, Veit is sitting next to the animal, stroking its shoulder. 'It's nearly dead,' he says. 'But not from the puppies. It's old. Look. There are sores everywhere.' Veit lifts the wallaby and carries it into the bush, lying it down on a bed of leaves to die in peace.

Pia returns looking pleased with herself. 'All calm up there now,' she says, dusting her hands.

I put the puppies on their leads and Pia and I go up to Tarrangaua to see Barbara. I'm distraught about the whole episode. To my horror, I sit by her bed and burst into tears.

'God. I'm so sorry,' I say. 'This is appalling.'

Barbara smiles and pats my hand. 'Tell me what's wrong,' she says.

And I blurt it all out. Ashamed of burdening her with triviality compared to a life that's shutting down. And yet unable to stop myself.

'Talk to Bob about it,' she says. 'He'll know what to do.'

Bob is waiting for me in the kitchen. Pia has filled him in.

'What do you think I should do?' I ask. 'Do you have any ideas?'

'Only one,' he replies, 'and you won't like it.'

'What?' I ask defensively.

'Find a new home for one of the puppies. Together, they're a pack. Alone, they become a pet,' he says.

'No way! Absolutely no way!'

I storm into the sitting room and tell Pia I'm going home.

'Lovely cup of tea, thanks, Robert,' she says, getting up to follow me. 'So it's fishing tomorrow, is it?'

Bob nods. 'On the incoming tide. I'll give you a call,' he says.

Outside, I explode. 'Fishing! How can you think about fishing?'

'Oh, get over it,' Pia says, not unkindly. 'Come fishing. At least the puppies won't be able to get into any mischief on the boat.'

She's wrong, of course. First they eat all the bait. Then, when Bob hauls in a big octopus, red with fury and fear, they hunt it around the boat until it scrambles up Pia's leg. She's torn between laughing and screaming until Bob yanks it off, its little suction cups popping.

'This will make terrific new bait,' he says happily.

I burst into tears. 'You can't kill it! Octopuses are great mothers, you know. She may have babies waiting for her to come home.'

Bob starts to look trapped. He looks at the octopus, which is going redder and redder, then chucks it overboard just as Pia catches a fish.

'Should I whack it on the head?' she asks, pleased with herself.

Before he can answer, the puppies leap for the wriggling fish and land in the tackle box. Hooks, sinkers and paraphernalia go flying.

Bob tosses the fish back in the water. 'Too small to get much meat off.' He starts the engine. 'Let's call it a day, shall we? Looks like a storm might be coming in.'

Pia and I look up. The sky is spotless.

At the pontoon, we invite Bob in for a drink. He shakes his head. 'Think I'll go home. Give Kelly a break.'

'Is there anything we can do?' Pia and I ask, almost in unison.

'Nothing anyone can do, is there?' He turns towards the steps, three fishing rods and a tackle box in his hands. He looks beaten.

'Think it was all a bit much for him. On top of everything else,' I say.

'Who told you octopuses are great mothers?' Pia demands.

'Barbara.'

'Oh.'

About three months after I quit my job, the news editor calls and asks me if I'm well enough to take on a little work from home, and it suits me magnificently. Write. Rest. Reread. One or two stories a month and a little income starts to dribble in. And I can see the sky from my desk.

Bob invites me to join his crew, sailing on his boat, *Larrikin*, for the Woody Point twilight races on Wednesday evening. The Woody Point yacht club is a local institution, created about twenty-five years ago by a group of 'social drinkers with a boating problem'. Not one of the original members even owned a yacht. It is not a swish yacht club. It is not even a very organised yacht club. Basically, you can sail anything that floats, and if you want to protest about someone else's behaviour in the race, your protest has to be delivered to the commodore along with a slab of beer. No slab, no protest. By the time the twenty-fourth bottle is finished, no one remembers what the problem was in the first place.

Larrikin is a racing yacht, the kind that is all about speed and wind and testosterone. There is no femininity here at all, just winches, rigging and enough hardware on the deck to make it difficult to know where to put your feet. It is as cheeky as its name.

The first time I sail on *Larrikin*, it's a sauna of an evening, thick and still. There's five of us on board but only three skilled sailors. I'm a novice and I've brought a friend who's never been on a boat before. We're trapped among nearly thirty boats stalled at the start line. There's not enough breeze to fill a handkerchief and we're all slopping around pushing away from each other with our feet. To ease the boredom, people are jumping overboard for a swim. Or having a beer. Or both.

There are still about ten people swimming when movement trickles across the water like a gentle breath blown over a hot cup of tea. By the time we all register the change in the weather, a hard and fast wind has blown up out of nowhere and black clouds are boiling in the south. People are yanked on board and the race is under way.

'Jesus! Where did this come from?' I call.

'Concentrate. Just concentrate,' yells Bob.

The boat is knocked hard and we all go flying while Bob struggles to control the tiller. There's noise everywhere. The howling wind, sails cracking like whips, stuff crashing around the cabin. Bob's yelling instructions, Nick, Konrad and I are struggling to control the sails.

'Get back there,' Bob tells my friend, pointing at the stern.

She stumbles back and we race straight up the middle of Pittwater at a forty-five-degree angle. At Stokes Point we set for a tack around the marker buoy as a gust hits the boat and the headsail gets wrapped round the mast. We're sailing into a bay where hundreds of boats are moored and we've got no control. About thirty feet from disaster, Konrad manages to untangle the sail and Bob regains control. It's the kind of race that can put you off sailing for ever.

The home leg is a hard beat with tack after tack, until it feels like our arms will fall off. Halfway home, the clouds split open and thunder and lightning ignite the sky. Rain pelts down and it's impossible to see through the squall.

When we're about two hundred feet from the finish, the wind drops to a breeze and a vivid red sunset breaks through the clouds. Out of nowhere, little black heads pop out of the water.

'Penguins!' shouts my friend. 'They're lucky, aren't they?'

They dip and dive, quacking with a joy that's contagious, and we all laugh. Then, when we look behind us, we see we've won the race.

'God, it's good to be alive,' Bob exults.

We troop up the hill and give Barbara a detailed report.

'It makes me feel part of it,' she tells me when I ask her if she's really interested or simply being polite. 'It makes me feel as though I'm out there on the water with you all.'

Christmas unfolds in steamy, overcast days, leaving me feeling like a hot reduction. It seems incredible to think I've been at Lovett Bay for nearly a year and my second Pittwater Christmas is approaching. So much has happened. And my view of the world will never be the same.

I start making the puddings in the weeks leading up to Christmas Day, to give them time to mature. The kitchen fills with the sweet, boozy smell of dried fruit soaking in brandy. And every time I see someone new arrive at the boat shed, I fly down with the bowl and demand they have a stir and make a wish.

In the final days of the second millennium, we are a small group of about twelve. There's Pia and her father Bill, my mother, Marty and Witch, and a few others. We initiate a tradition of bringing together separate family celebrations around the bays, for pudding. And because I am the only person who makes her pudding from scratch, it is decided the Tin Shed in Lovett Bay will be the place to gather.

At 7 a.m. on Christmas Day, Pia gets up to light the Weber for the turkey. She first consults the barbecue book, then counts the exact number of heat beads recommended to cook a ten-kilo turkey. She counts them out carefully until there are just four left in the bag.

'Chuck 'em in,' I insist.

'It says forty-two beads, not forty-six,' she says firmly.

'Four won't make a difference.'

I throw in the extra beads and light the fire starters. Pia throws up her hands, resigning from the future of the turkey.

Marty and Witch bring prawns, and we eat them on the pontoon at the foot of the garden. It's a hot summer's day with the humidity in the high nineties and we crack champagne and cool our feet by hanging them over the side in the water. Except for Marty. He keeps his shoes on.

'There are sharks, you know,' he says.

'Jesus, Marty, death's been stalking you for years. Don't you want to live a little dangerously before the grim reaper gets you?' As I say it, I realise with a jolt that I am feeling strong enough to joke about death.

Marty pretends to think for a while, his cheeks rosy-pink with health. 'I see no reason to tempt fate,' he says finally.

The turkey, when it's pulled from the barbecue kettle, is magnificent. A big, fat, golden bird glistening with juice and tender as a young chicken.

Pia gives me an accusing look. 'Seems all right, even though we didn't follow the directions *precisely*,' she says.

It's after 4 p.m. by the time we've waded through the turkey and ham. The Towlers Bay contingent arrives, wearing silly party hats and sillier grins, and our numbers swell to about twenty-four.

Pudding is served, we all search madly for threepences and six-pences, and then, when there are only about eight of us left, we climb those eighty-eight steps and lurch into Barbara's bedroom, where we sing carols until our throats hurt.

The house plans are finally approved by council just before Christmas and a starting date is set for the builders. I agonise over spending the money and ask sensible, steady Bob if I am being stupid.

'It's not the best investment you can make, but you won't lose money.'

I hold my breath and sign the contracts. All or nothing. As usual.

One morning, after taking Barbara a dish of tuna mornay, which I hope might soothe a tender stomach, I mention a meeting with the builders.

'I think Bob should be there,' Barbara says firmly.

'Absolutely not,' I reply. 'You've all got enough to do.'

'Men tend to listen to other men. That doesn't mean you can't handle it all. You can. But it will be easier if Bob is there. I've only got one bit of advice about the whole undertaking. Never think that you're stupid. If there's something that doesn't feel right, mention it.'

The builders arrive at 2 p.m. Bob arrives five minutes later.

'Go home,' I tell him, closing the door in his face.

'Barbara insisted,' he replies, unruffled, pushing the door back open.

I give up and we all sit down to go through the nitty-gritty of money.

Phil arrives with his bobcat, the builders lob up with their brawn and we are, at last, under way. The new foundation poles are buried, and at the end of the first day the front yard looks like a war zone.

About three weeks into the project, I notice, for the first time, six heavily inked black dots on the upper-storey floor plan.

'What are these?' I ask the builder.

'Poles for the supporting beams.'

'But they're right in the middle of the house.'

'That's how they'll be able to support the beams,' he says, giving me the impression he thinks I'm slow-witted.

'But I don't want them there! I want that all open and free.'

'Without them the roof will cave in,' he insists.

Duh! Should I feel stupid? No, bugger it. I don't want them and I know I won't be able to live with them. 'You can stop work now. I am not having six bloody great poles in the middle of the floor!'

The builder leaves. The boys look everywhere but at me. They are used to lemon cakes and cups of tea; any problems are sorted out 'man-to-man' with Bob, although I am always there.

Half an hour later, the builder calls. There is, apparently, a way round the pole problem after all. Reinforced steel beams. Harder for the builders, of course, and that is the crux of the issue.

'Great,' I say, putting down the phone with exaggerated gentleness.

I'd seen a magazine photograph of a house with a vast open space between beams, giving uninterrupted views. I knew it could be done, but not how. If I hadn't seen that picture I would probably have given in.

By mid-February, Bob's second daughter, Meg, takes leave from work to help her father and Kelly care for Barbara. The hub of the house moves from the kitchen and verandah to the bedroom. It's Bob's way of keeping Barbara in the loop of family life for as long as possible.

On an unseasonably hot Saturday night in late March, I come home from a dinner party at Michael's on Scotland Island at about 1 a.m. Bob is waiting on the pontoon in the moonlight. I know something's wrong.

'What's happened?' I ask.

'Can you come up the hill?' he says quietly. 'Barbara has died.'

He leads the way up that long, long stairway on a night so bright there is no need for a torch. Meg and Kelly are sitting round the table on the verandah in the cane armchairs. Nicole, Barbara's youngest child and now with two children of her own, is with them. She arrived a couple of days earlier. Scott, their only son, is on his way from the United States but won't arrive until morning.

Their faces are pale in the night, but the talk is loud and there is laughter as the kids talk about 'Mum'. I leave them reminiscing and go to the bedroom, where Barbara lies still, her hands folded neatly, the top sheet turned down and tucked in. I thank her for her friendship and say farewell. I do not ask why her and why not me. They are questions I will never ask again. What is, is.

At 5 a.m., the nervous energy of despair worn out, the kids file off to bed and I go home. In the morning, the undertakers arrive.

I will never forget standing on the lawn at Tarrangaua this bright Sunday morning as the Water Police boat, carrying Barbara and her family, makes its way towards Church Point. Meg still in her pyjamas, Kelly looking out to sea, Nicole leaning against her dad. Scott, whom Bob collected from the airport earlier, stands with his hand on the stretcher. Barbara, I think, was a lucky woman. She'd been surrounded by love until the last and was able to die in the home she loved best.

In the afternoon, a small fleet of tinnies noses quietly into Lovett Bay. their wakes streaking the bay with plumes of white. Friends climb the steps to the house. They stand on the verandah and tell stories about Barbara. After a long time, they make their way home, their boats slipping through the bay's still waters in gentle ceremony.

A week after the funeral, we learn we've won the Woody Point yacht race series. Bob stands to make a speech on the sloping concrete of the Lovett Bay boat shed, where the end of season Annual General Meeting is traditionally held.

For a moment, he cannot speak. Then he raises the heavy wooden trophy high and says: 'For Barbara.'

7

THERE IS A GREAT LOSS amidst our little enclave. Barbara was a wise, intelligent woman who steered and supported our lives in subtle ways. Now, there is no one to run to, to ask: 'What is that bird called?' 'Is this a weed or a rare and precious plant?' 'What tree should I plant next to the house?' No one to idle away an hour or two over a cup of tea and a slice of cake, talking about subjects that once would have seemed insignificant but now enrich each day.

'The glossy black cockatoos are back,' she said one afternoon. 'Casuarinas must have nuts.'

And her words turned my walks into an expedition in search of these magnificent big birds with a slash of vivid red under their tails. When I discovered them one exhilarating morning, alerted by the sound of nuts being loudly cracked, I rushed to tell her.

'How's the little fungi forest going at the turn by the big spotted gum?' she asked another time.

And I became her eyes and feet and searched beyond the boundaries of the track for her fungi forest. When I found it hidden in a damp, dark gully, a mass of tiered, pale brown mushrooms crenellated like an ancient castle, it felt like a grand achievement.

Barbara pushed me to see and understand detail when I'd made a career of skimming the surface. And it meant that my life, which was now mostly confined to Lovett Bay when once I'd strutted the world, did not feel diminished. It seemed, in fact, fuller than it had ever been.

One day I said to her that I realised people were wrong when they said we don't have distinct seasons here. When I see the escarpment foaming with pale pink wax flowers and deep pink boronia, I know it's spring. When the angophoras fizz, we're moving into summer. When the spotted gums disrobe and white ants hatch by the zillions, it's summer. By autumn, mozzies are on the wane, and the leopard moths are whirring along the tracks like frantic helicopters. The midges arrive in autumn, too, so it pays to keep your mouth closed when you're walking. In winter, the westerlies turn clean and cold and lose their toastiness. Seasons don't need to be marked by bare trees or snow on the ground. There's a million signs of change if you look for them.

Barbara smiled at me when I told her all this. 'So many people forget to open their eyes as they walk around,' she said.

And I am glad I remembered to thank her for opening mine.

In the weeks after Barbara's death, Bob and I fall into a routine. I cook and he brings the wine. The house up the hill is lonely, the memories of Barbara's presence too vivid and raw for solitary evenings. By coming to my home, he avoids those hours that seem emptiest—the times he and Barbara would have an early-evening drink and prepare dinner together.

As winter sets its course, my renovations move into high gear. Living in a house that's being ripped apart and resurrected feels like living in a derelict building. Mid-June, the front wall comes down. Stewart and Fleury offer their house in Towlers Bay and I gratefully accept.

'That's silly,' Bob says when I explain I'll be moving for a while. 'There's plenty of space at Tarrangaua.'

'People will talk,' I reply.

'Let them. This concerns only you and me. And anyway, I don't want to have to get in the boat every night to come to dinner at Towlers Bay.'

So I move up the hill for the next few weeks, with the puppies, of course. Bob builds a roaring fire every evening and we sit in front of it on different sides of the coffee table. He works, sketching ideas. I read. When I jump up and rush outside into the chill of the verandah to cool a hot flush, he gets so used to it he doesn't even look up. I prepare huge meals and fat begins to cling to my bones. My energy levels lift a little and work gets easier.

Without being conscious of it, my panic attacks fade away and I walk with dogged routine every morning through the national park, as I did when I first came here what seems like so many years ago.

Often I meet neighbours on the track. Maureen from Towlers Bay with her old border collie. Caroline from Little Lovett with a sweet-natured cattle dog cross called Figaro. Over time, I learn that Caroline has had two types of cancer, the first striking when she was in her early twenties, the second in her early forties.

'I survived the first diagnosis so I never doubted for a moment that I wouldn't survive the second time,' she says as we talk on our walk.

'I thought I was going to die,' I reply.

Because we have been through similar crises we understand the unspoken subplot of many of our conversations.

'Got a shocker of a pain in my knees,' I say one morning as we push ourselves to walk faster and faster up 'heart attack hill'.

She knows what I am *really* asking is whether I should worry about it. Any bone pain could be a symptom of the dreaded secondaries, cancer spreading to the bone. 'Both of them?' she asks.

'Yeah.'

'Arthritis, perhaps?'

And the fear, nearly always irrational, is sponged away.

Sometimes Bob comes with me on my walks and points out what is all around that I never much noticed until Barbara opened my eyes. The exquisite little white flowers of the blueberry ash trees in Towlers Bay. The vibrant yellow flowering tips of geebungs. I love the word so much, I ponder whether I'll name my house Geebung. Sounds joyful, with hints of amazement in it. And casual. Nothing grand about it.

One late afternoon, after a restless day, the sky is a mass of rainbows. More than I have ever seen at one time. A double rainbow stretches from the Elvina Bay side of the escarpment bang into the middle of Lovett Bay.

'I know exactly where to dig for the pot of gold,' I tell Bob as we look at the sight from his verandah.

He smiles, but his eyes are wet and I know he is thinking it is a sight Barbara would have cherished.

Without even noticing, I start adding Bob's washing to my own. And on days when I go off to do a story, Bob cooks dinner. Barbecued lamb chops, with the tails crisped. Four vegetables at least, of course. Oxtail stew is his favourite but, because he is a man who likes balance, he makes it infrequently so it remains a treat.

We always sit at the dining-room table with the fire burning in the background, and as we relax with each other, we begin to talk and talk. There is so much to sift through, in the months following someone's death. In the talking, it's as though an old skin is shed and a new one slowly acquired. The memories, once recounted out loud, are filed and stored, making room, eventually, for a future.

If the nights are filled with talk, the days are consumed by watching my house creep closer to completion. Sun is already spilling through the clerestory windows at the back of the house, and I visualise furniture in place. But deadlines for completion come and go, and I feel increasingly frustrated as weeks fly by. I wait for the corrugated-iron specialists to arrive and clad the outside walls. The man who is making the stairs is running behind schedule. The fireplace is the wrong size. I remind myself that they are little hitches, not life-threatening events. But I am impatient. I want my own home. Finally, it is time for the painters and the floor sanders to begin the final touches. Almost there!

One night, over a bottle of red, Bob tells me again that one way to solve the ongoing problem of the puppies running off when given the slightest chance is to find one of them a new home. 'Please think about it,' he says. 'Right now, you have two dogs that add up to less than one because they are loyal first to each other. If there is just one dog, all the dynamics change. You become leader of the pack and have some control.'

I know he's right. 'How can I choose, though?' I ask him. 'It's like deciding which child you love best.'

I delay making the decision for as long as I can but when I find a good home, it is crunch time. In the end, the decision-making is easy. Vita must be the one to go. She is the hunter, the ringleader.

When I pass Vita to her new owner at the Church Point ferry wharf, I am quite calm. He holds her up to his face. She covers him with tiny licks, her little pink tongue darting in and out.

Will he learn quickly that she only does that when she's frightened or nervous? Will he learn to soothe her fears with a tummy rub? Then I shut down these thoughts. *I am strong and my body and mind are strong.* This way, the puppies will both survive. If they stay here together, one day they'll find the fox baits in the national park and that will be the end.

'You'll be wonderful for each other,' I say, waving goodbye.

Bob is waiting at the dock with Dolce when I return.

'Do you think she senses Vita is gone?' I ask as he puts her in my arms.

Bob shakes his head. 'You're not going to like this, but she already seems pretty happy to be an only child.'

That night I jam my finger in a cupboard door, and although the pain is slight I sob and sob. Every past grief erupts and I feel like my world is caving in around me. Bob hands me a cognac, which I gulp down.

'I am so sick of bloody loss,' I say between sobs. 'Oh God, sorry. Sorry about Barbara. That's real loss. But Jesus. When's it going to end?'

'Never,' Bob says. 'Because that's the way life is.'

I keep crying until I fall asleep on the sofa. When I wake in the morning, Bob's put a cover over me. Dolce is curled in the crook of my legs.

'Hey, little puppy. There's just you and me now.'

Dolce doesn't stir.

'Do you miss your little sister?' I ask her.

Dolce's eyes don't open. When I rub her ears, she stretches happily and sighs. But her eyes stay closed. This is not a dog that's unhappy.

A few days later, when there's still no sign of any moping, I decide to rename her. 'I can't have a dog called Dolce without a Vita to follow,' I explain to Bob.

It takes a few weeks, but eventually, by a kind of osmosis, she is named Chip Chop from all the times I've called her chubby chops for the fluffy whiskers around her cheeks. And life becomes much simpler, as Bob said it would.

I love staying with Bob, but I am always a guest, mindful of keeping someone else's sense of order. I long to be in my own home, leave dishes in the sink and stay up all night playing music. Mostly, though, I want to be surrounded by my own past. Like the big, heavy table that every removalist has cursed, but I've kept it because when I am alone I can conjure up a memorable dinner or two and feel cheered by the images. And those wineglasses that are a bugger to wash but were given to me by my brother. They stand alongside the Limoges dessert plates my mother brought back from Paris and gave to me on the day she said, 'I don't think I'll be giving many more dinner parties.' The day I realise she is getting old and the fight goes out of me (and her!) and a new tenderness creeps into our relationship.

Odd, I think, as I pack away stuff so the builders can paint the walls and sand the floors, that I have so few framed photographs. So I go looking for old envelopes stuffed with prints and sift through them for a moment or two. Then I put them away again. They trigger the old, familiar anger of loss. No, it's better to stay away from photos.

It is my habit, every evening after the workmen have gone home, to do a tour of the house, getting a feel for how it will be to live in it. One afternoon I arrive a little early, just in time to see one of the painters slapping a second coat of high-gloss white paint on the bathroom door. Gordon Andrews's fabulous painting of a bright red rooster has been obliterated. I had told them *not* to touch the door. Now it is white.

'Oh, sorry, love,' he says, casually. 'Do you want me to see if I can get the white off? I don't think it will work, but I'll give it a go.'

Visions of an extra week spent trying to restore the rooster flash through my mind, so I shrug and tell him no. But I am incensed. I've already destroyed a lot of Gordon's touches in the frenzy of putting my own stamp on the place, and only quite late into the changes realise I am destroying some lovely, quirky work. Why do I always go like a bull at a gate? Why don't I see what's under my nose until it's too late?

Still angry and upset, I go into the bathroom to remove the mirror over the basin for the painters. So it takes me a couple of seconds to notice what is behind the mirror. In a few black lines, Gordon has drawn an irreverent self-portrait, full of humour and life.

I whirl on the painters. 'Touch that, and you will both be dead!'

The portrait is there now, hidden behind the mirror. A secret. Gordon's little joke. Later, I wonder if he drew the picture after I asked him, in the days just after I agreed to buy the house, to leave one small piece of his art behind.

After about five weeks, when I've decided the painters will probably live with me for ever, they pack up and leave. The renovation is over. The house is mine again. The freshly sanded and polished floors gleam like a golden lake, and the walls are flat expanses of pure white.

'It doesn't need a stick of furniture,' I say to Bob when he arrives with a bottle of champagne to toast the future. 'The bay comes right into the house and gives it life. And art. And warmth. And . . . it's great, isn't it? But I didn't expect to feel so nostalgic about Gordon's quirky details.'

Bob pops the cork and fills two glasses. 'Don't have any regrets,' he says. 'Before the renovations, it was essentially Gordon's house. But he doesn't live here any more. You do. You've made this your own home and it's great.' He clink his glass with mine. 'So here's to health and happiness.'

We wander out onto the new deck and lean on the rail. We're silent for a long time. The view is too gobsmackingly brilliant to disrupt.

'I've cooked dinner,' he says when it feels like an hour has passed. 'But it's easy to transport. Would you like me to bring it here?'

'Would you really *do* that?'

'I get the feeling you don't want to leave.'

'You're right. It's hard to explain. I feel like I've found where I belong and it's such a lovely, secure feeling I don't want to let it go.'

We dine on Bob's lamb curry, finish off the champagne and decide to leave the washing up for the morning. Chip Chop and I spend our last night at Tarrangaua, and I wake at dawn to rush down the hill to begin restoring order.

When I open the back door and look through the house to the bay and the ancient escarpment, I feel every hard-earned penny spent was worth it. My house embraces the water, the trees, the sky, and the whole, great big, bloody glorious outdoors. It's peaceful, spectacular, wonderful. Of course, there is bare earth all around, huge piles of it where the bobcat has made way for the building. It is rough and ragged and the work to get it into shape will be hard. But I don't care. I am quite simply overjoyed by *my home*. It is, without doubt, the most beautiful home I've ever owned—well, actually, the house is not beautiful. It is still a simple tin shed. But the way it incorporates its environment makes it sensational.

With a soaring heart, I begin arranging belongings. Bob helps me to move furniture around and saws off the kitchen worktop that sticks too far into the room. Every so often I stop and look at my new world and hours drift by. I feel like the luckiest woman alive.

We have returned to our old routine of dining at my home most nights. Bob arrives around 6 p.m. He watches the television news while I cook dinner. When the news ends, he turns off the television and puts on music. Which is the signal to open the wine. It is a routine that brings the pleasure of certainty. It is casual and familiar and makes no demands of either of us. But I am aware that his support is smoothing my life in many ways. Somehow he is always at the pontoon when I get home and he helps me tie the boat and schlep the shopping up to the house. He notices when the petrol is low and a full tank appears.

One day I return from an assignment and find him stacking timber offcuts neatly for next winter's kindling.

'Had a couple of empty hours,' he says when I thank him.

Which makes it no big deal. So I bake him a cake.

Sometimes he insists on taking me out to dinner to give me a break, he says, from the kitchen. After a while he stops suggesting restaurants because he realises that I would rather eat on the deck and tune in to the evening sounds of weary kookaburras, ill-humoured cockatoos, noisy miners, parrots, sometimes a whipbird. Often, a deep brown wallaby, her chest the same rusty colour as the local stones and with a joey in her pouch, hops across the front lawn. She is wild and beautiful and her joey is wide-eyed and curious.

If the evening is spectacular and the fish are jumping, Bob sets up the steel tub from an old washing machine by the edge of the water and we light a fire. We take down camp chairs, fishing rods and a big, black, cast-iron pot filled with meat and vegetables to cook over the fire.

Bob looks at the pot. 'Don't have much faith in me as a fisherman.'

'Just covering all the bases.'

The fire brings out the neighbours. Before long, there's a party. Well, not a party. A get-together. Everyone contributes something—wine, food, wood—and when a fish is caught, cleaned and cooked within minutes, we share it. We sit there late, with the fire throwing shadows across our faces and toasting our toes.

I get into the habit of calling Bob from Mona Vale on my way home, to ask if he would like me to pick anything up. Mostly, all he ever asks for is a newspaper. By now, there is not much we don't know about each other. He tolerates my mood swings, triggered by incessant hot flushes. I agree to pack a wound on his bottom for a couple of weeks so he can check out of hospital earlier than recommended. Wadding the bandage into a deep cut hurts him, which makes it a terrible job until I visualise his backside as a leg of lamb and pretend I am inserting cloves of garlic into it. When I tell him my method, he laughs so hard he cries.

'You wouldn't be this rough with a leg of lamb, would you?' he asks.

I slap his rump by way of an answer.

He is never critical of my more eccentric excesses but tries to influence me to use reason before plunging in. His quiet caution saves me from a couple of big mistakes. He talks about his life and his children, his love of sailing and his need of a challenge. I tell him about the lover.

'What did you get out of it?' he asks, genuinely puzzled.

'Respite, for a while, from grief. Then it turned into a grief of its own.'

'Are you glad it is ended?'

'Yes. I look back and wonder how I allowed it to happen.'

'It's in the past and it is always better to look forward,' he says.

There is a track, now, that runs from Tarrangaua to the back of my house. 'Sick and tired of going up and down all those bloody steps,' Bob explains when he asks me to come and look at the pathway he's cut. He's wearing goggles and protective clothing and there's a lethal, sharp-toothed blade on the machine he's carrying. I follow him up the hill behind my house.

'So now we have a back track.'

'It's not a new track. Once it was known as Lover's Lane.'

'Oh, Barbara's Lover's Lane. So this is where it was.'

He's slashed bracken and overhanging boughs are trimmed to English garden perfection. We walk the length of the track to where it ends near Bob's workshed. It's an easy trek, not steep enough even to increase our heart rate.

'Adrienne Howley says there was never a romance between Dorothea and the doctor,' I say. 'Bit sad, really, that he cut this path to her door and she had no time for him.'

'Dorothea lived a lonely life, I think,' Bob replies.

'Are you lonely, Bob?' I ask. And then I realise it's a dumb question. 'Of course you are. Sorry.'

'Are you?'

'Yes. Often. But I enjoy our friendship. It's the best part of my life right now.'

Bob pulls his goggles back on but I put a hand on the machine.

'Give it a rest. Come and have a cup of tea.'

He shakes his head. 'No, thanks. Want to get this done today. I'll drop by when I'm finished. What's for dinner? Should I bring red or white?'

Summer steams in and I join Bob's crew on *Larrikin* for Woody Point sailing again. Every Wednesday at 5.30 p.m., even in a gale or a storm, the crew meets at his dock. Nick and Ann from Little Lovett, who sailed here from England when their children were young, are regulars. Ann, who read to Barbara every Wednesday evening during her illness, sits with me up the back of the boat. And we chat while the boys tack and winch and bleed an extra puff of boat speed from the wind.

This year, the weather is frightful every Wednesday evening for weeks.

There are strong winds, rain, crackling storms and lots of frothy white-caps. It's too rough to take Chip Chop on board, and week after week she mewls plaintively, running along the shore, trying to keep pace with the boat. One Wednesday, Nick breaks. He leaps back into the tinny, charges for the shore, scoops her up and returns to the yacht.

'Here, Ann,' he says, plonking the dog in his wife's lap. 'You look after her.'

But it's a rough race in strong winds. The boat heels uncomfortably and the dog clings to Ann in fear. When we return to shore at the end of the race, she's the first off the tinny. For the next two or three weeks, she's nowhere around when we set off to sail. Smart dog.

We begin our regular post-race dinners at one house or another. The talk is invariably about who cut off whom, who doesn't know the rules, who's done the handicapping for the year (universally unappreciated).

About the fifth Wednesday into the series, it is a filthy evening. We march out in full wet-weather gear and flounder through the race. The power of the weather is awesome. Boats are knocked hard, the wind is frenzied. We slip and slide on a wet deck. One careless movement and we're overboard. Our bums are frigid and wet, our fingers stiff with cold. By the finish, one or two boats have been blown aground, and many are limping home, sails reefed to almost handkerchiefs.

'I can't believe I'm going to say this,' I tell Bob, 'but that was the most excruciatingly good fun! I know a bit more about sailing now. I'm feeling more confident. And much stronger. Every day, so much stronger.'

Dinner is at Stewart's house in Towlers Bay. Bob and I set off in his boat from Lovett Bay in heavy, stinging rain. The water is rougher than I've ever seen it in the bays so we motor slowly. We arrive cold, damp, and childishly excited in the way you are after you've done something really difficult and it's safely over. We race up the steps to the house and the blazing fire, carrying an apple cake, two bottles of wine and a jug of custard. Inside, we peel off layers of stinky wet clothes and grab a glass of wine. The house smells reassuringly of curry.

'Thought you knocked the marker but I didn't see you go round it again,' Stewart says to needle Bob.

He puts a couple of ladles into two big pots of curry and we all help ourselves. It is hot, spicy and perfectly cooked.

'Stewart, we were lucky to *find* the marker in that weather,' Bob replies. 'But we didn't knock it.'

The blokes rehash the race for an hour or so, and by the time dessert is served the weather has calmed to a shiny stillness. The moon rises, full and creamy, and sends a yellow glow across Towlers Bay. It has turned into a still, perfect night.

Bob and I head home, slightly tipsy. Behind us, a snowy swath stretches and melts into the water.

'Aren't we lucky? All this beauty,' I whisper.

At Woody Point, the long finger of land covered in young spotted gums that separates Towlers Bay from Little Lovett Bay, Bob slows the boat and cuts the engine. I look across at him, not understanding what is going on, and he leans forward and kisses me.

I feel a rush of tenderness for this man I have come to love and respect. Two words that rarely come together. And yet when they do, how much greater the possibility of lasting passion, because there is trust and knowledge *before* chemistry intrudes and explodes all reason.

'I am no great prize,' I tell him that night on the boat.

'I think you are.'

'I have one breast.'

'One is enough.'

'I don't know how long I will live, maybe months, maybe years.'

'I could walk under a bus tomorrow.'

'I am a risk.'

'Not to me.'

The relationship with Bob unfolds slowly and evenly, without drama or misunderstanding. Well, mostly. But then a little drama here and there never hurt anyone. We are both old enough to know what we want from each other and secure enough to articulate it instead of retreating to silent, festering corners. And there is love. Intensely physical, intensely satisfying and jammed with joy.

After a while, instead of trying to hide the scar on my chest, I turn on the bedside light and ask him to look closely at it.

'It is ugly,' I say, pointing at the jagged edges.

'Yes. It is. But it is part of you and therefore beautiful.'

'Why do you love me?' I ask time after time, seeking reassurance because I cannot believe a man who could choose anyone has chosen me. What do I have to offer? Just one breast and a risky future.

He never answers this question and I let it lie, until one day his silence stings and I invoke the name of his wife to make him take notice of my need: 'I can never replace Barbara. I am not like her.'

And he turns to me. '*Replace* is a terrible word,' he says. 'People can never be *replaced*. I don't want you to be a *replacement*! I came to love you for who you are. You alone.'

And I leap on his words, looking for phrases to sustain me when I feel insecure. 'So who am I, this person you love?'

But he grins because he sees my trap. 'You are . . . you.'

Exasperated, I demand more. 'Explain to me! I need to hear words.'

'I'm not good with words. They're difficult for me. Don't I show how I love you every day in the things that I do for you?'

And I am finally silenced.

I have used words all my life to create a desired effect, so I should know that words can be empty. Actions, as the old cliché goes, speak louder than words. That's Bob's maxim. But then I think about the way he uses words, sometimes hesitantly, sometimes in a rush, always sparsely, and I understand he is wonderful with words because he doesn't use them to achieve a result. He only ever says what he means.

Eventually I make *Poule avec sa mique*. Col, from the upmarket poultry shop, painstakingly bones the chooks for me. But when Bob goes in to the shop to pick up our order, Col is clearly not happy.

'Mate,' Col says. 'Mate, do me a favour, will ya?'

'Sure. What?' Bob asks.

'Burn the bloody recipe book where this business came from, will ya?'

On another occasion, Col delivers a box of spatchcocks late one Friday night when Bob and I are in our sunken bath with its floor-to-ceiling windows. When Col can't find us upstairs, he wanders onto the downstairs deck and sees us in the bath.

'Looks good, mate,' he says, leaning against the window.

Bob is laughing loudly. I'm trying to cover whatever bit of me I think is most vulnerable, which makes Bob laugh even more.

'Water looks good and hot. Any room for me? '

'Of course,' Bob says. 'Get your clothes off. Come on in.'

I finally find my voice. 'Go upstairs and drop off the spatchcocks. There's a beer in the fridge. We'll be up in a minute.'

He disappears and Bob and I collapse with laughter.

'I wouldn't want to live anywhere else in the world, would you?'

Not long after, Bob moves in, and so do the white cockatoos. They want my tender new lemons on the trees I planted only days after I bought the house when I was full of doubt and worry and with my father's words ringing in my head: 'A house is not a home until it has a lemon tree.' So I planted two trees, just to be sure. And after Tony died, I added a lime tree. Whenever I walk past it, I think of him. 'Gin and tonic, please, dear. Lime not lemon, if you don't mind.'

One early morning, when I'm just out of the shower, I glance outside and see lemons scattered all over the ground. The tree is thick with cockatoos taking a single bite, then dropping the fruit to pluck another.

'Get off, you bastards,' I shriek, racing out. 'Get away.'

Enraged, I pick up the damaged fruit and throw it at them where they hover in nearby gum trees, waiting for me to tire.

Jack walks past and says, 'Good morning. Real buggers, aren't they?'

'What can I do about them?' I wail.

'Not much.' And then I realise I'm standing there without a stitch on. 'Oh Jesus,' I say, looking down.

'What's the matter?' asks Jack, puzzled.

'Nothing.' And I flee inside.

Just as winter begins to cut short the days and the sun moves north, changing the pattern of light on the house, Bob leaves for a five-day business trip to Melbourne. I pack little containers of fresh and dried fruit, fill a Thermos with coffee, and make sandwiches. I am irrationally terrified that he, like my husband and brother, will be snatched away.

'Ring me often,' I plead. 'I want to know you're OK.'

'All right. But stop worrying. I've done this trip hundreds of times.'

'Yeah, but ring me anyway.'

Late morning, the phone rings. 'Next time,' Bob says emphatically, 'don't put in so many prunes!'

That night he rings from his daughter's home and we talk each other to sleep. Love doesn't change much, no matter how old you are.

On the day he is due home, I shop in Mona Vale for groceries to make a special welcome-home dinner. At the fruit market, I am pondering the flowers when an arm slips round my waist. I know who it is immediately from the scent. I kiss him hello, ridiculously happy to see him, grabbing a couple of bunches of flowers to hide my pleasure.

'Those flowers are awful,' Bob says. 'Put them back.'

'They're fine.' I put them in the trolley.

He takes them out. 'No. I really don't like them.'

His behaviour is so out of character that I shrug and let it go. We climb into our separate cars and go home. We pull in to the commuter dock to unload at the same time and he leaps out of his car, rushes to his boot and brings out a big, fat bunch of beautiful white lilies.

'These,' he says, his face gloriously smug, 'are better flowers.'

That night, after a dinner of roast lamb followed by lemon pancakes, we snuggle on the sofa.

'What would you say,' Bob murmurs, swirling wine in his glass and looking at it intently, 'if I asked you to marry me?'

'Why don't you ask me and find out, you dope?'

He looks at me for a second, then glances away. 'Well, will you?'

'Will I what?'

'Marry me!'

'*When?*'

And we start laughing.

'But,' I say, serious, 'not if your children don't like the idea. OK? We don't need the formality of marriage. Not if it's going to cause problems.'

Bob dials his kids. They are incredibly kind, wish us luck, and tell us it is wonderful news. Which must be difficult for them. Then Bob rings Barbara's mother in Melbourne.

'Oh, yes,' she says calmly, 'Barbara told me it would probably happen.'

Barbara's incredible generosity of spirit. She loved Bob enough to want him to be happy after she died. A rare woman.

That evening I felt settled in my mind and spirit. No more restlessness, no more searching for a place to set down roots. I was fifty years old, and instead of doors slamming in my face they were swinging wide open.

'There's just one thing,' I say to Bob. 'I do not want to move from my house. Can you live here, instead of Tarrangaua?'

'I think I could live anywhere with you.'

How do I explain the relationship with Bob? As I write this, it feels as though we have been together for forty years instead of, by the year 2005, four. Bob is my friend and our friendship is deep, forged in times that neither of us wants to remember but that we can never forget.

I feel comfortable whingeing about aches and pains when once I would have hidden what seemed like evidence of ageing, and I don't bother with stretchy fabrics and sexy shoes any more. 'I like what's underneath the clothes,' he says when I ask if he cares that I wear jeans and clumpy work boots now. I have put on weight and I like it because I am fit and healthy and that's all that matters.

I wake each day to a man who cares deeply about my happiness and does whatever he can to ensure it. What I love most is the way he notices. If I am tired after a long trip, the next time we have to travel a long way he invents a reason to stop halfway to rest. This is a man who puts himself between you and a cranky bison (which he did on a trip through Yellowstone National Park); who will chop parsley for two hundred people because you ask him to; who brings the dog when he picks you up after day surgery, even though he has to leap across three boats at the commuter dock, the dog in his arms, to reach the dock. But he does it because he knows the dog gives you joy.

This is a man who is tough but not afraid to be soft, a man who understands quite clearly the difference between right and wrong and, even if it costs him, will resist doing harm.

The greatest bliss is that when he says something it is the truth. Even if it's not what I want to hear. Which means, of course, that the trust is absolute. And that is the greatest of all gifts.

We are married in the middle of Lovett Bay on Perce's lovely old restored navy boat, *Perceverance*, which is also the Woody Point start boat. It's a splendidly sunny day in midwinter. Jack, our neighbour up the hill, fills the ferry wharf with fronds of fern so we walk through a delicate green arbour to climb on board, dogs and all (Chip Chop and my stepdaughter Lulu's dog, Bella), to meet the marriage celebrant.

We anchor in the heart of Lovett Bay and, after a glass or two of champagne, Bob and I stand together and, slightly red-cheeked with nerves, answer the questions until the celebrant announces us man and wife. My mother, dressed to the hilt, looks suspiciously like there is a tear in her sharp, old eyes.

After we sign the documents, we return to the house down the hill, the Tin Shed, where we live and where Sophia waits with a lunch pre- pared earlier. The table is set with the good silver cutlery, I've pulled out the crystal glasses. There are flowers everywhere. We feast on cold seafood and roasted spatchcocks and finish with a wicked cake layered with dark chocolate.

Long after everyone has gone to bed, Bob and I, with Chip Chop sleeping between us on the sofa, look into the flames of the fire, hold- ing hands. It is a day to hang on to for as long as possible.

'Happy?' he asks.

'I have never been happier in my life.'

And he sighs, as though he's done a good job.

The following night we decorate the pathway from the ferry wharf to the house with candles in paper bags weighted with sand. Their glow is festive and it feels like we're following a magical pathway to a carnival on the front deck. On the lawn, fires in old washing-machine drums warm the cold night air. Lisa from Elvina Bay, now a wonderful friend, has prepared enough food to still even my paranoia about not having enough, and we invite what feels like the whole of Pittwater to help us celebrate. I dance barefoot until my feet bleed.

EPILOGUE

I STARTED WRITING this book down the hill in the Tin Shed (I never did get around to renaming my house Geebung), where Bob and I lived when we returned from our honeymoon camping on Cape York Peninsula in Northern Queensland. Now, as I finish it, I sit in the room that was once Dorothea Mackellar's bedroom in the pale yellow house on the high, rough hill, looking through a forest of towering spotted gums across Pittwater to Scotland Island. We swapped houses, because I couldn't bear watching Bob run up to his shed whenever he wanted to fix something. I guess we *really* moved so Bob could get his shed back. I thought it would be a terrible wrench, but it was easy. Home is where Bob is. And Chip Chop.

Almost two years have passed since we first carried lots of boxes and armchairs along the back track—or Lover's Lane, as Barbara called it, and I now know why.

Pia has moved to a coastal town in northern New South Wales, where she works hard for charity and the local community. Lulu has a lovely, gentle, funny partner and they've been living together for a few years. Bella still drops twigs in your lap, but she's grey around the muzzle and her black fur is turning brown. In her heart, though, she still thinks she's a puppy.

My other stepdaughter, Suzi, has a child of her own, a smiley little boy with huge blue eyes and a passion for olives. She asked me to be godmother and it's a role I relish.

Our little ghetto in Lovett Bay has changed quite a lot since I moved here. Ken and his wife Jan have sold the Lovett Bay boat shed to Michael and Marybeth, a fantastic couple with big, generous hearts. Ric and Robyn have settled into the house next door to the Tin Shed and are great friends. The people who live in the Tin Shed, John and Terese, are a vibrant, engaging couple and wonderful to be around. And up the hill behind the Tin Shed, Jack and Brigitte have three boys instead of two. As the Buddhists say, change cannot be halted.

At first when we moved into Tarrangaua, I wanted to plant grand native gardens and tame the bush. But then the thought occurred to me that there was no way I could improve on nature. So it was better by far to let the burrawangs and xanthorrhoeas, the acacias, banksias and casuarinas, find their own places to set down roots. They are, after all, more suited to this rugged terrain than any strays I might bring in, native or not. In any case, wallabies soon devoured the few shrubs I planted in my first wave of creativity. So I am content, now, with a lemon and lime tree, and a few white magnolias in the courtyard at the back of the house. Barbara, I think, would be pleased with that.

The first Easter we lived here, we held an art exhibition of linocuts of Pittwater scenes and Pittwater's wonderfully quirky boat sheds by Katie Clemson, a friend. To open it, we invited Australian author Di Morrissey, who grew up in a house just beyond Frog Hollow. In her evocative speech, Di talked about the day she met Dorothea Mackellar. She was nine years old and a lonely child, living here at a time when there were few weekenders and even fewer full-timers.

'Dorothea, or Miss Mackellar—she was only ever known as Miss Mackellar—asked me what I was doing,' Di explained. 'I told her I was looking for fairies.'

Dorothea asked Di: 'Have you found any? May I help you?'

'And so we set off looking for fairies together,' Di continues. 'After a little while, when we returned to the house after hunting unsuccessfully, Dorothea asked me what I wanted to be when I grew up.

'"I want to be a writer," I told her, wide-eyed and innocent of her fame.

'"Do you?" she replied. "I write a little, too. Would you like me to recite a poem I've written?"

'"Oh yes, please," I said.

'Dorothea, in her lilting voice with its trace of a Scottish burr, began "The love of field and coppice" and did not stop until she'd recited every verse of her iconic poem, "My Country".

'When she finished, she smiled at me and I looked at her gravely and said, with surprise in my voice, "You know, that was really *quite* good."'

After her speech to open the art exhibition ended, I asked Di what Dorothea Mackellar had worn the day she met her.

'A long, dark dress and a hat, I think. Yes, that was it. A rather dull-coloured dress, navy or black, in a heavy fabric. The hat was quite big. Straw, I think.'

So Barbara's fleeting glimpse of a woman in a dark dress and straw hat, the roaming wraith, was laid to rest. I wish she had been able to hear Di's words.

Our life here is rich in all the ways that count. Rich in love, in family and friends, in community life, rich simply because we are able to live in such a stimulating and accessible physical world. When I look back, I realise that many of the times I thought were so tough that I might not recover taught me instead what I needed to know to grow stronger. They led me, eventually, to more joy than I ever thought existed. I guess what I learned above all else was never to give up, and to accept change instead of using it as a means to escape the hard episodes.

It is now six years since I was diagnosed with breast cancer and the great big crashing fear of those first days of diagnosis and chemo has abated. I know it will always be there in some form, although I do not think about cancer often, only if I find myself worrying about small problems and need reminding that life is finite.

As I write, it is raining, which is a blessing because we've had drought for four years and the bush is powdery and brittle. The lack of water has brought shy lyrebirds to the garden looking for food. Wallabies, skittish and unapproachable in good seasons, wait at the back door, swaying with hunger, for a few scraps. I find I cannot begrudge them food, even if it means letting them decimate the lemon tree and strip the herb garden until the plants give up and wither.

Today Lovett Bay is grey, like the sky. Every so often, when heavy black clouds roll in thickly, I cannot see beyond the trees. That's when I feel like I am sitting high above the world in my private paradise. Each day here holds some surprise. A goanna on the lawn, a python slithering along the hallway. Not a moment is empty or idle. There is not a day when I don't give a silent thank you for being alive.

And of course, there is Bob.

Treasured memories . . .

Left page: 1 'Tarrangaua', named by the house's original owner, poet Dorothea Mackellar. 2 Catching dinner at Cape Leveque in Western Australia—delicious mud crab, thrown into the billy to cook, then cracked open, peppered and dipped in melted butter and lemon juice. 3 & 4 Our wedding day in Lovett Bay and a rare night out—most nights are spent at home, watching the sun go down from the verandah. 5 With Bob on our honeymoon. He's a master on the barbecue. 6 Camping in Bell's Gorge in Western Australia, cool relief from 45 degree days. 7 Carving the Christmas ham with Chip Chop and Bob's daughter's ever hopeful hounds, Bear and Tali, waiting for a morsel to drop.

Right page: 8 Christmas Eve and the crowd is building for the Scotland Island to Church Point dog race. 9 The race to the finish line—it's a muddle of surfboards, kayaks, dogs, kids and the occasional owner who needs rescuing! 10 Sunrise in an isolated bush camp in Western Australia. 11 The sun going down at Cable Beach in Western Australia. 12 Winter at home and reading Bob the manuscript of *Salvation Creek* before sending it off see if anyone would publish it. Chip Chop in her favourite position—asleep on the sofa!

Susan Duncan